RHYS
OF
EARTH

The Falkrow Narratives
Book I

Kara D. Wilson

Rhys of Earth
The Falkrow Narratives, Book I

Copyright © 2015, 2023, 2024 Kara D. Wilson
www.karadwilson.com

First Edition.

Front Cover Image: Forplayday/123rf.com

ISBN-10: 0692476431
ISBN-13: 978-0692476437

This is a work of fiction. Names, characters, businesses, places, events, locales, and incidents are either products of the author's imagination or used in a fictitious manner. Any resemblance to actual persons, living or dead, or actual events is purely coincidental.

OTHER WORKS BY KARA D. WILSON

The Aurora Chronicles
The Empress' Consul
The Raven's Sister
The Assassin's Apprentice
The Emperor's Raven
The Dragon's Son

The Falkrow Narratives
Rhys of Earth
Rhys of Quadrant Six
Ronan of Space

Cardinal Zero

Breach Effect

Unbound

To My Husband.

For staying up with me late into the night to discuss absurd plot problems, unrealistic situations, character flaws, and the strength of the human heart. For always encouraging me to listen to my gut and follow my writer's intuition.

1
THE ESCAPE

"RHYS! WE'RE NOT SUPPOSED TO be here." Alina grabbed the nearest wall-mounted hand pulley and halted herself behind her older brother, Rhys. The hallways which were normally lit with yellow, ambient light were flooded with a crimson radiance. Overhead a low-pitched siren wailed rhythmically. In the distance, a dull roar caused the hallway to quiver beneath them. "We were told to remain in the lab," said Alina. "It's just a bulkhead breach."

"Come on," Rhys murmured, pushing off the wall and floating down the hallway.

"Rhys," hissed Alina.

At the end of the corridor, Rhys took hold of the next hand pulley and dragged himself to a stop. "It's no longer safe here." He looked at his sister.

Like the other females of the colony, she was slight in build with slender arms and delicate wrists. Her eyes, which mirrored his own, were a startling shade of blue and her long hair silver. Both were adaptations developed by the colony's geneticists centuries ago. Her gray stiff-collared, long-sleeved blouse marked her as belonging to the Genetic Manipulation and Modification Department.

"Even so, our orders were to remain in the lab," Alina replied.

Rhys glanced down the hallway and then lowered himself so their eyes met. Unlike Alina, Rhys was well-toned from his years working in the hangars. Though stronger than others his age who didn't do physical labor, Rhys was somewhat gangly. His arms were long and hands wide, making them slightly disproportionate to the rest of his body. His shoulders and legs were strong, yet he lacked endurance and the ability to continuously exert effort. Despite having just turned 18 years old, Rhys often felt stunted as though he was being physically held down by the very environment he called home.

Though many teased him about the length of his locks which he had allowed to grow out beyond the standard buzz cut, he was one of thousands of blue-eyed, silver-haired citizens; his overall appearance was not an oddity.

"Listen," he said. Alina gazed at him solemnly. "Doctor Falkrow asked that I retrieve you and leave the colony." Alina's eyes widened in disbelief and alarm. "We need to disconnect from the Core. Switch to silent AI communication."

Alina gently placed her hand on the small artificial intelligence unit locked to the apex of her temporal hairline just before her ear. Though the device's thickness did not exceed two millimeters, with ease she traced the switch along its length. Rhys did the same. Instantaneously, their digital presence and physical location disappeared from the colony's online network.

Whilst they stood staring at one another in silence, each sought out the other's coded identification and communication channels.

After a long moment of silence, Alina gripped her brother's sleeve. *Can you hear me?*

Rhys nodded, glanced over his shoulder, and then said, *We'll use AI communication until further notice. Come on.*

He took her hand and pushed off, their momentum carrying them to an intersecting corridor. Using the wall to slow them to a halt, Rhys strained his ears to listen. People were coming. He backed away from the intersection and pushed Alina from the glare of the emergency lighting into the shadows.

Momentarily a line of citizens dressed in variously colored blouses signifying the numerous departments on Caelestis appeared. In silence, they drifted down the perpendicular hallway toward the hangar. Only then did it seem to occur to Alina where Rhys was taking her.

The life pods? she asked.

It's our only chance to escape.

They'll know. They'll check our identification numbers. They don't allow siblings onboard, murmured Alina.

Your new number is 010354729.

It's illegal to steal another's identification code, whispered Alina.

I didn't steal it. Doctor Falkrow gave it to me.

Did he give you one as well?

Yes.

Rhys, we shouldn't be on the life pods, said Alina, gripping his sleeve. *It's not right. We weren't cleared. We're taking seats away from others who have been deemed deserving.*

No, we're taking Doctor Falkrow's colleagues' seats. Come on.

As the last person of the group passed, Rhys pushed Alina into the intersecting hallway. She grabbed hold of a pulley and took his hand, effectively redirecting his flight path into the line. With nervous glances, they followed the others down the crimson-lit hallway.

There will be two computers checking identification numbers. We'll part there. You go into one line and I'll take the other. This will put us on the same life pod but in different compartments. Rhys looked ahead over the other silver-haired individuals. Though he saw others wearing the gray blouses of the Genetic Manipulation and Modification Department, he was the only one dressed in the dark green of an engineer.

Suddenly, the line came to a halt before an airlock.

Stay calm, Rhys instructed.

Of course, came Alina's automatic reply. She was not one to panic unnecessarily.

Though two years his junior, Alina was an extremely competent individual. At nine years of age, she had tested higher than the other teenagers within her department and at 13, she had presented her first dissertation to the Universal Forum.

While there were many in their generation to specialize in genetic manipulation of the human body, Alina had been one of three who could, with ease, identify potentially problematic genetic codes and apply automatic corrections and repairs.

Since accepting an apprenticeship under Doctor Mohebbi, the colony's leading expert on Genetic Manipulation and Modification, Alina had become one of the top researchers in a new technology that would allow artificial intelligence enlightenment interface systems, or AIs, to commence development within the brain while in the false womb rather than wait for physical implementation after birth as was presently the case.

Alina was more qualified to be on the life pod than him. His 16-year-old sister was at the forefront of human genetic manipulation. She was an individual who could sustain mankind and create stronger, faster, and smarter humans. She was needed; Rhys was not.

Though he took pride in his sister, more often than not Rhys resented her for having received a better set of genes and being given a Logos AI, the most common AI computer delegated to Caelestis citizens.

While Alina was known as the charmed child of the highly esteemed and famous Doctor Severiano Falkrow, Rhys retained a lesser title—the Other Child. He was Doctor Falkrow's son but remained known only as the one who, despite scoring highly on his exams, took no interest in any of the illustrious departments that had offered him positions and instead chose to work in Spacecraft Engineering and Design. Though vital to the expansion of the human race, spacecraft design was not crucial like genetic modification.

Since leaving the Solar System, the cradle of humanity's inception, over 600 years ago, humanity had proven it could exist without extensive space travel. In fact, the last known expedition to the Solar System had been well over two centuries ago. The last report Rhys had read indicated that the place of man's birth had been depleted of all resources. Humanity had sustained itself living in colonies within Hyperes, another solar system located within the Orion-Cygnus arm of the Milky Way, for centuries and had been terraforming two planets there for the past century. The design and engineering of spacecraft were important to the expansion of the human race, but it was not vital like Alina's field of study.

Nevertheless, Rhys felt an oddly primal necessity to stand guard over Alina to ensure that her talents were used for the advancement of mankind and not thrown aside. It was this primordial desire that had driven him to leave his post in the hangar upon feeling the colony, Caelestis, quake violently and ushered him to Research and Development where he had run into his father, Doctor Falkrow.

Though the doctor rarely spoke with his offspring or even acknowledged them—as was customary on Caelestis—he had stopped Rhys with a firm grip and spoken hastily under his breath.

There was no bulkhead breach. Caelestis had been hit by a rogue asteroid whose trajectory had been predicted to bypass the colony. Caelestis was going to jettison quadrants two through four in an attempt to preserve air and resources, but it was unlikely it would prove successful.

"Board one of the life pods and leave Caelestis," Doctor Falkrow had murmured. "Take Alina and leave."

"We're siblings. The life pods are to preserve humanity. Siblings can't—"

"Take these identification numbers and board a life pod," interrupted Doctor Falkrow. "Same life pod. She's your responsibility now."

Standing in line, Rhys glanced at his sister. Her highly esteemed status had given her confidence, pride, and an uncanny ability to think on her feet. She was known for questioning orders and speaking her mind. Now though, Alina's usually stoic face was contorted in an expression he identified as fear. They had been born and raised on Caelestis as the 11 generations before them had. Caelestis was home.

Same life pod, different compartments, yes? asked Rhys in an attempt to calm his sister's racing mind.

Yes, she replied.

After 90 seconds of floating silently in a single-file line, they came upon the airlock and stepped in with the three passengers before them. The doors behind them closed, the room pressurized, and the secondary doors at the front of the pressurization chamber opened to admit the group into the attached spacecraft.

Keep your head down, Rhys murmured to Alina.

Ahead, the line split to filter into the two separate compartments of the spacecraft. As Rhys approached the scanner on the left—a small AI the size of a human's head perched atop a counter—he glanced at Alina. She swiftly entered her new identification number and passed through the scanner. Rhys punched in his and, with relief, was admitted into the first compartment.

The life pods were designed for long-distance travel with the primary means of propulsion being two centrally-located Eridanus engines that operated in tandem to achieve lightspeed. Because the engines were located in the center of the ship, the spacecraft was split into two compartments connected by a thin hallway near the cockpit. Within each compartment were ten seats equipped with short-term cryostasis masks to slow breathing and bodily functions for days and long-term cryo-pods to halt human activity for months or years.

It was only because Caelestis maintained well over 700 life pods that the boarding of such craft was limited to 20 individuals, the number sufficient to reproduce without genetic mutations or abnormalities given that all passengers were healthy and had no genetic deviations—as was the case for every inhabitant of Caelestis. Ten men, ten women—that's all that was needed.

Rhys seated himself in the last chair near the front of the compartment and glanced at the others who sat beside him and along the opposite wall. They were already buckling their five-star harnesses and checking the cryo-equipment, life-support AIs, and backup support units. Pushing Alina from his mind, Rhys did the same. The doors at the rear of the craft hissed shut and the chairs which had been facing the interior of the compartment spun forward and locked into place.

Rhys would like to have looked out a window at Caelestis to gauge the damage it had incurred, but there were no windows in the life pod. All that he found was the door leading to the other compartment a few paces to his right.

We're not ever coming back, said Alina. *What if we never wake up?*

Trust in mankind's ingenuity. It has yet to lead us astray, Rhys replied, though his heart wasn't in it. Hers was a legitimate fear that resonated deep within Rhys. What if they didn't wake up? What if they spent the rest of eternity wandering the galaxy looking for a suitable place to land?

The planets, which were in the process of being terraformed, would not be ready for several decades and the nearest colony, Zephyre, was already at capacity. Mankind could not risk endangering its brethren by overpopulating an already delicate ecosystem. Therefore, the life pods had been programmed to seek new inhabitable planets outside the Hyperes Solar System. Statistically, it was more probable that a ship would reach a planet rather than wander the galaxy aimlessly, but still, the idea frightened both Rhys and Alina.

The short-term cryomasks slowly lowered from the ceiling until they hovered just above their heads. Rhys gazed up warily at the unit. Already? They had not even left the dock.

Just as that thought passed his mind, the ship quaked violently and lurched sideways. As Rhys clung to his seat, a loud snap reverberated through the belly of both compartments and shook the floor beneath them. Knowing the sound all too well from having worked along the docks for years, Rhys pressed his head hard into the chair and braced himself.

The mechanic tethering arms snapped, and the life pod was hurled away from the docks into the black abyss of space.

Rhys gritted his teeth and silently bore the brutal, twisting ride. He strained to hear the stabilizers rush to life, but the comforting sound never came. Instead, the spacecraft continued to spin out of control farther and farther from Caelestis' perimeter docks.

What are the AI pilots doing? snarled Alina.

Rhys clamped his eyes shut. *The thrusters have been damaged. We can't stop.* With the thrusters malfunctioning and Caelestis dealing with its own problems, it was unlikely they would receive help.

Make it stop, please, murmured Alina. Unlike Rhys who had spent hours floating, turning, and maneuvering in zero gravity while working in the hangars, Alina was accustomed to artificial gravity.

Stay calm, said Rhys, still thinking. *I'm sure the pilots are—*

The spacecraft bucked downward and then rolled from side to side as the engines roared to life around them. The life pod shot forward, and the cryomasks lowered onto their heads.

Rhys! called Alina. Her voice cracked in fear.

Rhys didn't answer; he couldn't.

The cryomask, a large, bulky helmet, engulfed him and then locked into the chair's headrest. Restraints clamped onto Rhys' arms and lower legs.

Rhys... murmured Alina. For the first time in her life, she was near tears.

Rhys tried to turn his head and look at the person seated to his left, but his field of vision was limited. *Deep breaths, Alina. Deep breaths,* he said.

There was a sharp hiss and a cold gas began filling the helmet.

Rhys? Alina's voice was small.

I'll see you on the other side.

2
CRADLE

"… CONSCIOUSNESS REGAINED. VITALS: NOMINAL. Brain wave activity: nominal. Initiating secondary vitals analysis. Analysis complete. Nominal. Gravity equaling one g-force: detected. Remaining air supply at 64 percent and dropping. "

Rhys tried to move, but his body felt sluggish and his limbs heavy.

"Wake up," commanded Pathos, Rhys' AI.

Rhys opened his eyes briefly. He couldn't make sense of what he saw.

"Engaging electrical stimulation."

"Wait, Pathos… " Rhys managed to murmur, but he was too late. A jolt of internal electricity shook his core, tearing a sharp gasp from his lips. "Pathos!" he hissed.

"Your attention is required," replied Pathos in its usual gender-neutral tone.

Rhys shook his head and, finding himself free of the cryomask, opened his eyes. Once more his world was dipped in an eerie, crimson light. An alarm somewhere within the spacecraft wailed and all around him was a deep gurgling sound. "Water?" he mumbled in confusion. He moved his feet and squinted about the cabin. "Water?" Reality came into focus and Rhys' head cleared. "Water!" he shouted. He sprang from his seat but was thrown back by the harness. "Pathos!" He gathered his soaked legs into the chair.

"Four days after initial acceleration, our unit was pulled into an anomaly. Due to the damaged thrusters, we've just crash-landed. This spacecraft is filling with water," replied Pathos.

"It's filling with water?" Rhys ripped off the harness and stood in the ankle-deep water. It was warm. Frantically, he looked around but found he was the only one awake. The other passengers still wore their cryomasks. "Pathos? Why am I the only one?"

"You switched your AI offline before boarding. Because of this, you were not connected to the spacecraft's artificial intelligence. Therefore, it became my responsibility to awaken you."

Rhys staggered through the water to the nearest passenger—a middle-aged woman—and began searching for a switch to shut off the cryo-function. "Why isn't the spacecraft AI initiating reanimation protocols?"

"Unknown. It is hypothesized that the spacecraft AI was damaged during landing."

"Can we wake the others?"

"No, reanimation takes at least half an hour. The spacecraft will be fully submerged in four and a half minutes."

"So we're going to let them die?" Rhys looked at the line of seats stretching to the back of the spacecraft which rose at a ten-degree angle. It seemed they had crashed cockpit-first.

"It would be best to leave them in their cryogenic states," mused Pathos, "so they may not feel pain."

"Then... they'll stay like that forever?"

Rhys? came Alina's muffled voice.

He turned and began dragging himself through the rising water to the front of the spacecraft where the hallway connected the two compartments. "Alina!" he called, dropping unexpectedly into chest-deep water.

Rhys! Rhys! Alina cried through their AIs.

"Alina Falkrow is attempting to stand but is trapped and unable to move," reported Pathos.

"Alina!" called Rhys, swinging his arms wildly. Panting, he drew himself into the neighboring compartment and staggered up the aisle to Alina.

"Rhys!" she screeched, clawing at the helmet which was still on her head. "It won't unlock! The cryomask won't unlock!"

With frantic hands, Rhys began searching the helmet for an emergency override.

"Extraction must be completed by force," explained Logos, Alina's AI.

"Pathos, emergency supplies?" asked Rhys.

"Near the aft hatch," replied Logos and Pathos simultaneously. Rhys raced up the aisle to the stern of the ship. "All emergency supplies are to the right of the aft hatch," instructed Pathos. "Supplies contained in the emergency packs that could be of use include resonance knives and resonance cutters."

Rhys ripped open the side panels and began digging through the numerous packs. Though the supplies were kept for short exploration and expeditionary missions, they were easy to access. "Resonance cutters?" he asked of Pathos as he opened a heavy, black pack.

"Bottom right, outer pocket," Pathos replied. "Compartment one of the spacecraft has achieved full capacity. Complete spacecraft submersion in 125 seconds."

Rhys ripped the resonance cutters from the pack, turned on heel, and leapt down the aisle into the water which now covered his shoulders. "Alina!" he screamed, realizing her helmet was no longer visible above the waterline.

With expert hands, he depressed the safety button along the hilt of the resonance cutters and engaged the trigger. A brilliant blue laser materialized around the edges of the tool's main shaft and illuminated the darkening cabin. Rhys pushed himself underwater.

Providing a three-dimensional diagram for a most effective cut, hummed Pathos. A three-dimensional graphic of the helmet appeared on Rhys' retinas. *Perspective, curvature of the helmet, and light refraction have been accounted for.*

Rhys began tracing the diagram onto Alina's helmet. It took but three precise cuts before Alina's helmet split open. He jerked Alina upward from the seat, and together they hit the ceiling.

"Go!" Rhys kicked his sister toward the aft hatch. They could no longer stand on the floor; there remained only a quarter of a meter of air space.

"Unable to connect to spacecraft AI to acquire coordinates. Location: unknown. Depth: unknown," reported Pathos.

"So what happens when we open the aft hatch?" Alina sputtered.

Rhys stretched to find the floor below him but not even his extra height helped. "Grab the pack! Grab the pack!" he yelled as the bulk passed her underwater. Alina grabbed the top of a nearby chair and hooked the pack with her foot. Once even with her, Rhys pulled the pack to them, and together they kicked toward the aft hatch.

"Logos?" asked Alina, firmly pressing her fingers on the door.

"The pressure building on the hatch indicates that the ship is sinking, however, the depth we are at is escapable without suffering decompression sickness," replied Alina's AI. "Rerouting primary energy sources from the brain to increase muscle output."

"The emergency packs are equipped with compressed air," added Pathos. "Once the spacecraft has been cleared, release the compressed air using the valve located on the bottom of the pack."

"Alina, Alina, here," said Rhys, grabbing her arm and pushing the pack to her. He placed her other hand on the valve at the bottom of the pack. "Hold it. Be ready."

"Loosen the aft hatch wheel. You must wait until the entire spacecraft is submerged before opening the door," instructed Pathos.

"I know." Rhys maneuvered before the hatch wheel. Bracing himself on the side wall, he strained to break the door's seal. When he felt it finally give, he stopped and pulled her and the pack to him. "Deep, slow breaths."

"Logos and I will provide instructions once you are submerged," Pathos said.

"The craft will be completely submerged in ten seconds," reported Logos.

"Rhys, Rhys… " panting Alina, clinging to him.

"Deep breaths," he replied as the top of their heads touched the ceiling. The water was rising exponentially faster. "Breathe, breathe!" he exclaimed as they pushed their mouths above the encroaching water line.

"Rhys!" screamed Alina.

"Breathe!" he yelled. Together, they took sips of air. Within seconds they were submerged in the liquid coffin.

Pressure will be equalized in 12 seconds, notified Pathos. Rhys maneuvered around Alina and positioned himself at the door with his hands on the hatch wheel. *Start pulling,* instructed Pathos. Rhys strained against the wheel for a moment before it gave way and began spinning. *Kick it.*

Heart hammering in his ears, Rhys pressed himself against the nearest wall and kicked hard against the hatch. It cracked open. He wedged his leg through the opening and, using his body as a fulcrum, pushed at the door. With the resonance cutters still casting an eerie blue light, he motioned to Alina. Dragging the pack behind her, she exited the ship and pushed off the stern.

Fighting his panic, Rhys followed, grabbed hold of the pack, and then waved the cutters at his sister who, with fumbling hands, released the pack's compressed air. Instantaneously, they rocketed upward at a rate that made their ears squeal in protest and their bodies feel weak.

Surface breach in six seconds, reported Pathos.

Rhys squinted upward at the pink and orange light that shone through the water's depths. They couldn't reach the surface quickly enough. He wanted air; he needed air.

Surface breach in three, two, one.

The moment Rhys' mouth broke the surface, he inhaled deeply. The air could have been a poisonous, burning acid capable of melting their lungs, but for the moment, breathing was life no matter the composition of the atmosphere.

"Rhys," gasped Alina, flailing to hang onto the buoyant pack. He glanced at her and, seeing her gaze elsewhere, followed her eyes across the water's surface to land not ten meters from them.

"Searching historic documents, records, and media," reported Pathos. "Query: found. Swimming. Loading swimming skill set. Skill set acquired."

Rhys stashed the cutters in the top of the pack and began treading water. Though his limbs felt unbelievably awkward, the weightlessness reminded him of zero gravity and eased his anxiety. After checking on Alina, he looped an arm through the pack straps and began side-stroking toward shore.

"Where are we?" panted Alina.

"Coordinates unknown. Extensive analysis of the stars is required," replied Logos.

"Both of you work to acquire our position," said Rhys. "Pathos, transmit a rescue signal."

"Logos, what is the chemical composition of the atmosphere?" wheezed Alina.

"Nitrogen, Oxygen, Carbon Dioxide, and trace amounts of other elements. The air is safe for human respiration," Logos responded.

The moment their feet touched the sandy bottom and they were able to rest their weight upon their limbs, both Rhys and Alina collapsed at the waterline, wheezing. The pack lay between them. After a long moment of silence, Rhys dragged himself and the pack farther onto the sand and rock-speckled shore and rolled onto his back to stare at the sky.

"Where are we?" Alina asked, peering up at the pink, orange, and purple atmosphere above them.

"A single star," mused Rhys, spotting the small golden orb of light hovering just above the horizon. He sat up. Before them stretched a vast expanse of water. As far as the eye could see, water. Tiredly he looked over his shoulder.

"Vegetation—living organisms that absorb water and inorganic materials through roots and synthesize nutrients via photosynthesis," explained Pathos softly. "These are known as trees."

Rhys gawked at the multi-colored trees. He never imagined vegetation—plants—could look so beautiful. Perhaps it was just the tinting from the atmosphere, but the mixing of the trees' natural greens and yellows with the sunset's pastels was magnificent.

"Why are they so tall?" asked Alina. "Gravity is at one-g."

In the distance somewhere deep in the forest, a single call rose and fell in a sweet, delicious melody. It twitted and tweeted and then called-called-called. So delicate, so heart-wrenchingly warm.

Sensing his curiosity, Pathos whispered, "A bird—Aves Class. A warm-blooded, feathered creature with a beak, two wings, and two feet. It uses songs to communicate."

"You're... sure?" asked Rhys, straining to hear the song as it grew faint.

"Affirmative," replied Pathos. "I can present to you a better evaluation of the song later once I have calculated our coordinates."

Rhys rolled onto his knees and pulled himself to his feet. It seemed they were on a peninsula. Opposite the glowing orange orb hovering low in the sky, land stretched in both directions. "What now?"

Alina joined him to hold onto his arm. "What are we going to do?"

Rhys glanced back at the spread of water and then bent down and lifted the pack onto his back. "We find shelter."

"But what if our rescue beacons are heard and someone comes for us? Shouldn't we wait here?"

"No. We need to move out of sight," he replied. "We don't know what inhabits this planet." Rhys swung the pack forward and began going through the front pockets. The pack, like their clothes, was drying rapidly thanks to the synthetic materials from which it was made.

"How do you know... so much?" Alina murmured, squeegeeing the water from her long ponytail. "Only those who were designated as life pod passengers were supposed to receive survival training."

"Their training occurs regularly in the hangar," Rhys explained. He withdrew an arm-gun, closed the pack, and heaved it onto his back. Having watched others do it before, he expertly slipped the firearm onto his arm and wrapped the neurotransmitter bands tightly at his elbow. "Pathos, link-up." The weapon began humming with power.

Rhys glanced at his genius sister who seemed thoroughly offended he was holding a weapon and then entered the line of vegetation.

"It's… warm here," said Alina after several long moments of silence. "We could be on Trilon."

"Trilon has two moons." Rhys pointed overhead at the single, pale moon in the sky.

"Then, Mereena?"

"Mereena does not have water in such abundance," replied Logos.

"Pathos, what temperature do you estimate the nighttime lows to reach?" asked Rhys, gingerly pushing aside a large, thorny shrubbery. He held it away until Alina passed.

"It's difficult to say as I do not yet know our coordinators. It is my speculation that nighttime temperatures will not fluctuate as they do on other planets, however, influential factors such as the terrain of the surrounding area may cause my analysis to be incorrect."

Sensing that there was more Pathos wanted to say, Rhys prompted the AI. "What is it?"

"Logos and I have scanned the surrounding area. In a little over a kilometer, the vegetation will give way to open land, much like a desert," said Pathos.

"Would you suggest that we stay in the vegetation?" asked Alina tentatively.

"At least until daybreak," replied Alina's AI. "The scans indicate that there is life in this length of vegetation."

"How long does this stretch of forest go on?" Rhys stopped to touch a tree. The bark was rough, quite unlike the synthetic materials he was accustomed to on the colony. He moved his hand to a leaf and rubbed his thumb down its middle.

"The ground scan has reached its maximum range of 40 kilometers. Magnetic north has been identified. The line of vegetation continues beyond our scanning range for more than 40 kilometers west and east. South of our position is nothing but water. North is a desert," reported Pathos.

"The sea and desert both exceed our scanning ranges," added Logos.

"So, we literally dropped into the middle of nowhere," mumbled Alina. "You mentioned there was life here? Intelligent life?"

"We have picked up numerous heat signatures, but we are unable to determine if they are dangerous," replied Pathos.

"Is there anything you *can* tell us?" snapped Alina.

"Lower your voice," replied Rhys, regarding the darkening forest. In the time they had been walking, the sun had faded below the horizon and dipped the land into purple shadows. "Pathos, engage nighttime vision. Logos, you too."

"Acquiring data for nighttime vision installation," whirred Pathos. "Data acquired. Installing. Installation complete."

Rhys blinked rapidly to initiate the ability. When the forest and its shadows swam back into his field of vision, he looked at Alina. She nodded and he motioned for them to continue.

We'll communicate using internal communication from now on, Rhys said. *We have no idea who or what inhabits this planet. We don't want to give our position away. Not until we have more information.*

Rhys, look, said Alina. Rhys glanced at her and, finding her gazing upward, also turned his eyes to the sky. *Switch your night vision off and look.* Rhys did as he was told and gazed at the billions of stars. Though they were quite accustomed to looking out at the black abyss that was space, gazing up at stars through an atmosphere was something quite different.

This is how... our ancestors saw the skies, Rhys said in awe. *I'm sure they looked at the stars and wondered what's out there.*

It's possible they didn't even know what stars were, replied Alina.

It's possible but doubtful, Rhys murmured. *If they never knew what stars were, how did we end up where we were? Someone had to have made that leap of faith and jumped from the ground to the sky. Do you not feel that sense of innate nostalgia looking up at the stars through an atmosphere?*

No. How can one feel nostalgia if one's never experienced it before?

Rhys began walking again. *Come on. We need to make it to the desert before we settle for the night.* Just as his night vision re-engaged, he plowed headfirst into something solid. Rhys stumbled back, heart in his throat. Whatever he had just hit was cold and swinging before him from the force of his blow.

Rhys? Alina gripped his arm, frightened. *What is it?* Her internal communication was a whisper.

Rhys studied the black, shapeless mass swaying before them. It hung from a low-level branch. *Pathos?*

The mass' chemical composition and organic materials indicate that it is a human cadaver, replied Pathos matter-of-factly.

Rhys stared at the back of the body for a long moment before lowering their pack to the earth. He inched toward the mass, Alina gripping his arm with icy fingers. When he could no longer move properly, he extracted his arm from his sister's death grip and shifted around the obstacle. From the front, it was certainly a human body. Though he could discern very few details of the man's face, it was clear the man had been strung from the tree and hung. His hands were knotted together with thick rope and a dark mark decorated his forehead.

What… is it? asked Alina, joining Rhys.

Pathos, the symbol on his forehead—what's its meaning?

Unknown, replied Pathos. *The symbol is not in our database.*

What do you think happened? Alina once again took her brother's arm. He could feel her trembling.

Pathos? Logos? asked Rhys. He certainly didn't know.

The symbol could indicate that this man was part of a ritualistic sacrifice, said Logos, *however, it could also indicate that this person was a criminal or an outlaw.*

What's an outlaw?

Someone who lives outside the law, Pathos explained.

How can someone live outside the law? Alina looked at Rhys. *I don't understand. Laws are implemented to protect us and society. How does one live outside the law?*

Let's keep moving, murmured Rhys.

I suggest an alternate route, interrupted Logos. *Our scans indicate there are more bodies ahead.*

There're more? Rhys noted the black masses hanging from the trees farther ahead.

They extend from here to the desert. If you don't wish to come across anymore, move west first by half a kilometer, and then continue northward, replied Logos.

Rhys exchanged looks with Alina, shouldered the pack, and turned westward. It took almost an hour to reach the northern edge of the vegetation line. Only when they cleared the plants Pathos had identified as trees and walked onto the open plain did Rhys drop the pack and sit. Alina stood beside him and gazed out at the vast, scrub-inhabited wasteland.

Do you have coordinates yet? Rhys stared up at the stars.

We need more time, replied Pathos.

What are we going to do? whispered Alina. Hearing the fear in her voice, he looked at her. *There are other humans here.*

Rhys folded his arms behind his head. *Shouldn't that be a good thing?* When Alina didn't reply, he tapped her leg. *What?*

They're a different species, she said. *Their hair and skin are dark.*

That doesn't mean they're a different species, replied Rhys. He sat up and stared at the ground. *But that's not all, is it?*

Alina shook her head. *Did you notice anything about the man's skin?*

Other than the pigmentation, no.

I noticed it when we were walking away. It shines. Their skin shines in the starlight.

Shines? asked Rhys incredulously.

It reflects the light.

It wasn't something he wore?

No. The light of the moon was reflecting off his cheek, replied Alina firmly.

Pathos, Logos—you scanned the body. Was there anything unusual about it?

The body had more elements than either of yours, however, our scans were not efficient enough to identify the other chemicals. Alina is correct in positing that they are another species, replied Logos.

More elements than ours? wondered Rhys.

Even with the inorganic compounds present that allow you to sustain artificial intelligence, it would seem the chemicals that make up the cadaver outnumber your own. This could indicate that the intricacy of the human body on this planet is far greater than ours and thus requires a more diverse group of chemicals to sustain it.

I see. Rhys rose to his feet and pulled the pack onto his shoulder. *Let's find somewhe—*

A call rang out from behind them. Rhys startled horribly, and Alina staggered backward in surprise. Belatedly remembering his weapon, Rhys brought his firearm to the ready and armed it. Though their night vision was engaged, it was difficult to discern the humans from the shadows. Why hadn't their AIs warned them of the interlopers' approach?

A sentence of unintelligible words flowed from the shadows to hang heavily in the air between them and the newcomers. There was a moment of silence and then an unfamiliar, metallic sound. Unable to determine what or who the sound was, Rhys fired a warning shot into the nearest tree. The poor sapling's base exploded and then burst into neon-orange flames, causing the thin tree to collapse in a flurry of branches and leaves. Rhys remained motionless. He could hear his heart thrumming in his ears. His senses were afire.

A thick quiet blanketed the area. Either the natives had fled or they were still standing in the deep shadows puzzling through his response. Rhys pushed Alina behind him and backed away.

Why can't we see them? murmured Alina.

Does it have to do with their skin? mused Rhys, searching the forest line with all of his senses.

I don't think their skin works like that.

Pathos, Logos?

It was Rhys' AI that spoke. *They have not moved. Scanners indicate that there are three of them. Two males, one female. They have the same chemical composition as the cadaver we found.*

Why can't we see them? asked Rhys.

Unknown, replied Pathos.

After another long moment, there came soft murmuring from the vegetation. Rhys readied himself.

Searching historic documents, records, and media, said Pathos. *Query: found. Hand-to-hand combat. Loading combat skill set. Skill set acquired.*

You too, Alina, ordered Rhys.

The brush parted, and the female stepped out into the open desert. Rhys directed his weapon at her while Alina settled into a defensive stance beside him. Though the human was clearly a woman by the slender shape of her body and the curve of her breasts and hips, the remaining details were hard to discern as her skin was covered in a thick paste that made their night vision ineffective. She wore something akin to goggles over her eyes.

She stretched her hands out before her to reveal that she held no weapons. Neither Rhys nor Alina moved. The woman pointed to the mask covering her eyes and then moved her hand toward it.

"Stop," ordered Rhys. Though he knew their language was not the same, the command in his voice transcended the language barrier. The woman froze.

Is she trying to take it off? asked Alina.

Or it's a weapon, replied Rhys.

Scanners indicate that it is not a weapon, chorused Pathos.

The woman pointed to the goggles again and said something.

I think she wants to take it off, said Alina. *Why would she show us she's unarmed and then trick us?*

Rhys lowered his firearm. Alina was the master of logic; there was no arguing with her observational and reasoning skills. The woman had shown them a universal gesture of harmlessness. Why would she then attempt to injure them? Still, Rhys remained at the ready.

The woman murmured something that sounded like a reassurance and then reached for her goggles. With a delicate hand, she pulled the goggles from her face to reveal her eyes and the bridge of her nose, which were not protected by the paste-like substance but appeared in their night vision as completely human. Rhys relaxed. One of the men from the vegetation said something to the woman. She nodded and pushed the goggles back onto her face.

The goggles must *give them night vision,* murmured Alina. *While the substance covering their skin masks them from infrared or other night vision devices. It's stealth camouflage.*

The woman pointed to the sky and then motioned for them to approach her, palm facing down. Rhys and Alina remained motionless. The men behind the woman said something; she began motioning again. This time, she pointed to the sky and moved her hand in an aircraft-like manner. She then pointed to Rhys and Alina and crossed her wrists before her as though she was being bound. She reiterated this movement many times and then motioned for them to approach her.

I think we should go with them, Alina finally said.

We don't know who they are or what they want, replied Rhys.

If we stay here, someone else will find us—someone who is not as understanding.

You obtained all of that from her sign language? mumbled Rhys.

I am inclined to concur with Alina, said Logos.

You're her AI. You're supposed to agree with her.

You know that is untrue, responded Logos.

Rhys gripped his firearm rhythmically. *Pathos?*

Your hesitancy is understandable. We do not know who these people are or what they want from us, replied Pathos. *The final decision is yours. In this situation, you have ultimate authority.*

And what is your analysis of the situation?

*I concur with Logos though mine is a hesitant agreement as it is also possible that these people are attempting to gain our trust to take advant—*Pathos stopped. Rhys felt the AI's attention shift. *An aircraft is approaching from the east. Distance: 4.28 kilometers and closing. Scanners indicate it is running on an unknown source of power. Aircraft unidentifiable.*

Logos, your scanners have more range. Anything else? asked Alina.

My scanners indicate two vessels, replied Logos.

Both aircraft have also entered my range, added Pathos.

We need to run, said Rhys. Not for the first time that day, adrenaline began pushing the fatigue from his body and heightening his thought processes. *We need to find cover.*

No, we need to go with them, said Alina. She pushed past Rhys and started toward the woman.

Rhys pulled her back. *Alina.*

Alina looked at him. Her stoicism had returned. Her uncertainty and fear had been replaced with the general emotionless that was quite common for her AI core. Logic had made her decisive and determined.

She knew the course of action she needed to take; unfortunately, Rhys did not feel the same way.

We should head back into the forest and wait until sunrise. We'll make a decision then, he said.

Alina escaped from his grip. *It'll be too late then.*

The woman waited until Alina was within arm's reach and then tentatively held out her left hand. Slowly, Alina did the same so their hands met in the middle. The woman pulled Alina forward slightly and then bowed her head.

A greeting custom, I assume. Logos' commentary was muffled.

Uncomfortably, Alina mimicked the gesture.

Aircraft are 1.3 kilometers out. They're moving fast, reported Pathos. *What will you do?*

Rhys looked up at the sky and then hesitantly approached. The woman held her arm out once more, but Rhys didn't take it. Instead, he pointed to the sky and cupped his ear. He moved his arm before him like an aircraft moving through the air. She nodded and then said something to the others waiting in the vegetation.

One of the men stepped forward and pulled his goggles off so both Alina and Rhys could see his eyes. He was tall and quite wide. Had there been more time, Rhys would have gawked at the man's physique, however, already the low rumble of the aircraft's engines was within earshot. The man slipped the goggles back on and held his hand out for Alina.

Before Alina could take it, Rhys intercepted and motioned for them to lead. The man nodded and returned to the treeline. The woman fell in behind Rhys and Alina.

Pathos, keep an eye on her, commanded Rhys.

Of course, came the comforting reply.

Once they were concealed by the vegetation, the men started jogging west. When the roar of engines overhead became deafening, the group halted under the protection of a cluster of leafy trees. The woman grabbed Alina and pushed her to the ground. The two men roughly shoved Rhys to the earth. Though Rhys managed to knee one of his offenders and punch the other, his pack hindered the majority of his movements. Swiftly, the two men covered him with their bodies and fell still. Breathing hard, Rhys peered out from under one of the men's arms at Alina who was buried beneath the woman and brush.

As the aircraft came into view, Rhys stared at them in confusion. They were not airplanes or jets or anything he had read about in the historic documents available in Caelestis' Core. They were great metal ships 15 to 20 meters in length with enormous fan-like engines that extended horizontally from their bows and sterns.

What are they? he asked of Pathos.

I do not have any historical records of such transportation, replied Pathos. *They aren't anti-gravity as they require fans to remain aloft. The technology they are utilizing, though foreign, is primitive. Perhaps the most accurate name we can give it, for now, is an airship.*

An… airship?

For a long while, the airships circled the area. Not once was light shed on the tree canopy or ground. Was that why he and Alina had been pushed onto the ground and covered? Perhaps the natives were using their bodies to protect him and Alina from the airships' sensors?

Eventually, the airships moved on, leaving the group in silent darkness. The men moved from Rhys first before the woman stood and helped up Alina.

We stand out, Rhys remarked as the men started once more westward. *Our pale skin and hair are like beacons.*

Our clothing doesn't help either, replied Alina.

Once we find a place to rest, I'll see what's in the pack.

As though she had read their minds, the woman murmured something to one of the men and withdrew a piece of cloth from her belt. She motioned to Alina who took it in mild confusion. The woman patted her head and motioned that Alina should wrap the cloth about her. Hesitantly Alina did as the woman instructed.

Rhys, murmured Pathos in an attempt to acquire his attention. Rhys turned to find one of the men holding out a piece of cloth for him as well. Rhys took it and copied Alina.

The group started again. They hiked for about a kilometer before the men turned and started south toward the sea. After another kilometer and a half, they breached the forest. Once again, Rhys and Alina found themselves on a rock-encrusted beach. The woman walked down to the waterline and sat down on a large boulder half buried in sand. The two men stayed at the treeline and spoke softly.

Alina, breathing hard, fell to her knees and sat limply, her eyes fixed on the horizon. Rhys dropped the pack which had been growing increasingly heavier. Where were they? Why had these people brought them back to the water?

What are you thinking? he asked of Alina.

That I've never been this exhausted in my life, came his sister's soft reply.

Physical exertion requires more energy than the mental effort you normally use, said Logos. *Also, you've made two major downloads today—swimming and combat.*

Rhys glanced at the two men who murmured near the treeline, surveyed the woman who was now lying face up on the rock with her night-vision goggles off, and then sat beside Alina. He pulled the cloth from his head and ruffled his pale hair into place.

They're waiting for something, murmured Alina, studying the woman.

Why out in the open? I thought we were trying to hide. Rhys disengaged his night vision and looked up at the stars. Alina followed his gaze. *Pathos, do you have coordinates yet? Where are we?*

We finished calculating the coordinates a few minutes ago, replied Pathos.

Rhys exchanged looks with his sister. *And? Where are we? Are we still in the Milky Way?*

We're in the Milky Way in the solar system named The Solar System, said Pathos.

Uh, is that an error in your records? asked Alina. *A solar system named The Solar System?*

We are in The Solar System, the cradle of humanity, Alina's AI asserted. *We are on the third planet from The Sun, the planet where humanity began—Earth.*

3
FIRST SLEEP

"What?" whispered Alina.

Rhys slowly stood, his eyes wide. The cradle of human civilization, the beginning of mankind. "There's a mistake," he said. "We… can't… "

Our calculations are definitive, replied Pathos.

The breathable air, the land, the water—this had to be Earth. "Alina… " whispered Rhys. He looked up at the stars. "Earth. We're on Earth."

"How? It doesn't make sense." Alina's voice was unexpectedly angry. "Rhys… we'll never return to Caelestis."

The thought had not crossed his mind but she was right. "Someone will receive our signal," he replied in an attempt to encourage her.

"No! They won't!" snapped Alina, kicking at the sand. "Do you know how far we are from home? It'll take *hundreds* of years for our beacons to reach anyone!"

"Then how did we get here?" argued Rhys. "We were in cryo for a few days! What happened? We traveled thousands of light-years in just a few days!" Panting, Rhys sat and folded his arms around his legs. "We can go home. It will just take time."

"How?" Alina mumbled hopelessly.

Rhys glared out at the water because even he couldn't hide the sudden painful loneliness and heartbreak that now shook his courage. He couldn't admit it aloud; he couldn't let Alina know she was right. There was no going home. They were here, forever. The full consequences of the decision he had made to leave Caelestis now threatened to engulf his entire being.

Rhys regarded the woman and then the two men. All had been watching their argument and hysterics.

Pathos, is there any possibility of returning to Caelestis? he asked.

At the moment, no, replied Pathos. *Logos and I will continue to seek solutions, however.*

Rhys nodded. For nearly half an hour, they kept watch in silence. He was sure Alina had fallen asleep. Her breathing slowed and her hands went limp. Unwilling to leave themselves helpless, Rhys fought off his own fatigue and stood guard over his sister. It wasn't until he heard footsteps that he looked over his shoulder to find the woman approaching them. She studied Alina for a moment using her night vision goggles and then sat beside Rhys.

Rhys watched her warily. If he needed to, he could push Alina aside and use his weight against the woman. They weren't going to be killed by some Earthling, not after the hell they had endured.

"Kallen." The woman laid a hand on her chest. "Kallen." The woman's voice was higher pitched than he expected. She was young.

"Kallen," he murmured.

The woman nodded and then reached between them. Rhys pulled his arm from her touch. It didn't seem to faze her. Instead, she pointed once more to herself and said, "Kallen." She motioned to him.

She's asking for your name, said Pathos.

I know, replied Rhys. *Is there any way you can start translating?*

I need to hear more. I have not yet been able to build a sufficient vocabulary. I am still deciphering their syntax and sentence composition.

How long will that take?

It depends on how much you can make them talk, replied Pathos.

Rhys placed his hand on his chest. "Rhys."

"Rhys," mimicked Kallen. She nodded in understanding. "Rhys."

Rhys motioned to his sister. "Alina."

"Alina." Kallen pointed once more to him. "Rhys." Then to Alina. "Alina."

Remember, make her talk, chided Pathos.

"What are we waiting for?" Rhys asked. "Why did you bring us here?" Kallen turned her head in confusion. Rhys continued. "To whom did those airships belong? Are they after us?"

Kallen answered, though Rhys suspected it was an attempt to explain to him that she didn't understand.

I need a basic sentence structure to begin analysis, reported Pathos. *By the way, she's preparing to touch you.*

Rhys struck her hand away. Frowning, the woman took her night-vision goggles off and looked at him. She wanted him to see her face. With her eyes unfocused, she pointed to the side of her head and asked a question.

What that is? translated Pathos. Kallen spoke once more and Pathos continued, *I feel can?*

Rhys shook his head, the universal signal for a negative response.

Kallen sat back and slipped on the goggles. She looked at Rhys and then at Alina before speaking once more.

What did she say? asked Rhys.

I don't have enough vocabulary yet, replied the AI.

"Kallen," called one of the men, leaving the tree line. He motioned toward the water.

Kallen made a sound and then stood. "Rhys." Though he had just taught her his name, the sound of it on her lips surprised him. Everything that followed his name, he didn't understand.

My scanners are detecting another ship, said Pathos. *It's large, much larger than the airships from earlier.*

I don't hear anything, said Rhys. He shook Alina and rose to his feet.

It's a seafaring vessel. It's riding the water, replied Pathos.

Alina, wake up, said Rhys, nudging her with his knee.

Alina looked about wildly, stood, and then leaned heavily on him. Rhys could feel her weakness. *What's going on?*

Something's coming, replied Rhys. He turned and picked up their pack.

"Rhys, Alina," called Kallen. She motioned for them to follow. Rhys exchanged looks with his sister before guiding her toward the water.

The water vessel has halted and released a smaller, secondary vessel, Pathos said. *It appears the secondary vessel is coming to claim us.*

Us or them? asked Alina.

"Both," murmured Rhys.

After a moment, a small, single-manned dinghy slipped through the shallow waters along the shore. Rhys' largest captor, the beast of a man, immediately leapt through the water and swung himself aboard. The other man and Kallen motioned to Rhys and Alina.

They're asking for a lot of trust from us, Rhys remarked.

Would you prefer we stay in the forest? asked Alina. Rhys looked at his younger sister. Her hair shined in the starlight. *If that's your decision, then we'll stay, but I don't think they will approve.*

You think we should go with them, don't you? Rhys glanced at Kallen.

I think, at the moment, they are our best hope for survival. If that changes, I'll let you know.

Rhys nodded and motioned for her to lead the way. Weakly, Alina joined Kallen. The second man, a young, lithe individual, positioned himself at the water's edge and held his hand out. Alina took it and tried to pull herself to him, but instead, weak with fatigue, fell toward the water. The man caught her and, with ease, hoisted her into the small vessel.

He held his arm out for Rhys, but Rhys ignored it, slugged through the water, threw his pack into the boat, and dragged himself over the edge of the vessel. Though it was a strain, he didn't let it show. They had to think of him as capable and strong. Both the lithe man and Kallen swung into the vessel after him with grace.

The boat rotated and began trolling into the darkness. Rhys leaned into Alina and held her close. Though the night air was warm, she shivered.

It was but a breath's moment before a looming black mass melted from the stillness into Rhys' night vision.

A ship, whispered Alina.

Length: 30 meters. Height: ten meters at the water line. Engine type and power source: unknown. It's different from the previous airships, said Logos.

Heat sources detected onboard, reported Pathos.

The forward hatch of the vessel has opened. Entering forward hatch, said Logos. Alina clutched Rhys' legs and tucked herself into his body. Their small boat slipped into the forward hatch of the ship and up a submerged ramp. They skidded to a halt inside a dimly lit cabin.

Kallen pulled her goggles off, leapt from the boat, strode over to a pipe clamped to the nearest wall, and opened the small piece of metal covering its end. She murmured something into it, closed the lid, and then watched the others climb from the dinghy. Rhys and Alina didn't move.

Though they now had light, they could hardly make out the details of the forward hatch. It smelled damp and, despite the warm outdoor temperatures, was surprisingly chilly. The metal walls around them were decorated with rust and dark stains while the floor was a strange, slick brown material. Along the walls were various pipes—used to communicate, Pathos explained—tools, chests, and crates. On the back wall of the cabin was an odd piece of machinery that looked as though someone had been working on it. Pieces lay strewn across a gray ground cloth; the machine itself was held in place by large black straps.

"Rhys, Alina," said Kallen. She waved them out of the boat. Rhys took a deep breath and with steady hands helped Alina step from the dinghy onto the level decking. Seeing her weakness, Kallen braced her and waited for Rhys.

As Rhys slid out of the boat, the docking beneath him began vibrating. Startled, he grabbed Kallen's shoulder. With surprisingly strong hands, Kallen held both him and Alina steady. She said something, but neither Pathos nor Logos were able to translate. After a moment, she released them and, with a small smile, mimed that the vessel was now underway.

We shouldn't be here, said Rhys. *This doesn't feel right.*

Nothing will ever feel right again, Alina replied darkly.

Where are we going? Pathos?

South, according to my scanners, however, there is no land in a six-kilometer radius, replied Pathos.

I hate the water, grumbled Alina.

"Rhys?" asked Kallen. She was studying Alina's AI.

Can you try to translate, Pathos? Rhys asked.

I cannot ensure perfect accuracy.

"That is Alina's artificial intelligence unit, Logos. Mine is called Pathos," explained Rhys slowly.

He waited as Pathos attempted to translate his words. Seeing Kallen's eyes widen, Rhys backed away. *What did you say?*

I do not yet have the words needed to complete a grammatically correct sentence, retorted Pathos. *I need more time.*

It seemed to Rhys though that Kallen's response was not to the translation of the words but to the AI itself. It was then that it hit him—they had not yet heard the AIs speak. This was the woman's first time hearing Pathos.

Before Rhys could determine how best to approach the situation, Alina beat him to it.

"Here," she said, taking Kallen's hand and drawing it near the small, silver AI just above her ear. Kallen touched the device and then quickly drew away. She murmured something and then looked at the three men standing in the doorway. They too had heard Pathos speak.

"They're harmless," said Alina, commandeering Kallen's hand and pressing their palms together so they stood staring at one another. "See? We're the same." As Logos spoke, Kallen listened. It didn't appear she understood the AI's words immediately, but after a moment, she nodded enthusiastically. Alina looked at Rhys. "See?"

Kallen gently pulled away from Alina, smiled slightly, and then turned toward the doorway. It was then that Rhys saw the shimmering Alina had mentioned earlier. As the dim light caught the uncovered skin just below Kallen's eyes, it glistened briefly. It was not a brilliant flash but a subtle flickering of light that could be mistaken as an illusion. His sister was right—these people were different.

They're talking about us, said Pathos softly. Rhys listened, but the words still sounded like monotonal gibberish. *It seems this will be a long journey.*

How long? asked Rhys somberly.

They haven't said, though I suspect longer than a single day.

That's nothing, said Rhys. He looked at his younger sister. Seeing her shivering, he took the cloth around her neck and wrapped it about her head once more. *Pathos, ask them where we're going.*

As Pathos interrupted the foursome's conversation, Rhys watched. Kallen seemed beyond intrigued by the AIs. The largest of the three men gazed at Rhys indifferently while the other two listened. After a moment, the third man who had been piloting the dinghy turned and left the cabin. The beastly man turned to Rhys and spoke. Pathos attempted to translate.

Home to south go. Three days.

Ignoring the broken language, Rhys pushed. "Who are you running from? Why did you pursue us?"

You don't expect me to translate that, do you? asked Pathos incredulously.

Try.

In horrifically broken syntax, Pathos attempted to ask Rhys questions. Once finished, Kallen and the two men spoke at length to make sense of the queries. It was Kallen who finally replied. Pathos translated.

The people had you for look. Star crash saw. We saw. Who there first get? We you... I'm sorry. I don't understand the word she just used, offered his AI. *One moment.* Pathos asked Kallen a question. Kallen repeated herself, adding hand motions for clarification. Pathos translated. *We you track. You, find. They, you no find.*

Everyone in a 160-kilometer radius probably saw our ship enter the atmosphere, surmised Rhys, looking at Alina. *It's been a race to see who can get to us first.*

The question is why, murmured Alina, turning to Kallen. "Why?" Logos translated.

Kallen started to speak, but the youngest of the men called her name and shook his head. Kallen bowed her head to Rhys and Alina

28

apologetically. She glanced at her crewmates and then pointed to the larger of the two men standing in the doorway. "Kashim," she said. "Kashim."

Kallen pointed to the younger man who had his night goggles perched atop his head. "Hodge."

The 20-something-year-old man, Hodge, smiled at Alina before meeting Rhys' gaze. Though the man was far taller than Rhys, he seemed approachable like Kallen. Despite Hodge's lean and muscular build, he had a soft face and warm eyes, both of which were emphasized by the rich mop of tangled, dark hair that covered his ears.

Kashim, the bulky man leaning in the doorway beside Hodge, was another story. While Kallen and Hodge seemed friendly, Kashim exuded suspicion. He sported thick, dark hair bound in a knot at the back of his head and a wiry beard that covered most of his face. His entire body, from bulky legs to rippling, muscled arms, was tense with distrust. His dark gaze was calculating and invasive. Rhys felt as though he were under intense scrutiny.

As Kallen moved into the light of the dim lamp to speak with Kashim and Hodge, Rhys stared. Until that moment he had assumed her to be in her late twenties, but now that he could properly see the shape of her face and its details, he was uncertain. She appeared closer to his age, 19 or 20 maybe.

Rhys, look. Around her neck, murmured Alina.

Rhys shifted his gaze to the thumbnail-sized, black disc dangling from a thin, leather thong around Kallen's neck. *That doesn't look like it belongs,* he replied. *Pathos, do you know what it is?*

A relic from our past, replied his AI.

That belongs to us?

So it would seem.

"Rhys, Alina." Kallen motioned for them, again with her palm down. With Alina clutching his arm for support, Rhys led the way. Kallen pointed to Rhys' AI and began speaking. Pathos translated.

I translate hope. Now, we room leave.

"Where are we going?" asked Alina. Logos translated her query. Kallen responded, and the process was reversed.

Ship other side of. To rest. Rooms are. Quiet be. Sound water over moves.

Kallen motioned them through one of two doors into the main cabin of the ship which had only a single light illuminating the entryway. Kashim and Hodge started up a short flight of stairs. With Kallen's help,

Rhys drew his sister up the stairs and into a dark cabin—the bridge. They were met by half a dozen crew members each as foreboding as the next.

A man sitting skivvy in a chair near the far side of the room motioned to the group. The darkened cabin was immediately soaked by red, floodlights positioned along the ceiling. Suddenly illuminated, Alina shied behind Rhys who squared himself and searched the room for the commander. Even on Earth, people needed leaders.

All those present were male. It seemed Kallen was the only female onboard. Like Kashim, many of the men were tall, in their mid-thirties, and astonishingly muscular. All bore night-vision goggles atop their heads. Only Kallen, Kashim, and Hodge were covered in the thick, dark-colored paste.

Rhys' gaze rested on the man sitting in the chair. He was different from the others. Not only was he young like Hodge, but his black hair was trimmed short close to his ears, emphasizing the pale scars which decorated the side of his head. With a sigh, the man stood, rubbed his face tiredly, and crossed the room. Rhys watched as the crew moved aside, an obvious sign of respect.

The man's clothes, like everything else about him, were different. While everyone else wore nondescript, dark blouses and pants, his clothes were light-colored in comparison—a green, short-sleeved blouse and tan pants. Gray chaps with dark streaks of a mysterious substance were tucked into thick, black boots and wound up to his knees where they parted to reveal the pants underneath. At his waist was a broad black belt with variously sized compartments and a firearm.

He studied Alina before setting his eyes on Rhys. It took Rhys a moment to realize the man's gaze was light-colored. The strange effect that had on Rhys was disconcerting. Seeing another individual with fair eyes should have made him feel safe, at home. After all, every person he had ever known had been born with azure eyes. It was a genetic mutation. So, why now did a man bearing that same trait make Rhys uneasy?

As the man spoke, Pathos translated for Rhys.

Others there were?

"No," replied Kallen. Pathos' translation skills were starting to mesh with Rhys' own interpretation of the language.

They new information have?

"They're not the same," said Hodge.

Pathos, what does she mean? Ask, instructed Rhys. Pathos translated Rhys' question, halting all conversation between the man, Hodge, and Kallen.

"See?" murmured Kallen. Rhys glanced at her and then looked back at the man who was staring at them incredulously.

"They speak… Who speaking is?" the man asked.

Kallen leaned forward and pointed to the AI on the side of Alina's head. The man nodded in thought; others on the bridge seemed thoroughly alarmed. Slowly, in the natives' language, Alina formed a question which Pathos then translated for Rhys.

"Who are you?" she asked. "Why you need us?"

The man standing before them glanced at Kallen, Hodge, and Kashim in mild disbelief and then replied. His response was immediately translated for Rhys.

"I am Vinz, the Overseer. This is my ship."

"Overseer?" asked Alina in confusion. Neither Logos nor Pathos understood this word. "What is that?"

Ignoring the question, Vinz leaned forward and studied Rhys' AI. "What is it?" he asked.

Rhys formulated a question and, with Pathos' help, spoke. "Answer, please. Overseer. What does mean?" Like Alina, he spoke haltingly.

Vinz folded his arms across his chest. "It means this my ship. Now, you answer. What is that?"

I don't know the vocabulary for our technology, said Pathos.

"I not explain. No words," replied Rhys carefully. "Why we here?"

Vinz looked to Kallen. "They tired are. Them below take."

Kallen rested a gentle hand on Alina's shoulder and tried guiding them from the cabin. Alina, however, who was unaccustomed to being ignored, slapped Kallen's hand away and returned to the Overseer. Vinz regarded her with mild interest. "Why are we here?" she asked clearly.

"You here because I told them," Vinz nodded to Kallen, Hodge, and Kashim. "Better here than elsewhere."

I would advise that we not push him, Logos suggested. *We do not yet have enough information. We may need him later.*

I agree with Logos, said Rhys. *As much as I want answers, we need to tread carefully.*

Alina, whose gaze had not left Vinz's, frowned. *I need answers. I need to understand his motives, otherwise none of this makes sense.*

Tomorrow, insisted Logos. *Not now. The crew is very tense. All have elevated heart rates which indicate a preparedness to fight.*

Rhys touched his sister's arm. *Come on.*

Alina hesitantly returned to Rhys' side. Kallen motioned for them to follow her.

"Hodge, Kallen, them with stay," said Vinz. Rhys looked back at the Overseer. Everyone there was dangerous, but none more so than that man. That man had knowledge and intelligence, forces far greater than weapons or strength.

Kallen led them to the door at the rear of the bridge and back down the set of stairs; Hodge followed. It wasn't until they reached the hallway that the red flood lights streaming down the staircase from the bridge were replaced by soft, pale white ones. As they walked through the narrow corridor, Rhys took the time to peer into the various rooms.

Though the corridor was tight, the rooms were spacious and neatly kept. With ease, he identified a galley, a cabin crowded with clothing and bunks, a washroom, a private cabin, and an engine room. At the end of the hallway, Kallen opened a door to another cabin and motioned for them to enter.

Rhys followed Alina into the room. There were two bunk beds though neither appeared to be in use. On either side of the door were closets as well as cubbies with netting. Rhys set their pack down and then helped Alina to the nearest bed.

"Where we going?" asked Rhys, looking between Kallen and Hodge. "This ship."

"Home," replied Hodge. "Three days away."

"Us for you here came?" asked Alina.

Hodge and Kallen stared at her in confusion. *Did I say it correctly?* Alina asked of Logos and Rhys.

You came here for us? corrected Rhys. *I think.*

"You talk now?" Kallen pointed from Alina to Rhys. "You talk together?"

"Yes, we talked," said Rhys. Kallen murmured something indiscernible to Hodge. He nodded, a smirk on his face. "You came here for us?"

"No, we were here for a different reason," replied Kallen. "Overseer saw your star. He told us to find you."

"Why?" asked Alina.

"Sorry. Cannot answer," Hodge said.

"Who were other ships?" Rhys motioned with his hand. "Bad people?"

Kallen mused over the question before deferring to Hodge. "Not bad people," replied Hodge. "Different people. We not agree them with. So, not bad, but not good."

Rhys nodded, grateful for the explanation. Not knowing the word used to show gratitude, Rhys murmured "thank you" in his own language and bobbed his head to Hodge.

Kallen clapped Hodge on the shoulder and murmured what she thought Rhys' translation was. "I know what he said!" Hodge crowed good-naturedly.

"Tired?" asked Kallen. "Rest. Room of bath is there." She pointed across the hall. "Nowhere else go. Understand?"

"If trouble, what do?" asked Alina.

"We will come," Hodge assured them. The certainty in his voice was strangely comforting to Rhys. Hodge turned for the door but stopped. "One question—who you are?"

"Who are we?" asked Rhys, searching for clarification. Hodge nodded. "From… " Rhys thought for a moment. With Pathos' help, he searched for a term that could mean space. Finding none in their current vocabulary, he said, "Far sky from. That is home."

"Ship bad," added Alina, miming with her hands. She lowered her gaze. "Never home again go."

Hodge murmured a word, and Alina and Rhys exchanged looks. *What does it mean?* Rhys asked of Pathos.

I don't know. There is no previous usage of the word nor contextual clues, replied Pathos.

"That word, meaning?" asked Alina.

Hodge thought for a moment. "Bad people. Escape home from? Criminals?"

Ah, he's asking if we're criminals, mused Rhys.

"No, not criminals," Alina corrected. "Uh, livers… People who live."

"Survivors?" murmured Kallen somberly. Both Rhys and Alina nodded. "Please rest. You tired." Hodge slid the door open and disappeared into the hall. Kallen gave them a sad smile, joined Hodge in the hallway, and closed the door behind her.

Rhys sat heavily on the bed across from Alina's and stared at the floor. He had a slight headache. His body felt heavy. "I'm hungry," said Alina after a long moment of silence.

Wearily, Rhys pulled their pack to the side of the bed and began going through its contents. "There should be some food tablets in here."

"And I'm so tired," Alina murmured, closing her eyes. As he continued to dig through the pack, she added, "We're alone, Rhys. This is the... first time we will sleep without being connected to the Core."

Though her words caused worry to blossom in him, Rhys hid his fear. "It's fine. Humans have slept without the help of technology for centuries. I'm sure we're no different." He pulled out a green container, kicked the pack aside, and examined the food rations. "It looks like there's... " Rhys counted the pill pockets silently. "Two hundred total. That's 100 each. Each food tablet lasts about three days. We have reserves for 300 days each. Pathos, what are the estimated time cycles for Earth? Daylight hours, night hours, months, years."

"According to the data I've collected since we've landed, daylight hours may be as long as 15 hours. A measurement of the Earth's rotation indicates that an average day-night cycle should last about 26 hours," said Pathos. "I do not have enough data to calculate the rotation of Earth around the sun to predict a year's time."

"Alina, here." Rhys waited until his sister sat up before tossing her a small, precisely packaged tablet. Rhys opened his, popped the green tablet into his mouth, and began searching the pack for water reserves. Finding four small pouches, he threw one to Alina before drinking heavily from another.

Tiredly, he replaced the pack's contents and lay back on the bed. For several long minutes, he stared at the bunk overhead. Though the ship still vibrated, the motion wasn't as noticeable as before. "Alina, do you think—"

Rhys glanced at his sister to find her curled in the fetal position asleep, her water pouch still in her hand.

Would it be safe for them to sleep without a connection to the Core? He had napped several times on his own, however, a deep sleep was something completely different.

Every night, each individual on Caelestis would connect their AI to the Core, a centralized unit that stored the colony's knowledge, data, and information. Everything from updates on genetic manipulation trials to mechanical conditions of the colony to astrophysics equations was stored on the Core. At night, the AIs uploaded the day's learned data and knowledge to the Core to be shared with the colony. If humanity was to continue surviving, mankind needed to share information like air. Nightly updates were crucial for the development and advancement of humankind.

There was no Core here. If they were to survive, they would have to start using Pathos and Logos as "cores" and share knowledge and data between themselves. In this way, they would be able to achieve quicker results and a more apt understanding of the environment.

In silence, Rhys thought of the day's events. To reassure himself, he clenched the firearm still strapped to his arm. He was lucky. No one, aside from Kallen, Kashim, and Hodge, knew what the small piece of technology on his arm was capable of. In fact, it seemed that most people were more concerned about the AIs.

Rhys rolled over to face the wall. A wave of fatigue crashed over him and his eyes lowered. *Pathos?*

Since the beginning of time, humans have slept without the accompaniment of a Core. Your logic is solid, replied Pathos comfortingly.

Keep an eye on things, murmured Rhys.

Always.

4
A NEW ALLIANCE

"RHYS? HEY."

Rhys cracked his eyes open and, finding the room unbearably bright, groaned and covered his face with his arm. It took him but a moment to realize he had slept through the night without being connected to the Core. He rolled over and looked up in awe at Alina who nodded enthusiastically in agreement.

"It's fine," she whispered.

"How did you wake up?" Rhys sat up.

"I just... woke up," she replied gleefully. She plopped onto his bed and hugged his arm. "And Rhys, I slept so well! What about you?"

"I... don't know. I just slept." Rhys gazed at his sister in thought. Her usually stoic face was bright and eager. Though they had faced death multiple times the day prior, it seemed this one simple realization about sleep had become their saving grace. "We should try to find some different clothes today." He pulled the pack to them with his foot and began going through it. "There really isn't anything here pertaining to clothing other than a few blouses."

"I want one of the soft ones," said Alina, pulling out a cream, long-sleeved blouse. Rhys ignored her as she unceremoniously stripped out of her light gray uniform top, slipped on the blouse, and began rolling the oversized sleeves. "Will you change?"

"No," replied Rhys. "I'm fine."

Alina shrugged, tucked her blouse into her slacks, and bounced over to the window. "You really should come see this. I've been looking at it since I woke up."

"I don't remember a window being here," mused Rhys, standing. He straightened his sleeves and ruffled his hair into place.

Alina stood on her tiptoes. "It was closed."

Rhys leaned around her. Before him was a vast expanse of emerald water. Overhead, a cloudless, azure sky. "Pathos, I thought historical documents indicated that... Earth was deemed uninhabitable because of radiation levels and a lack of resources."

"Yes, the documentation I have access to states this," replied Pathos. "Unanimously, historical data indicates that humanity was in danger of destroying itself. Resources such as food, clean water, and energy were running low. Additionally, all documents are undivided when it comes to the presence of geographical anomalies. This is unmistakable."

"Something happened to the planet," said Alina, pulling away from the window to sit down on her bed.

"Unfortunately, most of the historical records we have that document the exodus from Earth are either conflicting or missing," said Logos. "As you know, the people on Caelestis acknowledge this absence of information, so it is not as if it is intentionally being hidden."

Rhys leaned into the window to see down the side of their vessel but could discern only water. "Has anyone attempted to retrieve us today?"

"The woman, Kallen, stopped by at dawn," reported Pathos, "however, I did not feel you were in danger, so I did not wake you."

"That's fine. I didn't—Wait, where are you going?"

Alina, who had the sliding door propped open, looked back at him innocently. "Out."

Rhys kicked the pack under the bed and hurried after her. The hallway was a completely different scene from the previous night. Where it had been cold, narrow, and unwelcoming just hours ago, Rhys now found it warm and bright. All of the rooms that had been dark the night before now exuded sunlight from their open windows.

As Alina led the way, Rhys followed, glancing into each of the rooms. In the other cabin, he found crew members snoring softly. It wasn't until they reached the galley that they finally heard soft murmurs of conversation. Without hesitation, Alina strode in.

Kashim and another man barred their entry. Behind them was Kallen and Vinz, the Overseer.

"Did you door lock?" growled Vinz. Kallen started to stand, but Vinz motioned for her to remain seated. "Kashim, Lyruc," said the

Overseer. The two men stepped aside to allow Alina and Rhys entry and then disappeared into the hallway.

"How you feel?" asked Kallen. The question was directed more toward Alina than Rhys.

Rhys gazed at the young woman. It was as if he were staring at a completely different person. No longer was she covered in the thick, black paste. Her skin was smooth and tan. Her eyes, though dark in color, were intelligent and warm. She was slender but not like Alina. She had muscle which was made apparent by the sleeveless blouse she wore. Her raven-colored hair was short in the back and long in the front, with wispy bangs that framed her face. A tendril of hair was adorned with a decorative coil of leather. Rhys noted the dirty gloves dangling from her pants pocket.

Alina nodded. "Good. Thank you." There were two long tables in the galley made of the same mysterious brown material that comprised certain parts of the ship. Alina sat beside Kallen and ran her hand over the table's glossy surface. "What is this?"

"A table," replied Kallen.

Alina looked at Rhys who attempted to clarify. "No, what… What is this made—"

"Wood," interrupted Vinz, his eyes on Rhys.

"Wood," repeated Alina. "What is wood?"

"From trees," said Kallen. "Do you know trees?"

The tall vegetation from earlier, explained Pathos.

Pathos, what's your translation rate? asked Rhys. *Do you have enough data to convert it to knowledge? We need to be able to speak competently.*

My vocabulary is horrifically lacking, however, the information Logos and I have acquired should give you enough support to communicate effectively.

Rhys bowed his head politely. "Please, one minute." He saw Kallen exchange looks with Vinz. *Alina, download the linguistic data Logos has prepared for you. We need to be able to communicate.*

Initializing linguistic collection, murmured Pathos. *Records indicate that the language derives from another that once existed long ago. Pairing data. Analysis complete. Collection complete. Initiating installation of basic Earth language grammar, syntax, vocabulary, and tones. Installation complete.*

Thank you, Pathos, said Rhys. He glanced at Alina who was still staring blankly at the table before them. "Thank you for your time," said Rhys.

"What's going on?" asked Kallen.

"Language acquisition," replied Alina. She smiled at Rhys.

"Overseer," said Rhys, "I am Rhys Falkrow. This is my younger sister, Alina Falkrow. We are from the black sky overhead."

"I know where you're from," Vinz replied, leaning forward on his arms. "What I want to know is how did you do that?"

Rhys' brain strained to comprehend the foreign language. This was going to take practice. "We... uh... " Rhys turned his head and pointed to his AI. "This is me. This is my... "

We're still missing key vocabulary, explained Pathos. *They may not even have words for our technology.*

"It's a machine," said Vinz.

"No. A computer." Alina gazed at the Overseer. "A machine requires effort. This is a computer; it thinks by itself."

"It acquired our language so quickly?" asked Vinz. "What powers it?"

"Us," replied Rhys. Seeing the pure expression of excitement on Kallen's face, he asked, "What?"

"Calm yourself. You can ask them about it later," said Vinz. The Overseer sat back to survey them. "We're on our way to New Arbroath, our home port. We'll be there in two days' time."

"Can you explain Earth's situation? Our records indicate that Earth should no longer be inhabitable." Rhys looked between Kallen and Vinz. "We don't understand."

Vinz stood and shuffled out from behind the table. "I haven't the time to waste on a history lesson." At the doorway, he looked back at Kallen. "Watch over them. They need to dye before we get to port."

Rhys leapt up, his firearm charging; its barrel glowed a faint orange. To his surprise, Alina withdrew a knife from her pocket, grabbed Kallen, and held the knife to the young woman's throat.

"He said *dye*—to dye your hair! To color your hair!" said Kallen frantically. "To color your hair!"

Vinz glanced between them, unfazed, and without another word, left the galley.

Alina pulled away from Kallen. With an apologetic look, she sheathed the knife and returned it to her pocket. Rhys peered at Kallen in confusion. "Color our hair?"

"Your hair color is bright." Kallen touched Alina's platinum locks. "You'll bring attention. We don't want attention."

"No one here has uh... " Alina thought for the word. "Light hair?"

"No." Kallen leaned against the table. "Light hair and light eyes are rare. They can only be found in certain areas."

"The Overseer has light eyes," mused Rhys.

"And he has many scars," Kallencountered. "I will help you before we return to port—"

Suddenly, the entire vessel lurched, causing the galley to tilt violently. With a cry of surprise, Rhys slid into the hallway and hit the wall hard. Rubbing the back of his head, he scrambled to his knees in time to see crew members pouring from the cabins. He dove back into the galley doorway. More than one of the men glanced at Rhys as they passed to enter the bridge.

I have to know what's going on! he told Alina. Before Kallen could say anything, Rhys left the galley and took the stairs to the bridge two at a time.

"Let's go! Let's go! I want this ship moving!" roared Vinz, pacing the helm. "Now! Before they come back around!"

"Do we need to launch?" asked Kashim.

"Wait." Vince moved to the front of the bridge and looked out the glass screen. "I want a count. How many are we dealing with?"

Rhys' newly acquired linguistic abilities were barely keeping up with the flurry of commands, responses, and reports.

"Power conduits are green. Output at 98 percent," reported a man seated at the front of the bridge.

"Good, see to—"

As Vinz spoke, a golden blur passed over the vessel and darted into the sky. The Overseer leaned forward to watch as the mysterious object soared ever higher. After a moment, he slammed his fist onto the instrument deck.

"Kashim, you and Hodge, launch. Our radar isn't going to pick up sunboards." Kashim and Hodge left the bridge. "Cannons at the ready. No gunners. Leave the sunboards to Kashim and Hodge." Vinz pulled a pipe down from overhead and unlatched the metal piece covering its end. "Kallen, get to the forward hatch. Kashim and Hodge are launching." With force, he snapped the communication pipe back into the ceiling and turned for his chair. Only then did he spot Rhys. "No one said you could be up here."

"What's going on?" asked Rhys. "What was that thing?" He motioned to the glass. "It flew."

"Would someone please get this child off the bridge?" asked Vinz.

"Are we being attacked?" continued Rhys. "Who is attacking?" Rhys leaned forward to see out the glass paneling. He found nothing but blue skies and green waters. What was going on? Did he need to do something?

"Andy, come to a halt. As soon as Kashim and Hodge launch, bring us to standard." Vinz side-glanced at Rhys. "Get off my bridge."

"Tell me what's going on," demanded Rhys. All chatter on the bridge died and suddenly everyone was awaiting the Overseer's reply. "What just flew by?"

Vinz stood with a quiet sigh. "I will tell you once more—get off my bridge."

"Tell me what's going on!"

Before Rhys could finish his command, Vinz stepped into him. Nose-to-nose, the Overseer gazed at Rhys.

Combat data analyzed, began Pathos. *Initiating—*

No. Leave it, ordered Rhys. *I don't need another download.*

The power in the man's gaze was frightening. "This is my ship," Vinz asserted. "While you are on it, I am in command. Do you understand?" Rhys nodded. Vinz shoved him toward the door and turned to the others. "Kashim and Hodge?"

"They're launching now," reported another man. Rhys glanced over his shoulder in time to see two people appear along the bow of the ship. Forgetting his confrontation with Vinz, Rhys leaned forward and squinted to better focus on the figures. It looked as though they were riding the water just ahead of the ship.

What are they? asked Rhys. *Pathos?*

They appear to be boards comprised of a free-rotating universal joint, a sail, and a two-sided boom, informed Pathos. *The sail, however, does not match the historic information I have in my records. Their sails seem to be made of a special, solar paneling, hence the gold sheen.*

They've harnessed the sun's energy.

Perhaps these are what the Overseer was referring to as 'sunboards?'

What's their purpose though?

After a cursory analysis of the equipment stationed on the bridge, I posit that the purpose of the sunboards is to act as surveillance.

Rhys tilted his head, intrigued. *So they can fly?*

It would seem so.

Feeling a tugging on his shirt, Rhys looked back at Vinz who leveled a look of cold anger. Realizing he had overstepped his bounds, Rhys started for the door. "Forward hatch is closed. Bringing the ship to standard speed," said the man named Andy. Rhys rejoined Alina.

"Is it true?" gasped Alina who had been waiting at the bottom of the stairs. "They can fly?"

Rhys jumped down the stairs and landed next to her. "They can," he breathed. "Did Kallen—"

A force they knew all too well bore down on them, g-force. Rhys grabbed Alina, and together they hit the hallway wall. The ship was accelerating—hard. Before Rhys could grab hold of a doorway for support, they slid farther down the hallway.

Alina laughed in sheer glee; Rhys stared at the ceiling in awe. Humans were so amazing.

Although Rhys had heard Vinz give the order to prepare the ship's cannons, he never heard them. For what seemed like an eternity, Rhys and Alina sat in the hallway, their backs pressed into the galley doorway frame. He wondered what had happened. Numerous times Pathos and Logos attempted to report, but they were not able to with certainty accurately interpret the conflict.

"Is this all because of us?" wondered Alina. "Did we cause all of this?"

For the next hour, they saw no one. No crew members left the bridge; Kallen didn't reappear, and no one came to check on them. They were completely alone. After a while of sitting together, Alina pulled Rhys to his feet and motioned that they should go to their bunks. Rhys begrudgingly followed her.

It wasn't until midday that they heard anyone in the hallway. While Rhys had been reviewing the pack's contents and going through the recorded historical data Pathos had to offer, Alina had spent her time napping. Careful not to wake her, Rhys slipped out of their cabin. It seemed the crew was gathering in the galley. Curious, Rhys padded down the hallway.

"I told you not to push your unit," said Kallen. For the first time, she sounded angry. The power in her voice surprised Rhys. "The repairs I made from the other day were tentative. That stunt you pulled has undone all of my work!"

"What was I supposed to do?" snapped Hodge. "They were going to ram me."

"Then you should have let them ram you!"

"Enough," murmured Vinz. "Andy, what was our final energy usage?"

"We weren't fully charged from yesterday's excursion, so the sudden launch altered the energy consumption," replied Andy.

"Where does that put us?"

"We are down to 53 percent," came the response.

Vinz sighed. "Start charging immediately."

"Yeah."

"Kallen, how badly was Hodge's unit damaged?"

"It's not flyable if that's what you're asking," said Kallen. "He can surf, but that's it. The connection between the solar paneling and the energy converter is fried."

"So, we have one unit left?" mused Vinz.

"We could see if our newcomers can help... " offered Kallen. The hesitancy in her voice told Rhys that she was bringing up a sensitive subject.

"I don't know enough about them to let them yet," replied Vinz. "They've learned our language too quickly. And the boy... "

"He's protecting his sister," said Hodge. "I'd act the same way for my kin."

"Then let me ask Alina for help," suggested Kallen. "She seems bright. I'm sure either of them would be able—"

"No. As long as they have that black technology, we can't trust them," interrupted Vinz.

"You said it earlier, didn't you? We need more men!"

"Kallen." Vinz shut her down. "Remember, we did not take them because we needed more hands."

"I'm sure there are more," said Andy, "at their crash site. You know the Pantaraks will be searching the area thoroughly."

"But Rhys said they were the only survivors," replied Kallen.

"I'm sure there are others," agreed Vinz. "At the moment, however, we can only go by what those two have said. Someone, get me one of those machines they wear. I want to study the techn—"

"You can't." Rhys stepped into the doorway, and the entire crew looked at him. "You can't take our AIs."

Vinz gazed at him from the far side of the galley. "And you're going to stop me?"

Rhys held the man's gaze. "No. But it's my understanding that you want us alive, yes? If our AI is taken from us, we die."

"Can you eject it?" asked Vinz.

"Why do you need it?"

Before Vinz could reply, Kallen pushed her way between them. "Vinz is the leading expert on black technology. Much of the technology on this ship is because of him," she explained. "I am his apprentice."

Rhys looked between Vinz and Kallen and then shook his head. "I can't eject it. It's a... uh... "

"Biologically intertwined with Rhys," concluded Pathos.

"Pathos... " murmured Rhys. He wanted to limit the conversation his AI did with others.

Pathos, however, had a different understanding of the situation. The AI continued fluently. "When a human is born, they are injected with a substance that acts as a conduit. This substance grows and develops as the human does and soon becomes an integral part of their system, linking them to their computer. Weeks after birth, each child is matched to a specific type of computer. There are two types: Pathos and Logos. Each of these operates differently and learns as the child grows. The computer helps to dictate the human's thought processes, actions, and behaviors." Pathos paused. Rhys looked between Vinz and Kallen. Vinz appeared indifferent, however, Kallen was enthralled. "Because every human has a computer, they are able to collectively produce, process, develop, and manage technologies that would otherwise be difficult to comprehend."

"Thank you, Pathos... " murmured Rhys in his native tongue.

"Who decides the type of computer you receive?" asked Hodge, his arms folded across his chest. "I don't understand what the purpose is."

"The Assessor determines which computer each person receives. Their analysis is based upon each human's genetic code and those of their parents," explained Pathos. "The purpose of the computers is to connect people. The computers not only enable humans to work longer but to think more critically. All learned data and information is turned into knowledge and linked to the Core. At night, humans connect to the Core and upload the information they have learned that day. In addition, they download information others within their prescribed departments have acquired. In this fashion, ideas, concepts, and hypotheses become a collective product ensuring that humanity's advancement never slows."

"Is this true?" whispered Kallen, looking at Rhys.

Rhys had not intended for Pathos to release so much information, but he trusted his AI. Perhaps it was searching for answers just like he was. "Yes," he murmured. "Last night was the first night in our lives to sleep without being connected to the Core."

"Back to work, everyone," murmured Vinz. "Notify me once we're out of Pantarak territory."

As the galley cleared, Rhys remained silent. He was conflicted. Logic told him to stay quiet. The less they knew about him, the better. But something else told him that in order to survive, they needed to communicate and learn about each other. Perhaps Pathos had sensed this as well.

Those who remained were Vinz, Hodge, and Kallen. "Was all of that true?" Kallen asked again.

Rhys opened his mouth to reply, however, Vinz beat him to it. "You're just like us… products of our society." The man's gaze was set somewhere in the distance. Vinz leaned against the table. "Your computer mentioned the idea of a prescribed department—what did it mean?"

"We're each assigned to a department within the colony," replied Rhys.

"And you? What department were you assigned to?"

"Design and Engineering."

"And the girl?" asked Vinz.

"Genetic Manipulation and Modification."

"What's that?" asked Kallen excitedly. "Building things?"

Vinz leaned on the table. "Kallen, Hodge. Could you leave us for a moment?"

The smile on Kallen's face faded and she frowned. "You can't keep him to yourself."

Vinz motioned for them to leave. Disappointment coloring her face, Kallen shuffled from the galley. Hodge followed and slid the door closed behind him. Uncomfortable, Rhys fidgeted.

Vinz looked at Rhys solemnly. "I'm going to tell this to you straight because I don't want you two finding trouble once we're in port. Your kind is not welcome among most societies on Earth—at least the ones I've come across. Your appearance is too different; you're too foreign. Blue eyes and silver hair stand out here and garner unwanted attention."

"You sound as though you've met others like us before," muttered Rhys.

Vinz straightened himself. "Kallen will dye your hair before we reach port. Starting now, I don't want your computers to speak aloud. You are not to share with anyone anything about your technology or about your home. Keep information about your family, job, and social life private. If anyone asks, you're a relative of mine. Ask that they defer all questions to me."

"What are we running from? I don't understand."

"Pantaraks," replied Vinz. "People who worship the stars. Like us, they saw your ship crash. Throughout history, others of your kind have crash-landed on Earth. The Pantaraks worship them as white gods."

"And how are you and your people any different?" asked Rhys.

Vinz met Rhys' gaze. "Because I'm one of you." He turned his head slightly and ran his fingers along the hairline along his neck. Though it was hardly discernible, Rhys saw it—the slight blond sheen that shone through the black dye and caught the sunlight.

"You're... " Rhys stared openly.

Vinz straightened himself. "We are not welcome here. We are the unknown. We bring intelligence, technology, logic, and science. We bring a sign that humans can and have changed."

"How... I don't... " Rhys ruffled his hair in confused amazement. "You don't have an artificial... I mean, a computer, do you?"

"No, my lineage goes back further than that. Rhys, I want to make something perfectly clear—you are always safe on this ship. Every person onboard knows what I am and what I'm—"

"Which is what?"

Vinz held his hand out. "Sail with us and find out."

Rhys gazed at him. What game was the Overseer playing? *Was* there even a game? Perhaps he could be trusted. He had saved them from the Pantaraks, whoever those were. They shared the same lineage as well. Hesitantly, Rhys took Vinz's hand and they shook.

"Welcome aboard *Themis*," said Vinz.

Rhys nodded, though he didn't feel the gratitude that perhaps he should have.

"Please keep this conversation between just us," said Vinz. "Word travels quickly in port."

"Right... So, what is it that we're after?" asked Rhys.

Vinz clapped him on the shoulder and started for the door. "To bring peace to this hellish world." He opened the door and stood in the doorway. "You should get some more rest. I'm sure there will be more Pantarak attacks later this afternoon." And with that, Vinz left the galley.

5
THEMIS AND ABROAD

RHYS DID AS HE WAS told and returned to his cabin. Having some trouble clearing his mind, he lay down. Part of him really wanted to trust Vinz, but what human was foolish enough to believe that, in a place like this, peace could ever be attained? He admitted that it was possible on Caelestis, but the colony was different.

From inception, humans were given few decisions so as to help them not make mistakes. From genes to names to individual AIs—every aspect of their lives was carefully chosen for them. Only after they completed their exams were they given some choice as to what department they would enter, and even then, their options were limited according to their exam scores and the colony's departmental needs.

Caelestis lived in harmony. Its distribution of resources, especially food, though not equal, was extremely fair. Those working in laboratories required less energy and thus less food. For this reason, many who worked in the theoretical sciences eventually became thinner but not malnourished. Alina was a prime specimen. Though well-nourished, she was thin, whereas Rhys was well-toned and strong. He could have taken a less labor-intensive job in a quiet department, but he didn't. He worked with machines. He pushed crates to and from zero-gravity areas, regularly navigated the hangars and warehouses using self-propulsion, and worked on parts in artificial gravity labs.

Despite his lean frame, gangly arms, and sleek muscles, compared to the men on Earth, Rhys was sure he appeared slender, fragile. With the exception of Vinz, Rhys was half the size of the men onboard both in height and weight.

Rhys laid his arm over his eyes to block out the harsh sunlight beating in through the window. Eventually, he rolled his back to the sun and stared at the wall.

The Pantaraks worshipped the stars. That didn't sound so bad. After all, on Caelestis man still stared out at the dark abyss and wondered with awe what was out there. Worshipping burning balls of gas billions of miles away was what his ancestors once did. The concept, though ridiculous, wasn't evil. Vinz obviously thought otherwise.

What did the Overseer and the others know that Rhys didn't? Why had there been such a mad flailing from both sides to reach Rhys and Alina? Was it possible they had landed in the middle of a war and been picked up by the wrong side? What if Vinz's idea of spreading peace was a euphemism for extermination?

After reviewing all that had happened in the past 48 hours, Rhys felt a profound exhaustion blanket him and, without a second thought, he fell asleep.

Sometime later, Alina's voice woke him from his slumber. Rhys breathed deeply and with heavy eyes rolled over to sleepily greet his sister. His gaze fell on a young woman with long black hair and large, blue eyes. Rhys stared at his sister, his mouth open in slight confusion.

Alina bashfully sat along the edge of his bed. "How strange do I look?"

Rhys sat up and looked her over once more. "You're beautiful, Sister," he said. Alina beamed. "It suits you."

"It didn't take long. Kallen does it for Vinz as we—"

Realizing she had said something they had not yet spoken about—Vinz's heritage—she fell silent. Rhys nudged her. "I know."

"About Vinz?"

Rhys nodded. "What did Kallen tell you?"

Alina stood and went to the window. It was midafternoon and the sun was high in the sky. "Vinz is one of us," Alina said. She pulled her freshly dyed hair over her shoulder and began braiding it. "Well… not pure, but… " She sighed softly. "His parents were killed when he was young. His mother was a doctor. At least, I think that's what she was. Kallen gave me a different name, but the meaning was the same." Alina pulled a hair tie from her pocket and tied her braid off. "She was killed, as was his father."

"What happened?"

"The Pantaraks killed them. That's all Kallen told me." Alina sat on her bed and smiled incredulously. "The entire story is so ridiculous. I mean, who kills in the name of religion?"

"Did Kallen say that's what happened?"

"She indicated that an old religion guides the Pantaraks to seek out Fallen Stars—our people." She laughed grimly. "Rhys, we are *so* far from home."

Perturbed by Alina's news, Rhys studied his hands. So that's what it was. Religion. The word was foreign to him. On Caelestis, there was sometimes talk of whether a higher deity presided over the universe, but the idea of organized religion did not promote human technological advancement. For that reason alone, religion was a nearly forgotten concept.

"At any rate," continued Alina, "there's not much more to the story. Kallen spoke on a variety of topics but nothing of consequence."

"Kallen is rather loquacious around you," mused Rhys.

Alina shrugged. "I like her. She's loud."

"Loud?"

"Everyone in the labs always spoke quietly. The atmosphere was forever one of grave seriousness or silent contemplation. I like Kallen. She's loud and says what she thinks. I need to do that more."

"When have you ever *not* done that?"

Alina frowned good-naturedly and then looked up at the window. Though they had been speaking in their native tongue already, Rhys felt Alina trigger their internal communication link. *You should know, there's a piece of technology in the forward hatch that Kallen's been working on. She mentioned it in passing, but while I was down there, I caught a glimpse of it.*

And?

Alina shrugged. *I have no idea what it is.*

And the material?

Made using very fine instruments and materials available only in space.

Rhys sighed. *That's a very... ambiguous explanation.*

Of course, it is! I'm not an engineer! I couldn't even tell you what our spacecraft was made of. "Kallen will be looking to dye your hair soon."

"Alina, when you're not with me, stay with Kallen," said Rhys, standing.

"She's the only one I feel safe around." Alina rose and reached between them to adjust his collar. "I don't like being such a weak individual." She ruffled his hair into place. "Perhaps I should have gone into engineering like you. At least I would have gotten to b—"

A deep rumble from outside the ship reverberated through their cabin. Both dashed to the porthole to find a smoking and fiery wreckage sinking into the sea. Without another word, Rhys turned on heel and ran for the bridge; Alina followed.

The entire crew except Hodge was on the bridge. Loitering in the doorway, Rhys looked for Vinz. "What's going on?"

"Pantaraks," replied Vinz, gaze unwaveringly set on the forward instruments. "Kallen, any luck?"

Kallen, who sat in Vinz's chair, shook her head. "None. I don't have the parts necessary to fix the sunboard."

"Kyo, how many more do we have incoming?" asked the Overseer, shifting his gaze to his crew members. Taking this as their cue, everyone returned to work. Rhys exchanged subtle looks with Alina.

"I'm only picking up one airship to our east," replied Kyo, one of the ship's apparent helmsmen. "But there's no way to know how many sunboards are in the air."

"And how far are we from port?"

"About 96 liretems."

"And where's Hodge?" asked Vinz thoughtfully.

Kyo leaned forward and looked out the glass pane. "Twenty to port. He's prepared to bring the next one into range."

Vinz nodded. "Do it. We can't afford to leave any in the air."

Kyo began tapping a switch on the instrument board in a rhythmic pattern. After a moment, Hodge's sunboard crossed over the bow of *Themis* and disappeared.

"Lyruc, ready the next shot," instructed Vinz, pacing.

"Hodge is coming down starboard," Kyo announced.

"Tracking," replied Lyruc, studying the dim screen before him. "Locked on."

"Fire at will," said Vinz. A loud *thwack* reverberated throughout the bridge, and *Themis* quivered.

"Direct hit," called Lyruc.

"They're withdrawing," Kyo reported. "Enemy ship is changing trajectory."

"Don't give chase." Vinz leaned forward to peer out the glass paneling. "Let them withdraw. Our priority is reaching New Arbroath."

Kallen leapt up to leave the bridge.

"Leave him," ordered Vinz. "I want Hodge to scout ahead. Kyo, relay the message. Kallen, once we're sure the enemy is no longer in range, go to the upper deck and check that we didn't incur any serious damage. Andy, bring us to full speed. The Pantaraks are too close to New Arbroath."

Hands on their arms, Kallen ushered Rhys and Alina from the bridge. At the bottom of the stairs, she parted from them and disappeared outside the ship. In silence, Rhys and Alina returned to the galley and sat beside one another.

Half an hour passed before Kallen reappeared with Hodge who was sweating profusely and still panting. The man's tan face and arms were thick with drying salt. Without a word, Hodge crossed the galley and drank deeply from a jug of water.

"He's fine," said Kallen, seeing Rhys and Alina's worried looks. "Just tired." As if nothing had happened, Kallen casually sat across from Rhys and leaned back in her chair. Studying him, she asked, "You're an engineer, right?"

"Yes," Rhys replied uncertainly.

Her gaze enchanting. "How are you with machines?"

"Why?" interjected Alina.

Kallen folded her arms. "We're one sunboard down."

"Hodge broke it," Alina concluded slowly. Rhys expected some sort of scoffing response from Hodge, but the young man was bent over the galley sink, seemingly unaware of their conversation.

"Right." She nodded to Rhys. "I want you to look at it."

"But I thought you said you're missing parts to repair it," replied Alina.

"I did, but maybe I missed something."

"Unlikely," murmured Alina. She glanced at Rhys. "I know that Rhys is very tired. I have never seen him sleep so much. Perhaps later?"

I don't mind looking at it, muttered Rhys.

I'm not keen on giving them anything until we have more information, replied Alina.

Kallen looked between them. She clearly knew something was going on, but she shrugged. "That's fine." She threw a flippant hand toward Rhys. "Shall we dye your hair?"

"Shall? I don't understand this word," replied Rhys.

"Let's dye your hair," Kallen corrected.

"I want to see this," said Alina, pulling Rhys toward the door. With Kallen in the lead, they left the galley and started down the hallway. Instead of taking the stairs up to the bridge, she stepped around the staircase and pushed open the door to the hangar. "There are two ways to enter the forward hatch," explained Alina. "Via the outside staircase and through this door."

The forward hatch was lit well as opposed to the other night. He found the room surprisingly bright and airy with windows decorating both the port and starboard walls of the tall cabin. To his immediate right were crates, boxes, and barrels as well as a variety of tools, small weaponry, and the outer door. Beside the crates was a machine partially covered by a drop cloth.

That's our technology, Alina remarked.

Rhys glanced at the machine furtively so as not to draw Kallen's attention and then gazed about. Overhead hung two sunboards chained to a pulley system. The dinghy from earlier was strapped on the wall above the hatch.

Yawning, Kallen went to the nearest crate and withdrew a wooden mug of black goop. She stirred it viciously with what appeared to be a wide brush and then gestured to Rhys. "Sit please." He seated himself cross-legged on the floor and looked up at the mug. "And hold your breath," added Kallen. "This smells." Rhys looked at Alina. He expected her to be smiling at him, however, her gaze was set on the mysterious machine.

Figure out what it is, he said.

I'm trying, came his sister's sharp response.

Rhys grimaced as he felt the cool goop drop onto his scalp. A noxious odor wafted over his face. He coughed, and Kallen chuckled. "I told you to hold your breath." Rhys opened his mouth and proceeded to breathe in that manner. "Your hair will be much easier than Alina's." Kallen drew his silver hair to the top of his head and rolled the goop over his scalp.

"Do you do this often for Vinz?" asked Rhys. Never had anyone laid hands on him in such a manner.

"Yes. I tell him that no one onboard cares what color his hair is, but... so much has happened to him that he can't believe anything else." Kallen traced her fingers along Rhys' hairline and up along his ears. Carefully she pulled the hair near Pathos away and upward. "Besides, he worries what those in port will think."

"Surely they know though," replied Alina. "He has light eyes."

"They may suspect, but no one is brave enough to confront him. Not after everything he's done for them." Kallen added more dye and then circled around and knelt before him. With steady hands, she applied a line of the dye to his eyebrows. "This ship acts as one of the major deterrents for Pantaraks. When it's in port, Pantaraks don't draw near."

"Why?" asked Alina.

"Because we're the best. Kashim and Hodge—I don't know of any other sunboarders who can fly like them. They do surveillance and exploratory assignments. Andy is an expert cartographer. He makes our maps, plots our courses, and pilots the ship. Lyruc is in charge of the ship's weaponry. Kyo assists Andy in energy management and consumption, though his primary job is to analyze the data provided by surveillance and monitor radar and the other bridge instruments. Vinz is the Overseer. He built this ship and knows it from bow to stern." Kallen laughed. "And I'm the chief mechanic. He and I work together to keep *Themis* running."

"*Themis?*"

"The ship's name," explained Kallen. "It's a god from an ancient religion or… something. I don't know. Vinz never explained it to me."

Pathos? asked Rhys.

Themis: an ancient Greek Titaness who was said to have been the personification of divine law and order.

That's an odd name for a ship, mused Alina.

I suspect there's more to Vinz than meets the eye, Rhys replied.

"Are you two talking to one another?" asked Kallen.

"Uh, yes," replied Alina. "How did you know?"

Kallen wiped her hands on a towel slung over a nearby crate and sat on a barrel. "When you two speak using your computers, both of you have strange expressions on your faces. It's like, facial expressions you'd make for a normal conversation but no words are heard." Kallen chuckled. "It's funny to watch. Oh, Rhys—that has to stay on you for about half an hour." She leaned on her knees. "So what were you talking about?"

"We were wondering if you could tell us more about your world," said Alina. "What is it like?"

Kallen leaned back and gazed about the forward hatch in thought. "Describe your world… " She laughed softly and looked at Rhys. "That's easier said than done."

"What happened to Earth after the exodus?" prompted Rhys. Alina nodded enthusiastically to show her approval of his question.

"Ahhh." Kallen thought for a long moment and then said, "I don't know much about history. Very few common people actually do. Only those who are rich or powerful have access to historical documents and information. And even then… many of our records have been lost. I do know that just before the exodus, Earth experienced some major environmental changes that ultimately changed its climate."

"Like what?"

"Oh, I don't know. Of course, everyone has their own theories— humans caused it, a deity caused it, war caused it, volcanoes caused it. Whatever the case… that's how Earth ended up like it is today."

"Which is how?" asked Alina. "Our experience here on Earth thus far has not been a very informative one. We've spent the majority of our time attempting the primal instinct of survival."

Kallen blinked at her and then shook her head incredulously. "Ehhh, it's very hot here." She thought and then added, "You two are going to have a hard time acclimating."

"I haven't been hot," admitted Rhys.

Kallen shook her head. "At night, it's very pleasant. During the day though… You two must *always* keep your skin covered. Every piece of it."

"But… you just said it's very hot," said Alina. "I don't understand. Wouldn't the excessive temperatures require that we wear less clothing to allow the effects of perspiration to be felt?"

"Yes, you will see many people who wear very little, however, you two don't get to do that." Kallen held her arm out and then motioned for Alina to do the same. "Do you see how different our skin is? The darker you are, the better chance you have at surviving the sun." Kallen pointed to Alina's pale, alabaster skin. "Your skin will burn. Even the top of your head where your hair is will burn." Kallen lowered her arm. "Vinz has the same problem. He isn't quite as fair as you two, but his skin is light enough that he burns if he stays in the sunlight for too long."

"Your skin—what do you have covering it?" asked Alina, touching Kallen's arm. "It's… not normal… "

Kallen laughed. "I can't believe no one's told you yet. We're born with it. Our second skin."

"What is its function?" asked Rhys, joining them. Curious, he also touched Kallen's arm. "It's… slick."

Kallen nodded. "Because it's so hot here, it helps us retain water and nutrition for longer periods of time. You two don't have it. Neither does Vinz."

"So, it allows you to go for longer periods of time without drinking or eating?"

Kallen nodded. "As we age, the second skin grows thinner and weaker. So, for instance, those in our town who are very old must eat twice a day! Can you imagine?" Rhys and Alina exchanged looks. Kallen quieted herself. "Right... you *do* eat like that... Which, by the way, aren't you hungry? I haven't seen either of you eat since we brought you aboard."

"We have some supplies in our emergency pack," said Rhys. "So, the second skin was developed to help humans survive here? If you have the resources, why not just eat and drink?"

"Earth's resources aren't slim," said Kallen, "but why waste them?"

"So, how long can you go without either?" asked Alina.

"The average is about three days," Kallen replied. She thought and then added, "It's different for everyone. The young and old eat more often, but the majority of healthy adults can go for about three days without food or water."

"And still function properly?" asked Rhys incredulously.

Kallen nodded. "I haven't eaten in... Today would be day four."

"Don't you feel dehydrated though, or sick or weak?"

"Maybe a little tired." Kallen shrugged. "We have food and water if you two ever need it. Don't force yourselves to suffer just to fit in." Kallen motioned upward to the bridge. "Vinz eats throughout the day. When he's not on the ship, he carries a canteen of water with him at all times. You may look into doing that as well." Kallen scrutinized Alina's outfit. "We have some spare clothes. They may be a bit large, but you'll need them. Your clothes won't protect you for long in the sun. Your hands will always be exposed as well as your neck, face, and head."

"What will we do once we're in port?" Rhys leaned against the wall. "What's there?"

Kallen's face became solemn. "Some of our people were captured four days ago by Pantaraks. We were notified and asked to investigate. By chance, your aircraft crashed near where we were patroling."

Hesitantly—for he knew the answer—Rhys asked, "Did you find them?"

Kallen grew grim. "Only after tracking you two."

"The bodies in the trees... " murmured Alina.

"We had to leave them," Kallen explained darkly. "You two were more important."

Of course, this very poignant statement warranted intense questioning, but Rhys remained silent. He needed to know who the

Pantaraks were, *what* they were. He needed to look one in the eye to determine for himself the evil residing within these people.

"Come on," said Kallen after a long moment. It was obvious she was trying to keep her emotions in check. "Let's get that off you."

After rinsing the noxious paste from his hair—and being silently mocked by Alina for his new black locks—Rhys followed Kallen to her room. He was surprised to find that five others, presumably the rest of the crew, also called the large cabin their quarters. For several minutes, she tore through chests and duffle bags. She pushed armfuls of clothes aside and even sat on her bunk to think. It was Alina who finally broke the quiet.

"What are these?" Alina held up a small, tightly bundled pack of soft, brown pieces of cloth. She gazed at them in confusion. "They don't look like the others."

Kallen stared at her for a long moment before glancing at Rhys uncomfortably. "They're underpants for when, ehhhh... you're bleeding." Rhys, not understanding, shook his head. Alina examined the bundle further. "*Alina...* for when *you're* bleeding."

"Bleeding?"

The expression on Kallen's face changed to one of intense curiosity. "How old are you?"

"Sixteen."

"Have you started bleeding?"

Alina chuckled nervously. "Why would I want to bleed? That sounds painful."

Kallen looked at Rhys who, seeing that this was an important topic, silently asked Alina to direct her full attention to Kallen. His sister put down the "underpants" and looked at Kallen innocently. "Does the word 'menstruation' mean anything to you?" asked Kallen.

Pathos? asked Rhys.

Menstruation: a process the female body undergoes once puberty is reached. Menstruation is the discharging of blood and other materials from the uterus in preparation for pregnancy. Throughout history, female humans on Earth have menstruated in intervals following Earth's lunar cycles. Female humans residing on Caelestis, however, do not.

Rhys looked at Alina in utter confusion. She was obviously receiving the same information from Logos. *I don't understand,* said Rhys. *Why would the human body bleed for no reason? What's the purpose?*

To allow the female human to carry within her a child, replied Pathos. *On Caelestis, the Department of Extracorporeal Sciences was charged with the preservation and continuation of the human race, therefore, females born on the colony never experienced menstruation. In this way, humans could maintain a homeostatic environment wherein every individual could continue working and not be bothered by the production and rearing of children.*

"I... "

Rhys looked at Alina who was gazing glassy-eyed at the floor.

"I knew that we... " she murmured in their native tongue. After a long moment, she looked at Rhys. "I knew what we were doing, but I was never told we could reproduce... ourselves."

"Maybe we can't," muttered Rhys.

"Logos says that female humans my age typically have already been bleeding for several years. Why haven't I? I don't... understand. My body can make a baby?"

Rhys, not knowing what to say, only looked to Kallen. Despite the dark truth they had just uncovered, he felt hope, for the look on Kallen's face was not one of confusion or bewilderment, but of compassion. He didn't understand why this particular truth hurt Alina so badly, but Kallen obviously did.

Kallen reached over the piles of clothes and touched Alina's leg. "Everything will work out," she murmured. Alina nodded and returned the bundle to the piles of clothes around them.

For the next 45 minutes, Kallen attempted to cheer up Alina. She shared with them short, entertaining stories and explained how to wear certain pieces of clothing. Though it was an obvious attempt to busy Alina's mind, she was only partially successful. Alina, despite being receptive and attentive, remained sullen.

After a while, Rhys left the room to change into his new clothes—a pair of brown pants, shin-high leather boots, a cream-colored blouse with long sleeves, and a pale head scarf. Rhys dressed slowly in his cabin, examining each article of clothing.

You are bothered by Alina, said Pathos.

Rhys stripped out of his uniform shirt and tentatively slipped on the new blouse. Although worn, it fit well. It smelled faintly of mold and cologne. *I don't understand her reaction,* he said, pulling at the blouse to straighten it. *Logically speaking, Caelestis needed to be able to exercise some sort of population control, otherwise, resources would have been stretched thin. Why is she so upset?*

Alina's reaction, as a female human, is acceptable.

Rhys sat on his bunk in confusion. *What do you mean?*

All humans on Caelestis are sexually controlled through the Core. As you know, all knowledge in the Core is available for download and installation. Information concerning sexual reproduction, including certain aspects of anatomy, biology, and physiology, however, are accessible by only a few, primarily those who work in the Department of Extracorporeal Sciences. Additionally, the primal instinct to reproduce that is present in all living species—especially humans—is controlled through the Core. Nightly connection with the Core allows certain chemicals and hormones to be tweaked within each individual, allowing for complete control of human reproduction.

What happens when we stop linking to the Core? asked Rhys.

Hypothesis: the human body will once again activate those instincts and resume the search for a mate.

Hypothesis?

I do not have access to official records that would indicate otherwise.

Rhys dragged his pants on and then once more sat on his bunk. He stared at the rays of sunlight filtering through the porthole. For having shared so much information with the people of Caelestis, he knew less than he thought. He had never questioned the authority that had guided his day-to-day activities; everything was for the advancement of mankind. It wasn't his place to question, to wonder. Thousands of generations before him had done that so he wouldn't have to.

Why didn't you ever share this information with me when we were on Caelestis?

Pathos' reply was instantaneous. *The information was irrelevant.*

And it's relevant here?

Yes.

Rhys stuffed his feet into his boots, knocked the heels to settle the shoes, and then stood. *And Alina has reached the same conclusion?*

Uncertain. Logos has not transmitted any data in the last half hour.

Well, how am I—

"Approaching port! All hands to the bridge!" called Vinz over the communication pipe in the hallway. "New Arbroath is under attack."

Rhys rushed into the hallway. Kallen dashed from her cabin, said something over her shoulder to Alina, and then disappeared into the bridge. "Alina?" he called. She appeared in the doorway of Kallen's cabin, a wild expression on her face.

"The port, New Arbroath," she said.

Rhys motioned to her and together they went to the bridge. He expected the helm to be chaotic. He expected to hear reports coming in from Kyo or Vinz issuing commands. He expected to hear the engines slowing or to see Kallen slip below deck to the forward hatch. When they entered, however, he found the bridge silent. All eyes were set forward, trained on something beyond the windscreen.

Slowly, with Alina close behind, Rhys approached the front of the bridge and looked out. In the light of the afternoon sun, Dark, black smoke rose in thick columns to choke out the sun. Numerous buildings and trees were ablaze; rubble, debris, and wreckage were piled everywhere.

"What do you want to do?" asked Andy.

Vinz returned to his chair. "Kallen, prep the remaining sunboard. Hodge, you're scouting. Survey the area." Vinz looked at the lanky man. "Be careful." Hodge nodded, and he and Kallen disappeared below deck to the forward hatch. "Kashim, Lyruc—once Hodge has made his report, disembark. Check that the warehouse is intact. Take weapons and medical equipment with you." The two broad men hurried from the bridge to prepare. "Andy, once we're in port, can we dock?"

"Unsure." Andy leaned over his workstation and put a monocular to his eye. "It looks like docks three through nine have been damaged. I can't see one, two, ten, or eleven."

"If need be, we'll send Kashim and Lyruc out on the dinghy. Andy, Kyo. You two stay onboard."

"Of course," replied Andy. Kyo nodded.

Vinz stood, studied Rhys' freshly dyed hair, and then said, "Once we've determined the attack has passed, you two will come with me." He looked at Alina. "You've worked with doctors before? Studied medicine?"

"Not really, but I can learn it all very quickly," replied Alina. "I have access to the databa—"

"Do it. We'll need it," interrupted Vinz. He nodded to Rhys. "Come with me."

Rhys glanced at Alina. By the intense expression on her face, it seemed she was already attempting to download and install the necessary data and information to be of assistance. Rhys followed Vinz from the bridge to the forward hatch where Kallen and Hodge were preparing the final sunboard for launch.

The Overseer reached behind a stack of crates, withdrew a surprisingly heavy, black tool, and threw it at Rhys who only barely caught it. "Fire first, ask questions later."

Rhys studied the piece of equipment. It was made of silver and black metal, perhaps steel—he wasn't sure—and fit well in the palm of his hand. "I don't... " He looked at Vinz. "What is it?"

Vinz slung one of the black pieces of technology over his shoulder and started for the door. "A gun. Let's go."

Gun: any weapon which propels from a metal tube bullets, missiles, or other projectiles using an explosive reaction, explained Pathos. *A gun is the equivalent of your plasma beam firearm.*

"Rhys," whispered Kallen, urging him to follow Vinz. With a final glance at Hodge and Kallen, Rhys left the forward hatch and caught up with the Overseer who was returning to the bridge.

"Finished?" asked Vinz as Alina turned to meet them.

Alina nodded tiredly and then looked at Rhys. *I never want to do that again,* Alina murmured. *That was... way too much.*

Vinz pulled a communication pipe down. "Kallen, get Hodge out there!" With a flick of his wrist, the pipe whizzed back to the ceiling.

"We're in port," declared Andy, leaning against the polished wood before him. He gazed out the glass. "What's left of it... "

"Where're Kashim and Lyruc?"

"Here," replied Kashim, entering the bridge. Both he and Lyruc were armed.

"Be ready. You're off as soon as we find a place to dock," said Vinz.

"What do you want from us?" asked Alina. She braced against the Overseer's chair.

Vinz looked at Rhys. "Your job is to protect her while she provides medical support."

"Don't you have your own doctors?" asked Rhys.

"Not anymore," Vinz replied somberly.

As Andy docked the ship, Vinz left the bridge through the side door. "Put that on," advised Kyo, pointing to the headscarf Rhys had tied around his neck. "You'll be burnt."

Begrudgingly, Rhys wrapped it around his head and over his chin. He turned to Alina and helped her. As he tucked the cloth this way and then that, he murmured in their own language, "Can you do this?"

"I don't have a choice," she replied.

"You always have a choice," he said.

"If I have the power to make a difference, I should use it." She turned to Kyo. "Do you have medical supplies onboard?"

"Not ones that you'll need. I suspect Vinz will take you to the warehouse," said Kyo. He glanced out. "He's only using you right now because we're in a dire situation. Keep your eyes down. Don't let anyone get a good look at you."

"What did he mean 'not anymore?'" asked Alina. "I don't understand. Where are your doctors?"

Kyo pointed at a part of the flaming rubble farther inland.

Rhys gently pulled at Alina's arm. "Come on."

"Hodge is launching," announced Andy. "Kashim and Lyruc have disembarked."

Kyo picked up what appeared to be a radio. "This is Kyo. Over."

"We're en route to the warehouse," came Kashim's immediate response.

"Keep us updated."

Rhys glanced back at Kyo and Andy and then slipped outside using the door Vinz had. The air reeked of smoke and something else he knew instinctively though he had never before smelled—human flesh. He turned and began coughing violently, pulling his headscarf over his nose to block the horrific odor. Alina tucked herself into his shoulder but remained silent.

"Let's go!" shouted Vinz from the dock.

"I can't do it," murmured Rhys.

In the distance, a woman began sobbing, wailing. Her shrill cries rolled over the crackling of the flames. Goosebumps spread over Rhys' body, and a fevered shiver ran up his spine.

"Rhys," whimpered Alina.

A rough hand grabbed hold of his shoulder and whipped him away from the door. Blinking against the harsh sunlight, Rhys met Vinz's gaze. "There are people down there who need help," the Overseer said. Rhys tried to look around, but the sunlight was blinding, the heat overwhelming. Vinz's hand slipped to the back of Rhys' neck. He lowered his voice. "Shallow breaths. Keep your nose and mouth covered at all times." Vinz lifted Alina's head and pulled the lower part of her headscarf over her nose. "Don't look upward—ever. You'll burn your eyes." Vinz met both of their gazes. "Let's go. I want you with me at all times."

Rhys double-tucked the fold of his headscarf and squinted after Vinz as the Overseer strode down the outer staircase and leapt onto the dock. Vinz pulled out his own headscarf, wrapped it about his head expertly, covered his nose and mouth, and then looked back up at them. "Come on," said Rhys, pulling at Alina.

Alina sunk to her knees. "I can't... It's too much."

Rhys knelt beside her. "Come on. People need you."

"Rhys, I can't do it." She folded herself around her knees and pressed her headscarf to her face. "I can't breathe. I can't!" Rhys looked back at Vinz who had begun pacing the dock.

"Alina, come on!" snapped Rhys. "People need you!"

Alina squinted at him. "I want to go home. I don't want to be here anymore. I can't... "

"Alina, humans are dying," murmured Rhys. "They're dying, and you're not doing anything to stop it." Alina frowned and then pushed herself to her knees. Rhys helped her up. "Together," he said quietly.

Alina readjusted her headscarf and followed him down the stairs. Rhys met Vinz's gaze to let him know they were ready. The Overseer led them off the docks. It seemed people had been waiting for Vinz, for as soon as he set foot on solid ground, a group of seven men and two women flocked to him.

"Pantarak attack?" he asked.

"Yeah. They came from the northeast about two hours ago. Bombed us," replied one of the men. "At least a third of the town was destroyed."

"How many dead?"

"Not sure yet," answered a woman. "We're still finding bodies."

"We've lost two schools, the hospital, numerous homes, and the town market," reported the man nearest Rhys.

"Crops?" asked Vinz.

"We didn't lose any crops, but we lost all the food being sold at the market."

"And the armories?"

"Safe."

Vinz thought for a moment. "What actions have you taken?"

"We have sunboarders in the air. There have been no other sightings of the Pantaraks. We've set up triage near the water's edge on the other side of the docks. We're using pumps because the main plant was damaged in the attack."

"Is it still functioning?"

"Somewhat. We have people working on it now."

Vinz withdrew a handheld radio from his pocket. "Kashim, what's your status? Over."

"Approaching the warehouse. It appears undamaged," crackled the radio.

"Check it out. If it's undamaged, head to the main water plant. See if you can help there. Over," replied Vinz.

"Who are they?" asked one of the men.

Rhys, who had been staring at the ground to keep the sun from his eyes, squinted up at the others. Stunned silence followed.

"The young man is Rhys. This is his sister, Alina." There were no greetings, introductions, or welcoming comments. Everyone simply stared. Vinz cleared his throat. "Rhys is an engineer. Alina is a doctor."

"A doctor?" One of the men approached Alina and looked her over. "That true?" Alina averted her gaze and nodded. The man glanced at Vinz incredulously. "They're kids—the both of them."

"Get her to triage. She's more than capable." Vinz pushed Alina toward the man. When she clung to Rhys, he slipped his arm from her grasp and stepped away. His sister gazed at him, an indiscernible expression on her face. "Alina, this man is named Trenton," said Vinz. "He works... *worked* at the hospital. Trenton, this is Alina Falkrow. She is an expert doctor and trauma surgeon."

"You know I don't believe you, right?" murmured Trenton. Like the others Rhys had seen, Trenton was tall, dark-haired, and tan. He wore a blue bandana on his head. With a heavy sigh, Trenton motioned for Alina to follow him. Alina threw Rhys a fleeting look before trailing after the man.

"We'll be joining her later," assured Vinz. "Trenton's a good person. He'll take care of her."

Rhys remained silent. He felt horrible pushing Alina away like that, but she needed to take her place in helping humanity. She had been the one to take on the downloading and installation of medical knowledge— not that he could have done it anyway. Pathos didn't have access to such information in the database. Nevertheless, he couldn't allow Alina to become a burden to society. Her talents and skills had always been necessary on Caelestis, and they would be here as well.

"Marii. Where's Tessa?" Vinz looked about. "I don't see her."

"She's fine, don't worry. She's in triage," replied the woman named Marii. "She's been there since the attack."

Vinz gently clapped Marii's shoulder. "Thank you." He motioned to Rhys. "Come on."

Instead of heading to triage as Rhys hoped, Vinz led him through rubble, flaming debris, and chaos. For nearly three hours they explored the ruins of New Arbroath, climbing over collapsed fences and clambering up enormous piles of rock and wood. They helped groups of haggard-looking, soot-covered citizens dig out others and organized rescue efforts farther in the town.

"Are you looking for something?" asked Rhys, sitting atop a pile of debris. He glanced at Vinz who was attempting to kick aside a large rock. Rhys lowered his head so his scarf provided some shade. He sweated profusely and his breathing rasped. His ears rang.

Vinz finally joined him and handed him a canteen. The Overseer was also layered in a heavy sweat. From under his hood, he regarded Rhys. "Do you see now why our kind don't belong here?" Vinz murmured. Rhys didn't reply. "Not everyone is as civilized as we are. Though there is plenty of land and resources, people still quarrel and... for what?" The Overseer looked about and shook his head. "I don't know."

Rhys gazed at Vinz. "Is that what we've been looking for? Reasons? Clues as to why the Pantaraks attacked?" Vinz's face contorted into a pained expression and he nodded. After a long moment, Rhys said, "Is it because of us? Is it because they know you have us?"

Vinz shifted his gaze back to the ruins. "Most likely, but I was hoping there was something else. Whatever their reason, they felt compelled enough to attack schools and a hospital."

"They've never done that before?"

"We've had our docks bombed a couple of times and our ships attacked, but... nothing like this."

"Vinz!" called a woman, jogging down the rubble-strewn street.

Vinz slid from their pile of debris and ran to meet her. Instead of stopping to talk as the others had done, the woman threw herself at the Overseer. Vinz's arms enveloped her. Torn between embarrassment and intrigue, Rhys fought to pull his eyes from the two, but he couldn't. He could only stare at how their bodies touched and fit so perfectly together, how the woman's arms laced around Vinz's neck in desperate need and how Vinz buried his face in her shoulder.

"I thought you were dead," Rhys heard the woman murmur.

Vinz kissed the top of her head. "I'm fine. We're all fine."

The woman slipped her hands to his face, fondly caressed his cheek, and then kissed him firmly on the lips. Rhys finally looked away, his heart hammering. Humans never interacted in such a manner on Caelestis. Perhaps young children would hold one another while joking amongst themselves, however, once puberty was reached, all physical contact was frowned upon. But here, physical contact seemed acceptable, even necessary.

"Rhys," called Vinz. Rhys shakily made his way down the rubble pile. He stopped before the woman. Like the others, her clothes were torn and filthy. Blood stains colored one side of her short-sleeved, midriff-showing blouse while dirt shaded her pants. She had an aging cut across her forehead. Her black hair was pinned in a loose horsetail and stuck to the sweat along the back of her neck. Her face was round and sweet and her eyes warm. "Rhys, this is Tessa. Tessa, Rhys Falkrow."

Tessa's lips parted in surprise, and she looked at Vinz, who nodded in understanding. Tessa reached through the space between them and lifted the hem of Rhys' headscarf. She studied his eyes for a long moment and then slipped her fingers into his hair. Rhys remained motionless; he hoped she couldn't hear his heart. Tenderly, Tessa touched a lock of his hair and rubbed it between her fingers. Her mouth widened to a smile, and she looked at the Overseer in wonderment.

"We found Rhys and his sister, Alina, a couple of days ago," Vinz murmured.

Tessa's hand slid down Rhys' face and hovered around his eyes. "Where are they from?"

Vinz motioned to Rhys who replied, "Caelestis."

"You speak our language?" whispered Tessa, enthralled. She drew away and laughed. "They speak... they speak our language!" She fell into thought. "Wait, so the new girl... She has your eyes too?" Rhys nodded. "I can't... She's... " Tessa looked at Vinz excitedly. "She's amazing! Trenton brought her in a while ago. She hasn't stopped working."

"Tess," said Vinz. The woman quelled her excitement. "I need to speak with Joss. Do you know where he is?"

"No, but we're having a town meeting in an hour. He'll want you there."

"What do you know?" asked Vinz.

The smile faded from Tessa's face. "They attacked using sunboards and an airship. I couldn't count the sunboards." She traced her finger through the sky. "They made a direct line for the hospital and inner town. Everything was so quick. There was nothing we could do. There was no time to evacuate or run. It just happened." She glanced at Rhys. "Is it because—"

"They saw Rhys and Alina's ship crash just like we did. It was a matter of who could get to them first."

"So they know we have them," concluded Tessa.

Vinz's face turned dark. "Yes."

Tessa pursed her lips. "This is retaliation then."

"We don't know for certain that that was their motive," Vinz countered. "We'll go to the town meeting, learn what we can, and then call a council meeting. This attack needs to be met with appropriate action." Tessa nodded solemnly.

Without another word, Vinz led them back through the wreckage toward the docks. Just as before, people stopped working to acknowledge Vinz or to ask him how he was. Vinz nodded to them and held short, encouraging conversations as he passed. Tessa followed with Rhys, smiling and acting just as warmly. By the time they made it to the triage area, Rhys was exhausted, soaked in his own sweat, and light-headed. He had lost too much water. The intense heat was wearing him down.

Wearily, he followed Vinz and Tessa into the shade of a tent. Eyes cast downward, he could only move his feet.

"Rhys!" cried Alina. Rhys looked up in time to see his sister fling herself into his arms. He tripped over his foot, and they collapsed to the hot earth. It took Rhys a moment to realize Alina was crying, sobbing. "Rhys... Rhys... " From her position over him, she punched his chest, hard. Each time she raised her hand to hit him though, the force that came down was less and less. Soon, she simply lay atop him, crying.

Rhys stared up at the tent ceiling. "I'm sorry," he murmured.

"You left me... " she whimpered in their native language. "You left me!"

"I'm sorry."

Alina slid off him and knelt in the dirt. Groaning, Rhys sat up. His vision tunneled. He held his head and clenched his eyes closed. He could feel his heartbeat in his ears.

You are extremely dehydrated, reported Pathos. *You need to replenish your fluids and rest.*

"Dehydration," whispered Alina. Her hands wrapped around his arm, and she pulled him to his feet.

Rhys leaned heavily on her as the world around him spun. "I think I'm going to be sick."

The tone of Alina's voice changed. "Vinz, help me. You there, grab fresh water, a wet cloth, and a waste bin." With Vinz's help, Alina guided Rhys to a small cot on the far side of the tent. His head felt as though it was going to burst. "Take one of the fans and bring it over here. You, check on patient number four."

Rhys squinted up at Alina. *Our bodies are so fragile here.*

I know that more than anyone right now, replied his sister. Her tears were gone. All that remained were tracks down her cheeks. *Why did you let them push you this hard? What were you doing?*

We surveyed the entire town. Rhys laid one of his sweat-soaked arms over his eyes. *I feel so sick.*

"Here," said Alina. She pushed his arm from his face and rested a wet cloth on his head. It wasn't cold, but the water drew away some of the heat from his face. "Can you sit up for a moment?" Alina pulled his headscarf from his head and pushed his hair around Pathos' unit. As he sat up, she cradled him and held the wet cloth to his forehead. "Hand me that other cloth," she murmured to someone. Water dripped down Rhys' back as his sister placed another wet cloth along the back of his neck. When she presented a pitcher of water, Rhys eagerly drank.

"I wish you had told me the heat was stressing you," said Vinz.

Rhys finished half the pitcher before Alina took it from him and made him lie back. *Alina,* said Pathos, *I am overriding Rhys' basic functions and placing him in a state of suspended consciousness to allow his body to rest.*

Alina gazed down at Rhys. *Is that really necessary? He'll cool down.*

Normally, the human body would cool itself, however, there is little data describing the reaction to heat that humans from Caelestis elicit, replied Pathos. *If you feel strongly that such precautions do not need to be taken, you may override my decision.*

Alina sighed. *Fine, put him to sleep. No more than three hours though.*

Understood.

Orders from the presiding doctor, confirmed, said Pathos. Rhys glanced at Vinz and Tessa who stood at the end of his cot watching. That was the last thing he remembered.

6
THE FACE OF HUMANITY

"O, WHEN THE SUN IS A' FALLING,
And the war pipes are calling,
Look here, my love. Look here.
O, when you've lost your way,
And you feel you cannot stay,
Look here, my love. Look here…"

Rhys opened his eyes. It was dark save a lamp resting on a nearby table. He rolled his head toward the soft, lilting voice. To his surprise, he found Kallen tilting precariously in a chair next to his bed. As she whittled a palm-sized block of wood, she alternated between humming and singing.

"And when your hope is gone
And you feel you can't move on,
Look here, my love. Look here…"

As her words trailed into a distant humming, something stirred in Rhys, something foreign but not all unwelcome. Whatever it was she was doing with her voice, the sound she was creating, it enthralled Rhys. Never before had he heard someone manipulate the human voice in such a manner.

It's called singing, explained Pathos.
I didn't know our voices could do that.

Not all humans have the gift to hold a melody on pitch. You have never been exposed to such a skill because it has no purpose. It is a forgotten skill on Caelestis because it does not advance the human race. It is not necessary.

Rhys stared at Kallen in awe. *But it's so beautiful.*

He must have unintentionally made a sound because Kallen looked up from her work. Her eyes brightened, and she smiled warmly. "Hey, how are you feeling?" She let her chair fall to the ground and leaned forward on his bed.

Suddenly aware of how close she was, Rhys turned away. "I… uh… Where's Alina?"

"Still working," replied Kallen, pointing across the tent. Rhys sat up—his head didn't spin—and looked. Even in the shadows, Alina was easy to spot. Her skin glowed like the moon. She stood at a bed with two other doctors, a man and a woman, listening to a patient. "I've only seen her off her feet once."

"And Vinz?"

"At the town meeting. Apparently, one of the Pantaraks' sunboarders was caught, but no one knew until about an hour ago."

"What will they do with the captive?" Rhys swung his feet off the bed; his boots had been removed.

Kallen straightened herself and started whittling again. "Don't know. Torture him for information and then kill him."

Rhys fell still. "You're not serious?"

Kallen shrugged. "I am. It's very likely. That's what they've done in the past. Vinz doesn't approve of it, but really… there's no other way to get information from them." Rhys laced his boots and started to stand. Kallen's hand fell on his arm, startling him horribly. "Be careful. Not everyone here can be trusted." She nodded toward Alina. "Trenton has been with her all day acting as her bodyguard."

"And… I get you?" asked Rhys. He didn't mean to sound ungrateful.

Kallen stood. "I surprise most people. Come on. Vinz told me to take you to him once you woke." Kallen lifted her rifle with ease and shouldered it. Rhys took a swig from the nearest pitcher and followed her from the tent. As they walked, he rolled his salt-laden sleeves. "Keep that computer-thing of yours hidden."

Rhys pushed his hair over Pathos' unit and glanced at Kallen. For the first time, he realized she was almost as tall as him. Additionally, now that she was visible in the light of the town's multitude of lamps, Rhys could see that she had exchanged her blouse for a sleeveless, dark purple crop top. Trying not to stare at the sliver of bare flesh above her hips, Rhys cleared his throat and attempted conversation. "You have a nice voice."

"My mother had a much lovelier one," Kallen remarked.

"Where is she?"

"Dead."

"Oh... " murmured Rhys.

"I'm fine. It was long ago."

"Was it because of the Pantaraks?"

"Fortunately, no. A virus swept through our town, and she just couldn't get over it."

"And your father?"

"He's here with another woman. I have a half-sister, but we don't get along." She glanced at him. "And you? What about your... I'm so sorry."

Rhys shook his head. "It seems people here cherish those who birth and raise them. Alina and I never experienced such a relationship."

"What does that mean? You don't... have a mother and father?"

"Alina and I are half-siblings."

Kallen stopped and looked at him in surprise. "Really?"

"Our father was the same, but we had different mothers. My mother's genes were not what they were looking for, so they used another woman to create Alina."

"What?" whispered Kallen.

Rhys regarded her, alarmed by her reaction. He had obviously said something offensive. He tried to save the conversation. "We are an oddity on Caelestis. Most people don't know who their siblings are, much less—"

Kallen pulled him into the shadows of a still-standing wall. She leaned into him and whispered fiercely. "Rhys, listen to me. Don't ever, *ever* tell anyone—*ever*—what you just told me." Rhys just stared at her. She swallowed visibly. "Rhys, you two were *created*."

The panic he felt suddenly vanished. That's what she was concerned about? "I don't understand," he murmured. "Humans are created eve—"

Kallen shook her head. "Don't ever," she whispered breathlessly. "Rhys, people will *kill* you. You must keep this to yourself. Even Vinz. Do not tell anyone else."

"I don't... understand."

"Here, life is sacred. Life cannot be created. Such talk is blasphemous."

Rhys gazed at her in desperate confusion. "Then how are you here..." Suddenly, the conversation they had had earlier with Alina slipped into his mind. "You mean... that wasn't a lie? You can carry a child in your body?" He lowered his voice. "That's how humans reproduce?" Kallen just gazed at him. Rhys thought for a moment before saying, "I won't tell another person."

"Don't mention your parents or you being half-siblings either," added Kallen. "Don't give anyone any reason to ask you questions, and if they do, lie." Rhys He. "I'm sorry, Rhys." Kallen's almond eyes softened, and she tried to smile. "If you're ever uncertain about anything, please ask me. Don't hesitate. I don't want something to happen to you, or Alina."

Rhys held her gaze for the longest moment. With the fear and confusion leaking out of him, he could more clearly comprehend just how close she was. A soft breeze brushed his cheek, and her scent, faint but sweet, swept across his face. His every instinct until that moment had been to pull back from any person who had drawn too close. Now though, all he could do was stand motionless and gaze at Kallen.

His own physical reaction to her nearness was disconcerting enough, but Kallen's response made his heart quicken. Instead of stepping away as most would have done, she also remained unmoving. Her eyes held steady on his, unwavering, as though she was intrigued and enthralled by everything that he was.

At that moment, Rhys forgot where he was. Never before had he gazed so intently into another human's eyes. Never before had he shared such a long moment of intimate silence in his immediate space.

Kallen finally cleared her throat and looked away. "I, ehhh... We should go to the town meeting." Rhys nodded. And just like that, the moment passed. It was gone—whatever *it* was.

In silence, they walked around the rubble, down the street, and into the town square where throngs of people stood in hushed silence.

Kallen tapped Rhys' arm and nodded to something beyond the crowd. On a dais some distance away stood a tall, middle-aged man with a round waist and neatly trimmed hair. Though he leaned casually on a podium, his dark eyes were sharp as he gazed out at the crowd. "That's the judge of New Arbroath, Joss," whispered Kallen.

"Is that it then?" asked Joss, looking about. There was silence. The judge nodded and then motioned to someone. Quiet murmurs broke out within the crowd as Joss stepped down and pulled the podium from the stage.

"What's going on?" asked Rhys. Kallen stood on her tiptoes. "What are they doing?"

"I don't know," she replied. "Here, this way." She drew him from the crowd to a tall lamp post set in stone. Gracefully, she swung herself atop its base and gestured for Rhys to join her. Once settled, Rhys turned his eyes back to the dais. "It looks like they're bringing out the Pantarak captive."

"Why?"

"To get information from him," she whispered.

"Here? Now?" gasped Rhys. Kallen nodded. Worriedly, Rhys searched the many heads in the crowd. Surely Vinz was there. He wouldn't allow anything to happen to the captive. Pantarak or not, the captive was human. Vinz craved peace. He wouldn't let anything happen.

A group of people emerged from a nearby building. There were six in total—five guards and the prisoner. Rhys craned his neck to get a better look. The man they escorted into the light of the town square appeared normal enough. Though his head was shaved bald and his scalp decorated with a variety of intricate, black tattoos, he appeared ordinary. It wasn't until he was fully illuminated and upon the dais that Rhys realized the prisoner wore shackles on his wrists and ankles.

Anxiously, he glanced at Kallen. Why was the man shackled, tethered like a beast? It didn't make sense! He was a man standing trial, not a wild creature. This was inhumane, savage. Wasn't anyone going to say something in the man's defense?

The Pantarak's guards locked his shackles to the dais and then positioned themselves around him. Joss once more took center stage. A man in white carrying a cloth-covered tray followed. Rhys recoiled in visceral disgust as the cloth was removed to reveal multiple tools. Even from a distance, he saw the judge's lips purse and his eyebrows furrow. Many of the women in the crowd began leaving, ushering their children with them. Rhys' heart leapt to his throat. He meant to ask Kallen what was happening, but his voice was caught between his lungs and his tongue. He couldn't speak.

"Why did the Pantarak people attack New Arbroath?" asked Joss, turning to the captive. The man remained silent, his eyes cast downward. "What was the purpose of the attack?" The judge waited for an answer and then continued. "Your people killed innocents. You destroyed a hospital. Murdered children who were in school." Joss leaned down. "What was the purpose of the attack?"

Rhys waited with bated breath. Why wasn't the man answering? Didn't he realize what would happen to him if he didn't? Surely he knew!

Joss grabbed the prisoner's chin and drew it upward so their gazes met. "You murdered innocents, children, women. Why? What was the purpose of the attack?" Defiantly, the man jerked out of the judge's grasp and spat.

Joss didn't react at first. He simply stared at the Pantarak. Finally though, the judge stood, took a cloth from one of the guards, wiped his face, and went to the man dressed in white. He pulled a knife the size of his forearm from the tray and returned to the captive. In a slow motion, Joss cut across the man's bare chest. The Pantarak groaned as rivulets of blood began weaving down his naked torso. The judge asked the question again; he received no answer. Once more he cut the man, this time vertically. Again, the Pantarak gave no response.

"Rhys," murmured Kallen, sliding down from the lamppost. She held her hand out to him. "Come on." Although shaking, Rhys remained where he was. Where was Vinz? Why was no one stopping this?

Joss returned the knife to the tray and then approached the man, bare-handed. He asked the question again. When the prisoner remained silent, Joss nodded to one of the guards who stepped onto the dais, jerked one of the man's hands forward, and opened his palm. In a swift movement, Joss broke the man's fingers.

Rhys's vision dimmed, and he slipped off the lamp post. Kallen broke his fall, and they collapsed to the ground. His legs were weak. He could hear his heart thrumming in his ears.

"Rhys, come on," Kallen murmured, holding his face. Distantly, Rhys heard the man gasp and groan. "Rhys." She pulled his chin up so their eyes could meet. "Rhys, come on. Let's go back."

"What was the purpose of the attack?" yelled Joss. The sound of bones snapping reverberated throughout the town square. "Answer!" Rhys buried his head in his hands and covered his ears. He sank further onto the ground until his head was centimeters from the broken stone beneath him. Another crackle of snapping bones rang out.

Kallen pulled his head to her chest and covered him. Too distraught, Rhys didn't resist. Instead, he clenched his eyes shut and pressed the palms of his hands against his ears. Kallen's arms tightened around him. Suddenly, a strangled cry tore from the captive's throat. Rhys curled into himself.

Where *were* they? This wasn't Earth. This wasn't the cradle of humanity! No human would inflict such atrocities on another. They weren't on Earth. He couldn't believe that after thousands of years, this was what the human race resorted to—torture, flogging, breaking bones. What kind of species could behave so savagely? Could purposefully injure and maim? What planet was this?

"O, when the sun is a'falling," whispered Kallen. "And the war pipes are calling... " Her voice though soft, ghostly, pervaded the palm-lock Rhys held over his ears. "Look here, my love. Look here." She lowered her mouth to his ear and gently pried his left hand away. "And when your hope is gone, and you feel you can't move on—look here, my love. Look here."

Rhys peered up at her through his tears and distress. He could hear only his own heavy breathing and her singing. Kallen hummed for a moment longer and then drew him to his knees. Adrenaline surging through him, Rhys clumsily rose, turned from the town square, and ran. Though his legs threatened to give out, he pushed onward down the disheveled, stone road toward the docks. He tripped over rubble and slid on loose gravel but never did he stop; never did he look back.

It wasn't until he reached the docks that he finally slowed. Only when he reached the end of the wharf and could go no farther did he stop and stare out at the black sea, wheezing.

"Why?" he shrieked in Interstellar Nefegian. "Why are we... here?" He grabbed his hair in distress. "What is this?" Why had they landed in such a savage, unforgiving land? These people were not human. They were, as Alina had said, a different species—an off-branch of mankind.

"Rhys?" Kallen's voice was small.

Wide-eyed and wind-swept, Rhys turned to look at her in the dim lamplight. Kallen seemed speechless. Angrily, Rhys turned fidgeted along the edge of the wharf. He could still hear the man's screams in his ears, in his mind.

For several long minutes, they stood in silence. Only the sound of the water lapping along the pier disturbed the quiet between them.

"I should have warned you," Kallen lamented.

Rhys just glared at the black water below. "How can... How can humans... " Realizing he was speaking in his mother tongue, he corrected himself and started again. "How can humans do that to one another?"

"This is the true face of humanity," Kallen murmured sullenly. "This is what humanity is."

Rhys shook his head. "No. You're not human. This isn't... This isn't Earth. No human would... " He took a slow breath. "I don't understand... I can't comprehend... " Unable to continue in Aabesh, he switched to his native tongue and allowed Pathos to translate for him as he spoke. "What is the point? If humans kill and torture without restraint, then what hope does humanity on Earth have? What hope does anyone have?"

"We aren't all like that," replied Kallen.

Rhys' throat was thick. "But no one stopped him."

"He is the scapegoat." Kallen joined him on the edge of the wharf. With a pained expression on her face, she explained, "Children died today. Were crushed, killed. The sick, the old, the injured—they were killed. Those in the town square right now are looking for justice for the loved ones they lost. It's the man's misfortune to have been caught."

Kallen's rational demeanor forced him to calm. After a moment, he asked in Aabesh, "How... are you not bothered by this? Your people are—"

"I am," interrupted Kallen. "But this is justice. Every man who goes into battle knows that there is a chance the enemy will take him... and make him pay for the sins of his comrades, his people, and his superiors. This is justice."

"That's savagery," replied Rhys. He reverted to Interstellar Nefegian and continued; Pathos translated aloud. "If you return blow for blow, where does that get you? Where does that take the human race? What becomes of humanity if you cannot discuss your differences, your problems, your political differences sensibly?" Rhys pointed vehemently toward the town square. "That! That is what mankind becomes."

Kallen considered him. "What would you do then? Alina is killed. What would you do?"

"She wouldn't be killed. Logos—"

"Alina is killed when they bomb the makeshift hospital. What do you do?"

Rhys stared at her. In fact, he had no idea what he would do.

"Would you go search for their leader and ask for an audience with him? Would you kill every enemy scout you got your hands on? Would you bomb them back? What would you do?" asked Kallen. Rhys remained silent. "You would want revenge, answers, reasons—something to validate her death. Right? But the reality is you will never know or understand. You will never find what you're looking for. Very few ever do."

7
DILEMMA

AFTER COAXING ALINA AWAY FROM her duties, they returned to the ship. Despite twilight's dim light, Rhys and Alina were finally able to see *Themis* in all of her glory. Though she was small compared to the enormous fishing vessels stationed at the remaining docks, *Themis* was sleek and showcased a hard, metal exterior intertwined with well-polished wood. Her build was composed of three levels stacked atop one another. The main cabins comprised the first level and the bridge made up the second and took up the entire bow. The third level was the upper deck which covered the top of the ship from bow to stern.

Most of the fishing ships in port had only one primary mast; *Themis* had two—a forward mast and a smaller rear mast. Both were equipped with solar-paneled sails to collect energy for the three motors the ship boasted on her stern. Vinz truly was a genius engineer. Compared to the other rusting ships in the port, *Themis* looked like a spacecraft.

Without a word, Kallen led them to their cabin, bid them goodnight, and left. Once alone, Alina crossed the hallway, took a bath, dressed, and immediately went to sleep.

She had said little since that afternoon's outburst. Whether she resented Rhys for abandoning her or was actually exhausted, Rhys didn't know. He would have asked Logos, but Alina had shut off her internal communication link. After taking a bath, examining his strange, new black hair in the mirror, and dressing, Rhys lay back in his bunk and stared at the ceiling. He had never been alone with his thoughts; he had never *not* been connected to others.

Long into the night, he tossed and turned, never truly falling asleep. His mind was overwhelmed, troubled, and restless. It wasn't until he finally sat up that Pathos said anything.

The memories of the events from earlier today can be suppressed if you would like.

Rhys considered Pathos' offer. He wanted to continue just as he had, but somehow, that didn't feel right. He couldn't disrespect the captive like that; he couldn't un-remember something so life-altering.

No, leave it. I'll work it out, he told Pathos. After a moment, he asked, *Do you know if Alina turned Logos off? When did you lose connection?*

Shortly after you went to sleep in the makeshift hospital, replied Pathos.

Was... there a reason?

Logos was overwhelmed, explained the AI. *By diverting the energy Logos required to communicate internally, Alina was able to focus more intensely on what she was doing.*

That wasn't the reason, Rhys muttered. He stood, glanced out the black porthole, put his boots on, and left the room.

Where are you going?

Pathos, remain quiet until I specify otherwise, he instructed.

Understood. Silencing internal voice simulator.

Rhys stood motionless in the hallway and listened. He could hear the soft waves lapping at the boat. In the cabin to his right, snoring permeated the door. Rhys padded down the hallway to the galley. Unsure of what he was searching for, of what he needed, he climbed the staircase, entered the empty bridge, and left through the outer staircase. The breeze that struck his face was cool but refreshing. Squinting against the lamps on the docks, he slipped down the staircase to the wharf.

He expected he would stop once his feet met the shifting dock, but he didn't. Instead, he continued onward toward the treeline at the edge of town. It wasn't until he stood just beneath the treetop canopy that he finally urged himself to halt. Breathing hard, he stared into the darkness. He could hear nighttime insects rhythmically chirping. The tree limbs overhead shifted in the breeze, a pleasant sound. Rhys breathed deeply and closed his eyes.

Eventually, he settled himself beneath a tree and observed the town illuminated by the stars' cold, indifferent light.

Gradually, his mind cleared and his eyes grew heavy with fatigue. The breeze was agreeable, the nighttime sounds oddly comforting, and the solitude soul-affirming. Only when he began to doze did he contemplate returning to *Themis*.

As he stood to make the return trip, he heard a rustle in the vegetation somewhere down the treeline. He engaged his night vision and searched the trees. To his great surprise and alarm, he found not one, but two men entering the forest. In complete darkness, they pushed through the vegetation to a small glade. Rhys knelt and squinted in an attempt to focus, his heart in his throat. One of the men had his arm in a sling and white bandages about his torso. His head was completely bald. The other had dark hair and alabaster skin. Reeling, Rhys sat in the grass.

Vinz and the Pantarak captive?

Surely not. The captive had been heavily guarded. There was no way he could have freed himself! And what of Vinz? That *couldn't* be Vinz. Someone else was helping the man escape. Rhys peered over the bushes. The two men were talking softly. Certainly the bandaged man was the Pantarak captive, but…

A breeze swept through the canopy and the wind carried their voices to Rhys' ears; he recognized Vinz's voice. What was going on? Where was he when the man was being tortured? Had he sneaked in and rescued the man? Was he working with the Pantaraks?

Rhys saw the Pantarak captive bow to Vinz and then sprint into the darkness. For the longest time, Vinz stood in the clearing, gazing into the shadows as if to make sure the man escaped without hindrance. Afterward, the Overseer started for the docks. Rhys slipped behind the tree he had been sitting under and watched as Vinz crossed the wharf and disappeared into *Themis*. Rhys waited half an hour before returning to the ship.

Sometime before dawn, loud, clanging bells woke Rhys. Their sound reverberated and rolled over the town of New Arbroath. It seemed the guards had discovered their captive was missing. Rhys sat up when he heard footsteps in the hallway but relaxed when he realized no one was scrambling for the bridge. The bells finally quieted, and he went back to sleep.

Though his sleep was heavy, it was troubled—something he had never before experienced. Images of blood, trees, crowds of people, and rubble plagued his mind's eye while Kallen's lilting tune filled his ears. No matter how he tossed, how he rolled, he could not quell his restlessness. Eventually, Alina entered his dreams. She smiled at him, gave the same chuckle she had the moment she had seen his new black hair, and then lithely danced away. Rhys called to her as she ran into the crowd of people, but his voice was swallowed.

He thought to go after her, but the sudden sound of crunching bones made his knees buckle beneath him. Distressed, he grabbed at what he could to help him rise. His hands fell on Kallen. She smiled affectionately and slowly leaned into him. Her breath was warm, intoxicating. Rhys stared at her lips. He couldn't bring himself to look away. His heart hammered, slamming painfully against his chest. He didn't understand. She made him feel a different type of weakness—a sweetly confusing emotion.

Rhys.

Hm? murmured Rhys, leaning into her. Kallen wrapped her hands around his face.

Rhys.

As Kallen's fingers laced around his head, his hands wound around her back. His breathing was coming in rasps now. For some unknown reason, he needed to touch her face, to feel her odd but beautiful skin. He needed to caress her black tresses.

Rhys!

Overriding sleep function. Exiting Rapid Eye Movement. Engaging consciousness.

Rhys! Rhys! screamed Alina.

In a mad flurry, Rhys rolled out of bed and crashed to the ground. Wildly, he looked about the room. Alina wasn't there. "Alina?" He stuffed his feet into his boots. "Alina?"

Rhys!

Pathos, find her! ordered Rhys, rushing through the door. He darted from his cabin, slammed into the wall, and raced down the hallway. Before he could stop himself, he ran headlong into Hodge who was shuffling from his cabin. Without a word, Rhys shoved the man aside and sprinted up the stairs to the bridge. He wasn't sure how he ended up on the wharf. Adrenaline powered him. Hands cold and clammy and heart thrumming, he tore across the docks into town toward the makeshift hospital.

Rhys! Alina's voice cracked. *Help!*

I'm coming! As he rounded one of the many tall piles of rubble, he spotted a struggle underway outside the makeshift hospital. Amongst the flailing was Alina. Though she was fending off her attackers well enough, she was losing ground. Skill couldn't always conquer brute strength which is what the three men who were trying to pin her had. Rhys saw Alina land a punch on one of the men and then turn and block another attack. In the split instant her back was unguarded, however, the third offender rushed her and slammed her to the ground.

Rhys' mind cleared, focused. Instinct took over. His senses heightened. His vision narrowed and became keener. His legs churned hard under him; his arms pumped.

With all his strength, Rhys lowered his right shoulder and rammed into the man who was atop Alina. Like a raging bull, Rhys exploded in every direction. His fists hit everything within reach. His feet drove into chests and sides, his elbows into faces. The pain that radiated through him after each strike only drove him onward, prompting him to hit again and again. Though the fight seemed to take hours, within seconds the men dispersed, leaving a crimson trail in the early morning light. Rhys didn't give chase. Instead, he stood glowering after them, panting. It wasn't until he realized his hands were still clenched in iron fists that he relaxed and looked for Alina. She had a nasty scrape across her left cheek and her hair was ruffled, but she seemed otherwise uninjured.

Nevertheless, Rhys still felt compelled to ask, "Are you hurt?" Alina's gaze filled with tears and she looked away ashamedly. "Hey... " He went to her and pulled her into his embrace. "Are you hurt?" Alina burst into soft sobs. As she cried, Rhys glanced into the hospital tent to find several of Alina's patients sitting up in bed, watching the scene. Fury boiled in him. They had sat motionlessly while she had attempted to fend off three men triple her size.

Sniffing, Alina finally pulled away and swiped at her tears.

"What did they want?" murmured Rhys in their native tongue. Alina pointed gravely at Logos' unit. "They said that's what they were after?"

She nodded. "They asked me to give it to them. I... told them I couldn't."

"And your patients whom you've spent *hours* caring for couldn't bear to call for help for you," snarled Rhys.

Alina gripped his arm and shook her head furiously. "There's no one here to call to. I shouldn't have come alone."

Rhys nodded to the people in the tent. "Do you need to care for them?" Alina looked at him in surprise. "Go. I'll stay with you."

"You're not angry?"

"Of course, I'm angry. Just go," he replied perhaps a little too harshly.

"Then let me treat you first," she offered. She took his arm and led him to a stand just inside the doorway. She cleaned the blood from his knuckles, hands, and elbows, and bandaged them. Afterward, Rhys left the tent. He settled himself against one of the awning poles and gazed darkly out at the world. From within the tent, he could hear Alina's patients asking about her wellbeing. Though his heart softened, his soul remained shackled to hatred.

There was no one he could blame. He couldn't blame Trenton, the man in whose care Alina had been placed. He couldn't blame Vinz for not noticing her leaving the ship. He couldn't blame anyone except the men who had come after her—which made him wonder... Why did they want her AI? What did they think it was? Were they trying to collect it for someone else? Certainly it wasn't worth any value here, though perhaps they thought otherwise.

He would speak with Vinz and Kallen about the matter. There had to be a better way to hide their AIs. As of the moment, the units were matte gray, a flashy statement against their now black locks. Kallen could probably paint them black. There really was no other option.

It wasn't long before crew members from *Themis* joined him. Though Vinz was with them, he seemed preoccupied with speaking with Kashim. Only Kallen, Hodge, and Andy showed any concern for Rhys' freshly bandaged hands.

"What happened?" murmured Kallen.

Hodge squatted in front of him and began examining his wounds. "What's wrong with your hands? Were you in a fight?" Rhys nodded. Hodge looked about. "With who? This pole?"

Kallen hit Hodge and opened her mouth to object, but a voice from within the tent stopped her. "He single-handedly fought those three from Armory West," croaked an elderly man. Rhys leaned back and looked into the tent to find Alina's patient sitting up on one of the cots. He had a perfect view of the open doorway where the fight had occurred. The old man nodded to Rhys. "She's your sister, right?"

"Yes," replied Rhys.

The old man looked at Hodge. "There's nothing stronger than a man protecting his family. I'm proud to have witnessed the fight myself." Recognizing the odd comment as a compliment, Rhys bowed his head in acknowledgment and then sighed. He was suddenly very tired.

"You all, come with me," called Vinz. It seemed he had been completely oblivious to the conversation. "You too, Rhys."

Rhys didn't move. Instead, he asked, "Where are we going?"

"To report our findings," Vinz replied.

"I can't leave Alina."

Vinz nudged Andy. "Stay with the girl."

Rhys pushed himself to his feet, glanced at Vinz, and then left the cover of the awning. The morning sun had been tolerable, but now, its brilliance and heat were overwhelming.

"Rhys," called Alina, trotting out of the tent. She held out a headscarf. Her eyes were still red from crying, but she seemed otherwise unbothered. Rhys passed her an appreciative smile, wrapped his face and neck, and then looked to Vinz. The Overseer motioned the group onward into town.

Make sure Andy is with you at all times, murmured Rhys. *And keep your internal communications on.*

I will, replied Alina.

As Vinz walked in silence, Kashim and Hodge ignited a conversation about sunboards. Rhys fell to the rear of the group. He just couldn't bring himself to focus on anything at the moment. He was tired, overwhelmed, and angry, emotions he had never before felt. It troubled him how deeply anger had anchored itself in his heart.

"Hey," whispered Kallen, falling into step with him.

Rhys glanced at her. Seeing the concerned look in her warm brown eyes, he sighed. "I'm tired. I don't feel well. I want to... "

Kallen glanced at the others and then gently pulled him to a halt. "What?"

"It's nothing."

Kallen lowered herself to catch his gaze. "Are you sick? You said you don't feel well."

"I'm... No. I'm not sick."

"I'll cook for you when we get back to the ship," she said. "How does that sound?"

"Cook? What does that mean?"

"Ehhh, food. I'll prepare food for you. I'll *cook.*"

"Hey, come on!" called Hodge.

"Coming," replied Kallen. She waited until Hodge had continued before gingerly slipping her hand around Rhys' arm. The sudden electric charge that snapped through Rhys caused him to jerk away in surprise. "Sorry!" she murmured. Rhys stared at her, his heart hammering painfully in his chest. "I, eh..." She cleared her throat. "Let's go." Without another look, she jogged after the group.

Pathos? asked Rhys shakily.

A natural response to physical contact with the opposite sex, his AI explained matter-of-factly. *Increased heart rate, heightened senses.*

Why?

Because you obviously view her as a potential mate and are sexually attracted to her.

What? Rhys stared incredulously after Kallen. Sensing Pathos had no more to explain, Rhys hurried after the group.

After a long walk through the rubble-encrusted town, Vinz eventually led the group to a still-standing, brick-and-mortar, three-story building. Though the outside was austere, the interior of the building was decorated with polished wood floors, glass lamps, and cushioned chairs. Even the people there were well-dressed in long-sleeved blouses, nice slacks, and dresses.

A woman seated at a table near the front door looked up from her writing and smiled charmingly at Vinz. "Joss is in his office. He's been waiting for you."

Joss? Rhys halted in the doorway. Unfortunately, no one seemed to notice, not even the woman seated near the door. Rhys watched as Vinz, Kallen, Kashim, and Hodge disappeared up a grand staircase to his left. He pulled his headscarf from his head and shifted anxiously in the doorway.

Finally, the woman looked up from her work. The expression on her face, initially one of exasperation, changed to surprise when she saw the color of his eyes and the paleness of his skin.

"Rhys," called Kallen. A moment later, she hurried down the staircase. Rhys met her at the bottom. "What are you doing?"

"I can't see that man," Rhys told her, gazing about the carpeted entryway.

Kallen looked at the people who were slowly stopping their daily activities to stare at him. "Come on." When she tried to persuade him up the stairs, he remained stubbornly immobile. Kallen passed him an emotion-loaded look. It was an expression of hopeful trust and silent pleading. Rhys couldn't help but acquiesce and follow. The staircase gave way to the second floor which showcased an extensive hallway of offices and a variety of nondescript paintings.

"Listen," murmured Kallen. "The judge wants to meet you."

"I don't want to meet him."

"You don't have to say anything. Just… "

"Why is this so important?"

"Because he's the one who gives us assignments," Kallen explained. "He's the one who commissioned Vinz to sail. Without him, there would be no *Themis*."

"What does that have to do with me?"

"You're part of the report. You are what led to us finding our murdered people."

Rhys looked down the hallway. All the doors were closed save the last one which was occupied by Hodge who was clearly waiting for them. "I'll stay here," said Rhys quietly.

"Rhys… "

"I'll be right here."

Kallen sighed, defeated, and joined the others. As Rhys watched her leave, he felt a twinge of guilt. Kallen had been nothing but caring and accommodating. He hated to upset her, but this was not up for debate. He would not meet with a man who had beaten and tortured another human.

Nearly half an hour passed before Rhys heard the door to the judge's office open. By then, he had examined every uninteresting painting and vase the second floor had to offer and even poked his head onto the third floor. Hearing voices, Rhys stopped his pacing. Vinz entered the hallway first, glanced at him, and then stepped aside for Joss.

Rhys didn't move, though instinct told him to dash down the staircase and sprint back to Alina. Pathos' information, however, indicated that doing that could be perceived as a sign of weakness. Conflicted, Rhys waited for the judge. Neither Vinz nor any of the other crew members followed.

Joss came to a stop before Rhys. Per Pathos' instruction, Rhys held the man's gaze. The judge appeared just as he had the previous night—middle-aged, tall, and untouchable. He had slightly sagging cheeks and bags under his eyes, which, according to Pathos, was indicative of poor sleep patterns. When he smiled, Rhys found his teeth yellow but relatively straight.

The judge held out his hand, but Rhys ignored it. "Master Falkrow," said Joss, relaxing. "It's a pleasure to meet you." Rhys glanced down the hall at the others who were watching the interaction with interest. "It is my understanding that the actions I took last night against the Pantarak captive upset you. Perhaps it will bring you some comfort to know that the prisoner escaped in the night. He injured two of our men in the process."

Rhys remained silent. He truly didn't understand what Joss wanted from him.

"Vinz tells me you have a younger sister," Joss continued in an attempt to push the conversation forward. "And that she's been volunteering at the makeshift hospital. I would very much like to meet her. I've heard great things about the new doctor. And you, I've been told that you're an engineer. What do you specialize in? Machinery, solar energy, building construction?" Joss waited for Rhys' reply. When Rhys said nothing, the judge's nostrils flared and he sighed. "I've given Vinz his new assignment. You're welcome to go with him or stay here and work. Either way, you will be graciously compensated."

This conversation was over, that much Rhys had decided. "Excuse me." Calmly, he turned and walked down the staircase. Without looking back, Rhys crossed the first floor and stepped outside.

A short time later, the others from *Themis* joined him. Though each glanced at Rhys, none spoke directly to him. "We're leaving tonight," concluded Vinz after shading his eyes against the high sun. "Kashim and I will secure armaments. Kallen, take Hodge and Rhys with you. Look into purchasing a new sunboard."

Was that it? They weren't even going to talk about what had happened?

"How much are you willing to spend?" asked Kallen as he handed her a small bag. "You know the good ones aren't cheap."

"I'll leave that to you." Vinz's gaze passed over Rhys before he and Kashim set off.

"Let's go see the Old Man," said Kallen.

Hodge laughed, following her. "I'm doing the haggling this time. Last time—"

"You're remembering that wrong," scoffed Kallen. "I got us the best deal. You were the one who told the Old Man we didn't need the spare part."

"I wouldn't have told him that. That sounds like you trying to save money."

"Right, so I could later stress about not having a spare connector? I'm doing the haggling. You just stand on the board and look pretty," countered Kallen.

As the two continued to bicker, Rhys trailed behind. Vinz hadn't said anything to him. In fact, the Overseer had completely ignored him. Rhys squinted ahead at Hodge and Kallen. Everyone else seemed to be disregarding him as well.

Even though the judge had meant for it to be a compliment, Joss' comment regarding Rhys' sister had made his skin crawl for reasons he didn't understand. Perhaps it had been the way the man had delivered the line or the way his eyes had glinted in the light as he had said it. Whatever the case, Rhys was determined to never let Alina near him. Ever. The man had far too much blood on his hands and malice in his heart.

Kallen led them down the docks, past *Themis,* to a ragged shop propped up by barrels and strategically placed wooden boards. In the slips near the shop floated several sunboards, two of which had their sails set at full mast. It looked as though they were charging.

A loud sound echoed over the wharf, and a large creature bound out of the shop toward them. Rhys stopped where he was, alarmed. The creature had four legs, soft yellow hair, and an extra limb-like structure that curled over its back.

Canis lupis familiaris, explained Pathos. *A canid known throughout history as 'dog.' It played a crucial role in man's development during humanity's earliest years and is considered to be man's closest non-human companion.*

As Kallen greeted the dog enthusiastically, Hodge studied the moored sunboards. Pointing to one, he called, "This one's not bad."

Kallen joined him. "That's the most expensive board he's got." Rhys wanted to follow but found his way blocked by the dog. It was a pretty creature with lush, golden fur, a small black nose, and round ears, but something in its eyes made Rhys feel as though it was more intelligent than it seemed. "Rhys?"

Rhys looked beyond the dog at Kallen. Both she and Hodge were watching him with expressions of amusement on their faces. Realizing he must appear both silly and incompetent, Rhys gathered himself and approached the dog with the intent to pass. The dog however backed away a few steps and emitted a low, foreboding sound. Rhys froze. Stiff-legged and tail wagging ever so slightly, the dog shifted on the dock.

"He's not going to hurt you!" called Hodge.

"Right," murmured Rhys. With more assertiveness, he stepped toward the dog who immediately let loose a series of barks. Rhys startled horribly. Over the dog's cries, Rhys heard Hodge howling in laughter.

"Mister Jon, here," commanded Kallen. "*No.* Here." The dog, Mister Jon, turned and trotted to Kallen happily. He sat at her feet and looked up at her, his tail thumping against the docks. "Come on, Rhys."

Humiliated, Rhys joined them. Mister Jon continued to wag his tail. "What is it doing?" Rhys asked warily.

"Haven't you seen a dog before?" Hodge folded his hands into his pockets. Rhys shook his head, studying the creature. "Not ever?"

"When dogs are happy, they wag their tails. It's how they tell humans and other dogs how they feel," said Kallen, regarding Rhys. Her warm smile made a jolt run through Rhys' chest. "You can pet him." Kallen knelt beside the dog who began licking her.

"I don't want it to do that," said Rhys.

"Look, just pet him. Like this," instructed Kallen as she slid her hand down the dog's broad head. Rhys hesitantly held his hand out. Mister Jon turned his attention from Kallen and leaned toward Rhys' hand. Certain the dog was going to bite into his flesh, Rhys jerked away. "He's going to smell you. Their sense of smell is better than ours. This is how he learns about you."

Rhys returned his hand before the dog's nose and allowed the beast to sniff him. Intrigued, Mister Jon stood and inched closer.

"Talk to him," said Kallen. "They like that." She scratched Mister Jon's head. "Don't you?" Mister Jon squinted his eyes at her, laid his ears back, and wagged his tail fiercely. The dog's physical change was astounding. How could a creature of limited intelligence communicate so well and understand human words?

"Hey, Kallen," murmured Hodge. Both Kallen and Rhys followed his gaze to a sunboard trolling back into port. Even from a distance, Rhys could see the person piloting the craft was an elderly man. He was lean, as brown as the earth, and wiry.

"Hey!" called Kallen, standing. She waved to the man. "JiJi!"

Mister Jon barked in glee and began pacing the docks excitedly. Kallen followed the dog to the edge of one of the wharves and waited for the man. "Who's that?" asked Rhys.

"Reza—he's New Arbroath's lead engineer in solar energy. He builds all of our sunboards and solar paneling," explained Hodge. "He's so old some say he was alive before the exodus." Rhys looked at Hodge incredulously. "It's a joke, Rhys."

As Kallen helped pull Reza into a slip, Rhys studied the man. How was someone his age still functioning? Though Hodge had been exaggerating, his words appeared closer to truth. The man, Reza, was ancient. When were the people of New Arbroath going to end his suffering? To be so old and still be given work—these people clearly had a different set of ideals. In addition, they made him dress in nothing but a tattered pair of pants so his bare, extremely dark chest took the brunt of the sun.

As Reza stepped onto the docks, Mister Jon pushed past Kallen and, whining, greeted him. The elderly man petted the dog and began speaking to Kallen. It took Rhys a moment to realize he no longer understood what they were saying.

"Don't worry. I can't understand them either," said Hodge. "Why do you think Vinz always sends Kallen?"

"But you were arguing earlier about haggling. That implies you are able to communicate with him."

Hodge nodded to Reza. "He speaks Aabesh too. Elali is his native tongue though."

"How does Kallen know it and you don't?"

"That's her grandfather."

"Grandfather?"

"Ehh, her father's father." Hodge led Rhys to them. "Old Man," he greeted with a friendly wave.

Reza, Kallen's grandfather, glanced at him and then looked at Rhys. Unlike everyone else who stared unashamedly at his light eyes and skin, the old man smiled and said, "You've brought someone new."

"JiJi, this is Rhys." She grabbed Rhys' arm and pulled him forward. "He's very interested in sunboards."

"Uh, hello," Rhys murmured awkwardly.

"A pleasure," said Reza, resting his hand on Mister Jon. "Let's get out of the sun." As he turned, he said something under his breath to Kallen who bashfully nudged her grandfather.

Once under the canopy of the shop, Rhys pulled his headscarf off and looked about. Sunboards hung from the ceiling while shelves crammed with parts, tools, and material adorned the walls.

"So, you're looking for a new board?" asked Reza, seating himself on a homemade workbench propped up by two cinder blocks.

"Hodge broke ours," Kallen asserted flatly.

"I didn't *break* it," retorted Hodge.

"As usual, you don't get a discount just because you're my granddaughter," said Reza. He looked at Rhys. "And what is your purpose here?"

"Purpose?" asked Rhys.

Reza pointed to Kallen. "Mechanic." He pointed to Hodge. "Pilot." He then pointed to Rhys and gave him a questioning look.

"Oh, I'm... "

"He's an engineer," provided Kallen. "He wants to become a pilot too just in case something happens to Hodge or Kashim."

Reza considered him. "You have any experience flying?"

"No."

"You have any experience working on sunboards?"

"No."

Reza stood and ushered Hodge out. "Go out and look at the three on the other side."

"Why not the two over there?" asked Hodge.

"Because you can't afford those," the old man replied smartly. Hodge growled under his breath and meandered out of the shop down the docks. Reza turned to Kallen. "Now, what's this really about?"

"Really, we need a board," explained Kallen. Reza pointed to Rhys. "And he needs a job."

"A job?" asked Rhys. "I didn't ask for that."

"Vinz told me you must have a job in order to stay on *Themis*. Unless, of course... you don't want to stay with us." Kallen's face fell slightly. "You could stay in town if you want. I know a few people who could use your expertise."

"What about Alina?"

"She'll be coming too. She's a medic after all, and we don't have one of those."

"A job then?" asked Reza. Rhys nodded. "Kallen, if he's going with your crew, what are you wanting from me?"

Kallen grinned. "Teach him."

"When do you leave?"

"Tonight."

"Kallen," wheezed Reza, sitting heavily. "It took years to teach you."

"Then let him look through the manuals you've written," argued Kallen. "Let him study the boards, your notes, anything."

Reza glanced at Rhys and then continued the conversation in Elali, leaving Rhys to guess what they were saying. Finally, Reza sighed and went out to join Hodge. Kallen folded her arms behind her back and smiled proudly. "What?" asked Rhys not understanding the expression on her face.

"He's going to teach you, well... I mean, you're going to teach yourself. He's letting you borrow his materials." Kallen pointed to the shelf lined with bound manuals, books, and notebooks on the far wall. "Read those by this evening."

"Understood," replied Rhys. Kallen's smile faded and her mouth opened in surprise. "What?"

"I was... joking, but can you really do that?"

Rhys gazed at the shelf. "Once I'm able to translate the text. Could you translate a couple of pages so I can begin the process?"

"Uh, sure. Let me choose a new board and then I'll come back and start translating," said Kallen. Rhys looked about the shack thoughtfully. "Did you want to come with me?"

"No, I'll stay here."

Kallen flitted from the shop. Rhys waited until she was out of sight before diving for the manuals. *Get to work, Pathos,* he instructed.

Start with this book, said Pathos. Rhys, sensing which book his AI was talking about, leaned forward and withdrew a slender manual third from the end. *It appears to have been heavily used, implying that it is important.*

I need Kallen to translate this. I can't work off of nothing.

Open it, ordered Pathos. Rhys opened the book and turned the first two pages. *Aabesh is a syllabic language meaning that it has more words, characters, and symbols than Interstellar Nefegian. It'll be more difficult to translate.*

Rhys studied the pages. Every so often, an intelligible word leapt from the page at his eyes. *This is all you have so far?*

Words, implied meanings, and characters have been accumulating in the database since we arrived. This method can only provide a very rough translation of a select number of words.

Then that's what we'll have to do, replied Rhys. He set the book down and picked up another. Quickly he flipped through it. There were sketches with arrows pointing at various machines as well as extensive lists of words he couldn't understand.

Perhaps if Logos is willing to data-share, the translation process can be completed more quickly.

I get the feeling Alina is not willing to do that right now... His sentence faded as more of the words began appearing comprehendible. Suddenly, 50 percent of the page was legible. *Pathos! What are you doing?*

Comparing Aabesh to ancient languages found in the database.

Keep doing it!

Return to the initial book. It has the most necessary information.

Rhys obeyed and began flipping through the pages. Nearly every word was translated now. *Very good, Pathos. Preparing for data extraction.*

Standby... Preparations complete. Initiating.

The entire page was imprinted on his mind. He turned the page and repeated the action. Again and again and again. Within minutes, he completed the first manual, withdrew another from the shelf, and began reading it. When he finished, he selected another. He chose the shortest manuals, the thin notebooks written only in Aabesh. If he picked up a book written in Elali, he traded it for another.

He stood at the shelf deep in a trance for an unknown amount of time. His mind was moving, dancing. Even working for the engineering department on Caelestis, he had never felt such an intense passion for something. He just wanted to keep turning the pages—he *needed* to. Engines, solar paneling, batteries, wind shifts and currents, thermal pockets, drag, lift, thrust, stall out, ailerons, stabilizers. It was all so familiar. The ideas were new but the concepts weren't. He understood the mechanics of the machines. He knew how they flew, how they worked. He needed to understand how they worked on Earth though.

"You better finish up."

Rhys startled, nearly dropping the notebook he was reading. He grimaced as his knees knocked and his back strained. His neck hurt. He expected to see Hodge—they had had more than enough time to choose and purchase a new sunboard. Instead, he found Reza sitting in the shadows of a dim lamp. It was dusk. Rhys looked from the old man to the waterfront.

"They'll be casting off soon," said Reza. Rhys looked about forlornly, perplexed by the passage of time. "Did you learn what you needed to?"

"Yes. Thank you," replied Rhys, bypassing the old man. Reza nodded. "Elali. That's your native language, right?"

"It's a dying language. Many of the manuals I wrote when I was younger are in Elali because I wasn't proficient enough to write them in Aabesh."

Rhys glanced back at the shelves. "I'll translate them for you."

"I was going to get to it eventually."

Rhys gazed at Reza and then said, "No, you weren't." The old man stood and approached Rhys, an indescribable expression on his face. "They've been sitting on that shelf for years." Rhys held up his hands to show Reza the brown ink and dust that covered his fingertips and palms.

The old man turned to the shelf and began gathering various books. When his arms were full, he handed them to Rhys and continued to withdraw more. "Finish them before the next time I see you."

"Thank you," said Rhys, stretching to see over the books.

Reza motioned for him to leave. "Mister Jon will see you to *Themis*."

Rhys glanced at Mister Jon who sat beside him happily wagging his whip-like tail. "Come on, Mister Jon."

"Ehh, Rhys?"

Rhys looked over his shoulder at the old man.

"Take care of my granddaughter. With you and your sister here, tension will be high at sea."

Rhys nodded and left the shop. In dusk's light, he returned to *Themis*, climbed the stairs, and entered the bridge. Vinz glanced at him from his chair and then said to the others, "We're launching. Let's go."

Rhys hurried to his quarters. His arms were starting to hurt. He found Alina sitting on her bed folding clothes. When he entered, she looked up but remained silent. With care, Rhys set the books and notebooks on the floor at the end of his bed and pushed them against the wall. "How are you?" he asked, settling on his bed.

"Fine," replied Alina tonelessly.

"What have you been doing?"

"Waiting for you."

Rhys smiled and lay back. "Sorry. I couldn't pull myself away from the books. It was so strange. I've never felt so, uh, accomplished." He chuckled to himself. "This goes way deeper than intellect or knowledge. It's... I don't know what it is. But, it's amazing."

"I'm glad."

Sensing something was wrong, he sat up and looked at his younger sister. "What have you been doing? You haven't been waiting here the entire time have you?"

Exasperated, Alina set the clothes on her lap and glared at him. "Yes. We've been waiting. For *you*. The ship wasn't going to launch until you returned."

"What's wrong?"

"Maybe I don't want to be here," murmured Alina, playing with the hem of her blouse. "There are people who need me in New Arbroath."

"We need you."

"Not the same. I don't know what this new assignment is, but this ship is asking for trouble. The people injured in town weren't. They were innocents just caught in the middle." Alina glared at her hands. "A woman started crying because Hodge came to retrieve me. They need me, Rhys. I shouldn't be here."

After a moment, Rhys murmured, "I can't let you be alone. You saw what happened this morning."

Alina dumped all her clothes on the floor in a sudden rage. "This isn't about me! There are people dying. Why am I here? Why am I on this *ship*?"

"Because they want us to be." Even as he said it, he knew it was the wrong answer.

Alina turned her brilliant blue gaze on him. "We're here because Vinz wants to keep his eye on us. Rhys, our talents can be used elsewhere!"

Rhys glanced at the pile of books. "Alina… my talents are needed here. I think."

"For what? Are you saving lives? Are you preventing disease? Are you rebuilding homes?"

"No. But this is—"

Alina crossed the cabin and sat next to him. "Rhys, please. I am needed in town. Not here."

"Alina… I can't. Wherever you are, I must be."

"Then come with me. I can give you my data. We could work together and heal people." She pulled his hands into hers. "We didn't have doctors on Caelestis because we don't become sick or diseased. There was no purpose. But here—Rhys, *here* we have a purpose!"

Utterly torn, Rhys remained silent. Alina had a point. He had been studying, but for what? Sunboarding? What good was that when they could be saving lives and healing others? He could let Alina have her way. They could return to the docks, disembark, learn medicine, and work as doctors for New Arbroath. They could save lives.

"Rhys?" murmured Alina.

He should tell Vinz. They needed to get off. They needed to return to town. Alina was needed. Her talents couldn't go wasted.

Alina stood and pulled at his arms. "Come on. We can't let them get too far from shore."

Rhys strained against her. "I'm sorry," he said softly. "I feel… I feel strongly that I need to be here. I can't go back. Not this time." Alina opened her mouth, but no words came from her throat. "Not this time." Rhys stood, brushed past her, and left their cabin. He closed the door behind him and leaned against it. "I'm sorry."

8
THE MEAL

"RHYS?"

Rhys turned to find Kallen standing in the hallway outside the galley. He hoped she couldn't see the distress on his face.

"Are you hungry? I've started cooking. We're going to eat tonight. Would you like to watch?"

Rhys glanced at his cabin door before following her into the galley.

"You didn't seem to know what cooking was, so I thought I'd show you." Kallen picked up several bags from the floor. "Can you get the rest?" Rhys carried the remaining three to her and watched her unpack them. As she organized the foreign vegetables and animal carcasses, she said, "I tried to tell you we were leaving, but you were enthralled with your work. I thought you said you needed help translating?"

"I thought so too, however, my computer was able to match the characters to others from history."

"So, you're proficient in Aabesh now?"

"It would seem that way."

Kallen glanced at him. "What's wrong?"

Rhys leaned against the nearest table. "Nothing. I'm fine." In an attempt to change the subject, he asked, "Where are we going?"

Kallen chuckled. "That's difficult to explain." She counted the plants resting on the counter. "It would be best if Vinz told you."

"The judge gave us an assignment?"

"He did." Her face darkened. "There's a chance we may have to fight."

"Pantaraks?"

She nodded.

"Why?"

"Joss told us it's in an attempt to make peace." She began withdrawing pots, pans, and cutting boards from the cabinets with a sigh. After a moment, she stopped, her thoughts obviously elsewhere. "Vinz wants to meet with the Pantaraks to talk with their leader."

"Is that possible?"

"As far as I know, all attempts to speak with Pantarak leaders have been met with violence."

"How will our attempt be any different?"

Kallen pulled a knife from a drawer, aligned a leafy plant on the cutting board, and began cutting. "Up until now, we've had no one to vouch for us. We've had nothing they want." She nodded to herself. "This time it will be different. I can tell."

Rhys crossed the space between them and gently stilled her hand. Kallen didn't look at him. "It will be different this time," he said, "because Alina and I are here?" Kallen pursed her lips and nodded. "Is Vinz planning to pass us over to the Pantaraks in exchange for a truce?" When Kallen didn't answer, Rhys gripped her hand tighter and placed his fingers on the knife's handle. "Kallen," he murmured. "Is Vinz planning to give us to the Pantaraks?"

"No. No, he's not."

"Then what is he planning?"

"He's going with you," she whispered.

"He... What?"

"You three are going to go talk to the Pantarak high priest."

Rhys released her and leaned against the counter. "If he's not giving us to—"

"That's all I know," interrupted Kallen. She finally met his gaze. "I don't want you or Alina hurt. I've told Vinz that from the beginning."

Rhys regarded her. Her words sounded sincere. "What do you want from us then?"

Kallen continued cutting through the greens with a satisfying crunch. "You will be a part of this crew. You will help me with maintenance, act as a sunboard pilot, and take care of your crewmates. In exchange, you will have a home, a place to sleep, food, and a family. You will be strong and do what is required of you to survive and to achieve peace. That is this ship's mission, to create the best possible world wherein people can live together as one and collectively work toward a better future."

Rhys stared at her. The advancement of the human race, the will to survive, even here it was strong. There were people looking to accomplish the same mission as those on Caelestis. That had been humanity's charge since the dawn of mankind. It hadn't been lost on Earth. It was just at a different stage!

Kallen passed him a nervous smile. "What's... that strange look for?"

"Uh, nothing." Clearing his thoughts, Rhys straightened himself to move away, but Kallen stopped him with a tender touch.

"Stay. Please."

For the next 20 minutes, Rhys watched as Kallen cut and diced, poured substances from pan to pot, skewered meat that belonged to an omnivorous animal named a jerabo, sprinkled mysterious powders, stirred, and repeated. All the while, she described what she was doing and what she was cooking. She even let him taste certain items. By the time the meal was ready to eat, Rhys could hardly contain himself. Never before had he smelled such an interesting and enticing aroma. Just watching the boiling pot of thick broth made his body quiver in excitement.

Crew members eventually began wandering into the galley. Hodge, who was among the first, stepped into the galley, inhaled deeply, and growled, "Yes."

Rhys grinned as Kallen rolled her eyes.

The lanky man seated himself at the table and eyed the pot. "I haven't eaten in three days."

"I haven't eaten in four," snapped Kallen, stirring the pot's contents. "And Rhys' last meal was in space."

"Yeah, how *have* you been able to go so long without eating?" asked Hodge.

"Emergency rations," Rhys explained.

"So, you *have* been eating."

"No. It's... a type of pill. It slows—"

Hodge slumped over the table dramatically. "Kallen... I'm dying."

"Rhys," said Kallen. She ladled some of the pot's contents into a bowl and handed it to him. "Take that to Hodge."

Though Rhys was tempted to down the entire bowl himself, he obeyed and deposited the culinary gift before Hodge. The man grinned foolishly at Rhys and then said with sincerity, "Thank you, Kallen."

Kallen tapped Rhys on the shoulder and gave him a bowl. "Eat. I'll retrieve Alina."

Though he had watched Kallen strip the vegetables, cut the meat, and cook the broth, Rhys cautiously sniffed the bowl's contents and sipped. He couldn't help but close his eyes in utter delight and satisfaction. He brought the bowl back to his lips and took a deep gulp. He felt aglow.

"Good, right?" hummed Hodge.

At that moment, Kallen, Alina, Kashim, Lyruc, and Vinz entered. Rhys joined Hodge at the table and watched the others while he inhaled the stew. Kashim received his meal and seated himself at the other table. Alina guardedly took the bowl Kallen offered her and sat near Kashim.

Rhys wanted to yell at his sister to eat the stew—eat it!—but they were quarreling. In addition, she had severed her internal communication link with him. Instead, Rhys watched from the corner of his eye as his sister sniffed the food and then politely sipped. He saw ravenous hunger awaken in her just as it had in him. Furtively, she glanced at him and then at Kashim before taking several long gulps. Pleased, Rhys returned his attention to his bowl which was rapidly becoming empty.

Hodge's beckoning hand appeared before him and, somewhat ashamed, Rhys passed his bowl to him. Only as Hodge claimed second helpings did Rhys realize Vinz and Lyruc were gone. They had taken meals and disappeared. His disappointment was brief, however, as Kallen joined him, beaming.

"Is it good?" she asked.

Hodge set Rhys' bowl on the table. "Second bowl," he announced to Kallen.

"I'm so glad," breathed Kallen. "I tried to choose something I felt would be easy on your stomach."

"Easy... on my stomach?"

"Ehh, it won't make your stomach ache," clarified Kallen. "Is this food very strange?"

Rhys shook his head. "It's very delicious."

"What type of food do you usually eat? Meats? Vegetables? Grains?"

Rhys glanced at Alina who was still viciously attacking her bowl. "We never ate like this. It wasn't necessary. All of our food was placed in capsules. We received the same caloric intake and nutrients but bypassed preparation and cooking."

Kallen, Hodge, and Kashim exchanged looks before Kallen said, "You've never cooked or eaten a meal like this?" Rhys shook his head. Kallen bit her lip in a half-smile and then drank deeply from her bowl. She seemed proud.

As Rhys finished his second bowl, he looked over its rim at Kallen as she spoke between bites to Hodge about their new sunboard. Her eyebrows were expressive and moved in rhythm with her words. Her voice was melodic; her smile was endearing. The elegant curve of her throat to her collarbone was striking. Why couldn't he take his eyes off her?

Rhys glanced at Alina once more—she was speaking with Kashim—before flicking his eyes back to Kallen. He was startled when her dark, almond gaze met his. It seemed she had been studying him as well.

"So, tomorrow we do a test flight of the new board," said Hodge, killing the moment. "Kashim." Kashim finished what he was saying to Alina and looked at Hodge. "Is that fine?"

"Just let me know when," replied the burly man, stroking the scruff along his jaw.

"There's only one board. Why do both of you need to be there?" queried Rhys.

"You're going to be there too," said Kallen, leaning on the table. "You're going to become our backup pilot."

"We need everyone involved with the sunboards to be there," said Hodge. He tilted his chair back and balanced it against the wall. "Kashim has to see how it flies. It's my new board, but he has to work with me."

"I thought the two of you just provided data for the bridge." Rhys looked between Kashim and Hodge. "Isn't that right?"

"We do, but we often have to work together to fend off incoming attacks or position enemies for gunfire from the bridge," explained Kashim. The man's dark eyes rested on Rhys. "Could you do something like that?"

"Of course, he could." Kallen flashed Rhys a smile. "We just have to get him in the air first."

Alina stood, placed her bowl on the counter, thanked Kallen, and returned to their cabin. Silence ensued until the sound of their cabin door closing reverberated softly down the hallway.

"Is she ill?" fretted Kallen. "Was it the food? I can make something else."

Rhys twisted his bowl in his hands. "No. It's not the food."

"Are you sure? It's no problem. I can make something else. I know your stomachs may be sensitive."

Rhys stood with a smile. "Thank you. It was delicious." Trying to cover his eminent dismissal to go after Alina, he added, "I suddenly feel very tired."

"From the good food," offered Hodge.

"Yes—and the eight hours of nonstop studying. Thank you, Kallen." He placed his bowl on the counter as well and went after his sister.

He found Alina sitting on her bed with her back pressed against the wall and her knees to her chest. "You insulted Kallen," he said in Nefegian. "She was worried you were sick because of her food." Alina made a face but remained silent. "Alina, there may be people you can help in New Arbroath, but you have to think—"

"We're here, Rhys, because we're following what *you* want to do," interrupted Alina. "You were just thinking about yourself. You're here because you want to become a mechanic and a pilot. Rhys, how is that going to help people?"

"Think about the grand scheme of things," argued Rhys. "You're not doing that. You're too tied down to everything. It's affecting your logic."

"It's affecting… my logic?" The anger in Alina's voice was chilling. "My work is affecting my logic? You're the one who's trying to live out a lifelong dream of becoming useful. Rhys, my skills and talents—they can save lives! And you? Why are we here?"

Hurt on so many levels, Rhys just glowered at her.

Alina threw herself down and rolled over to face the wall. "Just leave me alone."

9
EVER DEEPER

THAT NIGHT, RHYS SLEPT FITFULLY. For several hours, he wrestled with unpleasant and nonsensical dreams. Finally, sometime in the middle of the night, he rose, glanced at Alina, and dressed. Barefooted, he left their room. The ship was silent save the distant rushing of water beneath them.

Like a ghost, he padded down the hallway, passing the other cabins, and up the stairs which he took to the outer deck. He slid the door open and stepped into the cool, nighttime air.

He leaned heavily against the railing, breathed deeply, and looked up at the billions of stars overhead. Without asking, Pathos provided him with the ancient names of constellations. Rhys stayed on the deck until his legs grew weary from standing.

Feeling more at ease, he returned below deck. As he strolled down the inner staircase, a high-pitched shriek pierced the silence. Rhys nearly slid down the stairs in surprise, his heart racing. A wailing of sorts rose from the hallway followed by a series of panicked yelps.

"Kallen! Kallen!" called Hodge. "Hey, hey. Kallen. Wake up. Wake up." Feet like lead under him, Rhys stumbled to the crew's cabin. There he found Hodge, a tangle of sheets, holding Kallen in her bed as she cried. She was covered in a heavy sweat; her skin glistened in the lamplight. Her hands, which were clenched at her chest, shook horribly.

"Deep breaths," instructed Kyo, leaning over the top bunk. "Deep breaths."

Kallen braced on Hodge, sobs racking her body. "Same dream?" Hodge muttered, clinging to her. Kallen nodded.

"Hey." Kyo motioned to Rhys who remained in the doorway.

"Uh… " Rhys studied the situation. "What's wrong?" He felt as if he were interrupting a very private moment.

Kallen didn't look up at him like she usually did. Her crying only quieted. "Bad dream," explained Hodge. "Go back to bed."

Rhys hesitated. Kallen's scream had made the hairs on the back of his neck stand on end. That kind of scream, his instincts told him, was from someone in horrific pain. Just like with the Pantarak man, his body had recoiled at the sound.

Hodge nodded to him. "Go on."

Rhys imparted Kyo a worried glance and then returned to his cabin. He felt in the last five days he had grown close to Kallen, but apparently, not close enough. He still knew nothing about her or anyone onboard. Rhys slipped into bed and stared at the ceiling. For as long as he lived, he would always remember the sound of Kallen's screams.

It was shortly after dawn when there came a knock on the cabin door. Rhys glanced at Alina, who was still asleep, and then slid out of bed. Dressed in only his pants, he answered the door. He wasn't sure who he expected, but it certainly wasn't Kallen. Squinting against the bright morning light, he mumbled, "What's wrong?"

Kallen glanced at his bare chest bashfully and then peered into the room at Alina. "We're going to be doing a test flight in the next hour. If you want, I can cook something for you and Alina before then."

Rhys' immediate inclination was to decline, however, the hopeful look on Kallen's face forced him to say, "Please. If you don't mind."

Kallen smiled proudly and turned on heel. "I'll start cooking."

Rhys closed the door behind him. "You heard her." Though he hadn't seen Alina wake, he had sensed her. "You want food?"

"No."

"You should try to eat something. It's going to be a hard day."

Alina rolled away so her back was to him. "For you maybe… "

"You'll offend Kallen. She wants so badly to cook for us."

"No, she wants to cook for *you*."

Rhys pulled on his blouse and grabbed his headscarf. "She was worried about you last night." Alina didn't reply. He laced up his boots, threw his scarf around his neck, and left for the galley. He found Kallen standing before the stove in thought while Hodge lay stretched out across three chairs.

"Where's Alina?" she asked.

"She's still asleep," lied Rhys.

"We usually don't eat meals in the morning." Kallen leaned against the counter. "We only eat every three days in the evening."

"You don't have to cook anything big."

"JiJi... I mean, my grandfather, he eats meals every morning because of his age. Ah!" she exclaimed, turning and throwing open a cabinet. She withdrew a large bag of grain, poured some into a clean pot, and set the bag aside. She went to the cool larder bolted to the floor near the stove and began rifling through its contents. Eventually, she pulled out a small jug of liquid as well as an odd fruit.

"Am I allowed any of that?" asked Hodge despondently.

"No," replied Kallen. "It will throw you off our schedule."

Hodge groaned. Intrigued, Rhys inquired, "You mean eating another meal so soon after last night will cause him to depart from the rest of the crew's eating schedule?"

"It will make him want to eat more, yes." Kallen held the jug of liquid out for Rhys to smell. "Jerabo milk."

"Milk?"

Kallen thought for a moment while Hodge chuckled. "The animals produce it," she said. "It's very good for you."

Milk, said Pathos. *A white liquid produced by the mammary glands of mammals to feed their young. Humans also are capable of producing this liquid.*

Rhys peered into the jug and then looked at Kallen incredulously. "It's... from the animal?"

"You can drink it. It won't hurt you." Kallen glanced at Hodge. "It's really nutritious."

"Uh... But we produce it too... "

Hodge burst into laughter and sat up. Kallen's face turned a shade of pink. "Yes, but... Hodge, help me explain!"

Hodge grabbed hold of the table to support his mirth. "No. You got yourself into this one."

Pathos, asked Rhys.

Only female humans can produce milk to feed their young. The liquid, which is expelled from the woman's mammary glands, has an intense blend of antibodies to help offspring develop stronger immune systems.

Rhys glanced at Kallen, who was still trying to figure out how to best explain where milk came from, before his eyes slipped to her chest. That's what breasts were for? How odd! How utterly ingenious.

His gaze must have stayed on her chest for too long because Kallen frowned and turned away to the stove. Rhys looked to Hodge in confusion and disbelief. Hodge, still laughing, stood and put his arm around Rhys. "Women are a never-ending supply of mysteries."

Though Rhys didn't fully understand what he meant, blood rushed under his skin and his ears felt as though they had been set aflame. Hodge laughed harder and shook Rhys fondly.

After devouring his meal, which Kallen called "frumenty," Rhys followed her and Hodge to the bridge. They found Vinz once again sitting skivvy in his chair, his leg hanging over the side. He wore only pants and an open cream-colored blouse that revealed flesh nearly as pale as Rhys'. Kyo and Andy were on deck as well. Lyruc had taken the night watch and was sleeping.

"Ready?" asked Vinz, going to the paneling at the front of the bridge. "We'll drop the anchor. Once we're stopped, I'll let you know when you can open the forward hatch."

"Where's Kashim?" asked Hodge.

"Checking the sails. I'll have him meet you in the forward hatch." Vinz passed an appraising eye over Rhys. "You're up to this?"

"I'm just watching for now, right?" Rhys looked between Hodge and Kallen.

"For now, yes," assured Kallen. She led them down the inner staircase to the forward hatch where she and Hodge began opening all of the portholes to allow in natural light. Rhys watched as Hodge placed his hand on a metal wheel, looked up at the ceiling, and began cranking. Kashim's sunboard dropped to the platform below where Kallen guided its keel to a sheath.

Both she and Hodge checked the board. As Kallen examined the connector and the board's steering mechanisms, Hodge withdrew the sail from its stow. Spotting his chance to be of some assistance, Rhys moved forward to help pull the sail to its full length parallel to the board.

"Kallen, we're anchored," came Vinz's voice over the communication pipes. "Whenever you're ready."

"We'll launch once Kashim's here," shouted Kallen.

A breath's moment later, Kashim entered the forward hatch through the outer door. "Here," he said. He crossed the cabin and placed his hand on a lever. "Ready for float?"

"Almost." Kallen pulled her boots off and rolled up her pants. Hodge and Kashim did so as well. Unsure why he should be doing it, Rhys also ripped his boots off, threw them toward the back door, and jerked up his pant legs. Kallen ran her eyes over the board, glanced at the sail, and then pointed to Kashim. Kashim pulled the lever and the forward hatch opened. Water spilled up the launch ramp. Rhys wanted to back away—it reminded him too much of their spacecraft flooding—but he forced himself not to move.

As Hodge and Kallen moved about the submerged ramp, Rhys circled them on the dry docking area, fascinated. "So this is flight capable?" he murmured in his native tongue.

"Hm?" asked Kallen.

Rhys glanced at her and then pointed to the sail which was lying folded parallel to the board. "This form won't generate enough lift to allow a human to become airborne. It must transform."

"Right," said Hodge. He pointed to the sail and used his arm as a diagram. "It begins perpendicular to the board, however, once it's reached flight speed, it can shift so it's parallel."

"The sail becomes the unit's wings," concluded Rhys. He leaned forward and ran a thumb along the sail. "And the material is solar paneling?"

"It's layered solar paneling and batteries," Hodge continued. "The paneling is made of cells that convert sunlight into energy. Once there is enough energy to power the board, the batteries layered underneath each of the panels store the energy for later use."

"How do you steer the board once it's in the air?" mused Rhys. "While in the water, the force on the keel allows you to direct the energy, but once in the air… "

"The sails you're thinking of," said Kallen, "are those used long ago. These are not cloth. They are far more rigid." She placed her hand fondly on the mast. "When vertical, they are flexible and create a balance between drag and thrust. When turned horizontal, however, thrust exceeds drag and allows the unit to go airborne.

"At any rate, the fin—the sail—once horizontal, has connectors within the mast that become active and allow the pilot to control ailerons." Kallen heaved the sail up and pointed to a long rigid structure along its hem. "Those are the ailerons." She went to the board and ran her hand over its smooth surface. "While on the water, the board remains free of cluttering controls, but when the pilot shifts the fin horizontal, that changes." She pointed to a small panel near the front of the board. "A pulley system controls the ailerons." She slid her hand midway down the board to two more panels positioned at an equal distance from one other. "These open and allow the pilot to control the rudder."

All of the information Kallen was sharing with him Rhys knew from Reza's notes, but her words solidified the knowledge. He nodded in understanding as Kashim brushed past him and waded onto the ramp.

Hodge steadied the board while Kallen held the majority of the sail out of the water. Kashim started the fan motor, a deathly loud ruckus, and then hoisted himself onto the board. He motioned to Hodge once he was situated. Hodge reached under the board and released the sheath holding the keel. The sunboard rocketed forward; the sail flew from Kallen's hands. By the time it was erect, Kashim was outside *Themis*.

Kallen and Hodge turned to prepare the new board, but Rhys watched with intense interest as Kashim pulled himself to his feet and balanced his unit. Rhys stepped aside so Kallen and Hodge could keep working, but his eyes never left Kashim.

"Rhys," said Kallen. "Can you lift this?" Rhys pulled his gaze from Kashim and went to help steady the new sunboard. "No, here." Kallen handed him the sail. Rhys held it out of the water and watched as she moved to steady the board. Hodge jerked his shirt off and rerolled his pants' legs. "Go easy on it. It's new. I know we did a test flight yesterday before we bought it, but you still don't know this board."

"Yeah, yeah," replied Hodge. "Ready?" Kallen started the fan motor. Hodge swung himself onto the board so he sat on his knees. Once he was balanced, he motioned to Kallen who released the keel from its sheath. As Hodge's new board sprang forward, Rhys freed the sail just like he had seen Kallen do. With even more grace than Kashim, Hodge shot out of the forward hatch and stood up the same moment the sail reached its full height.

Kallen crossed the hangar. "Rhys, help me. We're launching the dinghy." She pointed to the other side of the cabin. "Get the fan motor there." As Rhys obeyed, Kallen climbed above the open airway, unhooked the dinghy's chain, and kicked the craft to the launch ramp.

Rhys grabbed the fan motor and waded to the boat. Before Kallen could climb down, he had it mounted. After pulling the dinghy farther onto the launch ramp, he looked to Kallen for guidance. Seemingly impressed, she checked his work, loaded a light tool kit and numerous spare parts, and then climbed into the small boat. Rhys leapt in behind her, and they shot out of the forward hatch into the hot morning sun.

Kallen motored out not even a full kilometer and cut the engine. "Put your hood up," she instructed as the dinghy settled on the waves. "You'll burn." As Rhys wrapped his headscarf around his head and neck, Kallen pulled out binoculars and knelt on the side of the boat. "You see them?" She pointed to the two dots riding along the waves. Rhys squinted, but the sun was blinding.

She withdrew a wood and metal tool from her pocket, brought it to her lips, and blew on it. A shrill, piercing cry emanated from the instrument, prompting Rhys to cover his ears. Kallen blew it rhythmically until, in the distance, the two dots—Kashim and Hodge—changed their boards' directions and started back for *Themis*. Kallen stashed the whistle and binoculars and started the engine once more. They met Kashim and Hodge halfway.

"This thing is so smooth!" shouted Hodge, riding the waves alongside the dinghy.

Kallen cupped her mouth. "Kashim, any problems?" Kashim, who was farther out, motioned in the negative and then did a series of complex hand movements. "Right." Kallen looked back at Hodge who was behind the boat now. "Hodge, take off."

In a single motion, Hodge swept his right leg out, hooked his foot onto the conversion lever, and rotated the fin horizontally. As it passed over his head, he lowered himself to his knees and pulled up on the two hidden compartments at the front of the board. He locked the sail into place and then stretched himself along the board, pushing his feet into the rudder pedals. The fan which had been quiet until then roared to life, and his board screamed across the open sea. After several meters, the unit lifted out of the water, gained more speed, and then whipped into the air. Rhys, heart beating hard, stood up in the dinghy, shaded his eyes from the sun, and followed Hodge. A moment later, Kashim also took off.

Kallen pulled on Rhys' shirt to make him sit and then throttled the fan engine. As the dinghy bounced over the waves, Rhys gaped up at Hodge and Kashim.

He needed to be up there.

For nearly an hour, they tracked the two pilots as they dove, circled, and weaved. Kallen explained in intervals what they were doing. Though the dexterity of the boards was not what Rhys had hoped for after studying Reza's manuals, they were fast and could be precisely operated. They were perfect for data collection and scouting. A good pilot could possibly even use them for battle.

Eventually, Kallen turned the dinghy back for *Themis*. As she drove, she motioned for Rhys to join her near the fan. Once he was beside her, she leaned into him and shouted, "See the wake behind us?" Rhys nodded. "To them," she pointed to Hodge and Kashim, "it's white. So, they can see us moving. They can see we're heading for *Themis*. We'll dock the dinghy and then wait for them. Our docking procedures are reverse of the launch. Unless there's major damage to one of the units. We'll dock, then Hodge, then Kashim."

"Does Kashim always go out first?"

Kallen nodded. "He's not as skilled a pilot as Hodge. If someone is going to be shot down or run into danger, we want it to be him, not Hodge."

"And he knows this?"

"Of course. Every person plays an important role onboard. Kashim knows that, if we enter a dangerous area, it's his job to make sure Hodge can safely launch. He's also responsible for helping Hodge dock unharmed."

"How many people does it take to dock a sunboard?"

"Two for the dinghy, three for a sunboard," replied Kallen over the roar of the fan. "Normally, we don't have three for a sunboard, so Lyruc comes down to help." She smiled. "With you here, it evens out!"

Once on the launch ramp, Kallen leapt out of the boat and began dismantling the fan motor. After disengaging the motor, Rhys took it so she could hook the raft to the ceiling chains.

"Help me," she commanded, straining against a metal crank. Rhys deposited the fan motor where he had originally found it and joined her. Together, they drew the dinghy to the ceiling. "Hold it there." Kallen released the crank, climbed the wall expertly, and pulled the boat to her. "Good. Lock it." Rhys did as he was told. Kallen finished chaining the dinghy, shimmied down the wall, and jogged across the cabin to speak into the communication pipes. "Notify Hodge. We're ready for docking."

"Notifying Hodge," replied Vinz.

Kallen returned to the ramp and stood in the water. "Hodge is going to return to surf. Just before he enters the hangar, he will unlock the sail and push it back into its storage position. He has to still be moving fast though to make it into the hatch."

"So he has to move the sail into its storage position just before entering the hangar, but if he does it too soon, it will hit the water. So, our job is to stop his unit but also catch the sail?"

Kallen nodded. "Exactly. You must slow his entrance. I'll grab the sail."

"Does his keel have to be locked in the sheath?"

"No. We need to stow the sail, chain the board, and lift it to the ceiling. For now, it doesn't matter how quickly we do it, but in desperate situations, how fast we move his board out of the way can determine whether Kashim lives. Ehh, ready? Here he comes. Watch out for the keel sheath on the ramp."

Rhys pulled his headscarf away from his face and looked out the forward hatch. Hodge was already on the water and had converted the board to its windsurfing mode. Rhys positioned himself next to Kallen near the entrance. The water was up to his thighs.

"Strong hands, Rhys," reminded Kallen as Hodge unlocked the sail. Rhys braced himself to catch the board. Muscles tight, he grabbed hold of the nose of the board—and was promptly carried backward. The board was heavier and much more difficult to stop than he had originally thought.

Hodge flung himself off and grabbed hold of the rim. The board came to a halt. Rhys gave Hodge an apologetic look. Hodge shrugged. "It's heavy."

"Let's get it stowed," said Kallen, folding the sail and pushing it into its storage compartment along the side of the board. "Hook it up." Rhys grabbed the chain hanging overhead and passed it to Hodge.

"It goes here and here." Hodge showed Rhys exactly where to connect the locks. "And then we hoist it."

Once the sunboard was docked, Hodge notified the bridge, and positioned himself on the launch ramp. Rhys watched as they worked together to receive Kashim.

"Woo!" cheered Hodge as he finished hoisting Kashim's board to the ceiling. He hugged Kallen and then clapped Rhys on the shoulder. "That went really smooth!" He shook Rhys. "You. If you're going to be a pilot, you have to become stronger."

"How do I do that?" Rhys glanced at Kallen. For some reason, he was embarrassed Hodge had said that in front of her.

"We'll work on it."

"Raising the hatch door," announced Kashim. Everyone backed out of the water and waited as he closed the hatch.

"Bridge, we're finished," reported Kallen into the communication pipe.

"Launching *Themis*," came Kyo's reply.

"Is that it?" Rhys asked.

"For now." Hodge laughed. "I'm tired. Flying that thing is hard work."

"*You're* tired?" asked Kashim. "You're 24. Say that again when you're my age." Hodge followed Kashim out of the forward hatch.

"Eh, Rhys?" asked Kallen. She nodded for him to stay behind. Rhys closed the door and looked at her. "I wanted to show you something."

She went to the far side of the cabin where the foreign piece of technology sat. Kallen pulled the drop cloth off the machine. It was definitely technology from space. It looked like a sunboard, but one that had been made by an incredibly advanced human race. Its materials were too well designed, well made. It was sleek, dynamic.

Rhys knelt to look under its belly but could discern nothing special. It was too dark and the machine was propped strangely against the wall. It was a meter and a half long, much shorter than the normal sunboards, and lacked a keel. The entire unit was black and silver.

He studied the creation and then looked to Kallen. "Well?" she asked.

"What?" asked Rhys.

"It's yours, right? Your people's?"

"Maybe. The materials look like something our ancestors used, but I have no idea what it is or what it does. It's a sunboard?"

"That's our best guess."

"Where did you find it?"

Kallen sat back. "Vinz inherited it from his parents."

"So, why doesn't Vinz know what it is?"

Kallen sat beside him. "He doesn't know what to do with it. Both of us have worked on it for ages. Its design is extremely precise. I can't get a tool between its seams to peel it apart and see what's going on inside."

Rhys glanced at Kallen. His eyes slipped to her low-cut blouse where the black disc on the leather thong hung. Hesitantly, he reached through the space between them and touched it. "And this?"

Kallen pulled the thong over her head. "Vinz gave it to me for safekeeping. Why? Do you think it has anything to do with it?"

"It's made of the same material." Rhys studied the piece. "Have you tested it?"

"Vinz has. I don't know what he's done with it, but he says that the machine doesn't react to the piece at all."

"It's made of the same material, but how does he know it is a part of the machine?"

"I suppose it's what he was told."

Rhys studied the square disc on the thong and then looked the machine over thoroughly. "Have you tried putting it in the water?"

"Once, but it sank on the launch ramp. It looks like a sunboard, but it isn't built to be on the water."

"Or at least, not on the water for long." Rhys glanced about the cabin. They were alone.

He didn't know why that thought crossed his mind, but it did, and suddenly he became hyperaware of Kallen's presence. Kallen must have had the same realization because she began studying the drop cloth with hollow intent. Not knowing what he should do, Rhys took the necklace and slipped it back over her neck. His skin burned where his fingers touched her flesh.

As he pulled his hands away, Kallen touched his arm. Rhys' breath caught in his chest. She languorously slid her hand down to his and intertwined their fingers. Rhys resisted the urge to jerk away as white fire torched his skin. Her eyes were entrancing, her skin soft. She smelled warm.

Kallen cleared her throat, ran her thumb along the top of his hand, and said, "I, ehh, I know this is difficult for you, ehh, being so close. Alina explained... that neither of you is very comfortable being physical with others." Kallen chuckled. "She doesn't like it when I touch her either." Her smile faded slightly. "We're going to be sailing for a while. I would like to get to know you better."

Rhys began to draw away. He had no idea what he was doing. He didn't understand anything his body was telling him. His mind was foggy, his throat tight. "I... " Rhys cleared his throat. "I don't know... "

Kallen leaned forward. Rhys jerked away warily—her face was too close. "Rhys."

"Kallen, I... " He couldn't form a proper sentence. It was becoming harder to translate. "I don't know... what... "

The look in Kallen's eyes changed, and Rhys realized he had spoken in his own tongue. Frustrated, he pulled away. He didn't understand any of this! What was happening to him?

Kallen sat back and regarded him thoughtfully. She kept his hand trapped with hers resting on her leg. For several long moments, they sat in utter silence. Eventually, Rhys' heart slid back into his chest. He could feel the blood, which had been warming his face, slowly recover its usual circulatory routines. He swallowed—there was still a lump in his throat—and took a deep breath.

"Better?" Kallen asked, amused.

Rhys nodded and then glanced at their hands still intertwined. "I'm sorry," he murmured. He felt humiliated, embarrassed.

"Like all things, it takes practice." She unfolded his hand and traced the lines running across his palm. "Maybe later this afternoon or tomorrow Hodge will take you out on the new board. You've got to fly sometime."

"Would that be possible?" asked Rhys.

Kallen ran her fingers along his wrist. "It won't be as smooth as a solo flight, but it's possible. That's how he taught Kashim. JiJi taught me long ago, but I don't have the strength to move it as smoothly as Hodge does. It takes more than just skill." She nodded to him. "That's why you have to get stronger. Hodge will help you. In the beginning, you'll be sore, but you'll become accustomed to the new tasks you're asking of your body."

There was a moment of silence before Rhys softly said, "May I ask you something?" Kallen nodded. "Last night… " The look on Kallen's face dimmed; her lips pursed. "I'm sorry. I shouldn't have asked. I apologize."

"No, you shouldn't be sorry. I woke the entire ship." She began to pull her hand away, but Rhys stopped her. "I would rather not talk about it, if that's fine. I'm sorry, Rhys. It's just… bad things happened, and I don't want to remember them. Do you understand?"

"Can you forget them?"

Kallen gazed at him in confusion.

"Can you forget them, the bad things?"

"Some things… No, you can't forget them." Kallen rose to her feet and straightened her damp clothes.

Rhys glanced at the machine and then stood as well. "Kallen?"

"Hm?"

"The bad things, you can tell them to me. I can hold them for you."

Kallen's mouth parted and an indescribable expression passed over her face. Rhys, unsure as to why he had just said that or what it even meant, tried to change the subject. "I should, uh, go check on Alina."

Kallen nodded, and Rhys left the forward hatch.

He didn't go straight to his cabin as he had told Kallen. Instead, he went to the bridge to confront Vinz. Wherever they were going, whatever they were doing, he needed to know. He needed to prepare himself physically and mentally for the future.

Unfortunately, Vinz was not on the bridge. He found only Andy and Kyo. "Where's Vinz?"

Andy swiveled in his chair. "His cabin. He and Kashim are talking. Do you need something?"

"I just want to talk." He left the bridge and stalked down to Vinz's cabin at the end of the hallway. Kashim opened the door to his stiff knock.

Rhys peered past him at Vinz who leaned against a dresser. "May I speak with you?

After a quick nod from the Overseer, Kashim left the room. Rhys entered and casually looked about the cabin. It was larger than the others but packed with shelves, crates, a cluttered desk, a bookshelf, a bed, a chair, a dresser, and a chest.

"Rhys," said Vinz.

"You've been avoiding me." Rhys didn't expect those words from his own mouth, yet there they were, hanging in the air.

Vinz folded his arms across his chest. "Yes. I've been avoiding you."

"Why?"

"Why do you think?"

Rhys remained silent. The correct answer could be any number of social faux pas he had committed.

Vinz cleared his throat. "You offended me. We've clothed you, fed you, taken you in, and you can't muster some strength to speak to my commanding officer who, by the way, has the power to decommission this ship and exile me. You're lucky Kallen was with you. She explained to me everything that happened at the town hearing. I understand it was a gruesome sight, but that doesn't excuse your behavior."

"I didn't think I would be able to civilly speak with the judge," stuttered Rhys.

"Then you should have said something before we went."

"I didn't have a chance because no one tells me anything. I didn't know where we were going or what we were doing. I was told while on the staircase in the judge's building that we would be meeting with him. You share no information with me at all." Rhys motioned to the rest of the ship. "Everyone here knows what we're doing, where we're going. Alina and I are left in the dark."

Vinz regarded him and then said with a shrug, "You're not wrong."

Not expecting that response, Rhys fought to regain the upper hand. "So, where are we going?"

The Overseer straightened himself. Although he was taller than Rhys, it wasn't by much. "We're heading for Paducah to speak with the priest there. Paducah is where the terrorists are coming from, so I figure we should start there. If that doesn't work, then we'll head for Brechin, the Pantarak capital."

"And... why do you think the people in Paducah will want to see you?"

"I've got a contact that—"

"The Pantarak man you helped release."

Vinz stiffened. "How do you know about that?"

"I was in the forest that night. I saw you."

Vinz sighed. "Very well, Rhys. Yes, I was the one who released the Pantarak man. Kashim distracted the guards and I led the man into the forest. The only people who know are those onboard right now. My *contact* has sworn to pass word along to the priest in Paducah."

"And you think we'll be openly welcomed because you released him? Because you freed one of their warriors?"

Vinz shrugged. "I suppose we'll find out once we get there. It is my intention to meet with the priest and negotiate a truce. I don't want any more attacks on New Arbroath."

"Why don't we just go straight to the capital? That city, Brechin?"

"There are several factors hindering our entry into Brechin. This includes a lack of communication. We would be sunk before we entered their port without representation. I released the Pantarak captive in New Arbroath with the assurance that he would send word to Paducah. If we can *reiterate* that message through the surrounding villages, then we'll be able to access the capital without being sunk."

"Joss asked you to do this?"

"No. He wanted us to put a dent in the Pantarak population."

"Kill the Pantaraks?"

"I would prefer we didn't lose human life needlessly. So, we're taking a more ambitious route."

"Does everyone else know what we're doing?"

"Yes."

Rhys felt the fight rush out of him. He thought for a moment and then asked, "So, what are you wanting from Alina and me?"

"Competent crew members who can help this team achieve its goal. Alina already has field experience working in emergency medicine. She's ready. You aren't. Kashim and Hodge are starting a training regimen with you tomorrow. We need to have a spare pilot in the event something happens to one of them. Kallen will continue teaching you about the boards and *Themis*. The stronger our team is, the better chance we have of coming out of this mission alive."

"Why didn't you ask us if we even wanted to be a part of this assignment?" Rhys quietly countered. Vinz just gazed at him. "Five days.

We've been on this planet for five days. You know nothing about us. You don't know who we are, where we come from. You don't know our people, our customs, our culture. And just like that, you can use us. Like tools."

"What's your point, Rhys?" asked Vinz. "Time isn't on our side. It never has been."

"Then… " Rhys sighed and considered giving up. But a thought occurred to him. "What about Kallen?"

Vinz shrugged. "What about her?"

None of it really made sense. The crew seemed happy, well-organized, at home. How could their leader be so cold and emotionally distant? How could he so blatantly place them in harm's way? "I don't understand," he finally murmured.

"Rhys, you and Alina are a part of this crew now whether you like it or not. You being here is non-negotiable. For so long as this ship runs, you will be aboard her." Vinz lowered his voice. "This is the burden we bear."

"We?"

"You, Alina, and I. People on this planet instinctively look to us for answers because they sense we're different. We are leaders of men, Rhys."

"In order for humanity to succeed, however, man must first understand that no one person is better than the next. He is as talented, as well-studied, as his brother. Only when people understand that and learn to cooperate will there be peace," said Rhys.

"That may work where you're from, but here, man needs leaders to guide him."

"I don't agree with you," acknowledged Rhys, "but I understand your philosophy." He held out his hand as was customary on Earth. "Let us make a pact. Alina and I will do whatever we can to support this crew. In exchange, you must share with me everything you know. Plans, assignments, problems, victories, everything."

Vinz took Rhys' hand and bowed his head. "From here on out, I will consider you and Alina vital members of this crew and share all that I know." Vinz released his hand and straightened himself.

Emboldened, Rhys asked, "Kallen. Why does she have bad dreams?"

"She was captured by Pantaraks five years ago to be used as a live sacrifice during their annual celebration. She was raped and tortured. Reza and her father managed to sneak into Paducah and rescue her."

"I'm sorry, one moment," said Rhys as Pathos explained to him what rape was. Rhys' mouth fell open. "She... "

Vinz went to his desk. "We're going back to the village she was held captive in." He began shuffling through papers and manuals. "She was given the option to stay in New Arbroath with her grandfather. She declined—because of you. Apparently, she likes you."

Pathos forced him to continue asking questions despite his sudden urge to run to Kallen. "Uh, the board in the forward hatch. The one you and Kallen have been working on. What is it?"

"A board. You know about as much as I do."

"Kallen said it was yours. Where did you get it?"

"My parents. And they got it from their parents." Vinz stopped his fidgeting and leaned against the desk. "It didn't exactly come with an instruction manual though. My parents didn't know how to use it either. It's old. Generations old." Vinz pointed to Rhys. "And now, if you want, it will be yours. I've done what I can with it. Maybe your knowledge and your computer-thing can figure it out."

"I'll work on it."

"I want to—"

Vinz was interrupted as an announcement echoed through the communication pipe in his cabin. "Vinz, can you get up here? We've got weather heading in," said Andy.

"On my way." Vinz ushered him out of his cabin. "Let's go." Rhys followed Vinz down the hallway, past Kallen who was speaking quietly with Alina in the galley, and up to the bridge. "What is it?" Vinz asked Andy, Lyruc, and Kashim.

Kyo pointed straight ahead at the sea before them. Along the horizon was a wall of red clouds. "Sandstorm. It'll be here in the next two hours."

"How big do you estimate it to be?"

"Too big to bypass," Kashim asserted. "We'll have to go through it."

"The winds will start getting rough in the next hour."

"Kashim, Lyruc. Bring in the sails," said Vinz. "Rhys, take Hodge to the forward hatch and secure every crate, board, and tool barrel down there. Tell Alina and Kallen to prepare the cabins. Andy, when the waves start becoming intolerable, boost the engine and keep us straight into the wind. Let's go. Once the waves are bad, we won't be able to get much done."

Rhys left the bridge and rushed down the stairs to the galley. Alina and Kallen looked up at him. "There's bad weather coming. Secure the cabins. Where's Hodge?"

"Asleep in his bunk," replied Kallen. She was already moving the tables against the wall.

Rhys crossed the hall. "Hodge, hey. Bad weather. Get up. We need to secure the forward hatch."

Hodge rolled out of his bunk, grabbed his shirt, and together they went to the forward hatch. Within the half-hour, *Themis* began rocking. For a while, they were able to continue working, but before long, Rhys found himself stumbling backward and rolling forward.

"That's it! That's it," called Hodge, hooking a chain around a set of barrels. He sidestepped several paces toward the wall as *Themis* pitched forward. "Let's get out of here. I'm getting sick." Grabbing hold of one another, Rhys and Hodge staggered from the forward hatch into the main hallway. "Check to see if the girls need help with the cabins. I'll talk with the bridge."

Rhys teetered down the hallway. He checked the galley, the crew cabin, and his cabin. When he heard Alina's voice in Vinz's cabin, he turned on heel and pushed at the door. It didn't open. "Alina?" he called.

"We can't get out," said Kallen. "Vinz's bookcase fell over."

"Is that what's against the door?" asked Rhys, holding on to the wall to keep himself from sliding down the hallway. "Kallen? Alina?"

"Yes!" called Alina. "Here." Suddenly the internal communication link between him and Alina snapped on and images filled his head. It was exactly what she was seeing. Books, papers, manuals, and notebooks were strewn everywhere. "See? The bookcase."

Can you pick it up at all? he asked. *How heavy is it?*

Alina instructed Kallen to attempt to lift it. Together, the two girls strained against the bulky piece of furniture. It budged, barely.

Hold on! I'll be right back. Rhys turned, ran down the hallway, and ducked into the forward hatch to search for tools. He was halfway through a barrel when he realized something—he had resonance cutters in his cabin! Groaning, he slid across the forward hatch and stumbled back to his cabin. He tore open their emergency pack, which was strapped to the bunk, grabbed the resonance cutters, and skated to Vinz's cabin.

I have the resonance cutters! You two step back! Rhys waited for Alina to pull Kallen away before he activated the cutters. The glowing technology in his hands made him feel powerful. He flipped the cutters in his palm and dug the tool into the wood. With little force, the cutters sliced through the door. Rhys edged along the entire door frame and then cut out a chunk near the top so he could reach his hand through and pull the door away. He carried the door into his cabin, laid it on the floor, and returned to the hallway. "Can you two clear the area around the bookcase?"

The door at the top of the stairs opened and Hodge staggered down to him. "What are you doing?"

"They're trapped." Rhys motioned to the inaccessible doorway. "Vinz's bookcase fell." Hodge regarded the shimmering, blue cutters and then looked at the door. "It's too heavy for any of us to pick up and it's wedged against the doorframe."

"So you're going to cut through it." Hodge held onto the frame to steady himself. "I always told him that *gawan* bookcase was going to kill someone. It was one of the only things we never got around to bolting down."

"Ready?" asked Rhys, sliding down the hall as *Themis* tilted. Hodge grabbed his free hand and held him still.

"Almost, one moment!" called Kallen.

"Ready!" said Alina suddenly.

"I'm cutting." Rhys looked to Hodge. "Steady me." Hodge dug his foot into the doorway, gripped the frame, and then wrapped his muscled arm around Rhys' middle. Rhys accelerated the cutters and began slicing through the bookcase.

As soon as the furniture was halved, he instructed the girls to back away. He leaned back and kicked the top of the bookcase. It didn't move. "Again," said Hodge, stepping back with him. Together they slammed into the bookcase. It budged. "Again." They kicked it once more. The top slid forward into the room. Hodge wedged himself into the doorway and slammed the loosened bookcase with his hip. It gave immediately to reveal Kallen and Alina.

He helped Alina out and then pulled Kallen through the narrow opening. Rhys grabbed his sister as the ship pitched forward, disengaged the cutters, stuffed the tool into his waistline, and anchored himself to the doorway. Hodge wrapped his hands around Kallen and pulled her close to keep her on her feet.

"All of the other rooms are secured," panted Kallen, clutching Hodge. "It's just Vinz's."

"Then Vinz can take care of his own *gawan* cabin!" growled Hodge. "Let's go." They wobbled down the hallway, up the stairs, and into the bridge. Hodge and Kallen both turned to the back wall of the bridge and began unhooking latches from the wall. Jump seats sprang down. "Sit," Hodge ordered. Alina obeyed, and Hodge strapped her in.

Rhys grabbed Kallen, pushed her into a chair, buckled her in, and sat beside her. Once secured, he glanced around the bridge. Vinz stood before the glass screen, rocking back and forth with the ship; Andy and Kyo were strapped into their chairs; Kashim and Lyruc stood on either side of Vinz.

Great waves smashed into the glass screen as wind tore at the ship. *Themis* moaned and creaked in agony.

Rhys glanced at Kallen who was holding her head. Aside from Kashim, Kyo, and Vinz, everyone else appeared to be suffering from some level of nausea. Even Alina had her knees pulled against her chest, and her face pressed in her hands. Rhys suspected he personally had not succumbed to sea sickness because of the years he had spent in zero gravity twirling in a constant state of disorientation.

For the next three hours, the sandstorm raged. Mud repeatedly accumulated on the windscreen and was washed away. The ship pitched in every direction. By the time the winds began to die, both Alina and Andy had vomited. Though Kallen complained of a headache, she didn't throw up.

After another hour, Hodge unbuckled himself and helped Alina to her feet. Rhys offered to help Andy back to the bunks, but the ship's pilot refused and instead flopped down on the hard floor of the bridge. Rhys escorted Kallen down the stairs and into the main hallway.

"Thanks," she breathed, holding herself in the doorway of her cabin. She pressed her head and clenched her eyes. "Why is Alina sick and you aren't?"

Rhys shrugged. "I worked in zero gravity. She didn't."

Kallen flinched. "I need to lie down... " She turned and disappeared into her quarters. Rhys sidestepped several paces and looked into his own cabin. He found Hodge seated next to Alina who was lying prone in her bed. When she started to roll toward the edge of the bunk with the ship's rocking, Hodge blocked her with his body and chuckled. Alina smiled for the first time in days.

Rhys returned to the crew's cabin where he stood in the doorway and gazed into the darkness at Kallen's form. He contemplated checking on her, but something told him that he shouldn't enter her quarters uninvited. Instead, he backed away.

"Rhys," called Kallen.

"Hm?" Rhys looked back into the room.

She sat up with a grimace. "Is something wrong?"

"No. Can I get you something?"

"A wet cloth," she replied.

Rhys slipped into the washroom, wetted a washrag, and returned. Tentatively, he entered her room. Although the others also slept there, the cabin felt like her private quarters. Rhys handed Kallen the wet cloth, and she promptly placed it on her forehead. "Thank you." Her response was a rush of relief.

Rhys started for the doorway.

Kallen made some sort of noise, and he looked back at her. She motioned for him to return. Heart starting to beat faster, Rhys approached her bed. He felt awkward, confused, excited, scared, and worried—all at the same time. Kallen reached between them and tugged at his sleeve, a clear invitation to sit. Rhys didn't move. "I... " Kallen cleared her throat. "I don't want you to leave yet."

The pressure, the overwhelming myriad of emotions that now battered Rhys, was almost too much. "Why?" he said, truly confused. He couldn't look her in the eye. "I don't understand. I don't understand any... of this."

Kallen sat up, holding the wet cloth to her forehead. "Understand what?"

How was he supposed to explain everything he felt? Unable to voice what was going through his mind, he simply said, "You."

He felt Kallen's eyes on him. "What about me?"

Rhys fidgeted under her scrutiny. "Why do you... " He felt uncomfortable talking about it. Perhaps he wasn't supposed to say anything.

"Why do I give you so much attention?" concluded Kallen. Rhys looked at her in the dim lamplight. She smiled and laid the wet cloth on her knees. "Because I like you. I like who you are." Her voice was almost indiscernible. "A lot."

"Like?" This was an odd expression, one that didn't at all explain to Rhys why it was that, of all of the crew members, she focused on him the most. "You enjoy me?"

Chuckling, she reached between them, took his hand, and laid her forehead on her knees so her eyes were hidden. "Yes."

Rhys stared at her, unsure of how to proceed. She liked him? She enjoyed him? What was there to enjoy about him? He wasn't anything special; he had been told that all his life. After a moment, Rhys leaned forward slightly. "Uh, Pathos tells me that when... "

Kallen looked up at him, and his words caught in his throat. The glow of her skin in the lamplight was stunning. The expression on his face must have changed because Kallen's lips suddenly parted in a most attractive way and her eyes focused intently on his.

"Tells me... that... " he continued in Interstellar Nefegian. Why was this woman so intoxicating? Why did the mere presence of her make him lose all control of himself? What ancient, primal power did she possess? He had never felt this way around the other females in the colony. So why now? What did she have that the others didn't?

Kallen swung her legs off the bed and stood with the intent to meet him. But dizziness must have gotten the best of her and she wobbled. Rhys stepped into her, his arms going around her shoulders. The instant his skin touched hers though, electricity shot through him. Eyes clenched, Kallen held her head before resting against him.

Rhys froze. Aside from Alina, he had never before felt the warmth of another woman. Though he could feel the heat of her cheek through his blouse, it was her weight against him that tore at his most primal instincts, those which Pathos would have to explain later in private.

Despite the pain she was obviously in, Kallen smiled wearily. "I can hear your heart."

The profound statement shook Rhys' core. Until that very moment, he had viewed himself as a biological machine, one intertwined with synthetic materials to create a human specimen capable of supporting artificial intelligence.

She could *hear* his heart.

Unsure of how to reply, he said the next logical thing. "What... does it sound like?"

Kallen sighed contently. "Like mine."

Highly aware that Kallen could hear his racing pulse and shaky breathing, he asked self-consciously, "What... am I supposed to do?"

Kallen pulled away to meet his gaze, but their coming together was ruined as the ship tilted precariously to starboard. Rhys ushered her back to bed, relieved—and disappointed—that he was no longer holding her. As Kallen curled up, he retrieved the wet cloth and placed it once more across her forehead. Kallen trapped his hand along the cloth and then brought his fingers to her lips. She kissed his knuckles and then gently pulled. Rhys allowed himself to be drawn downward, a simmering mixture of confusion, excitement, and eagerness. Kallen rose up on her elbows so their faces were centimeters apart.

Rhys could hear his own ragged breathing. He didn't know what to do, he didn't know what to touch! Kallen's gaze flickered between his eyes and his mouth. The cue was so obvious, yet he hesitated. After a moment's reflection, he lowered his gaze and started to draw away.

"Nu-uh," whispered Kallen, taking hold of his shirt collar. This time, she didn't stop. She slid the wet cloth from her forehead and touched her lips to his. Rhys fell motionless. While a war raged inside him, his body remained still. Her breath was hot, her skin warm.

Kallen pulled away and lay back, her eyes searching his face. Rhys stared down at her. He couldn't comprehend what was happening. Why had she pressed her lips to his? What meaning did it have? And why did that simple gesture carry with it such power?

Enthralled, Rhys lowered himself to her, this time of his own accord, and stiffly pressed his lips against hers. Kallen's mouth yielded to his, causing the breath to catch in his chest. Startled, he jerked away. Kallen peered up at him innocently, her long eyelashes striking in the light. He... liked this. He liked being close to another human. He liked touching her. He liked the way she made his heart hurt and his body weak.

A hunger awakening in him, Rhys leaned down and kissed her. Although he was ready for her mouth to open and yield to him, the action still shocked him. Moving her lips, Kallen began teaching him the unfamiliar motions.

Rhys couldn't breathe, couldn't think. His mind was dark. Pathos was nonexistent. Logic didn't exist; reason didn't exist. He was nothing but a moldable mound of mush. All he wanted was her. He *needed* her.

Panting, he followed Kallen's mouth; he mimicked her every movement. Though the first several kisses were awkward and bumbling—at least from Rhys' perspective—the subsequent ones grew in fervor. When they pulled apart to breathe, Rhys wound his right arm around her shoulders and neck and brought her back for more. Grinning into his mouth, Kallen explored his face, neck, and shoulders, curling against him so their bodies were closer.

Finally, she pushed him away with a soft smile. Rhys gazed down at her; she was glowing. "Too fast," she murmured.

Rhys opened his mouth to say something, anything, but a sharp force jerked him backward out of the bed. Before he knew what was happening, he was being dragged out of the room by his shirt collar.

"Kashim!" shouted Kallen. "Stop it! Kashim!"

Fearing for his safety and driven by his already pounding heart, Rhys swept his leg out, catching Kashim behind the knee. In a single motion, he knocked the enormous man to the floor.

"Kashim!" screamed Kallen. Rhys spun on his back and crouched against the wall. Kallen flew from the cabin and planted herself between them as Kashim drew himself to his knees. "Stop, stop, stop. I'm fine. I'm fine. I... " Kallen looked at Rhys. "I asked him to... "

Kashim looked between Rhys and Kallen. "You're sure?" he asked. "I'll bash his head in right now."

Kallen grabbed Rhys' arm and pulled him to her protectively. "It's fine. I'm fine. I asked him to."

Kashim gazed at them as if he didn't believe her and then relaxed. He rubbed his hip which had taken the brunt of the fall. "Sorry," he murmured. "I thought you were—"

"I know," interrupted Rhys. "I wasn't."

The enormous man glanced at Kallen and then awkwardly walked down the hall and up the staircase to the bridge. Kallen breathed deeply and rubbed her head. "Sorry," she murmured. "Ehh, everyone here... "

"I'm fine," interrupted Rhys. The moment was gone. "They're just watching out for you. Uh, you should probably rest. I'm sure... you're still not feeling well."

Kallen frowned. He didn't know what that meant. "What are you going to do...now?"

"Reza's translation materials."

"You could work in my cabin," Kallen offered. Rhys felt heat rise in his face once more. It took all of his willpower to refuse. He wouldn't complete any work with her so nearby. "Are you sure?" she whispered.

Still bewildered, Rhys held her gaze. Though he knew he probably shouldn't ask, he needed clarification. The nonverbal cues Kallen was sending weren't meshing with what she was saying. She wanted him to work, but she didn't. He glanced at the doorway and then pulled her deeper into the cabin. "I'm sorry. I don't understand," he said lowly. Kallen's face folded into worry. "Do your words hold any sexual implications?"

Kallen smiled. "Yes. They do." Her gaze found his once more. "My words hold sexual implications."

"I see," replied Rhys clumsily. He thought for a moment. He needed to go this alone; Pathos could only help so much. "Uh, what is expected of me then... "

Kallen chuckled. "It's not an obligation." She folded her arms to herself. "I don't expect anything from you."

"Do you want sex?" clarified Rhys.

For the first time, Kallen's face flushed. "I want what you want."

What did that mean? Was it a trick? Was there a correct response? "I... " he began.

"Rhys," interrupted Vinz, appearing in the doorway. The Overseer looked between him and Kallen. "Come with me."

"Vinz," said Kallen, stopping Rhys. "He didn't do anything."

"I know. I still need to talk with him."

Rhys started to pull away, but Kallen clenched his arm. "Whatever you have to say to him can be said in front of me."

Rhys didn't expect her logic to sit well with the Overseer, but Vinz sighed and said, "Very well." He entered the cabin and closed the door behind him. Sensing that something bad was about to be said, Rhys steeled himself. "As you know, I allow relationships on the ship under two conditions."

Rhys glanced at Kallen. As you know? Why would Vinz use those particular words?

"So, I say this more for Rhys' benefit than yours." Vinz leveled his blue gaze at Rhys. "The two conditions are as follows. One, you cannot get pregnant."

"I'm... male," murmured Rhys. "I don't think I can physically bear a child, can I?"

Vinz sighed and continued. "Two, you cannot let it affect your work." Vinz nodded to Kallen. "If you get pregnant, I'm kicking you off at the next port. Am I understood?"

"Yes," replied Kallen.

"You cannot let your relationship affect your ability to work together or work with others on the crew," said Vinz. "You may sleep in the same cabin if you need to, however, keep all sexual activity under control."

Rhys gaped at him. So casual, so nonchalant. "I... " He glanced at Kallen in utter confusion. "I'm sorry. What's happening?"

"I've done my job as Overseer. Close the door next time." And with that, Vinz left the room and shut the door behind him.

For a long moment, neither of them said anything. Finally, Rhys looked at Kallen. "I... don't understand."

Kallen sat on the edge of her bed. "I'm sorry, Rhys."

Confused, Rhys remained silent. Why was she apologizing? What had she done?

Kallen sighed. "Go do your work."

"Are you... sure?"

She nudged him toward the door. "Go on."

10
DISCUSSION

For the remainder of the afternoon, Rhys sat in the galley and worked on translating Reza's manuals from Elali to Aabesh. Every so often someone would poke their head in and ask what he was doing, but for the most part, the crew kept to themselves. Whether that was because they were tired from the storm earlier or because they were purposefully avoiding the cabins for fear he and Kallen would be engaged in some illicit sexual activity, he didn't know or care. All he could think of was Kallen.

The idea of an individual's sexuality being a topic for conversation was bizarre and disconcerting. This was especially so when nearly six days ago, Rhys didn't know that he had a sexual identity or that humans could even reproduce! Here, at least aboard *Themis*, it was treated as a normal concept. It was something humans engaged in. It wasn't taboo or kept secret. It just was.

And what had Vinz meant by "as you know?" That implied Kallen was already familiar with his rules, meaning that there had been sexual relationships on *Themis* beforehand. But there was one woman onboard—Kallen. Were humans allowed more than one partner? Was that biologically and socially acceptable?

It was well into the evening before Kallen woke. Though she saw him in the galley, she disappeared down the hall to speak with Alina.

"You've been here for hours," said Andy, materializing in the galley doorway. "Aren't you tired?"

"No. I've made progress." Rhys held up a manual. "I've completed half of this one."

As Andy joined him at the table and began reading the material, Rhys studied the man. Like the others onboard, with the exception of Vinz, Andy was taller than Rhys. He did not appear extraordinarily muscled like Kashim nor were his shoulders broad like Lyruc's. If anything, Rhys thought his build resembled Hodge most closely—lean and toned. He had dark eyes, but the tone of his skin was lighter than the others', perhaps because he spent much of his time on the bridge shaded from the sun. Hodge had the most untidy hair aboard; Andy came in at a close second. While the majority of the crew members had their hair clipped short or pulled back in a horsetail, Andy kept his wavy, shoulder-length black locks half-drawn from his face. Like Kashim, Lyruc, and Hodge, a thin layer of scruff covered his lower jaw.

"You understand all of this?" asked Andy, flipping through the pages. From what Rhys had seen of the man and his interactions with Vinz, Andy was a serious individual who expected much of himself. It seemed that, while Kashim was Vinz's right-hand man and confidant, Andy commanded the bridge in the Overseer's absence.

Keeping his observations of Andy in mind, Rhys said, "There are some words I can't translate properly because they don't have a linguistic equivalent in Aabesh, but yes, I understand all of it."

"How long do you have to complete this?"

"Until we return to New Arbroath."

Andy set the manual aside. "What's the point? Are you being paid?"

"Paid? As in an exchanging of labor for viable currency?"

An amused look on his face, Andy nodded.

"No. I'm not being paid. It's for the advancement of mankind. Sunboards have played a crucial role in espionage, hunting, and exploration. To further their use, all of the research which has been written must be made available for the masses." Rhys shuffled through his notes. "Sharing knowledge is the only way true peace will ever be reached."

"Until our enemies acquire that information and use it to kill us," Andy countered matter-of-factly.

Rhys looked at him. "Would not your enemies be seeking peace as well? Humanity is an endangered species. Why would man actively seek to destroy his own?"

"Because man has wants and desires and different ways to achieve those." The First Mate leaned back in his chair. "Consider the Pantaraks with whom you're most familiar. Their goal is not to consolidate mankind and create peace or continue the human race. From the day they are born, they are taught that their lives are meaningless."

"In the grand scheme of things, all lives *are* meaningless," interrupted Rhys.

Andy shook his head. "Their goal is to expand their empire and gather a unified state of worshipers. This ideology is promoted not only by the priests in each of the towns but encouraged by the high priest in Brechin. All people who do not believe in the power of the white gods and their priests are apostates, people who renounce the truth. The Pantaraks do not want peace. The high priests want power, wealth, and eternal obedience."

"People such as these exist?" asked Rhys incredulously. "But it doesn't make sense. They defeat the purpose of survival." He thought. "So, the Pantaraks worship white gods? People like Alina and I?"

"Correct. Of course, there are various levels of purity. You and your sister are pure. Vinz isn't. He's what they would call a half-blood."

"How do they even know of our existence?"

"Ehh, thousands of years ago, humanity fled Earth in an exodus— you are a product of those people—but some humans were left behind. We are those people. Because all technology was essentially wiped off the Earth, humanity was forced to start anew. Cultures, civilizations, states, everything. Well, your people started showing back up. When they did, they brought with them advanced technology—sky craft, weapons, and the like. The people here could only explain their presence as gods. I mean, isn't that how man has always explained things he doesn't comprehend? He doesn't understand why the rivers flood, so he blames it upon gods or god-like beings. If a woman dies of disease, she did not follow the wishes of the white gods or their messengers, the priests. She rightfully deserved it."

Rhys regarded Andy. "We are human. All of us. And until every person understands that and grasps it, there will never be peace."

"How then do you posit we go about achieving such a phenomenal realization?" asked Vinz, slipping into the galley with Kallen and Alina. "As you speak, we are sailing toward Paducah, a town of the Pantarak people. How do you propose we teach them the concept of equality?"

"We're going to talk, right?" asked Rhys.

Vinz nodded. "And when that doesn't work, what will we do?"

"You're assuming it won't work from the beginning," argued Rhys.

"Yes. Assume it doesn't work. Everything falls apart. What then? How do you keep the peace when everyone here is captured?"

"Stop," chided Kallen softly.

Vinz glanced at her apologetically but continued. "We appeal to their nonsensical religious beliefs and show them something they cannot explain."

"Like?" asked Rhys.

Vinz shrugged. "The Pantarak people in Paducah have never seen a *true* white god." A dark shadow passed over the Overseer's face. "One look at you two and they'll think they're standing in the presence of the stars themselves."

"Which will do what to advance our cause?" Rhys glanced at Alina. "They will want to use our abilities."

"And mate with you," added Vinz.

Alina began to object, but Rhys beat her to it. "So they will want to use our abilities and mate with us. Again, how does this advance our cause?"

"We won't let them. They have to sign a truce. They know you are here. Not *here* on this boat, but on Earth. They saw your craft just like we did. They knew what it meant."

"So they sign the truce, then what? You forfeit Alina and me?"

"We leave."

It was Hodge who spoke next. "They won't like that."

"No, they won't. But they won't have a choice. They wouldn't dare kill a white god without the priest's command," replied Vinz.

"Much of what you say is based on speculation," mused Alina. "You have no real idea what will happen nor the consequences."

"That's why we're testing the theory first in Paducah and not the Pantarak capital, Brechin," said Vinz.

To Rhys, Alina affirmed, "We should have stayed in New Arbroath," and then left the galley. For the first time in days, Rhys agreed with her.

"We're three and a half weeks from Paducah," explained Vinz. "Once there, you and I will go ashore. We will speak with their priest and tell them our intentions."

"And if they refuse?" asked Andy.

Vinz leaned in the doorway. "We can't let them refuse."

"Does the town have advanced technology?" asked Rhys.

"No. They have two airships. That's it. They are armed but with weapons that break or malfunction often. They are not as readily connected to the capital and so don't have access to a constant supply of materials."

"Do they have white go—our people in their village?"

"No. None of them have ever seen someone who looks like us. The man I rescued in New Arbroath seemed utterly alarmed at the sight of me."

"You're hoping our presence alone will cause change?"

"Correct," replied Vinz.

"And if they decline and instead try to capture us?" asked Andy.

"Then we engage in appropriate countermeasures and escape."

Why Rhys personally felt responsible for Alina—and Kallen's—safety and that of the crew, he didn't know. Perhaps it was Andy's words that had burrowed deep in him. He had the power, the skills, the abilities. He could make a difference. Nevertheless, he had no idea what he was going to do. He didn't understand what Vinz had planned. He doubted just his presence could alter an entire town's perception of the outside world.

Vinz cleared his throat and nodded to Andy and Hodge. "You two are on the bridge. Go relieve Lyruc and Kyo."

Hodge stalked out of the galley with a groan. Andy smiled at Rhys and pointed to the scattered papers. "Take a break. You'll burn yourself out." He followed Hodge.

"Are you hungry?" asked Kallen.

"Kallen," scolded Vinz as he left the galley, "make sure you aren't neglecting the machines."

"No, I'm fine," lied Rhys. "You tend to whatever you need to." He dragged his pen back to his fingers and picked up where he left off. He saw Kallen frown before leaving.

When he could no longer hear her footsteps, Rhys threw his pencil down and watched it roll across the table and clatter to the floor. For longer than he should have, he stared at the papers in thought.

What had they gotten themselves into? What had *he* gotten them into? He had placed Alina in danger because he had wanted to be of use. Well, here he was! Tiredly, he folded his arms on the table and laid his head there. Almost instantly, he was asleep.

"Rhys? Hey. Wake up."

Rhys tried to lift his head, but he felt insufferably heavy. Kallen shook him gently and then ran her hand down his cheek. That jumpstarted his slow heart rate. Rhys willed his eyes to open. It was dark out.

"Hey, you need to go to bed," she whispered, sitting beside him. She began collecting the paperwork and manuals. "Everyone else is asleep except Hodge and Andy. You start training tomorrow morning."

"Why do you follow him?"

Kallen tapped the papers into place and looked at him. "Who?"

"Vinz."

She continued cleaning up his mess. "Because I trust him."

"Why?"

"I just do. He took me in and taught me. He's been through a lot and knows a lot about the world."

"Do you like him?"

Kallen looked at him. "What do you mean?"

Rhys finally sat up. "Never mind."

"He's family to me," replied Kallen. "He took care of me when I was in a bad way."

"How?"

"Rhys, why do you need an answer for everything?"

"I didn't realize… I'm sorry." He stood, collected the papers and manuals Kallen had placed neatly on the table, and left for his cabin.

Despite the fact that he could hardly keep his eyes open, the moment he lay in bed, his mind awakened. Suspecting he was too warm, he stripped out of his shirt and spread out on the blankets. It helped but did nothing overall. He briefly thought of asking Pathos for help, but couldn't bring himself to do it.

For another hour, Rhys tossed. He stood in the middle of their cabin, stared out the porthole, and even paced the room, glancing at Alina who slept soundly. How she managed to sleep so well every night, he didn't know. Perhaps she was using Logos to help her forget about the day's stresses.

Rhys wandered into the hallway. He meandered to the porthole at the end, looked out, glanced into Vinz's open cabin, and then turned for the staircase. Like the night prior, he bypassed the bridge and instead went outside. The moment the cool wind hit him, every bothersome thought and worry drained from his mind. Before he had even shut the door behind him, he shifted his gaze to the stars overhead. Leaning against the outer railing, he took a deep breath, filling his lungs with life.

He didn't ask Pathos to identify the constellations. Instead, he only gazed up at them in wonder and longing. There was something about looking at the stars through the atmosphere that increased their beauty tenfold but portrayed them as distant, untouchable. He supposed to the people on Earth—and now to him and Alina—they were unreachable. They were never going home.

He sat on the top step of the outer staircase. Did Caelestis even still exist? Had the asteroid completely wiped it out or had their father and the others been able to save it?

Defeated, he stared out at the eternal expanse of water. If only he had stayed on Caelestis. He should have just gone about helping the others secure the hangars, but *no*. He had had to go search for Alina to make sure she was safe. That's when their father had told him to run, to leave the colony. Why? Why save both of them? He should have just told Rhys to plant Alina on one of the life pods. It would have been easier and more logical. He wasn't needed; his life wasn't necessary for the advancement of mankind. Alina's was.

But did that philosophy and mindset work here? Alina was certainly skilled in medicine and had the ability to save lives, but perhaps here he could also be of use. The crew certainly acted like it, but that was because he was a "white god" like Vinz. There was no telling what Alina thought.

Since he had abandoned her at the field hospital those days ago, she had been a simmering being of anger, frustration, and hostility. As siblings went, they had been considered close on Caelestis because they had shared thoughts and data, but here, he had learned that their relationship was nothing. There were other facets of the human psyche that warranted attention. Both he and Alina were being exposed to characteristics of their human identities that neither had known existed. It was only natural they withdrew into themselves.

A soft weight dropped onto his shoulders and he looked up to find Kallen wrapping a light blanket around him. She sat beside him and stared into the distance. Rhys glanced at her—and at the thin blouse she wore—and then returned his attention to the stars.

Why had the government on Caelestis decided to nullify the human sex drive? Why had it stripped its citizens of their rights to feel sexual frustration and reproduce? Had it truly been for the advancement of mankind? He understood that it had been a system implemented generations before he was created to control the population, but it seemed wrong. He and the rest of the citizens of the colony had lived in blissful ignorance. They had trusted full-heartedly in the government and had believed the government would provide and take care of them so long as it was for the good of mankind.

"I couldn't sleep," whispered Kallen. Rhys looked at her and seeing that, in fact, all she wore was a thin blouse and a set of underpants, he offered to wrap her in part of the blanket. She accepted and closed the gap between them. Her skin was chilly. Rhys swaddled her in the cocoon and they sat in silence.

Heart beating hard in his chest, Rhys wondered if Kallen was expecting something from him. She seemed to be already sexually experienced. Would she expect the same from him? And why did he always think about sex when she was around? What mysterious power did she have? Did everyone feel this way all the time? It was exhausting! Did the other males on the ship feel such an intense desire? Did Vinz?

"Hey," he murmured. He wanted to ask about her relationship with Vinz, but he wasn't sure how to broach the topic.

Kallen's face appeared much closer to his than he expected, and his thought faded. His fingers itched to touch her. It took all of his willpower to keep from leaping upon her in a most predatory-like fashion. Instinct knew what he wanted, what he needed. Only common sense and the threads of his self-control kept him from obeying his primal cravings.

A sudden thought struck him, and he looked away ashamedly. He was no better than the Pantaraks who had attacked her. Disgusted with himself, Rhys fell still and stared into the darkness.

"What?" she whispered.

"Nothing."

Kallen didn't push it. He was sure she thought she had done something to offend him, but how could he tell her the truth?

Eventually, Kallen laid her head on Rhys' shoulder and closed her eyes. After a few minutes, he felt her body start to go slack. Before she slid back onto the platform, he shook her awake and encouraged her to return to her cabin. Kallen kissed him on the cheek as he helped her stand. To protect her modesty, he slipped the blanket around her and then hesitantly touched his lips to her forehead. Such a kiss seemed more chaste than the one they had shared earlier. They returned to their separate quarters.

11
CHANGING LIVES

RHYS WOKE THE FOLLOWING MORNING to the smell of food. The ravenous hunger he had felt the previous evening returned and he sat up. Surprisingly, Alina was not in bed.

He changed into the pair of pants he had worn while on Caelestis and a short-sleeved shirt. Barefooted, he left for the galley. He expected to see Kallen standing before the stove; instead, he found his sister leaning against the counter as she studied a book, her hair pulled into a high ponytail and sleeves rolled above her elbows.

Rhys hesitantly entered. Alina glanced at him, stirred a pot, and then continued reading.

"Morning."

Rhys turned to find Hodge sitting at one of the tables. Kyo sat beside him reading a book.

"Did the smell wake you too?" chuckled Hodge.

Rhys crossed the galley and peered over Alina's shoulder. "It'll be finished in a few minutes," she murmured. "Go sit." Rhys caught her eye and smiled. She didn't smile back, but she didn't ignore him either. He tugged the tip of her ponytail and joined the others at the table.

"So." Hodge began shuffling a deck of cards. "Once you eat, I'm taking you out on the sunboard."

"The new one?" asked Rhys.

"Kashim's board is old. I don't trust it carrying two people." Hodge placed the cards on the table between them. "Here's the catch though. I haven't surfed tandem since I was a kid."

"Technically speaking, there shouldn't be any problems with the board lifting off. The trouble we're going to have," said Rhys, "is being able to windsurf. It doesn't matter who you have on the board."

"Which is why the new board will be equipped with a larger sail," replied Hodge, leaning back in his chair. He tilted it against the wall and braced his foot against the table. "With the larger fin though, it's going to take more manpower to move that beast."

Alina joined them and placed two bowls in front of Rhys. Casually, she pushed Hodge's foot off the table so his chair collapsed to the floor. "Do either of you want some?"

Hodge glanced furtively at the doorway and nodded.

"Hodge… " groaned Kyo, setting aside his book. "Don't do it. You'll be hungry by this evening."

"We're eating the day after tomorrow. What's the harm?"

Alina gave him two bowls as well and stood beside the table, expectedly. Knowing what she was looking for, Rhys sniffed each bowl. The first one was similar to what Kallen had made the day before—frumenty; the second bowl, however, contained a goopy, red mixture with lumps of plant in it. Rhys sipped at the first bowl and then nodded his approval to Alina.

It's fruit, she explained, seeing him eyeing the vivid concoction. *Mixed fruit. It's supposed to be healthy for you.*

Why is it… red?

That's the color of the fruit. It's to be served in a glass. You drink it, but I couldn't find the cups.

Rhys glanced at Hodge and then cautiously sipped the fruit mixture. It was sweet but refreshing. *It's really good!* he told her. Alina breathed out in relief and then retrieved food for herself. *Did Kallen teach you how to cook?*

No, replied Alina, returning with food. *I found her stash of books.*

You could have asked for my translation data. It would have been easier to read them.

As Alina ate, she explained, *If you were able to translate Aabesh so quickly, then there must be information in our database. Logos paired Aabesh to the ancient languages we have on file and translated everything.*

Still, you could have asked.

I wanted to do it myself, she murmured. She looked up from her bowl ruefully. *I've missed you.*

Stop turning your internal comms off then, replied Rhys. *We should be sharing everything we're learning; instead, we're quarreling.*

Alina stared at her bowl of frumenty. *I started my cycle, the menstruation.*

Rhys looked at her in surprise. *Really?*

His sister nodded. *Kallen's been helping me.* She smiled slightly. *I was... so scared. I thought I was dying.*

Why didn't you tell me?

I felt that I shouldn't. That... you wouldn't understand. You're a man.

That logic doesn't make sense.

It doesn't, does it? laughed Alina. *Kallen said that it is customary here to not discuss menstruation with men.* Her smile faded as she looked at her bowl. *Because it means that I can create a human now.*

You can... Rhys gawked at her. *Alina, you can create a human now! You can carry a human child. That wasn't taken from you!* Seeing her forced smile, he calmed himself. *What's wrong?*

The start of menstruation means that the woman is physically ready to be sexually active, said Alina. *That's what Kallen said. And... if some men find that out...*

"I'm sorry," interrupted Hodge. "What's going on? You two look absolutely ridiculous. This back and forth."

Alina glanced at Hodge but continued eating. "Internal communication," Rhys provided with a grin. "We were speaking to one another. I'm sorry. We didn't mean to leave you out of the conversation."

Hodge shrugged, exchanged looks with Kyo, and then said, "That's fine. Your facial expressions are entertaining." He pointed at Alina's AI unit. "What's the range on those things?"

"I don't know... " Rhys looked to his sister for an answer, but she didn't know either. "We've never needed to know that. Not even the computers know."

Hodge nodded thoughtfully before standing. "Right, I'm going to grab Kallen, and we can head down to the forward hatch. Kyo, tell Vinz we're starting the training."

Kyo folded his book under his arm. "I'll let you know once we've anchored."

"Is Kallen still asleep?" asked Rhys.

Hodge placed his dishes on the galley counter. "This trip is stressful for her, so she sleeps often. I'll meet you in the forward hatch.

As Hodge and Kyo left the galley, Rhys glanced at Alina, whose teasing gaze was fixed on him. *What?* he asked.

You really like her, don't you?

Yes, replied Rhys. He took his empty bowls to the sink. *Does that bother you?*

It only bothers me when I see how you become around her.

Which is what, exactly? Rhys leaned on his chair. Alina shrugged. *I see you with Hodge often. Do you like him?*

Alina's face flushed. *No! And even if I did, that's none of your business.*

Rhys straightened himself and headed for the door. *Exactly. Thank you for the meal. It was good.*

As he strolled down the hallway, Alina grumbled, *Give me all of the translation material you have. I want to know too.*

Here. Rhys opened the streaming knowledge and shared it with her. *Thanks.*

Kashim was already in the forward hatch opening all of the portholes to let in the natural light when Rhys entered. He greeted Rhys, and together, they worked to lower the old board to the launch ramp. By the time Hodge and Kallen joined them, *Themis* was anchored and the forward hatch had been opened to submerge the ramp.

"That was quick," said Kallen, stretching her neck as she entered the cabin. She wore a sleeveless crop top that showed just a sliver of midriff and a pair of shorts that revealed strong, tan legs. Today her hair was pulled back by a scarf. It was the first time Rhys could clearly see her entire face as well as the piercing along the cartilage of her right ear. "I heard Alina taught herself how to cook." Kallen waded onto the ramp and began examining Kashim's board. "It smelled good."

"It was good," replied Hodge. Kallen passed him a sharp look. "I mean… that's what Rhys said."

"You ate, didn't you?"

Hodge moaned. "I couldn't help it. It smelled *so* good."

Kallen continued working. "You'll regret it. Once you get into the habit of eating every day, that's what your body expects."

"I'm just going to become fat then because *they* have to eat every day," argued Hodge. "I can't just ignore food, especially when it smells good and is prepared by a cute… " Hodge began sifting through the tools to his left. "You need the lincer?"

"Yeah, to change the sail on your board."

As Kallen withdrew the sail from Kashim's board, Rhys entered the water and steadied the board. "It's a clip," the burly man explained. "The sheath, it's a clip. It just takes your thumb to unlock it."

"Right." Rhys balanced the board and looked to Kallen who was holding the fin. "Ready?" She glanced at Hodge and nodded. Kashim started the fan motor, waited a moment to let it warm up, and then heaved himself onto the board. Kneeling, he found his center and then motioned to Rhys. Rhys slipped his hand into the water, grabbed the clip of the sheath, and released it. Kashim's board rocketed forward. The moment the board hit the open water, the sail popped up and expanded. Kashim rocked onto his feet and grabbed hold of the sail's railing.

"Quicker or you'll lose your face," advised Hodge, wading across the ramp. "Look." He placed his thumb on the side of the keel sheath and flicked it. "It just takes that."

"I'll be faster next time," Rhys assured him.

Once they loaded Hodge's board on the ramp and added the sail extension, the process was repeated. Rhys steadied the board, Kallen worked the sail, and Hodge activated the fan.

After allowing the motor a moment to warm up, Hodge climbed onto the board and motioned to Rhys. "Don't take too long to get out there. I can surf this board, but with the bigger sail, it will take more strength," he shouted over the fan. Rhys nodded and prepared to release the sheath. Hodge balanced himself and then nodded when he was ready. Rhys flicked the sheath clip open and the board shot from the hatch.

"Let's go!" called Kallen, skipping across the ramp to the ladder along the wall. While she unchained the dinghy, Rhys collected the boat's fan motor. Once it was ready, Rhys hopped in and seated himself beside the motor. Kallen grabbed a headscarf from one of the crates, jumped into the boat, and handed it to Rhys. As he tied it about his head and neck, she started the fan. The boat reared out of the forward hatch and jetted across the water.

Headscarf pulled taut around his face, he squinted out at the emerald waters. It took him a moment to realize that he was wearing a short-sleeved shirt; his arms were going to fry. Scolding himself, he searched the waves for the pilots. Hodge was easy to find as the sail on his board was enormous; Kashim surfed nearby.

Kallen steered the dinghy ahead of Hodge and cut the engine. "You have to swim to him. He can't stop it. You're up-current of him. Uh... you can swim, right?"

Rhys glanced at her, pulled the headscarf from his head, and dove over the side. With strong strokes, he swam toward Hodge and positioned himself so he would come down along the side of the board.

"Grab my ankle," instructed Hodge, "and then the fin's beam."

Rhys waited until Hodge was within reach and then grabbed his ankle. So as not to put his full weight on Hodge, Rhys flung himself onto the board and then pulled up using the fin's beam.

"Good, good. Now stand up. Spread your feet apart. Hold the railing." Hodge kicked Rhys' feet apart. "Don't fight the lean. You will never be directly vertical. Don't fight it. Just move with the board."

Rhys held the fin's railing and positioned himself at the same angle. Hodge moved forward on the board so they were more evenly spread out.

"Normally, you would be near the middle or rear of the board but because there's two of us with a larger sail, we have to spread out our power." Hodge was winded, and Rhys could see why. Already, his own arms were straining against the weight of the sail. Though Hodge was taking a larger portion of the weight, Rhys could definitely feel the sail's power. "Do you see how fast we're going? We're not even using the fan right now," said Hodge.

"Why don't you install a harness to help take some of the force off your arms?" asked Rhys.

"Most boards that are used for just surfing do have a harness, but ours don't because they can fly. If we're engaged in some sort of battle and something happens to our board in midair, then we go down with the board. We have a better chance of surviving a fall into the water if we aren't attached."

"You could just unhook yourself as you're falling," replied Rhys.

"You're going to be more worried about other things than unhooking yourself," said Hodge. For the next hour, Hodge taught Rhys how to tack and jibe according to the wind. Though it was difficult to move the sail due to its enormous mass, together they managed and were able to change directions numerous times.

"Ready to fly?" asked Hodge. Rhys nodded. Hodge motioned to Kashim and Kallen who had been skimming alongside them and then said, "When you prepare to change the fin to a wing, it's crucial that you complete the motion smoothly. If you hesitate and the wind catches the sail at a bad angle, you're going down. So, if you're going to fly, commit to it."

Hodge pointed to a lever near the bottom of the vertical beam. He continued. "When you're ready to shift, smash that lever down with the heel of your foot." He pointed up the beam. "That's going to allow the fin to rotate on the hinge up there. See it? Once you've released the lever, the wind will kick the sail into the wing formation. Always, *always*, use the wind to move the sail. Don't do it yourself."

"Yeah."

"As the sail moves into the wing formation—you'll feel it catch—lower yourself on the board. When the wing snaps into place… " Hodge pointed to several spots on the board. "Those will open giving you a place for your hands, knees, and feet."

"Ailerons," said Rhys, gesturing to the forward compartments. "And rudder."

"Right. Now, because there are two of us, it will take longer for us to get in the air."

"Where do you want me to be?"

"Once I'm down, kneel on either side of the rudder pedals." Hodge looked at him. "If you fall from the board, keep your arms and legs together. Cross your arms over your chest and cross your feet. If you fall from any great height, the force of the hit can snap your limbs. Got it?" Hodge smiled. "Your arms are so red right now." Rhys frowned. He knew he was sunburned; his skin stung. "Ready? Let's go."

Hodge kicked the lever at the base of the beam. Rhys felt the board quiver under him so he lowered himself. Hodge knelt and watched as the sail swung over them and locked into place. There was a snap and the compartments along the board opened to reveal a pulley system. Hodge lowered himself and then looked over his shoulder at Rhys. Taking that as his cue, Rhys positioned himself over Hodge's legs and grabbed the sail's beam. Under him, Hodge's feet hooked over the rudder pulleys. The fan motor automatically roared to life.

At first, Rhys felt nothing. It was as if they were still surfing. But that changed as their speed dramatically increased. Soon, they were skimming along the waves instead of slugging through them as they had been doing for the past hour. It took a few seconds thereafter before Rhys suddenly felt that familiar drop in his stomach. He couldn't hide his smile.

As Hodge's board lifted off the water, Rhys clenched the beam. He couldn't believe it. They were flying! They were really flying. "Hold on," instructed Hodge. "Big jump here."

Rhys lowered himself onto the board as it leapt into the air and soared upward in a rush of heated wind.

"Look down," called Hodge. Rhys cautiously peered over the side of the board. Kallen sat in the dinghy below, shading her eyes against the sun. They were high enough now that he couldn't discern her face.

"This is amazing!" Rhys exclaimed, beaming. He looked over his shoulder and found Kashim soaring behind them.

"Keep yourself down," shouted Hodge. "You'll create too much drag." Rhys lowered himself once more and watched as Hodge manipulated the pulleys. Slowly, the board ambled left. "Do you see why you have to stay low?"

"How steeply can this bank?"

"A normal sail can bank as steeply as, ehh, 50 keis. This one can only do about 20 though."

"With a normal sail, it can complete 360 keis though, right?" asked Rhys. "In an emergency."

"Yeah, but you can't hold on."

"The force of the turn would keep you from falling," said Rhys.

"I don't think so," replied Hodge.

Though Rhys was certain Caelestis' laws of physics also applied here on Earth, he didn't push the matter. Hodge had already shown him a whole other world. If need be, he could experiment later and find out the answers himself.

They flew past *Themis* twice before a high-pitched whistle rose above the rush of wind. Recognizing the rhythm, he looked over the board at Kallen who was waving to them.

"Ready to give landing a try?" Hodge asked over his shoulder. Rhys leaned forward to hear Hodge's next lesson. "We now have to slow the board to trim speed."

"The speed just before stall out," clarified Rhys.

"Right. So, to do that, we need to pitch up to create drag." Hodge adjusted the ailerons and sat up on his elbows. Rhys looked up at the sail as it angled upward ever so slightly. The board's speed began to decrease. "Always keep *Themis* in sight. In some situations, you may need to land on the water and surf right back into the forward hatch, but if you're not lined up appropriately, then that can waste time." Hodge pointed his hand directly in front of him. "We're down *Themis'* port side. Once the tip of the ship passes this mark... *here!*" Hodge tapped the thin black line on his board. It looked as though it had been drawn there with a pencil. "Once the tip of the ship passes that mark, you bank." He pointed to another mark on the other side of the board. "It works for approach on either side of the ship."

As the board began to tilt precariously once more, Rhys clutched at the fin beam and leaned with the unit.

"You absolutely must get the board's speed down to trim speed or you'll hit the water hard," explained Hodge, sitting up so he could see over the board's edge. "If you're coming in too fast, then pull up and do it again. Better to miss a landing than destroy the board and yourself." The board was nearing the sea's surface. "Once we've touched down, give it a moment to stabilize. Then we'll swing it back into its surfing position."

The board touched the sea surface and began skimming across it. Hodge moved to his knees, manipulated the rudder briefly, and then waited for the unit to balance. He then motioned to Rhys who kicked the lever along the fin beam. Instantly, the wing folded in on itself and then snapped into its vertical position. Hodge grabbed the railing; Rhys was not so quick.

He hit the water hard and skidded on his back before plowing into the waves and somersaulting. Though he had managed to take a deep breath, he felt water invade every orifice. His sinuses burned horribly; water drove into his stomach. His butt stung. Mind whirling, Rhys kicked. The moment his mouth breached the surface, he began coughing and sputtering to clear his sinuses of liquid. When he could properly breathe, he squinted against the sun and looked about.

"She's coming," called Kashim who surfed past him. A moment later, the dinghy materialized along Rhys' field of vision. Kallen slowed the boat and pulled it alongside him.

"You hurt?" she asked, offering her arm. Rhys grabbed her wrist and heaved himself into the dinghy.

"I'm fine." He slid into the boat and gazed up at the sky, panting.

"You're sure?" asked Kallen. "You two were going well over 40 niks."

Rhys sat up, ruffled the water from his hair, and chuckled. "It hurt, but I'm fine."

She gave him an amused look and then headed for *Themis*. After they hung the dinghy on the wall, they worked together to dock Hodge and his board. Because the board was using the larger sail, the process took much longer. After several failed attempts to enter the cabin, they eventually caught the fin tip and slow the board to allow Hodge to dock. Afterward, Kashim's docking sequence was simple.

"Well?" asked Vinz, appearing in the doorway of the forward hatch as the group finished locking the machines into place. "How'd it go?"

Rhys glanced at Hodge and smiled. "It went well."

"You're sunburned. Badly," replied Vinz. Rhys glanced at his arms. "And your hands and feet. The feet will hurt the worst."

Rhys ruffled his hair once more. "I'll manage."

"Alina's preparing a meal. Once you're dried off, come eat." Vinz glanced at Hodge. "No food for you. With three of us eating, we're already putting a strain on our food supply. We don't need another hungry mouth." Hodge groaned.

After gorging himself on Alina's cooking, Rhys took a nap and then worked on translating Reza's manuals. He allowed Alina to treat his sunburn with a burn ointment she found in the pack. Early evening, Hodge diverted him from his work to participate in various exercises on the upper deck. By the time they were finished, Rhys could hardly move. Body limp with exhaustion, he bathed and went straight to bed. Even Kallen couldn't rouse him from his fatigued stupor.

For the next 23 days, Rhys' schedule remained as such. Every morning he, Hodge, Kashim, and Kallen launched the sunboards. Though he still rode with Hodge, he was given more control each day. Afterward, he would then come in, eat, take a nap, work on the translations, train with Hodge, eat again, and then go to bed.

Though it was hard work and tiring, he could think of nothing that made him happier. He was using his body and mind in ways he never knew he could. Every day he discovered something new about himself. He could make decisions. He could do what he wanted *when* he wanted.

His relationship with Alina seemed to repair itself. Though she spent quite a bit of time with Hodge, she often sat with Rhys and read books borrowed from Vinz's library. When Rhys was too tired to move, she would finish his chores and prepare the next meal. She read late into the night and woke in time to cook breakfast for Rhys and Vinz every morning. She often shared with Rhys the information she pulled from Vinz's books, both fiction and nonfiction. Though Rhys listened politely, he was uninterested in what she had to share. All he could think about were three things—sunboarding, Kallen, and when the next meal was. He loved all three.

The night the entire crew was to eat, Kallen and Alina worked together to prepare a hearty meal comprised of a type of meat called liiman Rhys had yet to eat, vegetables, and a grain-based soup. By the time the meal was ready, Rhys could hardly contain himself. Since starting sunboarding and Hodge's training, he was constantly hungry. It was as if his body was attempting to make up for all that he had missed while growing up on Caelestis.

"Yes... " growled Hodge as was his customary response to smelling good food. He stalked into the galley, surveyed the pots, and then sat at the table. Rhys was right beside him. Once everyone was gathered, Alina presented plates of food to Kyo who took them to Andy and Lyruc on the bridge. Afterward, Rhys and Hodge were given their meals. He was pleased to know that Hodge was also extremely hungry. Despite his friend's second skin, Hodge had been working just as hard.

With everyone eating, Kallen and Alina joined them at the table. Lively conversation broke out and soon Hodge was telling a story about his wild years as a freelance carrier pilot for New Arbroath. Rhys listened raptly, all the while inhaling the meal.

"More?" chuckled Kallen. Rhys glanced at Alina and then nodded. He was so hungry his stomach hurt. As Kallen took his plate to retrieve more food, Rhys watched Andy tease Hodge about a particularly nasty accident that had occurred years ago. Rhys tried to laugh when Hodge objected to Andy's accusations but found his throat a little tight. He coughed to clear what felt like a mild obstruction, drank water, and then swallowed several times.

"Rhys?" asked Alina between bites. She seemed to be the only one who noticed his discomfort. "What's wrong?"

The conversation at the table grew quiet. Rhys glanced at the others and tried to pull air into his lungs, but it was becoming increasingly difficult. "I can't... I can't... " He wheezed, touching his throat. He looked to Alina and tried to speak in Interstellar Nefegian, but his throat was closing.

"Hodge, move him," ordered Alina, shoving the table away with her hip. She and Hodge slid him to the floor. Rhys closed his eyes and wheezed. He couldn't breathe!

"Attention, anaphylaxic shock has been detected," alerted Pathos in their native tongue. "Heart rate: 112 beats per minute. Blood pressure: 160. Oxygen intake decreasing to 40 percent."

Alina knelt beside him. Rhys felt her hands checking his pulse. He heard her say something about their pack, but he couldn't focus on the words.

"Rhys? Stay with me," said Alina, opening his eyes to check his pupils. Rhys tried to look at her, but his throat felt constrained. His head hurt. He could feel his heart fluttering against his chest. "Pathos, prepare for epinephrine therapy."

"Oxygen intake: 22 percent," echoed Pathos.

"Here, here, here," said Hodge. Rhys felt the pack scrape his arm. Alina tore the bag open and began throwing its contents aside.

"Loss of consciousness in 15 seconds," reported Pathos. Rhys felt his mind darkening. All of his senses were numbing, dying. He felt flushed, heated, as though his entire body were sunburned.

Suddenly, a sharp pain struck his thigh. Fire roared through his limbs and shook his core. A sharp gasp tore through his throat and warm air filled his lungs. Rhys panted. His head throbbed, his heart pounded.

Rhys felt Alina's fingers on his eyes as she pried open his eyelids and flashed a brilliant light at him. He jerked his head away and then looked up at her. "Hey," she whispered. "Move your arms for me. Can you do that?" Rhys lay back, breathed, and then shakily moved his arms and hands. "Good." Alina's voice was soft. The room was silent. "Move your toes too. Good. Can you breathe now?" Rhys nodded. "Pathos, report."

"Heart rate: 121. Blood pressure: 130 over 90. Oxygen intake: 90 percent," said Pathos.

"Monitor his vitals for the next three hours. Alert me if there are any changes. Rhys, can you talk to me?" Alina leaned over him. "Does anything hurt?" Rhys shook his head and blinked up at the lights. "You have to talk to me."

"I'm fine," he murmured.

"Can you breathe?"

"Yes."

"Tell me what you're feeling."

Rhys gauged his body. "Cold. My hands and... feet are cold. My heart hurts... "

Alina sat back and nodded. "It's the epinephrine. Slow breaths. Keep moving your hands."

Rhys looked about the galley to find the entire crew standing around him. No one said a word. Kallen's eyes were moist while Hodge and Andy looked horrified. Vinz, as usual, wore a mask to veil his emotions. Kashim studied Alina.

"What happened?" Kallen finally whispered.

"Anaphylaxic shock. It's a severe allergic reaction," replied Alina.

"Allergic reaction?" mused Vinz.

"When the human body can't digest or break down a substance, it releases a mass dosage of a chemical to combat the substance. The dosage causes the throat to close up and breathing to become impossible." Alina sat back. "I gave him epinephrine, a different type of chemical, to fight the reaction."

"So... something in the food made this happen?" asked Hodge incredulously.

Alina nodded. "All of his symptoms matched the information in the database. We're lucky our pack has an assortment of medicines."

Rhys felt Kallen touch his hair and he looked up at her. "I didn't mean to... kill you with my food," she murmured.

Rhys smiled weakly. *Pathos, have you identified the source?*

Yes, it was the liiman, replied Pathos.

"It was the liiman," said Alina, having heard Rhys' AI. "He can't eat it or touch it."

"What about you?" asked Vinz. "Are you having any type of reaction to the meat?"

"No. I feel fine."

Vinz nudged Kallen. "Take care of him. If his condition worsens, let me know." Vinz motioned to Kashim, and the two stepped into the hallway.

"Do you think you can sit up?" asked Alina, feeling his forehead and cheek. Rhys took a deep breath and pushed himself upright. Kallen supported him while Alina checked his heart rate and temperature.

Hodge knelt beside them. "How long until he's recovered? We're entering Pantarak waters."

"He should be fine by tomorrow morning," Alina asserted.

"I'm sitting right here. I can speak for myself," muttered Rhys.

"You're not the doctor," replied Hodge. "You're the one who almost died because of *food*."

Rhys frowned. Kallen chuckled and ruffled the hair along his neckline. With a sigh, Hodge grabbed his plate from the table and sat on the floor beside Rhys.

"Would you not bring that near him?" insisted Alina. Hodge winced at her tone and inched away.

Rhys leaned forward to stand, but Alina and Kallen pushed him back down. "Wait a little while," suggested his sister. She glanced at Kallen and then began repacking the contents of their emergency supplies. "Kallen, can you help me clean the galley?" Alina closed the pack, pointed to Andy to move it aside, and began picking up dishes.

With Hodge and Andy's help, the galley cleanup was quicker than usual. Before long, Rhys was lying in his bunk. He still felt light-headed, but it was better than not being able to breathe. Once Alina retired to their cabin, she asked Pathos to report to Logos every hour on Rhys' vitals. Though slightly annoyed by her over-cautiousness—he felt fine—

he allowed Logos and Pathos to communicate freely. As Alina read by lamplight, Rhys drifted off to sleep.

It wasn't but three hours later when Kallen's hysterical screaming jarred him from his unconscious state. He rolled out of bed and started for the door.

"What was that?" whispered Alina, sitting up in bed.

"Kallen," he murmured. He slipped into the hallway and went to her cabin where he found Hodge sitting in bed with her; Kyo was also awake. Lyruc remained fast asleep. Without a word, Rhys entered the cabin. Hodge looked up at him but didn't say anything. "I'll take her," Rhys said, extending a hand. Hodge nudged Kallen to her feet.

Ignoring her scant attire, Rhys took her icy fingers, grabbed her blanket, and led her from the room. On shaky and weak legs, Kallen followed him down the hallway to the outer deck. He didn't look back at her, though he could hear her trying to stifle her crying. At the top of the stairs, he opened the outer deck door, let the wind sweep across his face, and then pulled her outside. He closed the door behind them.

Kallen turned away from him as she wiped her face. Rhys wrapped the blanket around his own shoulders and then enveloped her in his cloaked arms. As if a dam had burst open, Kallen's crying became more passionate, and she began sobbing. He just held her; he knew of nothing else to do. Kallen turned in his arms and laid her head on his bare chest.

After a minute, Rhys leaned against the door and invited her to sit with him. Wiping her eyes and nose, Kallen fitted herself between his legs. She lay against him and pulled the blanket around them.

Although Rhys felt aroused by her nearness and bare skin, his exhaustion was more than he could handle. Kallen sensed this too for she immediately settled against him and forced herself to breathe deeply. Rhys nodded off several times, jerking Kallen as he did so, but she never objected to him continuing to hold her. Eventually though, she turned, kissed his jaw, and whispered, "Go to bed. I'm fine."

Rhys nodded and together they went inside. When Kallen pulled away to reenter her cabin, Rhys stopped her and led her down to his and Alina's quarters. He felt her hesitation, but he didn't care. He wanted to sleep; he wanted her to sleep; he wanted everyone else on the ship to sleep.

Alina sat up when they entered. In silence, she watched as Rhys motioned Kallen to his bed. Kallen glanced at Alina and then crawled into Rhys' bunk. With a heavy sigh, Rhys flopped down beside her, murmured an apology to Alina, and promptly fell asleep.

12
WHITE GOD

AN ABRUPT KNOCK ON THEIR cabin door woke Rhys the next morning. "We're meeting on the bridge. Get up," called Vinz.

Rhys breathed deeply and opened his eyes to find the back of Kallen's head. It took a moment for him to realize two things. Firstly, that his hand was wrapped tightly around her right breast. Heart racing, he withdrew his grip. Kallen chuckled sleepily and rolled over to greet him. Rhys sat up and rolled to the edge of the bed with the blanket to hide his second realization.

As Kallen stretched, Rhys looked across at Alina who was watching the interaction with interest. "Feeling better?" his sister asked.

"I'm sorry for having caused you trouble," Kallen replied, scooting out of the bed.

Alina folded her legs to herself. "It's fine."

Kallen stood, revealing bare thighs, and went to Alina. Rhys looked away modestly. "I don't want this to be awkward," she said. "Are you sure you're not bothered?"

Alina began re-braiding her hair. "It's fine." The tone of her voice startled Rhys. He expected it to be cold and stoic to show her lack of care or to hide her real emotions. Instead, his sister sounded truly accepting of the situation and of their blossoming relationship. "I can't always look after him."

Beaming, Kallen flitted from the room. Rhys glimpsed her naked legs before she disappeared down the hall.

Alina began dressing. "Don't apologize. I saw how she reacted last night when you had the allergic reaction. She was in tears." His sister grinned as she slipped into yesterday's shirt. "Besides, I enjoy watching you. It's interesting."

Rhys lay back in bed and waited for Alina to finish dressing. Once she left, he dressed and followed after. Though he had no residual symptoms from the previous night, the place where Alina had stabbed him with the epinephrine shot ached. He found the entire crew on the bridge. Kyo and Andy sat in their normal seats, while Hodge sat sideways in Vinz's chair. Everyone else stood around the Overseer.

As Rhys closed the bridge door, Vinz nodded and looked about. "We're entering enemy territory. We'll be at Paducah by early afternoon. I want everyone to be armed. We are searching for peace, but it doesn't mean that we won't put bullets in them if they attack. Assuming we are allowed past the water gates, only a few of us will go ashore. Those people are Hodge, Kashim, Rhys, and myself." He looked at Alina and Kallen. "You two are to remain aboard *Themis* at all times." Both girls nodded gravely. "The rest of you are to defend this ship. No one is allowed inside the bridge or in the inner hallways. They may patrol the outer deck, but do not let them inside."

"And if they enter?" asked Andy.

"Shoot them. This ship doesn't belong to them. We must draw a line somewhere," replied Vinz. "Unfortunately, we have timed this expedition so we make landfall in the middle of one of their most important, religious celebrations—Trukuula." Lyruc and Hodge groaned. "Do not take *anything* that is given to you, not even food." Vinz looked at Rhys. "Many of the foods and drinks will be laced with a hallucinogenic drug as a part of the celebration. Do not take gifts, money, jewelry, pottery. Nothing. Our goal is to meet with the priest of Paducah."

"Once we're docked, how quickly are you disembarking?" asked Kyo.

"Immediately. Make sure the cannons and gunners are prepared and the emergency firearms ready."

"Question," Hodge raised his hand. "If it's Trukuula, should we really be bringing Rhys?"

Vinz regarded Rhys thoughtfully. "I was wondering that myself."

"What?" asked Rhys. "Why?"

"Trukuula is an annual religious celebration for the Pantaraks. They gorge themselves on food and drink and celebrate for many days." Vinz paused. "The celebration is intertwined with rituals—dancing, music, dramas, sacrifices."

"Sacrifices?" Rhys waited as Pathos expanded upon the idea for him.

"Human sacrifices," clarified Vinz.

"Death means nothing to them. There is life after it." Andy reminded quietly, seeing the look of horror on Rhys' face.

"The sick, the old, and a collection of young girls—that's who they sacrifice."

"For what reason?" asked Alina. "I don't understand. What do they hope to gain by killing other humans?"

"The killings are to honor the white gods. The old and sick are sent ahead so they no longer have to suffer. The virgins are sacrificed to satiate the gods' lustful tendencies as I understand it." Vinz thought. "Though I think it also has to do with something about how the virgins will erase the sins of all those under the priest's power." He looked between Alina and Rhys who were gaping at him. "I don't really remember the details. I've seen it twice. It's not a pleasant experience."

Kallen left the bridge.

"Rhys can stay here," said Hodge. "I'm sure we could use another hand guarding the ship."

"Why don't you ask me if I want to go?" asked Rhys.

"Rhys," murmured Alina, touching his arm. "Don't."

He held Vinz's gaze. "I'm going."

Vinz gave a nod. "We will attempt to return to the ship every night."

"How long do you foresee us staying in port?" asked Kyo.

"No longer than three days. I don't want to grow comfortable there." Vinz leaned against the console. "Keep the ship on constant lockdown. Prepare nighttime watches; set shifts." He looked at those who would be going ashore. "We must work together if we are to come out of this alive. Redirect all questions to me. Do not give away information about yourselves." Vinz's blue eyes focused on Rhys. "Once we arrive in port, you are a god."

"What about you?" countered Rhys.

Vinz shook his head. "If I was alone, they would treat me similarly, however, *you* will be there. You are more valuable. I'll be surprised if they even look at me."

"We appear the same."

Everyone on the bridge shook their heads in collective disagreement. Hodge chuckled. "You two may have the same eyes and skin tone, but there's no denying it—you and Alina are from a different world." Hodge pointed to the others. "Right?"

"It's the way you look at us," said Andy, "as if you're trying to solve a puzzle. Your eyes are intelligent but ehh... innocent and curious." He motioned to Vinz. "He just looks angry all the time."

"So... you're saying they will notice?" Rhys asked.

"Immediately," Vinz assured him.

"What should I do? How should I behave?"

"Remain stoic. Don't let anything they say or do affect you. You mustn't allow them to see that their worldly, trivial actions can reach you. Stay aloof, distant. Do not directly reply to their questions. I'll answer." Vinz pointed to Hodge and Kashim. "You are not to let anyone touch him, not even in a non-threatening manner."

"They're going to try," mumbled Hodge. "They won't be able to resist."

"Don't let them. If it happens, make a big commotion about it. They've desecrated a living white god. It's possible they'll be punished by the priest."

"We should get that taken care of," said Kashim, nodding to Rhys and tapping his temple.

"Right. Kallen—"

Vinz, realizing she had left, continued.

"Have Kallen paint your computer. You'll be standing out plenty. We don't need them to see that metal plate on your head." He folded his arms. "The dye she used for your hair will probably work though I don't know how long it will stay on the metal." Rhys nodded. "Questions? From anyone?"

Kyo hesitantly raised his hand. "Ehh... " He glanced at Hodge. "What do you want us to do about Kallen?"

It was Alina who spoke. "I'll take care of her."

"Any other questions?" Vinz peered out the bridge glass. "It's possible they'll send an airship to survey us. Do *not* shoot unless they shoot first. Like I said, we have to draw a line somewhere."

"I have a question," said Andy. "How are you expecting us to pass through the water gates?"

"The Pantarak captive in New Arbroath, the one I freed—he's our key to entering Paducah," concluded Vinz.

"How do you know he's given the message?" asked Hodge.

"I told him a new god has come to Earth," Vinz replied, "and that if they wanted to witness his miracles, they would need to allow our ship to pass and dock in port."

"*Gawan*," cursed Hodge as Andy declared, "That's a gamble."

"So, what miracles are we going to give them?" asked Hodge.

Vinz motioned to Rhys. "I'm leaving that to him. Let's prepare *Themis*."

Rhys felt Alina's hand on his arm and together they left the bridge. They found Kallen sitting at the bottom of the inner staircase scuffing her bare feet along the floor. Alina squeezed his arm before joining Kallen.

"Kallen," his sister chirped, sitting beside her. "Will you do something for us?"

Kallen glanced over her shoulder at Rhys. "Sure."

Alina leaned her head toward Kallen and pointed to Logos' unit. "Can you paint these for us? Don't they look ridiculous now? Our hair was silver, so the units matched, but now that it's black, don't you think they should be also black?"

Kallen chuckled. "They do stand out." She motioned them to the forward hatch. Alina followed immediately, however, Rhys hung at the top of the stairs for a long moment.

Although he could grasp all that had been said, he wasn't sure what he was supposed to do. He needed to come up with a miracle— something that would appear miraculous to people who were unfamiliar with his technology.

"You coming?" called Kallen from the open door of the hatch. Rhys jogged down the stairs and joined them.

It was midafternoon when Vinz called for everyone to reconvene on the bridge. Rhys was not surprised to find every person armed and dressed for battle. Rhys glanced down at his own attire which Vinz had lent him—a button-down, beige, long-sleeved blouse, khaki trousers, and a royal blue sash tied about his waist. His headscarf hung limply around his neck.

I feel ridiculous, Rhys murmured to Alina who stood near Hodge.

You shouldn't. Kallen keeps looking at you, replied Alina. Rhys glanced across the bridge at Kallen whose gaze had been set on him. When their eyes met, she smiled.

"We're nearing the water gates," announced Vinz, leaning against the forward paneling. Rhys looked out the windscreen. Rising from the green waves to greet the hot, afternoon sun were four stone pillars. Protruding from their sides were great gates of wood and metal. He could see nothing beyond them. "Bring *Themis* to one-third speed. Kyo, what's our charge?"

"Full gauge," replied Kyo.

"Kashim, Lyruc, bring in the sails," commanded Vinz. Kashim and Lyruc disappeared outside. "Ready forward thrusters. If the gates don't open once we're 20 retems out, bring us to a halt." Vinz looked at Alina and Kallen. "Secure yourselves."

Alina took Kallen's hand, glanced at Rhys, and then pulled her toward the door. Rhys stopped Alina. *If there's trouble, tell me*, he said. *Alina. We're here now. This world is different, but the people are still trying to attempt the same thing as those of Caelestis. We—*

I know, interrupted his sister. *We have to do what we can to support their efforts.* She lowered her voice. *That's our responsibility.* Rhys nodded. The girls left the bridge.

"The gates are opening," said Andy in a hushed tone. Rhys looked over his shoulder as the enormous wooden gates slowly pulled apart. Waves splashed upon the pillars and rocked *Themis*.

"Continue at one-third speed," commanded Vinz. "Kyo, any signs of aggression from the gate turrets?"

"None," replied Kyo, reading the units before him. "None."

"I wish there were," murmured Andy. "I would feel better."

Vinz pulled one of the many communication pipes down from the ceiling. "Kashim, Lyruc, sails done?"

"Almost," replied Kashim.

"Get down here immediately. Leave the rest." Vinz slid the pipe back to the ceiling and once more gazed anxiously out the windscreen. "Boats are waiting beyond the gates."

"I don't think their port can hold *Themis*," said Kyo, standing with a spyglass. "The water may be too shallow."

"Once we're clear of the gates, anchor us outside the docks. They're going to want to board the ship." As Kashim and Lyruc returned from outside, Vinz turned to Rhys and asked, "Weapon?"

Rhys reached into the collar of his blouse and withdrew the resonance cutters which he had strapped to his back using one of the many sheaths available in their pack. "And... the miracle," he said. "They can cut through anything. Any material."

Once he was reassured that everyone was armed, Vinz motioned for Kashim, Hodge, and Rhys to follow him onto the outer deck. Before the sun could touch his face, Rhys pulled his headscarf around his head and tied it off. He checked that the resonance cutters' holster was secure and then looked out at Paducah.

The port was nestled inside the narrow mouth of a cove. While *Themis* remained anchored away from the docks, smaller boats and dinghies motored to and from the wharves and shore. Vinz pointed out that many of their sunboards and larger boats had yet to return to port from the attack on New Arbroath. The treeline, which had been a key indicator of life since Rhys and Alina had arrived, was manicured and pruned so its vegetation leaned away from the town's major, dirt roads. Despite them having just arrived, the shoreline was rapidly becoming crowded with intrigued Pantaraks.

Vinz cleared his throat to redirect their attention to the group of dinghies approaching *Themis*. The Pantaraks wore familiar clothes like collared blouses and trousers but had nothing on their feet to protect them. All of the men's heads were shaved bald to reveal black, intricately designed tattoos.

One of the dinghies pulled alongside *Themis* and two men jumped onto the lower deck. Vinz started down the stairs with Kashim at his side. Hodge discreetly took Rhys' arm and guided him after them, making sure he stayed between Rhys and the newcomers.

"You are Vinz?" asked one of the men.

The Overseer stopped at the bottom platform. "I am."

"And the new god you promised?"

Vinz stepped aside to allow Hodge to present Rhys. Aware that all eyes were on him, Rhys squinted up from the shadows of his hood. Both men gaped and then bowed their heads and stepped away.

"Son of the Heavens, God of the Stars," murmured one of the men. He motioned for Rhys to board the dinghy.

Vinz barred his way. "This god is kin, therefore, he goes nowhere without me or his bodyguards." The two men looked between themselves and then bowed their heads once more. Vinz motioned for Kashim to lead the way. As Hodge passed them, Vinz leaned into Rhys. "They will try to separate you from us. Do not let them." Rhys acknowledged Vinz's words with a subtle eye flicker. Feigning respect, Vinz bowed his head to Rhys and motioned that he should board the dinghy.

Rhys stepped into the boat and seated himself next to Hodge. The Pantarak man at the motor kept his head bowed during the entire boarding process. As Vinz sat at the bow of the boat, the dinghy pulled away from *Themis,* leaving the two Pantarak men on the lower deck. Rhys could feel his heart in his throat. Kallen and Alina were in danger. Everything inside him told him to stop the boat, board *Themis*, and kick the men into the water.

The dinghy motored to the docks where already people dressed in flamboyant robes of orange, yellow, and red waited. The boat docked, and Vinz stepped out. Kashim followed and turned to help Rhys. Though he was more than capable, Rhys accepted Kashim's strong hand and pulled himself onto the docks. As he looked about at the people, they bowed.

"Son of the Heavens, God of the Stars," murmured the onlookers in intermittent chants. "Son of the Heavens... God of the Stars."

After a long, uncomfortable moment of hushed chanting, a man in a flaming orange robe stepped from the crowd. He was thin, thinner than most, and wiry. Despite his frail stature, however, Rhys was sure he was only middle-aged. Perhaps an illness or disease had formed him into such. His head, like the others, was tattooed with black ink as were his hands. He wore no shoes but had rings on his fingers and bracelets on his ankles. "Son of the Heavens, God of the Stars, welcome," the man said with a bow. Rhys expected him to smile in greeting, but the man's lips never once twitched. "I am Saccui Mazatl, priest of the town of Paducah." He raised himself and looked between the others and Rhys. "I am honored to be standing before. Truly, honored."

"Saccui Mazatl, Honored," said Vinz. Normally, Rhys would have gladly stepped aside to allow Vinz control, however, he had been told to remain stoic. "I am Vinz Blacksky Amadorri."

"Blacksky, yes. I see, I see," said Saccui. "You are the one who rescued one of our men from the pagans. Yes?"

Vinz dipped his head. "Yes, Honored." Rhys watched, intrigued. He had never before seen Vinz act so demure, so humble.

"And you bring to us the new god?"

"I bring him to you so he can bless your people before traveling to the capital," replied Vinz.

Saccui didn't seem as enamored with this response, but he let his displeasure show only briefly. "Come, let us speak in private." He glanced at Rhys, bowed deeply once more, and then motioned for the sea of people around them to split.

Vinz led the procession from the docks, up the road, and into town, following several paces behind Saccui. Though Rhys tried to remain emotionless, he couldn't help but let his gaze wander to the shops, people, and homes. Vinz and Andy had told him the Pantaraks were advanced technologically and that they were intelligent people, but he couldn't help but think poorly of them. No one wore shoes. Everywhere he looked, there were filthy feet. He didn't understand how their feet didn't burn on the hot ground or become scarred or cut on the rocks. Why didn't they wear shoes or some sort of protection?

As they walked up the narrow, winding streets, Rhys had another realization. Thinking himself wrong, he glanced about at the gawking individuals. In the doorways, on the streets, along the docks, outside the shops—there were only men. He hadn't seen a single woman. Baffled, he continued to survey the area. There were children but no female children. Where were the women?

Eventually, Saccui escorted them into a gated garden, over a small creek, and up a set of marble stairs to a decorated doorway. The priest glanced back at them, bowed once more, and then opened the carved door. It was then Rhys realized the door opened into the side of a grassy knoll. He froze. That doorway led to a prison.

"My Lord," murmured Saccui, bowing once more. It was an obvious invitation to enter. Sensing Vinz moving to pass him, Rhys stopped him. "God of the Stars, what troubles you?" Though the question was meant for Rhys, he directed it to Vinz, assuming Rhys could not understand Aabesh. "Please tell this one."

Rhys shared a dark look with Vinz and then shook his head.

"Please, what troubles you?" asked Saccui once more.

"As a god of the black sky, he does not feel comfortable going underground," lied Vinz.

"Through this door is our sacred, private temple," explained Saccui.

"I hope you can understand and respect the god's wishes," said Vinz with a polite bow.

Saccui considered them and then made a motion with his hand. Three men dressed in nothing but crimson slacks emerged from the darkened entryway. Rhys forced himself to remain still and be undisturbed by their nearness. The three men passed him and took hold of Vinz, Hodge, and Kashim. Without force or aggression, they pulled them away from Rhys.

"What is the meaning of this?" fumed Vinz, planting himself so he could no longer be moved.

"You have brought to us the new white god," said Saccui. "Now, I must ask that you leave as this is sacred ground."

Vinz jerked his arm free from his captor and rushed toward Rhys. Two more men appeared and tackled him to the ground in a single movement. Vinz struggled momentarily on the grass and then, with his face half-buried in the earth, growled, "Release me."

Saccui ignored Vinz and instead motioned Rhys to the door. "Son of the Heavens, God of the Stars."

Rhys ignored him, choosing instead to approach the men holding Vinz. "You will release him, immediately." The men simply stared at Rhys, eyes wide. Rhys looked back at Saccui. "Release him." Saccui motioned for his men to free Vinz who stood and brushed himself off. "The man who the people of New Arbroath captured, where is he?"

Saccui approached Rhys and lowered himself to see into the shadows of Rhys' hood. "Show your face."

"Why?" asked Rhys. He wasn't opposed to the idea—they were in the shade—but he didn't like being ordered by an individual who so clearly did not deserve respect.

"No white god has ever come to our world speaking our language. Even the great prophet was unfamiliar with the mother tongue." Saccui motioned to his red-clad warriors. "You're an imposter."

The men present grabbed Vinz and dragged him to the ground. Kashim managed to rid himself of his captors in time to free Hodge, but three more emerged from the doorway in the hill and, with ease, toppled them both.

Rhys successfully danced away from a pair of hands only to be knocked sideways. Sensing another incoming blow, he blocked the attack with the back of his arms and then swung out with his leg, downing one of Saccui's warriors. Despite Pathos' warning, his body didn't move fast enough and another man drove him to the earth. Rhys struggled to defend himself and his face, but the man atop him trumped him in size and strength.

Unable to fight back, Rhys struggled as a fist collided with his cheek. The solid and rock-like heel of another warrior connected with his gut. Rhys pulled himself into the fetal position, gasping in pain. His face throbbed fiercely, and his lungs screamed for air.

Suddenly, a horrifying sensation shot through him as a foreign hand touched Pathos' unit on the side of his head. "No!" Rhys barked, jerking away from the hand. "Pathos!"

Charging emergency deflection system. Charged.

"Do it!" Rhys screamed in Interstellar Nefegian.

Initiating.

Rhys felt a jolt of electricity leap from his body. The warriors atop him yelped in pain and confusion and rolled off. Panting, Rhys drew himself up and glared at Saccui.

Emergency deflection system operating at 95 percent power, reported Pathos.

Create a barrier around the external unit. Don't let anyone touch it, ordered Rhys, looking at Vinz and the others. Vinz and Hodge both had two warriors on them; Kashim warranted five. Rhys turned on the priest and pulled his hood clear of his head. "I am Rhys Blacksky Falkrow of Caelestis, born of the honored Severiano Falkrow and Yadhira Brauner. I command you, release them."

No one moved. Rhys forced himself to remain fierce, unyielding. They couldn't know that he was having trouble standing.

Saccui approached Rhys and studied him. "Your tricks do not scare us."

Rhys stepped closer to the priest. He hoped the man couldn't see how frightened he actually was. "Step down," murmured Rhys, searching the priest's gaze. "Or I will make you." The man didn't move. Rhys reached between them and rested his hand on the priest's shoulder.

The priest crumpled to the ground, his muscles clenched from the electrical shock. Rhys gazed at the man through tunneled vision. That one had been much stronger than the last. He hadn't killed the priest but had given him enough of a shock to render him disabled. In return, Rhys could now feel his knees threatening to buckle under him. After all, Pathos was rerouting biological energy to create an electric pulse. "Release them," Rhys demanded without looking at the others. He couldn't afford to move; he might fall.

There was movement, and suddenly Vinz was at his side.

Emergency deflection system going into standby. Disengaging.

Vinz lowered himself to meet Rhys' gaze. Rhys, exhausted, nodded encouragingly. A strange look entered Vinz's eyes; he smiled and then turned to the others. Calmly, the Overseer asked, "And where will we be staying until the festivities this evening?"

Half an hour later, Rhys found himself in a secluded building on the outskirts of town. Its purpose was to hold religious trials but, Rhys had been told, it could house a god if need be. Unlike the other buildings, it was built of marble and variously handcrafted stones and boasted vaulted ceilings. It was well-lit by the numerous windows which adorned its pristine walls.

The moment the warriors closed the door behind them, Rhys teetered over to a pile of cushions and collapsed. He took a long, deep breath and then fell asleep.

13
PADUCAH

RHYS FELT HIS BODY SHIFT as someone sat beside him. He opened his eyes and looked up at Hodge. "Hey," murmured his friend. Rhys sat up and looked about the vast room. By the lack of natural light, he had to guess it was nearing dusk. "How are you feeling?"

Rhys ruffled his hair into place. "Sorry for worrying you."

"You could have at least given us some warning," replied Hodge, fondly nudging him. Hearing their conversation, Vinz and Kashim joined them. "What was that? What happened?"

"An emergency deflection system. It repels anything that tries to touch Pathos," said Rhys.

"What does it do, exactly?" asked Vinz.

"It amplifies the electrical currents in my body to deliver a shock or provide a physical barrier around Pathos."

"You didn't kill the priest, did you?" Vinz seemed more concerned about that than Rhys' wellbeing.

"No, I didn't kill the priest. I don't think I could deliver a shock large enough to do so and remain conscious."

"Well, it seems that little stunt earned their faith," mused Vinz. He nodded toward the door. "People have been gathering outside for the past two hours."

"Why?" asked Rhys.

"To see you," replied Hodge.

Vinz smiled grimly. "You struck the priest of the town for blasphemy."

Rhys stared at the floor. "When are we returning to the ship?"

"Not for several more hours." Vinz knelt before him. "Trukuula is a five-day celebration. This is night number two. And with your arrival, it's only going to become more intense."

As if to emphasize the point, a thundering boom shook the building. The ground beneath them quivered. Rhys gawked at the large temple door before clambering to his feet. A series of blasts followed. Hodge covered his ears and frowned deeply at Vinz.

The Overseer leaned into Rhys and raised his voice. "Drums. They're calling for you."

"What do I do?" shouted Rhys.

"We won't be given the opportunity to discuss peace with them tonight. They're too riled up. For the moment, be stoic and distant. Don't let anyone touch you. *Don't* make another scene. One miracle is enough."

Vinz motioned to Kashim and Hodge, and together they approached the front door. Hodge wrapped his arm around Rhys' shoulders. "Stay calm," he murmured. "Don't let anything you see affect you."

Vinz opened the door and stepped aside. The thunderous drumming outside stopped and silence blanketed the area. Rhys passed Hodge, Kashim, and Vinz and stepped into the lamplight. The sight that greeted him was one he would never forget.

A sea of people—men and boys—stood silently before him, bowing, their hands folded across their chests. Every one of them, save the young children, had a bald head decorated with intricate tattoos. Their clothes were worn and ragged and showcased varying levels of grime. The air was heavy with thick incense, a caustic stench that accosted Rhys' nose, burned the back of his throat, and caused his eyes to water.

Though it was completely silent, there was an intense sense of apprehension in the air. Even Rhys could feel the excitement and focus of the people standing before him.

"Son of the Heavens," came a voice from his right. Rhys turned to find Saccui and his subordinates bowing. "God of the Stars." The sea of people straightened themselves, but their arms remained crossed. Saccui approached Rhys, knelt, and firmly planted his forehead on the ground. "Please, forgive this one! This servant doubted you, denied you. This servant looked upon your face with distrust. Please, forgive this errant servant."

Rhys remained silent. To the crowd, he was sure it appeared as though he were deliberating upon the priest's fate; he was, in all honesty, trying feverishly to decide how best to respond. What type of reply would be best?

Despite the fact that Pathos had made available to him information concerning ancient religions from Earth, he could not find a decisive answer. Every mythical god or divine being had their own way of responding to petulant worshipers. Mercy, death, exile, understanding, discipline. What was expected of him?

"You are forgiven," said Rhys. He thought for a moment and then added, "It is your job to protect your people and guide them along the path to the stars."

Saccui made a sign above his head and then rose to his knees. Rhys was startled to find the man teary-eyed. "This servant will never doubt again. This servant will forever praise you and give thanks to your brethren." Rhys didn't respond; he was too uncomfortable and anxious. Saccui rose to his feet. "We praise you!" he shouted suddenly, holding his arms above his head.

The people behind him cried out, "We praise you!" and raised their arms into the air as well. Again, Saccui called out and once more the people repeated the cheer. Thunderous applause ensued accompanied by wild, joyous calls.

The sea of boys and men parted, and Saccui entered the crowd. Sensing that they were to follow, Vinz, Kashim, and Hodge joined Rhys; together, they walked down the temple stairs and fell in behind the priest.

As Rhys passed, people bowed and murmured prayers and blessings. He couldn't tell the difference. The foreignness of it all was unsettling. The smells, the sounds, the sights—he had a hard time comprehending it all. He couldn't understand how so many people could so blindly follow an authoritarian figure, a divine being whose very existence they had never seen until then. How did any of it advance the human race? How did it bring about peace?

For more than two kilometers, they followed Paducah's priest. Despite Vinz's prediction, no one in the crowd tried to touch him, though many reached out in longing. He was untouchable, unattainable like the stars overhead. He saw it in their eyes. He was something they yearned for but were too afraid to near.

Saccui led them through the streets to the middle of town where there stood a large dais decorated in lush white cloth, colorful flowers, and a cornucopia of food. Warriors in red stood stiffly around the dais.

After a quiet conversation with lower-level clergymen, Saccui motioned for Rhys to step onto the dais. Rhys tensely obeyed and looked out over the town. Thousands of people stood before him; all eyes were trained on him.

"Let Trukuula truly commence!" shouted Saccui.

The crowd's eruptive cheers were drowned out by drums and a menagerie of horns exuberantly bugling. Rhys fought to recover his composure. The sea of people became a flurry of activity and soon there were several groups of men and boys rhythmically dancing in a circle while chanting incoherent words. It took but a few moments for the groups to expand and merge effortlessly with the hundreds of people moving around them. As far as Rhys could see, the people of Paducah became a single, unified wave of motion.

In time with the drum-heavy music, they circled clockwise in a unique jump-step, bobbing as if they were riding a wave. Without a signal, without a leader, the mass of people slowed and then came to a halt but continued marching in time with the drums. For several measures, they rocked back and forth and bobbed to the beat before suddenly turning in the opposite direction and moving the circle counter-clockwise.

After some time, great bonfires began cropping up around the edges of the town's square and many of the people within the circle lit torches and lamps to illuminate their feet and those of their neighbors.

For the first time since he had arrived on Earth, he called to Alina and shared with her what he was seeing.

What... are they doing? she whispered. He could sense she was just as captivated.

I have no idea. It's been going on for... 45 minutes now. What's the purpose? What do they hope to achieve?

Ask someone.

Can't, replied Rhys.

Why not?

Because all of this is for me, he explained darkly.

Eventually, a high-pitched horn entered the fray of rhythmic music and everyone began clapping in time. The bobbing and measured pacing stopped; all stood still. In a final cacophony of drums, the song ended, and silence blanketed the town. All that Rhys could hear was the ringing in his ears.

Saccui appeared and motioned for him to sit. Rhys numbly acquiesced and stared at the ground. He was so tired. Emotionally, physically—he wanted to be left alone. But the look in Vinz's eyes told him this was far from over.

As the great sea of sweaty people dispersed, a new group appeared on the scene. Rhys glanced at the clergyman leading the group and then shifted his gaze to the ground. Whatever was next, he hoped it was quick. The soft tinkle of metal caught his ears. It was then that he noticed a line of women behind the clergymen. The collection stopped before Rhys, bowed deeply, and then sidestepped to give Saccui center stage.

Rhys tried not to openly stare. He attempted to avert his eyes several times, but he couldn't help but glance at the young, nearly naked women standing before him. While the major erotic areas were covered by a thin, black material, the majority of their skin was bare. On their wrists were tinkling jewelry; their ankles were decorated with chunky anklets of glittering stones. There were five in total, but each wore her long, brown-black hair differently. Like their hairstyles, the looks in their eyes varied.

"Son of the Heavens, God of the Stars," said Saccui, bowing before Rhys. He motioned to the young women. "In anticipation of your arrival, we have gathered a selection of the most beautiful women."

Rhys' eyes slipped to the girl at the end of the line. His eyebrows furrowed slightly as he realized the bone structure of her face differed from the other girls'. Discreetly, he studied the young women. The texture of their hair varied as did their heights, breast sizes, hip widths, and statures.

"So you may not be alone during this time of great thanksgiving and celebration, please feel free to use them as you will," said Saccui.

The young woman on the end has similar facial characteristics to Kallen, said Pathos, picking up on Rhys' suspicions.

I thought so, replied Rhys. He glanced at the priest and then stepped from the dais. Everyone bowed. Rhys moved down the line of women to the last girl. He stopped in front of her.

She was young and petite with small breasts, slender hips, and lean legs. Though she wore clothing identical to the others, the arch in her nose and the shape of her cheekbones were eye-catching. He saw Kallen in her.

Rhys cleared his throat in hopes she would look up at him, but the girl kept her face turned downward. "How did you get here?" he finally asked in Elali.

The girl's head snapped up; her eyes widened. Rhys waited for her to respond, but she remained silent.

Perhaps she does not speak Elali? offered Pathos.

She speaks Elali, affirmed Rhys, holding the girl's frightened gaze. *She's scared. I'll try again.* "I said, how did you get here?"

"Me?" she whispered in Elali.

Rhys nodded. "You're not Pantarak, are you?"

She shook her head and looked at the ground.

"Are any of these girls?"

"Three of them are."

"Who's the other non-Pantarak woman?" asked Rhys.

"The girl in middle with her hair pulled back."

Rhys met her gaze. "What's your name?"

"Miuna."

"Where are you from?"

"Durslade."

"Miuna?" asked Rhys. The girl nodded once more. "I'm Rhys." He glanced at Saccui who was fidgeting. "I'm going to put my hand on you and bring you up on the dais with me. I'm going to do the same with the other girl." He lowered his voice. "What's the other girl's name?"

"Ceit," whispered Miuna.

"Does she speak Elali as well?"

"Yes."

Rhys put his arm behind Miuna and gently pushed her from the line. Her feet moved hesitantly. "Trust me, Miuna," Rhys murmured. Rhys passed Saccui and released Miuna beside Vinz. He then turned for Ceit.

"I know you don't belong here," said Rhys in Elali. Ceit's gaze found his, and he startled. Her eyes were not brown, but honey-colored. "Come with me." Ceit stared at him, frightened. Her hands shook visibly. "I'm not an enemy," added Rhys. "Trust me."

Tears swelled in the girl's honey-colored eyes and her lip quivered in fear. Not wanting to keep Saccui waiting any longer, Rhys reached for her wrist. Ceit snapped her hand away and cried out in terror. Though her reaction surprised Rhys, Saccui's immediate response startled him even more. In a single motion, the priest stepped between them and slapped Ceit across the face. With a whimper, Ceit stumbled back, tripped on her feet, and fell to the ground.

Something snapped in Rhys, a rage and fierce hatred he had never before felt. Instinctively, he turned to strike Saccui, but Kashim's strong hands stopped him. Panting with fury, Rhys freed himself from Kashim and then planted himself between Ceit and the priest.

"This servant apologizes!" said Saccui. "She will be punished further."

"Don't lay another hand on this woman," seethed Rhys. Saccui bobbed his head and backed away. To Ceit, he said in Elali, "If you want to live, get up." Ceit glanced at Miuna, crawled to her feet, and joined her friend. Rhys looked at the other girls and then returned to the dais. He sat in his plush chair and glowered into the distance. Miuna and Ceit sat on either side of his chair.

Saccui ushered the other girls from Rhys' sight. The area before the dais was replaced with a squad of dancing Pantarak women dressed in vibrant gold and yellow. As the music flowed, Rhys shifted his gaze to the ground. He was seeing too much, learning too much about Earth's human race. He didn't like it. He felt physically sick and emotionally perverted.

For the next two hours, he sat in silence. He didn't look at Miuna and Ceit, who he knew were frightened, nor did he talk with Vinz, Kashim, or Hodge. With Pathos' help, he blocked out the majority of the sounds and disengaged his peripheral vision so as not to be continuously overwhelmed. He kept his gaze straight ahead, staring into the dark distance. If Saccui and his minions wanted to provide hours of uninterrupted entertainment, food, beverages, and prayers, he wasn't going to stop them. Humans were such foolish creatures with narrow minds.

It was near dawn by the time the festivities died down. Saccui eventually bowed deeply to Rhys and then spoke with Vinz at length. Rhys numbly stood and dropped from the dais.

"Contact your sister. Send the dinghy," instructed Vinz under his breath. "They're allowing us to return to the ship to rest."

"What about them?" asked Rhys, nodding to Miuna and Ceit who were watching them.

"What about them? They're yours." Vinz motioned to Hodge who was wobbling precariously on exhausted legs. Unlike Rhys, the others had not been given the luxury of sitting.

Rhys turned to Miuna and Ceit. "Come on," he murmured in Elali.

They waited at the docks surrounded by warriors. When Lyruc arrived with the dinghy, Rhys could hardly contain himself. He knew nothing about Lyruc except the man's name and his duties aboard *Themis*, but he was relieved to see a familiar face.

In silence, the group rode back to the ship and entered through the forward hatch. As the hatch closed behind them and the water drained, everyone slid out of the boat. Rhys landed on unsteady legs. Instead of holding himself up, he sat on the ramp and stared blankly at the wall.

"Rhys?"

Rhys looked up to find Kallen and Alina standing in the doorway. His eyes became clouded with tears and his throat tightened. Before Alina could get to him, he was crying, unashamedly. Overcome, he groped for his sister and clung to her. Alina held him. No one else could understand because no one else knew what they knew—humanity on Earth was doomed.

14
THEIR RESPONSIBILITY

"RHYS," SAID VINZ AFTER A long moment. Everyone in the forward hatch fell still. Rhys gazed tiredly at the floor. "Get some rest. It starts all over in a few hours."

"Do it yourself," spat Rhys. "We're leaving."

"Where?" asked Vinz exasperatedly. "You've nowhere else to go."

"Anywhere!" snapped Rhys. "Anywhere but this hellhole!" He stood. "I'm leaving!"

"Calm down," murmured Alina, gently taking hold of him.

Rhys jerked his arm out of her grip and glared at Vinz through tears. "You didn't tell me everything. You swore you'd tell me everything. You didn't."

"What are you talking about?" grumbled Vinz. "I've told you all that I know."

Rhys pointed vehemently at the two new girls who stood near the back wall. "You didn't tell me about them. You didn't tell me about the mindless rituals. You didn't tell me *anything*!"

"You're right," said Vinz coldly. "I didn't tell you anything. Do you know why? Had you known what was going to happen, what you would see and hear, you would never have gone." Vinz motioned toward the town. "You would never have stepped foot onto land."

"You're right. I wouldn't have!" argued Rhys. "You're foolish to believe that there could ever be peace between your people and the Pantaraks. How blind are you to have even thought that?"

"Rhys!" hissed Alina.

"How foolish! You—none of you—have any idea how to go about finding peace. How could you? You've never known it! You've never known what it's like to live and work in perfect harmony with a unit of humans! To have the same goals and desires. You know *nothing*!" Rhys caught his breath, glanced at Vinz, and then said, "You were foolish to have ever believed you could cause change." To Alina, he said in Interstellar Nefegian, "*I* was foolish. I was foolish to have believed any of this. Sister, forgive me. Forgive me."

"Anything else to say?" asked Vinz.

Disconcerted by the Overseer's calm response, Rhys shook his head.

"Good. Go rest." Vinz turned and left with Kashim.

"Can… I ask your names?" asked Kallen, joining Rhys. The two girls, who had been silent until that moment, exchanged looks. "I'm Kallen."

"I'm Miuna, and this is Ceit." Miuna glanced at Rhys and then whispered, "What's going on? Who are you people?"

"Take them to our cabin and find them something to wear," said Hodge.

Alina took his arm and pulled him upright.

"Ehh, Rhys?" asked Miuna. Rhys looked at the two girls. Miuna shifted her gaze from Alina to Kallen then back to Rhys. "You two… really are white… gods."

"We're not from here," corrected Alina.

"You're the real thing," whispered Miuna.

"We're not gods!" snarled Rhys. He pushed past Hodge and left the forward hatch. Angrily, he entered their cabin, slammed the door, and dropped on his bunk. The tears returned. Bitter, he rolled over and went to sleep.

He woke several hours later to the smell of food. Late afternoon sunlight seeped through the porthole. Though Alina's bed was made, the bunk above hers was occupied.

There was a knock on the door and Kallen appeared. She glanced at him, looked at the two upper bunks, and then crossed the room. Kneeling beside his bed, she whispered, "Are you hungry?"

"Kallen, what I said… "

Kallen leaned forward and wrapped her arms around his neck. "Thank you," she whispered. "Thank you, thank you." She kissed his cheek. As she pulled away, Rhys peered at her in confusion. "You saved them."

"Who? Vinz?" asked Rhys, baffled.

Kallen embraced him once more. "No, Miuna and Ceit. You saved them." Her voice shook. "You saved them, Rhys. Thank you."

"There were four others... "

Kallen looked at him. "Did they belong to the Pantaraks?" He nodded. "So these were the only two who were kidnapped? How did you know?"

Rhys stared at Kallen, slowly piecing together the information. "You... you were one of the tributes," he whispered, "taken for Trukuula." Kallen nodded solemnly. "If I hadn't chosen them... they would have undergone the same thing you had?"

"Yes," whispered Kallen.

Rhys' gaze shifted to the bunk above Alina's bed. "But this is the first time these people have seen someone like me, right?"

Kallen sat on the bed beside him. "Yes, but the celebration happens no matter what."

"What happens to the women who are chosen as tributes?"

"The priest and clergymen take turns raping them," murmured Kallen.

"What was the priest's name?"

"What do you mean?"

"The men... What were their names?"

"I don't remember."

Rhys looked at her. "You're lying."

"Saccui Mazatl." Kallen grabbed his arms and held him still. "You *finish* your job. Don't go looking for revenge, Rhys. Not now. It will come but not now. We need this to succeed." Rhys forced himself to relax and nod. Kallen released his arms and kissed his jaw. "Take a bath and then come eat. Alina's been cooking for hours. She wants the whole ship to eat."

"Why?"

"She thinks it'll bring us together."

Rhys stood and began untying the sash around his waist. "I'm not going to just forgive Vinz. He's manipulative and—"

"I'm not asking you to forgive him," interrupted Kallen. "I'm asking that you continue acting in the capacity that you have been." As Rhys untucked his shirt and ruffled his hair, Kallen watched him. "This isn't futile. It's true we don't have much experience with peace, but we know we're moving in the right direction."

"I just need some time," whispered Rhys. "I just need to be given the opportunity to... comprehend everything."

Kallen stepped into him and ran her hand through his hair. After a moment, she scrunched her nose. "You stink."

"They were using incense last night."

She smiled. "The silver in your hair is starting to shine through." She pulled the shoulders of his shirt upward signaling Rhys to raise his arms. She slipped his blouse off and then pushed him toward the doorway. "Go. Take a bath. I'll set out clean clothes."

Rhys gave her an appreciative look and crossed the hall. After a quick bath of furious scrubbing, Rhys dressed and went to the galley. He was surprised to find not only Alina and Kallen, but Hodge, Miuna, Andy, and Kyo.

"Heeeyyy," said Andy. "You're hair's showing."

Rhys fluffed his drying hair. He had seen it in the mirror before leaving the washroom. After his bath, the dye in his hair had thinned considerably, leaving his untidy locks a dark gray. Alina passed him a smile before continuing to stir the pot on the stove. Kallen motioned toward Miuna.

The girl looked quite different than he remembered. Dressed in slacks and a loosely-fitted blouse, she seemed plain. The thick makeup which had shaded her eyes the night before was gone and her long hair was curled in a horsetail at the back of her head. "Hello," Miuna greeted quietly. Without the makeup and costume, she looked to be Alina's age, perhaps a little younger.

"Hi, Miuna," said Rhys.

Miuna glanced at Kallen. "I wanted… to thank you."

Not wanting to be reminded of everything, Rhys sat heavily at the nearest table. "Please don't."

"May I ask one thing though?" murmured Miuna. "How did you know we weren't Pantarak? We have nearly the same skin color and eyes. We look very similar."

"Your face," said Rhys. He motioned to Kallen. "It looks like hers."

Hodge and Andy leaned forward to study the women. "I don't see it," admitted Andy. "I really don't."

Rhys pointed to Miuna. "The shape of her forehead and how her nose arches. It's the same."

"Where are you from Kallen?" asked Miuna.

"New Arbroath," replied Kallen.

"No, your family."

"Durslade." Kallen looked at Miuna. "Is that where you're from?"

Miuna smiled at Rhys. "He spoke to us in Elali. It wasn't perfect, but I could understand him."

"He's been translating my grandfather's sunboard manuals," explained Kallen proudly. "He taught himself Elali."

"It's a dying language. Aabesh is far more universal now, but there are still some who use it." Miuna beamed at Kallen. "Did you have to learn it in school?"

"Of course, and I hated it," replied Kallen, holding a bowl out for Alina.

Rhys sat back and looked at Hodge who had yet to say anything of substance to him. Though Rhys didn't regret what he had said, he didn't want it to dampen his relationship with his best friend. "Did you sleep?"

Hodge sat across from him. Rhys expected him to smile and brag about how well he had slept, but Hodge's face remained grim.

"He didn't mean what he said," said Kallen, sensing the tension between them.

"Yes, I did," replied Rhys. He glanced at Hodge who was gazing at him solemnly. "But... I didn't mean for it to sound so blunt. I was upset."

"We all were," replied Hodge. "I've never witnessed Trukuula. Vinz and Kashim have, but I haven't. It was exhausting and trying." Hodge paused in thought, his eyebrows furrowed. "But... that doesn't give you the right to call what we're doing foolish. You can't trivialize something we're so desperately fighting for. We're going about this the only way we know how—by ourselves... because no one else believes in the cause. And now, not even you believe in what we're doing?" Hodge shifted his gaze to his fidgeting hands. "It's not fair."

Rhys glanced at the others in a quick read of the room. Though he could sense Alina was firmly sided with him, the expression on Kallen's face was less discernible. He did not regret all that he said, but he sensed he needed to show remorse. He didn't want his relationship with Hodge and Kallen to sour. "I was emotional. I apologize for my words. They were inappropriately stated. I'm sure there was a better way to address the issue."

Hodge gazed at him for the longest moment and then said, "That was the worst apology I've ever heard." A slight smile broke across his friend's face. "I guess that's the most I'm getting out of you." He took a deep breath. "We need to teach you tact." Kallen set a bowl of food in front of Hodge, patted his shoulder, and then retrieved more.

Though the meal was meant to be shared by the entire crew, only those present ate. As usual, Rhys and Hodge inhaled the food in unison. After the meal, Kallen spoke at length in Elali with Miuna and Ceit about Rhys and Alina. Not wanting to hear the story again, Rhys helped Alina clean the dishes and the cooking area.

What will you do? she asked, handing him a towel.

I don't know, replied Rhys.

Kallen told me Hodge was very upset after you yelled at everyone this morning. He was slamming doors and kicking things. Alina smiled. *You've become more of a crew member than I have. He was so angry.*

Rhys paused in his work. *What I said... Was I right?*

Alina nodded. *You were right.*

Alina, what are we doing here?

I think you're more well-equipped to answer that question.

I want your opinion.

Alina continued to wash the bowls. *We are, at the moment, the sum of humanity—you and I and all the people on Caelestis. How did we reach Hyperes? How were we able to leave the Solar System? Because our ancestors spent centuries staring up at the sky wondering, theorizing, planning, designing, and building. You and I stand upon hundreds of thousands of years of human development and advancement. Them—the people here—they aren't. After the exodus, all of that advancement disappeared. They're starting from the ground-up. So, from our point of view, of course they seem barbaric. Look at everything that is presented in our database from history. Violence, religious rituals and sacrifices, wars, disease, corruption, mass genocide, famine. All of these were a part of our ancestry.*

All of that is easier to accept when you say it like that, but when you see it... It's different. Rhys thought for a moment. *When you do though, you wonder, how can they not see that what they're doing is morally wrong? How can they not see that their species is nearing extinction?* He looked at her from the corner of his eye. *It brings out things in you that... you never knew you had.*

Alina set down the bowls. *What do you mean?*

There were times last night when I really did feel that I was a god, as though I was better than them. Smarter, stronger, faster. I deserved more respect because I was above everything they were doing. I knew it was wrong. He chuckled nervously. *The priest hit Ceit. That's why she has the welt across her cheek. When he hit her... I almost lost control. I was ready to do to him unspeakable things. I was upset, emotional, angry, hurt, betrayed.*

What happened?

Kashim stopped me. He caught my arm before I struck the man. Rhys bowed his head over the sink. *Alina, I disengaged my sensory functions last night. My hearing, I disengaged it completely. I brought my sight down to simple processing. I couldn't... couldn't take it. It was too much.*

Rhys, that's dangerous, scolded Alina though her heart wasn't in it. *But... I understand. I probably would have done the same thing.*

Is it possible that a perfect world doesn't exist and Caelestis... was a fake utopia?

There was no fighting over resources, jobs, property, or land. Everything was taken care of for us. We just had to function as a part of a colony and support mankind's advancement to the best of our abilities, said Alina. *But at what cost? We weren't allowed freewill or the ability to make decisions. We weren't even given the right to bear children. Our sexuality was taken from us.* She leaned against Rhys, seeking comfort. *Maybe... we're the fools. Maybe there is no such place.*

That frightens me, whispered Rhys.

Me too.

Just as they finished the dishes, Vinz appeared in the galley. He handed his empty bowl to Alina and then looked at Rhys. "We're leaving for shore in three hours."

Rhys' reply was stoic. "Fine." The Overseer nodded, smiled at Alina, and then left.

"You're going back?" gasped Ceit.

Rhys glanced at Alina. "Yes."

"I'm coming with you," Miuna asserted. "They'll want to see us beside you." She looked to Kallen. "Right?"

Kallen nodded slowly. "She makes a good point."

"I'm not leaving this ship," said Ceit.

"That's fine," replied Rhys. "Kallen, do you have anything that is... more... uh... "

Kallen nodded. "I can take care of that."

Rhys glanced at Alina and then left the galley and returned to his cabin. Vinz had known all along; he had known Rhys would not abandon the mission. How? Why? Was it possible he understood Rhys more than even Alina?

Rhys lay down on his bed. He frowned as the smell of incense from the night before wafted over him. Angrily, he ripped everything off the bed and threw it into a pile on the floor. He flopped back down on the bare mattress, covered his eyes with his arm, and rested.

It wasn't long before someone knocked on the door and entered. Rhys peeked up at Kallen who stood at his bedside. "Too hot?" she chuckled, spotting the pile of bedding.

"Thank you," he murmured.

He felt Kallen sit at the end of his bed. "Rhys?"

"Hm?"

"I was wondering something."

"What?"

"Ehh, can... " Kallen laughed nervously, causing Rhys to look at her. She fidgeted for a moment, her eyes darting toward the door. Recognizing her behavior, he sat up, took her arm, and pulled her to him. The invitation was enough. Kallen straddled him and pushed him back onto the bed. She planted her hands on either side of his head and stared down at him with the oddest expression on her face. "I need you to keep it together," she whispered.

Rhys tried to calm his racing heart. The look in her eyes was not one of hunger or lust, but of pain. This was a serious conversation.

"I need you to be strong," Kallen repeated. "You have to make this work. We're counting on you. I'm counting on you."

Rhys rose on his elbows and kissed her gently. "I know."

Smiling, Kallen settled herself atop him firmly. "Are you tired?"

"Yes," replied Rhys, bewildered by her question. Of course he was. Though he had slept deeply, tired didn't begin to describe his mental exhaustion.

Kallen leaned into him and kissed his lips sweetly. When she pulled away, he saw the look in her eyes change. "Are you too tired for sex?"

"Now?" he whispered. Kallen nodded. "I, uh, I don't know what to... do."

With an impish grin, she began stripping out of her shirt to reveal a thin undershirt. "You have to be quiet," she hummed. Rhys couldn't answer.

What was he supposed to do? Where should he put his hands? What should he say? Was he supposed to take her clothes off? What if he hurt her? What if he did something wrong? Maybe he wasn't supposed to touch certain areas. What was the protocol? What was polite? Did she expect him to help her?

"Rhys," said Kallen. His eyes snapped up to hers. Though the hunger was still there, her face was scrunched in silent humor. "Calm down." She touched his cheek. Her fingers felt cooler than his skin. "We have time."

"I don't... I don't know what to do."

"I know," replied Kallen, smiling fondly at him.

"But you know... and I don't. I should know how to at least... "

Kallen scooted off his lap and pulled at the hem of his shirt. "Take it off," she instructed. Shakily, Rhys obeyed. Kallen's fingers ran over the expanse of his chest and wound around his neck. She leaned into him. "We'll go slow," she murmured into his mouth.

They kissed leisurely at first, allowing Rhys the chance to once more learn the movements. It wasn't long though before Kallen had him pinned against the bed, her lips moving feverishly against his. Yearning to feel her skin under his hands, Rhys tugged at the hem of her thin undershirt. Her response was to rip it over her head and continue to kiss him. Rhys moaned at the electrifyingly new sensation of her breasts against his chest.

"Ssshhh," hissed Kallen between breaths. Rhys nodded and ran his hands down the length of her back. Kallen pulled his right hand from its course and, with surprising directness, wrapped it around her bare breast. She looked down at him. "No sound."

"Sorry," he breathed, rolling his palm over her breast. Kallen sighed in pleasure, an extremely erotic sound. Unable to contain himself any more, Rhys slipped his hand between them, forcing Kallen to lift her hips to give him access to her pants line. As his hand glided across the sensitive skin along her abdomen, Kallen's breathing began coming in gasps.

Without warning, a harsh pounding on the door sounded. "Hey, we're leaving," said Vinz. "Get dressed and get out here. A Pantarak party has left the docks."

Rhys lay back and stared up at the bunk overhead. He hated Vinz so much.

Kallen pulled Rhys' hand away and intertwined their fingers. For a long moment, they stared at one another, each mesmerized by the other's mere presence. Finally, Kallen nodded toward the door and slid off. She picked up her undershirt and began dressing. Rhys slipped back into his shirt, his eyes lingering on her.

Kallen cleared her throat. "I need to find you something suitable to wear." She hastily left the room. Rhys sat against the wall and took a long breath. He couldn't help the dumb smile on his face.

A soft noise from the hallway pulled his gaze to Alina who leaned in the doorway, smirking.

"What?" he asked.

"You are flushed," she teased in their native tongue. "And your hair—"

"I know." He stood and swiped at his disorderly locks. "Does everyone know?"

"They will once you step outside," giggled Alina. "Your face is quite pink."

"Here," said Kallen, rushing back into the room with clothes. "The Pantarak party is here. Hurry." She dressed him in a green long-sleeved blouse and tied another sash around his hips.

"Was all of this planned?" asked Rhys, frowning at Kallen.

"Yes and no." Kallen looked at Alina who appeared amused by the situation. "We needed to get your mind off the situation. I only told Alina."

"Vinz seemed to know," said Rhys, pulling at his clothes.

"I wasn't supposed to let anyone in," Alina defended. "He figured out the rest."

"Rhys!" called Hodge down the hallway.

"Coming!" replied Rhys.

"Rhys," said Kallen. She pressed his headscarf in his hand.

"I know," he said. He kissed her on the cheek and rushed past Alina. Walking backwards, he said in their native tongue, "Thank you, Sister."

"Be careful," Alina replied solemnly. Rhys nodded to her and jogged down the hallway and up the stairs.

15
HOMILIES AND HALLUCINATIONS

THEY WERE ONCE AGAIN GREETED by warriors dressed in red. According to Vinz, they had come to retrieve Rhys early because he was needed to preside over several ceremonies before the festivities of that night.

Once on the docks, Rhys locked his face into a stoic expression and prepared himself. The men led them down the road once more to the center of town where already people had gathered. Though the crowd was certainly not like the size it had been the previous night, there were still well over a hundred people present. Rhys noticed women now interspersed amongst the sea of moving bodies.

Saccui met them, announced Rhys' return, and parted the people so they might pass. With Vinz in the lead and Kashim and Hodge flanking him, Rhys felt protected but not invulnerable. He glanced under his lashes at Miuna who was demurely trailing him.

Kallen had dressed her in a sleeveless pale yellow dress. Why someone like Kallen had such an article of clothing, Rhys didn't know, but he had to praise her choice. The front of the dress was modest and hung just below Miuna's knees while the dress' rear hem flowed out behind her. He vaguely wondered what Kallen would look like wearing it.

Rhys shifted his attention to the people around him. Men and women alike bowed and folded their arms across their chests as he passed. Children bowed their heads as they clutched at their parents' clothes. Several young men Rhys' age, who appeared to be a part of a special faction, knelt on the ground as he passed and pressed their foreheads to the earth.

Eventually, the group made it to the dais at the center of town; Rhys' entourage settled around him. Once more, Rhys seated himself on the dais and gazed out at the crowd.

After a prayer of admiration directed toward Rhys, Saccui led the people in the cheer of "we praise you!" He then made a motion, and the people backed away from the dais, creating a large area. Men laid blankets on the ground, three in total, and then bowed to Saccui. "Let the mothers come!" called Saccui.

Women pulled away from the crowd carrying small bundles in their arms. One by one they placed the bundles on the blankets. It wasn't until one of the mothers passed before Rhys that he understood what they were—babies. Having never seen a human baby in his life, Rhys rose, his eyes locked on the infant in its mother's arms.

Vinz cleared his throat and motioned for him to sit. "I want to see," murmured Rhys, stepping from the dais.

"Woman," barked Saccui. The mother, whose back was to Rhys, startled horribly and looked at the priest. "Bow before your god!" The woman whirled around and nearly dropped her babe in an attempt to kneel.

Rhys held his hand up to Saccui and motioned for the woman to return to her feet. The woman obeyed, her eyes flickering between the priest and the ground. Rhys stared at the infant, mesmerized. This was what a human child looked like. Round, wide-eyed, pink cheeks, pudgy arms and legs, little hair.

"God of the Stars," murmured Saccui, approaching Rhys. "Does this child displease you?"

Rhys shook his head. "I've... never seen a human child before." He studied the infant. "It's beautiful."

"Thank you, my god," breathed the babe's mother, her head bowed. "I praise you. Thank you. I praise you."

"Does it have a name?" asked Rhys, entranced.

"Her name is Yesui," replied the mother.

"Give the babe to him," said Saccui. Rhys glanced at the priest. The child was intriguing, but he didn't want to be responsible for something so important. With no inhibitions, the woman pushed the baby into Rhys' arms, her head still bowed. Awkwardly, Rhys took the infant and held it as he had seen the mother do.

The baby blinked up at him with enormous, brown eyes and then scrunched its face into a sour expression. It began wailing. In a first, Rhys looked to Saccui for direction. He hated the man, but right now, the priest was his only salvation. Saccui simply smiled. "Very nice," said Rhys after a long, agonizing moment of listening to the screeching. He handed the baby back to the mother, who bowed deeply, and then returned to the dais.

The mother, along with the other women, laid their infants on the blankets in neat rows, five or so to a blanket. Rhys truly hoped these people weren't about to do something barbaric, not after that magical encounter. Saccui motioned to the crowd and a line formed several paces from the blankets and infants. The priest took a preparatory step back and then sprinted toward the infants. The line followed. Rhys jumped up in horror.

With Saccui in the lead, the people leapt over the first blanket of infants, the second, and then the third. Again and again, people jumped over the blankets like hurdles. Several times, Rhys flinched as someone's foot came perilously close to an infant's head but not once did anyone misstep.

As the long line of people continued to leap over the infants, Rhys sat. "What are they doing?" he asked of Vinz who stood nearby.

"Leaping over the infants who were born in the past year."

"Why?"

"To rid them of evil spirits and allow their souls to be as free as the adults'," Vinz explained under his breath.

Rhys glanced at Miuna, who was watching the event with some concern, and then exchanged bewildered looks with Hodge. The baby leaping continued for the next 20 minutes as what seemed all of Paducah leapt over the oblivious infants.

When Rhys thought the events concerning babies were finished, two lines formed across the center of town. Without explanation or preparation, one person from the first line picked up an infant while the other line took more blankets and spread them taut between themselves. In something that could only be described in Rhys' mind as sheer stupidity, the infants were tossed between the lines, a whole three meters, before they landed in the blanket held by no less than five people. The babies were picked up by their mothers who disappeared into the crowd. Rhys only stared in disbelief and confusion. By the time the entire infant event had finished, the sun had set.

"Son of the Heavens, God of the Stars," said Saccui, presenting himself to Rhys. "If it would please you, you may retire to the public temple whilst the festivities are prepared."

"Yes," said Rhys. "I request only that my men come with me."

Saccui bowed in acknowledgment. Rhys turned to Miuna and held his hand out to her. She took it and pulled herself to his side all the while keeping her eyes downcast. With Vinz in the lead as usual, they followed Saccui east of the town's center down a narrow road overshadowed by tall trees. Unlike the rest of Paducah, this area was not populated by housing or stores but by fields of crops which could be seen in the dimming light beyond the trees. Not long after, they came upon a tall building with great pillars of marble and stone etched into the entryway. Saccui led them up a few steps into the grand foyer.

The temple was lit by a multitude of lamps, torches, and candles, casting the entire building in a warm, welcoming glow. A menagerie of elaborately crafted carpets covered the temple's floor. Beyond the foyer was a great expanse of space also fully carpeted. Rhys gawked at the vaulted ceiling and the intricate paintings along the walls which depicted stars, planets, and a variety of other celestial scenes. At the front of the cavernous room was a small stage dripping with a variety of colored fabrics and cushions.

Saccui motioned for Rhys to sit on the largest pillow. As Saccui settled himself near Rhys, the others stood beside the stage in silence. "What do you think so far of our celebration?" asked the priest joyfully. "The babes who underwent the ceremony will forever be reminded that they were cleansed under your merciful and watchful gaze. We praise you."

"I'm glad I could witness such a momentous event," said Rhys.

"I felt so full and overcome with emotion as I watched you study the infant." Saccui shook his head in disbelief. "It is as it has been told to us—the white gods are fascinated by the offspring of humans."

Instead of focusing on the content of that statement, Rhys asked, "And where did you hear that from?"

Saccui stood and went to a beautifully garnished chest stationed against the wall at the rear of the stage. He opened the chest, pulled aside multiple layers of cloth, and withdrew a large book. He returned and handed it to Rhys. "The Hallowed *Magris*."

Rhys stared at it. *Magris*. That was Interstellar Nefegian—his language. The Hallowed Book. Slowly, he cracked it open. The first yellowed page was blank. The second, however, had neatly scrawled handwriting in old Interstellar Nefegarian.

To the Son of Mankind Who Next Finds These Writings:

This is an account of my journey from Mereena in the Hyperes Solar System of the Milky Way Galaxy to Earth, the third planet of the Solar System.

Included in these writings are my own observations and understandings of this new world, as well as instructions for future generations who happen upon this miraculous planet. I have included in this account stories, parables, and lessons so, should the people of Earth need a guiding light, this book may be used as such.

My testimony has been written in the native language, Aabesh, in hope that it will help the Earth natives better understand what it means to be human.

Leaving my life's work entirely in your hands, I am, forever your friend,

Ramsen Amadorri

Rhys rested the book on his lap and stared at the page. He wasn't alone. There *had* been others. Well, of course there had been others—how else would this ridiculous religion have started? But this was concrete proof!

"Son of the stars, what ails you?" asked Saccui.

Rhys pointed to the scrawl on the second page. "Can you read this?"

"No, no one can understand it. It is the language of the gods." Saccui studied Rhys for a moment and then asked, "Can you... understand it?"

Rhys nodded.

"Though it is a copy, it was printed exactly as the original. What does it say?" Saccui fell off his cushion and knelt before Rhys.

"It's a preface," lied Rhys, "foretelling of eternal peace between all people on Earth, no matter creed, political beliefs, skin color, language, or descent." He collected his thoughts before continuing. "It reminds all readers that harmony comes through peaceful conversation, understanding, and acceptance." Rhys looked at Saccui. "Do you agree with and follow these ideals?"

Saccui bowed. "Of course!"

Rhys solemnly gazed at him. "Do you lie to me?"

"Son of the Heavens, God of the Stars—no! I would never!"

Rhys closed the book and placed a reverent hand on its weathered cover. "I heard there was an attack on a small town named New

Arbroath recently. On my journey, I heard from many that it was you who destroyed the hospitals and schools and killed hundreds."

Saccui prostrated himself before Rhys. "The apostates, of course, would blame our people!"

"There were eye-witness accounts. Now, tell me! Did your people attack New Arbroath?"

"Yes!" shouted Saccui.

"Why?"

"To give them a warning!"

"About what?" snapped Rhys.

Saccui buried his face into the carpet. "Our people saw you descend to Earth on a burning star, but when we arrived at the place of your new birth, we could not locate you. We saw a ship leaving that night and tracked it. We knew it was this man's ship." Saccui pointed at Vinz. "We knew he had you. But the ship was well-defended, and we are ill-equipped for sea battle."

"So you bombed New Arbroath?"

"We did it in your name! If you saw the destruction, you would be prompted to come to us—and look! Here you are! We praise you. We praise you."

"You killed hundreds of innocent people."

"It was for the white gods. The apostates do not believe in the power you possess. They do not believe that your kind has the ability to raise empires from the sea or control the sky. We do. You are our white god, and we belong to you."

Rhys stared at Saccui, awe-struck. He could have easily smashed the priest's face into a bloody pulp or screamed obscenities at him, but he refrained. Instead, he took a long breath and said, "You are not to kill in my name or in the name of the white gods ever again." Saccui looked up at him, gaping. "You have misinterpreted The Hallowed *Magris*. Continue your celebrations and rituals, but do not kill." Rhys held Saccui's wide-eyed gaze until the man once more pressed his forehead to the floor. "See to it that your clergymen are informed of this development." Saccui didn't move. "Go."

The priest leapt to his feet, pulled his clothes into place, and rushed from the temple. Rhys looked down at the book. "Don't speak to me," he said to Vinz and the others. "I need to memorize this."

"Rhys, that's not necessary," started the Overseer.

"Just let me do it," replied Rhys. He opened the enormous, perfectly bound book. *Alina, I found this book. This is their holy book. It's written by one of our people. I'm going to start sharing the pages with you.*

I'm ready, replied Alina.

Rhys began scanning the pages using the same technique he had back at Reza's sunboard shop. He wasn't sure how long it took him, but by the time he closed the book, Miuna was dozing along the stairs and Vinz, Hodge, and Kashim were standing in the foyer quietly speaking.

He could sense Alina processing the data as well. Both were in stunned disbelief. Everything in The Hallowed *Magris* was as if they had written it themselves. The author, Ramsen Amadorri, had also been sent out on a life pod as a part of an emergency protocol. The artificial intelligence which had controlled the life pod could not comprehend the anomaly that had led him to Earth, though Ramsen himself suggested it was the work of a wormhole. He had been immediately picked up by the Pantarak people and proclaimed a god who had descended on a falling star.

In stunning detail, Ramsen explained the rituals he saw, the sacrifices he witnessed, and the acts of utter brutality he observed. He explained how he felt, his own understanding of the situations, and the actual meaning behind the rituals which were created for him on the spot. The man's writing changed over the course of the work. While the first half of the book was written in awe, confusion, and disbelief, the second half presented a deep, philosophical perception of the world around him.

Though the book was a detailed report of his observations and the lessons he learned, Rhys found very little information in it that he and Alina could readily use. Time had moved on and already many of the ideas he had suggested in his text were no longer viable. Rhys had conclusively found a simple journal which held great importance to the Pantaraks but no helpful information for him.

He returned The Hallowed *Magris* to the chest, covered it with cloth, and closed it.

"Done?" asked Vinz from across the room.

Rhys nudged Miuna awake and crossed the foyer to join the others.

"The festivities have already begun," remarked Vinz.

"I know," replied Rhys, passing through the enormous doors. The moment they stepped from the temple, warriors bearing rifles straightened in attention. Rhys exchanged looks with Vinz who took the lead and the group started back to the center of town.

Even from a distance, Rhys could hear music swelling into the sky. When they reached town, they found people dancing exuberantly, laughing, and cheering. Vinz led them discreetly along the outskirts of the festivities back to the dais in the center of town. The moment they broke from the crowd, Saccui, who had been waiting at the dais, clapped his hands joyfully and rushed to Rhys.

"Lord, you were so entranced in the teachings of our prophet that I didn't dare interrupt," explained Saccui. He motioned to the great sea of moving bodies. "What do you think?"

"It's quite a sight!" shouted Rhys over the rumbling of the drums. "I've never seen anything like this."

Saccui nodded enthusiastically and escorted Rhys to the dais. "You three should go enjoy yourselves," the priest gestured to Vinz. "Your lord is safe here."

"With all due respect, Priest, we will keep our watch," replied Vinz.

Men and women gathered around Rhys, offering him great trays of food and tall mugs overflowing with a strong-smelling but sweet liquid. Rhys turned the food away but gratefully took a mug. As he sipped at the saccharine substance, he gazed out at the people.

For a moment, he forgot that these people had murdered hundreds of innocents. He forgot where he was; he was in another realm—a happy, joyful one alive with the rhythm of music and smiles. Unable to withstand the festively infectious atmosphere, Rhys eventually found himself tapping his feet in time with the pulsing music.

Someone brought him another tall mug of the sweet cocktail. The crowd parted to allow several women, clad in very little, to dance about in coordinated step and rhythm. With a precision Rhys didn't know humans could achieve, the women moved as one. Each motion, every step, was synchronized perfectly. They twirled, gyrated, spun, pranced, and swayed. Rhys couldn't help but feel the emotion from their dance and applauded with the crowd when they finished their choreography.

Several more routines followed the women's performance including a comedy sketch. As three men argued over who would best be able to deliver a pastry to a beautiful woman in town, Rhys watched in amused confusion. Comedy and humor had no place on Caelestis, but here it brought people together. After spending some time reviewing the material in his head to comprehend the subtle nuances, Rhys found he quite enjoyed comedy. By the third sketch, he was laughing with the crowd and chuckling at the slap-stick antics of the three men.

When the music finally restarted, Rhys reclined heavily in his chair and breathed deeply. His stomach hurt from laughing. Was something so ridiculous even possible?

After draining another mug of the sweet potion, he looked at Miuna. She glanced at him and immediately averted her gaze. The shape of her face reminded him of Kallen, but also of a woman he used to work with on Caelestis. What was her name? Annalise. She had been one of the deputy directors for the Design and Engineering Department. Like Alina, Annalise had scored high on her exams and had been designated as an assistant overseer. By the time Rhys entered the department, Annalise had been deputy director for nearly three years.

What had happened to her? The last time he had seen her had been two weeks before the accident. Was she even still alive? What about the director of the department, Povl Henningsen? Had he survived the collision? Rhys thought. He had seen Doctor Henningsen a few hours prior to the accident because the old man had given Rhys and his fellow crew members updates on one of the ships they had been repairing.

What was the ship? What had they been doing? Rhys grew motionless in deep thought. There had been several tasks needing completion. Rhys had been charged with taking the engine apart, rebuilding a converter, and connecting it. He startled in his chair. He had finished building the piece but had not taken the engine apart yet! When was that task due? Had he passed the due date? Doctor Henningsen was an understanding man, but that ship was needed for maintenance. They only had a dozen or so maintenance craft. With even one down, problems would begin to backup.

What was he doing sitting? He needed to get back to the hangar. Shakily, Rhys stood and leapt off the dais.

"What you doing?" came a voice.

"I have to get to the hangar. Craft Seven still needs to have its converter replaced. It was due… " Rhys thought. He couldn't remember when the assignment was due. "I just need to go. If there is a problem, please direct all concerns to Doctor Povl Henningsen, Director of Design and Engineering." Rhys turned and hurried off. There was distant shouting and a cacophony of sounds, but he was accustomed to the noise in the hangar.

As he ran, he wondered if one of his teammates had covered for him. He both hoped and dreaded the possibility. Craft Seven needed to be returned to service, there was no doubt about that, but that would mean that he had left his job incomplete. Someone else had had to pick up his slack. Rhys cursed under his breath. How could he have been so foolish?

As the sound around him faded, he slowed. Was he near the decompression chamber? Was he even going the right way?

"Rhys!" called a voice. Rhys turned and looked at four people he recognized but couldn't put names to. "Where you go?" They must have seen him running and were worried something was wrong in the hangar.

"The hangar," he breathed. "I haven't completed—"

"Rhys, stop."

Rhys stared at the people, three men and one woman. Ah, the woman—Annalise. "Deputy Director, would you please explain to them that I forgot about an assignment?"

The woman, Annalise, stared at him in confusion. One of the men murmured something and, the largest member of the group turned and disappeared into the dark. "Rhys, me you understand can?" asked the man.

Rhys looked at Annalise and then nodded. "Why are you speaking like that?"

The man who, for some reason, had scars on the side of his head, sighed exasperatedly. Rhys peered anxiously over his shoulder. He needed to get to the hangar. He had left a project with his name on it unfinished. He was Doctor Falkrow's Other Child; this was unacceptable!

"I'm sorry. I really don't have time for this. Deputy Director, please." Rhys turned to walk away, but the gangly man with a mop of dark hair grabbed Rhys' arm.

The scarred man leaned into Rhys. "Machine-thing, me hear can? What happening is?"

"Rhys Falkrow is hallucinating," replied Pathos. The AI's accent was strange and foreign to Rhys. "Right now, he believes he is returning to the hangar on Caelestis to complete a project he was assigned by the director of the department. Rhys believes the assignment is past its due date. He does not know any of you except Miuna who resembles the deputy director of his department."

Rhys gazed at the people in confusion. Why did these people care where he was going? He was an engineer, a technician—and not even one of the important ones. He was a foot soldier in the neverending battle against repairs. His job was to complete as many repairs, routine checks, and construction projects in a day as possible. He wasn't important, not like the deputy director or Alina. Someone could easily do his work. He was replaceable.

"I'm sorry. I need to get to the hangar," said Rhys, suddenly somber. This feeling of hopelessness and infinite despondency was familiar. He was Doctor Falkrow's Other Child; Alina was the chosen one. She had been given the Logos AI, after all. "Please excuse me." He turned and started walking again.

"Rhys," called the scarred man. "The hangar this way is."

Rhys stopped and looked about. "Is it?" He heard Pathos say something, but he couldn't quite understand his AI.

"I certain am," asserted the scarred man. "Right?" Annalise nodded and motioned him in the opposite direction. Rhys considered his confusion and then followed. It was possible he was turned around. On multiple occasions when he first started working, he had become lost amongst the labyrinth of corridors in Caelestis.

Recognizing the familiar sound of docked craft, Rhys nodded in approval. It was true. He had been going the wrong way. Pathos spoke to Annalise and the two men before the deputy director approached Rhys. "Decompression Chamber enter," she said.

Rhys stepped into the chamber. Suddenly, wind rushed across his face.

"Here are," Annalise announced. Rhys stood and began climbing stairs. He could feel someone touching him as if to brace or balance him.

The scarred man stopped him at the top of the staircase. "Hangar this way is," he explained.

Rhys followed him down another flight of stairs into the hangar. Lights flickered on and Rhys gazed about. Why was it so small? Very few craft could fit there.

"Rhys," said the scarred man, crossing the hangar. He pointed to the converter. "This yours is."

"Ah!" exclaimed Rhys in relief. No one had moved it! Pathos murmured something as Rhys knelt beside the converter.

"It not complete is," said the man.

"I know, I know. I'll finish it by morning. I apologize for my tardiness," replied Rhys, running his hands over the converter. It didn't look like he remembered, but what did he truly remember? He had gotten lost on his way to the hangar. Perhaps there had been a glitch in his Core connectivity? That would explain the mix up. "I'll finish it by morning."

The scarred man sighed heavily, said something to the deputy director, and then left the hangar. Rhys glanced at Annalise, smiled, and got to work.

16
ALINA TAKES A STAND

RHYS WOKE. HIS HEAD FELT heavy and his body weary. He rolled over and winced as a hot pain shot through his neck. Groaning, he closed his eyes. He felt sick. After several more minutes of lying in silence, he attempted to sit up. Rubbing his aching neck, which seemed permanently set to the left, he looked around, perplexed. Why was he on the floor of *Themis'* forward hatch? He studied the menagerie of tools and disorderly piles of paper scattered around him. What had happened?

A glimmer caught his eye and Rhys peeked over his shoulder. There, propped between two barrels, was the sunboard that had been passed down to Vinz. "What?" he whispered, realizing the machine looked different.

He stood and shakily approached the board. No longer did it look like a hunk of metal. It *looked* like a working, ready-to-launch sunboard! How he had managed to unlock it, extend the board, and prep it, he didn't know.

Rhys circled it. The unit didn't have a fin. Was it possible it wasn't meant for the water? It also wasn't equipped with a propeller, fan, ailerons, or... anything that would allow it to go airborne. If it wasn't meant to be on the water or in the air, what was the board's purpose?

Rhys knelt to study the underbelly of the board. It took him a moment to realize what he was looking at. In awe, he dropped to the floor and gaped. "Are you serious?" he murmured. The board had a magnetic converter. It didn't need an engine! It utilized magnetic waves. "Are... you... serious?" He laughed in disbelief—the pounding headache that ensued quickly quelled his glee. Rhys flopped back and stared at the ceiling. "I can't believe it."

"I thought I heard you," chirped Kallen, appearing in the doorway. Her eyes flickered to the board, and her mouth fell open. "You… " She rushed to the board. "You figured it out!"

Rhys closed his eyes. "And I don't even know how."

Kallen circled the board. "Of course it extends," she mused. "That's why it kept sinking when we put it in water. It wasn't fully extended." Rhys sat up and watched her. He was waiting for her to ask how it flew. "It doesn't transform and… there aren't hand or footholds to control the board while in flight." Her excitement faded. "It doesn't fly?"

"It flies," said Rhys, moving to his feet. He gripped the side of the board to brace himself as his head reeled. "It flies using magnetic waves."

"Using what?"

"Magnetic waves. The planet gives off magnetic waves which the board can ride along." He pointed to the underbelly of the board. "The amplifier. It takes the magnetic waves and amplifies them, allowing the board to move along them."

"How do you steer and maneuver?"

Rhys regarded the board. That was a good question.

"I mean, magnetic waves aren't like wind, right?"

"Right."

"So, how do you control where the board goes once it's in the air?" Kallen caressed the board. "I… don't understand. No motor, no sail. Why doesn't it have solar paneling like the other boards?"

"It doesn't need energy," murmured Rhys.

Unable to fully understand the concept of magnetic waves, Kallen left him to his thoughts, and together they cleaned the area. After gathering the majority of the tools and returning them to their rightful places, Kallen said, "Last night, you kept dropping things."

"I did?"

"Often. But it wasn't like you were being clumsy. It was as though you were purposefully setting them aside, but… you just dropped them instead."

Rhys remembered thinking about his work on the colony and attempting to return to a project that was long past its due date. He also remembered seeing the deputy director of his department. Everything from the night prior was a blur. "I wasn't… thinking much last night."

Kallen joined him. "That's not it. You were dropping tools on purpose. I saw you pick up the lincer, study it, and then drop it over your shoulder. You did that with many of the tools."

"I think… I thought I was in space," mused Rhys.

"Vinz told us that you thought you were back on the colony," Kallen offered.

Rhys nodded. "That explains why I was dropping tools then." Seeing the confused expression on Kallen's face, he explained, "I thought I was in zero gravity."

"You've said that word before. What does it mean?"

"Everything floats in space. Your body, tools, everything. When we work in the hangars where everything floats, we can simply let go of a tool. It just hangs in the air until we need it again." He nodded once more to confirm his thought process. "I'm sorry I was so loud." Kallen brushed off the apology.

Once the board was stored and Rhys' notes put away, they left the forward hatch.

While Kallen returned to the galley to finish cooking, Rhys shuffled to the washroom and bathed. Once rid of the previous night's odors, he dried off and padded down the hallway to his quarters.

He expected Alina to be asleep. He didn't anticipate finding Hodge stretched out beside her shirtless and snoring. After a moment, Rhys dropped his dirty clothes into a pile at the foot of his bed, picked up the clean shirt Kallen had laid out, and left the cabin. He entered the galley and awkwardly sat at the table.

"What's wrong?" asked Kallen, looking up from a book. Rhys pointed over his shoulder toward his cabin.

"Oh, Alina." She leaned against the cabinet. "It's been hard on her having both of you in Paducah. She worries often."

"Both of us? Hodge and I?"

Kallen set her book aside and joined him. "Don't worry. Vinz spoke with her and Hodge the other night." She chuckled. "I think he's growing weary of repeating himself." Her laughter faded. "Are you worried? Hodge won't hurt her."

Though it was certainly odd seeing his sister asleep next to a man, Rhys wasn't sure that it worried him. "No, I don't guess it bothers me."

"You know, Alina stayed up with you all last night."

"She did?"

"And Hodge stayed with her. She was upset seeing you the way you were. Once you fell asleep shortly before dawn, she came and got me and they went to bed."

Rhys gazed at the table. "Seeing me how I was... What do you mean?"

"You were stoic, emotionless. It was like… your mind wasn't really working. Your demeanor changed too. You were timid, humble, and willing to do whatever anyone told you." She paused and then added lowly, "It was disturbing to watch. It wasn't who you are. It bothered me but… I think it really upset Alina."

"I'm sorry."

Kallen returned to the stove with a shrug. After some time, she said, "You should see if Alina wants to eat while it's hot." Rhys hesitated, causing Kallen to wave him out of the galley.

He reentered his cabin. Hodge and Alina hadn't moved. *Logos, would Alina like to eat?*

Negative, replied Logos. *She has not yet even reached hour three of her sleep cycle.*

I see. When she wakes, let her know that there will be food ready for her. Rhys gazed at them for a moment longer and then reported to Kallen that Alina did not want food.

After taking food to Vinz, who was in his cabin, Kallen sat with Rhys as he ate. She tried to keep the conversation light, but the heavy silence and tension on the ship threatened to swallow them both. "The… Pantarak people aren't pleased," she said finally. Rhys stopped mid-bite. "You ran off in the middle of the festivities last night. They've taken it as a bad omen."

"How?" asked Rhys, distraught and incredulous. "If they were drinking the same stuff I was, how were they still coherent to notice?"

"Not everyone was drinking," Kallen chided. "And Vinz… "

Rhys slumped against the back of his chair. Another bout with Vinz was inevitable. "So, no one's happy?"

"Yeah," murmured Kallen.

"Can anything be done?"

"Not that I know of."

"What do people here normally do when they've made a mistake?"

Kallen thought. "Apologize."

"Would an official apology work?"

"Perhaps. People sometimes give gifts too."

"An apology and a gift to the priest… " Rhys frowned at the ceiling. "I don't want to apologize to that man, much less give him a gift."

"I'm not really the best person to help with this," Kallen began. Rhys stood. "Where are you going?"

"Ashore," he replied.

She tangled her hand around his arm. "Talk to Vinz first. You don't know what kind of damage control he's already done. You don't want to contradict his work."

Rhys frowned again. Vinz was quickly becoming his least favorite person. "Fine." Kallen kissed his cheek and pushed him out the galley. Rhys slipped down the hallway and stood just out of sight of Vinz's open cabin doorway—they had yet to repair the mangled doorframe. After a few calming breaths, Rhys knocked on the frame.

Vinz, who was seated at his desk, looked over his shoulder and, seeing who it was, sighed and closed his book. "What?"

"I'm going ashore," said Rhys. "I understand that my sudden disappearance last night caused some misgivings about myself and this ship. I want to rectify that."

Vinz stood and leaned against his desk. "How many times did I tell you not to drink or eat anything they offered?"

"I forgot."

Vinz shook his head. "That's not good enough."

"I'm going to speak with Saccui right now."

"That won't be necessary." The Overseer's face was dark, and his eyebrows furrowed in a mixture of stress, anger, and exasperation. "They've already punished those they thought most contributed to your dissatisfaction with the festivities last night."

"What... do you mean?" Dread churned in Rhys' stomach. "What does that mean?"

Vinz gazed at Rhys for a long moment and then said, "You're learning what I learned several years ago. Mistakes made by a god or a son of a god have consequences. Therefore, we must be infallible. We are not given the same freedoms as others. We are held to a higher standard. We warrant stricter consequences." Vinz paused and then added, "They sacrificed the musicians and the performers who performed. If you go into town now, you will find their bodies resting in the center of town."

Rhys stared at Vinz in horror. "I told them... I told them they couldn't kill in my name... "

Vinz gazed at him gravely. "They don't listen."

"Did you know?"

"Know what?"

"Did you know they wouldn't listen to my words?"

"I hoped I was wrong," remarked the Overseer. "Historically, they have not listened to anyone." Rhys gaped in despair. "Think about it, even The Hallowed *Magris* indicates that the Pantarak people are bullheaded and unwilling to listen to logic or reason."

Rhys nodded in agreement. The Hallowed *Magris'* author mentioned multiple times how—His train of thought shifted and he looked at Vinz. "How do you know what's in The Hallowed *Magris*?"

Vinz crossed the room to his bookshelf and pulled a large leather-bound book from its lopsided shelves. "Because I have the original copy." He handed it to Rhys. "The author, Ramsen Amadorri, was my great-great-great grandfather."

Rhys handled the book with care. "If you had it, why did you let me spend an hour speed-reading their copy?"

"I thought maybe you would find something in it at that moment to help us better deal with what we were to face." Vinz took the enormous book from Rhys and returned it to the shelf. "Instead, you drugged yourself." Vinz looked at him. "We leave tomorrow. Until then, however, we must endure whatever the Pantaraks are preparing for this evening."

"They're not going to kill more, are they?"

"Don't know. Usually, the fourth night includes self-mutilation in remembrance of one of the fallen white gods—one of my ancestors—but for you, they may just throw in something special."

"I understand!" fumed Rhys. "I messed up."

Vinz hit his desk. "That's not good enough, Rhys! Listen to what I'm about to say, because I'm going to say it only once. You are *here* now. You are never, *ever*, going home. Earth does not have the resources, and its people do not have the technology. This is your home now, so start giving a *damn* about it." Vinz breathed deeply to calm himself. "*This* is our home. Change starts with us."

The Overseer held his gaze for a long moment and then sighed. Rhys didn't wait for the encouraging statements that were to follow. Instead, he turned and strode from the room down the hallway. Kallen, who was standing in the doorway of the galley, opened her mouth to speak, but no words followed. "I'm going ashore. Come help me launch," he demanded, stalking past her.

They worked swiftly to prepare the dinghy. As Rhys lowered the hatch door, Kallen climbed up the wall and dislodged the small craft. Together, they mounted the motor.

"I'm coming."

Rhys looked up at Alina who stood in the doorway of the cabin. Behind her was Hodge.

"No, you're not," replied Rhys.

Alina approached the dinghy. "I'm tired of sitting by and waiting for you to fix everything. I'm coming."

"No. You're. Not." Rhys turned to continue their preparations.

Alina grabbed his arm and whirled him back around. "I am not some person to be ignored," she said in Nefegian. "I am your sister. Just as it was on Caelestis, we are equal."

Rhys laughed dryly. "Equal?"

Alina shoved him. Rhys stumbled into the water and glared at her. "I am your sister! We landed on this hellhole *together*. We are in this *together*. How *dare* you talk to me like I am just some woman!"

"You *are* just some woman!" Rhys barked. All anger dropped from Alina's face and she gazed at him, hurt. Rhys sighed. "I... Alina... I didn't mean it like that."

"Then what did you mean?"

Rhys wavered. "I don't feel connected to you. Ever. We no longer link with the Core, so it's difficult to share data and information. Without that, I don't know you. I don't know who you are." He leaned against the dinghy. "They're all wanting some sort of miracle from me, but I'm so overwhelmed I can hardly understand what's before me." He looked at her. "How am I supposed to change the world? Vinz doesn't know how. He thinks he does, but he doesn't. No one knows how to connect with these people."

"Then we make a pact," said Alina. She stepped into the water and approached him. "Heretofore, we will share everything with one another. What we've seen, heard, felt... All of it."

"I... " Rhys considered her. "I don't want that. And neither do you."

Alina didn't seem taken aback by his words. "We can't continue in this manner." She glanced at Kallen and Hodge. "We're making fools of ourselves."

Rhys sighed. "Maybe... we should just talk more."

"That seems like a very human thing to do," Alina softly replied. "Fine, we'll talk more." She heaved herself into the dinghy. "Let's go."

Rhys frowned. "You don't want to do this, Sister."

Alina settled herself on one of the benches and pulled her headscarf around her neck and head. "I can assure you, I do. Now get in the boat."

Rhys looked at Hodge. "Are you coming?"

Hodge withdrew a rifle from one of the crates and leapt into the dinghy. Rhys settled himself beside the engine, waited for Kallen to back away, and then started the fan.

As they motored toward the wharves, Alina leaned against Hodge briefly for emotional support. When they reached the docks, Hodge grabbed a rope, pulled the drifting boat to a halt, and helped her disembark. They were immediately met by two clergymen and four warriors. Rhys stepped before Alina to address the men. "I need to speak with Saccui."

"He is busy at the moment, however, you may wait for him in the public temple," replied one of the clergymen.

Before Rhys could stop her, Alina pushed past him and slipped her scarf from her head. "You will fetch him at once," she commanded. The men gaped at her before one of the clergymen turned and ran.

"Son of the Heavens, God of the Stars," breathed the other clergyman. He bowed deeply. "Please, follow me to the public temple."

"No. Take me to the center of town," said Rhys.

"Yes, Lord," murmured the clergyman haltingly, exchanging looks with his brothers.

I don't want you seeing this, said Rhys.

I had four people die under my hands in New Arbroath, replied Alina. *Stop protecting me.*

It seemed the first clergyman who had ran off had signaled the arrival of another god because by the time they reached the center of town, people had gathered. Though they whispered and clamored to see the new god, no one ventured near the rows of bodies laid under the hot sun. There were 14 in total—11 men and 3 women. Each was dressed in white and laid so their arms were crossed over their chests. There was no evidence of wounds, blood, or torture.

While the warriors and clergyman stopped several meters from the bodies, Rhys, Alina, and Hodge approached the corpses. Without warning, Alina knelt beside the nearest one and touched the man's forehead with the tips of her fingers. She moved methodically down the line, repeating the motion again and again.

Once she made it to the end of the line, she rose and looked out at the crowd. "These people were slain." Her voice echoed against the buildings. "They were slain by kin—by their own blood—to appease gods who do not care one way or the other. The next time you decide to kill, remember this: we do not care about your lives. They are nothing to us. Your sacrifices and ritualistic ceremonies, they mean nothing to us. They are foolish, human acts. They are desperate cries for attention."

Alina pivoted, passing an appraising eye over the crowd. "For generations, we gods have spoken amongst ourselves and shaken our heads in disgust as on Earth, brothers killed brothers and fathers killed sons. So *easily* you humans murder one another. Do you want salvation, deliverance from this world? Do not kill in the name of your gods or in the name of your priest. Do not murder in the name of ritual and ceremony. Murder *not* so when you die and are set forth to be judged, you may be judged based on how you lived your life and how you helped your fellow man step forward." Alina pointed at the bodies. "This—this is *not* how you should treat your fellow man."

Alina rejoined Rhys and Hodge, pulling her headscarf back over her delicate scalp. She was sweating. Rhys met her gaze, nodded in acknowledgment, and then stepped forward. "Who among you will claim these bodies?" he called. For several long moments—moments that stretched into infinity—there was silence. No one moved.

Finally, five men separated themselves from the crowd and approached the bodies. They knelt beside the first corpse, picked it up, and carried it off. Another handful of people left the safety of the crowd, gathered a body, and followed. Again and again people extracted themselves from the multitude, respectfully took a body, and left. As the last group of people collected the remaining body, Saccui approached Hodge, Rhys, and Alina.

The priest bowed before Rhys and then timidly looked at Alina. "Priest," said Rhys, "May I introduce my sister." Saccui nearly went prone. He seemed at a loss for words. "Saccui. My sister has been unwell the past few days and has therefore been unable to attend the festivities. We will be taking our leave tomorrow to continue to the capital, however, she would very much like to see all that you have to offer by means of music and dance. Is that something you and your people would be willing to show her?"

Saccui straightened himself. "I... ehh, yes," he stammered. "We will begin preparations immediately."

"I would very much like to look around," said Alina, "and visit with your people."

"We would be honored," effused Saccui.

Alina smiled sweetly at the priest. "Thank you." She looked to Rhys. "Brother." With Hodge at his side, Rhys followed Alina from the center of town. The crowd of people broke apart to allow them passage.

Rhys would have preferred that they had a moment to talk about what had just happened, but Alina had other ideas. She stopped before a mother and child, smiled at the mother, and then crouched before the child. It was then Rhys remembered that his sister had never before seen a human child.

Fascinated, Alina studied the little boy. "What's your name?"

The child ducked behind his mother's legs. The mother bowed deeply to Alina and then pushed her child forward against his protests. "Tobo," said the woman. "His name is Tobo."

"Tobo," repeated Alina. She smiled at the little boy and then stood. "He's beautiful."

"I am honored," murmured the woman.

For the next hour, Alina flitted from one person to the next, speaking softly and asking questions. Rhys offered her information when necessary but remained silent otherwise. Alina knelt in the dirt numerous times to speak with children. Rhys wondered if her fascination with them was as evident to Hodge as it was to him. She was enamored.

Rhys, look at this one, his sister said, moving aside so Rhys could behold a little girl. *She's six years old but look how big she is!* Alina's eyes shifted to Hodge. An odd expression overcame her, and she returned her gaze to the child.

"Daughter of the heavens," said a young man no older than Rhys. Alina stood and looked at the newcomer. Beside him was a feeble, old woman. "I am honored to be before you." He looked to Rhys. "And you, Son of the Heavens." He bowed to them both.

Though Rhys was inclined to remain where he was, Alina approached the young man. "You come to ask of us a request?"

"Yes," he replied. He bowed once more so the sun shone off his bald, tattooed head. "My grandmother is ill. I know... you care not about our meager human lives, but—"

Alina knelt before the old, wrinkled woman who immediately bowed. "Please, if you do that, I cannot properly see you," chided Alina softly. The old woman straightened herself, and Alina studied her. "Tell me what ails you."

The old woman opened her mouth and pointed to her bloody and swollen gums with a shaking finger. Rhys looked at Alina to gauge her reaction. Was it a disease? Had something happened?

Alina studied the woman's blistered gums. "Is it very tender?" The woman nodded. "And are you experiencing any other symptoms?"

"My knees... and elbows hurt," the senior mumbled.

"She also has these," said the woman's grandson. He pulled her collar from her neck and pointed to a collection of pin-point sized red dots.

Alina studied the woman's skin and then leaned back. "What do you normally eat?"

"She doesn't eat much," the young man provided. "Grains, whatever broth I cook her."

Alina stood, wiped her hands on her pants, and looked at the young man. "I assume you have access to physsels?" He nodded. "She needs to start eating at least three a day. She won't be able to eat the actual fruit, so you need to ground it into a thin mush and mix it with water. Her gums should stop bleeding within the next day or so. It will take a little longer for the effects to become apparent in her joints however."

"Just physsels?" asked the woman's grandson. "That's it?"

Alina nodded. "She must eat as least three daily, if not more. Even once she's better."

The young man bowed deeply to them, his arms folded across his chest. "Thank you. We praise you. We praise you. We praise you." The old woman bowed before her grandson gently ushered her away.

Did you just make that up? asked Rhys.

No, replied Alina. *She has a very old sickness, one that has plagued the human race for thousands of years. A vitamin deficiency. It's evident by her gums.*

My genius sister, teased Rhys, observing the people around them.

"Daughter of the heavens," beckoned another man.

I'll retrieve your medical supplies, said Rhys. When he returned with a small bag, he found a line of people stretching through the middle of town with Alina seated in a tent at the end of it. Hodge stood near her, his rifle slung over his shoulder. It appeared to Rhys that Hodge was rather enjoying himself watching Alina work.

"Brother," bubbled Alina, standing. Rhys handed her the bag and seated himself in the corner of the tent. He and Hodge watched Alina work for the next few hours as she met with families, husbands, daughters, and grandfathers inquiring about a loved one's health.

Alina diagnosed each individual's ailment and offered treatments that were easily accessible such as a change in diet or an addition of a supplement. She performed half a dozen minor surgeries, including the removal of a rotten toenail and the suturing of a leg wound. After the second hour, doctors arrived from the town's medical clinic to learn from the white god.

As the line of people waiting outside Alina's tent dwindled, Vinz, along with Miuna and Kashim, appeared. The Overseer watched as Alina examined a baby's eyes and then looked at Rhys. "Lord, may I have a word with you?"

Rhys followed Vinz from the tent to the shade of the nearest building. They were alone.

"Have there been any problems?"

"None," replied Rhys. "Alina is very good at what she does."

"Which is what... exactly?" asked Vinz. He didn't sound mad, only interested. "I heard she gave a rather rousing speech earlier."

Rhys glanced back at the tent. "Like I said, she's very good at what she does... She's good at everything." Sensing Vinz's gaze on him, Rhys looked at the Overseer. "What are you doing here?"

"We came to check on you. Have you seen Saccui?"

"Not since earlier. Why? Is that bad?"

Vinz shrugged. "His doctors are here to study with the female white god. I thought he would be here as well."

"Should we look for him?"

"It wouldn't be a bad idea," grunted Vinz. "I would hate for him to be scheming without our knowledge."

"Alina is almost done. Once she is, we'll return to *Themis*."

Vinz nodded. "And I'll look for Saccui."

Rhys returned to the tent to find Alina studying a very fat woman. He halted in the doorway, perplexed. He didn't understand how someone so petite could have a stomach that enormous.

Rhys, said Alina. Her hands were on the woman's abdomen. Alina looked up at him, smiling widely. *She's pregnant. This is what... a woman looks like when she is carrying a human child. Look, look.* As intrigued as his sister, Rhys joined her and gawked at the woman's round, bare stomach. Alina cupped both of her hands around the woman's bump. *Can you even believe it?* His sister startled and looked between Rhys and the woman.

"What?" asked Rhys in their native tongue.

"You felt him kick?" asked the mother.

Alina laughed elatedly. "It did! It kicked! Rhys, Rhys." Alina grabbed Rhys' hand and pressed his palm to the woman.

For several moments, they remained motionless. Rhys began to pull his hand away thinking Alina was joking but stopped as something very blatantly kicked his hand. He let out an amazed chuckle. A series of motions rolled under his palm. Both he and Alina broke into joyous giggles. "It's true," breathed Rhys. "It's really true."

The woman, who had watched their reactions in mild amusement, cradled her stomach fondly. "He's very excited to meet you. Thank you, God of the Stars. I'll try the remedy you spoke of." She bowed to Alina and left the tent.

Rhys and Alina exchanged looks and then broke into laughter. They were beside themselves in shocked disbelief. Humans were truly amazing creatures.

"You two are ridiculous," muttered Hodge who had been sitting in the corner of the tent with Miuna. Rhys saw his eyes fall on Alina which, to his surprise, made her shyly drop her gaze.

"Are you finished here?" asked Rhys. "We're to return to *Themis*."

Alina gathered the handful of tools and medicines they had brought. "I am now."

17
BETRAYAL

THAT EVENING AFTER HAVING EATEN and rested, Rhys, Alina, Hodge, and Miuna rode back to the docks. Vinz and Kashim had returned to *Themis* briefly a few hours prior; however, they had immediately left for shore again.

"I wonder where they are," Rhys mused aloud as they tied the dinghy to the docks.

"Kashim mentioned something about meeting with the clergymen," replied Hodge, pulling Miuna ashore. "But that's all I know." He held his hand out to Alina and, with much more care, withdrew her from the dinghy.

Rhys stared at the empty docks. "Where are the guards?"

Alina drew even with him. "Perhaps they didn't know we were coming."

Rhys shook his head. "No, they always have guards posted." He looked back out at *Themis* and then, shifting his eyes to utilize focused night vision, studied the enormous water gates. All was silent. The gates were closed as usual. "Hodge... " murmured Rhys, feeling that something was wrong.

"I know." Hodge pushed Alina and Miuna behind them and readied his rifle. Rhys rested his hand on the resonance cutters which remained permanently sheathed under his shirt.

"What's going on?" whispered Alina.

"Engage your night vision," advised Rhys in their tongue. "Something doesn't feel right."

"I don't feel anything," she whispered.

"What do you want to do?" Rhys asked of Hodge. "We haven't seen Vinz or Kashim in four hours."

Hodge nodded. "If something's wrong, we can't leave them."

Rhys exhaled as a breeze played across his face. He could smell nothing but the sea. He could hear nothing but the sound of the water lapping at the docks. He frowned. All of his physical senses told him nothing was wrong, but his gut said otherwise. "Miuna, Alina. You two stay with the boat. Stay low." Rhys went to the nearest lamp and switched it off. The area fell into complete darkness. "Stay here."

"No," replied Alina. She moved beside him.

Miuna was right beside her. "I'm coming too."

He didn't argue; it was futile. Together, they crept off the docks and up the road toward town. As they neared the first set of buildings, Rhys withdrew the resonance cutters from its sheath and gripped the tool in his hand.

They made their way to the center of town. If anything was happening, that's where it would be. It was the only place large enough to hold thousands of people. Even the public temple couldn't accommodate all of Paducah.

As they turned onto the main street that led into the town square, they halted. Before them was a silent, solid wall of people. What was going on? What were they watching? What had their attention?

A sudden moan of pain rose into the air, causing the hairs on Rhys' neck to stand on end and his heart to leap to his throat. He could feel Miuna's hand on his arm. Mustering both strength and courage, Rhys approached the blockade of people. "Move," he ordered. The people glanced behind them and, seeing who it was, immediately stepped aside. A pathway emerged. Shoulders squared and gaze set unwaveringly ahead, Rhys stalked through the crowd.

No one bowed or moved to make any respectful gestures. Instead, they stood in complete silence. When Rhys finally broke through the never-ending conglomerate of people, he stared. He had prepared himself, steeled his heart, and collected his wits, but he was still shocked to find Vinz and Kashim kneeling in the dirt shirtless with their hands bound by chains. Vinz had several seeping cuts to his face while Kashim's back was covered in blood.

Rhys didn't know Kashim very well, and he didn't like Vinz, but they were his crew members. They were a part of his crew and to see them helpless and bleeding awakened something unholy within Rhys. Shaking in fury, Rhys jerked his arm from Miuna's grasp and strode from the crowd. Vinz looked up as he entered the circle; Kashim's head remained bowed in submission. The clergymen standing behind them stopped their preparations. Saccui was among them.

The priest of Paducah, who held a short whip, ran his hand over its tails and threw the blood that had gathered there to the dirt. "Son of the Heavens," he said, nodding to Rhys. "I was wondering when you would show."

Rhys stopped before Vinz and Kashim and studied the two men. Vinz looked beaten but functioning. Kashim, however, was unconscious on his knees. He had been whipped hard. "What's going on?"

The priest handed the bloodied whip to one of his men and circled Kashim and Vinz. "I had an interesting conversation with your envoy earlier." He halted before Rhys and folded his bloodied hands behind his back. "He spoke of a world where the Pantarak people might live peacefully with his own." Saccui nodded to Rhys. "This is reminiscent of what you and your sister preached, is it not?"

"Why are they bound?" growled Rhys.

Saccui cleared his throat and turned to Vinz and Kashim. "In exchange for a truce with the city of New Arbroath, they offered you."

Rhys remained expressionless. "And?"

Saccui pursed his lips. "That's not enough." He breathed deeply and said, "We would consider peace if you *and* your sister were to live among us. Your envoy disagreed and… " Saccui motioned to the scene. "Now we are here."

Rhys glanced at Vinz. "Let me make sure I understand. You are torturing these men so they may acquiesce to your request that both my sister and I be handed over to you?"

Saccui nodded. "Yes."

"And what if my sister and I are not for sale or bargaining?"

"There are ways to assure—"

Rhys switched on the resonance cutters. "I said, what if my sister and I are *not* for sale or bargaining?"

Saccui gazed at the instrument. "You are a white god," he said. "You would not hurt your worshipers, your people."

"You are not my people," Rhys replied darkly. He motioned with the cutters. "Now, release them." Saccui didn't move. Rhys turned and, in a single, smooth motion, cut first through Vinz's chains and then through Kashim's. Before Kashim collapsed, Vinz caught him. Rhys turned on Saccui. He wanted to say something to damn the priest, to scorn him, to anger him, but he could think of nothing.

Vinz lifted Kashim to his feet. "You will not be leaving," affirmed Saccui. "You, your sister, and your envoy. None of you are leaving."

Before he could stop himself, Rhys leapt at the priest. As he pushed the man back, he swept Saccui's ankle, driving the priest to the earth. Panting with wrath, Rhys pushed the resonance cutters to the man's throat. "We will leave. And no one will stop us." Saccui squirmed as the heat from the cutters began to eat at his flesh. Rhys held the man's dark gaze for a long moment before rising to his feet to look out at the people.

"That method may work with me, but it will not work on the rest of the town," said Saccui, holding his raw neck. "You cannot fight a thousand men."

Rhys didn't look back at him. Instead, he followed behind Vinz and Kashim as they stumbled away. Alina, Hodge, and Miuna ran to them. Hodge drew Kashim's other arm over his shoulder as Alina began examining Kashim's back. "Let's go," Rhys said, nodding to the docks.

"The people," whispered Miuna.

Rhys passed their group and went to the blockade of Paducah citizens. He expected a fight, an argument, a definitive stating of their beliefs and their willingness to die. Instead, the crowd parted. Every person bowed.

Rhys motioned for Hodge and Vinz to hurry. As the others of his crew passed, he looked back at Saccui who had not moved from the center of town and then at the people around him.

From the moment they cleared the crowd, it was a mad dash to the dinghy. Already Kashim had lost a lot of blood; Vinz and Hodge were covered in it. Once everyone piled into the boat, Rhys started the motor and they sped back to *Themis*. As they hit the launch ramp and came to a halt, Rhys leapt out, raced over to the communication pipes, and began disseminating orders.

"Everyone's on board. Kallen, get down to the forward hatch and dock us. Andy, weigh anchor and start the engines. Lyruc, get down here. Kashim is wounded. He needs to be carried."

Kallen and Lyruc appeared in the forward hatch. As Vinz and Hodge dragged Kashim from the boat, Rhys began dismantling the dinghy's engine. He passed it to Kallen when she entered the water. She didn't ask questions. She didn't cry out in shock at the blood in the bottom of the dinghy. She worked, exactly what he expected of her.

"Alina, I'm leaving him to you," said Rhys, rushing out. He hurried up the stairs to the bridge.

"What's going on?" asked Andy as Rhys flew in.

"Vinz and Kashim are wounded. I'm taking control."

"We can't launch!" said Andy. "The water gates."

"Start the engines. Prepare the cannons. We're taking the gates down."

Andy and Kyo exchanged looks and then began working. Rhys pulled Vinz's communication pipe from the ceiling. "Kallen, are we sealed?"

"Yes," came the reply.

As *Themis'* engines roared to life, Andy reported. "Energy levels at 100 percent. Anchor is weighed."

"Come about 90 keis. Engines at five percent," said Rhys, bracing himself against Vinz's chair. "Kyo, cannons?"

"Double-shot cannons prepped. Targeting water gates," replied Kyo, standing at Lyruc's station.

Rhys approached the bridge glass and watched as the water gates came into view. "Maintain speed at five percent. Kyo, standby. Prepare to fire on my mark." Rhys studied the gates. "In three. Two. One. Fire."

Themis quivered from the cannons' blasts. The water gates were illuminated in a brilliant explosion. As debris rained around them, Rhys leaned forward, shifted his sight to night vision, and studied the gates' remains. There were none. "Andy, one-third speed through the gates. Once we're clear, standard speed."

"Coming to one-third speed. One-third speed achieved," reported Andy. Rhys glanced up at the remaining fragments of the water gates. "Coming to standard speed." Rhys began pacing the bridge, his eyes on the dark horizon. "Standard speed. Energy levels at 99 percent. Engines satisfactory."

"Set a course, north-by-northeast, 15 keis. Get us as far from Paducah as possible."

"Setting course," said Kyo, moving back to his station.

"Anything on radar?" asked Rhys, continuing to pace.

Andy leaned over the panel to his left. "Nothing on radar. That doesn't account for sunboards though."

"Do they usually launch sunboards at night?"

"No. Not for long-distance attacks. It requires too much energy," replied Andy.

"Load the next cannon shells and prepare the gunners. Can the sails be opened from the bridge?"

"No, but I would advise keeping the sails stowed," offered Andy. "If there is an attack, they would be damaged." Rhys acknowledged the counsel and continued to pace. "What happened?"

"I'll let your Overseer tell you." Rhys drew a deep breath and slumped into Vinz's chair. He held his head. He couldn't dwell on Vinz's betrayal. He needed to make sure the crew was safe first and away from Paducah.

For the next hour, they sat in tense silence. Rhys expected an attack at any moment; he expected to be hit by cannon fire or sunboard rockets, but nothing ever came. Radar remained silent. Eventually, he gave the order to stand down and disengage all weapons. A half-hour after that, Kallen and Lyruc joined them on the bridge. In silence, Lyruc went to his station and sat down. Kallen leaned against Vinz's chair where Rhys sat but didn't say a word.

Through the early morning hours, they stayed vigilant on the bridge. Several times, Rhys nodded off. The drama of the day coupled with the loss of adrenaline he had experienced was making it difficult to remain awake.

Sometime around four in the morning, Vinz finally appeared on the bridge. Rhys, who was slouched in the Overseer's chair, only glanced at him. With the blood gone, he could discern the numerous gashes and cuts on the Overseer's face, two of which had several stitches.

"I'll take command," murmured Vinz without looking at him.

Rhys stood, nudged Kallen, who was asleep on the floor, and, with her at his side, left the bridge. As they passed the galley, Rhys looked in at Kashim who was limp on a table, his back in stitches. Alina stood beside him checking his pulse. Hodge was sprawled out nearby on the floor, asleep. Rhys' sister glanced at him and then motioned for him to go.

When Kallen pulled away to go to her cabin, Rhys stopped her, and they entered his cabin where Ceit and Miuna slept. Once the door was closed, Kallen began dragging his shirt over his head. Rhys fell into bed. Kallen pulled her filthy pants off and climbed in beside him. Rhys felt her kiss his chin before he fell unconscious.

It was dawn when he woke next. Though he had slept for only three hours, he was wide awake. He glanced at Kallen who was motionless and then slid out of bed. He opened the porthole in the cabin and gazed bleakly out at the early morning light. *Themis* was still moving.

He wanted to go back to sleep—Pathos indicated he needed more rest—but his mind was too busy. Did the others, those who had been with them last night, know about Vinz's betrayal? Did *everyone* on the ship know what the Overseer had had planned? Rhys leaned against the porthole and glowered out at the water.

"Rhys?" whispered Kallen, sitting up. "What's wrong?"

"I'm fine. Just restless."

Kallen lay back down, but her eyes never left him. For a long while, Rhys pondered on what he should do. Perhaps the others hadn't heard what Saccui had said. There was a chance they didn't know that Vinz had betrayed him and Alina. What if Kashim and Vinz were the only two who knew what had transpired last night? Since no one in this world seemed to be trustworthy, could he use that information as leverage against them?

Or maybe the entire crew knew, even Kallen? Perhaps she was a distraction for him, and Hodge was a distraction for Alina.

Rhys began pacing the space between the door and the porthole. Was there a possibility he and Alina had fallen in with the wrong people? But who were the other options, the Pantaraks?

What was his next course of action? Undoubtedly, he needed to speak with Alina on the subject, but beyond that, what could they do? If he assumed worst-case scenario and everyone on the ship knew of Vinz's plans, then they could leave. But how? He was sure they were kilometers from land by now. Besides, even if they escaped, where would they go? They could live off the land and learn to survive by themselves, but truly, what type of existence was that?

"What's going on?" Kallen asked with a sigh.

Rhys regarded her. As a female, she was certainly attractive, especially with such little clothing on, but at the moment, he was unsure of how he felt. He doubted her and everyone on board.

This must have shown on his face because Kallen asked, "What's wrong? Why are you looking at me like that?"

Not wanting to confront her just yet, Rhys began searching for a clean shirt amongst the pile of clothes stacked at the foot of his bed.

"Rhys," said Kallen, standing. She touched him. "What's wrong?"

Rhys jerked his arm from her. "Just... Don't... " Kallen froze. He grabbed a blouse, slid it over his head, and left for the galley. He found Alina and Hodge sprawled out on the galley floor, asleep. Alina's medical tools were in a pile nearby. "Alina," he said. Hodge stirred, but neither woke. *Alina,* called Rhys.

His sister groaned and opened her heavy eyes. *What?* she hissed.

He nodded toward the forward hatch. *We need to talk.*

Now?

Yes, now, he replied.

Alina slid away from Hodge, briefly examined Kashim who was still unconscious on the galley table, and then followed Rhys to the forward hatch. *What is this about?* she asked. *I just went to sleep two hours ago. I'm exhausted.*

Logos, divert power to fully awaken her, commanded Rhys.

Rhys, groused Alina as her AI raised her heart rate.

Once in the forward hatch, Rhys closed the cabin door. *Last night,* he said, turning to his sister. *What did you hear last night?*

Not much, replied Alina, now fully awake. *It was difficult to hear what Saccui was saying.*

Rhys considered this before saying, *Vinz tried to sell me. He made an offer to Saccui to hand me over, but the negotiating turned dirty. They wanted both of us, but Vinz wasn't willing to give you up. That's why they were being tortured last night—to make them agree to hand us over to the Pantarak people.*

Alina gaped at him. *No...*

We were always supposed to be bargaining chips. And if a truce couldn't be agreed upon in Paducah, then they'd try in Brechin.

Who else knows? asked Alina. Her mind was logically processing the information much faster than his. *Just he and Kashim made the offer, so at least they know, but did everyone agree to the plan?* She frowned. *But he only offered you. What does that mean?*

Perhaps he was saving you to bargain with the capital, mused Rhys. *That's his ultimate goal, isn't it? Making peace with the high priest in the capital?*

Why am I more important?

Because you're a woman, replied Rhys. *You can make more of us.*

Alina frowned. *I don't think the rest of the crew knew.*

Are you saying that because of your relationship with Hodge? Both Hodge and Kallen could be distractions, methods to keep our attention diverted elsewhere so we're not following the inner workings of the ship's crew.

Alina looked as though she was going to contest his argument but stopped. *I'm having a difficult time...*

Let me deal with the sense of betrayal, said Rhys. *Logically, what's our next move?*

Alina looked around the hatch. *Clearly, Vinz and Kashim spearheaded the idea, but who else knew about it?*

And you truly couldn't hear what Saccui said last night?

No. We couldn't hear what either of said. Alina gazed at him. *I'm glad you were there. I didn't know what to do, how to react. I was so surprised.*

I didn't know what to do either, but I felt that I had to intervene.

Hodge told me he's frightened of you.

Rhys looked at her in surprise. *Why?*

I believe Miuna is also afraid of you now.

Why? I didn't do anything.

I know you, said Alina. *I know how you think, how you act. I know what will infuriate you and what will make you happy. I know that you despise me sometimes and that you have always been told you're not good enough, or that you're the Other Child. I know what you think of me, how you feel about me. How you feel about others. So, when you reacted last night, I understood. I expected such a reaction from you.* She paused and then said, *No one else understands you. They cannot read you. They don't know what to expect from you.*

And you? What about you?

I am a woman. Here, that means something. I am not as much of a threat, explained Alina. *Though, if it makes you feel better, Hodge has told me that he never knows what I'm thinking. You are a young man with intelligence beyond those around you and strength and speed. You are experiencing things for the first time and engaging in an unknown world. No one knows how you will react to anything, except me. I am never surprised by you.*

You are my sister, replied Rhys fondly, kicking her pants leg.

Alina smiled. *We need a better understanding of what we're up against. If we face the entire crew, then we must flee.*

And if it's just Kashim and Vinz?

Then we use their betrayal as leverage. I'm not sure how though.

Rhys leaned against a barrel. *Can I tell you something?*

Hm?

Since we've been here… I've never once really wanted to go home. Not once. I've pondered on the reality, that we'll never return to Caelestis, but I've never wished to return to the colony.

I have, said Alina. *I've wished to return home. But… when I'm with Hodge, that desire goes away and it's like I've always belonged. Is it the same when you're with Kallen?*

I don't want to say, murmured Rhys. *It will hurt that much more if it turns out she knew about all of this.* Sensing Alina's intense gaze on him, Rhys looked at her. *What?*

I'm having a difficult time comprehending what you're calling betrayal. I understand the logic, the reasoning behind him. I understand the idea. I don't understand the feeling. It hurts?

Rhys nodded. *When Saccui told me about Vinz's offer, my heart… my heart hurt. I did everything I could to remain stoic, to not show my surprise or pain, but it hurts. Even now. And I don't even like the man.*

Does it hurt more when you think of Kallen?

What does it feel like when I tell you that Hodge is using you? He's not romantically, sexually, or emotionally interested in you. He's only keeping you distracted so we won't spoil Vinz's plans. How does that make you feel?

Alina thought for a long moment and then said, *Disbelief. I think. I can't put the words to it.*

Does it hurt? When you think about it, does it hurt?

Logos says intricate human emotions like betrayal are difficult for me to process. I can understand the eight primary universal human emotions but nothing beyond those.

The cons of having a Logos AI, said Rhys softly.

Would you want me to experience such emotions?

Rhys chuckled darkly. *Ask me again later.*

Your answer will change?

Inevitably. In seriousness, he asked, *How should we find out whether the crew knew?*

Question them.

Rhys motioned for Alina to lead the way out of the forward hatch. As she reentered the galley, Rhys returned to their quarters. He found Kallen lying in his bed, an arm over her eyes. "We need to talk," he told her. "Would you come with me?"

"Why?" Her voice was thick with sourness.

"Something happened yesterday. Alina and I need to speak with you. In private."

Avoiding his eyes, Kallen dressed and followed him to the galley. Alina already had Hodge seated at the second table. Rhys closed the door behind them, glanced at Kashim who was still unconscious, and then gestured for Kallen to join Alina and Hodge.

Once all four of them were seated, Rhys exchanged looks with Alina and then said, "Last night was a trying time for everyone. As you know, both Kashim and Vinz were badly injured. We escaped from Paducah by luck."

"What's this about, Rhys?" prompted Hodge.

"What did you hear last night when I spoke with Saccui?"

Hodge gazed at him in confusion. "I couldn't hear either of you. Why?"

"I asked the priest what was going on. He informed me that Vinz and Kashim had come to offer a deal." Rhys looked between Hodge and Kallen. "He would hand me over to Paducah in exchange for a truce with New Arbroath. Saccui indicated that I was not enough, however, if Vinz were to give both myself and Alina to Paducah, they would agree to the proposal. Vinz refused, and they tortured him and Kashim. Comments?"

Hodge and Kallen gaped at him. "I… He wouldn't… " Hodge stammered. He looked to Kallen who shook her head. "From the moment we brought you two on board, we've told Vinz that you were not to be used in bargains."

"Why?" asked Alina coldly. "It would have been beneficial to everyone. You didn't know us. What did you have to lose?"

"Our humanity," Kallen argued. "We are not Pantarak. We do not bargain using people." She glared at Rhys. "And you… You thought I was a part of it? That I would betray your trust?"

"We don't have an outstanding record here on Earth," provided Rhys. "It's difficult for us to know whom we can trust and—"

"You can trust *me*." Kallen's voice cracked.

"Hodge?" asked Alina.

Hodge slumped in his chair. "I echo Kallen's thoughts, but I understand why you came to us. You are strangers to our world. It's been weeks since you arrived here, but you are still learning. You do not know to whom you can turn other than each other."

"Precisely," replied Alina. "Which is why as we discuss with you this matter, Rhys and I are having a separate conversation concerning the validity of your statements." Seeing the look on Kallen's face, Alina added, "Please understand. Neither of us is equipped to independently judge the situation. We are relaying our thoughts to check for symmetry."

Rhys glanced at Hodge and then met Kallen's gaze. Silent tears hung in her eyes. A part of Rhys wanted to reach between them to comfort her, but he refrained. So far, he and Alina both agreed: based on facial expressions and nonverbal communication, Kallen and Hodge were innocent and had been unaware of Vinz's plan. As usual, Alina felt more ready to forgive and forget than Rhys who, despite their probable innocence, still felt betrayed.

"And how are we faring right now?" asked Hodge.

"We concur that neither of you knew of Vinz's plan," said Alina, "however, Rhys is still unsure whether to trust you."

Hodge motioned between them. "I don't understand. If you have the same thoughts, why does he feel differently?"

"Our AIs—our computers," said Rhys, pointing to Pathos' external unit along his temple. "Her unit, Logos, focuses the individual's mental processes on logic and computation. Mine, Pathos, applies more mental effort to the processing of emotional stimuli. Very few have my type of unit as it is not necessary for the advancement of mankind. It has its pros—I have more empathy than Alina and am able to experience the emotional scale in its entirety. I cannot, however, separate what I feel from logic."

Kallen stood and left the galley. Rhys gazed at her empty chair despairingly.

"We had no part in his plan," asserted Hodge. "Please, believe us."

"I believe you," said Alina. She looked to Rhys. "Brother?"

"Not yet," he murmured.

"You need to speak with Vinz," pled Hodge. "He will clear our—"

At that very moment, Kallen returned, dragging Vinz by the arm. When the Overseer saw who was in the galley, he tensed considerably. Kallen closed the door behind them. Rhys saw resolve settle on Vinz's face.

"Tell them," said Hodge, standing. The sudden hostility in his previously unemotional voice startled Rhys. "Tell them we knew nothing of this!"

Vinz cleared his throat, glanced at Kallen who was glaring at him, and then looked at Rhys. "I never intended for it to work out this way."

"How did you intend for it to work out?" asked Alina. Rhys was glad his sister had decided to take the lead. He wasn't sure how civilly he could act toward Vinz right now.

"I went to speak with Saccui about options for peace," said the Overseer. "He ignored me and my efforts. Finally, I mentioned you." Vinz met Rhys' gaze. "It was a mistake, one made in desperation. For New Arbroath."

"Who all knew about this plan aside from yourself and Kashim?" asked Alina.

"No one," replied Vinz. "It was ours alone."

"Had you passed both of us off, how do you feel your crew would have reacted?" Alina nodded to Hodge. "How would you have told them?"

"We would have immediately left. My crew would have been under the belief that you two had been captured."

With surprising speed, Kallen slapped Vinz across the face. "Don't you *ever* resort to such measures again!" she screamed. "Do you know what you've done?"

"We were running out of options!" snapped Vinz, rubbing his cheek. "And our departure was set. There was no time left. I needed to make a move."

Rhys spoke for the first time since the Overseer had entered the galley. "The peace talks weren't going poorly. They just weren't going as quickly as you wanted."

"Were you in the same town I was?" asked Vinz. "Did you not see the entire town observe our beatings in silence?"

"I saw. I also saw them let us leave against the direct command of their priest. Religion is power, and those who rule in the name of a god are like kings. Their word is ultimate. I saw an entire town intentionally disobey its ruler, its king and priest. That, Overseer, is progress."

Vinz gritted his jaws but remained silent.

"May I ask," said Alina, leaning forward. "Why?"

"Why what?" asked Vinz.

"Peace is an admirable ambition. It has been sought after by many throughout the history of mankind and achieved only by a few. Why do you want it so desperately?"

"So no one else must suffer what I have, or what Kallen has, or Kashim, or my parents," said Vinz. "I want a world where everyone knows their place, where there is no indecision or chance to make horrible mistakes like war." Vinz looked at Alina and Rhys. "I want a world like where you came from."

"No, you don't," said Rhys. "You don't want that."

"You two embody an ideal world—protected, safe. You are biologically, physiologically, and psychologically superior because you had the time to develop the means to alter your environment. You were given—"

"Nothing," interrupted Rhys. "We were given nothing. We were given no freewill, no freedom. All decisions were made for us. We were given a sheltered cocoon in which we remained ignorant from humanity's greatest achievements—music, art, dance, song, poetry, literature. Our sexuality was taken. True, we were given an environment void of confrontation, but we were given it without knowing. We lived in ignorance."

"Then what's the point?" asked Vinz. "What's the point of all of this if we don't have a goal to reach, a plan of an ideal world we want to create?"

"You are thousands of years away from achieving something akin to our world," clarified Alina. "You are at peace's inception." Alina thought for a moment and then added, "Why did you offer to exchange Rhys instead of me?"

"You are too valuable," said Vinz.

"Because I'm a woman?"

Vinz nodded solemnly.

"Were you going to use me as a bargaining chip later at the capital?"

"If it came to that, yes."

Rhys stood and approached Vinz. "I propose we continue to the capital."

"We need to resupply at Firekli," said Kallen. "That's eight days out."

"Fine. We resupply at Firekli and then continue to the capital. Once there, Alina and I will meet with the high priest."

"The capital is unlike Paducah or any of its sister towns," remarked Vinz. "I have been there once. It is far more advanced. They will be less impressed by your tricks."

"We'll figure that out once we arrive. By then, Paducah will have sent word to the high priest." Rhys looked at Alina. "Hopefully our work will not go unnoticed."

"What stake do you have in this?" asked Vinz.

"It's as you said, Overseer... This is our home now," said Rhys. "Even if we left *Themis* and set off into the wilderness, it would still be our home and we would be caught in the middle of the great war."

Alina nodded in agreement. "As humans from a more technologically advanced civilization, it is our responsibility to shepherd our brothers in the right direction."

"You've talked about this before," said Hodge, smiling.

"And what of this?" asked Vinz.

"Of what? Your plan to turn us over to the Pantaraks?" asked Alina. She exchanged looks with Rhys. "You are in our debt, Overseer."

Vinz nodded. "I am in your debt."

"No one is to speak of this to the rest of the crew," said Rhys.

"They will want to know what happened," said Hodge. "I would."

"Tell them the priest wanted us," said Alina, "but Vinz objected. A fight broke out, and Vinz and Kashim were overpowered and captured."

"I am an educated man and pride myself in making decisions that reflect well on my scholarship," said Vinz, "so it is with difficulty that I admit my mistake."

"Let your actions prove your words," Rhys advised darkly. "I could have left you two to die there."

"But you didn't." Vinz glanced at the others and then left the galley. Kallen closed the door behind him and leaned against it.

"What now?" asked Hodge in an attempt to break the silence.

"I'm going to check on Kashim and then go back to sleep," said Alina. *Brother, are you satisfied with all that you found?*

No, replied Rhys. *He's broken our trust too many times.*

And what about the woman gazing at you so forlornly? asked Alina, moving to Kashim. Rhys looked at Kallen. *Take her somewhere and apologize. Then go to sleep. We do not deal with stress well.*

Rhys approached Kallen. "Would you come with me?" She nodded and they left the galley. Rhys led her to the forward hatch and closed the door behind them. Kallen turned to start opening the porthole windows, but Rhys pulled her roughly into his embrace and buried his head into her neck. Without hesitation, Kallen's hands weaved around his back. For several long moments he held her. "I... couldn't bear to look at you... thinking you had betrayed us," he whispered into her hair. "It... made my chest hurt."

Kallen pulled away. "How could you think so poorly of me?"

Sensing that perhaps this was a rhetorical question and not one that warranted an answer, he kissed the side of her head.

Kallen pulled from his embrace and looked at him. "Do you trust me?"

"Yes," said Rhys hesitantly.

"Then listen to what I am about to say—Vinz is not a bad person. He is not evil as you may call some of the Pantaraks. He is an ambitious individual, intelligent, and devoted to his cause." She studied him. "I sense that you are a vengeful person, someone who does not let go of grudges. Do not bear ill will toward Vinz. He made a mistake in a time of desperation."

"Why are you protecting him? Kallen, he tried to *sell* Alina and I."

"Because I know him. I know his past and I know him."

"If you know him, why didn't you guess that he'd do something like this?"

Kallen frowned. "I didn't think he would become so desperate. Rhys, promise you won't harbor any ill-will against him."

Rhys released Kallen. She wasn't telling him something. She knew information about Vinz, intimate information, that she wasn't sharing. "Tell me," he said.

"Tell you what?"

"What is your relationship with him?"

"He's our Overseer," she replied.

Rhys considered her. "Why did you slap him earlier? Why didn't you punch him?"

Kallen remained silent.

"Kallen, tell me."

"Because a slap from a woman hurts more than a punch," she murmured.

"That doesn't make physiological sense," replied Rhys. "A balled fist has more—"

"It hurts more when it's from a woman you're close to."

Rhys stared at Kallen, allowing what she said to process. Finally, he said, "Were you and Vinz sexually intimate?"

"Yes."

"Are you still?"

"No."

"Then why are you defending him?"

Kallen leaned against a barrel. "You know what happened when I was captured and taken into Paducah," she said. "And... how Father and JiJi rescued me... "

"You don't have to tell me this," said Rhys. They were quarreling, but he didn't want to dig up any painful memories.

"Yes, I do." She went on. "When JiJi and Father brought me home, I couldn't function. I didn't want to be around anyone. I didn't want to talk. I wanted to be left alone. By chance, I ran into Vinz while in town. He was looking to put a crew together. He had purchased sunboards from JiJi for the past two years, so he was familiar with my family's work. News travels fast in town, and I guess he heard what happened. He saw me at the shop one day and offered me a job as his mechanic. I couldn't... take it though. I didn't trust anyone. I turned him down and continued my work with JiJi. The next day, he returned and asked me again. I turned him down again. Soon, he was coming by the docks every day just to speak with me.

"Eventually, he invited me to see *Themis* and work on her engines. I visited the ship infrequently at first, but after a while, I grew comfortable being alone with Vinz on the ship. We spent hours finetuning the engines and installing the technology he developed." She took a breath. "Then, one day, he asked me about what happened... " She took another deeper breath. "And I told him. I expected everything to change after that day, but it didn't. He continued asking for my help on Themis, and we continued to work together as if nothing happened.

"For the next several weeks, we acted like nothing existed between us. But... I was in the process of healing and I wanted to know what real sex… was like. So, I asked him. I explained myself to him, and he agreed."

"Why didn't you continue?"

"Tessa," explained Kallen. "The woman you met in New Arbroath."

"She is his mate?"

Kallen nodded. "She knew about my history and knew what Vinz was doing. When Vinz started courting her, she allowed him to continue being, ehh, sexually active with me. Eventually though, she wanted him to commit fully to her." Kallen shrugged in an attempt to show Rhys that she didn't care, but something on her face made him doubt that. "Our relationship was purely platonic. We didn't see each other as mates. Still though, he took me in, helped me, gave me a job, and got me back on my feet. He's not a bad person. He just needs guidance from someone who can see beyond his field of vision. He needs you, Rhys. You and Alina." She waited before asking, "Are you angry at me?"

"I don't know how I feel right now," Rhys said. "Could I… be alone? For a little while?"

Kallen slipped out of the forward hatch. Rhys gazed at the floor where she had been standing. The cabin felt much colder with her gone. Feeling emotionally overwhelmed for reasons he didn't understand, he leaned against one of the crates.

Kallen had been by his side from the day they had been found. She had helped him, taken care of him, fed him, and tended to him emotionally. But he didn't feel right. She had done nothing to him, yet he felt like targeting her. She seemed like a suitable scapegoat for the inner turmoil he was experiencing.

He was angry, livid like a stormy sea. He felt helpless and without reason or purpose. Despite Alina's nearness, he felt alone.

Pathos, explain this to me, he murmured. *I don't understand my state of mind.*

You are currently struggling to decide a course of action, but you do not have the necessary data to make an informed decision. In addition, you are wavering in your trust of those around you and are therefore lashing out in an attempt to defend yourself from any further hurt.

I'm angry. Rhys looked about the forward hatch. *I want to throw something.*

I advise against doing so as physical embodiments of negative emotions such as anger and fury are frowned upon here, especially when they are not necessary. Perhaps putting your mind to work will ease the stress you feel.

Rhys' gaze shifted to the sunboard he had been working on.

Deep breaths. You will calm, said Pathos.

Rhys went to the board, examined it for a moment, and then pulled it from its position against the wall. Eyes heavy, he reviewed his handwritten notes and then knelt below the board. *Would you guess this to be the primary computer unit?*

Touch it so I may collect readings.

Rhys pressed his fingers against the compartment.

The components residing in the compartment, said Pathos, *are, in fact, the hardware for a computer.*

Rhys sat back on his heels. *If the board is magnetic, it has to have the ability to read the magnetic waves. This computer does just that, but how would a human read such waves? AIs were only recently introduced into human biology. A computer of some sort is needed in order to visually see the waves otherwise, the board would be un-pilotable.*

A connection between the board's computer and the human would need to be established, asserted Pathos. *In humanity's past, this has been accomplished through multiple methods.*

Rhys examined the board's computer compartment, running his hands along the edges. *There is no way to open it.*

Perhaps it opens not from the bottom but from the top, suggested Pathos.

Rhys traced the compartment's edges a moment longer and then stood. He ran his hand along the side of the board until his fingers touched a piece that was smoother than the rest.

This is a tracer, said Rhys more to himself than to Pathos. *And if I run my thumb... along it, the board will snap back into place.* Carefully, he withdrew his hand. *But I don't want that. I want to open the board's computer.*

Rhys thought for a moment and then replaced his fingers on the board's tracer. What if that was the only way to access the computer? He slid his thumb down the tracer. With a soft hiss, the rear-half of the board glided into the front half which wrapped around it like a sheath. "There," he breathed. He slid his thumb down the tracer once more and then depressed it. Something inside clicked and the computer compartment dropped open to reveal a palm-sized, black box. Rhys laughed and lay down under the board. *What is it, Pathos?*

An old reader from a life pod. Its primary function was to sense the magnetic waves prevalent on inhabitable planets.

The builder tweaked it though, mused Rhys. He touched the computer and then traced a silver wire running into the depths of the board. He reached in. *What is it?*

Another computer, Pathos replied. *Perhaps it requires two computers, one to process the magnetic waves and another to transmit the data to its pilot.*

How aware were our computers then? Were they capable of learning?

They were, said Pathos. *But, to what degree, I cannot confidently say.*

Whoever had the board last and could properly pilot it... do you think the board was able to learn from him?

It's a possibility.

Could I gain access to that information?

Not without connecting to the computer yourself.

Is that dangerous?

I can connect with the unit by tracing its electrical signal when in operation, however, I would not recommend doing so until we know more about its history. The interfacing of your Pathos unit with one so old could cause corruption.

Rhys carefully ran his hand through the innards of the board until his fingertips touched yet another mystery. *There's a port here with something in it.*

Based on the data you've collected so far, it could be a relay port used to transmit the magnetic readings to the pilot.

So, the computers were capable of transmitting data in real time. Rhys pulled his hand out and sat up. *If that's the case, then I can connect to it as well.*

Yes, you can. However, once more, I would advise that you research this board further before exposing yourself to the dangers of technological tampering.

Rhys closed the compartment and stood. Pathos was right. He felt calmer but still miserably tired. After securing the board against the wall, He left the forward hatch to return to his cabin. He saw Hodge and Alina speaking softly in the galley but refused to join them. Ceit passed him in the hallway with a smile and disappeared onto the bridge.

Rhys' cabin was empty. He supposed Miuna was also on the bridge. He had seen no sign of Kallen. Exhausted, he lay down and, with some difficulty, went to sleep.

18
THE TRADING PORT

THE SMELL OF FOOD WOKE Rhys some hours later when the sun was high in the sky. He was surprised to find Alina asleep in her bed. Groggy, he left their cabin and went to the galley where Kallen stood before the stove, twirling a knife between her fingers as she watched food cook. Kashim was nowhere to be found.

"Where is everyone?" asked Rhys, entering the galley.

"Asleep, on the bridge, or working outside," she replied without looking at him. "You have an incredible talent. Somehow you always manage to wake when I start cooking."

"I'm always hungry," chuckled Rhys. He leaned against the counter, glanced at the bubbling pots, and then looked at Kallen. "I'm sorry." Kallen stilled the knife. Rhys took her free hand and intertwined their fingers. "I should never have doubted you."

Her response was tempered. "No, you shouldn't have." She dipped her knife into the pan and stirred. After a long moment, she asked, "What will you do to win back my favor?"

"What will I do? I do not understand. Is there more I must do than apologize?"

Kallen took the small spoon resting on the counter, drew liquid from the pan, and offered it to Rhys. "Blow first. It's hot."

Rhys did as he was told before sipping. "It's good. As usual."

She gave him another spoonful, stirred the pan again, and then leaned against the counter. "I didn't like the look you gave me... earlier. No one will tell you this, not even Hodge, but when you're angry, your eyes change." Rhys scoffed. "When you came in the other night after rescuing Vinz and Kashim… your eyes were frightening. Hodge told me that when you were in town, they were like the color of the night sky."

"And… what color are they now?"

Kallen studied his gaze. "Blue." She leaned forward, kissed his cheek, and then continued to stir the pan's contents.

"Miuna and Ceit, how have they fared?"

Kallen pulled a plate from the cupboard and began dishing food onto it. "Miuna has taken everything in stride. Ceit… not so much. We'll be dropping them off in Firekli. They can get back to Durslade from there." She handed the plate to Rhys. "Miuna likes you."

Rhys blew at the steam. "How do you know?"

"She asks about you often. I've already told her that you're in a relationship."

Rhys paused in his eating. "With… you?" Kallen nodded. "Does that mean we are mates?"

She pushed the pan from the burner. "What do you think?"

Rhys took another slow bite. He knew the answer, but he wasn't going to give it to her so readily. Kallen smiled and folded her arms across her chest as he mulled the thought—and his food—over. Kallen raised an expectant eyebrow when he acted as though he was going to reply and then unceremoniously stuffed another spoonful into his mouth.

"I know what you're doing."

Rhys shrugged as he had seen her do many times. "Eating?" Seeing the look on her face, he snickered, set the plate aside, and pulled her to him. "I would like very much to be… in a relationship with you."

"Good answer," Kallen hummed. She kissed him lightly on the lips and returned his plate. "I'm going to take some food to Vinz. Would you wake Alina? She needs to eat." Kallen slipped out of the galley.

Rhys tapped Alina's AI. *Hey, food. Come eat.*

I'll be right there, came the reply.

After lunch, Rhys retrieved Reza's manuals from his cabin and spread them out on the tables in the galley. Kallen went outside to work on the sails with Vinz while Alina played a card game with Hodge in his cabin. Late into the evening, Rhys translated the manuals. He breaked only to relieve himself and to briefly visit with Andy who had come in to read.

The next day, the schedule the crew had set prior to their visit to Paducah resumed. Rhys was awakened by Hodge, and, with Kallen, they launched the dinghy and new sunboard. After reviewing techniques for two hours, they returned to *Themis*. He ate midday meal, took a nap, worked on the translations, trained with Hodge, ate again, and then went to bed.

For the next eight days, this regimen continued. After working with Hodge and Kallen in the mornings, Rhys spent the remainder of the day occupied by Reza's manuals. At night, Kallen kept him company. Though they were never alone long enough to complete the deed, each night proved more educational than the last. With Alina, at least Rhys could warn her, but Miuna and Ceit's unexpected returns to the cabin were unavoidable. Rhys figured he would remain virginal for the rest of his life.

As for Vinz, Rhys saw very little of him. Kallen worked with the Overseer daily on ship maintenance and claimed Vinz was in a bad way mentally, but Rhys saw no evidence of this. On the rare occasion that Vinz did happen to run into Rhys, he was his usual stoic self. When he addressed Rhys, he did so as if nothing had changed between them.

Though Rhys spent most of his time translating, training, sleeping, or surfing, he managed to catch glimpses of the crew engaging in normal activities. Often, Andy joined him in the galley to read while Rhys translated. They said very little to one another, but Rhys noticed that each day Andy had a new book. When Rhys inquired about the daily change in reading material, Andy indicated that Vinz wasn't the only one with a stash of literature.

Rhys learned that Lyruc and Kyo, despite the vast differences in their physique and personalities, spent much time together discussing maps, the stars, weather, and courses. Rhys also learned that Kyo was musically gifted and could play the piax—a sort of lute. Very rarely did Kyo play for anyone onboard, but Kallen managed to coax a few songs out of him.

Kashim grew stronger over the following days. Alina saw him twice daily and tended to his wounds as any professional doctor would. Unlike Vinz, Kashim seemed thoroughly ashamed of himself and openly admitted so to both Alina and Rhys. As if some sort of barrier broke between them, Kashim became a much more approachable person. To Rhys' surprise, he even began joking with them.

Late in the afternoon on the eighth day, *Themis* pulled into Firekli's port. There were no welcoming parties or groups of gaping people. Instead, a few nondescript dock hands helped them moor. Though the wharves were busy, no one paid them heed.

"Trading ships," said Kallen, joining Rhys on the outer staircase. Miuna and Ceit were behind her. "As we get closer to the Pantarak capital, we'll come across more trading ships."

"But these are not Pantarak people," said Rhys.

"No, only a few ships are actually Pantarak. Traders live by a separate code than those on the mainland. Rarely are there disputes like the ones we had in Paducah."

"Why aren't we a trading ship then?" Rhys mused.

She nudged him. "Because we don't trade."

Vinz appeared behind them, Kyo with him. "Let's get moving. I want to drop you two off at Primary Hall before dark."

Miuna and Ceit glanced at one another and then turned to Rhys. "Thank you," said Miuna. "We are eternally grateful to you for having saved our lives." Unsure of how to respond, Rhys nodded. Miuna looked to Kallen. "Take care of him."

"I will," Kallen assured her. Miuna smiled fondly at Rhys and then touched Ceit's arm.

"Thank you," said Ceit. "Truly, thank you."

With Vinz and Kyo in the lead, Miuna and Ceit followed them onto the docks. Rhys leaned against the staircase railing and watched. He was glad they were on their way. At least someone was able to go home.

"You're a good person," said Kallen.

Rhys glanced at her. Her raven hair looked purple in the light of the setting sun. As usual she wore a sleeveless top and dirt-streaked pants. "You're beautiful," he murmured. Kallen grinned in pleasure. "So, when are we going into town for supplies?"

"Tomorrow morning. It'll take a while. Between you, Alina, and Vinz, our food supplies are almost nonexistent. You three eat too much." Kallen straightened herself. "When are you going to work on your board?"

"I've been meaning to talk with Vinz about it. It has a computer that I could possibly link to, but I first need to learn where it came from or otherwise risk being corrupted."

"Corrupted?"

"The computer could damage Pathos," clarified Rhys.

"Ahh. Well, I figure you'll eventually need this." Kallen reached into the depths of her shirt. She withdrew the square, black disc on the leather thong, pulled it over her head, and slipped it onto Rhys. "I have no idea what it is, but you'll have better use for it than me."

"And Vinz gave this to you?"

"He told me to keep it safe. That's it."

Rhys folded a hand around the black chip, allowing Pathos to examine its material. "I know what it is, but I don't understand its function," he said after a moment.

With a ginger hand, Kallen pushed his freshly dyed hair from his eyes. "You'll figure it out. Ehh, I have to work on the sails before the sun goes down. Help me?"

Though Kallen asked for assistance, Rhys ended up doing very little as most of her work had to do with fine-tuning single panels. Instead, Rhys lay on the top deck and stared up at the purple, pink, and gold sky. When it was finally too dark to continue working, Kallen joined him under the stars.

"Tell me about your home."

"Why?" He was genuinely bewildered.

"I want to know where you come from. Tell me about your childhood."

Aware that she had explicitly told him not to talk about his life on Caelstis with anyone else, Rhys shifted languages and began speaking in Elali, the region's least known language. "Like all colonies, Caelestis had one goal—to preserve and advance mankind. We believed, as did generations before us, that nothing remained of Earth, humanity's home. We had to continue onward. We had no other choice."

"Describe Caelestis to me. What does it look like?" Kallen whispered eagerly.

"The entire colony was cylindrical-shaped with levels stacked upon one another. Think of this ship but thousands of times larger."

"How many people lived on it?"

"Caelestis' population was precisely 63,402," replied Rhys.

Kallen gasped. "So many?"

"And we were but one colony. There were others we traded and worked with but... for the most part, if something happened, we were on our own."

"Where did you get your food from? Your water?"

"We grew it. In fact, many of our levels were allotted for production and distribution of food throughout the colony. All forms of food were compacted into pills. We harvested water from ice in space."

"And you and Alina... everyone was created?"

"The design and creation of humans belonged to a single department in the colony. I don't personally know the details as to how it was decided whose genes, sperm, and eggs would be used—Alina could tell you—but they were hand-selected."

"What happened to the child? You didn't just become a working member of society the next day, did you?"

"No, children were kept separate from adults in the colony to be educated and raised. When they turned nine, they were given a series of exams to test their aptitude. Depending upon your scores, you were given the option of three different departments best suited for your proclivities. Afterward, you attended schooling within the department and became a member."

"And Alina was in… "

"Genetic Modification and Manipulation."

"What does that mean?"

"She worked on the things that make humans who they are." Rhys struggled to explain the complex subject. "She could manipulate genes to make a specific type of person or to rid a person of sickness or a genetic defect. There is no sickness on Caelestis because our bodies have been perfectly engineered to withstand illness or adapt to overcome it."

"Does that mean neither of you can become ill?"

"Correct."

"*Gawan…* Has anyone ever become sick?"

"No. This also means that we heal at a much, much faster rate."

Kallen thought for a moment and then said, "So, you and Alina are half-siblings. If you never meet your parents and are kept separate from the adults in the colony, how did you find out?"

"Our father," said Rhys. "He was… a pioneer of sorts. He worked in genetics like Alina but studied different concepts."

"Like what?"

"He researched the effects of genetics on human sociology and kinship. In other words, how an individual's genetic build affected how they interacted socially."

"How was he able to achieve any type of viable data if all Caelestis citizens were socially formed to interact as one?"

"He didn't," said Rhys. "Alina and I were the first."

"What do you mean?"

"We were the first of his experiments to come of age, to know of our lineage and of each other."

Kallen rolled onto her side to regard him. "Is that why you were given different types of AIs?"

"We weren't told specifically, so it could be pure coincidence, but he probably had his hand in it."

"Does it bother you not knowing?"

"It used to."

"It doesn't now?"

Rhys studied the stars overhead. "Alina and I see the world differently. Since we've been here, our experiences have varied. We decided a while ago not to connect with one another like we did on Caelestis."

"Connect? You mean share data?"

"No, we still share data and information. We agreed we wouldn't mar each other's personality or thought processes by synchronizing our AIs at night."

"I didn't know you could do that."

"We've done it a few times since we've been on Earth but no more. It's not good for us."

"Why is that? It sounds smart—knowing how the other is feeling."

"We can't process each other's emotional and logical data effectively because of the differences in our AIs. So, the un-processable data becomes an inaccurate interpretation of the world. Besides, we both agreed that our thoughts and memories and emotions are our own."

"Everyone on Caelestis was connected, right?"

"Correct. When the majority of the colony rested, we connected to a core computer. This organized, shared, and transferred data. But you were only permitted access to information that was relevant to your department or field."

"That sounds efficient."

"It was very efficient, but... looking back, it was like a prison. We knew nothing outside of our work. The most exciting thing that happened to me in my entire life was the day the asteroid hit Caelestis and I had to drag Alina into the life pod."

"Did she not want to leave?"

"That wasn't it. We weren't *supposed* to leave," murmured Rhys, reliving the experience. "We had not been named to be placed in the life pods. Besides, we were brother and sister. Family members weren't allowed on the life pods."

"You were supposed to remain on the colony and die?"

"It wasn't an exact death sentence. It's possible Caelestis survived the collision, but we had never experienced anything of that caliber before. Rather jettison five percent of the population than risk the human race being obliterated."

"But why weren't you and Alina chosen to be on the life pods?"

"Neither of us was valuable enough," replied Rhys. "I most certainly wasn't. I think Alina may have been considered for the life pods, but it was decided that she would need to stay behind in the off-chance that Caelestis remained functional. They would need people to take over abandoned positions and she was a prime candidate."

Kallen curled into him. "Can I tell you something?" Rhys looked at her. "Please don't tell her this. I think Alina is incredibly intelligent and caring, but between the two of you, you seem much more approachable. You're more aware of people's facial expressions and the emotions behind them. Sometimes, I feel like I'm talking to a wall when I talk to Alina."

Rhys chuckled. "That's Alina's AI. She may not be as perceptive, but she has ten times my intelligence and can work—"

"Can she pilot a sunboard?"

"If she practiced, I'm sure—"

"Does she ask Kyo to continue playing his piax late into the night?"

"Well, no."

"Do you ever see her out here staring up at the stars?"

"No."

"Alina is smart, but she doesn't have the emotional intelligence you have," said Kallen. "The ability to see and understand with your entire being—she can't do that."

"That's nothing really against her. She was highly respected on Caelestis, much more so than I ever was."

"We're not on Caelestis."

Rhys fell silent. He didn't like hearing negative words against his sister. It made him feel uncomfortable.

"I don't say this to be cruel." Kallen caressed his arm. "Just... you think too much of her and not enough of yourself."

Rhys stared up at the stars. "Alina has been commended for her work and recognized numerous times by various department heads for her forward thinking and progress in genetic modification. She is nothing short of a genius."

Kallen rolled onto her back but kept her hand on his arm. "I know."

After stargazing for another hour, they retired to his cabin where Alina and Hodge slept. With Kallen tucked against him, Rhys tried to sleep, but rest never came. Instead, he stared at the wall for some time and then, after making sure Kallen was asleep, stood and paced the room.

Take the manuals and go translate in the galley, instructed Pathos.

Rhys paused in step. *Why?*

Because your brain wave activity indicates that you are restless and need something to busy your mind.

Rhys collected the manuals and slipped out to the galley. He worked by lamplight for two hours before resting his head on the table and groaning. *What's the point of this work? It doesn't require thinking any more. I know the language so well now that I don't have to concentrate. It's just another task to complete.*

Perhaps that in itself is the challenge, Pathos suggested. *You lack discipline.*

You know that's not true.

It's true when you're bored, his AI retorted.

Why do I go through cycles of insomnia? Some nights I fall asleep immediately, and others... I feel like I need to be working, planning, reading, something!

It has to do with your stress levels. When you're at sea away from people you don't know, your stress levels are minimal. You're in port now and that makes you anxious, especially after everything that happened in Paducah.

Is what Kallen said about Alina true?

Which part?

That she is unable to fully experience the world.

In a sense, yes. Alina cannot experience certain emotions because of Logos. She can only feel surprise, disgust, joy, anger, sadness, fear, and love. Intricate emotions, secondary emotions, like betrayal, guilt, contentment, and wonder are unachievable by her AI. Her inability to comprehend these emotions, however, enables her to more readily problem solve. She can look past what others can't—the logic, the reasoning.

Between the two of us, who is more equipped to survive on Earth?

That is dependent upon what should happen in the coming months, replied Pathos.

I see, murmured Rhys. He collected the manuals and papers and returned to his cabin. After stashing his translating materials, he lay down beside Kallen. *Put me to sleep, Pathos. Allow any of the other crew members to wake me.*

Understood.

It was early morning when Kallen shook him awake. She kissed his cheek, slid out of bed, and dressed. Alina sat cross-legged in her own bed; Hodge was nowhere to be seen. "We're leaving in half an hour for the market," his sister mumbled.

"I have to help Vinz repair a malfunctioning solar plate." Kallen adjusted her shirt. "I should be done before then." She hurried from the room.

"What's wrong?" asked Alina in their native tongue.

"Just tired," Rhys mumbled, standing. He ruffled his hair into place and began dressing. "Are you coming?"

"We need as many hands as possible. Besides, I need to restock our medical supplies."

Once dressed, Rhys sat back down and stared blankly at the floor. "Do you use Logos to help you sleep?"

Alina paused braiding her hair. "Sometimes. Why?"

"I was just wondering."

"Do you?"

"No."

"That's a lie."

Rhys frowned and Alina shrugged. "There's no reason to be ashamed of it. We're in a new land facing different stressors than those who live here. Sometimes sleep doesn't come as naturally as it should."

Once dressed, they joined Kallen and the others on the outer deck. Though Alina had said they needed as many hands as possible, only Vinz, Hodge, and Kallen were there. Including himself and Alina, that made five.

"Are we waiting on anyone else?" asked Alina uncertainly.

"No, this is enough," replied Vinz, pulling a headscarf over his head. "You two, cover up."

The group disembarked *Themis* and started along the docks. Unlike Paducah, the docks of Firekli were crowded with clamoring sailors, traders, and merchants working to load and unload cargo. A variety of people stalked the docks, keeping Rhys' head on a swivel. Though he was accustomed to seeing people who were extremely tan, he had never before seen people whose skin was as black as night.

"What?" asked a short, ebony-colored man.

Rhys snapped his wandering eyes back to the docks to avoid trouble, but within seconds he was people-watching again.

"This is a trading port," explained Kallen. "There are people and goods here from all over the region." She pointed to a four-story building beyond the docks. "Because of this, the economy is stronger. People are better off here."

"This is... much nicer than New Arbroath," said Rhys, noting the stone roads leading into town. As they drew farther from the docks, men in cropped pants and sleeveless shirts became less common, and soon Rhys found himself surrounded by citizens in intricately designed jackets and long, color-accented dresses.

"Don't stare," hummed Kallen.

"Why are they dressed this way? It must be very hot," said Rhys under his breath.

"Women are expected to wear long dresses to cover their ankles," Kallen replied, glancing at a middle-aged woman dressed in a soft green and cream dress. "And men are to look presentable in the event that their power is questioned."

"That... makes no sense." Rhys studied another woman's dress for a moment and then looked at the man she was with who had his dark hair pulled in a tight horsetail at the back of his head. He wore pants, a long-sleeved blouse, and a vest. "How is there such a wealth gap between New Arbroath, Paducah, and Firekli?"

"Trade," interjected Vinz. " It accounts for nearly 70 percent of the income here."

"And these people... are Pantarak?"

"Some are, but the overwhelming majority are Aabeshian like us."

"And the difference between the two?"

As they climbed the gradual hill to the town square, Vinz continued, "The first Aabesh people existed in the Southwest about five centuries ago. They began trading with the area that was originally known as Elal— now it's Durslade. It turned out that the two groups meshed well, so the two became one. This is the reason that Elali is a dying language and that only those from Durslade who are direct descendants speak it. Aabesh is the primary language in Durslade, New Arbroath, and a number of other ports now. "

"And the Pantaraks?"

"They originated from the Southeast. Their ancestors were from a landmass called Pantarak. Pushed by religious zealousness, they began spreading west until they ran into the Aabeshians whose social, political, and economic orders vastly differed. Until they hit Aabeshian forces, the Pantarak people were a powerful civilization. They had the man power to take down towns and cities and build anew. It continues, even now."

"Sounds like a militaristic venture," remarked Alina.

"It is," Vina assured her.

"I have seen no evidence that a single military unit exists on Earth." Alina looked to Rhys. "Right?"

"It's true," Rhys said.

"That's because all of our military power is geared toward halting the Pantarak capital's progress westward. We have limited people, so most towns that are not Pantarak must protect themselves from invasion and attack. Hence the reason New Arbroath was so easily targeted." Vinz nodded to a passerby. "As we draw closer to Brechin, the Pantarak capital, we will probably be stopped by Aabeshian forces and questioned."

"Does Brechin engage in trade with outside ports?" asked Alina.

"Yes," replied Hodge. "But it's heavily sanctioned."

"So, some of the ships in port right now—you said they are Pantarak?"

"They are," said Vinz.

"Does Firekli not worry about conflict? It seems that by allowing Pantaraks the right to trade within Firekli, its government is opening itself to internal issues."

"That's an astute observation, however, the Pantarak government—chiefly, the high priest and his clergymen—know that Brechin flourishes through trade. If they attack a powerful trading port like Firekli, they would be dooming themselves."

"They're not as moronic as we thought," murmured Hodge with grim humor.

"Why wouldn't they overtake it and claim it as their own?" Rhys glanced at a couple passing by. "I don't understand. If they're so worried about maintaining trade, wouldn't it make more sense to claim Firekli as theirs and have it nested under their empire?"

"Not necessarily," replied Alina. "People who aren't under the rule of an unwanted power tend to be more willing to acquiesce to political and economic requests. They think they have a choice. If they were subjugated and simply forced to continue trade, this would cause a great upset. People have the power, at least here in Firekli, to hold off a regime. The Pantarak government would gain briefly from its exploits if it attempted to overtake Firekli, however, in the long-run, it would not be a wise decision."

Rhys saw Vinz nod in approval before turning onto another thoroughfare. After peering about at the numerous shops and stores, he circled the group together. "Kallen, Rhys—you're with me. Alina, Hodge—look for the medical supplies necessary to replenish our stock and then go to the solar paneling store. Let's see if we can build up our supply of spare plating. We'll meet you back here."

For the next hour and a half, Rhys trailed behind Kallen and Vinz as they entered and exited stores and shops. He didn't mind holding the increasing number of bags and small boxes. Both Kallen and Vinz had brought over-the-shoulder bags to help with the load, so the weight was tolerable. Though Rhys should have been paying attention to what they were purchasing and to whom they were talking, he couldn't. He was completely absorbed in studying the people and buildings.

Firekli was like another world. It was clean, quiet, relaxed. The roads were flagstone while the streets were well-kept and free of mud. All of the stores and shops were indoors with the exception of a flower stand. Each building had electricity and used energy provided by solar paneling. To Rhys' astonishment, several of the stores even had running water which he had only briefly seen in New Arbroath.

Houses that stretched beyond the main street and far into the town were comprised of stone, mortar, and wood. Many of the homes stood two or three stories tall with open glass windows and heavy, intricately-decorated front doors.

The people were just as interesting. Though Rhys had initially taken interest in their fashion, he soon found their faces just as fascinating. Standing patiently inside shops, he studied those around him.

"Vinz," said Rhys as they stood outside a meat store. "Some of the people here have light-colored eyes. Why?"

"Trading port," Vinz replied flatly as he studied his list of goods. "Kallen, we need two more things—spices and textiles."

Kallen took a bag from the Overseer and told Rhys, "Don't think about it too much. You see?" She nodded to a young woman walking with her child down the street. "It's not just the color of their eyes. Their hair too."

Alina, their hair, murmured Rhys, gawking at the woman whose hair, although mostly brown, had streaks of red weaved through its tresses. *I don't understand this.*

Kallen's right. Don't try to think about it. The concept of human genetics cannot be so simply explained.

Leave it to people like you, right? murmured Rhys.

After purchasing spices, Vinz led the way to the textile shop which, Kallen explained, was where they bought the majority of their clothes. While Kallen looked for new articles of clothing to fit herself and Alina, Vinz took Rhys to the shop owner and had him measured. Until then, he had been borrowing clothes from Vinz because his were the only size that fit Rhys properly. After purchasing several pairs of pants, various shirts, and a pair of boots, the items were wrapped in a thick linen and added to Rhys' load.

"We have one more place," said Vinz. "I need to check on something."

As they followed Vinz down the street, Kallen took some of the more cumbersome bags from Rhys. "What else do we need?" he asked, straining slightly.

Kallen shrugged. "I don't know."

Vinz led them back toward the docks to a small shop along the waterfront. He stepped inside briefly before reappearing and nodding toward the ship.

"What did you ask?" asked Kallen.

"I'll show you once we're aboard," replied Vinz.

After chatting with a handful of sailors loitering on the docks, they boarded *Themis* and entered the bridge. Kyo and Lyruc were the only two there.

"Where is he?" asked Vinz.

"The galley," said Kyo.

With some difficulty, Rhys followed Kallen and Vinz down the stairs to the galley. "You take the food," instructed Kallen, stopping him in the hallway. "Give me the clothes." They exchanged bags, and she went to her cabin. Rhys repositioned a particularly heavy duffle bag of food and waddled into the galley behind Vinz. He stopped just in the doorway. Beside Andy and Kashim was a teenage boy of perhaps 16 or 17 years of age.

"I... was not expecting this," mumbled Vinz, also regarding the newcomer.

Rhys moved past Vinz and set the heaviest of his bags down. Rubbing the stiffness from his shoulder, he turned to survey the teen. The boy was young, like Alina, but his blue-gray eyes were solemn, grave even. The sides of his head were shaved close to the scalp while the top showcased a strip of ash-brown hair decorated with gold streaks. He wore clothes similar to their own and flaunted an elaborate, leaf-shaped earring that wrapped around the outer rim of his right ear and connected to a stud at the earlobe.

The boy smiled. "You're the Overseer?"

Vinz nodded but didn't answer, obviously taken aback.

The boy ran an appraising eye over Rhys. "Who're your parents?"

Rhys glanced at Andy in confusion. That was an odd first question.

"Where is Jovo?" asked Vinz. "I asked for Jovo."

Andy, who was leaning back in a chair, said, "He claims Jovo shipped off with someone else."

"I *specifically* asked for Jovo," fumed Vinz. He set his bags down.

"Yanamichin said for us to take the kid," Andy explained. "I've been told he'll be just as useful."

Vinz approached the boy. "Who are you?"

"It depends." The boy nodded to Rhys. "Who are his parents?"

Vinz exchanged looks with Kashim who swiftly withdrew a knife from his belt and held it to the newcomer's throat. The boy didn't move; in fact, he didn't even flinch. "I'm going to ask once more—who are you?" Vinz folded his arms across his chest. "You have to be someone to come recommended by Yanamichin."

"Sorry, friend," the boy replied. "I don't play unless I know who I'm working with."

Kashim caressed his knife along the boy's neck.

"Of course, I know of you, Vinz Amadorri. I've heard everything from Jovo." He looked at Rhys. "What I want to know is who is the pure-blood?"

At that moment, Hodge and Alina appeared in the doorway. "What's going on... " hesitated Hodge. Their eyes fell on the newcomer.

The boy looked between Rhys and Alina, alarmed. "This is a set-up."

"What? No," groaned Vinz.

Before another word could be said, two knives appeared in the boy's hands.

"Wait!" shouted Rhys. "Wait, wait." Everyone fell still. "Kashim. Let him go." Kashim glanced at Vinz and then stepped away.

"To what family do you belong?" The boy leveled a knife at Rhys.

"Falkrow," replied Rhys. Utter confusion tugged at the boy's brows. "We're not from *here*."

The boy retracted his knives into the secret sheaths within his sleeves, his eyes shifting between Rhys and Alina. "So, you really are... pure, *pure* bloods."

"They've been here a couple of months," Vinz offered.

The boy chuckled. "*Gawan.* You two are what the uproar has been about."

"Uproar?" queried Rhys.

"You were just in Paducah, yes?" The boy presented his left hand. "Leo." Rhys took his arm, and the young boy bobbed his head. "And you?"

"Rhys." He nodded to Alina. "And my younger sister, Alina."

Leo smiled charmingly at Alina and then glanced at Kallen. "Ladies," he acknowledged.

"Leo—uproar?" asked Rhys. "What do you mean?"

"Word has spread to the capital that two white gods were brought to Paducah by apostates." Leo motioned to the group. "I can only guess they mean you."

Vinz nodded, glanced at Kashim, and said, "Yanamichin seems to think that, once we cross the Aabeshian line of defense, you can guide our ship to Brechin's port safely. Is this true?"

"Of course," Leo confidently avowed. Rhys didn't miss the subtle glance the teen passed Alina and Kallen. "It's not a problem. I have contacts everywhere."

"And in Brechin?" asked Vinz.

"Yes. I am known."

"And what is it you're known for?" Alina brushed past Vinz to join Rhys.

Leo smiled mischievously. "Why are you so eager to know?"

Alina sighed. "I'm sure this bravado has worked on the countless ladies you have tricked into your bed, however, it won't work on me. Now, if you would, please answer my question. What is it that you are known for?"

Leo gaped and then broke into laughter. "This one!" He pointed to Alina. "This one I like."

Rhys exchanged looks with Alina and then the others. Though he didn't care for his advances on Alina or Kallen, Rhys liked Leo. He seemed outgoing and personable despite his unwillingness to directly answer questions.

Leo cleared his throat and, with the utmost seriousness, claimed, "I can get you to Brechin. I can get you into the temple at the center of the capital. Like I said, I have contacts from here to Maliyansa."

"In exchange for what?" asked Vinz.

"Whatever you were going to pay Jovo."

"And?"

Leo shook his head. "That's it. I am Jovo's substitute. Nothing more." With a cocky smile, the kid asked, "So, where is my cabin? If need be, I can bunk with the ladies."

Kallen shared a disgusted look with Rhys, grabbed her bags, and began storing the supplies.

"Hey, hey." Leo gently took hold of Kallen's arm as she passed.

Rhys tried to warn Leo, but Kallen was fast. In a swift movement, she flung the bag from her shoulder and unfurled a punch. The boy stumbled backward holding his bruised cheekbone. "Touch me again and I'll break your jaw," Kallen snarled. Leo tried to smile, but his swelling face made it difficult. Instead, he bowed his head in acknowledgment.

"Leo, this way. I'd like to speak with you." Vinz led Leo and his bruised ego out of the galley; Kashim followed.

After Alina wrapped Kallen's hand and they stored the food, they worked together to prepare a meal. In the meantime, Rhys and Hodge organized the new supplies Andy and Lyruc had brought in to fix Vinz's cabin door, checked the sunboards to ensure they were ready to be deployed, and prepared Alina's medical supplies in the new bag they had purchased.

Kallen took meals to Lyruc, Andy, and Kyo, who were lounging on the bridge, and then called Vinz to eat. Rhys was halfway through his meal when Vinz, Kashim, and Leo returned to the galley.

"We set sail for the capital at dusk," Vinz announced, sitting across from Rhys and leaning on his elbows. Kallen presented the Overseer with a plate of food and then seated herself beside Rhys.
"It is as we've planned—word has spread."

"Thanks to Alina," said Rhys.

Vinz nodded. "Yes, thanks to Alina." He motioned to Leo. "He will be our chief guide. He says he knows the ports and has contacts."

"Can we trust him?" asked Kallen.

"Of course—"

Vinz cut Leo off. "That has yet to be determined, however, I have threatened him with his life, so… we have that."

"Which means nothing if he's Pantarak," retorted Alina.

"So what if I am?" asked Leo, suddenly serious.

Taken aback by his change in attitude, everyone fell silent.

Leo cleared his throat. "Before we leave, I want to make myself clear. I'm Pantarak, yes. I was raised in the religion of my fathers, but I am not my father."

"What does that mean?" asked Kallen. Rhys could hear the animosity in her voice.

"It means my father's wars are not my wars."

Kallen started to reply, but Rhys placed a gentle hand on her arm. "Thank you for clarifying. We will respect you and your religion so long as you respect those onboard."

Leo nodded in agreement but didn't say anything.

"Once we're in Brechin, we will request a meeting with the high priest," continued Vinz. "We may or may not be refused; it will depend upon how magnanimous His Grace is feeling on that particular day. If we are refused, Leo will find us a way in. We will ask that a truce be enacted between New Arbroath and Paducah."

"What will we use to bargain with?" asked Hodge.

"We can bargain our medical expertise," the Overseer suggested, nodding to Alina, "as well as technological services. I have several historical documents, as well numerous artifacts from the Old World, I'm sure would excite."

"I doubt books and artifacts will be enough." Kallen looked between them. "Witnessing the presence of two white gods wasn't enough for Paducah."

"In regions like Paducah," said Leo, "a viewing of the white gods is rare. But in Brechin, there are generations of white gods. People such as myself stroll down the pristine streets daily. You are not a rarity."

"Does our appearance not give us any leverage?" asked Rhys.

"You have pure eyes, but so do many others within the capital. Your appearance will help you in so far as to gain favor with the nobles."

"Nobles?"

"Descendants of the white gods," explained Leo.

"We don't just have light eyes," said Alina. "Our hair... it's silver."

"It looks black to me," said Leo.

Kallen forced Rhys to turn his head and she ran her hands through his hair near the nape of his neck. "See?" she asked. "We dye their hair to keep attention from them."

Leo nodded thoughtfully. "Again, this would only help you gain favor with the nobles. I don't believe you will impress the high priest."

"What do you suggest then?"

"Technology. Machinery they don't have." Leo nodded to Rhys. "Like the thing on your head. What is that?"

Rhys tried not to sound too defensive. "It cannot be separated from us."

"Then you could bargain yourselves. It would be a good trade," said Leo. "You and your machines for peace."

Instead of immediately objecting, Rhys glanced at Alina whose eyes were trained on Leo. When put like that, the bargain seemed more than acceptable.

"Your job is to get us into port and take us to the high priest." Vinz's voice was low, dark. "We'll take care of the rest."

Perhaps they had been too quick to judge Vinz's logic. Two people for the sake of several nations was acceptable. Had they been on Caelestis, the decision would have been finalized within seconds. The sacrifice of a few for the lives of many was worth the loss. Alina met his gaze. They didn't have to use their internal connection to know they were thinking the same thing. The grave expression on her face was enough.

After that, conversation died. Hodge attempted to regale everyone with a tale of his adventure on the docks that afternoon, but his heart wasn't in it. Rhys thanked Alina and Kallen for the meal and, for the first time, left the table before anyone else. Stressed and distraught, he climbed the stairs to the outer deck and leaned against the railing.

Just when he thought he had everything figured out, planned, something changed. He just wanted to quietly live out the remainder of his days in this hellhole. Perhaps that meant resigning himself to live in Brechin under the watchful eye of the high priest. If Kallen and Vinz and the others could live without bother or worry, then wasn't that worth it?

He laid his head on the railing and watched as several men used a pulley to haul a large crate onto the ship in the next slip.

He could run. He could board another ship—a non-Pantarak ship—and run. He and Alina could escape and leave the world to fend for itself. Though they had discussed at length their responsibility as non-Earthlings, Rhys felt he could convince Alina. They could run right now. Before *Themis* left port, they could board another ship or disappear into town and never be seen again.

Stop, scolded Alina suddenly.

Rhys sighed. *Why can't you let me play out one of my fantasies just once?*

Because they're nonsensical, his sister replied. *Now, get to the forward hatch and start figuring out how to use that magnetic board.*

Hm? Why?

Because that will be our offering to the high priest, said Alina.

You really want to give them such a valuable piece of equipment?

We could give ourselves to them if you would prefer.

Rhys thought. *What do you suppose happened to Vinz's parents?*

They were killed by Pantaraks.

Why? What did they do? If we know the answer to that, then perhaps we'll have a better understanding of what we're going into.

I'll leave that to you. You are on better terms with him than me.

Are you serious? Rhys muttered incredulously.

Yes. He may have betrayed us, but you two have more in common than you think. Besides, he watches me too much. It makes me uncomfortable speaking with him about consequential matters.

Fine, I'll do it.

Soon, added Alina.

19
NIGHT AT SEA

BY DUSK, THEMIS WAS OUT at sea churning through the waves. After several hours of studying the magnetic sunboard and attempting to tear it apart, Rhys finally gave up for the evening and retired to his cabin. To his displeasure, he found Leo there.

The newcomer, who sat on the bunk above Alina's bed, looked over his book but didn't say anything. Tiredly, Rhys flung himself onto his bed and stared at the wall. He would like to have lay out under the stars with Kallen, but she was busy working on the converter in the engine room. With a sigh of annoyance, he rolled out of bed and gathered his translation work. Having made little progress on the sunboard, he needed to occupy his still restless mind.

"What's all that?" Leo set his book aside.

"I'm translating manuals for a friend," replied Rhys, organizing the piles around him.

"Manuals about what?"

"Sunboards," replied Rhys. There was a long moment of silence. Sensing Leo's gaze, Rhys looked up at him. "What?"

Leo grimly regarded him. "You're different. You and your sister."

"Can I ask, when was the last time a white god—someone like us—crashed here?"

Leo shrugged. "I don't know, but it's been a while. You two are definitely an oddity." He sat back and continued to read. Uncomfortable with the conversation, Rhys took his materials and went to the galley to wait for Kallen. Andy was already there.

Two hours into his work, Rhys looked up at the ship's First Mate. "Do you feel that?"

Andy paused in his reading. "I do. The waves are kicking up." He set his book aside and stood. "It's almost time for my watch anyway. I'll check the bridge."

Becoming increasingly aware of the ship's rocking, Rhys returned to his cabin to stash his work. He was surprised to find the door closed with a shirt hanging between it and the doorframe. Had he carelessly dragged the shirt behind him when he left earlier? He opened the door and started to bend down to retrieve the shirt; movement across the room stopped him.

For the longest moment, he stared. Alina's naked back was to him, her black hair spilling around her shoulders in long, thick waves. Under her was Hodge who, from Rhys' position in the doorway, appeared just as naked. Flustered, surprised, and caught off guard, Rhys tried to stumble back into the hallway but hit the doorway. Alina spun around. Their eyes met.

"I... " murmured Rhys in Interstellar Nefegian. "I'm sorry!" He rolled into the hall and slammed the door behind him.

He and Alina had discussed human sexuality on a number of occasions and accepted that they were both in the process of discovering their sexual identities, but... seeing Alina naked atop Hodge brought new meaning to it. The image of her naked back and small but round hips was burned into his mind.

Rhys hurried down the hallway, dumped his work in the galley, and went in search of Kallen. He found her on the outer deck studying the sails through night-vision goggles. She covered her glasses when he came out so the light from the inner cabins wouldn't destroy her sight. Despite the rocking of the ship and the rising wind, Rhys managed to find her arm in the darkness and grab it.

"I... Uh... " he stammered. "I, uh, accidently... Alina... and Hodge... " Why was it so difficult to say? They weren't doing anything bad. There was nothing wrong with them expressing their interest in one another sexually.

"Ah," said Kallen. She pulled the goggles from her eyes and hung them around her neck. "You walked in on them?"

"Uh... yes."

Kallen chuckled and held Rhys' arm. "Is that the first time you've walked in on them?"

"Yes."

"Was there a shirt wedged between the door and the frame?"

"But... I thought I had dragged it out or... something." Kallen kissed his cheek. "Wait... What do you mean is it my first time? You've walked in on them?"

"Twice," said Kallen. "Both times were in my cabin."

Rhys gaped into the darkness. "I... How?"

Kallen laughed and then groped for the railing as the ship rolled steeply to port. "They've just had more time alone than we have. Don't worry about it."

Rhys frowned. He didn't like that answer. It had never been a race to see who could engage in the human sexual experience first, but somehow Alina having sex before him made him feel inadequate.

"Come on. The wind is picking up. I've finished working. I just wanted to check on the sails to make sure the adjustments we made the other day were holding." Kallen ushered him inside to the forward hatch where she began putting away the goggles and tools she had strapped to her waist. "Why are you sulking?" she asked over her shoulder.

Rhys, who was gazing morosely at his sunboard, shrugged. He knew the reason, but he felt silly explaining it aloud. Kallen turned around to scold him good-naturedly, but a deep rumbling suddenly permeated the ship. Alarmed, Rhys froze. "What was that?"

"I think... it's thunder," murmured Kallen.

"Thunder?" Was that an enemy? Was that the name of another ship? What did it mean?

"Come on." She ducked out of the forward hatch and climbed the inner stairs to the bridge. The wind had definitely picked up. *Themis* was swaying ever deeper. "Is it—"

"A storm," concluded Vinz perched at the helm.

Kallen hugged Rhys excitedly. "From where?"

"From the northeast," interjected Leo, leaning against the back wall. "It's a big one."

Rhys looked about the bridge at the meters and gauges. Everything appeared normal.

"Kallen, take Lyruc and bring down the sails," instructed Vinz. "Make sure both of you are secured to the deck. I don't want bodies in the water." Kallen squeezed Rhys' arm fondly, motioned to Lyruc, and disappeared downstairs. "Andy, bring the engines to full speed. Keep us east-by-northeast. Kyo, prepare an alternate route. If the storm worsens, we'll need an escape. Where is Hodge? Rhys, check the forward hatch. Make sure the crates and boards are secure." Vinz pulled the communication pipe from the ceiling. "All hands, we're entering a storm. Prepare the cabins for turbulence."

A flash of green light blinded Rhys and a crack of what Kallen had called "thunder" shook the ship. Rhys startled horribly, and a cold sweat broke out across his body. Reading his sudden adrenaline levels, Pathos set up a barrier around the AI's external unit. "Danger," the AI reported in Aabesh so all could understand. "High-voltage electricity has been detected. All personnel should move away from metal objects and seek shelter immediately."

"What's happening?" Rhys quavered. "I don't understand."

"It's a thunderstorm," replied Leo matter-of-factly.

"What's a thunderstorm?"

"An Earth phenomenon," explained Vinz. "It happens rarely now because the atmosphere is so dry, but when water collects overhead, clouds form. Eventually, those clouds become too heavy and a storm occurs. When charges in the clouds grow large enough, lightning is created."

Another crack of eerie green lightning split the sky, illuminating the wind screen. Rhys stumbled toward the door.

"Calm down," murmured Leo, amused.

"What can we do? Will it hit us?"

Vinz peered over his shoulder at Rhys. "Don't worry. We're fine." Rhys and Pathos could not disagree more.

Themis lurched to the side and then dipped steeply, causing Rhys and the others on the bridge to grope for handholds. Another bolt of lightning fissured ahead of the ship and the hair on Rhys' arms stood on end. Thunder broke directly overhead, shaking the ship.

"We need the sails in," said Andy over his shoulder. "They'll be fried."

Rhys fell still as the realization of what Andy said settled on him. Kallen was in danger. He rushed out of the bridge onto the outer platform. He slammed the door behind him and, shifting his eyesight to night vision, climbed the ladder to the upper deck.

Lyruc was nearest pulling at a crank while Kallen balanced on a beam three meters overhead. Rhys watched them for a moment and then looked up at the sky as flashes of green light sparked between clouds and darted from heaven to sea.

"Kallen!" he shouted as a gust of wind tore at his clothes. "Lyruc!" His voice was thrown to the water. Rhys pulled himself onto the deck and, wobbling, took hold of the railing. "Kallen! Lyruc!" Both turned to look at him. Neither seemed perturbed by the lightning or the wind or the deep rumbling that shook the ship.

"We're fine," called Kallen, guessing why he was there. "Almost finished!"

Rhys stared up at the black skies in awe and fear. Never in his life had he felt so small and insignificant, even while living on Caelestis. How could something so powerful, so vast like the sky above, come to life?

Another horrific but awe-inspiring crack of lightning flashed overhead and thunder followed. The deep boom shook Rhys' core. As if to reiterate Earth's fury and power, a gust of wind whipped his clothes around him and clawed at his hair. *Themis* rolled steeply to port and then jerked upward onto the crest of the next wave.

"Lyruc!" screeched Kallen over the chaos.

Rhys looked up to find Lyruc dangling off the side of the ship, his safety line pulled taut. Using a swift calculation, Rhys stood, slid down the deck, and wrapped his arm around Lyruc's safety cord. Kallen leapt from the beam overhead, landed beside him, and took hold of the cord as well. Together, they began pulling.

They strained against the man's weight. Lyruc was not the largest crew member, but he was heavy enough to prevent them from reeling him back in.

"Stay locked!" shouted Rhys to Kallen. Kallen braced herself. Rhys glanced at the coming waves and, in motion with the boat, slid down the deck to the outer railing using Lyruc's safety cord as a guidewire. He hit the metal bars, reached over them, and began pulling. At first, he could do nothing but strain; he found, however, that if he pulled when the ship rolled to starboard, the water took some of Lyruc's weight off the cord. He didn't need to explain to Kallen to gather the slack.

For several long minutes, Lyruc struggled but, despite the distance they made, he still couldn't reach the railing. Groaning, Rhys held the rope taut until *Themis* pitched to starboard again. When Lyruc's weight briefly lessened, Rhys heaved.

Lyruc's hand shot from the black water and took hold of the railing. Once Rhys saw that Lyruc had a secure grip, he released the cord and began hauling the man onto the ship by his arms and clothes. Kallen appeared beside him. With their combined strength, they dragged Lyruc away from the railing toward the masts. Kallen shortened both her safety cord and Lyruc's and then collapsed on the deck, panting.

Rhys took hold of the metal safety railing positioned at the primary mast's base. "Are you hurt?" he shouted over the storm's fury.

Lyruc shook his head. "Thanks—"

Themis rolled forward violently and then bucked, stripping Rhys' fingers from the safety railing and tossing him down the length of the deck. Kallen's shrill screech followed him.

Thinking quickly, he turned on his stomach and groped for anything—wood, metal, rope, cord. His fingers momentarily caught something hard, but his momentum snapped his grip. He slammed into the outer railing on the far end of the deck and flew into the sea's foamy embrace.

Rhys tossed and tumbled in the black abyss. He rolled and flipped under the waves before his face finally breached the surface. He took a gulp of air and attempted to steady himself, but another wave pounded him back underwater. He scrambled for air only to be beaten back down.

Twirling and rolling, he remained just under the water's surface. Head-over-heels, he somersaulted through the violent tumult of water, fighting with all his strength to reach the surface.

No matter how he and Pathos attempted to read the wave patterns and coordinate his movements, the force of the storm's fury managed to find him and pummel him back into the black depths.

The sea was merciless. Not only did it strip him of air but of his clothes. His shirt was ripped from his body and his pants torn from his hips. He was a defenseless human against one of man's greatest nemeses.

Time ceased to have meaning. Exhaustion plagued him and his body ached. His lungs were tight from swallowing so much water. He wanted to quit. Every time he went under, he told himself to stop fighting—he just wanted the tortuous struggle to end—but something kept pushing him. It wasn't Pathos. No matter the data downloaded on oceanic survival, Pathos could do nothing to control the waves around him. His will to survive was his alone. The AI, which had functioned as a support system his entire existence, could not offer any support against the sea and its elements.

Again and again, he resigned himself to his fate and accepted his death. But it never came. He kept fighting and struggling, clawing his way back to the surface. Instinct took hold of his mind and body and soon became the only thing driving him, powering him through the waves.

His mind shut down. No thoughts passed between him and Pathos. He could feel nothing, see nothing, hear nothing. All life-support energy was directed to his limbs and lungs. The sea had him in its claws, but instinct had a vice-grip hold on his life.

He thought he spotted a beam of light searching the waters, but lightning flashed overhead and he was reminded once more that he was alone in the watery grave.

Hours passed.

How long had he been in the water? How long could he keep going? Eventually, the skies lightened and the waves began to come over Rhys in patterns Pathos could read. Allowing the AI full control of his body, Rhys rose and fell with the waves, breathing at the trough and swimming at the crest. His body fell into a meditative and automatic rhythm; his mind shut off, and he focused on survival, whatever that meant.

When he next looked at the skies, the storm clouds had moved to the horizon and the heavens were a faint blue. It was dawn. Though the waves were still enormous and required his full attention, he couldn't help but feel some happiness knowing that, at least for now, he had defeated night. Rhys fell back into his automatic swimming and breathing pattern. He needed to keep going.

Something touched his back; suddenly, hands began dragging him from the water. He couldn't still his arms and legs. He had to keep swimming.

"Rhys, Rhys!"

Rhys snapped from his trance and, realizing he was no longer weightless, heaved for air. He could finally take a full breath! Dizzy, exhausted, and weak, he fell backward into the dinghy. Blankets wrapped around him, and Kallen held him fast to the boat. He could see others in the dinghy with them but couldn't make out who they were. He was safe. He could breathe, he could stop moving. Pathos knocked him unconscious.

In his dreams, he swam. His body moved and rocked with the waves. He gasped for air and struggled. He felt hands on him, but he could see no one, hear no one. All he knew was the raging sea.

When he finally opened his eyes, he thought he might have died. All he saw was black. It was silent. Adrenaline filled his aching and weary body, and he began flailing fiercely. He was not going to drown, not after fighting for so long!

"Hey, hey, hey... " came a man's voice. A light flicked on and Rhys grimaced against its brilliance. Vinz peered down at him worriedly. "What's wrong?"

Rhys looked about. He was in his cabin. Leo, who was asleep in the top bunk, appeared to be the only other person in the room.

"I... " Rhys' voice cracked and he coughed.

Vinz sat back down on the floor. It appeared the Overseer had been there for a long time as he had a nest of blankets around him, reading materials, an empty plate, and a pillow. "How are you feeling?"

Rhys tried to swallow but found his throat tight. He had survived?

"I'm sorry. We couldn't get to you sooner. We were tracking you, but the waves were so bad, we couldn't launch the dinghy. Anything we would have thrown at you would have been swallowed by the sea."

"This... is real?" The question seemed silly when said aloud.

"Yes," Vinz replied. "You've been asleep for nearly a full day."

Rhys tried to sit up. His entire body ached horribly. His shoulders were weak. Vinz told him to remain still and then went to the door.

Momentarily, Alina appeared. "How are you feeling?" She took his hand and placed her fingers at his wrist.

"Uh... tired," he replied in their tongue.

"You were in the water for 11 hours." Alina released his hand, withdrew a small light, and tilted his head to the side. She studied one ear and then the other. "Does anything in specific hurt?"

"My... chest." He started to sit up, but Alina stopped him.

"Your ribs are bruised." She leaned down and kissed his forehead. "I'm glad you're safe. You can't leave me here alone."

"I know," Rhys breathed.

Alina sat back as Kallen, Hodge, and Lyruc entered. Leo rolled over in his bunk to watch. "Hey," greeted Hodge. Kallen exchanged places with Alina. "How are you feeling?"

"Tired," replied Rhys once more in Nefegian. He corrected himself in Aabesh.

"How... did you not die?" asked Hodge as Kallen leaned down to kiss him. "We saw you get swallowed by hundreds of waves."

"I don't know," mumbled Rhys.

Lyruc pushed past Hodge and offered his hand to Rhys. "Thank you." The large man smiled. "You saved my life. Thank you." Rhys took his arm in the universal sign of friendship. "Thank you, Rhys."

Not ever been given such gratitude, Rhys only nodded. He had saved someone's life?

"When can he get up?" Kallen asked of Alina. "I'm sure he's starved."

"He can stand now; he just needs to take it slow," his sister replied.

"Do you want to come to the galley while I cook? It's late, but I don't mind."

Rhys gripped her arm and Lyruc braced his back so he could sit up. The pain was dull, but it was there. His chest hurt.

"Everyone out," instructed Kallen. Rhys looked down at the blankets barely covering his naked lower half. Everyone except Kallen filed out of the cabin. She closed the door behind them and began digging through piles of folded clothes. She withdrew a large, loose shirt and a pair of shorts. "Raise your arms."

Rhys obeyed, and she slipped the shirt onto him. With her help, he stiffly moved to his feet. Rhys groaned as pain punched him in the chest. Kallen pulled a new pair of shorts on and then stood to set his hair in place. Her hands slid from his hair to his face, and she leaned onto his shoulder. "I should have put a safety line on you. But... I didn't... I wasn't thinking."

"It's not your fault. I shouldn't have been out there to begin with."

"Rhys, if you hadn't been there... Lyruc would... There's no way I could have pulled him back by myself. And by the time I had gone to get help..." She sniffed loudly. "One moment you were there... and the next you weren't. I don't ever want to experience something like that again."

Rhys kissed her hair. Kallen eventually pulled away, and together they went to the galley. Andy, Kyo, and Kashim met him there to welcome him back.

"We searched for you with a spotlight," divulged Andy, "but the waves were just too high and violent. The only reason we knew where you were was because of Alina. She operated the engines and kept *Themis* near you." Andy nodded to Rhys. "I'm glad you made it. *Themis* would have been less exciting without you."

Rhys grinned. "Uh, thank you?"

Andy and Kyo passed him warm smiles and then left for the bridge.

"I wish I could have been on the boat that rescued you," said Kashim, sitting across from Rhys.

"You're still healing," said Rhys. "It wouldn't have made any sense."

Kashim chuckled. "Sure." His face became solemn once more. "Don't try to leave again." He nodded to Kallen who was leaning against the table. "She had a near hysterical breakdown and your sister stopped talking." Kashim patted Rhys' arm. "Take care of them."

Kallen glanced at Rhys shamefacedly and then went to help Alina cook. Kashim stood and left the galley. All who remained were Rhys, Alina, Kallen, Hodge, and Vinz.

The girls cooked and served the food and, just as quietly, the small group ate. Afterward, Vinz escorted Rhys back to his cabin. "Kashim's right," the Overseer said, watching Rhys as he sat on his bed. "When you get the chance, spend some time with Kallen and Alina."

"Kallen is fine," asserted Rhys, gingerly touching his ribs.

"I'm more concerned about Alina." Vinz closed the door behind him. "It's true, Alina piloted *Themis* during the storm. But... "

"But what?"

"She's stopped communicating with anyone. She hasn't spoken to any of us since you went overboard."

Rhys held his arm out for Vinz to help him stand. The moment he was on his feet, Rhys was down the hallway and back in the galley. He went to Alina, who was washing a pan, and pulled her to him. He pressed his forehead against hers and opened all communications between them.

Rhys, please don't, murmured Alina.

Rhys held her face and made their eyes meet. *I'm here. I haven't left you.*

Alina's lip trembled, and she looked away. *When I... tried to contact you... I couldn't. There was no connection.*

Hey, I'm here. I haven't left you.

Tears began falling down Alina's cheeks. *Rhys... I was alone. I couldn't talk with you. I couldn't see you. I was... the only one.* A sob erupted from her throat. *I was the only one here.*

I know, I know. I'm here.

Alina sobbed into his shirt. *I was the only one!*

Rhys held Alina's head. *I'm sorry, I'm sorry.* Her crying coming hard, Alina slipped to the floor. All the while, Rhys held her in his arms.

They stayed that way with the others looking on for several minutes. There was nothing he could say to comfort Alina. All he could provide her was the constant reminder that he was safe and that they had each other; they were not alone.

Eventually, Rhys nodded to Hodge who gently pried Alina from him and escorted her to the cabin across the hall. Kallen pulled Rhys to his feet, kissed him, and took him to his quarters. Exhausted by everything, Rhys lay down—with Kallen's help—and, after reminding himself that he was safe, fell asleep.

20
SOLO FLIGHT

RHYS WOKE WITH KALLEN THE following morning and, after dressing, followed her into the galley to help her cook. When it became obvious his help was redundant, he sat at the table and thought to himself.

They were three weeks from Brechin. He and Alina had two options. Firstly, they could offer themselves as bargaining tools in hope their presence could bring peace. He had heard numerous times that Brechin was unlike the other cities they had come upon; it was technologically advanced and comprised of people from Rhys' heritage. What they could offer that the city didn't already have was a mystery. If they considered this option, however, it was vital that he and Alina be taken together. One leaving the other was not possible.

The second option was that they offer a technologically-advanced piece of equipment. The only item he knew that fit that description was the magnetic sunboard which he had yet to pilot.

After eating, Rhys went to Vinz's cabin.

"Rhys," acknowledged the Overseer, reclining on his bed, a book on his knees.

Rhys wished the repairs to Vinz's door were complete. "I want to talk with you about the board."

Vinz sat up and laid his book aside. "What about it?"

"I know how it works. I think I know how to operate it… I just… I need to know where it came from. I need to know it's history."

"And why do you need to know that?"

"Because, in order to operate it properly, I will have to connect to its computer using mine."

"You talk as if you're a machine," scoffed Vinz.

"That's the part of me I'm worried about. If I connect to the board, there is a chance my computer will become corrupt in the process." Rhys gazed at Vinz solemnly. "So, I need to know everything about it before I risk myself."

"My father used to tinker with it. I remember him becoming exceptionally frustrated with it and going through piles and piles of books, hoping to find answers."

"Nothing was ever said about how to operate the board or pilot it?"

Vinz shook his head. "Not ever."

Rhys withdrew the necklace he now regularly wore. It had been the only item to remain with him during his night at sea. "And this?"

"I was told it's vital to the operation of the board. That's it."

"And your parents," said Rhys. "They were both pure-bloods?"

"No," replied Vinz. "My mother was. My father was a native of New Arbroath."

"So, the generations before you, there were more than just two?"

"Yes. There was a handful of people who had settled on this planet after they were forced to crash-land here. They were captured or killed off," said Vinz. "My parents included."

"Why?"

"If you do not assimilate to the Pantarak world, you are eventually killed. Once my parents were captured, my mother refused to assimilate according to the Pantarak way, and she was killed."

"Assimilate. What do you mean?"

"Mate, become integrated into the system. My mother was killed because she would not bow before the high priest and adhere to the societal rules she was placed under. My father was killed because he was her husband."

"And your grandparents? Did you know them?"

"I met them twice before they were both assimilated into the Pantarak capital. I'm sure they're probably still there."

"And their parents?"

"I don't recall," replied Vinz.

Sensing the Overseer was becoming bogged down with memories, Rhys changed the subject. "So, once I turn on the computer, I will be able to link with it, however, that's just the first of the problems. I still have to learn how to pilot it."

"You're on your own," Vinz admitted. "I've sunk countless hours into that thing. It's yours now. Why the sudden interest in its operation?"

"Because it will become a bargaining piece once we reach Brechin. I doubt they have something like it."

"You'd be surprised what they have," mumbled Vinz. "At any rate, our first challenge will be to pass our own troops. Merchant ships are allowed entry into Brechin with the proper documentation, but we are not a merchant ship."

"We're diplomats," said Rhys.

"Diplomats without documentation," corrected Vinz.

"Will they try to sink us?"

"No. They will most definitely stop us though and ask that we turn back. If we don't, *then* they'll sink us. After all, there's no telling what our actual business is in Brechin. For all they know, we could be planning to incite war anew."

"And what happens if we get through?"

"They'll pursue us for a short while but eventually give up. Tension is high right now between our troops and the Pantaraks'."

"Will we face much trouble from the Pantaraks once we enter their waters?"

"No, because we look like a merchant ship. I can only hope that Leo can get us to the proper people once we dock."

"One problem at a time," concluded Rhys.

Vinz nodded in agreement. "Getting past our own troops comes first."

Rhys looked at him incredulously. "Why go through all of this? Why put yourself at risk? What do you get out of this?"

Vinz chuckled grimly. "I never tire of your straightforwardness." He thought for a moment. "For peace. War is cyclical. If we don't do something or try to change the status quo, who will? We have the power and the resources. It's possible we can't make a big difference, but maybe we can push others in the right direction."

"Does this have to do with your family?"

"Everyone I've ever known has hated the Pantaraks for their religious zealousness and their narrow-mindedness. Generations of people have killed in the name of religion or to acquire freedom from the oppressive regime. Many believe that everyone willingly becomes Pantarak. The empire has absorbed countless towns, but in truth, there are thousands of people who are under Brechin's rule simply because they can't fight the empire's military. So, they carry out the Pantarak expansion in order to live in pseudo-peace." Vinz wearily stood. "I have the knowledge and the background, I have the crew, and I have you and Alina. I can make a difference."

"Why don't you… want revenge for your parents?"

"One problem at a time, right? Sometimes that's all we can handle. Oh, and Rhys? Would you tell Hodge to pick a time and meet here to rebuild my *gawan* door?"

That afternoon, Rhys, Hodge, and Vinz sat on the upper deck to calculate, cut, and install a new sliding door for Vinz's cabin. Once it was placed, they cleaned up and went to the forward hatch to discuss the boards. Rhys explained to Vinz all that he had discovered but didn't go into detail the exact pieces of equipment that came with the board.

Later that evening, as Rhys sat in the galley watching Alina cook, he asked in their tongue, "Have you seen Leo?"

"He spends most of his time outside on the upper decks." Alina stirred the contents of a pot. "I'm surprised you didn't see him up there while you were working on the door."

Rhys made a mental note to check on the newcomer and then sat and translated while Alina cooked. Andy joined him later to read and Hodge silently played cards on the floor. That night when Leo finally returned to the cabin, Rhys sat up and looked at him.

"Did you wait up for me?" Leo laughed, swinging himself onto the top bunk.

"Why do you spend so much time on the upper decks?"

"You aren't my crew." Leo leaned casually on his elbow. "I have no need to become acquainted with you. I'm going to be paid either way."

"Would it not be more enjoyable to spend time with others?"

"The women, yes. But it turns out both are taken, though I'm sure your woman would be interested in a more *open* relationship."

Rhys ignored the comment. "What do you do all day? How are you not bored?"

"Honestly, I just can't be locked away with you people. You make me insane with your sanctimonious talk. You speak incessantly about what is morally right, but not a one of you has the power to change an empire."

"Is that why you stay outside all day? To be away from us?"

"Yuh," replied Leo, lying back.

The next morning, the crew fell back into their daily routines. Rhys rose with Kallen and prepped the sunboards for launch. After breakfast, Hodge, Kashim, and Rhys met in the forward hatch. Once the ship was anchored, they lowered the hatch door.

As Rhys helped Hodge prepare the new board for launch, Kallen and Leo joined them. "So which of you is the pilot?" quizzed Leo.

"Hodge and Kashim," said Rhys.

"Not today," replied Hodge.

"What?" Rhys looked between them. "Why? Is something wrong?"

Hodge and Kashim exchanged looks before Kashim said, "You're taking my board today."

"Are you sure?"

Hodge kicked water at Rhys. "You'll be fine."

"Don't worry, we'll be right below," assured Kallen, motioning to the dinghy on the wall.

Rhys glanced between Hodge and Kashim. "So... who's launching first?"

Hodge grinned wolfishly. "You are."

"It'll be best if Kashim and Hodge stabilize your board instead of me," Kallen explained. "Wait for us to launch before you take flight."

"What's wrong? Haven't you flown before?" interjected Leo.

Rhys tied his headscarf around his neck and kicked off his boots. As Hodge and Kashim worked to prepare his board, Rhys watched. He was ready. If he was ever going to figure out how to fly the magnetic board, he first needed to know that he could fly a normal sunboard. For his and Alina's sakes, he needed to succeed.

When Kashim motioned that the board was ready and balanced, Rhys swung up and positioned himself in a crouch as he had seen Hodge and Kashim do numerous times. He spread his feet apart and felt the board shift under him. He knew that the moment he left the hatch, the fin would spring up and he would have seconds to grab hold of it before toppling into a heap. Kallen stepped forward and started the fan.

Rhys steadied himself once more and then motioned to Kashim. The board flew from *Themis'* forward hatch. Rhys rotated, grabbed the fin's bar, and pulled it toward him. The fin swung upright and then strained against the wind. Rhys' muscles pulled taut as he leaned to counteract the fin's drag.

It was different not being with Hodge. Not only did it respond more quickly, but the tilt of his body made a bigger difference; he seemed to go much faster! Rhys glanced over his shoulder at *Themis* and then out at the vast horizon.

A few minutes later, Hodge launched. Once Kallen and Kashim joined them in the dinghy, Hodge began discussing flight with Rhys.

"Watch your balance," his friend shouted over the waves. "Don't assume the fin will do what you want." Rhys nodded. "Ready?" Rhys nodded again. "Whenever you want."

Rhys glanced down at the marks on the board where he was to place his elbows, knees, and feet once prone. He could do this. He and Hodge had done it numerous times.

He unlocked the fin and swung it overhead. He moved to lower himself but suddenly found the board floundering on the water's surface.

"The fin!" called Kallen.

Rhys leapt back up to lock the fin into position, but it was too late. It was already leaning precariously out over the water completely out of his reach. Rhys swiveled on the board, cut the engine so as not to drag the fin through the water, and waited for the board to come to a halt. Frowning, he glared at the sail. The latching mechanism wasn't as accepting on Kashim's board as it was on the new sunboard. He hadn't properly locked it into its wing position.

"What happened?" inquired Kallen, bringing the dinghy to idle beside him. Kashim slipped into the water.

"The fin didn't lock into place." Rhys watched as Kashim repositioned the sail.

"I didn't warn you," the large man admitted. "New locks are easier to use than old locks." He pushed the fin out of the water so Rhys could grab hold of the lateral bar. "Lock it into the original position." Rhys did as he was told. Instantly, the fin caught the wind, and he sailed off.

After a moment of smooth surfing, Rhys peered up at the lock that had foiled his first attempt at flight. He needed to become airborne!

Again, he kicked the locking mechanism, swung the fin overhead, and jerked it into place. There was a faint click and the board shuttered. Rhys dropped down and placed his elbows, knees, and feet into their assigned compartments. When he was balanced, he sat still for a long moment to feel the board. He wanted to remember what perfect conditions for flight felt like without Hodge.

When he was confident, he began manipulating the rudder and ailerons. The board leapt from the water and rushed upward in a draft of heated wind. As he gained altitude, he looked down at the dinghy. Hodge was soaring farther below him.

Rhys looked back out at the horizon. He was doing it; he was flying! With a triumphant cry, he banked the board to port to circle around. He couldn't stop smiling. He was flying.

Hodge eventually joined him. They motioned to one another before Hodge indicated that he should follow. Rhys waited for Hodge to bank once more and then followed him back to *Themis*. For the next half hour, they circled the ship, skimmed along the water's surface, attempted two high maneuverability techniques, and chased Kallen and Kashim.

By the time they returned to the water, Rhys was fatigued. His muscles shook in an effort to keep the board at the proper angle. Kallen and Kashim docked the dinghy followed by Hodge who once more demonstrated to Rhys the process. Rhys cut the fan engine and then placed his foot on the fin lock to prepare its dismantling. As he neared the forward hatch ramp, he swung the fin backward and crouched. Like a veteran, he skidded the board onto the ramp where Kashim and Hodge halted him.

Wind-whipped, he beamed at them. Kashim laughed while Hodge reached down and splashed water onto him. Rhys tried to swing off the board expertly, but the moment his legs hit the solid ramp, his knees collapsed and he plunged into the water.

"A little… tired?" crowed Kallen.

Rhys stood, pulled his sopping shirt off, and threw it at her. Kallen swatted it away and flung herself into the water. With surprising strength, she tackled him and pushed him underwater. Not to be outdone, Rhys grabbed her and dragged her onto the submerged ramp. Shrieking, she slung water at his face and tried to scramble away. Rhys crawled after her, jerked her back down, and sat on the ramp with her.

Kallen glanced up at Hodge and Kashim, who were chaining his sunboard, and then kissed Rhys' forehead. "What did you think?"

"I want to do it again," Rhys declared.

Kallen stood and pulled him to his feet. He could feel his thighs trembling. "When you can walk, huh?"

Once the boards and dinghy were put away and the forward hatch closed, *Themis* got underway. Rhys ate a hearty midday meal, took a nap, worked on his translations with Andy as company, ate dinner, and then retired to his cabin. As usual, Alina was not there—she had taken up sleeping in Hodge's cabin—and Leo was hanging out on the upper deck.

After a trip to the washroom, Rhys flopped into bed. If every day was like the day he just had, he wouldn't mind living on Earth. Though he knew it would have to end, he allowed himself to relive the experience of flying.

It was just before midnight when the door to the cabin opened. Rhys glanced up expecting Leo; instead, found Kallen. He was happy to see her because most nights she came in after he was asleep. Rhys watched as she searched the room.

"What is it?" he asked, sitting up.

She picked up a dirty shirt and slipped it between the door and the frame. Now completely aware of what the simple gesture meant, Rhys slid to the edge of his bed, heart pounding. Kallen glanced up at Leo's bunk before stripping out of her shirt, pushing Rhys' legs apart, and placing her knee on the bed. Hungrily, Rhys kissed her. His body hurt all over from the day's activities, but he would manage!

Kallen pushed him back on to the bed, kissed him for a moment, and then stood and slipped out of her dirty pants. Completely naked, she went to his belt and began undoing his shorts. With his clothes on the floor, she moved to the bed and straddled him.

The overwhelming desire for sex that he had kept at bay for weeks broke its bonds, and his hands went to her body.

21
BEST METHOD OF
COMMUNICATION

THE NEXT FEW DAYS WERE as if Rhys existed in a dream world. Despite his aching muscles, he flew every day without Hodge's aid. While the first two days consisted of one learning experience after another, Rhys found he had a proclivity for flight. By the fourth day, he could move with as much ease as Hodge and could bank tighter due to the weight difference between them. After the morning sunboard exercises, he ate, worked on the manuals, helped with chores around the ship, slept, ate, and then retired to his cabin. Kallen joined him an hour or so later to continue his learning of the human sexual experience.

In his spare time, he visited with Alina who had taken it upon herself to become proficient in everything she touched. She learned from Lyruc how to properly use firearms and accurately hit targets without the aid of Logos. She also spent time with Kyo during morning flight sessions fishing off *Themis'* stern and learning to butcher her catches.

Vinz introduced her to his favorite strategy game in which players tested one another's ability to formulate battle strategies and trap their opponent's flagship. Always eager to engage in logic, Alina enthusiastically threw herself into the game, beating every person onboard including Rhys. The only person she couldn't trap was Vinz who, by some miracle, always managed to keep her forces at bay. Often, the two could be found in the galley midafternoon staring intensely at the game board.

Everyone on *Themis* had their own schedule, their own pattern of behavior. It surprised Rhys how, despite the diverse set of activities he engaged in daily, he was still able to fall into a routine. On Caelestis, he did the same work, said the same things, and reviewed the same information habitually. He had a routine but was significantly less happy. Here, surrounded by people he liked and doing things that made his heart happy, he was content with his "routine" because it didn't feel like a routine. It felt like a home.

He enjoyed being around each of his crew members. Andy treasured silence just as Rhys did and could be counted on to serve as good company when work needed to be completed. Kyo began to open up to Rhys, which meant more late-night music sessions on the upper deck of the ship and even short-lived lessons. Lyruc took it upon himself to teach Rhys all that he could about the ship and even took Rhys diving to check on the ship's hull. Kashim, though silent and brooding, offered to teach Rhys navigation by stars and how to read weather, wind currents, and temperature fluxes. In all things relating to the environment, Kashim was expert.

Of course, Hodge was Rhys' companion in crime. Together, they raced recklessly through the skies, pushing one another to go faster, turn sharper, or descend quicker. They trained together, roughhoused in the galley, wrestled on the upper deck, and pondered the mysteries of Earth while watching the sun set. The man had the reckless fire of youth still raging inside him but years of experience guiding his common sense. He and Hodge were not rivals nor were they master and student. They were friends; it was as simple and as complex as that.

When Rhys wasn't with Hodge or working by himself, he was with Kallen. Each night, they engaged in sexual activities; his adoration for the woman grew. A deep need to be with her rooted within him and it became difficult to remember his life as a sexually ambiguous virgin. He had an intense desire to be everything she needed, to be the only person upon which she relied. On the now rare occasion that she had a nightmare, he woke her and wrapped her in his arms. When she smashed her fingers in the engine room door, he sat with her while Alina bandaged her wounds. And when Kallen lay in her bunk curled in the fetal position because her monthly cycle was wreaking havoc on her body, Rhys brought her warm broth and kept her company.

Kallen did things to him he didn't understand. She made him want to be strong, to be able to care for her and the others on the ship. She made him more patient, more level-headed, more caring, and more comfortable with his faults. The transformation in Rhys was almost immediate. He could feel himself changing, moving to a different rhythm.

Alina was his sister; she was the moonlight that guided him along the dark path. But Kallen was the sun. And just like all life, Rhys couldn't live without the sun.

Leo, the ship's newcomer, remained aloof as always. He spent much of his time on the upper deck lounging in the moving shadows of the sails, sleeping in their cabin, or scribbling at the notebook he kept tucked in his waistband. When asked what was in the notebook, he explained that he was an aspiring writer. No one believed him but, not wanting to cause trouble, the crew let the boy be.

Rhys' relationship with Vinz steadily improved. Having finally decided that he would forgive Vinz, Rhys made an effort to get to know the Overseer. When Kashim taught Rhys star reading and navigation, Vinz lay out on the upper deck and listened. Rhys tried on several occasions to engage Vinz in conversation or playful banter but found it difficult. The man had the very unique ability to keep himself emotionally detached from others. Rhys brought it up to Kallen on two separate occasions, but she brushed the subject aside explaining that was just who Vinz was. He asked Alina if she had noticed the Overseer's talent to remain distant, but she had replied indifferently. She wasn't concerned about his emotional availability, only his skills of logic.

Nine days into his new schedule, Rhys decided he was content to sail Earth's seas forever. He loved the water and he loved *Themis*. The only thing he didn't love was knowing that it would all come to an end once they reached Brechin. The life he and Alina had built on *Themis* was more than anyone from Caelestis could ever ask for.

As the sun set on another busy day, Rhys stretched out on the upper deck. A gust of wind buffeted the solar-paneled sails and rushed over Rhys. He took a deep breath and closed his eyes. He never wanted to go back to Caelestis; he never wanted to go back to space. Who would want to live in a black abyss when one could be surrounded by a spectrum of colors, smells, and sounds?

Attention, said Pathos. Rhys startled as it was the first time Pathos had said anything in the past three days. *Unidentified ship. Eleven degrees off the port bow.*

Rhys stood and looked out at the horizon where an almost indiscernible, black pinprick hung in the brilliant orange light of the setting sun. *What's its direction and speed?*

Rhys stood in silence as Pathos calculated the unknown ship's speed in relation to *Themis'*. Pathos finally replied. *It's unmoving.*

They're anchored? We're nearing the primary waterways only merchants use. Why would they be anchored? After a moment of deliberation, Rhys climbed down the deck ladder and entered the ship. He found Kallen lying flat on her back under the paneling at the front of the bridge. Vinz leaned over the top, studying the gauges. Andy sat at his station reading while Lyruc lounged in Vinz's chair. "Uh," said Rhys. Everyone looked at him. He pointed out the bridge. "There's a ship."

Vinz shifted his attention to the windscreen. "Where?"

"Off the port bow. It's difficult to see, but it's there. It looks like it's anchored."

Andy set his book aside, grabbed a pair of binoculars, and gazed out. "Yeah… he's right. There's a ship."

"They have merchant markings?" asked Vinz, snaking a wire down to Kallen's waiting fingers.

"Can't tell. We're too far out. It looks like a merchant ship though." Andy glanced at Rhys. "It's not moving?"

Rhys tapped Pathos' external unit. "I calculated it. They're not moving."

Andy leaned against his chair. "Why do you think they're anchored? We're nearing the primary waterways."

"Don't know," murmured Vinz, straining to hand another wire to Kallen. "Lyruc, inform the ship. Put everyone on alert. We're almost finished here."

As Lyruc reported the find through the pipe communication system, Rhys gazed at the vessel. It didn't make sense. Why would a ship anchor in the middle of the sea? Momentarily, Leo entered the bridge. "We should bypass it," he asserted, gazing at the ship through a monocular.

"Why?" hummed Lyruc, his eyes on Leo.

"Because no good can come from a ship that's camped out in the middle of nowhere."

"We do it all the time," argued Kallen.

Leo motioned toward windscreen. "There's smoke coming from the ship."

Rhys squinted, allowing Pathos to focus for him. Though he couldn't detect the smoke with his bare eyes, Pathos could. "He's right. The ship is smoking."

"Two possibilities." Leo passed the monocular back to Andy. "They really are in distress, or it's a trap."

"Who would have attacked them?" mused Andy. "We haven't seen another ship in days."

Kallen pulled herself out from under the paneling. "Pantaraks?"

"Why do you people always blame us for everything?" growled Leo.

Instead of snapping back, Kallen began helping Vinz reassemble the display. "Then what do you think happened?" the Overseer prompted.

"Nothing. It's a trap." Leo started for the door. "But this is your ship, Great Overseer. Do as you like."

Once Leo was gone, Lyruc offered, "If you want, we can dump him with the other ship."

"No, we need him," replied Vinz. "We'll circle the ship, get a better understanding of what's going on, and then decide. Perhaps once we're closer we'll be able to see more."

As they neared the distressed ship over the next hour, it became evident that something was, in fact, aflame, though the source of the fire was not visible from *Themis'* point of view. They circled the ship keeping about 200 meters between them.

"There are people," murmured Alina who had joined them a few minutes prior.

"I wish I could see what was on fire," Vinz remarked. "I don't understand. If they've been out here for so long, why hasn't the ship just burned to the water?"

"And no other ships have crossed our navigational field either," added Rhys. He looked to Vinz. "Trap?"

"Possibly," replied the Overseer. "But... if we were in the same predicament, I would want someone to help us. Bring us in by 150 retems."

Rhys watched as several people on the upper deck frantically waved their arms and articles of charred cloth. Others drew water up the side of the ship to throw at the flames.

"Entering striking range," reported Andy. "Distance—"

Themis quaked and then lurched. Vinz grabbed Kallen before she slammed into the chair while Rhys and Lyruc clung to one another for balance. A series of alarms began sounding.

"Engines one and three, offline," reported Andy, gripping the ship's wheel. "Engine two at 30 percent and dropping. The rudder's seized."

Vinz gazed down at the newly-repaired energy sensor. "Power levels decreasing. We're at 12 percent." He growled. "They've got us." The Overseer whirled around. "Lyruc, arm the crew. Alina, go with him." As they left, Vinz turned to Rhys. "Lock all external doors and bar the portholes. Hide anything valuable in the storage unit under my bed. Go."

Rhys sprinted from the bridge. He locked the outer doors and went through every cabin, barring each of the portholes with reinforced wood. He grabbed the most valuable medical supplies in his emergency pack, as well as a handful of Vinz's books, and threw them in the storage slip in the floor boards under Vinz's bed.

By the time he returned to the bridge, two men-filled dinghies had gathered around *Themis*. "Who are they?" Rhys asked, watching as people began climbing the stairs up to the bridge.

"Not Pantarak," said Vinz. The entire crew was on the bridge. "We armed?"

A loud pounding shook the outer bridge door followed by a rough voice. "Open up!"

Vinz approached the door. "What do you want?"

There was a long moment of silence before a dull humming began grinding at the door.

"Kallen, you and Alina get down to the forward hatch. Prepare the dinghy for launch," ordered Hodge, grabbing Alina and pushing her toward Kallen.

"Nobody is leaving the bridge," declared Kashim. "The bridge doors are stronger than the ones leading out the ship. If they have cutters, the other doors will be child's play to them."

Hodge pushed Alina into the corner behind him and readied his short rifle. Rhys glanced at Kallen, worried. He didn't want her hurt, but he knew she was a fighter. If there was going to be a battle, she was going to be a part of it. Rhys positioned himself by her side, linked the plasma firearm he had strapped on his arm to Pathos, and prepared himself. The others pulled away from the door and racked their rifles and short arms.

"Do not fire unless we are fired upon first," said Vinz. His voice was more tense than usual.

The locking mechanism, which kept the outer door sealed, dropped onto the floor, allowing sunlight to filter in. The door swung open to reveal a group of five armed men. They stared at *Themis'* crew for a long moment, their eyes passing over each person.

"Him," said one of the men, standing in the doorway. He pointed to Vinz. "And him." He nodded to Rhys. The invaders shouldered their weapons and barreled through the open door.

"Don't shoot!" commanded Vinz as the men grabbed him and shoved him toward the doorway. Andy and Kashim leapt at the men in an attempt to pull them off Vinz, but they were met with gun barrels.

The two men deposited Vinz onto the outer platform and then reentered the bridge. Rhys backed away, his heart hammering. He wasn't frightened—though he probably should have been. He was angry. He felt violated. These men had trapped his ship, boarded uninvited, and were now picking crew members out for slaughter.

"Rhys!" barked Vinz from outside.

"Come on," said one of the men, motioning for Rhys.

"Get out," Rhys snarled.

The man pushed past Kyo. Rhys sensed Kallen move beside him, and suddenly the man lurched back, yowling, a knife in his arm. Frantic to keep Kallen safe, Rhys shoved her out of the fray and leapt for the swarthy man nearest him. With ease, the interlope blocked the blow and struck Rhys in the stomach with metal-covered knuckles.

An electrical wave of energy rushed through Rhys' gut. He opened his mouth in a silent cry and collapsed onto the floor, completely paralyzed. His eyes were clamped shut; his lungs were still, shocked into submission. He could feel no air entering through his nose or mouth. He could hear nothing. He felt conscious but not present. For how long? He couldn't tell.

In the darkness where his mind's eye slept, Pathos' voice, though distant, filtered through the murk. *Consciousness regained. Electric stimulation successful. Vitals: elevated. Brain wave activity: nominal. Initiating secondary vitals analysis. Analysis complete.*

Rhys' eyes snapped open. His limbs flailed momentarily as he tried to grab what he could to stabilize himself. Gasping, he sat up. He was surprised to find himself on one of the foreign dinghies. Blinking, he looked at the boat's occupants—three men, himself, and Vinz. Rhys met Vinz's gaze. What had happened?

The Overseer glanced at Rhys, defeated. His shoulders were slack; his posture indicated that he was a prisoner, that he had no power.

Rhys looked at the three foreigners. All of them wore rags as clothing. One was completely shirtless. Their hair was dark, their eyes black and almond-shaped. Their second skin gleamed in the light of the setting sun. All three watched him warily.

Rhys found his hands bound with cord. Frowning, he peeked over his shoulder at the enemy's ship. From afar, the vessel appeared like a merchant ship; however, close-up, it obviously belonged to no port, nor did it belong to any merchant guilds.

The ship itself was about the same size as *Themis,* but its shape was less aerodynamic. Rhys concluded it had to be a slow-moving craft. It had two masts, but its sails were missing. Smoke still poured from a mysterious source on its upper deck.

Rhys? Rhys? came Alina's distressed calls.

I'm awake, murmured Rhys, watching as their dinghy approached the ship from the rear.

Are you hurt? What happened?

The shock knocked out Pathos, replied Rhys. *Is everyone fine?*

Yes. They didn't touch anyone else. Why did they take just you two? I don't understand.

We'll find out.

The dinghy turned toward the stern of the new ship and blasted up the ramp hanging in the water. Rhys rocked forward and then slid into Vinz. Rough hands jerked them from the boat and dragged them up a flight of stairs to the upper deck. There, a large barrel of old solar panels burned, producing black, billowing smoke that rose high into the sky.

The men shoved Rhys to his knees on the deck and brought Vinz to his side. Rhys glanced at the Overseer and then at the men. One of the men, who had been standing at the ship's metal railing watching *Themis,* approached them. Like all men on Earth, he was tall. His thick, black hair was dreaded and pulled into a horsetail at the back of his head. His jaw had a long scar etched in white while the side of his head showcased another old battle wound. Though his face appeared middle-aged, his body was young and fit. This was made extremely apparent by the vest he wore which revealed a broad, hairy chest, muscled shoulders, and toned arms.

The man, presumably the ship's Overseer, chuckled. "Knew we'd find some." He studied Rhys. "I didn't believe they could be so fair." The man's eyes slipped to Vinz. His mouth curled into a wicked smile. "And this one was already someone's catch. He's got the markings to prove it. How'd you manage to get away?" Vinz grimly gazed at the deck. "I asked you a question," growled the man. "From whose care did you escape?"

Rhys started to stand, but hands pushed him back down. Tired of being maltreated, he lashed out with a kick. His strike didn't connect, but it cleared the space around them. Off-balance, he stumbled to remain standing. "What do you want?"

"This was the one you claimed was dead?" asked the brawny man.

"We pulled him from the ship, but he didn't have a pulse," replied one his subordinates. "And then he seized in the boat and woke up."

The man approached Rhys, his gate a swagger. He passed an appraising eye over him. "Where are you from? Brechin?"

Rhys remained silent.

"Not Brechin, eh? That's surprising seeing as your hair is gray like an old man's." The man leaned forward and touched Rhys' hair near his brow. Rhys jerked away, pivoted on his foot, and slammed his heel into the man's gut. The man didn't flinch. "Sit down, boy," he growled, knocking Rhys' knees forward. Unable to stop his fall, Rhys smashed his chin on the deck. Simmering in pain and rage, he glowered at his captors. "And you?" The man moved to Vinz. "Where're you from?"

"New Arbroath," muttered Vinz.

The man raised Vinz's chin so their gazes met. "Whose care were you under before you settled in New Arbroath?"

"Yeeta Barail."

The man nodded. "Not many men escape her alive."

Vinz's response was solemn. "I am aware."

In thought, the man rubbed his scruffy chin. "Perhaps I should return you to her."

Rhys saw Vinz turn pale. "Please... don't."

"Hey!" shouted Rhys, struggling to his knees. "Bastard! Don't touch—"

The man leapt forward, grabbed Rhys' shirt collar, and jerked him from the deck. "Boy, don't you *ever* address me like that again!" The Overseer threw Rhys back to the deck where he landed in a crumpled pile. "You Pantarak scum don't deserve to breathe the same air as us."

Wheezing, Rhys drew himself up. "We're not Pantarak!"

"You're sailing toward Brechin," replied the Overseer. "Only people who go there are merchants, Aabeshian military, and Pantaraks."

"We're not Pantaraks," snarled Rhys. "We're diplomats en route to the capital!"

The man burst into laughter. "Diplomats? Two young fellers like yourselves?" There were calls of agreement from the man's crew. "You should have just said you were paying homage to the capital or some bullshit."

Rhys pushed himself to his feet, and the laughter died. "We are *not* Pantarak!"

"Easy boy. We got others on board. You'll be joining them. Best not to let them hear you denying the great gods of the stars."

"It's the truth!" Rhys shouted.

Vinz called, "Rhys… Just leave it."

Rhys stared at Vinz incredulously. "No! Get up, Vinz. Get up!"

"Restrain him," ordered the rogue Overseer.

Hands grabbed Rhys' shoulders and pushed him down. *Pathos,* cried Rhys.

Charging emergency deflection system… Charged.

Rhys felt energy jolt through his body. The two men, who had their hands knotted in his back, yelped and rolled off him. Rhys stood and glared at the rogue Overseer. "Touch me again and see what happens."

Rhys, said Alina suddenly. *I'm ready.*

Rhys glanced at *Themis* and, seeing several figures atop her upper deck, smiled grimly. "You're at a disadvantage here, Overseer," he said. "Start providing information, or your men will start falling."

The rogue Overseer spat on the deck. "What is this *gaw—* "

There was a sudden *thwack,* and the man nearest the outer railing of the rogue ship stumbled and fell to the deck, his leg gushing blood.

"Prepare to fire," shouted the rogue Overseer as his men scrambled for their weapons.

Rhys charged the man and slammed into him. Another jolt of energy left his body, shocking the Overseer into submission. Heaving, Rhys knelt at the man's head and placed his knee on his neck. The ship's crew, which had been rushing in all directions, came to a standstill—all weapons pointed at him.

"I can kill him," Rhys warned. "You know it wouldn't be hard." He added pressure to the Overseer's neck. "Stand down." When no one moved, Rhys shouted, "I said, stand down!" The crew lowered their weapons. "Put them on the deck. Do it!" He nodded to the nearest man. "Unbind me. Now." The man approached Rhys. "Touch me wrong, I'll have you on the deck unconscious as well."

Momentarily, his hands were free. He pulled the Overseer's rifle to his shoulder but kept his knee on his captive. "Now, tell me—who are you people?"

"Slave traders," supplied Vinz.

"Slave?" Rhys waited for Pathos to explain the concept. "You abduct people and then sell them into slavery?"

"They specialize in selling and trading Pantarak slaves," Vinz continued, his voice low.

"To whom?"

"People who hate Pantaraks."

Rhys relaxed his hold on the rogue Overseer's neck. He had thought only the Pantaraks were evil. He had thought only *they* were his enemy.

"The world isn't so black and white..." muttered Vinz.

"But for what reason? Why would... I don't understand. What purpose has the human race for enslaving one another?"

"Why... do you... " whispered the Overseer under Rhys' knee. "Why do you talk as if you're better than us?"

Rhys rose to his feet. "Because this bullshit... this is something humans on Earth do." Rhys glanced at the Overseer who was watching him from the deck. "No civilized race would enslave one another, murder one another... torture one another." Rhys crossed the deck and pulled Vinz to his feet. Once Rhys untied him, he turned to the rogue Overseer. "Bring your prisoners up here."

"No."

"Rhys," chided Vinz.

Rhys couldn't understand. The world he had come to know had just been flipped upside. All at once he both hated everyone with the deepest of loathing and wished them peace.

Rhys, please come back, said Alina. *Leave this for another day.*

Disgusted, enraged, and unsure of how to continue, Rhys started for the ship's ramp where the dinghies were docked. He sensed Vinz behind him.

"Hey! Kid," called the Overseer. Rhys looked over his shoulder at the man. "Where are you from?" Rhys glanced at Vinz and then pointed upward to the heavens. "You know how much we would be paid if we brought you to either the Pantaraks or the Aabeshians?"

Vinz rested his hand on Rhys' shoulder as a warning.

Unwilling to accept anything Vinz had to say anymore, Rhys strode back across the deck. The entire crew stiffened at his sudden approach. "You seem to be a man who knows a good trade," Rhys began, planting himself before the rogue Overseer, "so I offer this challenge."

The man smirked. "A challenge?"

"A fight. Your best man against myself. If I win, you give up your trade and come with us."

"And if *I* win?"

"Without struggle, I become your prisoner and you can take me to Brechin."

"Rhys," barked Vinz the exact moment Alina did through Pathos.

Rhys held his hand out. "Do you accept?"

Without hesitation, the man shoved his hand into Rhys' and they shook. Grinning wolfishly, the Overseer nodded to one of his subordinates. "Adasi." As the slave traders' fighter lumbered forward, the Overseer said, "We may be slave traders, but we honor our word. A fair fight using no weapons, only skill and strength. And... you can't do that thing you did earlier."

Rhys slipped the stolen rifle off his shoulder and passed it to Vinz. Knowing his Overseer wanted to stop the wager, Rhys pushed him away. *Don't interfere, Alina,* said Rhys.

You're stupid, she fumed.

Rhys rolled his neck and pulled at his arms. *Use what energy you need to protect the external unit,* he told Pathos.

Thirty-six other queries concerning stylized fighting, grappling, and combat are available for download, replied Pathos. *Would you like to access them?*

No, I don't have the energy to accept so many and still fight. Not after utilizing the deflection system. Just focus on protecting the external unit even if it means rerouting biological energy reserves and knocking me unconscious.

Understood.

"This man is Adasi," explained the rogue Overseer, moving across the deck to the ship's railing to give them room. "He is a war veteran, expert sharpshooter, and this ship's primary tactician. What about you, Grayhair? What's your story?"

Rhys pulled at his legs and then knelt to re-lace his boots. "I am Rhys Falkrow from Caelestis, a human colony outside of this solar system. I have neither studied martial arts nor engaged in war." He stood and gazed at Adasi.

Unlike the rogue Overseer who was a rather lean man, Adasi was broad-chested, burly, and layered with muscles. His nearly black skin was riddled with a variety of scars, scrapes, and old cuts. He too had a thick horsetail of black dreads knotted at the back of his head. He wore no shoes, only a pair of cut-offs and a loose blouse. He was at least twice Rhys' size and three times his weight.

The man, Adasi, despite his horribly intimidating appearance, regarded Rhys in confusion and wonder. "Why did you choose this then if you've never studied or fought?" he asked.

"Because I know that that's what will speak loudest to you people," said Rhys.

"Boy, before your internal organs are smeared all over the deck," said the rogue Overseer, "you said you two were diplomats?"

"We're on our way to Brechin to meet with the high priest."

"And why would they listen to someone like you?"

"Because I have something they want," replied Rhys.

"Which is?" asked Adasi.

"Myself and my sister."

The rogue Overseer who, until that point, had been leaning against the deck railing, stood. "Wait, you're willingly going to give yourself over to the nobles in Brechin?"

"I'm going to Brechin to bargain for peace."

"You don't *bargain* for peace," countered the rogue. "You fight for it. Besides, there's no talking with the Pantaraks. They're illogical people. It's not in their nature to question."

Rhys grinned. "Then you can help me negotiate with them once I win this fight."

The rogue Overseer burst into laughter. "And what part does this man play? What use have you for a former slave?"

Rhys motioned to Vinz. "He is our Overseer and our primary tactician. He's an engineer, mechanic, and scholar. His ideals are what will change the world."

"Adasi," chuckled the rogue Overseer, "shut this naïve kid up."

Instead of moving into a fighting position as Rhys did, Adasi continued to stare.

"Let's go," the rogue Overseer barked.

Adasi looked at his boss. "I don't want to."

"Humor has never been your strong suit."

"I can't fight him," replied Adasi. "I'll lose."

"Don't bullshit," said the rogue Overseer. "Do it."

Adasi backed away, shaking his head. Rhys saw no fear or regret in Adasi's gaze, only intrigue and solemn respect. "Can't do it. Sorry."

"Hanu," called the Overseer.

Another man drew away from the crew and approached Rhys. He glanced at Adasi and then prepared himself for a fight. The man, who Rhys recognized as one of his capturers, was tall and lanky, taller even than the rogue Overseer. His skin was tan and pock-marked, his eyes a muddy brown. His hair was cropped close to his scalp to reveal two separate scars. Another scar in the shape of a half-moon decorated the upper half of his left arm.

The man pulled himself into a fighting stance with both fists held out before him. Though Rhys didn't know the fighting styles of humans today, he knew what they had been and intended to draw upon that knowledge. He positioned himself into his stance—one fist at his cheek, the other outstretched before him. He spread his feet apart and relaxed his knees. If he was going to win this fight, he needed to move without hesitation, think, and be deadly accurate. As much as he hated having to place his hands in a violent fashion on another human, he knew that in this world it was what communicated loudest.

His new opponent, Hanu, studied Rhys for a moment and then feigned an attack. Rhys didn't move. It would take more than a poorly executed bluff to force him to counter. This seemed to concern Hanu because the man drew away and changed his fighting stance. Rhys remained motionless.

Hanu once more faked an attack to the left and then leapt at Rhys. With a sharp strike, Rhys blocked his punch, exchanging the blow with a knee thrust. Wheezing, Hanu grabbed Rhys with surprising strength and weaved his arms around Rhys' shoulders, effectively trapping Rhys in a hold.

Rhys struggled for a breath's moment before judging that he would be unable to break the embrace. This man wasn't simply a fighter; he was a grappler, someone who specialized in holds and take-downs. He had misjudged his fighting style.

Gathering all of his strength, Rhys lurched downward to loosen the man's grip and then sprang up into his gut. Though the motion wrenched both of Rhys' shoulders, it was successful. The moment the pressure on his neck and shoulders came off, he pivoted on his foot, whirled around, and smashed his heel into Hanu's upper thigh.

He couldn't give the man time to grab his leg! Rhys shifted his balance and then lunged. Despite the crippling blow to his thigh, Hanu blocked Rhys' advance and delivered a series of rapid-fire punches. As Pathos read the trajectories, Rhys dodged.

When Hanu fumbled in his volley, Rhys saw his chance. Spinning, he whirled his heel around and upward, forcing his torso to dip toward the deck. He felt his boot brush Hanu's face, but there wasn't a definitive connection. Using the momentum, Rhys rotated his body again and struck with the other leg. The toe of his boot caught Hanu's jaw.

As Hanu toppled backward, Rhys drew away and poised himself for another attack. Exhaustion was starting to seep into his movements. He wasn't a fighter. Even if he was in the best shape of his life, he was not trained to move in stylized combat. In addition, he had shocked two people earlier.

As they drew closer to one another, Rhys kept his gaze fixed on the spot between Hanu's eyes, allowing his periphery—and Pathos—to detect motion.

Hanu threw a punch, which Rhys dodged, and then reached between them to shove him. Rhys drove his arms down to prevent the man from grabbing his clothes, but he was a fraction of a second too slow. Before he could comprehend what had happened, he had been flipped over Hanu's shoulder and thrown to the deck. He felt energy leave his body as Pathos emitted a light screen around the AIs external unit.

"Stop!" ordered the rogue Overseer.

Panting, Rhys drew himself up.

"No cheating!"

"I-I'm not cheating," panted Rhys.

"What was that light just now?"

"A shield," replied Rhys. He pushed his hair away from Pathos' external unit. "To protect this. That's it. I swear."

"What is it?"

Rhys shook his head, wheezing. "I'll tell you if he beats me."

The rogue Overseer motioned impatiently for the fight to continue. Rhys only barely made it to his feet before Hanu was bearing down on him. He swung tiredly at Hanu, but victory seemed to be escaping his clutches. Pathos was wearing him out.

Rhys' foot connected with Hanu's thigh once more before the man grabbed his leg and dumped Rhys at his feet. More energy left Rhys as Pathos shielded its external unit. Determined to end the fight, Rhys pushed his left heel behind Hanu's left knee and swung his right foot.

Although his attempt to sweep his opponent's legs out from under him resulted in Hanu being sent to the deck, it was enough. Rhys spun on his back to his knees and, once his feet were under him, lunged at Hanu. With his elbow, he slammed into the man's face, sending Hanu sprawling.

Rhys took a few more steps after the attack and then collapsed to his knees, breathless. He couldn't keep going. He needed to rest, to sleep. Pathos had used too much biological energy. Wearily, he looked under his arm at Hanu who was moaning but somehow still conscious. Rhys mustered the last tendrils of strength in his body and crawled to Hanu. He wrapped his arms around the man's neck and forced him into a chokehold.

"Call the fight!" Rhys shouted hoarsely, struggling against Hanu's strength. "Call it."

No one moved.

"I could kill him. Call the fight."

The rogue Overseer just gazed at him solemnly.

Rhys cranked down on Hanu's neck, cutting off the man's air supply. "He has.... about nine hits until he's... unconscious." He moved his head away from Hanu's frantically searching hands. "Five hits." Silence. Before Hanu's body went limp, Rhys released the man's neck, allowing his opponent air. Rhys laid Hanu's head on the deck and scooted away. Shaking, he pushed his legs under him and attempted to stand. The moment he put weight on his knees, they gave, and he collapsed back on the deck.

Remaining biological energy at 22 percent, reported Pathos.

Stay conscious, ordered Rhys.

Once biological energy falls below 15 percent, consciousness must be foregone in order to maintain regular functions.

Understood. Rhys pushed himself onto his heels. He felt light-headed.

"An admirable battle," said the rogue Overseer, approaching Hanu and Rhys. He held his hand out to his crewmate and pulled the man to his feet. "You do, of course, realize that having worn yourself out, you can no longer fight us if we decide to take you two prisoner."

Still winded, Rhys grinned. He wiped at the sweat running down his forehead and forced himself to stand. "However true that may be, you won't be able to."

Instead of being threatened, the Overseer chuckled. "And why is that?"

Rhys motioned to *Themis.* "My sister. You lost the fight; now, you're coming with us to Brechin."

"Why would *diplomats* need slave traders?"

"Because you're smart and you have something that we need," replied Rhys.

"Which is what?"

"The machine you used to trap our ship." Wearily, he approached the rogue Overseer and held his hand out. "Will you be honoring your word, Overseer?"

"You've shot one of my men, shocked me unconscious, and nearly killed Hanu." The Overseer took Rhys' hand. "I can't wait to see what you do in Brechin."

Alina, come take care of these people, ordered Rhys.

I'm on my way, came the reply.

"Our doctor is on the way to tend to your wounded man." Rhys withdrew and regarded the remaining crew members. "You men will remain under the command of your Overseer. Should any of you disagree with this arrangement, we will drop you off at the nearest port outside of Brechin."

"Your name is Rhys?" asked the Overseer. "I'm Irvine Clemons. This is my First Mate, Adisa Naram."

"I'm Rhys Falkrow." Rhys motioned to Vinz. "This is Vinz Amadorri."

Irvine looked between Rhys and Vinz. "Amadorri? Like the, eh, what's the word—the prophet? The one in The Hallowed *Magris*?"

"One of my ancestors," explained Vinz.

Irvine pointed to Rhys and then to the sky. "And you're from… up there?"

"Yes."

Irvine nodded, impressed. "So, you actually are diplomats."

"In a sense."

"And you two are hoping to prove *what* once you reach Brechin?"

"A couple of months ago, New Arbroath was attacked by Pantaraks," said Vinz. "We tried negotiating a truce, but that didn't work. So, now we're heading to the capital."

"That's very vague," murmured Irvine. "And you thought you'd just bring us along?"

"Yes," said Rhys with a small smile.

"Uh-huh… And why aren't you Overseer?"

"Because Vinz is," replied Rhys, peering over his shoulder. The dinghy from *Themis* had arrived.

Momentarily Hodge, Kashim, and Andy appeared at the top of the aft ramp, rifles drawn and ready. Kallen, who was also armed, and Alina followed. "The one who needs attention is over there." Rhys pointed to the man lying on the deck holding his leg. Alina glanced at the crew members and then hurried to the man, her traveling medical bag slung over her back. Hodge and Kashim followed.

Rhys turned to meet Kallen and Andy. As Kallen silently checked him for injuries, Andy tended to Vinz.

"I take it the doctor is your sister?" Irvine inquired.

"She is." Rhys glanced at the Overseer from under his lashes. "She's also the one who shot your man."

Again, Irvine did not have the reaction Rhys expected. Instead of being angry, he nodded, impressed. "She's a good shot. Very few can hit a target at that distance."

"Even fewer can do it and intentionally miss vitals," Rhys boasted.

Irvine rubbed his scruffy face. "What are ya expecting from us? Brechin is at least two weeks' travel, assuming we don't come across another storm."

"You will remain along our port and accompany us to the Aabeshian military line."

"Ahh... the Golden Corridor." Irvine nodded. "We could help you cross that. We're a slave ship after all, and the military uses our captives often."

Rhys held his tongue. He would fight for Irvine's slaves later. Right now, he needed to return to *Themis* and lay down before he passed out.

"Overseer!" called Alina.

Both Vinz and Irvine looked at her. She motioned Irvine to her. With the Overseer's attention elsewhere, Rhys let his fatigue show to Kallen. Under his breath, he murmured, "I can't keep standing. I've used too much energy." She nodded and glanced at Vinz and Andy.

Once it was determined that Irvine's man was in need of surgery to remove the bullet, the process of disembarking the foreign ship hastened. Within minutes, the injured crew member—whose name was Vega—was in the galley on *Themis* being prepped for surgery. Adisa, Irvine's First Mate, sat in the corner, silent and watchful. Hodge and Andy remained in the galley with Alina.

In the meantime, Rhys anchored *Themis* and monitored Irvine's ship *Grisle* for any suspicious activity. Vinz and Kallen worked on repairing the bridge door while Kashim and Lyruc brought in the sails. Kyo sat at his station on the bridge, surveying the maps before him.

Rhys looked at Vinz as he passed a tool to Kallen. "Are you going to tell me what that was about back there?"

"No," replied Vinz.

"You owe me an explanation," Rhys murmured. "Your inability to lead and act nearly cost us both our freedom."

Vinz remained silent.

Rhys wearily stood, waited for the room to stop spinning, and then stumbled from the bridge. Once off the inner stairs, he leaned against the wall, his head in his hands.

"Rhys."

He looked through his fingers at Alina who stood in the doorway of the galley. She wiped her hands on her bloodstained apron and went to him. With warm, gentle hands, she pried his fingers from his face and examined his knuckles. She studied his scraped elbow and then the bleeding gash on his chin.

"Come on," she said in Nefegian. She led him into the galley and motioned for him to sit in one of the empty chairs at the second table. Her bullet-wound patient, who was on the first table, watched him warily. Adisa's eyes also followed Rhys. "I'm sorry I didn't tend to you sooner," Alina murmured.

"That's a nasty cut," remarked Hodge, leaning against the stove.

Rhys ignored them all and closed his eyes. He felt Alina begin to wash off his chin. When she drew away, he said, once again in their mother tongue, "I feel so lost. What are we doing here?"

"I was hoping you would tell me," Alina softly replied. There was silence between them as she began applying a numbing agent. "You need sutures."

"Our journey—yours and mine—ends in Brechin."

"I know."

Feeling her hands tremble, Rhys looked at her. His sister was fighting back tears with a strong face. "You tried to die on me again," she continued in Nefegian. "You collapsed on the bridge, and they dragged you out... like it was nothing."

"The electric shock jolted Pathos and disrupted my biological-mechanized interface," explained Rhys.

Alina turned to prepare his stitches. "I don't care," she snapped. "You're reckless."

"Can... we not do this now?" Rhys glanced at the others watching their conversation with interest.

Alina stopped what she was doing and looked at him. "You are all that I have, Brother. If you leave me in this world alone... "

"You're not alone," corrected Rhys. "You have Hodge."

"That's not what I mean," replied Alina.

"Again... can we not do this now?" Rhys grimaced at the pain in his head. His eyes were heavy; he was dizzy. He slipped into a light doze within the next few seconds.

Before he knew it, Alina was tapping his face to wake him. "Don't touch them for the next two days," she instructed with little warmth. Rhys started to stand, but his knees buckled under him. He fell back into the chair.

Hodge gripped his arm and pulled him to his feet. "Slowly," his friend murmured.

Rhys felt his head loll to the side. He could no longer control his fatigue. Hodge dragged Rhys to his cabin and deposited him on his bed.

"Hey," said Rhys. He could no longer open his eyes. He hoped Hodge still stood nearby. "If... something happens to me... promise you'll take care of Alina."

Hodge took his hand and gripped it tightly. "You didn't even have to ask."

Rhys tried to smile, but he was already asleep.

22
MISUNDERSTANDINGS AND MISGIVINGS

WHEN RHYS FINALLY WOKE, IT was dark. How long had it been since Hodge had flopped him onto his bed like a dead fish? He went to rub his eyes, but his hand brushed his sutured chin. He flinched and sat up. He was the only one in the cabin. Alina was probably with Hodge, but where was Leo?

Rhys stretched and then went to the washroom to relieve himself and clean up. He emerged sometime later with glowing silver hair. The dye had completely worn off. Shirtless, he wandered down the hall, glancing into rooms as he went. From the sound of it, Alina, Hodge, Kashim, and Lyruc were asleep. Where was Kallen? He checked the galley, which was empty, and then the forward hatch. It too was dark. Growing worried, he poked his head onto the bridge. Only Andy and Kyo were in attendance, and neither acknowledged his presence.

He slipped onto the outer staircase and began climbing the ladder to the upper deck. He peered over the top of the bridge and surveyed the deck in the moonlight.

At first, he thought that perhaps what he saw was a trick of the shadows, an illusion caused by the half-moon's light reflecting on the deck or water. Only when Kallen pulled away from Vinz's embrace and kissed the Overseer's cheek did Rhys comprehend the situation.

For a long moment, he just stared, his hands clamped on the ladder railing. Something in chest felt as though it snapped; his heart thrummed in his ears while his stomach shriveled in on itself. He watched as Kallen whispered, held Vinz's arm to her, and then motioned to the horizon. Vinz chuckled—a warm, deep sound—and leaned in to kiss her face.

Rhys slid down the ladder and rested against the railing on the outer platform. He felt ill; his chest hurt. Was such a thing even possible? Physically, there was nothing wrong with him. He had only one minor injury but nothing that would result in his heart hammering against his ribs so very, very painfully.

Alina, he whispered, becoming increasingly worried.

Rhys?

Something's wrong, he wheezed.

What's wrong?

He entered the ship and leaned heavily against the door. *I don't know.*

He heard Alina roll out of bed and pad down the hall to him. *What's wrong?* She climbed the stairs and knelt beside him.

My heart, he murmured.

Your heart? she replied worriedly. *Pathos, report to me his vitals.*

Heart rate: 98. Blood pressure: 128 over 84. Oxygen intake: 97 percent, responded Pathos. *Beta brain waves are reading unusually high, indicating emotional distress and anxiety.*

Nothing's wrong with his heart?

No.

Alina's hands touched Rhys' face. *What's wrong? What happened?*

I don't know, replied Rhys, though he knew. *I'm sorry. I guess… I'm just really stressed.*

You're lying.

I'm just tired.

You've been asleep for a day and a half. You can't be tired.

Rhys tried to push himself to his feet, but Alina held him down. *I'm just stressed. I'm sorry for having woken you. I became worried when my chest started hurting.*

Brother, said Alina solemnly.

Rhys removed her hands from him and stood. *I'm fine. I'm sorry. I should have waited to see if it would pass before waking you.*

Please try to take it easy, said Alina, following him down the stairs. *You think you're invincible because we're—*

Thank you, Alina, interrupted Rhys as he stalked back down the hall to their room. He closed the door behind him and sat on the edge of his bed.

Perhaps what he had seen was a misunderstanding. Kallen had told him she was not sleeping with Vinz. They had always been honest with one another, so he trusted her.

Even so... the image of her kissing Vinz, the sound of Vinz's intimate chuckle, and the Overseer leaning his face to hers caused the edges of his trust to fray.

Rhys grabbed his chest once more. His heart felt like it was trying to either dive into his stomach or claw its way up his throat. Either way, it was excruciating. When he tried to breathe normally, he instead audibly sucked in air. What was this feeling? It tasted familiar, like something bad he had once eaten.

Betrayal.

The word struck his mind as hard as it slammed into his heart. Betrayal—it was the same feeling he had experienced in Paducah when Saccui told him that Vinz had attempted to use him as a bartering chip.

This hurt exponentially more.

The door to his cabin opened. Rhys looked up expecting Kallen. Instead, Leo entered and climbed into bed. Rhys wanted to ask him where he had been—after all, he had searched the entire ship for Kallen—but he couldn't bring himself to open his mouth. After a moment, Leo rolled over and looked down at Rhys. "Thought you'd like to know: your woman is alone with the Overseer on the upper deck."

"I know," replied Rhys, trying to hide his contempt.

Leo stared down at him. "Aren't you going to... go do something?"

"Like what?"

Leo lay back. "I don't know. Go interrupt them or... go push your Overseer into the sea. I don't really care. If I was in your situation, I would want someone to tell me though."

Rhys stood. "Thanks."

Leo grunted in acknowledgment and then rolled over. Instead of going straight to the upper deck, Rhys hung out on the inner stairs. He sat in silence for nearly half an hour, plotting, thinking, imagining, and planning. He ran through several mock conversations but never settled on one.

Eventually, he grew tired. The emotional trauma was making it difficult for him to think clearly and rationally. He waited another hour and then returned to his cabin.

He dozed restlessly for an unknown amount of time before rolling out of bed and going to the forward hatch where he memorized the magnetic board's extension system and build. He returned briefly to his cabin to retrieve the leather thong with the chip that Kallen had given him and attempted to tear the converter out of the board to better analyze it.

By the time dawn arrived, Rhys was ready to test the board. Despite having been able to study the converter, trace its wires, and gain a better understanding of the board's capabilities, he was frustrated. The magnetic board clearly needed to be connected to the pilot in order to transmit its readings. If he could complete a connection using Pathos, perhaps he would be able to pilot it. Of course, that brought him full circle to endangering himself and possibly corrupting his AI.

While sprawled out under the board, the forward hatch door opened to admit Hodge. "Thought I'd find you here." His friend surveyed the mess around him. "So... you've been here a while... " Rhys continued to study the underbelly of his board. Hodge joined him. "Do you know what you're looking at?"

Rhys pointed to each of the items. "Magnetic reader. Intake. Converter. Exhaust. Central computer. Converter."

"Please tell me we get to take it out soon."

Rhys sat up, rubbed his neck, and began collecting the tools around him. "Today or tomorrow."

"Finally," groaned Hodge, helping him. "I saw Vinz try to put that thing in water once. It sunk to the bottom of the ramp."

"I'm not Vinz," Rhys spat.

"No, you're not," replied Hodge warily.

Once the forward hatch was tidy, they went to the galley, all the while attempting to trip each other as they walked down the narrow hallway. Rhys couldn't help but laugh when he tagged Hodge's leg too hard and the man stumbled into the galley doorway. Alina, who was at the stove cooking, startled.

"Sorry," both mumbled through smiles. Hodge crossed the room, kissed Alina's cheek, tapped her butt fondly, and grabbed a slice of bread. He broke it in half and threw part of it to Rhys who only barely caught it.

"Rhys says we can test the magnetic board today," said Hodge.

"Really?" chuckled Alina as she added a liquid to her concoction.

"He even guarantees it won't sink."

"Have you considered how you'll pilot it?" she asked over her shoulder.

"I want to see what it does in the water first," replied Rhys. "I don't want a board that can't even float. If it crashes, I need to be able to retrieve it. I'm not keen on deep-sea diving."

"Then it's settled?" asked Hodge excitedly. "After breakfast?"

Rhys shrugged. "We probably won't be able to leave the ramp, but we can try."

"Have you thought of adding a fin to it? We have a spare fin and solar panels."

"Do we have a normal fin? A cloth one?"

"You'd have to talk to Kallen about that. If we do, it's somewhere deep in storage. None of our boards can really use it."

"Let's just see that it doesn't sink first," said Alina, setting the meal to cook. She wiped her hands and joined them at the table. "Hodge says that because we're moving further east, there's a possibility we'll find new fish."

"So long as it isn't *liiman*," muttered Rhys.

"Contrary to popular belief, Kashim is a good teacher. He's gruff, but he's a good teacher," Alina retorted. "We've not gone through our entire food supply like last time thanks to me and him."

"I'm horrible at fishing. I'm too impatient." Hodge mimicked the act. "Once I set the bait, something better be there. What's the point then?"

"It's man versus beast," replied Alina. "You have to trick the fish into wanting your bait."

"And how does one make one's bait appealing?" teased Hodge. Alina puffed her cheeks in playful contempt. "Do either of you know where Leo goes? The boy is missing most hours of the day. The ship isn't that big."

"The upper decks," replied Rhys. "He's a writer. He enjoys solitude." He thought for a moment. "Where was he when Irvine and his crew invaded *Themis*? He wasn't on the bridge with us, was he?"

"No," replied Hodge, rocking his chair. "He disappeared and stayed that way until the man Alina stitched up and his bodyguard returned to *Grisle*. He then casually emerged from Vinz's cabin."

"And what did he say?"

Hodge shrugged. "Nothing. He didn't offer any excuse for why he had disappeared during the raid."

"Does the earring he wears hold any significance for the Pantarak people?" mused Alina.

Again, Hodge shrugged. "I really don't know. You need to talk to Vinz. He's the one with that kind of knowledge."

Alina sighed. "That makes me wonder though."

"What does?" interjected Kallen, entering the galley dressed in her daily uniform of a sleeveless shirt and dirty pants.

Rhys glanced at Kallen and, finding it too difficult to look at her, shifted his eyes elsewhere.

"What makes you wonder?" Kallen repeated, looking between them. When no one answered, she fidgeted. "What?"

Alina cleared her throat, stood, and went to stir the bubbling pot. Kallen watched her before looking to Hodge and Rhys.

"Rhys? What's wrong?"

Alina filled two bowls of soup and set them on the table before Rhys and Hodge. When it became obvious he wasn't going to respond, Kallen crossed the room and rested her hand on Rhys' shoulder. Her touch made his heart hurt and his blood simmer.

"Kallen," warned Hodge.

She looked at him in confusion. "What? I don't... What's going on?"

The panic and concern in her voice both infuriated Rhys and made him want to reach out and embrace her. Instead, he avoided her gaze. If he just ignored her, she would leave, and they wouldn't have to discuss what he had seen.

Unfortunately, that was not what Alina had in mind. Rhys' sister wedged herself between them, pushing Kallen away. "What were you doing last night?" Rhys could hear no anger in her voice, but he could sense it in the way she stood firmly planted at his side.

"What are you talking about?" asked Kallen. "I haven't... " Rhys glanced at her in time to see something akin to realization cross her face. Her mouth fell open slightly, and she looked at Rhys. "You... saw us?"

Alina moved herself into Kallen's field of vision. "What were you doing?"

"I was just talking with Vinz. That's it. I swear." Kallen attempted to push through Alina, but Rhys' sister was stubborn. "Rhys. We were talking, that's it! I swear. Alina... move. Rhys."

Annoyed by her blatant attempts to once more protect Vinz, Rhys seethed, "Stop lying." Silence blanketed the galley. "I saw you two."

"Rhys, I'm not lying!" argued Kallen. She pushed Alina aside and grabbed his chair. "I'm not lying to you."

"I saw you two." Rhys peered up at her.

Flushed, Kallen fidgeted. "Rhys... that was nothing. *Please*, believe me."

"Kallen." Rhys stood. "Our rules of engagement were simple."

"Why don't you *ever* believe me?" cried Kallen. "Why do you never trust anyone?"

"I saw you kiss him!" barked Rhys.

"He was upset. I was talking with him and comforting him."

"Like he comforted you all those times before?" He immediately regretted saying that, but it was too late. Eyes moist and jaws clenched, Kallen ran from the room.

Rhys stared at the spot where she had been standing. He didn't like the emotions stirring inside him—anger, jealousy, rage, contempt. It made him feel like a completely different person.

After a long moment, he sat and attempted to eat the meal Alina had prepared for him. Despite forcing several bites into his mouth, he continued to shake with anger. Bowl half empty, he hit the table and stalked out of the galley, enraged.

For the next hour, he sat on the upper deck in the shade of the sails contemplating the tumult of emotions that had risen in him. The situation with Kallen upset him, but his own reaction to finding her alone with Vinz bothered him most of all. He had tasted these emotions briefly before, but the power they now possessed frightened him. He craved a fight with Vinz.

"Hey!" called Hodge from the deck ladder. "Are we going to try to launch your board or not? I got permission to test it. We're stopping for a bit."

"I'll be right there," Rhys replied. He looked off the ship's port side to find *Grisle* slowing to a halt as well. Part of him wanted to go meet with Irvine and Adisa once more to gain a better read of their characters, however, for the time being, he needed to concentrate on his board. If it wasn't operational by the time they reached Brechin, he and Alina would be used as bargaining pieces.

Rhys descended to the forward hatch where he found Hodge and Alina already lowering the hatch door. As Rhys and Hodge studied his board and talked about the plan, Alina sat on the ramp and dangled her feet in the water.

"Just put it in the water," she said, interrupting Hodge who was explaining to Rhys what had happened last time Vinz had placed the device in the water.

Rhys and Hodge exchanged looks, picked up the board, and waded onto the ramp. After checking that all of the compartments were sealed and the board was fully extended, they placed it onto the water. Hodge let out a loud whoop as the board floated between them.

Rhys firmly pushed the board downward to test its weight capacity. It didn't move. He smiled at Hodge excitedly. "Help me." With Hodge steadying him, Rhys swung his weight onto the board and knelt effortlessly on it. "Yes… " he murmured. He pumped the board several times to check its buoyancy and then stood up.

"How does it feel?" asked Hodge, balancing the board.

"Different than the others." Rhys took a step forward and then two back along the board.

"Next," cheered Hodge. "Let's run it through some water!" Rhys jumped off, dragged the board out of the water, and began preparing Hodge's unit for launch. Within minutes, Hodge was surfing off *Themis'* bow.

"Rhys," said Alina as Rhys waded into the water with his board. He took his shirt off and looked at her. "You're not going to connect to that thing today, are you?"

"No," he replied, adjusting the leather thong around his neck. "I'm just checking its buoyancy and how well it moves. Don't worry. I'll let you know if I decide to do that."

He took a running leap and dove off the ramp into the water, board to his chest. Once he was a short distance from the ship, he waved to Hodge who had been circling. Rhys knelt on his board and waited for Hodge to pass him.

"It's coming down your right," shouted Hodge, surfing past him. Rhys watched as the rope tied to the stern of Hodge's board skimmed under the water's surface. He traced it until he caught sight of the yellow cloth they had tied to the end of the rope. He slipped his hands under the water and allowed the rope to pass through his fingers. When the yellow cloth neared, he clamped down on the rope. He was violently jerked forward. Though he was prepared for the force, the motion still wrenched his shoulders.

His board began skimming along the water behind Hodge's unit. Laughing, he moved to his feet—and nosedived, plowing into the water and smacking his face hard. Sure that he had ripped the sutures on his chin, Rhys surfaced, checked his wound, and then searched for the board. He found it floating less than a meter away.

Within minutes, he was once more skimming across the water behind his friend. This time, however, instead of moving directly to his feet, Rhys spent time testing the board's balance and calculating where he should be positioned to optimize the board's movement.

Eventually, he managed to draw himself to a crouching position and then, despite his aching muscles, into an erect stance. He leaned back against the rope and widened his stance on the board. Wincing as the rope bit into his hand, he shifted his weight from side-to-side, causing the board to move accordingly. After a few attempts to move it a short distance, he leaned hard to the right. The board banked sharply and tore over the small wake Hodge's craft had created.

Rhys cried out in surprise but kept his balance. Though the water was rougher and he could feel Hodge's board straining against the force, he was freer to move. He stayed there just long enough to become comfortable before zipping back over the edge of the wake and flying across its opposite bank.

He landed on the rougher waters, hit a small wave, and rolled head-over-heels. He came up sputtering and frantically searching for the board. Again, he found the board a short distance away. Rhys swam to it, climbed atop, and looked about for Hodge. Already his friend was circling. Rhys pulled at his arms and gyrated his neck in an attempt to stretch. He was going to be sore later.

Despite being in Hodge's wake, it was, a hard ride back to *Themis*. Rhys' lower back and shoulder muscles burned and his hands bled from the rope. Hodge dropped him off at the forward hatch, and Rhys swam his board onto the ramp where Alina—and Kallen—waited. With Alina's help, Kallen lifted his board from the water and propped it against the wall while Rhys turned to wait for Hodge. No one said anything about the blood flowing freely from his hands into the water.

With little trouble, he caught Hodge's board and docked it. Realizing he was leaving bloody handprints, Alina stepped in to take control. Rhys waved his bleeding hands in the water. There were two or three semi-deep gashes across both palms and the padding on his lower fingers was raw.

"Not our smartest idea," remarked Hodge, lifting his board out of the water with the crank.

Rhys turned to reply but instead found Kallen standing next to him in the water. Their gazes met for a moment before she took his arm and guided him off the ramp. He wanted to snarl at her or to jerk away, but he was tired. Once out of the water, she knelt, wrung the water from his pants legs and rolled them to his knees.

"Let's get your hands looked at," said Alina, attempting to intercept.

Kallen, however, stood and gently removed Alina's hand. "Come on," she said, leading Rhys from the forward hatch. In silence, they went to the galley where Kallen motioned for him to sit. She retrieved the ship's medical tools and began withdrawing gauze, an antibacterial cream, and cloth wrappings. She sat on her knees before Rhys and studied his hands. "Does it hurt?"

"No," replied Rhys.

Kallen doctored his hands, wrapped them, and then sat back and looked at his stitched chin. "Alina will have to tend to that. It's not bleeding, but it is open."

Rhys gazed at her, hurt, angry, and tired.

"I'm sorry," she breathed, kissing his hands with tender lips. "I'm sorry. I shouldn't have been alone with him." Rhys shifted his gaze to the floor, but Kallen drew it back by touching his cheek. "Honestly—we only talked. I kissed him fondly, as you would... a brother or sister."

"Why were you so close to him?"

Kallen lowered her voice. "I can't tell you that."

Rhys didn't expect that answer. He peered incredulously at her. "Do you know how bad that sounds?"

"I do, I do. Rhys, please. Believe me," she said quietly. "Nothing happened between us."

"Why were you so close to him?"

"I can't tell you that."

Rhys stood, against Kallen's protests, and returned to the forward hatch to find Hodge and Alina quietly talking by his board.

"Help me dry it," muttered Rhys, grabbing a bit of cloth. Alina glanced at Hodge and then left the forward hatch.

"Don't," said Hodge as Rhys began wiping down the board. "You'll get your bandages wet."

Though Rhys wanted to do so anyway just to spite Kallen, he listened. After a long moment, Hodge asked, "Do you want me to talk to Kallen or Vinz?"

"No."

"Did she say anything just now?"

"I asked her why she had been so close to Vinz, and she told me that she couldn't answer that."

The subtle look on Hodge's face let Rhys know that had not been the correct response Kallen should have provided. "Sorry," he murmured. As Hodge worked in silence, Rhys despondently stared at the floor. Despite his great victory with the board, he felt more alone and defeated than before. Eventually, Hodge tossed the damp cloth into a bin and motioned them out. "Go rest. I'll let Andy know we're good to go."

Rhys followed Hodge from the forward hatch and then shuffled down the hall to his cabin. As usual, Leo wasn't there. Physically tired, not mentally, he sat in the floor and began working on his translation materials. After a few minutes of trying to clasp a writing utensil with his bandaged palms, he gave up. Instead, he began organizing the manuals and reviewing all that he had completed.

He managed nearly two hours of work before he stretched out on the floor and went to sleep. He woke sometime later to find Vinz standing in the doorway.

Rhys frowned at him, glanced at the porthole above him to check the time, and then sat up. As he cleaned the papers and manuals around him, Vinz watched. "What?" Rhys finally growled.

Vinz entered his cabin and closed the door behind him. Rhys stopped what he was doing and looked up at the Overseer. "We need to talk," said Vinz.

"About what?"

"Kallen," replied Vinz.

Rhys piled his translation materials in their designated corner and sat on his bed.

Vinz went to the porthole and looked out. "After my parents were killed, I was captured and put aboard a slave ship. I lived on the slave ship from the ages of 12 to 15 until a crew member, Kashim, recognized my potential and snuck me off." He paused, swallowed, and then continued. "My initial time aboard was… traumatizing." Vinz pointed to the scars on the side of his head. "From the ship's Overseer. Having decided to keep me for herself, she shoved my head into a metal grating when I disobeyed one of her direct orders." He traced a faint scar along his brow. "Also from her. One of her rings did that." He pointed to another along his chin. "One of her mates slammed me against a metal door frame. The hinge caught my jaw."

Vinz took a few steps back and sat on Alina's bed.

"I was physically, emotionally, and sexually abused until Kashim dragged me out one night, and we escaped on the ship's dinghy into a local harbor. I have worked diligently since that day to better myself and the world around me. I have read thousands of books. I have studied history, sociology, politics, engineering, economics, and linguistics. I've researched peace and conflict across a wide platform of cultures and civilizations. I have built a ship with my bare hands and maintained a crew of like-minded individuals. I have done *literally* everything in my power to better myself so I might be able to move on from the miserable person I once was." Vinz clasped his hands between his knees. "And all of that fell apart the moment the slave traders boarded *Themis*."

Rhys stared at Vinz in a mixture of horror and awe.

"When I finally began searching for a crew... I came across Kallen. Aside from Kashim, she was the first person I actively recruited to work directly under me." His lips pursed. "I had never seen a human so beaten and defeated. She was torn from the inside out. On the few occasions I saw her with her grandfather or father, she was jumpy. She shied away from anyone who got too close." He smiled grimly. "I wondered if I had once looked that way."

"So you took her in," said Rhys.

"Yes. I'm sure Kallen has told you about our relationship."

Rhys met Vinz's gaze. "I want to hear it from you."

The Overseer nodded. "I had had some time to heal, seven years about, but Kallen was fresh from the cutting board. After seeing her handywork on the Old Man's sunboards, I started teaching her engineering in an attempt to help her heal and to readjust to normal life. After a couple of months, I could see improvements, but she still wasn't functioning in society. One day when we were working on the ship, she asked if she could stay the night knowing that my cabin was my home. I agreed... Does that make you angry?"

"No," replied Rhys, though he did feel a twinge of jealousy. "This was before my time."

"Despite the years of healing I had managed to do myself, seeing someone in a more desperate situation and being able to help them did more for me than anything else. And I enjoyed her company. She was the first woman who actually liked being with me for me, not because of my lineage.

"Because of this, I feel very comfortable talking to her. We've been in similar situations and have been traumatized by our pasts. It's easy for me to share with her my weaknesses. When in port, I can't even do that with Tessa." Vinz nodded. "That's what you saw last night. I had barred myself in my cabin since leaving Irvine's ship because... my metaphorical wounds had reopened." Vinz looked at him. "She knows. And now you know."

"Why were you so close to her last night?"

"Because... I needed her," Vinz said.

Rhys gazed at him. "What does that mean?"

"It was wrong of me to be with her alone."

"Do you have romantic feelings for Kallen?"

"Yes."

Rhys thought for a moment. He had no idea where to take the conversation or even how to respond. Instead, he simply regarded the Overseer.

"Kallen, however, made it clear to me last night that she does not reciprocate those feelings. So, don't blame her for anything. Direct your contempt at me."

"How does this work then?" murmured Rhys.

"I maintain an acceptable distance from her unless she indicates that she wants otherwise," replied Vinz. He met Rhys' gaze. "But she won't change her mind. You're hers now."

Rhys wanted to hate Vinz and to give him a tongue lashing, but he couldn't find the words. Vinz and Kallen's history extended far back, and he couldn't change that.

"Kallen has had eyes only for you since the night we brought you two aboard." Vinz smiled. "After you and Alina went to bed that first night, she came to me and made me swear I wouldn't use you two. It was obvious even then that she was enamored with you."

Rhys considered Vinz's words. He hadn't known that Kallen's fondness of him had gone that far back. Of course, in hindsight, it was obvious. She had started flirting with him almost immediately.

"She started singing." Vinz nodded to himself and looked to Rhys. "I didn't even know she sang. It wasn't until you came that she began doing it."

Rhys took a deep, calming breath and said, "That's it then?"

"That's it," replied Vinz. An uncomfortable silence ensued before Vinz stood and went to the door.

Feeling obligated to say something, Rhys muttered, "Thanks." Vinz nodded and left.

23
THE INSIDE GUIDE

RHYS DIDN'T SEEK OUT KALLEN immediately. Instead, he reviewed all that Vinz had shared with him.

The Overseer's story certainly shed light on a lot of Vinz's behavioral issues and his inability to communicate his emotions to others. It also made two things clear to Rhys. Firstly, Vinz's weakness was captivity. That explained why the Overseer didn't fight or struggle when the priest, Saccui, captured and tortured him and Kashim in Paducah. It also explained why he simply crumpled when the slave traders boarded *Themis*.

Vinz had suffered at the hands of both Aabeshian people—slave traders—and Pantaraks. He was more motivated to bring about change than anyone else. He had the education, the equipment, and the willpower. He just needed someone to bring it all together, harness it, and utilize it effectively.

Rhys thought back to all of the time and energy he had invested into Vinz's cause. After a moment, he sat up in bed and stared at the floor, a revelation stirring within him. "Huuuh... " he breathed. "I think... that's me—"

"All crew members to the upper deck!" boomed Andy through the pipe communication system. "All crew members to the upper deck. Whales!"

Rhys stood in confusion. Andy sounded excited, elated even. By the time Rhys made it to the upper deck, *Themis'* entire crew was leaning over the railing chattering excitedly. Even the ship's two moodiest people, Vinz and Leo, were present.

As if sensing him, Alina turned and waved. "Rhys!" she squealed, pointing behind her.

Now curious as to what could cause Alina to become so animated, Rhys joined them at the railing.

His eyes fell on a pod of great, gray marine beasts as long as *Themis* gliding alongside the ship. Periodically, one breached the surface and exhaled loudly, shooting thick clouds of mist into the air before retreating below the water line once more.

Rhys leaned far over the railing, gaping. They were enormous! How could anything so massive exist?

"I guess they're as resilient as humans," remarked Alina, her eyes lit with awe.

"They survived the mass exodus and whatever followed. Ah, Alina! Look!" Rhys pointed to a whale as it broke the surface and then dove headfirst, allowing its immense tail to come completely out of the water. "Look, look!" he exclaimed excitedly in Nefegian.

"Look at that one," gasped Alina, grabbing his arm and redirecting his attention to another whale doing the same thing.

Just below, there came a loud exhalation. Both Alina and Rhys peered down at a giant which had just surfaced next to *Themis*. With another loud exhale, the whale rolled leisurely onto its side to survey them with a dark, intelligent eye. Satisfied with what it saw, it disappeared under the boat.

Alina touched his arm and nodded to *Grisle*. Though the slave ship was a good distance away, Rhys could clearly discern men standing on her deck also observing the whales.

Eventually, the pod dispersed, disappearing north. Like the whales, the crew returned to their work and chores. Kallen, who had been hanging laundry along the upper deck, continued her task. Sensing now was the time for a private discussion, Rhys waited for the others to disappear below deck before joining her.

"What?" she asked, shaking out a damp shirt.

"You saw the whales first?" he asked.

"What of it?" Kallen turned and hung up the blouse.

Rhys watched her for a long moment. He had been in the wrong. He needed to apologize. Not knowing what else to do, he touched her arm to make her stop moving. Kallen kept her gaze on the deck. "I'm sorry," he murmured. "I didn't know the whole story."

Kallen stiffly pulled her arm from him, picked up the small bag of damp clothes, and said, "No, you didn't." And with that, she walked to the other end of the deck.

Rhys stared after her, confused. He had apologized just as he had before. Why wasn't she accepting his admission of guilt? Should he try again? He must have stood there for a long while deciding what to do because eventually Kallen passed him carrying the empty bag.

He jogged after her. "Kallen!"

The hostility on her face when she turned around halted Rhys in his tracks. "I'm busy." She climbed down the ladder to the outer platform.

Unwilling to go inside where he might run into her again, Rhys remained on the upper deck until dusk. He slept in the shade, cloud-watched, pondered on the whales, and paced. Kallen made a brief appearance late in the afternoon to collect laundry but immediately returned below without a word. Leo joined Rhys about the time Kallen left, and together they sat in the shade of the sails in silence.

When the sun began to slip below the horizon, Rhys stood and stretched. He glanced over his shoulder at Leo who had been writing. "Are you coming in?"

"No. Not for a while," Leo replied without looking up.

"What are you writing?"

"Creative work."

"Creative work? What does that mean?"

"Poetry, short stories, fiction," explained Leo patiently. Rhys leaned forward to see. The young man sighed and closed the notebook. "You're new at this, so I'm going to tell you straightforward—you don't ever look at a writer's raw work."

"Why not?"

"Because it's unrefined."

"But you spend so much time on it. How can it be unrefined?"

Leo rested the book on his lap. "Weren't you leaving?"

"Sorry." Rhys turned to go but stopped as he caught sight of the innards of Leo's book. He squinted at it for a moment and then leapt at Leo.

"What are—*Gawan!* What are you doing?"

Rhys snatched the book from Leo and danced away with it. He wildly flipped through it, his eyes searching the young man's neat, perfectly legible handwriting. Leo hurled himself at Rhys, and together they collided onto the deck. The wind knocked out of him, Rhys released the book and lay staring up at the sky.

"What is *wrong* with you?" barked Leo, his hands flying to the book.

Rhys sat up. "You're literate in Interstellar Nefegian." Leo froze. "How are you literate in Interstellar Nefegian?"

"Why does it matter?"

"Because Alina and I are the only ones who speak it."

The young man's response was low. "No, you're not."

"There are others?"

"Many of the nobles in Brechin speak it. Some are fully literate, but the majority of them can only speak it."

"Was it your first language?" asked Rhys, switching to his mother tongue.

Leo thought for a moment before replying similarly. "Yes, but it varies greatly from your own."

Rhys dissected Leo's words, taking note of the different sounds accompanying the vowels and the boy's odd accent. He could understand Leo, but it was going to take practice. Leo's Interstellar Nefegian sounded old and not as refined as Rhys and Alina's version.

"So, it was your first language and Aabesh was your second?" Rhys continued in Aabesh.

"Listen, I really don't want to discuss this with you. I'm here to direct your crew once you reach Brechin." Leo shuffled back to the main mast and sat against it. Rhys turned to go inside. "Uh, hey?" called Leo. Rhys looked over his shoulder. "No one else needs to know that I'm literate in your language. Understand?"

"Can I tell Alina?"

"Only her," replied Leo.

Rhys descended into the ship. As soon as he entered, the smell of food hit him, and his stomach roared to life. He found Kallen, Alina, Hodge, and Andy in the galley.

"Good timing," chirped Alina. "Dinner's almost ready."

Rhys glanced at Kallen, who stood at the stove, and then sat across from his sister.

Hodge nudged his chair. "How are the hands?"

"Not bad. They'll hurt tomorrow, I'm sure," replied Rhys. *Leo can speak Interstellar Nefegian,* he said to Alina.

Alina appeared physically as though she did not hear him. Instead, she nodded and said, "We'll have to put more salve on them tonight before you sleep." *How did you find out?*

I saw his book. He can speak, read, and write it.

What does that mean for us? Alina asked.

293

"Hey, I meant to ask, how did your board work this morning towing me?" asked Rhys in an attempt to hide their private conversation.

"You're fat," joked Hodge. "My board was moaning the entire time. I thought the rope was going to snap when you went outside the wake, but it held. You've got hands of steel."

I guess this means we have to be more careful with what we say around each other. If need be, we can communicate internally from here on out, said Rhys. "The magnetic board moved well, but it's not meant for water."

My concern, murmured Alina, *is that there will be others.*

He said there were others, that many of the nobles in Brechin speak it, though not all can read and write it.

That indicates that our culture and ancestors have had—and continue to—influence on the capital. Perhaps this is a good thing.

"Why do you say that? Looked like it surfed well enough," queried Hodge.

"No, the material was created for space," Rhys corrected. "That's the reason it moves so well and with such little drag." Kallen placed a plate before Alina and then served him. Rhys looked up to thank her, but she had already turned away.

He, Hodge, and Andy continued the conversation between bites, though Rhys' heart wasn't in it. He really just wanted to be alone with Kallen, but it was obvious she was hurt. It also became apparent that she was angry at Alina who, on more than one occasion, had jumped down her throat in Rhys' defense. Therefore, despite their attempts to make the meal less awkward, it remained tense.

Rhys retired to his cabin afterward and stretched out on his bed. For the first time in several days, he took a moment to analyze everything from an objective point of view.

He had had no idea that one person could make the room so hostile. Human relationships were complex, something that he had never experienced while on Caelestis. Furthermore, while human relationships between friends and crew members were intricate, they paled in comparison to the bond shared between two people romantically and sexually involved. How was he supposed to know what Kallen was thinking, what she wanted? She never told him!

Rhys laid his arm over his eyes. It had only been a day, yet he felt worn, fatigued from the drama and constant tension pulling at him. It was painful to look at Kallen and even more so to speak to her. She exuded irritation.

There was a knock on his door; Vinz appeared.

Rhys sat up. "What's wrong?"

"I wanted to talk with you."

"If it's about Kallen, can we... just postpone it? Please?"

Confused, Vinz offered, "It's about Brechin."

"Oh... Yes, of course."

Vinz entered and closed the door behind him. "Have you still not settled this thing with Kallen?"

"Apparently not," replied Rhys.

Vinz seated himself on the edge of Alina's bed. "I want your honest opinion." He looked at Rhys. "Am I doing the right thing?"

"Going to Brechin?"

The Overseer nodded.

"Why does my opinion matter? You were going there eventually."

"Not for a very, very long time," Vinz replied solemnly. "You and Alina prompted me to make a hasty decision."

"Do you regret it?"

"That's not what I asked," said Vinz. "Am I doing the right thing? Was it the right choice?"

"How can we know until it's over?"

Vinz sighed. "In your personal opinion, am I doing the right thing?"

"No," replied Rhys.

"Why?"

"We're placing too much trust in Leo. If we get to Brechin and he betrays us, we are trapped. Besides that though, do you know anything about Brechin? Is it the place we need to be?"

Vinz leaned on his knees. "What do you know?"

"About Brechin?"

"No. I can tell—you know something. What?"

"I don't know anything. I'm simply asking you a question."

In thought, Vinz regarded him before saying, "I've been there twice while a slave, but I didn't see much of it. Only the docks."

"The political system—it's tied to religious law, right?"

"Correct."

"So, the high priest has supreme authority?"

"Yes," replied Vinz.

"Who is below him?"

"Other clergymen and nobles."

"And the racial make-up of the capital's citizens?"

"From what I've heard, it varies by class. There are the nobles who can trace their blood lines directly to 'white gods.' Commoners—Aabeshian, Garamites, and North Landers—make up the rest."

"And we're thinking that by presenting myself and Alina, we will be permitted an audience with the high priest?"

"That is the hope, yes."

"And what if that doesn't happen? What's to stop them from taking Alina and I hostage and sinking *Themis*?"

"Nothing."

"And what do you know of Leo?"

"He comes highly recommended from a trustworthy source in Firekli. I was told he is knowledgeable when it comes to navigating Brechin and that he's got valuable contacts."

Rhys stood. "Wait here." He slipped out of the cabin and went to the upper deck where he had last seen Leo. Rhys activated his night vision. Leo was where he had left him near the main mast. "Leo!" he called.

"What?" barked Leo.

"A word?"

Leo tucked his book into his beltline and followed. He groaned when Rhys opened the cabin door to reveal Vinz. "What's this about?" growled Leo.

"Come sit," Vinz instructed.

Rhys closed the door behind them and crossed the room. Since Leo was seated at the end of his bed, Rhys chose to stand. "We're devising a plan that will guarantee us an audience with the high priest," he explained. "You've come highly recommended as someone who has contacts within the government. How can we make this happen?"

Leo shrugged. "I don't know."

"So, what is your plan once we arrive in Brechin?" probed Vinz. "Have you someone waiting at the docks to meet us? Or will you be taking us directly to a governmental building?"

Though he hid it well, Rhys could feel Leo's growing discomfort. "I haven't really… I don't have that part worked out yet."

"Then what's stopping your people from sinking our ship and killing all of us?" Vinz growled.

"They won't do that, not once we're docked."

"Why do you think that?" asked Rhys.

"I'll just tell them—you're diplomats." Leo looked between Rhys and Vinz. "The people at the docks aren't the ones you have to worry about."

When Leo glanced down at the floor, Rhys and Vinz exchanged looks. Neither of them believed him. "Are you a noble?" asked Rhys in Interstellar Nefegian.

"No," replied Leo.

There was silence for a long moment before Leo realized what he had done. He warily peered at Vinz who had the oddest expression on his face.

"He speaks my language," shared Rhys.

"How?" Vinz mused. It didn't appear as though he was angry, only intrigued and concerned. "Why can he speak your language?"

"It's not the exact dialect. But it's close enough that we understand one another." Rhys thought and then added hesitantly, "I believe he is a Pantarak noble."

The Overseer raised a brow. "And what led you to that?"

"He speaks, reads, and writes our language. He told me himself that many of the noble families are capable of doing so. It's, therefore, not a common ability amongst lower-class individuals." Rhys gazed at Leo. "I'm sorry, but we need answers."

"And I can't give you answers," countered Leo.

"Why are you on this ship?" Vinz stood. "What purpose have you guiding a group of miscreant diplomats? What's in it for you?" Vinz advanced on Leo. "What do you get out of this?"

When Leo next spoke, it was with alarming authority. "Back up." Vinz didn't move. Leo threw Rhys a look of annoyance before saying, "I'm Leucetios Damian, youngest son of Saloman Damian."

"And Saloman Damian. What is his official title?" asked Vinz.

"Minister of Education. He's also a professor at the university."

Vinz backed away from Leo and sat heavily on Alina's bed. "You're nobility. You're one of the royal families. What are you doing outside of Brechin?"

"Research," replied Leo matter-of-factly.

"But you're a kid."

Leo shrugged. "No one else would go."

Rhys cocked his head. "So it was an assignment?"

"More like a challenge."

"What was the challenge?"

For the first time since the conversation had started, Leo smiled mischievously. "You."

"Me?"

Leo leaned back on his hands. "The royal court received word regarding the appearance of two white gods and a half-blood in Paducah. Each of the 15 heads of the royal court wanted to send a representative to meet you, however, that would be too obvious. When single representatives were chosen for the job, they declined as what you had done in Paducah had also reached the court's ears." He shrugged. "I volunteered."

"And what is the court hoping to achieve by sending you?" asked Vinz darkly.

"Think of me as their welcoming gift. Once you get past the Golden Corridor, you're in my territory. I have power." Leo turned his head to show the cuff-earring outlining his ear. "Royalty wear these when they come of age."

Vinz opened his mouth to speak, however, Rhys interrupted him. "That's why you disappeared when the slave traders raided the ship."

"If Irvine and his crew found out I was onboard, they would tear this ship apart to get to me," said Leo. He smiled arrogantly. "So, take care of me."

"Well, this changes things," said Vinz.

"Yes," Rhys mused, "but in our favor. They *want* to meet us. They've sent a representative. Once we pass through the Golden Corridor, we shouldn't have any trouble meeting the high priest."

Leo made a sound, drawing attention back to him. "Meeting the high priest directly might be... difficult. He doesn't meet with anyone outside of the royal family heads and temple priests who preside under him."

"Then who would we be meeting?"

"The royal family heads," Leo asserted.

"Do they have the ability to declare war?" asked Vinz.

"They themselves cannot as that power belongs solely to the high priest, however, they have the power to persuade him to do otherwise. They hold more power than the nine temple priests do anyway." Leo sat up. "Is there any way we can keep this information between just us?"

Rhys glanced at the book tucked in the boy's belt. "Fine. We won't tell anyone about you. However, once we're in Brechin's waters, they have a right to know."

Leo nodded and stood. "Are we done? I haven't eaten yet."

The Overseer waved him off. "Yes, go."

Once he was gone, Rhys murmured, "This has worked in our favor." He looked at Vinz. "I feel good about this."

"I wish I could say the same." Vinz rose to his feet with a sigh unbecoming of his age. "Keep an eye on him." He clapped Rhys on the back and crossed the hall to his personal cabin.

24
MEETING ABOARD GRISLE

RHYS WOKE TO KALLEN'S SHRIEKS of terror. Flailing wildly in an attempt to grab Kallen from what he thought was an attacker, Rhys rolled out of bed and hit the floor hard. It was then he remembered Kallen was in her own cabin. He groaned and untangled himself from the blankets.

"What was that?" quavered Leo, sitting up in bed. Even in the dim moonlight, Rhys could see his eyes were wide.

"Kallen," Rhys explained. He slipped out the open doorway and padded down the hall to the other cabin. Everyone in her cabin was already awake; Alina sat in Kallen's bed. She returned to Hodge when Rhys entered the room.

Kallen seemed unaware of him, hugging her knees to her chest; a thick layer of sweat covered her from head to toe, and her clothes and hair stuck to her skin. Alternating silent sobs and heaves wracked her body.

"Hey." Rhys leaned forward to touch her.

"Go... away," she growled pitifully.

"Kallen." Rhys touched the side of her head in an attempt to comfort her. Instead, she startled horribly and glared at him through tears. Rhys held her fiery gaze for a long moment before sliding his hand to her arm and pulling. "Come on."

Kallen wrenched her arm from his grip. "I said *go away.*"

In a single motion, he leaned forward, slid his arms under her, and lifted her clear of the bed. To his surprise, Kallen didn't struggle or say anything. Rhys made sure he had her firmly in his grasp and then started down the hall to his cabin. In the darkness, Kallen slipped her arms around his neck and pressed her wet face into the curve of his neck.

When Rhys entered, Leo was standing near the bunk beds. "What's going on?" he asked.

"Bad dream," replied Rhys, placing Kallen on his bed. She rolled away to curl against the wall. Sensing Leo's gaze, Rhys added, "Everything's fine. Honest. It was a bad dream." Leo hesitantly climbed the ladder to his bunk.

Rhys lay down and breathed deeply. His heart still raced. He didn't like hearing her scream. Feeling Kallen's shoulder shaking as she tried to quell her crying, Rhys spooned her. He rubbed her shoulder and then slithered an arm around her and clenched her icy hands.

Kallen hugged his knuckles to her chest and relaxed, allowing her form to mold to his. Rhys buried his head in her shoulder, breathed in her scent, and kissed her hot cheek. "Would you like to go outside?" he murmured in Elali. "Would that help?"

Kallen shook her head. "I'm sorry," she whispered. Rhys kissed her shoulder and, with Kallen pressed comfortably against him, he fell asleep.

Despite once again being in the same bed, Kallen fidgeted the rest of the night. She grew hot and then cold, broke into sweats, and rolled from side-to-side in an attempt to become comfortable. Rhys gave her the majority of the bed and dozed in intervals. An hour or so before dawn, she disappeared into the washroom. When she didn't return, he tiredly crossed the hall and knocked on the door. "Hey," he murmured.

"I'm fine," came the immediate reply.

"Can I come in ?"

"Ehh, yes."

He opened the door. Kallen sat on the floor with her back against the wall. Her arms were wrapped around her stomach and her legs scrunched to her abdomen.

"What's wrong?"

"My... cycle," she murmured shamefacedly.

"Do you want me to make something warm?"

Kallen nodded. Rhys pulled her to her feet and guided her to the galley. He retrieved a blanket from their cabin and wrapped her in it. While he heated water on the stove, he leaned against the counter and gazed at her. She looked absolutely miserable. Her eyes were bloodshot from lack of sleep and heavy with the pain. Her hair, which was normally neatly pulled back from her face by a kerchief, was glued to her forehead and neck by old sweat. Her glossy gaze was set on the table.

Rhys added special leaves to water as he had seen Alina do, brought the brew to a simmer, and then served Kallen a hot mug. He sat beside her and watched as she wrapped her hands around it and put her face over the steam.

They sat in the galley for another half hour before she set her empty mug aside and tapped Rhys' arm. He woke from his doze. "Come on," she whispered.

Rhys stood, and together they returned to his cabin. Although hints of dawn peaked through the porthole, Rhys lay down beside Kallen, rested his arm across her hips, and immediately went to sleep.

It was not the crew that woke Rhys nor the smell of food wafting through the hallway but the ship's rocking. Squinting, he rolled his head back to look out the porthole. Where there should have been blinding sunlight, there were blue-gray clouds. He moaned, rubbed his face, and looked at Kallen who was stretched out across him.

Still tired from the night's action, he lay in bed and stared at the ceiling thoughtlessly. It wasn't until the ship finally dipped a little too steeply that he woke Kallen. With a foot placed against the bunk railing to keep them from rolling out, he caroused her from her sleep.

Feeling the ship's lurching, Kallen groaned. "I don't want to get up."

"They'll be needing our help," replied Rhys, though he agreed with her. He kissed her cheek and stood. Holding onto the bed railing, he dressed. He threw Kallen one of his blouses to cover her thin nightshirt.

Semi-dressed, Kallen climbed out of bed and held onto Rhys. "Stay inside the ship this time."

"Don't make me come get you then," he retorted. Kallen patted his butt and hurried from the room. Rhys heard her hit the doorway as the ship rolled one way and then the other. Quickly, he stuffed his feet into boots and jogged from the room. He stopped in the galley to find Alina, Kyo, Kashim, and Vinz. Bewildered by their calm demeanors, he asked, "Are we not... worried about the storm?"

Vinz, who was studying The Hallowed *Magris,* shrugged. "Kyo and Andy both agree it won't be bad. We've already brought the sails down and locked the engines. We just have to wait it out."

"Hungry?" asked Alina, holding a pan over its burner. She caught a jug with the other hand as it slid off the counter.

"Uh, yes. Please." He sat across from Vinz, glanced at the ancient book, and then at Kashim. "You're sure we don't need to be doing anything?"

"It's fine," Kashim assured.

Kallen joined them momentarily, as baffled as Rhys as to why no one was scurrying about in preparation for the storm. "Come eat," beckoned Alina, handing Rhys a plate.

"Where's Hodge?" Rhys asked between bites.

"Cleaning up the forward hatch and locking everything down," replied Alina. "I'll get him in a bit." She leaned against the counter. "Can anyone tell me why it is that since we've been farther out to sea, we've experienced more turbulent weather?"

Rhys nodded in agreement. "I don't understand either. The port cities all flourish because they live near the water, but it's my understanding that farther inland there are desert-like landscapes. At least, that's what Pathos reported."

"Earth is drying," Vinz solemnly explained. "It was once three-quarters covered by water but now, that is about 43 percent, roughly. This means that although the seas provide life for the port towns, those farther inland experience drought. Storms form primarily out here because they have the necessary forces and elements." Vinz pointed over his shoulder. "Inland, storms can't form. Due to a variety of factors like wind, sunshine, heat thermals, and a lack of moisture to absorb, it's just simply impossible." He looked back down at The Hallowed *Magris*. "Some people go their entire lives never seeing rain."

"Could we flee Earth?" asked Kallen, unusually pensive. "Would it even be possible?"

Rhys glanced at Alina who appeared amused. "No," he replied. "Not for our generation."

"Don't be so quick to judge," chided Vinz. "You haven't seen Brechin."

"They have technology to reach space?"

"Possibly," replied Vinz. "Their entire religion focuses on the civilization's ability to track and assimilate 'white gods.' They have technology that you're probably more familiar with than we are."

"Even so," said Alina, "once they reach space, they need to be able to go somewhere. If they have not been able to send probes, satellites, or machines to space thus far, they have no idea what is waiting for them outside the galaxy, much less Earth's orbit."

"Like I said," mumbled Vinz, "don't be so quick to judge."

Rhys shared a dubious look with his sister. *Surely not. There's no way.*

What if they were able to retrieve our ship? challenged Alina. Her eyes widened. *If they have others' ships, it's entirely possible that technology can be used to launch a spacecraft.*

Rhys slumped against his chair. *Would you really want to go back to space though?*

Alina's response was immediate. *Yes.*

I don't, Rhys murmured.

You've just forgotten how peaceful it was, said Alina. *If others were here and we had the capability, you would do it.*

Rhys shook his head. *I wouldn't.*

Alina began cleaning the dishes with a shrug. Rhys glanced at Kallen who had been watching the conversation. Even if it was possible, he would never go back to space.

The storm passed within the hour, and the sun triumphantly burst through the clouds. Kyo received a message via shortwave radio that Irvine wanted to meet. Kashim, Vinz, Hodge, and Rhys piled into *Themis'* dinghy and set off for *Grisle.* The entire ride over, Vinz rhythmically clenched and unclenched his hands in his lap. Rhys exchanged looks with Kashim who was at the motor.

Once at *Grisle,* they motored around back and skidded onto the rear ramp. Though they were supposed allies, everyone was armed. Rhys hopped out of the dinghy and casually adjusted the firearm attachment at his wrist. Hodge shouldered his rifle and stoically regarded the slave trader ship's crew. Vinz and Kashim followed.

Taking the lead, Rhys stalked up the ramp. The traders' ship crew moved with him warily. It seemed they had not forgotten his talent for turning the tables. Irvine and Adisa met him at the top of the ramp.

"Irvine," acknowledge Rhys. He held out his freshly bandaged hand, and the slave trader took it.

"Rhys," said Irvine. He looked to Vinz who appeared at Rhys' side. "Vinz." They shook as well. "Lucky there weren't nothing to that storm."

"Hopefully it'll bring some relief to a port though," offered Vinz.

"What did you do to your hands, boy?" asked Irvine.

"Sunboard practice," Rhys explained.

"Ah, that's what you were doing the other day. Didn't see but one sunboard though," chuckled Irvine.

"We're working on a new design, but it's slow-going." Rhys passed Adisa a silent nod of acknowledgment. "How's your injured man?"

"He'll be fine," replied Adisa. "Your doctor did professional work stitching him up."

"I'm glad to hear that. Alina will be pleased," replied Rhys.

"Ehh, yah yah yah," said Irvine. "I called you here because I want to know your plan. How do you plan to pass through the Golden Corridor?

I mean, we've got cargo to bargain with. The Aabeshian military can use bodies for a variety of tasks. What have you?" Irvine laughed. "Or are you going to just barrel through their ranks and hope they don't shoot?"

"How far out are we from the Golden Corridor?" Rhys inquired of Vinz.

Themis' Overseer thought. "Maybe four days depending upon the weather."

"We have some provisions we can bargain with, however, nothing as... *valuable* as a human life," said Rhys.

"Ehh, I'm sure you're hiding some cargo onboard that could be pawned off for passage," teased Irvine. "Your alternative is to fight through them, but it doesn't seem as though your ship is equipped for heavy sea battle."

"Don't underestimate my ship," Vinz suddenly countered. The rush of emotion and pride in his voice made Rhys smile. Vinz's most prized possession and greatest work floated in the water a short distance away.

"So you're going to push through the Aabeshian ranks?" Irvine asked incredulously.

"Perhaps," replied Vinz.

Irvine looked to Rhys for verification. Unwilling to cause Vinz to lose face before a possible enemy, Rhys nodded in confidence. "We're fast. Once we push through, they won't be able to catch up."

"And what about us?" asked Irvine.

Rhys exchanged looks with Vinz before they both smiled. "Please attempt to keep up," said Vinz.

"Mh-hmmm," mused Irvine. "I'll believe it when I see it, youngsters. You two are brave, I'll give you that, but brave doesn't get you to an old age."

"We're not trying to get to an old age," replied Rhys. He glanced at the other crew members, his smile fading. "While we're here, could I ask a favor of you, Overseer?"

"A favor?"

Sensing Vinz's sudden discomfort with the change in topic, Rhys approached Irvine to draw attention to himself. "I want to see the slaves."

"For what reason?"

"I just want to see them. Talk to them, maybe."

"They're Pantaraks," replied Irvine.

"I don't mind."

"What do you want with them?"

"To ask them about Brechin," said Rhys.

Irvine nodded. "Fine, but you disarm here. You leave all of your weapons with me and Adisa goes with you."

"Fair enough," replied Rhys, stripping out of his firearm and passing it and his waist knife to Irvine.

"Rhys," Vinz admonished.

"It's fine." They couldn't see the resonance cutters bound against his back under his shirt. There was no need to endanger himself entirely.

"Adisa, show him," demanded Irvine, nodding to his First Mate.

Rhys glanced at Vinz, Hodge, and Kashim before turning to follow Adisa below deck.

Unlike *Themis*, the slave trader ship had only one entrance below deck, a single door and a passageway located in the middle of the ship. With Adisa in the lead, they descended a flight of stairs into the light of solar-powered lamps. The moment they were out of earshot, Adisa turned and grabbed for Rhys' shoulder.

Rhys deflected his blow with a strong arm and drew back to strike. Adisa relaxed. "Why are you here? You shouldn't be here."

"To speak with the Pantaraks about Brechin," replied Rhys.

"What information do you think they will be able to provide?"

"Nothing," said Rhys.

This seemed to confuse Adisa because he slowly nodded and then continued to lead Rhys down the hallway to the belly of the ship. They passed a few cabins and even a washroom before Adisa stopped at the end of the hall, pulled at a trapdoor in the floor, and motioned to another staircase that stretched downward. Rhys gathered his courage and descended the steep stairs into the dim room.

"There should be a lamp above your head to the left," called Adisa. Rhys switched it on.

The room was small, cramped, and humid. Rhys covered his face as the smell of bodies and excrement hit his nose. He adjusted his olfactory settings and pulled his hand from his face. As he stepped forward, there was a slight shuffle of movement across the room. Realizing people were drawing away from him, he fell still.

There were six in total—four young men, a middle-aged woman, and a girl of perhaps 12. All wore clothes made of rags. Their shirts were virtually nonexistent and their pants and dresses torn, tattered, and filthy. Their hair was thick with dirt and their faces drawn and gaunt. They wore chains on their ankles.

"Adisa, could I have water and a rag?" Rhys yelled up the stairs. Surprisingly, he heard Adisa pad down the hallway. The First Mate returned momentarily, stepped down the stairs, and handed Rhys a small bucket and cloth. "Is it potable?"

"It is," replied Adisa.

Rhys crossed the room and knelt on the filthy, mold and dirt-encrusted floor. It pained his heart to see humans suffering, to see such wide, untrusting eyes. He swallowed his fear. "Do you see the color of my hair and the color of my eyes? I am Rhys Falkrow, a white god from Caelestis beyond the stars." No one moved. "After witnessing the horrors humans have done to one another, I am seeking an audience with the high priest in Brechin to ascertain a truce amongst all men. Can anyone here help me?"

"Why... should we help you," asked one of the young men, "when no one has helped us?"

"Why do you think I'm here?" Rhys moved to the nearest prisoner who was perhaps Hodge's age. The young man had dried blood on the side of his head as well as several cuts along his arms. Rhys dipped the rag into the water and reached for the man's arm. Before he could near, however, the man jerked his limb away and shuffled back. "Is there anyone here from the capital? Is anyone here a noble, a part of the royal families?"

Though there was silence, Rhys saw at least two of the captives glance toward the girl. The middle-aged woman drew the girl to her chest.

"Please trust me," said Rhys in Interstellar Nefegian. "Please, believe me when I tell you who I am."

The girl pulled away from the woman, her blue eyes intent on Rhys. "Why didn't you come sooner?" she whimpered in the same tongue.

"I'm being watched, even now," replied Rhys. "It has been a tedious game. What's your name?"

"Cantia Sorex," she replied.

"Sorex is a Nefegian surname," said Rhys.

"I am a direct descendent of Gaius Sorex, a white god."

"And who are your parents?"

"My mother is Daine Sorex, Minister of Justice."

Rhys refrained from gaping. "Have you told this to the slave traders?"

"No," replied Cantia. "I tell you because you speak the same dialect as the other white gods."

Rhys shifted to his knees. "Other white gods? You mean those who are descendants like yourself?"

She shook her head. "The white gods who recently joined the high priest in his temple."

"What do they look like?"

"Like you—silver hair, blue eyes. They were recently rescued."

"When did they arrive in Brechin?"

"I'm sorry. I don't know. I only met them twice."

"How many are there?"

"Three," replied Cantia. "Do you know them?"

"I... don't." Rhys held out his hand, and she joined him. He wiped at the heavy layer of dirt on her face, scrubbing her jaw and hairline to clear the muck away. Once done, he rubbed her arms and then examined the cut along her left shoulder. It appeared similar to Kashim's whip wounds. Finally, he looked at the others. "It is... unfair of me to say this," he murmured, "but I am going to attempt to free Cantia. I do not know if I will be able to come back for the rest of you."

"Please take her," begged the woman. "Take her back to Brechin so she may carry out the gods' wills."

Rhys looked at the others. "I will leave this here for you."

"Take it," murmured one of the men. "If you don't, they'll just use it to punish us."

Realizing the man was right, Rhys lifted the bucket and carried it across the room. He placed it at the bottom of the stairs and then returned to Cantia who stood in the middle of the cabin. Her chains were taut against her thin ankles. "Be still," he instructed, reaching into his shirt collar and pulling out the resonance cutters. Eyes set on the girl, he switched on the cutters, illuminating the room in an electric blue hue. While the others drew away, Cantia remained motionless. Rhys cut her chains to release her from the wall. "We'll remove the rest later," he murmured in Nefegian.

He sheathed the resonance cutters, took her hand, and looked at the others. "I'm sorry," he whispered.

"Go," replied the young man he had attempted to clean. "You're going to have a hard enough time getting out of here with just her."

Rhys turned and, with Cantia in tow, crossed the room. He didn't make it up the stairs before Adisa blocked his path. Shielding Cantia, Rhys commanded, "Move aside."

"The moment slaves board this ship, they are the property of our Overseer. You are stealing," replied Adisa.

"Surely you can release a single child. What good is she as a slave?"

Though Rhys was sure Adisa could have explained to him the many uses for a young female slave, he didn't. Instead, he asserted, "She will not be leaving this ship."

"Adisa. She's a *child*."

"People will pay a high price for a child."

Rhys considered him. "How much?"

Adisa seemed taken aback by the question.

"How much is she? I'll buy her."

Adisa withdrew from the stairs, and Rhys pulled Cantia into the hallway. Her thin arms wrapped tightly around his waist. Rhys felt a strange emotion course through him, one of protectiveness, a desire to defend that which couldn't. "Speak with the Overseer," said Adisa, motioning for him onward.

Rhys slipped an arm over Cantia's shoulders and guided her down the hallway and up the stairs. The moment sunlight hit her face, she flinched and buried herself in Rhys' shirt. Feeling her tremble, Rhys patted her comfortingly.

Adisa jogged across the deck to where Irvine, Vinz, Hodge, and Kashim talked and whispered into Irvine's ear. The Overseer shifted his dark gaze to Rhys.

"I won't let anyone hurt you," Rhys stated in Nefegian. "Trust me." Cantia nodded, and Rhys pushed her forward to meet the others.

In the sunlight, he could discern blond hair beneath the grime. Her eyes, which were heavy with fatigue, were a fascinating shade of green-blue. Her skin mirrored Rhys' save the remnants of filth streaked across her body. Her short dress was in tatters and hung off her shoulders.

Once before Irvine, Rhys declared, "I wish to purchase this girl."

"With what?" asked Irvine, amused.

"I'll trade you."

The Overseer chuckled. "You got a proclivity for bargaining."

"I have tablets on the ship that will cut your need for food in half. They lower your metabolism, allowing you to go days without food."

"Not enough."

Rhys thought of the other emergency equipment in his pack. "Fine. The tablets—there's about 150 of those—and a resonance knife. It can cut through anything."

Irvine waggled his fingers at Rhys indicating that he needed more.

"Those items and 4,000 klepira," interrupted Vinz.

Irvine looked between them and then shrugged. "Fine. I would have taken less, but the offer's set. Take her."

"Everything is on *Themis*," said Vinz.

"Then we will wait here. Take one of your men and retrieve the items," instructed Irvine.

Vinz motioned to Hodge, and together they jogged off to the ramp. Rhys heard the engine start and then grow distant as they returned to *Themis*.

"I'll be keeping this as part of the bargain," said Irvine, waving Rhys' plasma firearm.

Rhys shrugged. "It won't work for you, but that's fine."

Irvine examined the weapon and then attempted to fire it. Nothing happened. Growling, he tossed the firearm to Rhys who strapped it on and connected it to Pathos.

"You cut her chains off," Irvine remarked, leaning against the deck railing.

"Yes," replied Rhys.

"You didn't hand over all your weapons as I asked."

Rhys flashed a cocky grin. "You would have done the same had the situation been reversed." He glanced at Cantia to find her teetering on her feet. Realizing she was weak, he encouraged her to rest on the deck. She sat with some difficult and then leaned heavily against Rhys' legs. "So, I have to ask," he said.

"What?" said Irvine.

"Please don't take umbrage at what I'm about to say for I truly am naïve. How do you justify keeping your prisoners in such squalor? What is the point? Wouldn't it make more sense to feed them and keep them healthy so as to sell them for a higher price?"

"Sometimes," replied Irvine, "but these ones are destined for outlying cities. No one there cares if they're fed. They just want bodies."

"What determines where you sell them?"

"Demand. Just like crops, spices, materials, and textiles, cargo orders are filled and filed at the local ports. We pick them up and go hunt," Irvine explained. "The cargo's destination determines the level of care we provide them. If we can't afford to take on high-quality cargo, then we handle the orders that require fewer resources."

"And how did you get into the business?" asked Rhys.

"My father," replied Irvine. "Ah, *gawan*. That was quick."

Rhys looked up to find Vinz and Hodge zooming across the water to *Grisle*. They skidded onto the ramp and leapt out together. Rhys motioned for Cantia to rise, but she looked up at him pitifully and shook her head. Rhys squatted beside her to allow her to clamber onto his back. With Irvine, Adisa, and Kashim at his side, they met Vinz and Hodge.

The exchange was quick. Vinz handed over the packet of rationing tablets, Rhys' backup resonance knife, and a small bag of coins. Wanting this trade to be successful, Rhys set down Cantia and showed Irvine how to use the knife and then explained the rationing tablets to him. In general, Irvine seemed pleased with the trade.

"Once we have a firm idea of what we will be doing at the Golden Corridor, we'll let you know," said Vinz.

"Of course," said Irvine, toying with the knife.

Rhys lifted Cantia into his arms, and their group returned to the dinghy. It wasn't until they pulled into *Themis'* forward hatch that Rhys breathed a sigh of relief. He looked down at Cantia who rested against his chest. "Welcome," he said in Nefegian.

Kallen and Alina appeared in the forward hatch to help with the docking process. Rhys stood and, holding Cantia in his arms, stepped from the dinghy. Alina fell on them immediately.

"She's in bad shape," he said in Nefegian. "Malnourished and dehydrated. Also, she has a cut on her left shoulder that will probably need stitches." Alina studied the girl, checked her pulse, and then nodded for him to follow her to the galley.

Rhys set Cantia on the first table in the galley and pulled the edges of her ragged dress around her knees. "You're safe."

"Who is she?" Cantia asked in Nefegian, watching as Alina washed her hands.

"My sister," replied Rhys.

"She's pretty."

"I think so too."

"Rhys, can you uncover the shoulder wound?" Alina unwrapped her surgical supplies. Rhys gently rolled Cantia over and pulled the top of her dress away from her wound. "Cut it off," instructed Alina, handing him scissors. He did so, patted Cantia's arm, and then knelt beside the table so he could see the girl's eyes. "I'm going to clean the wound now. It will be painful so bear with me." Rhys offered his hands to Cantia which she gratefully took.

The entire process took no less than half an hour, but by the time Alina had finished, the girl was asleep.

"I hope she's worth 4,000 klepira," scoffed Vinz. He, Kallen, and Hodge had been sitting in silence for the past ten minutes watching Alina work.

"She's the daughter of the Minister of Justice in Brechin," said Rhys.

Vinz nodded, impressed. "I'm guessing Irvine doesn't know that."

"He does not."

"Was she the only one down there?"

"There were five others, but none of them were nobles." Rhys pushed Cantia's filthy hair away and studied her face. "She's one of us."

Kallen's voice was low. "She's Pantarak."

"Oh Kallen, will you help me get her washed up?" asked Alina, gathering her medical tools. "I don't want her anywhere near a bed until she's clean."

Though Rhys could tell Kallen didn't want so much as to even look at the girl, she nodded solemnly. Rhys nudged Cantia. "Hey," he murmured. "Wake up."

The girl stirred and opened her eyes. "Are we done?" she asked in Nefegian.

He nodded. "We're going to get you cleaned up and then you can sleep."

Stiffly, she sat up. Rhys helped to her feet and then pointed to Kallen. "This is Kallen. She and my sister, Alina, will help you."

Cantia gazed at Kallen and then looked up at Rhys. "I don't want her to touch me."

Rhys kept all emotion from his face. "And why is that?"

"Because she is not Pantarak. I would not take her even as a servant."

Rhys glanced at Alina who had stopped midway through packing. "You allowed us to handle you," his sister said. "We are not Pantarak."

"But you are white gods," countered Cantia.

"What's going on?" asked Vinz, looking between them.

Rhys glanced at Vinz and shook his head subtly. "Cantia, you do realize that the people on this ship rescued you and have welcomed you," continued Rhys in Nefegian.

"No," replied Cantia. "The white gods rescued me."

"It was a team effort," said Alina. "How do you think we were able to retrieve your purchase price so quickly?"

Cantia gazed at them for a long moment and then said, "I don't understand why this is a big deal. I don't want an apostate touching me."

"Cantia," came a new voice. Rhys looked up to find Leo leaning in the doorway. "Act your age, not your rank."

"Leo." Cantia turned and, with some trouble, wobbled to the doorway. She wrapped her arms around Leo and buried her head in his shirt. "Why are you here?" she murmured in Nefegian.

"I could ask you the same," he replied. Leo exchanged looks with Rhys. "She was on the slave ship?" Rhys nodded. "Thank you."

Cantia pulled away from Leo and looked at Rhys. "Leo, were you taken captive as well?"

Leo chuckled, "No," and untangled her arms from him. "Come on. Let's get you cleaned up."

Rhys exchanged looks with his sister who shrugged and continued to pack medical supplies.

"What was that all about?" asked Kallen.

"She didn't want to be with a stranger," Rhys lied. "That's it."

Kallen saw through it. "You mean because I'm not Pantarak."

"So what?" huffed Alina, leaning against the pack. "So she didn't want you to touch her because you aren't Pantarak? She's 12. Are you so threatened by her?"

"No," replied Kallen, standing.

"Good, you shouldn't be. You're twice her size and weight." Alina glanced at Rhys. "Besides, just wait until she finds out that you're the mate of a white god."

"Let's leave that for later," Rhys urged. Remembering what vital piece of information Cantia had shared with him earlier, Rhys looked at the others. "I'm sorry. I need to speak with Alina. It'll be just a moment."

"That's fine. I have other things to do." Vinz clapped Hodge on the shoulder and left.

Rhys glanced at Hodge and Kallen and then turned to his sister who was awaiting communication. *There are others. Cantia said there were others like us in Brechin.*

You mean ancestors, replied Alina.

Rhys shook his head. *No, like us. She said they spoke the same dialect as us.*

Alina thought, her brows furrowed. *But how? Unless another ship crashed… I mean, it's possible.*

What if they brought up our ship?

They would have had to locate our ship and dive for it.

If they have the advanced technology Vinz seems to think they do, it's entirely possible.

Alina made a sound of incredulousness. *Even if they dove for the ship, Rhys, what about the people?*

What about them? They were locked in temporary cryo.

Let's look past the fact that the Pantaraks would have to know how to disengage the temporary cryo units. The people we left down there, though very much alive, were essentially buried in a watery grave. The masks may have sealed off their faces, but their bodies were open to the elements.

What if they got to the ship within two to four days after the crash? asked Rhys. *Would the theory be viable then?*

Alina shifted uncomfortably. *Yes. But... I don't want to imagine that these people would go to such extreme lengths... to get their hands on... us.*

"Well?" asked Hodge. "Are you going to share?"

Once the door was closed, he and Alina rehashed the story of their escape from the ship. They spoke of the cryo-systems and the craft's shape and size. They shared with them the number of people and everything they had just discussed between themselves.

"Suppose the people the girl mentioned are, in fact, from your ship," speculated Hodge, "how does that affect you two?"

"Technically speaking, their survival should not affect us in the least bit," said Alina, "however, with them under the care and protection of the high priest... we worry about what they've been shown."

"We were impressionable when we first arrived," added Rhys. "We still are. Luckily, we've been shown an accurate picture of the world and been allowed to make decisions and come to conclusions by ourselves."

"If they have not been permitted the same," continued Alina, "it's entirely possible they could lead the Pantarak Empire to war given the power they've been handed."

"And they won't even know it," Rhys concluded.

"But if they are your people," murmured Kallen, "wouldn't that mean you can communicate and share with them the information and knowledge you've gathered?"

Rhys glanced at Alina. "You're absolutely right."

"Then our goal is *not* to meet with the high priest," said Hodge, "but to get you two to meet with the others of your kind. If you can influence them, then perhaps they can cause change from within."

25
THEIR OBSERVER

AFTER DECIDING THAT WAS THE master plan, Rhys separated from the group, found Vinz, and explained to him all that had transpired. By the time he left the Overseer's cabin, the crew had moved back into their usual patterns of activity. Kallen was in the engine room while Hodge tinkered with his board in the forward hatch. Kyo, Andy, and Lyruc remained on the bridge, and Kashim lay down for a nap. The only two who were not a part of that pattern were Leo and now Cantia.

After checking on the girl, who was asleep in Alina's bed, Rhys climbed to the upper deck in search of Leo. The young man was exactly where he expected him to be, sitting at the base of the main mast scribbling furiously in his notebook.

"Hey," murmured Rhys, sitting beside him. He found speaking in Nefegian when alone with Leo useful. He could grasp a much more precise reading of him. "How's Cantia?"

Leo rested his book in his lap. "She's asleep."

"Did she say how she was captured?"

"Her mother, the Minister of Justice, was visiting our sister port to preside over a town-wide hearing. Unfortunately, the Minister of Justice, despite her extensive education, has not imparted upon her daughter common sense. Cantia was picked up off the docks by the slave traders, not a soul in sight." Leo sighed. "Cantia is brilliant but still a child."

"You know her well?"

"The children of the royal heads look out for one another. Often, we are thrown into rooms with each other because no one else is qualified enough to look after us. So, yes. I know her well."

Rhys thought for a moment. "Can I ask, you told Cantia earlier to act her age, not her rank. What did you mean?"

"All of that drivel she was spouting, that's from her mother and the other highborn children."

"She doesn't think that way?"

"She does but only because her parents do."

"What do you think about us? Does it bother you that you're on a ship with apostates?"

Leo shrugged. "Not really. I've been around many types of people. What each of you believes is your own personal truth. Who am I to tell you otherwise?"

"Do you think Alina and I are white gods?"

Leo chuckled. "No. You're not. Anyone who spends more than a few days watching you two can see you're just like us."

"Does that mean you renounce your faith as a Pantarak?"

"The Pantarak faith is more than just believing in white gods. It's a way of life. It's believing in a life after death. It's believing that you will one day join the stars."

"But if you don't believe in white gods—"

"Just because I know you are people like us doesn't mean I don't believe that after I die my soul won't rejoin with the stars. I believe it will."

"I'm sure you are not the first to come across this revelation—that the white gods are just humans. What do others who have discovered the truth say?"

"To be honest, I don't know. I am more forward-thinking than the other highborns, mostly because my father is the Minister of Education. I've read thousands of books from a variety of cultures both past and present. I'm not arrogant enough to believe the Pantarak faith is our only means of salvation."

"Salvation? To be saved?"

Leo nodded.

"To be saved from what?"

"This world."

"Why would you want to be saved from something so beautiful?"

"Because not everything is beautiful."

Rhys peered up at the sails. "So, what happens when you achieve salvation?"

"Your soul goes to the stars to reside eternally."

Rhys chuckled. "I'm sorry. I don't mean to insult you but... if you knew the hell we lived in amongst the stars, you wouldn't want to be joining us."

"For many though, it is far better than the lot they were given in this life. By believing in a life after death, they are offered a second chance."

"Why don't they just try to make a difference during this life? That's what's going to matter. In the grand scheme of things... human lives are specks of dust."

"Who would be so cruel to think such a thing?"

"Anyone who has been to space and seen how vast the universe is." Rhys thought and then said, "Could I borrow a page from your book and your pen?"

Leo handed him paper and his writing utensil. Rhys knelt on the deck and began sketching out the Solar System. "This is us," he said, pointing to Earth. He continued drawing. "This is our Solar System. And... this is our Solar Interstellar Neighborhood. And this is the Milky Way, our galaxy. This is our Local Galactic Group and... our Virgo Supercluster. I could keep going, but I won't." He circled the tiny dot that was Earth. "So, you're telling me that humans are the center of the universe? Do you see how tiny we are?" Rhys pointed to a spot inside the Solar Interstellar Neighborhood outside the Solar System. "This is the Hyperes Solar System where Alina and I grew up. Do you see a problem here? Do you know how long it would take for a ship from Earth to reach Caelestis in Hyperes?" Rhys tilted his head. "Pathos?"

"Traveling at the speed of light, it would take 64 years," replied Pathos.

Leo pulled away from Rhys, his eyes wide. "What is that?"

"A computer," explained Rhys with a sigh. "I'm not trying to convert you from your faith. If that is what you believe and what makes you strong, then I won't take that away from you, but... I just ask that you look at how tiny you are in the grand scheme of the universe and realize that as a human, you and your people do not have all the answers." He chuckled. "I mean... my people, the people on Caelestis, don't even have all the answers though they think they do."

Leo settled back against the main mast. "I'll remember that." He fiddled with his book and then handed it to Rhys.

"I thought no one was supposed to read a writer's rough draft?"

"I lied," replied Leo. "It's not creative writing."

Rhys gazed at the front of the bound book. "What is it?"

"A report."

"About?"

"You."

Rhys opened the bound pages and scanned the first several lines.

I happened upon the ship, Themis, by chance. Her crew had put in an order for a Brechin guide days in advance. Upon her arrival in Firekli, I took it upon myself to meet with their contact, whose name will not be revealed in this report and, acting quickly, had their contact shift the currently assigned guide to another merchant's vessel. I waited at the target location for nearly an hour before being approached by two men from the ship's crew.

"To whom is this report going?" asked Rhys.

"My father."

Rhys flipped through a few more pages and continued reading.

I was struck with awe when I first laid eyes on the two white gods, a brother and sister, who were rumored to have thrown Paducah into upheaval. They were young, wide eyed, and distant. They seemed unreachable, as though despite their very presences, I could no more touch them than I could the stars. After being threatened by the ship's enforcer, I inquired after the siblings' family name. When provided the name 'Falkrow,' I immediately suspected fraud.

He skipped through several more pages.

Tension amongst Themis' crew members is tangible today. It undoubtedly stems from two sources. Firstly, the relationship of Rhys and the female mechanic, Kallen. After finding her alone with the Overseer, Rhys has since kept to himself and remained busy. He pours over materials and spends hours locked away in solitary confinement.

Unwilling to continue reading, Rhys closed the book and looked at Leo. "What purpose have you for taking such detailed notes on myself and Alina?"

"Alina is not the subject of my observation," said Leo, "though I have been watching her. Initially, I was to observe the *both* of you; however, I believe that... you are more valuable than she is."

"Because she is a woman?"

Leo shook his head. "Because you are a leader and she is not."

"She can be a leader if she wants," Rhys argued. "Alina—"

"I do not care about Alina," interrupted Leo softly. "You are the one who can move people. You are the one who can start change."

"Big words coming from a 15-year-old."

Leo chuckled. "I'm not 15."

Rhys pulled away to get a better view of Leo's face. "But you look so young…"

A dark smile spread across Leo's face. "Do you want me to tell you how young *you* look? It's our ancestry. I thought Alina was 14 because of how slight she is, but that's incorrect now, isn't it?"

"She'll be 17 next month."

"And you? Seventeen, 18?"

"Eighteen," replied Rhys.

"Eighteen and you still haven't grown any hair. All of the men onboard are showcasing varying degrees of scruff with the exception of your Overseer and you." Leo rubbed his face. "And me."

"So how old are you?"

"Nineteen. Come on…"

"What do you plan to do once we arrive in Brechin?"

"Those at the docks know who I am. I am friends with many of the slip owners."

"That's not what I mean…" Rhys waved Leo's book. "What will you do with this?"

"Give it to my father."

"And what will he do with it?"

Leo shrugged. "Read it, I suppose. That's typically what one does with reports. Does that worry you?"

"Only because I don't know you… and I don't know your father."

"My father will be the least of your worries. I may have power once we're in Brechin's waters, but within the royal family heads meeting chamber, I am nothing. The cabinet members—the family heads—they're the ones you need to be worried about."

"And the other people who look like us? What about them?"

Leo frowned. "What are you talking about?"

"Cantia told me there were others, people who look like Alina and myself. She said we had the same dialect."

"It's possible she knows information I don't. Her mother has more influence than me or my father. But she said there are others?"

Rhys nodded. "That's what made me pull her from the slave ship."

"I think it was more than that," replied Leo.

Rhys stretched his legs out before him and breathed deeply. "Can I ask you something?"

"Hm?"

"Why is it called the Golden Corridor? I don't understand. It's an absolute military line, right?

"You'll see when we get there. All of the ships have sails like this one—solar paneled. From a distance in the daytime, they appear as a solid line of golden-white light. Despite the fact that solar paneling reflects very little light... Think about it. To create that amount of light, there have to be hundreds of ships."

"How are we to get through it?"

"The slave ship won't have any problems. They regularly use slaves to bribe their way into Brechin. Your ship will be different. *Themis* isn't marked as a merchant ship or slave ship."

"Could we mark it?"

"It's possible, but those coming into Brechin always have their hulls filled with goods to be traded in the city. If we come in with nothing, the troops will be suspicious."

"Can we bypass the Golden Corridor then?"

"No, but if you can fight our way through and make it to Brechin's waters, they will stop attacking for fear of inciting war. Brechin has its own navy anchored near the Golden Corridor."

"Could we fight through the Aabeshian ranks? I don't want to hurt anyone."

"It's possible, but *Themis* will take damage."

"Would your status allow us to pass as a diplomatic vessel?"

"If I were higher born, maybe, but no, not for the son of the Minister of Education. *Please*... I'm a professor's boy." Leo tapped his booted toes together. "In fact, if they saw me... or you or Alina or even your Overseer, they would probably take the ship."

"Vinz has papers indicating New Arbroath citizenship."

"Fine, then it would be just you, me, and your sister. You two don't have papers and my origins are pinned to my ear."

"Take it off."

"Can't."

"Can't or won't?"

"Does it matter?"

"So we fight through the Aabeshian ranks," concluded Rhys.

"Tell me about the board you were riding the other day. It isn't a sunboard. What is it?"

"A magnetic board. It uses the magnetic waves in the atmosphere."

"So why weren't you *flying* the other day?"

"Because its initiation process will require me to connect my computer to the board's. I'm not ready for that."

"Will connecting with it hurt you?"

"I don't know. Yet another reason I haven't done so already."

There was silence between them before Leo took the book from Rhys. "I swear, there's nothing incriminating in here."

Rhys rose. "I didn't think there was."

For the remainder of the evening, Rhys alternated between working on the translation materials, listening to Kyo practice music, and playing games with Hodge, Alina, and Kallen. After losing almost every round, Rhys gave up and retired to his cabin. Finding Cantia still asleep in Alina's bed, he stripped out of his shirt and lay down. Half an hour later, Kallen joined him.

They snuggled in silence, listening to the ship's engines purr. Eyes closed, Rhys drowsily ran his fingers through Kallen's hair and breathed in when she breathed out. Despite all that had happened in the past few days and the quarreling they had done, he adored her.

Burying his face into her neck, he said in Elali, "May I ask you something?" He felt Kallen nod. "Is it acceptable for me to call you... by a title?"

"What do you mean?"

"Uh... " Rhys thought. He didn't want to keep calling her his mate. It was strange. "Well, you are my mate... but is there... anything else I can call you?" His sentence trailed off.

Kallen stretched her legs and wriggled close so her head fit perfectly under his chin. "Yes. I am yours."

Fire roared through Rhys' body and set his blood aflame. His heart pounded hard against his chest, and he felt heat flood his limbs and face. "You're... mine," he whispered. He couldn't wipe the stupid grin from his face. "You're *mine*." He kissed her hard. "You're mine."

Rhys enveloped her in a deep hug. He felt like they were one body, one person. He kissed the top of her head and then rolled on top of her. Heart hammering painfully against his chest, he stared down at her. He loved the woman so much.

Despite feeling as though he was the one in control, Kallen reached through the space between them, knotted her hand in his hair, and pulled his face to hers. They kissed for a long moment before she placed a ginger hand on his chest and lay back. "I can't," she murmured in Elali. "Not right now." Remembering she was on her cycle, Rhys sighed and laid his forehead on her chest. Not fair, not fair! He had forgotten.

"Aren't you going to punish her?"

Rhys looked at Cantia who sat in bed watching them. He glanced at Kallen and then, balancing his weight on his knees, sat up. "What are you talking about?"

"She denied you, a white god." Cantia nodded to Kallen. "She doesn't have the right. She should be honored to even be in the same room as you."

"She's not my servant," growled Rhys.

"Why else would she be in your cabin? I don't understand."

"Because... she's my mate."

"Because you asked her to be in your bed," Cantia clarified.

"No," he snapped. "Because she chose me."

Cantia gawked at them before a look of disgust crossed her face. "You would want *her* to bear your children?"

Rhys paused for a moment; he had never considered Kallen as a *mother* and he as a *father*. The idea, the concept, had never crossed his mind, but now that Cantia had mentioned it, wasn't that part of being mates? "Yes, of course," he said. He glanced at Kallen and found her hiding her face under her arm. Her cheeks flamed pink. Despite Cantia and her words, he couldn't help but smile.

"Does your sister know?" hissed Cantia.

Rhys slid off Kallen and leaned against the wall. "Yes."

"She must be humiliated."

Instead of feeling anger toward the girl, Rhys studied her, intrigued. "What have you been told? What is it that makes you hate people who are not highborn?"

"It's not just commoners," replied Cantia. "Non-Pantarak people as well." She looked at Kallen. "You're heathens."

Kallen laughed sarcastically and sat up. "Heathens?" Rhys laid his hand on her leg, and Kallen fell silent. He knew what she was going to say and, as much as he wanted to share with Cantia all that they had experienced under the hands of the Pantaraks, he couldn't expose the girl so quickly or else risk pushing her away.

"Why do you think you're better than her?" Rhys motioned to Kallen. "Is it because you have fair skin and light eyes? Or because you're Pantarak and she's not?"

"All of it," replied Cantia. "I'm smarter and stronger. I can make complex calculations instantly. I've been recommended as an understudy for the Minister of Finance." She smugly smiled at Kallen. "What have you done?"

"I helped build this ship," replied Kallen. "I'm a mechanic."

"A meager job for a meager person," said Cantia.

"Enough." Rhys slid out of bed. "While you remain on this ship, you will be courteous to all crew members, Pantarak and apostate alike." Noticing Cantia's fierce hazel gaze set on Kallen, Rhys snapped his fingers at her. "Do you understand?"

"Yes," Cantia growled.

Rhys glanced at Kallen and then said, "With that aside, Cantia, are you hungry?" The look in Cantia's gaze shifted before she eagerly nodded. With a sigh, Rhys passed Kallen a pitiful expression. "Can you help me cook something for her?"

"May I place poison in it?" muttered Kallen in Elali, padding from the room.

By the time Kallen finished cooking a small meal, Leo, who had been on the upper deck, joined them. He and Cantia spoke softly in Interstellar Nefegian, but Rhys chose to ignore it. Instead, he helped Kallen clean the dishes and put away supplies.

"Ignore her," instructed Leo once Cantia wobbled off to the washroom. "She's naïve and believes the world revolves around Brechin."

Rhys began to reply in Nefegian but, remembering Kallen, said, "She may be naïve, but her words still cut. If she keeps talking like she does, she's going to make enemies with the crew quickly."

"I'll tend to her," Leo assured them, standing. He pushed in all of the chairs and leaned against the table. "She knows only what is fed to her by her parents and the other nobles." He sighed. "She's all talk. She has no physical power or real courage. It's all a front." He looked at Kallen. "I'm sorry for her hurtful words. Please forgive her naivety." Kallen only nodded. "I'll stay up with her until she's ready to sleep. You two go ahead and rest."

"Are you sure?" asked Rhys.

"I'm sure," replied Leo. Rhys led Kallen back to the cabin, closed the door, and went to bed.

26
REST

THE NEXT FEW DAYS WERE trying. Upon his arrival, Leo had kept to himself and stayed out of the crew's way. Aside from letting Rhys know that Kallen was alone with Vinz, he had remained silent, a ghost of a passenger. If Leo was the equivalent to a lonely specter, Cantia was a screeching banshee. From the moment she set her feet on the floor in the morning until she crawled back into her nest-like bed at night, she was everywhere—on the bridge, in the galley, on the upper deck, in the engine room, in Vinz's cabin. Everywhere.

When she wasn't skulking around the bridge, she was tormenting Andy with questions while he read in the galley. She went through Kallen's belongings—twice that Rhys knew of—and left them scattered about the cabin. She threw Hodge and Kyo's clothes into the hallway, claiming they reeked and stuffed Kashim's in the washroom basin. When Hodge began cursing at her, she shouted at him in Nefegian and locked herself in Rhys' cabin. Even Vinz and his possessions weren't safe; he was a half-blood after all. By the end of the second day, Vinz had locked his cabin door with a padlock to keep her from destroying books and delicate research materials.

Rhys hoped her proclivity for destruction was limited to physical items, but he soon found the girl's malice had no limit. Aside from wreaking havoc throughout the ship, toying with the controls on the bridge, and mixing Kyo's maps, Cantia had the uncanny ability to target people's weaknesses and pit them against one another. In the first full day of her being aboard *Themis*, she managed to incite an argument between Kyo and Andy—the first Rhys had ever seen—and cause Hodge to yell at Vinz about Kyo and Andy's quarrel.

By the third day, aside from being in foul moods, the crew was exhausted. After so much drama when there had initially been none, every member wanted to be left alone. To their dismay however, seeing this as a success, Cantia remained ever-destructive, working overtime to cause problems and form rifts between crew members.

That afternoon, Rhys, Vinz, Hodge, and Kashim left *Themis* to meet with Irvine to once more discuss their plans for crossing the Golden Corridor. Though the meeting didn't take long, by the time they returned, Rhys was exhausted.

"Well?" prompted Alina as Rhys and Hodge trudged into the galley.

"We're going to fight our way through," said Hodge, "and hope we survive."

"Sounds foolish." Alina watched Rhys as she stirred the bubbling contents of the pot.

Hodge plopped down into a chair. "That's the short version. Rhys?"

"Irvine's ship will pass through the line first. He seems to think he won't have any problems. I'm doubtful." Rhys sighed wearily. "Once he's through, he's going to set up the energy snare that we ran over. Once it becomes apparent that we will be unable to pass peacefully, we'll make a break for the snare."

His sister frowned. "It'll hit us like before."

"The snare picks up systems that utilize solar energy. Irvine will give us the coordinates once its set up. We will still have to pass over it, but if we cut the solar energy system before we run over it, we shouldn't become trapped."

"We're taking a big risk trusting Irvine and his crew," murmured Alina.

"See?" Hodge motioned to her. "I've told both him and Vinz that near four times now, and no one listens!"

"We don't have a choice," said Rhys.

"This is bad," groaned Hodge. "I feel it. This is bad-bad."

"Speaking of bad, where is Cantia?" asked Rhys. "I haven't seen her all day."

Alina leaned against the counter. "I drugged her."

Hodge burst into manic laughter while Rhys gaped at her. "You-you drugged her?" howled Hodge. He leapt from his chair, flew across the galley, and lifted Alina into the air. "Oh you wonderful, wonderful woman!"

"What's going on?" asked Vinz, appearing in the doorway with Kashim and Lyruc.

Still holding Alina and beaming, Hodge cackled, "Alina drugged Cantia."

For the first time in weeks, Rhys saw a smile crack over Vinz's face. Kashim cleared his throat to hide his own mirth before disappearing into the bridge. "Huh, even our patient saint has her limit," Vinz mused.

Hodge set Alina down so she could stir her pot which was about to boil over. "I was tired of listening to her bad-mouth everyone," Alina explained. "Use the time while you can. She'll wake this evening."

Taking Alina's advice, Rhys set off to help Kallen who was checking the equipment in the engine room. Afterward, they replaced four panels on the rear sail and then sat with Leo on the upper deck and talked. At dusk, they joined the rest of the crew in the galley for dinner. With Cantia out of sight, everyone seemed relaxed. Rhys found that even Leo, who normally remained aloof, was smiling and laughing.

As Kallen, Alina, and Andy cleaned the galley, Kyo withdrew his piax and played for the crew, alternating between lively jigs and well-known traditional songs. Rhys' heart soared when, during the fourth song, Kallen sang the lyrics. Having never before heard an instrument mix with a human voice, he sat transfixed, his eyes glued to Kallen. He couldn't believe how indescribably beautiful it was. Why would humans ever want to forget the power of music?

After Andy and Kashim went to join Lyruc on the bridge, Vinz nodded to Kyo. "Do you know 'The Maiden's Call?'"

Kyo thought for a moment, tentatively plucked a few strings, and then broke into a rhythmic melody. Vinz stretched back in his chair and closed his eyes. Rhys watched as Kyo glanced at Kallen, played a few more chords, and then motioned for her to join.

O, when the sun is a' falling,
And the war pipes are calling,
Look here, my love. Look here.
O, when you've lost your way,
And you feel you can't stay,
Look here, my love. Look here…

Rhys smiled. It was the first song he had ever heard Kallen sing lo those months ago. It was the first taste of music he had ever experienced. She had brought him that joy.

And when your hope is gone
And you feel you can't move on,
Look here, my love. Look here.
All that you adore
All that you look for
Is here, my love. Look here.

Kallen glanced at him and smiled before her eyes flicked purposefully to the doorway. Rhys followed her gaze to Cantia who stood in the hallway. Though the girl was nearly indiscernible from the shadows, Rhys could make out her face and the look of utter confusion that colored it. Smiling, he returned his attention to Kallen who, it seemed for Cantia' benefit, was adding more emotion to her already glorious voice.

As Kallen turned on her heel to clap, Vinz clapped with her, signaling a change of pace and rhythm in the song. Kallen bounced her finger in time with Kyo's quickened accompaniment and swayed with the music.

Rhys glanced at Alina. While everyone else in the room seemed to be enthralled by Kallen and Kyo's performance, Alina's face remained expressionless. She studied Kallen and watched Kyo's hands, but never did the tension in his sister's shoulders disappear or a smile spread across her face. Thus was the downfall of the AI Logos.

Kallen sang another two verses and then waited beside Kyo as he plucked the final notes. Everyone in the galley broke into applause.

"Perfect," said Vinz as the noise died down. "Thank you." He stood. "And with that, I'm going to check on the bridge and turn in." He glanced at Cantia as he passed her in the hallway but didn't say anything.

"Cantia," called Alina, motioning to the girl. "Join us." All eyes turned to Cantia as she shuffled into the room, her gaze passing between Leo and Rhys before settling on Kallen. "You're awake. How are you feeling?"

"It's difficult to sleep when there's so much noise," she murmured.

"Don't complain," Leo scolded. He patted to the chair beside him, and Cantia sat.

"Kyo." Rhys turned to the man. "Can you play that one I really like?"

"'The Stars' Light?'" Kyo touched the strings just gently enough to make them ring.

"Yes. That one."

"Ahhh, that one?" groaned Hodge, slouching in his chair. "It's so slow and sad."

Rhys motioned for Kallen to come sit with him. She returned to her chair and nudged him lovingly.

As Kyo played the mournful tune, Rhys closed his eyes. He wished Alina could experience the emotions that accompanied the piece and comprehend the inherent story of how cold and unforgiving the stars were. Even if he told her of the nuances in the music that reflected the twinkling of the stars or the unrequited love humans felt toward them, she would never fully comprehend the power behind the melody. For the first time in his life, he found himself consciously thankful for his Pathos AI.

Kallen leaned against Rhys and stared at Kyo's hands as he released into the air the forlorn tune. Rhys kissed the side of her head and wished the evening could go on forever. Knowing the passage of time, however, Rhys prepared himself for the inevitable final chords. After soaring through the chorus one last time, Kyo concluded the song and sat in silence, allowing the ending notes to dissipate into the hallway.

Rhys opened his eyes and smiled. Kyo nodded in acknowledgment and stood. "I'm done," he announced. "It's hard to top something so perfect."

"But you didn't even play a *good* song," moaned Hodge. "At least leave on an upbeat!" Kyo traded a knowing smile with Rhys and slipped from the galley. "Come *on*," said Hodge. "We're losing people! It's not even that late."

"Some of us have been working," Kallen muttered good-naturedly.

"I've been working," snapped Hodge in mock umbrage. "I don't know about you other fools, but I spent the afternoon organizing our supplies and taking inventory." He pointed to Rhys. "He's the one who hasn't been doing anything!"

"Rhys helped me replace solar panels," affirmed Kallen. "Alina has cooked all the meals today, and Leo... " Kallen considered him. "Leo has been supervising all upper deck activities."

Hodge snorted. "Please, all he does is sit there and write."

"How did I get dragged into this?" asked Leo, bewildered but amused.

Alina chuckled, "Let's not drag in the newcomer."

"Stay out of their quarrel," jested Rhys. "You'll only make it worse."

"True." His sister glanced at Kallen. "Perhaps we should leave and just let them finish it by themselves."

"I don't appreciate your tone," said Hodge, wagging his finger at Alina. "Honestly, it sounds like you condone our fighting."

"You two quarrel all the time," chortled Rhys. "We don't condone it; it just happens."

Hodge stretched in his chair, tangled his foot around the edge of Rhys' seat, and began dragging Rhys alongside the table. "We're men. We have to... stick to... stick together," he explained, straining against Rhys' weight. Rhys turned in his chair and grabbed for Kallen who jerked her arm from his grip. "Hehehe, your woman has abandoned you! You are mine!" shouted Hodge in glee.

Rhys tried to kick Hodge from his chair but ended up tangling his own foot in its legs. "*Gawan.* Kallen, Kallen... Help. "

Kallen turned her back to him and folded her arms across her chest. "You knew the consequences of siding with him. You're his now."

Once Rhys' chair was within reach, Hodge grabbed the edge and heaved him to his side where he promptly wrapped a muscled arm around Rhys' shoulders. "See? Isn't that better?" Hodge pushed Alina's chair toward Kallen. "You belong over there." Unlike Rhys, Alina didn't resist.

"Leo!" laughed Hodge. He motioned to the vacant seat on his other side. "You. Here, now! Men against the womenfolk!"

"I do not want to be on either side of the quarrel," stated Leo. He appeared thoroughly amused.

"Gravel bar," murmured Hodge. "No matter. Ladies. Are you ready?"

Alina gave him a dubious look. "For what?"

Kallen leaned on her knees. "Chair battles. Whoever stays in their chair last wins. Hodge, I've already beat you four times."

"Uappp! Ssshhh!" interrupted Hodge with a wild flapping of his hand. "This time it will be different. We haven't played with these two. The tides of battle have shifted."

"You mean the tides of war," Kallen corrected.

"So, we have to knock the other person from the chair?" Rhys clarified.

"Using only your feet, you have to turn the chair over. You can't physically push them from the chair."

"That seems unfair... We weigh more than them."

Hodge leaned into Rhys and pointed vehemently at Kallen. "That *one* is especially talented! Beware of her magic feet."

"So we try to get them out of the chair without actually touching the person?"

Rhys was glad he wasn't the only one who still didn't fully grasp the challenge.

"Yes," mumbled Kallen whose gaze was set on Hodge.

"Ready... " Hodge stretched out his long legs. "Go!" As he wrapped his foot about the edge of Kallen's chair, Kallen blocked his other foot.

Now, said Rhys to Alina.

Simultaneously, they turned to their supposed teammates. In a single movement, Rhys looped one leg at the front of Hodge's chair and the other around the back. He jerked. Hodge tumbled to the floor. A breath's moment later, Alina did the same to Kallen. With both Kallen and Hodge on the floor, Rhys grinned at Alina.

"Rhys... Why?" howled Hodge, rubbing his lower back. "You were my teammate. I trusted you. I fought beside you... "

"We defeated both you and your strategies," Alina declared in mock triumph.

"It's not a strategy game," said Kallen, clambering back into her chair. She looked at Rhys. "*Not* a strategy game."

"Oh... " Rhys helped Hodge up. "Then what's the point?"

"It's fun," murmured Cantia from the corner of the room. Everyone turned to look at her. "Right?" she asked of Leo.

Leo glanced at Rhys. "Right." He stood and began rolling up his sleeves. "I'll join the boy's team if you'll be with the girls."

"Uh... " Cantia glanced at Kallen uncertainly.

"It's fine," said Kallen, putting on a brave face. "With another girl here, we can take them down."

Cantia slid out of her chair and followed Leo to the group. Once they were situated—boys on one side and girls across from them—Hodge explained the rules again. He pointed to Rhys and Alina. "No cheating."

"This seems unfair," said Cantia. "Can't Leo and I exchange places? I weigh less than all of you."

"Weight doesn't matter," said Kallen, her eyes calculating. "It's all about technique."

"Ready... " murmured Hodge, his gaze shifting between Alina and Kallen. "Go!"

In a flurry of motion, everyone threw their legs forward in an attempt to break the others' defenses. Though Rhys had meant to clash with Kallen, the person whose legs he had to defend against was Alina. Rhys' younger sister pushed hard, her jaws clenched. "Cantia!"

Rhys glanced at Cantia who had been play-fighting with Leo. The moment Alina called her name, Cantia turned sideways in her chair and drove at Rhys' chair legs. "What? No!" shouted Rhys. To his surprise, Leo cut in, grabbed Cantia's chair, and flipped her.

"One down!" whooped Hodge through gritted teeth.

"Together, together," Rhys said. He was struggling against Alina because of the strange angle. His sister was winning.

"Nope," replied Kallen, releasing her grip on Hodge's chair and wrapping a foot around the leg of Rhys'. With an unsurprising amount of strength, Kallen flipped Rhys onto the floor.

Not allotted the time to moan on the floor, Rhys slid out of the way. "Go, Leo," he said, thrusting Leo's chair toward Kallen.

"I don't want to fight her!" barked Leo, tackling the side of Kallen's chair with his feet.

"Kallen, deal with Hodge," panted Alina between breaths. Together, both girls managed to trap Hodge's feet between them and then tilt him out of his chair. Hodge toppled to the floor, wailing dramatically in defeat.

"I yield," said Leo when Kallen and Alina turned on him.

Kallen clapped hands with Alina and then turned to Cantia who had withdrawn from the mock-battle and was leaning against the counter. "We won. Good teamwork!" Kallen held out her hand to Cantia. The girl stepped forward tentatively, glanced at Rhys, and then accepted the gesture. Kallen nodded. "You were there when we needed you. Maybe you didn't take one down yourself, but you made it so others could. That's teamwork."

The uncomfortable smile on Cantia' face disappeared. She studied Kallen and then looked at Hodge. When she spoke, it was as if she had experienced a revelation of sorts. "We're the... same."

Kallen nodded. "Yes, we are."

27
NEW PLAN

JUST BEFORE DAWN, VINZ'S VOICE rang through the ship. "Everyone to the bridge. We're approaching the Golden Corridor. Let's go."

Rhys nudged Kallen awake. "Come on," he murmured. Cantia sat up in Alina's bed and rubbed her eyes. Leo didn't move. Frowning, Rhys grabbed a shirt and threw it at Leo's head. "Wake up. We're at the Golden Corridor." Leo groaned.

Together, he and Kallen dressed in their day clothing and, after making sure Leo and Cantia were awake, stumbled up to the bridge. Vinz, Lyruc, Kashim, Andy, Alina, and Kyo were already there. Hodge staggered in a minute later.

"We're about an hour from the Golden Corridor," Vinz explained. He pointed out at the dimly lit horizon. "See those black silhouettes? Those're Aabeshian war ships."

"What about *Grisle*?" asked Rhys.

"They passed through the Golden Corridor just after midnight," replied Vinz. "According to Irvine, they've already set up the snare. We received the coordinates last night by radiotelegraphy. So, theoretically, if we end up in a pinch, all we have to do is lead Aabeshian ships that are on our tail to it."

"You still thinking we'll attack a ship and slip through the hole we create?" asked Hodge groggily.

"That was the plan until Irvine reported that the Aabeshian navy has high-powered weaponry aboard many of its ships." Vinz leaned against his chair. "A head-on attack is plan number two."

"And our first one?" asked Lyruc.

Vinz pointed to Rhys.

"Wait… What?" Rhys glanced at Hodge.

"Your board," said Vinz.

Realization dawning on him, Rhys said, "You want me to connect to it."

"You connect to it, fly out, and cause chaos."

"It's just a board," countered Kallen. "It's not a weapon."

"No, but he has weapons that can be used against them."

Kallen scoffed. "You don't have to do this." The bridge door opened to admit Cantia and Leo. "Even if you connect with it, we have no idea how it'll function."

"You can't just send him out alone," added Hodge.

"But he has the weapons he used against us when we first met," replied Kashim solemnly. "Remember?"

"Those are handheld weapons. They can't possibly take out ships—"

"I don't need him to *take* out ships," explained Vinz. "I need him to *distract* and, if need be, *disable* them."

There was momentary silence before Kallen vehemently shook her head. "It's too dangerous. Come on. Vinz. If it were you carrying out the assignment, would you really want to be sent out by yourself?"

The Overseer's response was matter of fact. "I'm not him."

"Is no one else concerned," asked Andy, "about what will happen after Rhys attacks them?"

"That's why Rhys has to be quick."

"Others will come to help," murmured Kyo. "It's not your best plan."

"It's better than us trying to spring an attack on them," Kashim contended.

Kallen grimaced. "There has to be a better way."

"What's going on?" asked Leo in an attempt to follow the conversation.

"Vinz wants Rhys to fly ahead and divert the ships' attention." Kallen folded her arms. "Let's just send Hodge out on his board. It's the same difference."

"It *gawan* isn't!" huffed Hodge.

Leo peered between Rhys and Vinz. "How is he going to attack them?"

"He has his own weapons—"

"I'll do it," interjected Rhys. The bridge fell silent. The only person who wasn't surprised by his response was Alina.

Kallen slipped between him and Vinz. "You do *not* have to do this."

Alina gently tugged at Kallen's shirt. "It's his decision."

"Why are you supporting him?" growled Kallen. "You're putting your brother in danger."

Alina glanced at Rhys. "Of everyone here, I am the only one who understands that Rhys' greatest danger is not the ships. It's from the board itself."

Rhys smiled grimly at Alina; his sister gazed back at him stoically—her way of shielding herself from the emotions that conflicted with her logic. To Hodge and Kallen, he said, "Would you get the board and bring it to the upper deck?" They disappeared from the bridge. Rhys looked at Vinz. "What ships are you wanting to pass between."

Vinz directed Rhys' attention to a schematic on the small table near Kyo. "Here, here, here, and here," the Overseer said, pointing to the seven ships in the vicinity. Clear these three first so we can pass. The others will need to be handled quickly to keep them from attacking us."

"And Irvine's snare?" asked Rhys.

Vinz traced his finger just beyond the line of Aabeshian ships to a black circle sketched onto the map. "This is the snare zone. We will head for it with the hopes of drawing them in behind us."

"But they won't give chase forever, right?"

Vinz slid his finger roughly three kilometers east. "Until they reach here. It intersects with the northern commercial highway. Once we enter this area, they should back off. They don't want to incite the Pantaraks."

"And Irvine?"

"We'll meet them at the intersection."

"They could just run."

Vinz shook his head. "They ditched their snare for us. They're going to want compensation. That technology isn't cheap. It can be purchased in Brechin, but it's expensive."

"Anything else?" asked Rhys.

"No." Vinz lowered his voice. "You sure you want to do this?"

"Yes."

The Overseer regarded him. "Rhys. I'm not using you as a tool. I'm trying to find the best way to keep my crew safe."

"The sacrifice of one for the many," Rhys concluded. Vinz opened his mouth to object, but Rhys stopped him. "It's fine."

"I intend for you to return. Becoming a sacrifice is not an option."

Rhys nodded, glanced at the others on the bridge, and then left for his cabin. Alina followed.

Please ensure that Pathos does not have control of your vitals, warned his sister. *If the board's computer is corrupt, it will damage Pathos. I don't want the AI to have control of anything that could kill you.*

They entered their cabin. Rhys grabbed the plasma firearm which he kept hanging on the bunk post and strapped it on. *I'm going to back up vital information to you. Fighting, linguistics, engineering.*

Don't. Alina plopped onto her bed. *I don't want you to waste your energy. I can attain that information easily from the database.*

Rhys slid the resonance cutters into the special sheath he had made and slung it over his shoulder so the cutters rested along his back. After a moment of thought, he gazed at Alina. *If I don't come back, you absolutely must see to it that Vinz makes it to Brechin and speaks to our people.*

Instead of insisting otherwise, his sister only nodded.

Alina, don't do anything stupid.

I won't.

Take care of... Kallen.

It's possible that if the computer corrupts your AI, she said, *I will no longer be able to speak with you like this.*

I know, replied Rhys. He motioned for her to walk with him. *I'm leaving my wellbeing in your hands, Sister.*

Leo and Cantia, who were waiting in the hallway, watched them pass before following them to the upper deck. Under the sails, Rhys found Kallen, Hodge, and Kashim standing around his board.

For storage purposes, he had retracted it to its shortest form, leaving it as an unassuming piece of blank technology. Only he and Alina fully understood what it was possibly capable of.

With a deep breath, Rhys turned his eyes to the horizon glowing orange-pink and to the extensive line of Aabeshian ships whose sails reflected the faint gold of the sunrise. This wasn't going to be easy. Of course, when had anything on this planet been easy?

Finally he looked at his sister. *Ready?*

Alina nodded. *Ready.*

I trust you.

Alina glanced at the board. *Let's get this over with.*

Rhys peered over his shoulder. "Kashim, are we ready on the bridge?"

"Ready. Once you've cleared the first three ships, we'll follow behind," the man replied. "You absolutely *must* keep the remaining ships off our back until we reach the intersecting highway."

Rhys exchanged looks with Kallen and Hodge and then approached the board. *Pathos, confirm that you've been locked from accessing all of my vitals.*

Confirmed.

Ensure that Alina has full access to my data and can initiate override if need be, mumbled Rhys, touching the board.

Alina Falkrow has been given full access to your data. She has complete override authority, Pathos assured.

Rhys reached under the belly of the board, slid open a small hatch, and switched on the board's computer.

A weak signal has been detected.

Rhys took a deep breath. *Connect me to the board's computer.*

Preparing Pathos AI for intake of antique data.

Rhys closed his eyes in preparation.

AI unit ready for intake of antique data. Permission to initiate data-lock?

Permission granted, replied Rhys.

Initiating data-lock. Source confirmed. Engaging transfer of antique data in three, two, one.

Pain like that of thousands of stabbing knives suddenly drilled into his head, forcing Rhys to crumple to the deck. Panting and groping for something to hold onto, he curled into himself. His muscles spasmed violently along his back. Instantly, he became coated in a thick layer of sweat. And still the agony continued.

Rhys felt his hands clenched in a death grip around someone, but he couldn't force his eyes open. Through gritted teeth, he wheezed and groaned. He wanted to make it stop, make it all stop.

For several long moments, he writhed on the deck in an attempt to dull the pain, but it only seemed to increase. His head pounded; his face was hot. More than that though, he felt as though the side of his head was on fire, as though the skin under Pathos' external unit was blistering.

With a cry, he reached along the side of his head and groped desperately to eject the AI. Hands stopped him and pinned him down. "Get it off!" he screamed, fighting fiercely. Tears unashamedly streamed down his face. The pain was too much.

"Pathos!" shouted Alina. Her voice bore through the layers of pain that threatened to swallow Rhys.

"A-A-Alina... " cried Rhys. His entire body seized.

"Forced override. Knock him out!" commanded Alina.

Rhys dropped into darkness.

28
THE GOLDEN CORRIDOR

A SOFT BREEZE PLAYED ON Rhys' face, drawing away the heat from his skin. His head throbbed rhythmically with the beating of his heart, an unusual and disconcerting sensation. Another puff of air stirred his hair, and the smell of sea water wafted over his face.

He inhaled deeply before tentatively reaching for his aching head. His arms didn't move; they were pinned to his sides by a weight. Instead of panicking as would have been his normal response, Rhys relaxed and allowed himself to drift along the line between consciousness and coma. He could hear snippets of conversations but couldn't process them. He was too groggy.

For several long minutes, he lay motionless. It wasn't until the floor beneath him quivered that he finally attempted to open his eyes. With some difficulty, Rhys squinted against the harsh morning light. Where was he? The bridge? Why?

After trying to comprehend why he was on the bridge, he weakly looked to his left. A head came into view.

"Hey," Rhys murmured, recognizing Lyruc's short horsetail and crop of black hair. "I'm... awake." Lyruc didn't move. Rhys tried to sit up but found himself pinioned against the floor. "Lyruc." He shook him. When there was no response, Rhys gathered his strength and rolled Lyruc off of him.

The man slid limply onto the floor. His face lolled toward Rhys to reveal multiple shafts of wood and metal buried deep in his neck and chest. Rhys himself sat in a congealing pool of blood. Wide-eyed, Rhys looked about. He found only Andy and Vinz. Kyo was slumped in his chair, soaked in crimson.

Suddenly, everything came into focus, and a cacophony of sound struck him all at once.

"They're flanking us!" shouted Andy, bracing against the steering column. His left arm hung at a weird angle by his side.

"Where's Irvine?" asked Vinz, manning the weapons.

"Not here," Andy panted.

Another hot breeze swept through the bridge. How? The bridge was a locked cabin. Slipping in Lyruc's blood, Rhys clambered to his feet and gaped.

The entire port side of the bridge was gone. In its stead was a gaping hole of curled metal, splintered wood, and arcing wires. The pain in his head didn't come close to the panic and hysteria that now tore at his heart. Alina. Kallen. Hodge. Where were they?

Rhys steadied himself against the wall and took a deep breath.

"We can't keep this up," declared Vinz through gritted teeth.

Rhys stumbled to the front of the cabin and gazed out the horribly cracked windscreen. How long had he been unconscious?

He meant to dive headlong into the situation and provide immediate support for Vinz and Andy, but the moment he looked out the bridge, his attention shifted.

For as far as he could see, there stretched an endless field of fog, a mist that varied not only in density but in color. Brilliant reds blended with soft oranges to shimmer in the morning light. Perplexed, Rhys gazed upward out of the bridge. The colored fog was everywhere. Above *Themis* and high into the cloudless sky it sparkled in an astonishing mixture of bright hues.

Rhys peered over his shoulder. Though it hadn't been obvious before, the strange, scarlet fog hung even there in the bridge. Beyond confused, he set his gaze on Andy who gawked at him. "Your eyes," murmured the First Mate.

Vinz considered Rhys before saying, "Can you go?"

"I don't know... You don't see this colored fog, do you?" When neither replied, Rhys touched the left side of his face. It still hurt. *Pathos, what's going on?*

It took his AI a moment to respond which worried Rhys.

AI connection to the magnetic board was successful, Pathos finally replied. *Because the machine uses an ancient interface system, it needed to be adapted to your AI.*

So, all of these colors... These are magnetic fields?

I adapted your optical system to enable visual procurement of the magnetic fields. The readings are currently being reflected onto your retinas. The ability may be turned off at any time.

And the board?

Data downloaded from the board's computer indicates that the board will follow you so long as the following two conditions are adhered to, explained Pathos. *Firstly, the board must have access to adequate magnetic density, meaning it must be able to maintain altitude. Secondly, its pilot must always wear the tracking chip.*

Rhys looked down at the leather thong around his neck. It wasn't an initiation key as he had originally thought. It was a tracking chip.

Provided that the two conditions are met, you may call the board to you at any time. Only through your artificial intelligence enlightenment interface system is this capability available.

Rhys grabbed hold of Vinz's chair as *Themis* quaked from an explosion off her stern. *And the colors?* he asked of Pathos. *What do they mean?*

Unknown. Data must be acquired.

Rhys staggered over to the yawning hole along the port side of the bridge. *Come!* he shouted, using Pathos' connection to the board to issue the command.

The board appeared along the bridge's port. Rhys looked it over, his heart pounding. Despite having seen it fully extended before, there was something different about the machine as it hung in the morning sun. It seemed sleek, agile, and other-worldly.

He reached out. When his hand touched it, two compartments on the top of the board opened to reveal clasps.

Enemy is preparing another assault, Pathos reported suddenly.

Out of time, Rhys flung himself onto the board, his weight and momentum carrying the unit away from *Themis* and over the open water. Shakily, he pushed himself to his knees and then looked over his shoulder at *Themis*. The ship was wrecked.

Aside from the bridge, the stern mast had been snapped and one of its three motors destroyed. Rhys shifted his gaze to the attacking ships. Although it appeared *Themis* had destroyed one and disabled another, she was completely surrounded. Five Aabeshian military ships trailed in her wake, cannons bared.

A sudden burst of brilliant orange from atop *Themis'* deck drew Rhys' attention. To his surprise, he found Hodge, Kashim, and Alina mounting an offense. While Hodge and Kashim picked off people on the other decks using rifles, Alina sniped with the plasma firearm that Rhys had been wearing.

"*Gawan.*" Urging himself upright, he stepped into the clasps, right foot forward. When he settled his weight, the padded fastening snapped over the top of his foot and closed behind his ankle.

With his bare feet now completely clamped to the board, he looked out at the field of colors. It was going to take practice to read the flurry of reds and oranges that attacked his senses; it was like squinting through an eternal screen of noise.

He leaned his weight to the right and the board began drifting back toward *Themis.* He shifted to the left hard and the board banked suddenly, causing Rhys to yelp in surprise. Noting that the amount of force he placed on the board determined not only the direction but how hard it turned, he lowered himself to a crouch. The lower he got, the faster the board went. By the time he pushed himself back up to a standing form, he was already far from the battle.

He surveyed the oceanic battlefield briefly before leaning his weight to the right. Instead of zipping over the water as Rhys expected, the board sluggishly drifted through the air as though it was flying through molasses.

"What? What? What?" He looked about. "Why?" It was then that he realized the color of the fog around him. Orange. He looked over his shoulder and, spotting a field of red, shifted his weight toward it. The moment his board hit the red mist, it leapt forward in a great explosion of power. *You get all that?* he asked Pathos.

Yes. Red indicates a higher level of density in the magnetic field. Orange is a lower level.

A higher level of density means more power. He lowered himself to the board once more, and it picked up speed. Squinting against the wind, Rhys tore back to *Themis.* "Alina!" he shouted, coming alongside the ship.

Data collected thus far suggests that to make the board gain altitude, you need to put more force on the rear clasp, reported Pathos.

Rhys moved his weight to his left leg, and the board rose. He leveled off at the upper deck. Alina was already running toward him. When she was within range, she threw the plasma firearm. Rhys shifted his weight on the board, caught it, and then began ascending. Within seconds he was above the central mast.

He strapped the firearm on and connected it to Pathos. Though he would have liked the chance to become accustomed to the height, time wasn't on his side. He frantically surveyed the battle to establish which ship was causing the most damage. Determining that all were equally dangerous, Rhys banked to the left and took aim at the nearest ship's cannons.

One, two, three, four—four shots was all it took to disable the ship's port-side weapons. Rhys shifted his weight and began searching for his next target.

Before he could fire off another round, however, cannon fire exploded from one of the ships. Rhys had only a breath's moment to detect it and evade. Realizing that staying still was not an option, he lowered himself and rocketed toward a ship, staying low along the water. With the wind whistling in his ears, he purposefully edged back and forth along the magnetic waves to avoid the orange patches of weak force.

As he passed the ship, he fired at its cannons, causing immediate explosions and internal damage to the ship. He rose in a rush above his victim and then leaned hard to the right. Though he expected the tight turn, he didn't expect the speed. Gasping, Rhys grabbed hold of the board with his free hand and blinked to clear his vision of the gravitational forces.

"Let's go, let's go." He wasn't finished. He had already failed to protect *Themis*; he needed to make up for that.

He crossed the bow of another Aabeshian ship, took aim of her cannons, and fired. The plasma blasts melted through the weapon; a collection of delayed explosions created a fiery blaze that rolled across the deck.

Rhys banked hard. Prepared for the forces acting on his body, he squatted, held the board, and then leapt upward when the turn was complete. Though his vision had not tunneled, his muscles screamed. His legs shook horribly. "Come on!" he shouted to himself, punching the heel of his left foot into the board. He rocketed up and over the limping Aabeshian ship, leaving his stomach somewhere along the water's surface.

He passed over the next ship as a blur and opened fire on the main cannon located atop the ship's bridge. When a single shot did nothing to the enormous armament, Rhys fired multiples in an attempt to burn through the weapon's bracings.

Unaware the cannon's mountings had been disintegrated, the ship opened fire, causing the cannon to snap backward and topple from the top of the bridge to the middle deck. Its weight punched a hole there and bore it into the innards of the ship. Rhys didn't wait to watch the craft fill with water.

He glanced at *Themis,* which seemed to be gaining speed, and then tore toward his next target. As he prepared to fire at another ship's primary cannon, a rapid volley erupted from the vessel's stern guns. Rhys raced upward. He heard one or two shots ping off the underbelly of his board while the rest whizzed around him.

Teeth gritted, he banked hard and then dropped from the sky. His eyesight tunneled, and the air in his chest seemed to leave his body. Using Pathos to help lock onto his target, he fired at the stern gun; the ship's weapon melted and caught fire. Only at the last moment did he comprehend there was a human at its controls. "No," he murmured, realizing the man wasn't going to escape the growing inferno. "No!"

Without thinking, Rhys dove for the boat. When he was within jumping distance, he pulled his feet from the board's clasps and leapt onto the deck. His knees buckled beneath him. He staggered over to the uniformed man and, squinting against the heat of the fire, dragged the Aabeshian soldier from the controls of the stern gunner.

The right side of the soldier's face was burned as was his right arm. Struggling for strength, Rhys heaved the man across the deck until he could no longer feel the heat from the blaze.

"Sorry, I'm sorry. I'm sorry," he muttered. "I didn't mean to." Shaking, probably from shock, the man peered up at Rhys with his one good eye. "Medic!" shouted Rhys over his shoulder. "I need a doctor!" He clenched the man's uninjured arm. "They're coming. Hang on."

Voices rose on the deck as other soldiers appeared from their stations. Taking that as his cue, Rhys left the man, stepped back on his board—which had followed him up the deck—and lifted off. Not a single shot followed him.

Suddenly weary, Rhys gained altitude so he could study the battlefield. To his great relief, *Themis* was clear of cannon fire and blasting full-speed east toward the morning sun. Deciding that he didn't need to continue the attack, he followed after, minding the patches of orange fog that mingled with the red.

By the time he caught up with the ship, he could hardly remain standing. His legs threatened to give out beneath him and his back ached. He had a fierce headache. Flying alongside the ship, he surveyed the damage that had been done while he was unconscious.

Kashim was the first to spot him from the upper deck. He tapped Hodge, and together they rose to greet him. Alina wasn't there. Rhys stopped the board and gazed at them tiredly. Though they weren't as bad off as Andy and Vinz, Hodge had streaks of soot on his face, and Kashim's shirt was shredded down the front.

Rhys lowered the board to the deck and stepped out of the clasps. When his bare foot hit the deck, his legs gave. Hodge caught him, barely. "Alina?" asked Rhys. "Where is she?"

"She's tending to the wounded," Kashim explained lowly.

"Wounded… " Rhys leaned heavily against Hodge. "Who?

"We don't know."

Wide-eyed, Hodge asked, "Have… you seen yourself?"

"No," replied Rhys.

"Your eyes… are glowing. And… I can see the, eh, lines around them… "

"It's uh… " Rhys struggled to think of the words. "It's Pathos."

Kashim motioned to his board. "What do you want me to do with it?"

"I'll turn it off," said Rhys.

The pressure which had been growing exponentially behind his eyes lifted, and he sighed in elated relief. The distractingly bright array of colors was no longer a part of his vision. The world was as it should be.

"Hey… hey," said Hodge as Rhys' knees buckled.

Rhys grabbed for his friend. "Sorry. I need to lie down."

Hodge lowered him to the deck. Rhys tried to look up at them but found the simple motion impossible. He relaxed his neck, and his body followed.

Hours later, Rhys awakened in the shade of the main sail. For a long while, he listened to the water churn against the ship. Eventually, he opened his eyes and stared up at the azure sky. According to the sun's position, it had to be mid-to-late afternoon. He peered across the deck to find his board where he had left it.

Mustering his strength, Rhys struggled to sit up. He groaned as the muscles down the stretch of his back ached and burned. In the end, he rolled onto his side and then onto his stomach before pushing himself upright.

Flinching, wincing, and moaning, he clambered to his knees—his legs were in no better condition—and then rose to his feet. He stiffly shuffled the length of the deck to the ladder and entered the ship.

A trail of blood led from the bridge and decorated the inner staircase. Rhys stepped around the crimson trail and carefully hobbled down the stairs. He found Kallen sprawled out on the floor in the hallway outside the galley.

"Kallen!" he shouted, limping to her. He calmed himself when he realized she was asleep. Her clothes were brown with dried blood, and her face, arms, and hands were covered in soot and grease. Rhys looked over his shoulder and, finding blood leading into the galley, entered the room.

The galley was empty though it was obvious it had been used as a triage center. Soiled bandages, clothes, and napkins littered the room while all of Alina's medical supplies rested on a chair. Both tables were covered in streaks of blood.

Rhys turned to leave, but movement caught his eye. It was Alina. She had been sitting against the inner-most wall just beside where he stood. "Hey," he said, kneeling as swiftly as his legs would allow. "Hey."

Alina looked up at him. Her eyes were red. She had a large smear of dried blood on her forehead. She wore the apron she and Kallen normally used while cooking. Like the rest of the ship, she too was streaked in blood.

He held her face. "What happened?" Alina just stared at him. After a moment, Rhys tugged her into his embrace and kissed the top of her head. His sister began sobbing enormous, heaving cries of despair and sorrow.

He sat beside her for a long while and listened to her cry. Though she didn't say a word, Rhys understood enough. Their home for the past three months had been attacked. They had lost people, members of their crew. They could have lost each other.

He let his gaze fix on the soiled bandages scattered about the galley. He could have prevented this had he not been stunned by the board's computer interface. He should have connected to the *gawan* computer sooner. He had been foolish to think that the connection would happen effortlessly. He should have tested the board, learned more about it, flown it. He should have done everything sooner.

He could have stopped this—and that truth was going to haunt him for the rest of his life.

Sometime later, a small cough from across the hallway caused Alina to stir. Rhys heard a man moan. Alina disentangled herself from his arms and disappeared into the cabin across the hallway. He listened as she spoke to her patient, asking him questions and reassuring him. After a short moment, she reappeared. Tears gone, Alina took her bloodied apron off, draped it over a chair, and fetched water.

"Who is it?" asked Rhys.

"Leo."

"He was injured?"

Alina soaked a cloth in a small pail of water. "He protected Cantia when the engine exploded."

"How bad?" murmured Rhys.

"I've seen worse," was all his sister said as she left the galley.

Rhys struggled to his knees and then to his feet before stumbling into the hallway. After checking on Kallen, he made for the bridge. To his surprise, he found only Kashim. He noted the blood-drenched chair where Kyo had been sitting and the pool of brown blood which stained the area near the back wall where Rhys had been. Wearily, he looked at Kashim. So far, the man seemed to be the only one unaffected by the disaster. "What... happened?"

Kashim drew a long breath. "Irvine and his crew didn't set the snare."

Rhys thought for a long moment and then, unsure of how to introduce the question, said, "We lost people, didn't we?" Kashim nodded, his eyes set in the distance. "Who?"

"Kyo and Lyruc." He looked at Rhys. "Lyruc died protecting you."

"What... "

"The ship was shaking badly. He was holding you still to keep you from sliding about the bridge. The explosion came." Kashim nodded toward the hole behind Rhys. "He got on top of you. He saved your life."

Rhys looked at the brown, coagulated pool of blood near the back wall. A human had sacrificed himself for *him*.

"Total fatality count is two. Injured is three. Andy broke his arm in the explosion. Cantia was knocked out. I believe the word Alina used was 'concussion.' And Leo... " Kashim's sentence faded. Rhys waited patiently. "Alina is a miracle-worker. The boy should be dead."

"What happened to him?"

"Same as Kyo and Lyruc—he was hit with debris in an explosion. Punctured his innards."

"And Vinz?" asked Rhys.

"Physically, he's fine," concluded Kashim. Rhys waited for more, but Kashim remained silent. Taking that as his cue, Rhys left the bridge. He staggered down the stairs, passed Kallen, and looked into the cabin where Leo slept.

The room, which normally had clothes strewn on beds, was clean. Everything was piled in the corner of the room while Kallen's bed was stripped bare of blankets. Leo lay there, motionless. Rhys leaned in the doorway to study him. His entire torso was heavily bandaged. Alina sat at his head offering him water.

"Hey," murmured Hodge. Rhys looked at the bunk across the room. To his surprise, not only did he find Hodge but Cantia who was curled against him.

Rhys went to his friend. Hodge held out his hand, and they greeted each other warmly. Rhys sat at the end of Hodge's bed and gazed at Cantia. "How is she doing?"

"Alina says she just needs sleep," Hodge whispered. Like Kallen, his face, hands, and arms were soot-streaked. He had stripped out of his bloody shirt. "You? How are you?"

"Sore," replied Rhys.

Hodge lay back and rested his arm over his eyes. "What hell did we wake up to this morning?"

Rhys glanced at Alina and Leo and then stood. The guilt he felt overwhelmed him. "Is there anything that needs to be done right now?"

"Just rest," replied Hodge. Rhys left the room and stumbled down the hallway to his cabin. He entered, closed the door behind him, and then slid to the floor, tears gathering in his eyes.

29
SYNTHOCYTE COUNT

IT WAS SHORTLY AFTER MIDNIGHT when Rhys woke from his deep slumber. Kallen lay beside him naked as she had also stripped out of her filthy clothes.

Rhys rolled out of bed. He kicked his soiled clothes to the corner of the room, gathered clean ones, and crossed over to the washroom. As the wash tub filled, he studied himself in the small mirror. Aside from the pale, purple bags under his eyes, he could discern nothing out of the ordinary. Whatever Hodge had seen earlier had to have been purely from Rhys' connection to the board.

After scrubbing the dirt from his hair and the streaks of Lyruc's blood from his back, chest, and arms, Rhys changed into fresh clothes and stood in the middle of the darkened hallway. Dim lamplight shown from the table next to Leo's bed. The once-polished wood was blood crusted. Dark smears adorned the walls where people had braced.

Rhys returned to his cabin, pulled his shirt off, and rolled up his pants legs. Closing the door behind him, he padded down the hall, glanced into both the galley and main crew cabin—everyone was asleep, including Alina—and then slipped into the forward hatch.

He switched on the light and froze. There on the launch ramp were two bodies covered by a large drop-cloth.

They were dead. Their hearts no longer pumped blood and oxygen through their bodies; their brains no longer accepted or disseminated electrical signals to their limbs and muscles. They were plain, organic pieces of dead tissue now. They were nothing.

So why did the mere sight of Kyo and Lyruc's lifeless corpses tear a yawning hole deep within Rhys? Why did he feel the core of his being waver? Their lives were finished. They had been snuffed like a candle, never to be reignited again. Everything they stood for—their skills, talents, personalities, likes, dislikes, beliefs—all of it was gone. Was that it? If life was so fragile, what was its purpose?

Once more overwhelmed with guilt and shame, Rhys turned his attention to the supplies he had originally come to retrieve. He pulled a large bucket and several dust cloths from one of the crates and hurriedly left.

For hours, he scrubbed the blood from the inner platform, the stairs, and the hallway. He made numerous trips to the washroom to refill on soap and water and spent the majority of the time on his hands and knees despite his burning muscles. A little over two hours into his work, Alina appeared. She glanced at him, retrieved medicine and more bandages from the galley, and then returned to tend to Leo. Rhys worked through the night into the early morning hours before finally falling asleep in the hallway.

He woke midmorning to the smell of cooking food. When he sat up, blankets cascaded to the floor. He rubbed his face tiredly and then moved to his knees. As the muscles in his lower back seized, he groaned and flopped back. He rested his face on the blankets and stared at the opposite wall.

"You're awake," remarked Kallen, appearing in the galley doorway. Rhys glanced at her but didn't move. "What's wrong?"

"I can't get up," he muttered pitifully. Kallen chuckled. "No. I'm serious. I can't move."

"Oh. Hold on." Kallen disappeared into the galley and then returned. "Hodge," she called into the cabin, kneeling beside Rhys. "What's wrong?"

"My back."

Hodge joined them. "What?"

"Help me lift him," Kallen instructed, pushing Rhys onto his left side. Rhys hissed in pain as the muscles in his back spasmed painfully once more. "Hodge, on three. One, two, three." Together, they lifted him to his feet and kept him steady.

"You got it?" asked Hodge.

Rhys nodded and followed Kallen into the galley where he hobbled to a chair and stiffly sat. "I'll make some hot water for you in a bit, and we'll put it on your back," said Kallen. "It's from the board, right?"

"Mh-hm." Rhys searched the galley for remnants of blood but found none. "Who cleaned the galley?"

"Vinz," replied Kallen. "Kashim took care of the bridge."

"And Leo? How is he?"

"Doing better. Alina's an amazing doctor. He won't be allowed to get up for the next day or two, but he'll be capable by the time we reach Brechin. The emergency tools and medicines that came with you are absolutely amazing."

"How far out are we from Brechin?"

Kallen stirred the pan's contents. "Six days."

"And the others? Andy and Cantia?"

"Andy will be in a sling for a while. Cantia woke earlier before going back to sleep."

They sat in silence throughout the meal. As Kallen distributed bowls to the remaining crew, Rhys ate, his eyes set on the floor. Afterward, he helped Kallen clean the galley and then retired to his cabin where he found Alina asleep in her bunk. Kallen joined him a few minutes later with a pot of hot water and several clean rags. She helped him lie down and then roll over. Grimacing, Rhys tried to relax the straining muscles in his back, but it was no use.

After soaking cloths, wringing them out, and laying the hot rags across Rhys' back, she kneaded the strained muscles with strong hands. Aside from Rhys' intermittent hisses of pain, they didn't said anything because there was nothing to say.

"We'll send off Kyo and Lyruc this evening," Kallen eventually said, kissing his hair. "I'll wake you before then if you're asleep."

Rhys looked at her. "Send off?"

"Their bodies," she replied.

"What happens to their bodies?"

"Vinz wrapped the bodies this morning," Kallen murmured somberly. "We'll open the forward hatch and let them go to the sea." She picked up the pot and left the cabin. Rhys gingerly rolled onto his side—his back didn't hurt as badly now—and gazed at the wall.

Everything was his fault.

That evening, Rhys gathered in the forward hatch with the other crew members. Leo was the only one not in attendance. With morbid curiosity, Rhys watched as Vinz visited both bodies in silence and then, with Kashim's help, tied the cloth-wrapped corpses to a large chunk of metal Rhys recognized as a part of the destroyed engine mount. When they were ready, Vinz nodded to Hodge who cranked open the hatch. Water submerged the ramp and covered both bodies.

Eyes moist, Kallen waded onto the ramp and touched both Kyo and Lyruc fondly. She bowed her head momentarily and then returned to Rhys' side. Andy and Hodge did the same. Vinz glanced at Rhys as if to ask if he too was going to participate in the motion, but Rhys only stared. The action had no meaning, it had no purpose. Both were dead. Neither had a consciousness anymore. What was the point?

Sensing his confusion, Vinz grimly smiled and then motioned to Kashim and Hodge. Together they lifted the heavy engine mount and carried it to the edge of the ramp. Under Vinz's instruction, they dropped it and stepped back. In the blink of an eye, both Lyruc and Kyo vanished into the sea.

Standing on the submerged ramp, Vinz regarded the remainder of his crew. He appeared worn. Though, like Rhys, he was unable to grow much facial hair, the Overseer looked ragged and weary. His eyes were sullen.

"It is said that… time heals pain," began Vinz. He thought for a moment and then shook his head. "I disagree." His gray eyes passed over each person. "Time doesn't heal pain. Our minds, in fits of despair and grief, work to cover the wounds with scar tissue so the cut doesn't hurt as much. The wound never disappears. It stays with us for the rest of our lives, reminding us of our mistakes, of our regrets, and of our misgivings. Pain is wicked; pain is vile." Vinz paused briefly. "But pain is also powerful. It can create change and move people to action. It can strengthen resolve, fortify hearts, and illuminate minds. It can unify people. As we move forward from this point, let us not falter in what we must do; let us not be misled by revenge or rage. Our journey continues. Our objective remains the same."

The crew split from there. Kashim, Vinz, and Andy went up to the bridge; Hodge guided Cantia from the forward hatch with Alina close behind. Rhys remained behind to help Kallen close the door and organize the cabin.

Afterward, Kallen went to the engine room to check on her makeshift repairs and Rhys retired to his cabin. Though he passed Hodge and Cantia, who were in the galley playing a game, he didn't join them. He found Alina in their cabin perched on the edge of her bed. When he entered, she didn't look up. Rhys closed the door behind him and sat weakly on his bunk. He flinched as the muscles in his lower back pulled taut.

"I feel… as though much happened while I was unconscious," he murmured.

"Much did happen." His sister studied his face for a long moment and then said, "Why are you in so much pain?"

"I'm sore from piloting the board."

"Is that really it?"

Rhys thought for a long moment and then gaped at her.

Alina nodded, crossed the room, and knelt before Rhys. She dug her fingers into his wrist and examined his pulse. "Pathos, report to me Rhys' blood pressure and oxygen intake."

"Blood pressure is 119 over 81," replied Pathos. "Oxygen intake at 99 percent."

"Run a complete blood count on Rhys."

"One moment."

Rhys kept his eyes on Alina's bare feet, dreading the results.

"CBC complete," said Pathos.

"And the results?" asked Alina, sitting back on her heels.

"Red blood cell count, hemoglobin, and hematocrit levels: average. White blood cell count: above average. Platelet count: average."

Rhys looked to Alina to gauge her reaction.

"Provide details regarding the white blood cell count," ordered Alina.

"Neutrophils: 43 percent. Lymphocytes: 32 percent. Monocytes: 6 percent. Eosinophils: 2.5 percent. Basophils: 0.7 percent. Synthocytes: 44 percent," hummed Pathos.

Alina looked at Rhys. Mouth suddenly dry, Rhys asked quietly, "How bad is it?"

"Pathos, please run a complete scan on all synthetic synapses. Lie down."

Rhys attempted to do so with some grace. Instead, he collapsed unceremoniously onto his bed and stared at the top bunk.

"It's going to take a short while," Alina explained. "Aside from the synapses that all humans are born with, you and I are were given trillions of synthetic synapses which allow the processing of data acquired by our AIs."

"I see." Rhys looked across the room. "It's… bad, huh?"

Alina slid the cabin door closed with her foot and then moved to his bed. "I want my results to be conclusive."

"Will this test confirm your theory?" murmured Rhys.

"Yes."

Rhys laid his arm over his eyes. "If... my AI is corrupted... is there anything that can be done?"

His sister's response was soft. "No, not that I know of."

Rhys felt a tight pinch in his nose, and his eyes tickled. "Uh... if it's... " He cleared his tightening throat. "If it's corrupted, how long will it take before... "

"I don't know. I'll need Pathos to report on your CBC, specifically on your synthocyte count, daily. I'll check your synthetic synapses as well. Once we have a daily reading, I can calculate... " Her sentence faded.

Rhys nodded. He hoped Alina couldn't see his face flushing with fear and panic. "Well, we knew the risks... didn't we?"

There was a cautious knock on the door before it opened tentatively. "Rhys, do you want... " Kallen's voice faded upon seeing the grim expressions on their faces. "I'm sorry. I didn't mean to interrupt." She left.

"Pathos, what's your status?" muttered Alina.

"Status: 83 percent completed," replied Pathos.

Alina stood, retrieved one of Rhys' empty translation notebooks, and began scribbling notes in preparation for Pathos' report. With Alina's attention elsewhere, Rhys took the opportunity to swipe at the tears that had gathered in his eyes.

"Synthetic synapses scan completed. Total efficacy at 96 percent," reported Pathos. Alina quickly wrote the results and closed the notebook.

"Ninety-six percent," said Rhys, looking at her. "Is that... bad?"

Alina shook her head. "It's not bad. I thought it was going to be worse."

Rhys rolled onto his side and tried to push himself up, but his back spasmed and, groaning, he fell still. Alina gazed at him. "You're lying to me," he said finally.

His sister stood. "I'm not lying to you."

"Then why do I hurt so much?"

"Pathos runs through your entire body. The AI is intertwined with every system via nerves and synthetic materials. It took a hard blow. Of course your body will be sore."

Still unsure whether Alina was being completely honest, Rhys began to sit up; Alina helped him. "What can be done?"

"Medication. There's some in the pack meant specifically to ease the pain and slow corruption. Superficial methods to soothe the muscles and relax the nerves will also work."

"Can I still pilot the board?"

"Of that I am not sure. It's possible the damage your AI incurred is done. It's finished. None more can be received from the board as you are fully capable of communicating with the ancient computer and processing its data." Alina cocked her head. "Or, it could be that every time you use the board, the condition is exacerbated."

"And there's no way to know unless I pilot it again," he mused darkly.

"Correct."

"Am I... going to die?"

"I won't know until I have several days' worth of data."

Rhys nodded. "Please don't tell anyone. Not even Hodge."

"I won't." She glanced about the room. "We probably shouldn't utilize the internal communication system. Honestly, I think it would be fine, but on the off-chance that it affects Logos... "

"I understand," replied Rhys.

"I have to go check on Leo." Alina slipped from the room, leaving Rhys alone with his thoughts.

He didn't want Kallen or Hodge to know. They didn't need to know. It would only make them worry. Rhys moved to his feet and shuffled from the room across the hallway. He stood outside of Vinz's cabin for a long moment and then knocked.

"What?" came Vinz's muffled response.

"It's me," said Rhys. "Can we talk?"

"Does it... have to be right now?" Vinz asked.

"Uh, no. It can be later." He returned to his cabin, closed the door, and fell onto his bed.

30
DEAD ZONE

THE NEXT TWO DAYS WERE uneventful and boring. The battle with the Aabeshian military had crushed the crew's spirit; half of its remaining members were injured. Though some semblance of routine returned, it didn't feel right without Lyruc or Kyo. The ship seemed bigger, the cabins quieter, and the bridge emptier.

By the dawn of the second day, Leo was conscious and hobbling about with Hodge or Kallen's help. Alina was never far from his side, talking with him, checking on his wounds and wellbeing, and whispering to him in the night.

Since the battle, Cantia had not only stuck closely to Hodge but had begun hanging out with Kallen in the engine room. "What changed Cantia's attitude?" asked Rhys late in the afternoon on the second day as he and Kallen sat in the shade on the upper deck.

Kallen, who was preparing a solar panel for replacement on the main sail, smiled. "Because I saved her."

"When?"

"During the battle. When the third engine blew, it shot debris into the ship. Leo was hit. Cantia ran for help. She found me in the engine room trying to put out a fire." Kallen looked at Rhys. "One of the support beams against the wall came loose. I grabbed her just as it fell. Unfortunately, that's also how she got her concussion."

"And Hodge?"

"Hodge took care of Leo. He carried him to the galley, put pressure on his wounds, and watched over him until Alina arrived. She adores Hodge." Kallen shrugged. "She tolerates me."

Rhys stretched out on the deck and looked up at the azure sky. Thanks to the medication Alina had started giving him to ease the pain of the corruption, he could at least appear normal. "We're four days out from Brechin. Is that right?"

"There about," replied Kallen. "It's slow going. We're missing an engine, so our speed has been reduced dramatically."

"Are we expecting to run into trouble between now and then?"

"Kashim can answer that. I honestly don't know."

That night, Rhys approached Vinz once more but found the Overseer already asleep. Though surrounded by friends, Rhys felt utterly alone. He wanted to discuss with Vinz his own situation, but according to Hodge, the Overseer had taken the battle hard. It seemed Vinz, like Rhys, blamed himself for Kyo and Lyruc's deaths.

The following morning, after helping Kallen clean the galley, he waited for Leo. Though Alina felt perfectly comfortable helping him, there were some things Leo preferred to do alone—or preferred to *attempt* to do alone. Bathing was one of them.

"I'm not totally helpless," Leo muttered as Rhys closed the washroom door behind them. "I can wash myself."

"Alina said that I have to help you into the bathtub," replied Rhys. "Don't touch your stitches either."

Leo glanced down at the numerous wounds along his torso which were stitched closed and covered in a blue, goopy paste. He touched the glue tentatively. "What is this?"

"Sealant." Rhys checked the water temperature and then turned to Leo. "Strip."

"So romantic." The young man turned his back to Rhys. Once naked, Leo approached the tub. He lifted a leg but immediately teetered. Rhys supported his arms and slowly lowered him into the tub. "How pathetic am I?"

"Start washing," instructed Rhys. "That sealant won't stay on forever."

"I'm fine, I'm fine. Now go," growled Leo before pouring water atop his head.

"I'm outside. Call me when you're ready to get out. *Don't* try to by yourself." Rhys stepped from the washroom, closed the door, and leaned against the wall.

Caution. Extended radar has detected two airships moving west-by-southwest, alerted Pathos suddenly. *Course appears to be set for this ship.*

Rhys cursed and threw the washroom door back open. "Get out, now." Leo was covered in soap. "We have airships coming in." Leo grabbed a bucket of water, threw it over his head, and held his arm out to Rhys. "Alina!" shouted Rhys over his shoulder as he began lifting Leo out of the tub.

"What is it?" asked Hodge, appearing in the doorway.

"Airships," Alina replied, joining them.

"Can we please close the door?" growled Leo as Rhys helped him from the tub.

"Hodge, take him."

"No, I can launch," argued Hodge. "You and I can launch."

Rhys looked to Alina who grabbed towel and pushed into the washroom. Rhys passed Leo to her and then slipped out. He rushed to the bridge where Andy and Vinz sat. "We have airships coming in."

"They're not anywhere on our scanners," replied Andy.

"Not yet they aren't." Rhys looked at Vinz. "What do you want to do?"

"You're sure they're airships?" the Overseer queried.

"Two of them."

"They must have launched from Brechin," mused Vinz. He glanced over his shoulder as Hodge joined them. "Brechin's the only place around here with such technology."

"Why would they be coming out this far though?" asked Andy.

"For us," replied Rhys, glancing at Kashim as he also joined. "Pathos calculated their course. They'll be here within the half hour, if not sooner."

"It's possible word finally reached Brechin about the Golden Corridor," Hodge suggested with a shrug.

"Or that Irvine and his crew have made it to harbor and mentioned they had a run-in with pirates," said Vinz.

"We're not pirates," replied Rhys.

"On the other side of the Golden Corridor, Brechin polices the waters. If there are sightings of pirates or renegades, airships are sent out," explained Kashim. "Slave traders aren't pirates. They're businessmen. Our ship, on the other hand…"

"What will happen once the airships arrive?" asked Vinz.

"We don't know their reasoning. It's possible, like Hodge said, that they've only just been notified of the incident along the Golden Corridor. They may be scouting."

"They're not scouting," replied Rhys. "Their course is set for us."

"The only banner we have indicates we hail from New Arbroath," offered Vinz.

"We also have readings," said Andy, standing over the radar imaging screen. "He's right. There are two."

Vinz stood. "What's the likelihood of attack?"

"Again, it will depend upon what it is they've been told. If we're pirates, a direct attack is likely. If they are simply coming to investigate, then they could perform a fly-by," Kashim offered.

The bridge was silent for a long moment before Vinz looked at Rhys. "I want you to launch. Be prepared to use force to defend this ship."

Rhys nodded grimly and left the bridge. At the bottom of the inner staircase, he stared at the floor. *Can we do this? I don't… want to die.*

The decision is yours, replied Pathos.

As my AI, what do you suggest?

It is not my place to tell you that.

It is your place to advise me on matters pertaining to life and death. When Pathos didn't respond, Rhys asked, *What was last night's result for the synthetic synapses scan?*

Synthetic synapse efficacy was last measured at 94.4 percent, Pathos reported matter-of-factly.

"What did they decide?" asked Kallen, appearing from forward hatch.

Rhys wiped all emotion from his face. "I'm launching."

"Are you up to that?" Kallen followed him into the forward hatch. "I know you're still sore."

"I'll be fine," he replied, crossing the cabin. Kallen joined him, and together, they set the board on the upper edge of the ramp.

"We're ready for launch," called Kallen into the communication tube.

"*Themis* is stopped. Launch when ready," came Vinz's reply.

Kallen jogged to the other side of the cabin and cranked at the hatch chains; the hatch door opened, and water climbed the ramp. Rhys grabbed his firearm, connected it to Pathos, and slung the resonance cutters over his back. "Hey," said Kallen, stopping him.

Rhys looked at her. "What?"

Kallen seemed to push away whatever was on her mind and shrugged. "I just wanted to make sure that everything was fine between you and Alina. You've been speaking often—just the two of you— especially in the evenings."

Rhys knelt beside the board. "We're just discussing what we think is going to happen once we arrive in Brechin."

"We want to get moving," called Vinz through the communication pipe. "Rhys, launch!"

"Almost!" shouted Rhys over his shoulder. He reache under the board's belly, slid open the small hatch, and turned on the computer. "Pathos, connect me."

Data-lock initiating in five seconds, said Pathos.

Rhys prepared his mind and his body. Pain was inevitable.

Source confirmed. Data-lock, engaging.

Rhys groaned as pressure swelled behind his eyes. The left side of his head where Pathos' external unit connected burned horribly. Gritting his teeth, he clenched his eyes and resisted the overwhelming urge to claw at Pathos' unit. The pain in his back returned. Though it wasn't in full force, he could tell that soon it would be bad enough.

After a long moment, Rhys opened his eyes. The cabin was filled with orange fog. He blinked and then looked at the board which floated before him. Distantly, he sensed Kallen's eyes on him. He needed to do what he could and get it over with, *quickly*. He kicked off his boots and stepped lightly onto the board. The clasps appeared, and he settled his weight into their grasps.

Orange fog. This color indicated magnetic fields dense enough to carry the board and that was about it. Rhys wiggled the board's tail left and right and then pushed off from the forward hatch. The board sluggishly warbled out of the cabin into the brilliant morning sunlight.

Rhys looked about and, spotting several patches of red fog before him, steered his board toward them. The moment he entered the screen of red, the world turned into a solid blur. The board sprang forward like a fidgeting horse that had been asked to restrain its power and soared into the air. Rhys made a few passes across the bow and then retreated to the stern of the ship. He tried to ignore Alina who stood on the upper deck, her eyes set on him, and instead looked east. The airships would be making an appearance any moment.

No sooner had he thought it than two black dots appeared on the horizon. Rhys studied them, glanced at Alina, and then soared upward. Higher and higher he climbed until the air began to feel cool against his skin.

Keeping an eye on the two airships, he surveyed the magnetic fields around him. Though the majority of them shimmered red with glimpses of orange, every so often patches of black or gray caught his attention. If orange caused his board to operate sluggishly, he didn't want to know the effects of black or gray-colored magnetic fields.

Once he set his trajectory, he glanced down at *Themis* and then banked for the airships. Perhaps he could discern their purpose before they reached *Themis.*

Dodging the alarming number of gray and black patches, Rhys sped for the airships. They weren't as he remembered from their first night on Earth, but he had not gotten a clear view then.

They bristled with weaponry—six turrets and a forward-mounted cannon per ship. The airships were long and boasted four powerful fans, two small ones in the front and two larger ones in the rear. Despite Rhys' aerial view, he could very clearly make out numerous men clothed in black and orange riding atop the airship surrounded by railing and various types of barriers. All carried rifles and other weapons Rhys couldn't identify.

What could he do? Should he attack? What if they were just coming to check on *Themis?* He didn't want to kill anyone.

Injure, maim? Yes.

Kill? No.

But if he didn't do something, they could attack *Themis,* sink her, and kill her crew.

Still wavering in his decision, Rhys lowered his board steadily until he was directly above the ship. Heart in his throat, he pulled his feet from the clasps and jumped. The airship appeared under him sooner than he expected, and he collapsed and rolled across the deck. When he sat up, aching, he found his board hovering by his side—and a gaggle of soldiers gaping at him.

Using the board as support, Rhys pulled himself to his feet. "Your commanding officer, where is he?"

"Here," came a rough voice. A short man with a large mustache pushed through the soldiers and approached Rhys, his rifle ready. "Who are you?"

"I'm from the ship you're preparing to attack," said Rhys. "*Themis.*"

"You're a white god," muttered the officer.

"We're making our way to Brechin," continued Rhys. "We were forced to fight through the Golden Corridor and have taken on heavy damage."

"Why do you need to get to Brechin so badly?"

"I need to speak with the high priest."

The officer considered him and then said, "We're following information regarding the capture of Lady Cantia Sorex, daughter of the Minister of Justice of Brechin. We were informed she had been picked up by a slave ship out of Bathsgate."

"Though that might be true, we're not a slave ship," replied Rhys. "We sail from New Arbroath to inquire after an audience with the high priest."

"It is true, Lord," said the officer, nodding in acknowledgment of Rhys, "that you are a white god, however, your ship does not bear insignia that would identify her as a diplomat's ship. We still need to search her."

Rhys nodded. "Very well. I will add, however, that I am not the only diplomat onboard. We carry also my sister as well as Leucetios Damian, youngest son of the Minister of Education. Unfortunately, Leucetios was injured badly during the battle and has been under my sister's care for the past several days."

The officer lowered his rifle. "That's fine. Our search will be thorough but quick."

Rhys glanced at the soldiers. "I must warn you that we have taken causalities and are not in the mood to be trifled with. If you come with guns ready, you will be met in a similar fashion. We survived the Aabeshian army alone. Don't think we can't take you as well." He stepped onto his board, surveyed the magnetic fields around him, and then leapt from the ship.

Decision made, he rose sharply above the airship and then dashed back to *Themis*. They couldn't get a hold of Cantia! She was a key to unlock the many bureaucratic doors in the capital. Rhys glanced over his shoulder at the airships and then dove for *Themis*.

"Alina!" he shouted, banking hard and pulling up beside her. "Get me Cantia. Now. Hurry. They're after her. We can't lose her."

Alina slid down the ladder and disappeared into the ship. Rhys lowered himself onto the outer platform beside the ladder and waited, panting. Momentarily, Alina reappeared with Cantia who took one look at Rhys, screamed, and attempted to flee back into the ship.

"Cantia, Cantia," said Alina. "Listen." She held the girl firmly. "Men are coming for you. You're not safe on the ship. You have to go with Rhys until they leave."

Cantia peeked at Rhys over her shoulder, her eyes wide and mouth open. "What... happened to you?"

Alina lifted Cantia onto Rhys' board. "It's Rhys. This is Rhys. Go with him." Cantia wrapped her arms around Rhys' waist and buried her face into his shirt. Rhys exchanged looks with Alina and then, using *Themis* as a shield to block his movements, skimmed across the water.

For several long minutes, he soared just above the water away from *Themis*. Eventually, Cantia turned to watch, but she kept a death grip on him.

"Who's coming?" she asked when Rhys finally slowed to a stop. *Themis* was a black dot now.

"Soldiers," he replied. "They're looking for you."

Cantia wrenched her head back to glare at Rhys. "Why did you take me? They're looking for me!"

"Doesn't matter," he said. "We need you."

Cantia turned and began screaming. "Heyyyy! I'm here! I'm here!"

"What are you doing?" hissed Rhys, covering her mouth. She spitefully licked his palm. Rhys jerked his hand from her. "Listen, we need you. You're valuable."

"Because I'm the daughter of the Minister of Justice?"

"Yes, because you can vouch for us," replied Rhys. "You and Leo both."

"So why didn't you take Leo too?"

"Because I didn't buy him from a slave ship. He boarded our ship of his own accord."

Cantia gazed up at him with contempt. "Why do your eyes look like that?" she murmured. "And your face."

"It's the board," replied Rhys.

"How does the board make your eyes glow?" ·

"My computer, it reflects light onto my eyes so I can see the magnetic fields necessary to pilot this thing."

"And your face?"

"I don't know. What's it doing to my face?"

Cantia touched the left side of his face. "All of the veins, they're glowing, but they're also blue, which I don't understand."

Rhys tried to smile but only grimaced. "I must appear frightening."

Cantia nodded and then surveyed the water. "The soldiers aren't going to hurt anyone, are they?"

"They shouldn't." Rhys wanted to believe his own words.

For the next half hour, they drifted a few paces above the water, exchanging small-talk and stories. By the time Pathos informed him it was safe to return to *Themis*, he could hardly see straight. Beyond exhausted, head throbbing, and vision blurring, he started the journey back to the ship.

"Rhys?" called Cantia. Her voice seemed muffled to him. "Rhys? Rhys?"

He snapped out of his trance. "Hm? What?"

"I don't think... we're moving," she said, looking about. "I could be wrong because the water is shifting below us, but... I don't think... "

Rhys blinked and looked about. It took him a moment to realize that although there were patches of red or orange around him, the exact color that currently held his board was gray—gray fog. "It's a dead zone," he mused.

"Am I wrong?" asked Cantia.

"No, you're right. We're not moving." Rhys searched for the nearest patch of red or orange fog. Spotting a shimmering red patch of fog a few meters away, he sighed. "We have to swim."

"What? Why?" quavered Cantia.

He pointed to the red patch of fog which he realized she couldn't see. "We're in a dead zone. We need to get to an area that has a denser magnetic field."

"I can't swim," the girl admitted fearfully.

Rhys pulled his feet from the clasps. "I'm going to turn the board off, so it's going to hit the water."

"No, Rhys. I don't like the water. I can't swim."

"I'll hold you. Just stay on the board. Pathos, disconnect me," he breathed.

Disengaging data-lock.

The board dropped into the water. Despite his overwhelming fatigue, Rhys managed to trap Cantia on the board to keep her from rolling off. Panting from the pain he was now in, he asked, "You have a good hold?"

"Yes," she whimpered.

"I'm going to let you... go now. I have to push." Rhys released her and then weakly got behind the board. He started kicking. His legs and back spasmed simultaneously, and he flinched. Pushing through it, he ordered himself to kick, to propel them to the red fog. "Pathos?" he asked after a minute of kicking.

One more meter, replied Pathos. Gasping, Rhys frog-kicked the remaining distance. *Magnetic field is red.*

Connect me, said Rhys, lying his head on the board. The familiar pressure behind his eyes returned full force, and pain flared up his back to his neck.

"Rhys!" screamed Cantia. Distantly, he felt her hands on him, but he couldn't bring himself to move. "Rhys! Come on! Rhys!" A force hit him hard across the face, knocking him awake. Rhys opened his eyes and looked at Cantia. Her hand was poised to slap him again. "Come on!" she cried, swollen tears pouring down her face. She was terrified.

Rhys dragged himself onto the board and, legs trembling, pushed his feet under him. With Cantia's help, he stood and slipped into the clasps. The board began skimming across the surface once more.

Cantia gripped him tightly. "Rhys, come on."

Rhys widened his eyes to keep them from drooping and focused on *Themis.* "Crouch, Cantia." The board shot forward. "Lean left," he said, spotting a gray patch ahead. "Easy." As they approached *Themis,* he added pressure to his left leg, and the board climbed. They leveled out over the upper deck and landed.

Cantia stepped off and turned to help him, but Rhys was already going down. "Hey!" Cantia tried to grab him. He felt himself slip through her fingertips.

31
THE CURSE REVEALED

A LOUD THUMP SHOOK RHYS' bed, waking him from his coma-like sleep.

"He could have killed himself!" Kallen snarled. Rhys tried to open his eyes but found them insufferably heavy.

"Get your hands off of me," said Alina.

"Kallen, come on," murmured Hodge.

"Don't you dare tell me to calm down." Rhys felt his bed quiver again. "I know you're as pissed as I am!"

"The point of the matter is that he didn't kill himself," Alina continued stoically. "He's fine. Now, get your hands off me."

"Is he though?" asked Kallen. "That *gawan* board is killing him!"

"Kallen, enough," barked Hodge.

"I'll pound her face in!"

Mustering all of his willpower, Rhys forced open his eyes. The entire room was blurry. He blinked to clear his vision. Alina stood at his bedside, her brows furrowed in an indiscernible expression. Nearby, Hodge had Kallen pinned against the doorway.

"Get a hold of yourself," Hodge demanded.

Kallen glowered at Alina. "Were you ever going to tell me?" Rhys wasn't sure he had ever seen Kallen appear so fierce, so enraged. He tried to sit up, but nothing moved. His body felt like a lead weight.

"No," came Alina's eventual response.

Kallen strained against Hodge. "That thing… was going to kill him… and you weren't going to tell a single person!"

"I was told not to," countered Alina.

"Alina," whispered Rhys. The room fell silent.

Alina pushed past Kallen. "Hold on." Rhys closed his eyes and waited; everything on him hurt—bad. His sister returned with a metal injector which she had already loaded with an opaque vial. "I'm giving you a quarter vial," she told him in their native tongue.

"More," whispered Rhys.

Sensing Alina's hesitation, he looked at her wearily. Alina spoke lowly. "Monaxin is an emergency narcotic for AI corruption. It has addictive qualities. Plus, I don't have an infinite supply of it."

Sighing, Rhys closed his eyes. "Fine."

"I'm trying to protect you," whispered Alina. She loaded the injector, placed it under Rhys' chin, and pressed it firmly against his skin. He felt a collection of pinches as half a dozen fine needles punctured the soft skin along his jaw. A soft hiss ensued as the substance was released into him. The pain eating away at his back immediately subsided.

He drew a deep breath and stared at the bottom of the top bunk.

Kallen tentatively drew closer. "Rhys?"

"Give him a moment," instructed Alina, returning the medical supplies to the pack.

Rhys took several more calming breaths, feeling better each time he inhaled. After a moment, he pushed himself upright and gingerly touched the left side of his face. It was tender.

Kallen stood at his bedside. "Why would you hide something like this from us?"

"I didn't want to worry you. Not after the Golden Corridor," murmured Rhys. He glanced at Hodge, who leaned in the doorway, his gaze averted elsewhere in obvious disappointment. "It's not as bad as it seems."

"It isn't?" Vinz stepped past Hodge and entered the room. "This is what you've been wanting to talk to me about, isn't it?"

"Could everyone please... go away?" muttered Rhys.

Vinz turned to Alina. "How bad is it?"

Rhys sensed Alina's gaze on him, but he didn't look at her. He was too ashamed, too tired, and too distraught. He wanted to be left alone. He didn't want everyone fussing over him; it was humiliating.

"Every time Rhys pilots the board," said Alina, "his condition will worsen. We had hoped that wouldn't be the case, however, this last flight proved otherwise."

"And what exactly is happening to him?" asked Vinz.

"Alina." Rhys glanced at his sister and then looked at the others. "This has nothing to do with you. Any of you."

"His bonding to the board's computer has resulted in corruption," said Alina.

"Meaning what?" Kallen whispered thickly.

"I'm dying," snapped Rhys. "My AI has been corrupted. It's killing me."

Stunned silence ensued. Rhys glanced at his sister and then looked at Kallen whose eyes were filling with tears.

"It was my choice," Rhys continued. "I knew it was a possibility, but... I didn't want to be useless. I wanted to protect you, all of you. I wanted to do something because... "

"Because when we were on Caelestis," interrupted Alina, "he could do nothing."

Hodge motioned to Alina. "What's the medication you just gave him do?"

"It slows the corruption process of the synthetic synapses in his brain and eases the pain that it causes," Rhys' sister explained. "As I was telling Rhys though, Monaxin is a highly addictive narcotic. Although it's meant specifically to help slow the corruption process, those who use it become addicted to it because of the relief it provides."

"Are there no long-term solutions?" mused Vinz. "Nothing to halt the process?"

"Not that I know of. Short of separating Rhys from his AI, I don't know of anything that would stop the process." Alina gazed at Rhys. "Every time he pilots the board, the corruption process accelerates—at least during the time that he pilots it. So, the longer he spends on the board, the more damage it causes."

"So what did that little excursion cost me?" Rhys bitterly muttered.

Alina didn't answer.

"Answer his question," commanded Vinz grimly.

"Efficacy of your synthetic synapses is at 87 percent," murmured Alina.

Rhys held in the urge to cry. He couldn't let them see his panic, his hysteria.

"I could have gone out," seethed Hodge. He kicked the doorway. "I could have launched!" He disappeared down the hallway.

"I don't want you on the board anymore," said Vinz. "Don't connect to it, don't touch it, don't go near it." Before Rhys could argue, Vinz left the cabin.

Kallen closed the door. Her back to them, she took a deep breath and said, "When are you two going to learn? It's not you two against the world anymore. It's all of us."

"I disagree," Alina immediately countered. "It will always be this way. Rhys and I are not from here, and we never will be. The fact of the matter is that this is not home; this is not who we are. It is not what we were raised to be. When Vinz goes on his sanctimonious spiels about bringing peace and understanding between civilizations, we look at him the same way you look at the Pantarak peo—"

"Alina," interrupted Rhys. "Enough. That isn't true, and you know it. You're angry."

Alina started for the door. "I regret letting you talk me into participating in this journey," she muttered in Nefegian. "We're going to end up killing ourselves." She slammed the door open and stalked out.

32
EMOTIONAL TOLL

FOR THE NEXT TWO DAYS, tempers remained high on *Themis*. Even between himself and Kallen, Rhys could feel tension. He supposed it was because everyone was upset that he had kept such a devastating secret from them, but he couldn't be sure. Kashim, Vinz, and Andy stayed on the bridge most hours, exchanging shifts every so often with Hodge and Kallen to get some rest. Despite the atmosphere onboard, Leo continued to recover. Under Alina's watchful eye, he tormented Cantia and wrote in his journal when he felt well enough.

Unfortunately, Leo's rebounding energy seemed to only exaggerate the general unease and imbalance onboard. Kallen and Alina often passed each other looks but refrained from speaking. Hodge kept to himself and lay out on the upper deck in the evenings with Cantia. Andy remained aloof and unwilling to speak with Rhys—whether he blamed Rhys for Kyo and Lyruc's deaths, Rhys didn't know, but he suspected. Only Kashim and Vinz seemed unfazed by the unrest onboard. While everyone else walked on eggshells around Rhys, both treated him no differently. Despite Rhys' obvious fatigue, Vinz still asked him to help clean the ship daily and assist Kallen in maintenance.

On the eve of the sixth day, they finally limped into Brechin's port. After docking and registering *Themis* with the port authority, they locked the ship down and went to bed. Dawn the next morning, they found Leo gone.

"Did *anyone* see him leave?" sighed Vinz, standing in the hallway.

"Why didn't he take me?" Cantia plaintively asked.

"Hodge, you and Andy check the docks. He's still recovering. He couldn't have gone far." Vinz thought for a moment. "Kallen, take Kashim and start running through the supplies list. We're going to be here a while, but we have reparations to make and we need to eat." Turning to Rhys, Alina, and Cantia, he said, "And… that leaves the four of us."

"What's your plan?" asked Alina. "I'm tired of being on this ship."

Vinz gestured to Cantia "Who would be best to contact?"

She gazed at him in surprise. "You're asking my opinion?"

"You are our friend and guide," the Overseer humbly replied. "You know our situation and what we are in need of."

Cantia glanced at Alina and Rhys and then said, "I can contact my father. Mother will be too busy, however, Father will be able to provide aid."

"I know he does not carry a title, but would he be—"

"Overseer?" called Hodge from the outer staircase. Vinz turned and, with Rhys, Alina, and Cantia, climbed the stairs to the outer platform. "You'll want to see this." Hodge stepped aside for them to pass. Rhys peered around Vinz.

Standing on the dock dressed in an elegant, knee-length green robe and satin pants was Leo. Behind him were numerous soldiers and the crew of *Grisle*. Irvine, along with the other crew members, knelt on the docks, their heads bowed. The soldiers around them held rifles to their backs. Leo smiled smugly and leaned against a nearby crate. "Good morning, friends," he effused. "I brought you a gift. Think of it as a welcoming present."

Rhys exchanged looks with Vinz and, with the Overseer at his side, descended the outer staircase. "Leo, this is too much," he said in Nefegian.

Leo shrugged. "I know you promised no revenge, but I never vowed such a thing. Besides, I found their ship at the next pier."

"What are we under arrest for?" Irvine spat.

The noble motioned to Cantia who descended the staircase and hopped onto the docks. "For kidnapping this girl. Overseer, may I introduce Lady Cantia Sorex, daughter of the Minister of Justice."

"She doesn't belong to us. Your mate there bought her from us several days ago," replied Irvine, nodding to Rhys.

"You abducted her from Bathsgate. The abduction of a noble warrants death. Did you know that?" asked Leo coldly. "Not to mention, you made an oath to help *Themis* and you broke it. Do you see the state of her and her crew?"

Irvine gaped at *Themis* and then at Rhys. "You knew? You knew the girl was nobility?"

"That's why I bought her," Rhys affirmed.

"So," Leo looked between Vinz and Rhys, "what should I do with them? If you cannot agree upon a punishment, then they will be brought into the Brechin justice system."

Rhys glanced at Vinz. Both knew what the other wanted to say, but neither was willing to say it.

"Execute them," urged Alina, pushing past Hodge and the others. Everyone, including Leo, gaped. "For the pain they have caused the countless people imprisoned by their trade, for the damage they brought upon our ship, for the lives we lost because of them—execute them." Rhys passed his sister a bewildered look, but she remained unyielding.

"Are you in agreement then?" Leo ventured, looking to Rhys and Vinz.

Irvine pressed his forehead to the warped docks. "We beg of you. Spare our lives. Please!" The rest of the crew mimicked his display of earnestness.

Rhys stared. He wanted retribution, perhaps even revenge, but not at the cost of others' lives. It was pointless.

"We are in agreement," declared Vinz.

"Vinz," hissed Rhys under his breath. Vinz glanced at Rhys and then shook his head as if to say there was no changing his mind.

Leo motioned to the soldiers who dragged Irvine and his crew, many of whom continued to beg for their lives, off the docks. "I didn't think you had it in you," the noble scolded.

"We were worried you left us," said Vinz. Rhys couldn't believe the man's composure; Vinz had just sentenced men to their deaths.

"Nonsense. I got up early to survey the docks and happened to come across Irvine and his crew. I contacted my house, called guards, and here I am." Leo glanced at Alina and smiled. "As much I love living in filth with you, it's nice to be home."

"Kallen, Hodge, Kashim," Vinz motioned to his crew. "*Themis* is in need of repair." They started down the stairs. Vinz slipped money into Kallen's hand as she passed.

"Is there anything I can do to help?" asked Leo, his eyes falling on Alina once more.

Cantia weaved between everyone and punched Leo's arm. "You left me."

"I'm sorry. It wasn't my intent," Leo replied. "Ah, Vinz. I forgot to tell you. I also notified a family contact that you were in need of a rear mast. He'll be here this afternoon to examine *Themis*."

Surprise flickered across the Overseer's face. "Oh, thank you."

"If you don't mind, I'm going to take Cantia to her father. I'll return this afternoon." Leo glanced at Rhys, flashed a haughty smile at Alina, and then ushered Cantia along the docks. Rhys watched as the people Leo passed stopped and bowed their heads to him. Aside from the elaborate ear decoration, was his nobility really such an obvious quality?

Vinz sighed. "We still need food. Andy, Rhys—you two up to staying with the ship? I'll take Alina and go to the market."

"Sure," replied Rhys. Andy nodded.

Alina hurried into the ship, grabbed several cloth satchels, and returned. She followed Vinz off the wharf onto the flagstone road. Rhys watched them until they turned the corner and disappeared behind several well-kept buildings.

Andy nudged Rhys. "Hey." Rhys followed his gaze across the docks to find several port workers facing him with their heads bowed. Disgusted, Rhys retreated indoors.

For the next few hours, Rhys and Andy busied themselves. Because Andy's arm was still in a sling, his chores consisted primarily of tidying the bridge, checking the engines, and assessing inventory. Rhys handled everything else. He cleaned the cabins, washed every crew members' clothes, hung those to dry on the upper deck, cleaned the galley, organized and took inventory of the freezer, cleaned the washroom, and worked on repairing the solar panels on the main mast. Because *Themis* no longer had a rear mast to balance the power intake, the solar panels had shorted out quicker than they could replace them. It was while Rhys sat in the shade of the sail repairing solar panels that he heard a voice.

"Do you mind if I join you?"

He peered up to find a middle-aged man with flaxen hair pulling himself onto the upper deck. Although he wore normal enough clothes, his long hair, which rested in a horsetail on his shoulder, was anything but. "Uh... that's fine," murmured Rhys, studying the man. He was thinner than others he had met thus far on Earth and had willowy arms and hands. His face was fine-featured and his eyes hazel-green. He showed no evidence of possessing a second-skin.

The man folded his legs under him and sat across from Rhys. "I saw you from afar and wanted to know what a silver-haired youth such as yourself was doing on a bedraggled ship such as this."

Rhys laughed darkly and continued to unscrew the covering to the solar panel in his hand. "Just doing repairs. And you? I doubt a noble would be wandering the docks sightseeing."

"Why do you think I'm a noble?" the man queried. "Because of my hair?"

"The shape of your face." Rhys studied the inner panel and then rustled through a pile of spare parts. "Mostly though, I can sense it. You nobles don't have any grit."

"One would be inclined to think you are a noble," offered the man. "Your hair is far lighter than even mine."

"No, not a noble." Rhys popped out the burnt panel with his tool. "I would never want to be one of them."

"Oh? How bold."

Rhys knew he was speaking face-to-face with a high-ranking noble, but he didn't care. *This* noble was on *his* ship. "What were you doing along the docks?"

"I heard someone sentenced slave traders to their deaths for kidnapping Lady Cantia Sorex."

Rhys paused in his work. "It was for more than that."

"You were there?" asked the noble, intrigued. Rhys looked at him, and the noble's smile faded. "Nice eyes you have," the man said in Interstellar Nefegian. "They're old." With a frown, Rhys continued to work. "What's your name?"

"Rhys. Yours?"

"Sal," replied the man. He continued in Aabesh. "To whom do you belong, Rhys? I don't recognize your name."

"I don't belong to a family."

"Are you Pantarak?" asked Sal.

"No. Are you?"

"No," replied Sal.

Rhys met his gaze in surprise. "You're not?" Sal shook his head. "I thought everyone in Brechin was Pantarak."

"Most are. I would say perhaps 98 percent of our population is."

"And how does a noble get away with not being Pantarak? Isn't the Pantarak faith built into the political infrastructure here? The entire bureaucratic system is supported by the religion."

"It is. I've just learned to accept that and live with it. I most certainly do not have the power to change the minds of the family heads." The man smiled slyly at Rhys.

"Rhys!"

Rhys looked over his shoulder at Kallen, Kashim, Hodge, and Leo who were walking along the docks. Kallen waved at him and then hurried after Hodge.

"A friend of yours?" asked Sal.

Rhys stacked the repaired solar panels. "You could say that."

"She must be special to have earned your affection," Sal remarked, pushing himself to his feet. Rhys stood and stretched his aching back. Sitting for so long did not help the nagging pain. "I'm sorry your journey has been such a trying one."

"You speak as if you know," Rhys replied, watching Leo as he appeared on the upper deck.

"I hope your presence here can act as a cornerstone for change," continued Sal.

"I told you to wait until I got back," scolded Leo, joining them.

Sal smiled. "I couldn't resist. His silver hair stands out."

Leo sighed. "Rhys, this is my father, Saloman Damian, the Minister of Education."

"Sal for short," offered Leo's father.

Unsurprised, Rhys nodded in acknowledgment. "A pleasure." He looked at Leo. "You already submitted the journal reports, didn't you?"

Leo smirked. "First thing this morning,"

Rhys rubbed his neck absent-mindedly to ease the pain building there. "To him?"

"Only him," assured Leo. "I saw Alina and Vinz in town. Both were carrying their weight in food. They should be on their way back now. You've been busy." He pointed to the pile of repaired panels. "Did all those take long?"

"No. Just an hour or so. I thought I'd help Kallen." Rhys bent down to collect the panels but froze as his back spasmed. The pain was deep. It didn't feel muscular anymore. "Uh... " he drew a steading breath and dropped to his knees. "I'm... uh... You said Alina was... coming back? Is Alina?... "

"Can Kallen help?" asked Leo worriedly. "Help him lie down."

Rhys rubbed his back; it didn't help. "I'm fine. I just need to... go slow."

Despite his excuses, Sal helped him lie down. "Go get help," the willowy man instructed. Rhys heard Leo run across the deck. Rhys flinched as another sharp, gut-wrenching spasm shook his body. "Slow breaths," Sal murmured. Though Rhys wasn't happy a stranger sat beside him, he was grateful Sal wasn't asking questions.

"Rhys. Hey, hey," called Kallen, scrambling up the ladder. She ran across the deck; Hodge was right behind her. With searching hands, Kallen knelt beside him and brushed his hair from his face. "What's wrong? Your back?"

"The medication has worn off," he grumbled.

Kallen sat back. "So quickly?" she asked in Elali. "Your next dose was supposed to be this evening."

"I guess I did too much work this afternoon." Rhys closed his eyes and took a deep breath.

"I see Alina and Vinz," reported Hodge.

Kallen nudged him. "Go help them bring the supplies in." As Hodge jogged off, she turned to the noble. "Who are you?"

"Sal," replied Sal, unperturbed by Kallen's abrasive tone.

"Leo's father," replied Rhys.

Some of the hostility on Kallen's face faded. "I see."

"Is there something I can do to help?" asked Sal, hovering around Rhys.

"No, Alina is the only one who can do anything." Kallen touched his face. "I can't believe you did all the laundry. You didn't have to."

Rhys knew she was trying to take his mind off the pain, but he would have preferred complete silence.

"He fixed these things too," offered Sal, motioning to the solar panels.

"All of those? Rhys, those take me several hours. You should have just left them."

"Can you please be quiet?" Rhys hissed suddenly. "The both of you." Though Kallen didn't move her hand from his face, she fell silent. "I... " He groaned. "I'm sorry. I just... It hurts." Hearing footsteps, Rhys turned his head to find Alina running toward him, a small, portable medicine bag clutched in her hand. "Alina." He had never been so happy to see her.

His sister knelt beside him, opened the medicine pack, and began loading the injector. "How bad is it?" she murmured in their native tongue. "You're not due for another dose for six hours."

"It's bad," he replied. "Alina... "

374

Alina ran her hand along his wrist, checked his pulse, and then tilted his chin. The familiar hiss of the injector followed. She touched his hair and ran her hand over Pathos' external unit, an action only she and Kallen were ever allowed to do. "Pathos is warm," she murmured. Rhys nodded between breaths; the pain was dissipating. "Kallen, would you prepare hot water for him?" Kallen immediately left.

"Alina," murmured Rhys, pushing himself upright. "It's affecting Pathos."

Alina considered Sal for a moment and then said, "Help me get him up. I'd ask Leo, but he's still recuperating." Together, she and the noble hauled Rhys to his feet, where he swayed for several moments before leaning heavily on his sister. They guided Rhys back into the ship and deposited him on his bed.

"I can function now," Rhys groaned, rolling over to look at his sister. "The medicine has kicked in."

"Just lie there," ordered Alina, disappearing down the hallway. When she returned, Kallen was with her. "Undress." Now knowing Leo's humiliation, Rhys undressed and lay flat on his stomach. For the next half hour, they took turns soaking cloths in hot water, wringing them out, and laying them on his back, shoulders, buttocks, and thighs. Eventually, he lost the energy to feel embarrassed.

"I'm going to start dinner," said Kallen. "Tonight is a crew meal."

Once she left, Alina began gathering the cooling cloths. "What evidence do you see that makes you think the corruption is affecting Pathos' performance?"

Rhys, who had been staring at the same spot across the room, finally looked at her. "Because... I'm having a hard time controlling my emotions." He frowned. "I keep wanting to cry."

"It seems to me Pathos is doing an excellent job maintaining your emotions." She sat back on her heels. "Rhys, you're stressed and in severe pain. To put it in perspective, the level of pain you are achieving regularly would knock an Earthling unconscious. Of course, you're emotional. You're suffering."

"I don't want people to see me like this," he admitted.

"My greatest concern right now is finding another medication that can be used as a substitute for Monaxin. That's why we were gone for so long today. I dragged Vinz to four separate apothecaries searching for substitutes."

"Any luck?"

"Perhaps. I'm going to have to play with some of the ingredients I found." Alina stood and picked up the pot of water. "I'm assuming you can dress yourself." She left.

Rhys rolled out of bed and landed on all fours. He grabbed his shirt, slid it over his head, and then pushed himself to his feet using the bed. Once dressed, he padded down the hall to the galley where he could hear Leo, Sal, and Hodge talking.

"Feeling better?" inquired Sal.

Rhys sat beside Hodge. "Yes, thank you." He was surprised to find Andy, Kashim, and Vinz there as well. Quite literally, for the first time ever, the entire crew was gathered in the galley for a single meal.

"Ah, Vinz, I meant to ask," said Leo. "Were you able to meet with George?"

"I did. We spoke briefly about replacing the rear mast. I already had the designs ready for him, so the process was quick," replied Vinz. "Thank you. I appreciate your help."

"We ordered a new motor," said Kallen, cutting a variety of vegetables on the counter.

"Same model?" asked Vinz.

"No. They didn't have it, but I got the manager to find one in the same class. Same conversion speed and output." She smiled at Vinz. "I saved us money too."

"Kallen's always been our best haggler," boasted Hodge. "She haggled her own grandfather for us."

Sal laughed. "That's talent!" His mirth was brief however. "Vinz, your crew is strong. Steadfast. Determined."

The Oversse grinned. "I appreciate your words, but it wasn't me who brought them together." He pointed to Rhys and Alina. "It was those two."

"What are you talking about?" asked Rhys, abashed by the high praise. "This is your ship, your crew. Both existed long before Alina and I arrived."

"True, but it takes more than just people and a boat to make it go."

"It takes courage, teamwork, and comradery," Sal added. "That is how a small ship from New Arbroath can throw one of the Pantaraks' most defensive territories into absolute chaos and rebellion."

"Wait." Vinz sat bolt upright. "What?"

Rhys gaped. "Paducah."

"I told you," said Leo. "After you left, Paducah rioted."

"And the result?" asked Vinz.

Leo looked to his father. "The latest report as of two days ago," said Sal, "was that the priest there had been killed and the clergymen were being put on trial by the town. Unfortunately, despite the people's want for control, the family heads decided, after hearing that particular report, to send troops to Paducah."

"How are they going to do that?" asked Alina. "They have to cross the Golden Corridor."

"Airships," Leo's father explained.

"They're not going to kill everyone, are they?"

"I don't know. I suppose it will depend upon the people's willingness to cooperate with Brechin's military."

Rhys leaned on the table. "What are they hoping to achieve by sending military power to Paducah?"

"It's a means to keep the people under the influence of the Pantarak faith and Brechin's control." Sal thought. "It's possible the people will fight the military. From what I understand, Paducah also has airships."

"Two," Vinz solemnly provided.

"They will try to protect their newfound freedom, but they've been under Brechin's rule for too long. They may be able to rebel against their own government, but they don't have the power to fight off Brechin forces."

Hodge scoffed. "It sounds as though you approve."

"On the contrary," countered the noble. "Myself and three others voted against the movement to deploy. We were overruled. It's politics."

"So, they either die defending their freedom or give everything up and submit," said Rhys darkly.

"Save the murderous gazes for people who actually deserve them," teased Sal with a small smile. "I am not your enemy. Even the 15 heads of the families aren't your enemies. It is the high priest at whom you need to aim your anger."

A thought occurred to Rhys. "Sal, the high priest—is there anyone higher than him? Anyone who supersedes his word or commands him?"

"I am not sure what you mean," said Sal. "The title of high priest is our highest title."

Rhys studied his face and then, deciding Sal didn't know anything, dropped the subject. "Uh, never mind. I was confused," he lied. They would have to resort to Cantia's contacts if they were going to gain access to his people. "How is Cantia, by the way?"

"Ah, her father was so relieved to see her. Of course, he wants to reward you," mused Sal. "I wouldn't be surprised if she came to visit you tomorrow." He chuckled. "Honestly, I don't believe she wanted to return to Brechin." He nodded to Rhys. "She's a bright child and has a proclivity for financial work, but I get the sense she quite enjoyed being led on an adventure."

For the next two hours, they talked, ate, joked, and learned more about Brechin. Eventually, Sal and Leo left the ship to return to whatever extravagant abode in which they dwelled. Alina checked Rhys' CBC and synthetic synapses scan and, after declaring there had been no change, left him alone in his cabin.

Before bed, Kallen heated another pot of water on the stove and joined Rhys. She closed the door—Rhys saw her wedge a shirt between the door and the frame—and knelt at his bedside.

"I'm fine," he assured her, looking over his written translation work. "You didn't have to boil that."

Kallen reached between them and gently took the manual from his hands. She folded it and laid it atop the others like it in the corner. She turned to Rhys and gently coaxed him to his feet. Once they were level, she kissed him.

Rhys sighed under her lips; it felt like days since they had last kissed. Kallen's fingertips pulled at the hem of his shirt. He raised his arms, and she slipped it over his head. With soft eyes and hands, she leaned in, kissed him again, and tugged at his belt.

Rhys cupped her face and bent her strong form into him. He didn't kiss her hard as he might have done weeks earlier; that didn't express his current state of mind. Instead, he moved his lips tenderly, sweetly, so as to convey to her his absolute affection. He wanted her to understand that he was scared and worried, that he felt vulnerable because he was relying so heavily upon others. He wanted to communicate to her that, despite everything, he was still mad about her. He adored her.

As Kallen shifted between them, her cheek touched his; he was startled by the tears there. He pulled away and looked at her. Kallen leaned her head onto his chest, kissed the spot at her lips, and audibly swallowed. "Rhys." His name escaped her throat as a soft whisper and hung between them.

Rhys enveloped her. "I wish I could tell you that everything will be fine," he said after a moment. "But I can't... because I don't know."

Kallen swiped at her tears, cleared her throat, and set her face in a solid expression of forced courage. "I know." She attempted to smile playfully and tugged at his belt. "Come on. Let's get some hot towels on you."

"Kallen," he said, his eyes finding hers. The smile on her face faded. "I need you to take care of yourself." His words came out as a hoarse mess. "Can you promise me that?" Despite the heavy flow of tears that swam down her cheeks, she nodded. Rhys hugged her. "I need... to know that." He felt Kallen nod against his chest. "Promise me." She nodded again.

33
THE PANTARAK CAPITAL

IT WAS MIDMORNING WHEN CANTIA arrived on the docks. Unlike Leo and Sal, who had discretely come and gone, Cantia stepped out of a solar-powered carriage wearing an elegant, ankle-length, floral-patterned gown. Her brilliant, blond hair was swept back in an intricate hairstyle and held in place by a silver circlet. With four guards trailing her, she strolled along the wharf and, picking up her dress, climbed the outer stairs of *Themis*. Rhys, who had been standing on the upper deck surveying the area with Kallen, only stared.

"Rhys!" called Cantia from the ladder on the outer platform.

Rhys exchanged looks with Kallen. "Yes?"

"Come here."

They walked over to the ladder and peered down at the girl. She frowned up at him. "I've made you, Alina, and Vinz an audience with the family heads."

"Oh, thank you," murmured Rhys.

"With that being said, I'm to retrieve you three and prepare you."

"Hm? Can't they go as they are?" asked Kallen.

Cantia chuckled arrogantly. "Of course not."

Rhys climbed down the ladder, waited for Kallen, and then led them inside. He was relieved when Cantia ordered her guards to remain on the outer platform.

"What's going on?" asked Hodge, appearing in the hallway. He glanced at Cantia and his mouth gaped. "Whoa..."

"We have an audience with the family heads," Rhys explained when Alina appeared beside Hodge. She nodded and padded down the hall to Vinz's cabin.

Cantia gracefully waltzed down the stairs and approached Hodge. "I don't usually go for your type, but I could make an exception."

Hodge laughed uncomfortably. "You're... nine years old."

"I'm 12," she disclosed hotly.

Hodge glanced at Rhys, but Rhys only smiled. There was no way he was helping his friend out of this one. "Well, 12 is still... young, you know?" murmured Hodge. Kallen turned away to hide her mirth. "You should really go for someone maybe... Leo's age."

"Leo's 19," Rhys quietly corrected.

"What is it with you people?" barked Hodge. "None of you look the age you're supposed to be!"

"Lady Cantia," greeted Vinz, joining them in the hallway; Alina followed. "We have an audience with the family heads?"

Cantia, whose eyes were still locked on Hodge, nodded. "I got it just for you three."

"You're going with them though," said Hodge awkwardly. "You're not staying here... right?"

Cantia swung away from him with a growl. "Yes, I'm going with them. But I'm to escort you to the Damien residence first." Cantia began climbing the stairs. "We don't have much time. The audience is set shortly after midday, and you three are beyond disgusting."

Vinz and Alina followed. Rhys kissed Kallen's cheek before jogging after the group. They clambered into Cantia's solar-powered carriage and seated themselves in the back. The carriage whizzed off down the flagstone road. Rhys strained to see who was controlling the machine, but no matter how he craned his neck, he couldn't see the front seat.

"It's automatic," explained Cantia, hands folded in her lap. "I have it set to take me to the docks, Leo's residence, and then the temple."

"What do the family heads know about us?" asked Vinz.

"I've told them about you two," she nodded to Rhys and Alina, "and about you, Overseer."

"That doesn't answer my question,"

Cantia chuckled. "Rhys, what do you think?"

Rhys stared out the carriage's window. So much was passing by so quickly. He couldn't comprehend it all. He thought he saw a shop door open on its own but dismissed the idea. He caught glimpses of people wearing embellished clothing and children riding small, solar-powered carriages in an alley. The farther they ventured into Brechin, the taller the buildings became. Soon, Rhys couldn't see the tops of them no matter how far he leaned against the window.

As they moved from one district to the next, enormous screens featuring attractive, moving male models or fresh goods began appearing outside stores and in shop windows. Doors, in fact, *did* open on their own.

The quality of the buildings increased exponentially, showcasing various fine metals and stones as their cornerstones and borders. And the people… The majority of the men, women, and children sported varying colors of light-colored hair. Not once did he see a dark head, a disconcerting realization.

Nervously, Rhys looked at Alina. For the first time in his life, he found anxiety on her face. Her brows were creased upward in worry, her jaws tight. She met his eyes, and he knew instantly that, despite all of the talk about returning to Caelestis, Alina had grown accustomed to living in a non-technological world. Like him, she also feared being re-assimilated into the black abyss of a Core-like computer.

"What's wrong?" asked Cantia. She seemed genuinely concerned.

"It just reminds us of home."

"Oh really?" Cantia leaned forward enthusiastically. "Tell me!"

"We would prefer not to," said Alina, glancing outside the carriage once more. The remainder of the ride was in silence.

When the carriage finally turned off the main street and passed through rows of large, granite columns, Cantia sighed and unfolded her legs. "We're here. Leo and Lord Damien were more than accepting of your manners while aboard your ship, however, you should keep those uncouth behaviors at a minimum while here. They won't be the only ones present."

Rhys peered out the window at the enormous, granite pillars on either side of the driveway. The grass growing alongside the road was startlingly rich and green despite the dry climate. At the end of the pristine street was a white brick and cream-colored metal, three-story building. Numerous columns held up a north-facing balcony just above its main entrance. Flowers of varying species and colors flourished in the shade of the front patio.

Cantia's carriage stopped before the staircase, and she swung the door open. Rhys, Alina, and Vinz slid out and gaped at the building.

"What is this place?" asked Rhys.

"The Damien residence," Cantia replied matter-of-factly.

The luxurious white doors at the top of the stairs opened, and three people stepped onto the porch. Rhys immediately noticed their tan skin and dark hair and eyes.

"Where's the lord of the house?" Cantia climbed the stairs. "He should be here himself."

The three men bowed to her. "He's currently conducting a lecture," one replied. "We've been instructed to assist you in his absence."

"That was fast," Leo remarked, appearing behind the dark-haired men. "I didn't expect you to get here so soon." He motioned for them to follow. Vinz took the lead, and together they climbed the stairs into the mansion.

"This is where... you live?" breathed Alina as they stepped into the vast, marble-floored foyer.

"Members of the family of Damien live here, so, yes," replied Leo. He smiled charmingly at her.

Seemingly taken aback by the gesture, Alina frowned. "What?"

"It's strange seeing you outside the ship. That's all." Leo called into the next room. "Misha, Lilan? Can you come here?" Momentarily, two dark-haired and brown-eyed women appeared in the doorway. Both were young, perhaps in their thirties, and, despite their plain clothing, were rather attractive. "This is her." Leo motioned to Alina. "I've asked Misha and Lilan to help you. I hope you don't mind, Alina."

"Help me with what?" asked Alina.

Leo chuckled. "Help you dress."

"I don't need help dressing."

Leo glanced at Cantia, who immediately took Alina's arm and escorted her down the hallway with Misha and Lilan. "You two, with me," he called to Rhys and Vinz as he started up the grand staircase to their left.

"Where are they taking Alina?" asked Rhys.

"The same place I'm taking you," said Leo. "All of you stink." Leo led them upstairs, down another corridor, and into a large room with a vaulted ceiling. There they found another young man waiting. Though he didn't smile when they entered, Rhys could sense his curiosity and intrigue. "May I introduce my oldest brother, Terron."

Terron crossed the room and stopped before them. He appeared in his late teens, but Rhys knew better. More than likely the man was already well into his twenties. Unlike Leo, Terron's hair was blond with streaks of copper decorating his short tresses. His eyes were the same though—hazel-green. He wore modest clothes like Leo as well as the ornamental ear piece. Despite their similarities, however, Rhys found Terron far more willowy than Leo, a trait he undoubtedly inherited from their father.

"So this is them," said Terron, his eyes flicking between Vinz and Rhys. "And the girl?"

"With Cantia," replied Leo.

Terron smiled. "I feel like I know you personally thanks to Leo's journals. Why don't you get cleaned up, and we'll talk more in a little while?"

"Thank you for your hospitality," said Vinz.

Leo pointed them into an adjoining washroom, which was easily the size of *Themis*, informed them baths had been drawn, and closed the doors, leaving them alone. Rhys wandered about the washroom, studying the porcelain tubs of which there were three, the chrome sinks, and floral paintings on the walls. As he passed the sinks, a vanity light came on, illuminating him in a mirror. Rhys surveyed himself.

He didn't recognize the young man standing before him with intense, blue eyes and untidy silver locks. Pathos' external unit was almost indiscernible beneath Rhys' hair. His jaw line had become stronger, his shoulders broader, and his chest muscled. No longer was he ghostly pale. His skin had warmth. Had he grown? Was he taller? Rhys turned and viewed himself in profile. Why was he so tall?

"You look like a woman preening before a mirror," teased Vinz.

Rhys frowned. "When did I become so tall? And… " Rhys looked back at himself. "I'm bigger."

Vinz, who had already stripped out of his two layers of shirts, gazed at Rhys in amusement. "You've been growing since you came on board. That's one of the reasons you've been eating so much."

Rhys avoided gazing at the scars on Vinz's chest. "I thought it was just because I was working hard."

"Alina doesn't eat as much as you, but she can pack food away. She's grown too." Vinz tested the water in the tub nearest him. "It's like your bodies are trying to catch you up."

Rhys stared at himself for a moment longer and then pulled his shirt over his head. When he looked back in the mirror, he found muscled arms and toned pectorals. He gaped. Of course he wasn't burly like Kashim or as muscled as Hodge, but still, the changes he saw were shocking. When he heard Vinz slide into the water, he abandoned the mirror and began undressing. After testing the water of another tub,

Rhys clambered in and slid to the bottom, allowing the hot water to swaddle him.

"What are we doing?" Vinz eventually asked. Rhys blew on the water and watched as the steam puffed into the air. "What are we supposed to say to the family heads?"

"Stop killing people," Rhys offered.

"It's not them though. It's the high priest encouraging the spread of the Pantarak faith and calling for the killing of all non-believers... the creation of a Pantarak-dominated empire."

Rhys thought back to the night he and Alina had crashed on Earth. "Vinz, how did you get there so quickly?"

"Where?" mumbled Vinz.

"How did you get to us so fast the night we crashed?"

"We were already in the area." Vinz spread his arms along the tub's basin. "We had heard that some of our merchant ships were being attacked days prior and so had been lying in wait to ambush the airships."

"And what were the Pantarak airships doing there?"

"Attacking our merchant ships."

"And the airships were from Paducah?"

Vinz nodded. "Had they been from Brechin, they wouldn't have attacked us later with sunboards. Paducah has airships, but they aren't willing to throw them into battle unless it's absolutely necessary. They knew our ship and so left us and flew ahead to New Arbroath which was unguarded."

Rhys dunked himself underwater. Days of dirt and grit lifted from his head. He ruffled his hair and came up for air. They bathed in silence until Vinz hoisted himself out of the tub and began drying off. Rhys glanced at him and, seeing the numerous scars on his back, redirected his attention elsewhere.

Vinz wrapped a towel about himself and leaned against his emptying tub. "I thought back in New Arbroath that I knew what I wanted, that I knew what needed to be done—and with you and Alina, I thought I could do it."

"Look where we are. You got us here," said Rhys.

"No. *You* got us here. I was foolish to think I alone could bring us to Brechin. You've saved our lives on more than one occasion. And... " Vinz sighed. "I've risked the lives of my crew more times than I can count."

Rhys didn't object because it was the truth. Vinz *had* been a poor leader, but Rhys supposed he had his reasons. Only when they had been boarded by Irvine's crew had Vinz completely given up. He had always kept *Themis'* crew functioning like a well-oiled machine. The Overseer may not have spoken directly to Rhys often, but Rhys had seen how much time he spent on the bridge with Andy, Kyo, Lyruc, and Kashim. He had seen how well-liked he was, how much Andy trusted him, and how protective Kashim was of him. Vinz was loved, if not by Rhys, then by the other crew members.

Rhys shook the water from his hair, climbed out of the tub, and dried off. "I'm sorry," said Vinz suddenly. The solemn tone of the Overseer's voice worried Rhys. "I swore to never lie to you, but I did. Multiple times."

"I know," replied Rhys.

Vinz studied him and then said, "Do you hate me?"

"No, not hate," replied Rhys. "Hate is too strong of a word. I could never hate someone who is so obviously beloved by his crew. I dislike you. You have not made our lives on Earth easy."

"No, I guess not." He grinned morosely. "I am *very* glad though that you're here with me. I don't think I could do this alone. I had always thought Kashim would be the one by my side, but... I guess not."

"We're fighting for a common cause," said Rhys, leaning on the tub, "which is why we'll have to work together from here on out."

"Agre—"

"Are you two finished?" called Leo at the door.

Rhys glanced at Vinz, smiled, and said, "Yes."

Leo snapped the double doors open. "Good, let's go."

Half an hour later, Rhys found himself dressed in clothes similar to Leo's—a knee-length, high-collared green robe, pale satin pants, a wide golden sash, and slippers. His silver-gray hair was swept away from his face and his bangs combed neatly to the side. Awkwardly, Rhys surveyed himself in the full-length mirror. "I feel ridiculous," he muttered.

"You'll get used to it," Leo assured him. "We're running short on time." Rhys and Vinz were ushered from the room, down the staircase, and back to the foyer. Leo looked about anxiously. "Cantia said they were almost finished with Alina."

"We *are* finished," sang Cantia, striding down the corridor. She joined Leo and pointed behind her. "See?"

Alina stepped from the corridor and tiptoed over to the group. No one said a word. Rhys had heard Hodge tell Alina she was beautiful. He knew others thought so as well because of how their heads turned when she walked by, but he himself had never put much thought into noticing. She was his sister.

Standing before him now though was a young woman with soft shoulders, long, silver hair, and brilliant blue eyes. Like him, Alina was also dressed in green, but her wardrobe was more eye-catching. The simple dress she wore hung from her pale shoulders, accentuating her breasts, and flowed from a corset to the floor.

Alina turned away from them. "Stop staring!"

Rhys glanced at the others and found all of the men, including Vinz, gawking.

"Are you done undressing her with your eyes?" snapped Cantia. She took Alina's arm and led her from the foyer. Rhys had to hide a smile as his sister tripped on the hem of her dress.

"Good luck," bid Leo, holding his arm out to Rhys. "We're here if you need anything."

Rhys took his arm warmly. "Thank you." Vinz exchanged niceties as well before they jogged after Alina and Cantia.

The ride to the main temple was a long one. Rhys kept his head down to avoid the numerous screens, automated machines, and light-haired people their carriage passed; he noticed Alina did the same.

Cantia seemed to sense their apprehension and so silently stared out the window, her chin propped on her hand and a bored expression on her face. Vinz also gazed out the window, but instead of staring into the distance, his eyes jumped from one illuminated screen to the next.

When the solar-powered carriage finally came to a halt, Rhys was beyond anxious. Despite the heat of the day, his hands felt damp and cold. His throat was tight, and he felt that if someone pushed him, his knees might collapse under him.

As he stepped out of the carriage behind Alina, his eyes shot upward. The temple caressed the sky. Though the majority of the building was constructed of stone and marble, its top tiers appeared to be of metal and glass. Before them rose a great marble staircase encrusted with silver.

Cantia started up the stairs, daintily holding her dress above her feet. Rhys exchanged looks with the others and followed. The staircase gave way to a grand entryway with open walls, a vast ceiling, numerous windows, and marble floors. To Rhys' surprise, many people milled about in the enormous corridor, talking quietly or chuckling behind polite hands. To his even greater surprise, there were no monks or clergymen, none that he could detect anyway. Every person there appeared to be an aristocrat or a highborn showcasing elaborate dresses and opulent robes.

As Cantia led them through the busy entryway, very few people took notice of the newcomers. Leo had been right—appearances alone wouldn't have gotten them far in Brechin.

On the other side of the cavernous entryway rose dual staircases which stemmed as one and wound upward in opposite directions. Cantia led them up the left staircase to a pair of metal doors which opened automatically to reveal an elevator. Vinz studied the narrow room cautiously. As Rhys stepped in, he gently pushed the Overseer into the elevator and smiled to let him know the machine wasn't a trap. When it began moving, Vinz lurched.

"I forget you people have never seen such technology before," hummed Cantia. She turned just as the dark walls surrounding the elevator shifted to glass.

Vinz went to the sheer, outer wall and gaped as the elevator climbed ever higher alongside the temple. "What is this called?"

"An elevator," replied Alina.

"Oh? You know?" Cantia chirped.

The elevator slowed and the doors opened. "It was our technology to begin with," explained Alina, stepping out. Rhys glanced at Vinz before they followed Alina onto the fifteenth floor. Instead of a vast room as Rhys expected, they entered a long, narrow corridor lined with ornately crafted windows and flowers of varying species. The hallway was warm but pleasantly so.

"This is the fifteenth floor," announced Cantia, standing near the elevator. "I cannot go any farther because I am not yet a family head. At the end of this corridor, you will find a set of doors. Through those doors is the Tribunal Room where the family heads meet."

"Will the high priest be there?" Alina queried.

"I don't know. Only when important matters are being discussed does he seek the counsel of the family heads and his clergymen."

"Thank you, Cantia," said Vinz.

Cantia turned, and the elevator doors opened once more. "When you are finished, you may use this elevator to return to the entryway." She stepped inside and waved to them as the doors closed.

With less confidence than Rhys had hoped he would have, he made his way down the narrow hallway until he reached the doors. They were solid, black metal. He was sure the material had originally been used for space exploration.

"We come in together," said Vinz, looking between Rhys and Alina. "We come out together. Yes?"

"Yes," replied Rhys and Alina simultaneously. Vinz nodded to Rhys who stepped before the doors which silently slid open. They entered.

The Tribunal Room was surprisingly small for such an auspicious title. Though he knew they had just entered a sacred space, Rhys felt more as though he had just stepped into a cage. At eye level, all that met his gaze was polished wood adorned with intricate flourishes. The myriad of ornate carvings led upward more than two meters before giving way to numerous faces peering down at them. One-hundred-eighty degrees— they were almost entirely surrounded by members of the Brechin elite.

Though all that Rhys could see of the nobles were their heads and shoulders, he was certain each of them was dressed in clothing far more opulent than either he or Alina wore. All had varying shades of blond hair, ranging from gray-white to brilliant gold to strawberry-blond.

As Rhys turned to each person, his eyes fell on a familiar face—Sal. Leo's father smiled warmly and settled back in his chair. He spoke quietly with the person next to him, but his eyes never left Rhys, Alina, and Vinz.

Someone cleared his throat, and the room quieted. Rhys directed his attention to the older man perched nearby. Though he could see very little of the noble, Rhys could tell by the shape of his face that he was a rather robust individual. He had pink cheeks, a balding spot atop his head, and a gold and white beard. The plaque hanging on the polished wall before his seat read "Minister of State."

"The 15 family heads welcome you," the Minister of State said. "Present yourselves."

"Vinz Amadorri of New Arbroath and Overseer of the ship, *Themis*," said Vinz.

"Rhys Falkrow of Caelestis."

"Alina Falkrow of Caelestis."

The Minister of State leaned back in his chair. "Well, it wasn't a lie, Daine." He looked to the woman three seats to his left. Rhys was startled by how similar she appeared to Cantia.

The Minister of Justice, Daine Sorex—Cantia's mother—brushed her long, blond hair from her face. "Please, give my daughter more credit."

"Let's start with you, Overseer," said the Minister of State. "Your name proceeds you."

"I am a direct descendent of Ramsen Amadorri, the author of The Hallowed *Magris*," Vinz solemnly affirmed. Rhys detected no fear in his voice which made his own confidence swell.

"You're a half-blood, right?" asked another man.

"Eh... yes. My mother was a white god; my father was a resident of New Arbroath. I'm a first generation... "

"Have you proof?" asked the Minister of State.

"I have the original copy of The Hallowed *Magris*," replied Vinz. "It has been passed down in my family for generations." When silence followed, Vinz glanced at Rhys and then stepped forward. "We've traveled for weeks to reach Brechin so we might have an audience with the high priest."

"Yes," grumbled the Minister of State. "And, on your way, you incited a rebellion and prompted military deployment. Well done, by the way. We weren't expecting Paducah."

"It was not our intention to incite a rebellion," said Vinz. "We wanted to negotiate a truce."

"A truce? For what reason?"

A pregnant moment ensued. Rhys could feel Vinz winding up. "Your people are out of control," the Overseer stated. The humored expression on the Minister of State's face disappeared. "On more than one occasion, Paducah has attacked New Arbroath for the primary reason of religious differences. Nearly five months ago, they bombed the town, destroying schools and a hospital and killing hundreds."

"What Paducah does is none of our concern," said the woman to the Minister of State's right.

"Apparently it is," interjected Alina, "otherwise you wouldn't be sending troops there."

Sensing the tension in the room rise precipitously, Rhys said, "We're not looking for reparations or apologies. We've come because we know you have the power to change the minds of your people. If an order comes down from Brechin to cease all religious—"

"*This* is what you traveled here for?" the Minister of State huffed. "To tell us this?"

"The high priest is disseminating orders throughout his empire that promote religious warfare and the overtake of non-Pantarak territories," argued Vinz. "Thousands of people are dying, thousands more are being indoctrinated into the slavery system—from both sides. Brechin itself suffers from the high priest's orders. The Golden Corridor is reason enough to forego religious intolerance. It can't possibly be helping Brechin's trade."

"The goal of all Pantaraks is to convert as many people as possible and claim territory in the name of our white gods, our ancestors. The mandate comes from the high priest."

"Are there others whose will the high priest carries out?" Rhys interrogated. "Anyone else he takes into consideration when disseminating commands?"

"Rhys Falkrow, was it?" asked the Minister of State.

"Yes."

"You have no business with the white gods as—"

"We are them," snapped Alina in Interstellar Nefegian. "If you've others kept here in this gaudy building, then you had best bring them to us now." Unfettered chatter broke out amongst the family heads.

"Easy," chided Rhys under his breath.

"I'm tired of being trifled with," Alina continued in Nefegian. "You highborn aristocrats sit upon your elevated dais and judge the world below you, sneering at those who work along the docks or scoffing at the apostates you bring in to use as your personal servants." She turned and spoke over the hushed whispers. "I loathe you, all of you. Do you know why? Because everything around you comes from *our* people. You're entitled. You have our blood, and so you are privileged. You know nothing except of the little world you command."

"Quiet!" snapped the Minister of State.

"You know nothing of humanity!"

"Enough!"

Panting, Alina rejoined Rhys. Her chest and neck were flushed, and her hands shook.

"If you cannot control yourselves, we will have guards escort you from the room," warned the Minister of State. Rhys glanced at Sal and found the Minister of Education smugly smiling, his gaze set on the Minister of State.

"How did you two become involved with this one?" asked a middle-aged man to Rhys' left, pointing to Vinz. His plaque read "Minister of Labor."

"We were rescued by him and his crew," replied Rhys. "He was kind enough to take care of us and help us acclimate to this new world." The Minister of Labor only nodded thoughtfully.

"What you are wanting from us, to summarize," said another woman, the Minister of Transportation, "is to command a standing down of our people to further halt all religious warfare between Aabeshians and Pantaraks. Is that correct?"

"Yes," replied Vinz.

The Minister of Transportation looked at the Minister of State. "Many of our cities are far from Brechin. This leaves room for misinterpretation of announcements, orders, edicts. Perhaps we can make an effort to pass along a cease-and-desist to the outlying edges of our empire."

"Nonsense," replied the Minister of State. "This is not something to be decided upon lightly. The future of the Pantarak Empire rests with us."

"The future of the human race here on Earth," said Alina, "rests with you." She looked at Rhys indicating that it was his turn to speak.

"Where we're from," Rhys began, "human advancement is paramount. In space, there is no room for warfare, there is no room for mistakes, there is no room for hate. We've passed all of that and reached the point in human evolution where we do what is needed for the human race to survive. After all, to us, you are dead. Earth is dead. So, when we first arrived here, we couldn't comprehend why it was humans were killing one another so freely. We're an endangered species! Again and again, we witnessed humans brutally attacking one another, torturing one another, betraying one another. We couldn't understand it; we *still* don't understand it. If you do not pool your resources and knowledge and stop fighting with one another, humanity on Earth will end with you."

"Is that a bad thing?" came a voice from behind the Minister of State. All eyes turned to a man cloaked in white and orange as he appeared beside the Minister of State. He was older, just like the Minister of State, but slender with short arms and stubby fingers. His thinning, gray hair was cut close to his ears; he wore a golden circlet atop his head. His skin was decorated with pock marks and slight discolorations common for his age.

"High Priest," murmured everyone in the room, bowing their heads.

Rhys exchanged wild looks with Alina and Vinz.

"I asked, is that a bad thing?" repeated the high priest, his gaze set on Rhys. "Once we leave our physical bodies, we will join our ancestors in the stars. We will continue living as we always have. Why then should we not try to save as many people as possible? They need to be converted to the Pantarak faith, otherwise they risk no longer existing."

"You don't actually believe that, do you?" asked Alina in disgust.

The high priest studied Alina, Rhys, and Vinz and then smiled forlornly. "My apologies. I didn't mean to elicit such emotion from you. Allow me to introduce myself. I am the high priest, Michael. Speaker for the white gods and disseminator of their holy messages."

"What white gods?" prompted Rhys.

"The ones we rescued from their watery tombs."

"How?"

"We are a society of advanced technology. With ease, we were able to resurrect three of the mighty gods."

Alina's voice was small. "What happened to the others?"

"They wished to remain with their brothers and sisters," replied Michael.

"You're lying!" barked Rhys. He shifted into his mother tongue to better impress upon the high priest the gravity of the situation. "Every person on the ship was under short-term cryostasis. Without the help of their AIs, disconnecting from the systems would have been impossible."

"And yet, we were able to do it," replied the high priest in fluent Nefegian. Like Leo, Michael had a strange accent, one that pushed Rhys' comprehension to the limit. "We were able to revive three white gods."

Rhys glowered at him. "Prove it. Prove your technological advances. Prove that you *resurrected* white gods."

"Very well." The high priest turned and disappeared through the door behind the Minister of State, leaving the room in complete silence.

Rhys shifted nervously. He didn't like how calm the high priest was. He glanced at Alina and Vinz and then looked up at Sal who was speaking softly to the Minister of Finance. Leo's father caught Rhys' eye and shook his head to indicate that he didn't know what was going on. Was it possible there were family heads here who were unaware of the rescue operation from the spaceship wreckage?

As time passed, more and more Brechin elite began speaking softly to one another, discussing the high priest and the current situation. The only people who did not seemed perturbed by the high priest's words were the Minister of State, Cantia's mother, and the Minister of Defense.

Aline drew Rhys and Vinz close. "What happens if these people are real?"

"I think the more important question," whispered Rhys, "is, if they're real, why are they cooperating with the high priest? Anyone with a logic AI could easily understand the consequences of religion-backed world domination."

"You can share with them the data you two have collected," Vinz suggested.

"I can't, but Alina can," said Rhys.

Vinz gestured to Alina. "Then you can show them."

At that moment, the paneling under the Minister of State's desk slid open to reveal Michael. He smiled at them and then stepped aside. Rhys couldn't keep his mouth from gaping as three silver-haired, slender individuals—two males and one female—clothed in fine gray robes entered the Tribunal Room and stood before them. Murmurs of shock, awe, and confusion broke out.

Rhys felt himself torn. He wanted to leap at them in excitement, to touch them, to speak with them familiarly, yet something held him still. Even amongst the light-haired, fair-skinned nobles, these people were other-worldly. Their gazes were probing and distant, their postures stiff. When their blue eyes settled on Alina and Rhys, they stared blankly. Rhys wondered if that's how he and Alina had originally appeared.

Michael, the high priest, raised a hand to signal silence, and the Tribunal Room quieted. "The white gods," he presented. "Bow your heads in their presence." The majority of the family heads did so, though some obeyed hesitantly. Sal and the Minister of Finance were the only two who remained upright, their solemn gazes set on the newcomers. Michael looked to Rhys, Alina, and Vinz before speaking in Interstellar Nefegian. "Introduce yourselves."

Rhys stepped forward. "I am Rhys Falkrow of Caelestis in the Hyperes Solar System. This is my sister, Alina Falkrow. This man is Vinz Amadorri, descendent of Ramsen Amadorri, writer of The Hallowed *Magris.*"

The man nearest Michael gazed at Rhys and then shifted his hollow eyes to Alina. "The children of Doctor Severiano Falkrow," he said. "I am Etion." He motioned to the slight woman with short hair beside him. "This is Rullena." He nodded to the other man. "And Gealdir."

"Those aren't your birth names," Alina remarked.

"No, they are the names given to us by our worshippers," replied Gealdir.

Rhys studied them. They were clearly from Caelestis. The pronunciation of their mother tongue was too familiar. Though it was strange to hear it spoken by someone other than Alina, it was definitely Caelestis' dialect. "How did you escape the life pod?"

"It was thanks to this man's devotion and tireless work," replied Etion, gesturing to the high priest.

Alina gasped loudly, her hands flying to her mouth. Rhys himself tried to hide his shock, but he couldn't conceal the expression of horrified surprise on his face.

"Where... Where is your AI?" whispered Alina from behind trembling fingers. Where Etion's external AI unit should have been, there was nothing save a bare spot and two small, injector sockets.

"It was removed for my own protection," Etion explained.

Rhys turned on Michael, shaking with fury and horror. "What have you done to them?"

"It is as the lord, Etion, says," Michael confirmed. "We removed the parasitic attachment to give them the freedom of gods."

"Are you... " Rhys tried to summon the words, but his mind was blank. "Are you trying... "

"What have you done?" whispered Alina. She approached Etion. "How are you alive?"

Michael looked on. "The removal of the parasite kept these gods alive."

"Are there others?" Rhys asked.

Michael bowed his head. "No."

Rhys touched Alina's bare shoulder. Still in horror, she looked at him. "The others are dead," he murmured in Elali. "He killed them."

Alina glanced at Michael and then at the other three. "They tried to spare all the passengers on the ship, but couldn't detach them from the cryostasis system without killing them." She thought. "Removing the AI was the only way to completely disengage the system and withdraw the body. These are the only three left."

"Do you know where you are?" probed Rhys in Nefegian.

"Earth, the birthplace of humanity," Rullena promptly replied.

"Do you remember your lives on Caelestis?" Alina looked between them. "Do you remember your jobs, your identification numbers?"

"Of course," replied Etion. "Why wouldn't we?"

"We don't understand!" said Alina. "Why are you alive? Existence without the AI is impossible."

"On the contrary, Alina Falkrow. Life without our AIs is simple, quiet." Etion studied them and then said, "I do not understand why you two are here, however. If memory serves, your names were not listed for deployment. More importantly, even if you had been chosen to be placed on a life pod, you wouldn't have been placed on the same one. Explain this."

"Why does it matter?" countered Rhys.

Etion's stoic blue eyes fixed on Rhys. "I understand why Alina Falkrow would have been chosen for deployment, however, I am puzzled as to why the esteemed Doctor Falkrow's Other Child is here."

It was Alina who answered. "We were told by our father to board a life pod. We hijacked identification numbers."

"Identity theft and protocol violation," mused Rullena. "One is punishable by imprisonment and the other by death."

"This isn't the damned colony!" snapped Rhys. He could feel his blood simmering.

"I will not be spoken to by the Other Child in such a manner," Etion choked.

Rhys could hardly restrain himself. "Fuck off."

"Such language," purred the high priest, casually separating Rhys and Alina from the others. "Don't speak to your superiors that way."

"They are *not* my superiors," Rhys snarled.

"Gods, lords of man—these children before you," said Michael, "have come here today to request that the Pantarak Empire cease all warfare and violent activities that promote the persecution of non-Pantarak peoples and the hostile takeover of outlying territories. What say you on the matter?"

"Human and territorial conquest has been the cornerstone of mankind since the dawn of civilization," began Etion. "Great empires have risen, technology has been created, and humans have flourished as a consequence of it. Invasion, subjugation, and assimilation are the keys to the creation of a future as history has shown us."

"As keepers of knowledge, as humans of a higher consciousness," Alina seethed, "how can you justify these words? How can you not see that it is our responsibility to guide these people into the future so they don't repeat the mistakes of humanity's past?"

"Because we are gods," asserted Rullena. "We are exonerated from all fault. If humanity destroys itself, we will continue to live on."

"You are flesh and bone!" shouted Rhys. "You are like us, like every other person in this room."

"No," said Etion with a smile. "We are beyond that. We are gods born again to this world to bring divine retribution, to cleanse the Earth of its sins. Non-believers, apostates who claim we are not—they will perish first for they are the ones who will bring this world to an end. A world under one empire is a unified world. A unified world is a perfect world." Etion looked at Alina. "We want you to join us."

"No," seethed Rhys.

Etion's smile disappeared. "Not you. Her. We want her."

"I would never associate with such people. Not even if they were my own."

"Alina Falkrow, with you we would have the ability to start a new race—a new race of gods to preside over the humans here. Our genes are perfect." Etion held his hand out to her. "Make our new world a reality."

"I am not a broodmare!" She glared at Michael. "We're finished here. If you want a war with the Aabeshian people, you'll get one, but be warned, High Priest. You may have three *white gods* here, but we're out *there*. Two white gods who know the outside world, who can speak the languages, who can fight, who can negotiate, maim, and kill."

"Your number is about to be half that," replied Michael. He motioned with his hand, and the door behind Rhys, Alina, and Vinz opened. Several soldiers with armor entered the room and lined the walls.

"Objection!" called Sal from on high. "Use of inappropriate force and intimidation tactics!"

"Overruled," replied Michael. He looked to the nearest soldier. "I want only the girl."

Rhys grabbed Alina and forced her between himself and Vinz. "What's going on?" asked Vinz, having been unable to understand the Nefegian-predominant conversation.

"They want Alina," said Rhys. "Alina, charge Logos."

"I said objection!" shouted Sal.

"Objection!" came another voice.

"Objection!" said yet another.

Michael looked up at the family heads in contempt. "Stay out of this, or I'll have your posts."

"Rhys, I'm not going with them," said Alina. He could hear the growing fear in her voice.

"I know, I know," Rhys replied.

Michael motioned for Etion, Gealdir, and Rullena to retreat to safety. They disappeared into the corridor beneath the Minister of State's desk. Rhys heard a thud and turned to find Sal. It appeared as though he had jumped over the tall desks to join them in the eye of the Tribunal Room. "My son has grown fond of you," he said. "I promised Leo I would do what I could to support you three."

"Minister," said one of the soldiers. "Stand aside. We have been authorized to use force if necessary."

"Retreat from this room." Sal pointed vehemently at the door behind him. "No military is allowed within the Tribunal Room walls.

Force and intimidation tactics are not permitted here." The Minister of Education whirled on the high priest. "Get your men out of here at once!"

Michael gazed at Sal and then said, "This is going to come back to you, Sal." He left through the corridor under the Minister of State's desk.

The soldier nearest Leo's father popped open his belt loop, withdrew a pen-shaped item, and snapped it into a baton with a flick of his wrist. "Last warning, Minister."

"Rhys," said Sal over his shoulder. "Take your sister."

Rhys moved for the door, but two soldiers stepped into their way. He shoved Alina into Vinz's arms and charged. Before either could withdraw their batons, Rhys engaged them. With as much power as he could muster, he swung at the soldiers. Though his first fist connected, the second was dodged and exchanged for a strike to the gut. Wheezing, he stumbled back. On the ball of his foot, he whirled and then kicked, sending the second soldier to the wall. Rhys leapt for the first soldier who was wavering on his feet; instead, he was blindsided by another and thrown to the ground.

Charged. Initiating, announced Pathos instantly.

A jolt of electricity lurched from Rhys' body, causing the soldier atop him to scramble off, writhing. Rhys scrambled to his feet and held his hand out before him to keep the others at bay. With four soldiers surrounding him, he had nowhere to go. Panting, he glanced at Vinz and Alina. Like him, his sister had her hand outstretched threateningly.

"Want to find out... how much it hurts?" Rhys spat. He could feel his fingers shaking. He hoped it wasn't evident to the soldiers.

"Out of my way!" barked Sal, shoving a soldier. The soldier turned and, in a single motion, struck Sal in the face. The Minister of Education, a slender and willowy man, toppled backwards onto the floor and slid half a meter. Seeing his chance, Rhys tackled the soldier whose fist was still raised. Twice, he punched before being forced to defend against others.

Taking a direct hit to the face to shorten the distance between them, Rhys grabbed his attacker's opposite arm and wrenched it upward. In the same moment, he stepped into the second soldier and placed his hand on the man's shoulder. Rhys' body flinched as another shock of electricity leapt from his skin. Both soldiers crumpled to the floor, taking Rhys with them.

On his hands and knees, he panted. His vision tunneled, his back ached, and his hands shook beyond his control. Suddenly, a solid weight slammed into him, sending him sprawling across the floor into the wall. Distantly, he heard Alina screech.

Moving on pure instinct, Rhys tried to haul himself to his knees, but his vision blurred. The shooting pain in his back had returned. He felt hands on him.

Final charge will render you unconscious, said Pathos.

Rhys grappled with the soldier for a moment before being forced back to the ground. "A-Alina!" he groaned, fighting with all his strength.

"Rhys. Rhys!"

Alina's high-pitched screams tore at the darkness that threatened to consume him. Using his legs, Rhys kicked out at the soldier and then pulled himself up the wall. His back, the pain was swelling exponentially. Wildly, he looked about to get his bearings.

"Rhysss!" shrieked Alina. He found her halfway through the corridor's entryway, soldiers pulling at her and her dress. Like a wildcat she kicked, clawed, punched, and assaulted her captors with attack after attack. But there were five of them and one of her. "Rhys!"

Staggering, Rhys rushed the corridor. He didn't know where Vinz was. His only objective was Alina. Like a raging bull, he barreled into the soldiers. All technique was gone now. Only desperation and willpower kept him moving, swinging, and kicking. As the soldier to his left fell writhing from one of Alina's debilitating shocks, Rhys dove for her.

He felt a gloved fist connect with his face and a boot with his leg, yet he remained standing. In the midst of the brawl, his fingers found Alina's pale arm, and he clamped down on her. With all his strength, he jerked her from the corridor back into the Tribunal Room. Another fist connected with Rhys' face, and the world around him was dunked into an all-consuming darkness.

34
RHYS ON HIS OWN

HE WAS BOTH HOT AND cold. He felt sweat on his forehead slither down his neck and chest. His clothes stuck to his body, yet his hands and feet were icy. A shiver ran through his body causing the pain that had been simmering below the surface to break free.

Rhys rolled onto his side and clenched the lush bedding around him. Shaking, he buried his head in the blankets and tensed all of his muscles in an attempt to ease the pain in his back, neck, and legs. No relief came. Panting, he rested his cheek on the bedding and looked about. He was in the room at Leo's estate he and Vinz had changed in before leaving for the temple. According to Pathos, a full day had passed.

Rhys gritted his teeth and pushed himself upright. Nearly all of the blankets were on the floor where he had kicked them in fits of agony.

Alina. Where was Alina? Had she escaped? The last thing he remembered was throwing her back into the Tribunal Room from the secret corridor.

"Come on," he growled to himself, crawling to the edge of the bed. He tried to slide his legs off to stand. Instead, he rolled from the bed and landed on the floor in a crumpled pile.

He felt sick. He had exerted himself too much. Pathos had provided a handful of powerful electrical shocks. Normally, such feats would have left him fatigued but functioning. With the corruption spreading throughout his body, however, he had depleted everything.

Annoyed and seething, he drew himself to his knees and, using the bed, brought his feet under him. Legs quivering, Rhys collapsed on the bed once more and vomited. The pain was too much.

He thought to call out to someone and, on more than one occasion, he opened his mouth to, but nothing came from his throat. Finally, he mustered a hoarse, "Hello?" Silence ensued.

Where was everyone? Where was Alina?

"Hello?" he shouted louder. Again, nothing.

Mustering his strength and willpower, Rhys threw himself onto his feet, doubled over in pain, and then staggered across the large room. He leaned against the open doorway, wheezed for a moment, and then looked about the Damien mansion.

"Hello!" His voice reverberated down the corridor.

Steeling himself, he hobbled down the hallway until he reached the staircase which led to the main foyer. He studied the stairs, unsure if his legs would support him. Desperate, he forced some steadiness into his limbs and made it down three steps before his right knee gave out. Though he didn't topple down the rest of the staircase, he did slide a good meter before lying on his back, winded. It was when he began pulling himself upright that a voice at the bottom of the lengthy staircase rang out.

"Rhys!"

Shaking horribly, Rhys looked over his shoulder at Vinz. He had never been so happy to see the Overseer. Though the left side of Vinz's face was swollen and his head was bound with gauze and bandaging, he seemed functioning—unlike Rhys. Vinz hurried up the stairs.

Before the Overseer could get to him, Rhys was already reaching out in near-hysteric worry. "Alina." He grabbed Vinz's wrinkled clothes. "Alina, where is she?"

"Hey, come on. You shouldn't be moving right now," replied Vinz.

Rhys dug his fingers into Vinz's clothes and jerked the Overseer to him. "Where is she?"

"She's not here."

"Where is she? At the ship? Or... where?"

Vinz pulled Rhys' hands from him and straightened himself. With pursed lips, he said, "The high priest has her."

Rhys stared at Vinz. "What?"

"Sal and two other family heads are currently battling for her custody. They're doing everything they can."

"Custody?" Rhys' gaze slipped to the stairs. "She's... been taken?"

The Overseer's response was low, grim. "Yes."

"But... I-I pulled her from the corridor... " He couldn't remember the details. He was sure he had saved her; he had jerked her from the soldiers' grasps.

"They still got her."

"They... " He couldn't wrap his mind around it. "She... "

For the first time since he had connected to the board, he reached out for his sister using their internal communications link. *Alina? Alina?*

There was no answer.

"Rhys, hey. Rhys."

Distantly, Rhys felt Vinz shaking him.

"Come on. Hey... "

"She's... not answering," Rhys murmured. His head spun. "She's not answering. Where is she?"

"Rhys!" called a voice.

"He's just found out," explained Vinz as Kallen, Leo, and Hodge joined them on the staircase.

Kallen knelt beside him and wiped his wet cheeks. "Hey, hey." She tapped his cheek. "It's me. Rhys, look at me. Rhys." Rhys forced his eyes to focus on Kallen's face. "Everything will be fine. We'll figure it out." Kallen motioned to the others. "Help him. I need him to be somewhere where he can lie down."

Hodge, Vinz, and Leo pulled him to his feet, but his legs wouldn't support his weight. Between the three of them, they dragged him back down the corridor to his room and deposited him on the bed. Rhys stared at the white ceiling overhead.

"Rhys, I have the medication," Kallen said. "I've seen Alina load it, but I don't know how much to give you."

"All of it," Rhys murmured.

"Nope. Not the answer," replied Hodge hastily. "Alina told me—a quarter of a vial. That's it. It's habit-forming."

Kallen shuffled through the small medication bag. "Should I give him more though? He's in so much pain."

"Stay with the known dosage," Hodge advised.

Kallen loaded the injector and tilted Rhys' chin upward. A familiar hiss slithered into Rhys' ears. Immediately, his body relaxed. He took several deep breaths before closing his eyes. The sharp, stabbing pain that had been searing his back and neck began to recede. Rhys laid his arm over his eyes to hide his tears of relief. Kallen patted his leg.

"Any word from my father?" asked Leo.

"Nothing so far," replied Vinz.

"Can... someone tell me what's going on?" Rhys whispered hoarsely.

"My father and other members of the noble families carried you two out," said Leo. "They brought you here. Per Vinz's request, I went to the docks to retrieve your medication as well as anyone who knew how to help you." Leo looked to Vinz. "That's all I know."

Rhys sat up, wiped his face on his shoulder, and looked at Vinz. "And Alina is... with the high priest?"

"Yes," said Vinz.

Rhys thought for a moment and then swung his legs off the bed. "I'm going after her."

Both Hodge and Vinz stopped him. "Not right now you're not," asserted Hodge.

"You *don't* understand." Rhys pushed them aside. "She's not answering. She's not answering any of my internal communications."

"That doesn't mean much though," Vinz offered. "There could be interference."

"Nothing interferes with our AIs," spat Rhys, standing. The room swirled, and the floor leapt at his face. Hands grabbed him and set him back on the bed.

"Rest for now," said Kallen. "Let Sal and the others take care of it. We're in unfamiliar territory."

Rhys blinked to keep the spinning room still, and then held his head. "But it's so silent. She's not here. She's not anywhere."

"Maybe she just has her internal communications turned off," Hodge suggested. "She turned it off to keep you from accidentally contacting her, right? Because of the corruption?"

Rhys considered his rationale and, realizing it held merit, nodded in agreement.

"I'll send for food," said Leo. "Afterward, rest. Vinz, Hodge, come with me."

Rhys watched as the three men left the room; only Kallen remained. He hoped Hodge was right. Alina had her internal communications switched off. She had done so as a precaution to keep him from absent-mindedly contacting her. They didn't know what the corruption would do if he tried to link with her AI.

After trays of food were sent upstairs, Rhys stripped out of his clothes and stretched out to sleep. His body was exhausted, and his mind emotionally fatigued, so it came as no surprise when he finally woke several hours later, it was near midnight. He glanced at the moonlight filtering in through the enormous window to his right and sat up. Kallen was asleep beside him. Her hair was still damp from bathing. Stretching his neck, Rhys crawled out of bed and went to stare out the window. Beyond the great columns of granite, the city lights of Brechin glimmered.

Rhys?

Rhys startled horribly and then breathed in relief. *Alina! Are you hurt? Where are you?*

I'm uninjured. I'm sorry. I didn't contact you sooner. I thought you were unconscious, and then I checked my internal communications settings. I had the internal link switched off.

Rhys leaned his forehead against the window. *You're not hurt?*

I'm not hurt, replied Alina, *but I want out of here. I'm scared. Etion, Gealdir, and Rullena speak with me often about creating a new class of white gods. They're completely consumed with the idea. They believe they are actually gods.*

And the high priest, Michael?

He's asked me twice to remove Logos, but I've told him 'no' both times. He didn't push the idea, but... I get the feeling that he's just playing nice.

Rhys turned and began dragging his clothes on. *Where are you? What part of the temple?*

At the very top, she replied. *The top two or three levels are reserved specifically for the high priest and the white gods.*

So, the part of the temple constructed of metal?

Yes.

Are there soldiers? Guards?

Yes. At every entryway.

Rhys stuffed his feet into his boots. *And the top floors—are there windows?*

Yes. But the windows have sensors on them. They didn't tell me that of course, but I know what our sensors look like. If any of those windows are damaged, an alarm will sound.

Rhys gazed at Kallen in thought and then began searching her pile of clothes for the medication pack. When he didn't find it, he began scouring room.

What are you doing? asked Alina.

We're at Leo's estate, replied Rhys. *If I'm going to get to you, I need to be able to move freely. Kallen brought my medication here, but she's hidden it.*

Good, grumbled Alina.

Rhys frowned deeply. *You realize that with it hidden, I can't do much to help you, right?*

There was a long pause before Alina said, *It has to be somewhere in the room. She wouldn't have taken it far in case you needed it immediately.*

Rhys got on his hands and knees and looked under the bed. Using his night vision, he found the pack wedged between the railing and the mattress. He pulled it out and gave himself half a vial.

That's too much, chided Alina.

Not for what I'm about to do. Rhys slid the medication back under the bed and then sat down. *Pathos, initiate query search for combat data.*

Searching historic documents, records, and media, replied Pathos. *Query: found. Number of results found in database: 123.*

Refine: hand-to-hand combat, instructed Rhys.

Refining. Number of results found: 18.

Rhys clenched his jaws. *Load them.*

Initiating the loading of 18 hand-to-hand combat skill sets. Estimated time of completion: 20 minutes.

Rhys lay across the bottom of the bed and closed his eyes. Data began scrolling across the inside of his eyelids; information poured into his brain. His limbs twitched, his hands moved in sync with the skills being imprinted onto his brain, his legs grew stiff and tense with anticipation. Several minutes passed and though he could feel his mind becoming weary, he endeavored. He *needed* this information.

As the final bits of data were added to his repertoire, Rhys rolled onto his side and, rubbing his neck, sat up. His body was tight like a spring.

If I take another dose to get me through the night, said Rhys, standing, *how much would you recommend?*

You've already had half a vial. Probably another quarter, replied Alina. *Remember, you have a finite supply of Monaxin, Rhys. I found some herbs and other medications that could possibly be made into a weaker substitute to kill the pain, but Monaxin is the best you have right now.*

Rhys pulled the medication pack out once more, dosed himself, and then jumped to his feet.

Phase one was complete.

Phase two—start.

Connect me to the board, said Rhys to Pathos, jogging out the room and down the corridor. In mid-step, Pathos linked him to the magnetic board. He knew Vinz had left the board under a tarp on *Themis'* upper deck that morning in case of an emergency. *Come.* He felt the board tug at the link that bonded him to it.

Rhys hurried down the stairs, glanced down the expansive entryway, and then rushed outside. Once past the marble stairs, he ran down the long, pristine cobblestone driveway. His board met him just as he reached the outer gates of the Damien estate. He leapt onto the board, stepped into the clasps, and zoomed upward.

Despite the darkness, the colors indicating the magnetic field density in and around the city shone vividly in Rhys' vision. Using Pathos to guide him, Rhys flew directly to the temple.

For several long minutes, he soared around the skyscraper, surveying the building and searching for doors and windows. When he found no unmanned entryways, he climbed to the top of the temple.

Alina, he called. *I'm here.*

Where?

Outside the window.

Alina's dark form appeared, but it was on the floor overhead. Rhys ascended until he was even with her.

Where are the others? He peered into the darkness of the room. Alina had been stripped of her green dress and was now clothed in the gray and silver robes the other Caelestis survivors wore.

I'm the only one in this room. She pressed her face against the glass and gazed downward. *Any luck?*

No. That's why I'm going to bust the windows open.

Wait, wait! No, no, no. Alina stepped back and pointed overhead to metal blinds stored above the windows. *If that glass is broken, the shutters will come down and lock—and an alarm will sound.*

Rhys squatted on the board. Resting his arms on his knees, he sighed. *So, what do you want me to do? I have no weapons, except myself. I could go to the ship and retrieve them. The resonance cutters could easily take care of the glass and the metal shutters.*

Alina thought and then said, *If you do that, then you need to make sure that we can leave Brechin immediately. That means notifying Leo, retrieving everyone at his estate, getting them to the port, and shipping out for sea.*

My priority right now is you, replied Rhys. *If I need to, I can carry you to another port.*

And leave Vinz, Hodge, Kallen, and the others to fend off the high priest's wrath?

Rhys frowned. *Plan, Alina. What's your plan? Everything I've offered, you've shot down.*

Bathsgate, Brechin's sister port. How far is that from here?

I don't know. It's going to be more than a 30 minute flight though.

Alina paced before the window. Finally, she looked at Rhys. *Go to the ship, retrieve the resonance cutters, and get me out. We'll return to Leo's estate, warn the others, and then go into hiding. Warn Andy and anyone else on the ship.*

Rhys gazed at his sister. *I'm sorry. I should have fought harder.*

It doesn't matter how skilled a fighter you are, Rhys. If you're outnumbered, you're outnumbered. Alina studied him for a long while before smiling. *You're the only one I can depend on.*

If I fail, the others will come for you.

Alina shook her head. *It's true, they would probably fight for my sake, but... they can't do what you can. Even I, your sister, cannot do the things you do.*

Rhys stared at Alina. Never before had she said words so identity-affirming to him. Never before had she expressed those sentiments.

Go, Alina commanded.

Rhys shifted his weight, banked west, and headed for the port. As he neared *Themis,* the feeling of unease growing in his gut blossomed into crippling anxiety. Ignoring the dull pain in his back, he landed on the upper deck, jumped off the board, and descended the ladder to the bridge. Finding the outer door locked, he knocked rapidly. When the bridge door opened, he was met by a rifle.

"Hey, it's me," he warned, recognizing Kashim's burly form.

Kashim stepped aside to admit him onto the bridge. "Leo said you were bad off."

"I'm feeling better."

"And why are you here in the middle of the night? Where's Vinz and the others?"

Rhys started down the inner stairs and jogged to his cabin. He collected the resonance cutters and his plasma firearm. Kashim met him in the hallway. "I'm going after Alina and am probably going to make a scene. *Themis* needs to be prepared to leave at first sign's notice of trouble."

"And Vinz?"

"We'll warn them." Rhys strapped on both weapons.

"Do they know you're here?"

"No." Rhys rushed up the stairs. "Prepare *Themis* for launch. I want to know that at least you are—"

Rhys! Alina's shrill scream nearly cracked open Rhys' skull. He melted against the door frame holding his head. *Rhys!*

What? What's wrong?

Rhys! They're... Rhys, they're trying...

Hold on! Rhys scrambled up the outer ladder and leapt onto the magnetic board. Before he was fully clamped in, he was rocketing back toward the temple. *Alina, answer me! What's wrong?*

When Alina replied, her inner voice was strained. *They're coming for me. Please!*

I'm coming. I'm coming! Rhys leaned into the board, urging it faster. Squinting against the warm wind, he raced toward the temple. At a near vertical ascent, he climbed to the top of the skyscraper where he had last seen Alina. *I'm here!*

Rhys!

Rhys armed and fired the plasma weapon. The glass melted, setting off a loud, obnoxious alarm that echoed through the temple and rolled over the city. The metal, emergency shutters snapped down over the dissolved window, forcing Rhys to fire again. When the blast did nothing—the metal belonged to a past spacecraft—Rhys withdrew the resonance cutters and dove for the metal shutters. With ease, he cut a haphazard square into the metal and then punched his board into the center, causing the metal to snapped inward.

He caught a glimpse of Alina being restrained before he was met by gunfire. Rhys fired back into the room, unclasped his feet, and then lunged through the hole he had created. Using the resonance cutters as his primary weapon, he ran for the numerous soldiers that had piled into the room in response to the perimeter breach. He just had to get close to the soldiers; they wouldn't fire if their own men were in the way.

With deadly precision, Rhys threw the resonance cutters at a soldier and rushed toward the others. With the skill of an experienced fighter, he ducked and blocked. Using his momentum, he slammed into the nearest soldier, wrapped his arms around the man, and leveraged the soldier over his leg. Rhys pivoted on his foot, stopped another attack with the back of his arm, and then lashed out with his sharp elbow.

"Son of a bitch!" shouted Alina, kicking at the soldiers who were trying to pull her into the corridor.

Rhys dove for her but was hit from the side and sent sprawling to the floor. He rolled into a crouch and raised his firearm. Without thinking, without considering the consequences, he fired. The soldier before him crumpled to the floor, a hole in his chest. Rhys rose to his feet. All activity in the room came to an abrupt halt. Alina's captors fell motionless.

"Alina," he panted.

His sister attempted to pull away from the guards but before she could put more than a step between them, her arms were pinned behind her back and she was placed in a submissive hold. Alina kicked behind her, but her captor simply stepped aside before wrenching her arms upward. She fell to her knees and glared at the floor.

"Release her," growled Rhys. When no one moved, Rhys aimed for the soldier next to his sister and fired. The man collapsed, dead. "*Now.*"

A loud *thwack* tore through the stunned silence. Pain erupted along Rhys' left shoulder as the force of whatever had hit him carried backward into the wall. Alina's horrified gasp followed him. Shaking hard—from adrenaline and shock—Rhys touched his left shoulder. His fingers came away slick with blood.

Perplexed as to what had happened, Rhys glanced about the room to find Michael looming in the doorway behind Alina and her guards. In his hand was a silver handgun.

"Arrest him," the high priest calmly commanded.

"No!" Alina shifted her weight. With the dexterity and flexibility of a lithe dancer, she dipped forward and unfurled her leg. Her bare heel caught her captor in the jaw, and she was freed. With a ferocity Rhys had never before seen, Alina charged Michael and slammed him into the wall.

Before the high priest could regain his balance, she darted across the room toward the fallen soldier with the resonance cutters in his chest. With a snarl, she ripped the burning tool from his body and stood over him. "Everyone, back up!" she shrieked, her voice shaking. No one moved.

"Put that down," instructed Michael. The high priest pushed past his soldiers and pointed his gun at Rhys. "I have no reservations about sending your brother to rejoin the stars."

Rhys, murmured Alina. *You have to run.*

Not without you.

We're outnumbered and you're injured. Go.

Rhys stared at his sister. *What about you?*

I'll be fine. They won't hurt me. I'm too valuable.

I'm coming back for you, Alina, said Rhys. She met his gaze from the corner of her eye. *I promise.*

Alina switched the resonance cutters off and looked to Michael. "Fine. I yield."

Michael lowered his gun. "Good. Let's get this cleaned up. You there, detain him." Michael motioned to Alina. "Come with me."

Alina glanced between Michael and Rhys before throwing the cutters into the air. Mustering his strength, Rhys leapt forward, caught the tool, and then sprinted for the window. No gunfire followed. There was only silence.

Rhys stepped from the destroyed, twentieth-story window onto his board and knelt there. He shifted his weight to the front of the board and rapidly descended. He sheathed the resonance cutters and, gasping, looked about. *Get me back to the Damien estate,* he murmured to Pathos.

35
DATA DUMP

By the time Rhys landed on the veranda of Leo's mansion, he was dizzy and weak from loss of blood. It was by sheer luck that a servant happened to be meeting her late-night lover in the shadows of the front porch, saw him, and ran for help. As Rhys lay on the pristine marble veranda floor, blood-soaked and half-unconscious, he stared at the stars. Cold, indifferent—they had nothing to offer. Yet, for the first time in weeks, he wished to be back on Caelestis.

It didn't take long for news to spread through the mansion of Rhys' return, and soon lights all over the enormous building flickered on. When the female servant returned, Leo and Terron were by her side.

"*Gawan*, Rhys," Leo muttered, kneeling beside him. "Your *gawan* eyes—they're glowing! What's going on?" He leaned over him, searching for the source of the blood and then tore Rhys' shirt off his body. Distantly, Rhys heard Terron disseminating orders to servants. Leo placed his open palms on Rhys' bleeding wound. "What happened? Huh? Rhys? Hey, what happened?"

"I... was shot," whispered Rhys, his gaze still on the stars.

"By whom? Who shot you?"

"The high priest... "

"The high priest shot you?" asked Terron incredulously. "How? Why?"

"Alina." His sister's name stayed on his lips.

He had failed her yet again.

"Get Vinz. *Not* Kallen," Leo instructed over his shoulder. As Terron disappeared inside, Leo leaned over Rhys and forced their eyes to meet.

"Are you here? Are you with me?" Rhys nodded. Leo glanced up as a servant placed a basin of water next to him. "Prepare bandages to apply pressure." The servant knelt beside Leo and began unwinding gauze from a bag.

The young noble removed his bloody hands from Rhys' shoulder, checked the wound, and then began soaking cloths in the basin. Afterward, he wiped the wound and the immediate area and, with a dry cloth, continued to apply pressure. As he leaned on his hands, Leo examined Rhys' face. "Are you hurt anywhere else?"

Rhys felt his eyes roll into his head, but he managed to murmur, "No."

Vinz ran onto the veranda. "How bad is it?"

"Gunshot wound to the shoulder," replied Leo. "He's going to need a doctor. You know why his eyes are glowing?"

Rhys heard Vinz kneel beside him, but he barely comprehended it. Only when the Overseer tapped his cheek did some life flicker back into Rhys. "Hey, disconnect from the board. You're draining yourself," said the Overseer. Rhys just stared at him. Was that such a bad thing? Vinz made a soft sound and then said, "Pathos, disconnect Rhys from the board. Immediately."

"Override functions denied," replied Pathos. "All override functions have been set for Alina Falkrow."

"Rhys." Vinz leaned over him. "If you're going to kill yourself, that's fine. But this isn't the way to do it. Disconnect from the *gawan* thing."

Rhys gave the order to Pathos. He heard his board gently settle on the cobblestone.

Terron motioned to the servants. "You three, carry the board in. Leo, I just received word that a city-wide warrant has been released for Rhys' arrest."

"Vinz, keep pressure here," coached Leo. "Let's move him inside."

"As soon as he's inside, start cleaning the veranda," added Terron. "Make sure not a streak of blood is left. Let's move."

It took several long minutes, but Rhys eventually found himself in an empty room adjoining the entryway. Though he had remained conscious, he could hardly think straight. As Vinz leaned on Rhys' shoulder wound, the Overseer listened to what was being said in the entryway.

Data dump pending, Pathos suddenly announced.

Wait, what? gasped Rhys, lurching. Vinz startled.

Alina Falkrow is attempting to transfer a large amount of data to you. Data dump pending, explained Pathos. *Awaiting approval.*

Why? I can't take that right now!

Data dump denied. There was a momentary pause before Pathos added, *Alina Falkrow is pushing the data and is willing to execute a system override to force download.*

Fine, replied Rhys. He looked up at Vinz. "Alina is sending data to me... I will lose consciousness."

Vinz nodded. "We'll take care of you."

Pathos, initiate data dump. It took but ten seconds of the data transfer to knock out Rhys.

When he woke next it was midmorning. Squinting against the harsh sunlight, Rhys rolled his head away from the window and looked about the room. It appeared that he was in a study as there were numerous bookcases, a wide desk, and a board on the wall with notes scrawled in Nefegian.

Pathos?

Forty-three hours have passed since you last lost consciousness.

After several preparatory breaths, he tried to sit up. A sharp twinge in his chest forced him back onto the floor. Panting, he examined his shoulder which was thick with gauze and bandages. Whoever had doctored him had knowledge in the medicine field. It didn't appear to be haphazardly done.

It is advisable to rest, continued Pathos. *All biological energy has been redirected in an attempt to heal the damaged shoulder muscle and tissue, however, this rerouting has left you weak. Another 24 hours of sleep is recommended to accomplish at least 90 percent muscle reparation.*

Rhys thought for a moment reviewing the various muscles that had been damaged in his shoulder. Realizing he now had precise knowledge of the human body, he lurched onto his side and scrambled to his knees. *Alina? Alina?* He squeezed his eyes shut to ease his dizziness. *Alina!*

Your internal connection with Alina Falkrow is no longer valid, reported Pathos.

Rhys froze. *What do you mean 'no longer valid?' Does she have it turned off?*

No.

Rhys' heart sank. With renewed strength, he forced himself to his feet and staggered across the room to the door. It was locked. "No," he murmured, pulling at the bronze door handle. When it didn't budge, he kicked it angrily.

Rhys hobbled across the room and peered out the window. He was surprised to find soldiers stationed around the Damien estate. After several minutes of pacing and fidgeting, Rhys redirected his attention to Sal's desk where he found a tray of food and water waiting for him. Leaning against the desk, he ate the cold meal and drank all that he could stomach. In the meantime, he noted his own physical condition.

Thanks to Pathos, his shoulder was healing rapidly. Both he and Alina had always been astonishingly quick healers. His back didn't hurt, but that didn't mean the pain wasn't coming. Leo had ripped his shirt from him, and his boots were missing. All he wore were a pair of blood-stained pants and his bandages. To his chagrin, he realized he had also been stripped of his weapons. Both the resonance cutters and his firearm were gone.

After finishing his meal, he sifted through the desk's contents. He didn't need a key but something that he could use to pick a lock. When he found his tools—a small piece of sturdy wire and a long, metal shank used for opening boxes—he crossed the room and knelt before the bronze handle and its lock. With Pathos' expert instruction, Rhys picked the lock and inched open the door. He waited before creaking it wider. When he heard nothing, he tossed the wire aside, tucked the shank into his pants pocket, and crept toward the entryway.

When he saw not a soul, he stole across the vast foyer into what appeared to be a kitchen. Again, no servants. Rhys surveyed the stoves, ovens, coolers, and cabinets as he stalked through. He passed his hand over the burners of the stove. Two of them were warm.

When he reached the double doors on the opposite side of the kitchen, he paused to listen. He could hear murmuring. He glanced up at the hinges of the door and, realizing the doors could swing, crouched. He cracked one of the doors open.

Pathos, increase auditory capabilities by ten percent. The voices that had been indistinct came to his ears.

"When was the last time someone checked on him?" That was Leo.

"Vinz checked on him around six and told me he was showing signs of pain," replied Kallen. "I gave his medication about an hour ago."

"Has his conditioned improved?" said Sal.

"I looked at his wound this morning," Kallen continued. "Unsurprisingly, it's healing. I wouldn't be surprised if that's Pathos' work. Nevertheless, you did a good job."

Sal chuckled warmly. "My wife always encouraged me to learn a little bit of everything."

"Hodge, come eat," called Leo. He sighed. "So, what's the likelihood of Rhys trying to kill himself today?"

"I want to know how he just walked out the other night," Kallen huffed. "No one was standing watch. Not even your servants saw him."

"You were the one in bed with him," retorted Leo.

"You forget," said Vinz solemnly, "Rhys has every human ability at his disposal. He needs only to access them. If espionage, tracking, and combat is what he needs, he'll acquire those skills. It's simple."

"Do you think it's true what he said?" asked Leo. "That the high priest shot him?"

Sal's response was immediate. "Yes. I was at the temple when Rhys attempted to rescue Alina. I was three or four floors below the action, but it was loud. Gunfire, alarms, yelling. Soldiers swarmed the building. To be honest, I've never seen anything like it. It was quite terrifying."

"Surely that wasn't all Rhys though," Kallen breathed incredulously. "He's one person."

"Did you not hear what I just said?" asked Vinz. "The one person on this entire planet who knew him completely has been taken. I'm sorry, but Kallen, he has nothing left right now. Alina was everything."

"He's right," Hodge grumbled, joining the group. "They may not have always acted like it, but a day didn't go by when they weren't communicating either verbally or using their computer-things."

"Well, he can still talk with her through the computers, right?" asked Leo. "There's nothing stopping them."

"Unless the high priest has stripped Alina of hers," said Sal. Silence followed. "I think... that's why Rhys is so desperate to get to her."

"Agreed," said Vinz. "He's not going to stop. Nothing will stop him. Even if we lock him up and chain him to the floor—he'll find a way to escape."

"So, what's the solution?" Kallen wondered aloud. "We let him go?"

"Whatever Rhys chooses, I'm going with him," asserted Hodge.

"Not if he leaves you," replied Leo.

"He's not leaving me. Alina is mine too."

"Well, I'm coming too then."

"Leo, this isn't something you should tangle yourself in," scolded Sal half-heartedly.

"I became entangled in this mess the moment I agreed to track *Themis'* crew. If I have to, I'll leave Brechin and never look back," the young noble told his father.

"Bold words, Little Brother," chuckled Terron. "Why don't you go outside and tell the royal guard that."

"I mean it." Leo pushed his chair back and stood. "When this is over, I'm… leaving Brechin. The corruption here is unsettling. If you'll have me, I'll come aboard *Themis* as a crew member."

"I have no reason to deny you," said Vinz, "but why? You're leaving the comforts of home, status, title, money."

"Because what you're trying to achieve—peace between the Aabeshian people and the Pantaraks—won't come easily. I believe in your cause. It's just that simple." Leo began collecting dishes from the table. "Besides, you're short crew members, aren't you?"

Realizing that Leo was heading for the kitchen, Rhys leaned against the wall. Pushing the door open with his shoulder, Leo entered the kitchen and set the glassware on the counter. When he turned, his eyes fell on Rhys. Though surprised, he didn't startle or say a word. Instead, he smiled and returned to the dining room. "So, what's the plan? Hodge and I are willing to accompany Rhys in his endeavors. That makes three of us."

"I will join you," said Vinz.

"And me," added Kallen.

"You don't have to," said Hodge, his voice warm, soft. "Rhys wouldn't want you to be in danger. Not after what's happened with Alina."

"Before Rhys came, I regularly went out on patrols with you and Kashim, remember?" Kallen countered. "I can handle myself."

"Good, then it's settled," said Leo. "Now we ask Rhys what he wants to do."

"Right now?" asked Hodge. "He'll be out for the next two days."

"Rhys," called Leo, amused.

Rhys pushed the nearest door open with his good arm and gazed at the group.

"How did you… get out of my study?" asked Sal. "The door is double-locked."

"I told you," Vinz gloated.

"Son of the stars, what's your plan?" asked Leo, leaning against the table.

"Explosives," replied Rhys. "That temple is coming down."

"And how do you plan on getting Alina out?" asked Sal. "Also, there are innocent people in that building. You'll end up killing them in the process."

"I killed innocent people last night," Rhys replied darkly. "If anyone else gets in my way, I'll kill them too."

Kallen's eyes grew wide. "Rhys… "

"Explosives, huh?" mused Terron. He thought for a moment and then looked at Leo. "Charlie."

Leo nodded enthusiastically. "Of course—*Charlie!*"

"Don't get Charlie involved in this," advised Sal.

"Then what do you suggest?" Leo groaned.

"I can't get you explosives, but I can get my hands on weapons. Will that work?"

"Yes," said Rhys.

"What do you need?"

"Rifles, guns, grenades, plasma arms—"

"We don't have those," interrupted Terron.

"Then we'll make due." Rhys began pacing. "I'm going to need help bringing down the power system. Kallen—"

He stopped. Kallen was staring at the table, her brows furrowed.

"What's wrong?" asked Vinz.

Without a word, Kallen stood and left the room. Rhys suspected she was angry over a number of items, but he couldn't afford to waste time. "Once the preparations are set and we have what we need, I'm going to rewire the circuits on all of the temple's solar panels and cause them to short out."

"At least let me send a warning to the innocents there—"

Rhys stopped Sal. "Don't say a word. Am I understood?"

Sal frowned but nodded.

"Good. Now go."

"How are any of us supposed to leave the premises?" asked Vinz. "All family head residences have been put under the watch of the royal guard."

"Where's my gun?" asked Rhys.

Sal stood abruptly. "You're not killing the soldiers."

Rhys considered him and then shrugged. "Fine, you come up with a way to leave the mansion. You have until this afternoon otherwise, we're doing it my way." Sal's usually calm and good-natured disposition fractured. Angrily, he stalked out. "Terron, go with him," Rhys ordered. "He'll need help." Terron followed his father from the dining room.

"Hey… we're here to help you," mumbled Leo. "Don't be so angry."

Rhys began pacing once more. It seemed to be the only thing that kept the unease in his gut from consuming him. "Weapons, solar panels... " he thought aloud. "*Themis*." He looked at Vinz. "Get to the harbor. I stopped there last night and warned them it might get ugly. I told Andy and Kashim to leave the docks if necessary. If you can, prepare the double-shot cannons."

"Rhys, *Themis* is strong, but she's not equipped for a battle like the one you're getting ready to start," argued the Overseer.

"Your only target is the temple," replied Rhys. "That's it. Once you've hit it, go out to sea and stay out of the way."

Vinz stood and leaned on the table. "Look, we all want to save Alina, but it's going to take precision and skill, not plans thrown together."

"Which is why I'm asking you to go to the harbor and prepare the double-cannons," growled Rhys. Vinz didn't move. "If you want to be a part of this, then do as I say. I'll fire the plasma gun as a signal so watch for it around dusk. Go."

"Hey," murmured Hodge, "take it easy."

"I'm not going to take it easy!" cried Rhys, hitting the table with his good arm. The dishes quivered violently. "Alina's gone."

"We know. That's why—"

"No! You *don't* know! I can't reach her."

"Her internal communications are shut off," said Vinz.

Rhys shook his head. His hands trembled. "She did an emergency data dump last night. She gave me everything that she had... "

Leo lowered his voice. "What is the... significance of that?"

Rhys glared at the table. "They've stripped her of her AI or... they're in the process of it." No one said anything. When Rhys spoke, it was in Interstellar Nefegian. "That's why... I'm going to kill every last Pantarak piece of shit... that stands in my way." Rhys looked to Leo. "Including you or any of the nobles."

Face suddenly stoic, Leo started for the door. "Vinz, let's go."

In silence, Rhys watched them leave. Only he and Hodge remained. He expected Hodge to say something, but his friend remained quiet. "Come with me," Rhys eventually said.

Together, they went upstairs to the room he and Kallen had slept in the night before. Unsurprisingly, Kallen was already there sitting on the edge of the bed, crying. She looked up at them when they entered but didn't say anything.

Rhys gazed at her solemnly. "Are you coming with us?"

Kallen glared at him. "To kill more people?"

"To save Alina. If it comes to killing, then so be it."

"How can you… say it so calmly like it's something you do every day?"

"Because, I will do *anything* for Alina," avowed Rhys. "Just like I would do anything for you or Hodge. So, if killing another human will bring me closer to rescuing her, I will gladly bear that sin."

Kallen gazed at him for a long moment and then nodded. "What do you want me to do?"

36
RAID ON THE TEMPLE

IT WAS LATE AFTERNOON WHEN everyone reconvened in the dining room. Despite the numerous soldiers stationed around the Damien estate, Vinz and Leo had managed to sneak out and make a run for the harbor. According to Pathos, *Themis* was still in port. In the meantime, Sal and Terron had returned with crates of weapons and ammo. Leo's father indicated there were others in Brechin who did not agree with the high priest's international policies and wanted to help instigate change.

In the meantime, under Kallen's strict orders, Rhys had spent the afternoon sleeping—or trying to sleep—to allow Pathos to work on his injured shoulder. Though it was by no means fully healed, by the time Rhys reappeared in the dining room, he was able to move his injured arm with little pain.

Now, standing before the group strapped in his weapons and bandages, Rhys led a review of the plan. "Once Kallen and I have destroyed the solar panels, I'll signal Vinz who will strike the tower. Afterward, we'll go in through the front doors."

"I didn't get a chance to tell you this earlier," said Sal, "but that won't work. I mean… the solar panel destruction. The primary source of power for the elevators is the solar power. Destroy those and you have no way to the top."

"Stairs?" suggested Kallen.

"Climbing 20 flights of stairs is an option, but not one I would recommend. The staircases are narrow—very few people take the stairs. They're mainly there as emergency exits," said Sal. "If we get cornered in a stairwell, then it's entirely possible the military could hold us off indefinitely."

"Where would the high priest take the white gods—Rhys' people— in the event of an emergency?" asked Hodge. "Where would they go?"

"There are vaults within the temple," Sal explained, "but… that's the extent of my knowledge. It's possible they wouldn't go anywhere. Better to believe the white gods perished than allow the citizens see them running. Remember, there is life after death."

"But if the high priest is trying to create a pure-blood race of people, he can't afford to let them die," mused Rhys. "Therefore, he would need to protect them at all costs."

"I agree with Rhys," said Kallen. "He wants them alive."

"Then don't destroy the solar panels." Sal tapped his fingers on the table in thought. "Don't destroy them. Use the elevators to get to the top. Leave half your unit on a floor below as back up."

"That won't stop them from using the other elevator though. There are two," said Rhys. "The elevators alternate floors, right?"

"Correct, the elevator to the left is for high-level personnel only. The elevator on the right admits to inconsequential floors," replied Sal.

"Can we force *them* to come down the elevators?" asked Hodge. "What's Vinz firing at? Can he even reach the tower from the harbor?"

"Yes, he's within range," asserted Rhys. "He's firing several floors from the top, around the thirteenth or fourteenth floors. That's going to cause the most chaos." Rhys leaned on the table. "The double-shot cannon aboard *Themis* is powerful, but at such a distance, it won't bring the temple down."

"Perhaps then that's all we need," offered Kallen. "Give them a reason to evacuate."

"They still have the vaults," Sal replied, "maybe more. Again, I don't know."

"And I can guarantee those vaults are made of materials constructed by my people," said Rhys. "They're impervious to most destruction."

"You said 'most' destruction," said Hodge. "What aren't they protected against?"

Rhys motioned to himself. "The resonance cutters. It's a tool made specifically for space materials. It can cut through anything."

"Then we get you up to the vault and you break in," said Sal.

"Rhys is injured. He may be super-human," responded Kallen, "but even he has his limits."

"I'll be with him," Hodge countered.

Leo strolled into the room. "And me. *Themis* is ready."

"On my signal, Vinz will open fire on the temple," explained Rhys in an attempt to solidify the plan. "This will hopefully allow us the opportunity to climb the temple using the left elevator. Once up there, we will have to fight our way to the vaults. No doubt, there will be guards."

"When do we leave?" asked Hodge.

"Right now," replied Rhys. "Sal, have you come up with a plan to get us out past the soldiers?"

The Minister of Education nodded. "The same way I retrieved the weapons. The underground tunnel under the estate."

"And you have somewhere to go if things turn ugly?" queried Hodge.

"The high priest already indicated that I'm in danger of losing my post. With the conclusion of this mission, I'm going to join Sean in Bathsgate for a while. You take care of yourselves. Don't worry about me."

"Kallen, a word?" said Rhys. "The rest of you, arm yourselves."

Rhys led Kallen upstairs to their temporary chamber and closed the door behind them. "The medication. Give it to me."

"You've been doing really well," Kallen hummed.

"It doesn't cure me," replied Rhys. "It eases the pain." Rhys thought for a moment. The last dose he had had was nearly 12 hours ago. He still wasn't in pain. He looked at her intently. "What did you do?"

"I gave you a dose this morning."

"How much?"

"A vial and a half," murmured Kallen.

"Why... would you give me that much?"

"I know it's not a cure... but I'm so tired of seeing you in pain, always crippled in agony." She smiled grimly. "Right now, it's necessary. You need to be able to fight. You must fight."

"Kallen... There are only three vials left."

"I know." Resolve on her face, she nodded. "And you're going to use another tonight. Right now." Kallen went into the washroom and returned a moment later with the medication pack. She loaded another vial and motioned to Rhys.

Rhys gazed morosely at her. "I don't want you to come with us." She lowered the injector. "I don't think... I could bear it if something happened to you too."

"Nothing is going to happen to me." She put on a strong face, gently placed the injector under his jaw, and administered the dose.

Rhys sighed in relief as his body relaxed. After a moment, he took Kallen by the waist and pulled her to him. Forehead-to-forehead, they breathed in one another. "I want you to go back to *Themis*," he whispered. "Please."

"Rhys, I can fight. I'm not—"

"Kallen, *please*. I'm begging you."

"Rhys… "

"Kallen." Rhys kissed her forehead. "Please."

They melted into silence, each testing the other's will. It was Kallen who finally submitted with a soft sigh. "Fine." She leaned in, kissed him on the lips and then the cheek. "Come back to me."

"I'll do my best."

Kallen drew away and cleared her throat. "I'm taking your medication with me. It will be on *Themis*."

"My board. Where is it?"

"I saw Terron moving it earlier to the underground tunnel." She went to the doorway, gave a small wave, and then disappeared.

With one last glance about the room, Rhys swept down the corridor and returned to the dining room. He found Leo and Hodge inspecting a handgun. Both wore bullet-proof vests, rifles, and grenades on their hips.

"I'm not going to lie," grinned Hodge as he holstered a handgun. "Capital weapons are slick."

"Leo, you can still back out of this," said Rhys.

"You're giving him the option but not me?" Hodge grumbled.

Leo leaned on the table. "I made my decision a while ago." He looked at his father who was studying a gun. "Besides, it's our generation's time to fight. My father and the other family heads have done their time ruling the Pantarak Empire. It's our turn."

"Sal… " Rhys turned to Leo's willowy, light-haired father. "Thank you for your help."

"Change does not happen overnight, Rhys," he said solemnly. "It happens gradually."

Rhys motioned to his comrades. With Leo in the lead, they left the dining room and made their way to the underground tunnel via a staircase hidden under an expensive rug in one of the mansion's many back rooms. They found Terron waiting for them at the bottom of the stairs with a lamp. Leo touched his closed fist to Terron's and took the lamp.

"The tunnel will take you outside the estate grounds," Leo's brother explained. "Rhys, we already moved your board. It's at the end of the tunnel." Terron turned and climbed the stairs back into the Damien mansion.

"Let's go," murmured Leo. They walked down the dark, dirt passageway, Leo's lamp the only light to guide them.

"Have you been here before?" Hodge eventually asked. "It's... creepy down here."

"Terron and I used to play down here all the time," said Leo.

"You have another brother, right?" asked Rhys.

"Senantis, eh, Sean for short. He's studying at the university in Bathsgate." Leo chuckled. "He'll be surprised when Father tells him all he's missed." There was silence for a moment before Leo asked, "In all seriousness, what do we do once we've rescued Alina? Walking out of Brechin isn't an option."

"I haven't thought that far ahead," Rhys admitted.

"As long as we're being honest," said Hodge, "your shoulder, is it going to slow us down?" Rhys scoffed. "Hey, I had to ask. You're the one leading this raid."

After several more minutes of silence, they slowed to halt at the end of the tunnel. Rhys went to his board, which was propped against the wall, and looked at Leo and Hodge. "Ready?"

"We're walking, right?" asked Hodge. "All three of us can't fit on that."

"Right," replied Rhys as Leo climbed a ladder and pushed at the trap door overhead with his shoulder. *Pathos, connect to the board.* Rhys felt the pressure behind his eyes increase, and he blinked to adjust.

"Come on," Leo whispered after peering out the trap door and pulling himself from the tunnel; Hodge followed. Surveying the magnetic fields around him, Rhys crouched on the board and rose through the trapdoor. He set his feet on the grass and then pushed the board aside so Leo could close the door and conceal it.

Rhys looked about in surprise. They were in a large field of a tall, sweet-smelling crop. In the distance, the lights of the city illuminated the dusk sky. "Where are we?"

"One of the harvest fields," said Leo. "Stay down. There are sentries out here to keep thieves from taking crops." Leo lowered himself to the ground. "This way."

They stole across the countryside, pushing aside the crops until they reached a looming, metal gate. Leo looked to Rhys who slipped by Hodge and withdrew his cutters. Once a large enough hole had been created, they darted through the gate, and sprinted to the nearest alleyway. Rhys' board followed.

Panting, they peered at each other in the dim light of a streetlamp. It was another four kilometers to the temple. If they kept to the shadows and stayed off the streets, they could perhaps make the journey in under half an hour. With Leo once again in the lead, they jogged down the alley, across another street, and behind a row of homes and shops.

Now more than ever Rhys was thankful for the time he had spent on the ship and on the sunboards. Although still in recovery, he and Hodge maintained a solid pace. It wasn't until Leo murmured for respite that they slowed to a stop in the shadows of a government building. While Leo bent over his knees, gasping silently, Rhys examined the area. They were close. The temple entrance was another four or five blocks away.

"I'm going to send Vinz the signal," said Rhys, prepping his firearm.

Leo leaned against the wall, wiping at the sweat on his brow. "One more minute," he beseeched.

"If you come aboard *Themis* permanently," joked Hodge, "you'll have to get in better shape. You're pathetic."

"Some of us don't have super-human healing abilities," muttered Leo. "I'm still injured."

Hoping that Vinz was as watchful as he usually was, Rhys pointed his arm to the sky and fired three times. The orange blasts though small, were bright and illuminated the area briefly before disappearing into the nighttime sky. Heart in his throat, Rhys stared up at the stars. He strained his ears.

Suddenly, two deep belches of sound erupted in the distance. "Let's go, let's go." Rhys darted into the street. Overhead, Vinz's cannon fire whistled by; a split-second later, it bore deep into the temple. There was a delay before explosions tore at the right side of the building, and flames erupted from several of the floors.

People began filling the streets. Residents staggered from their homes to gape up at the glowing temple. Some sprinted toward it to offer help or support while others ran in the opposite direction. In seconds, the streets were a crowded mess. Caught in a throng of people moving away from the temple, Rhys began shoving them from his path. "Move!"

Leo raised his handgun and fired into the air. Screams erupted from the crowd and people ducked. "The royal guard will handle these acts of terrorism," Leo called. "Citizens should stay inside their homes. Now, move! Clear the roads for soldiers." The people stepped aside. Together,

Rhys, Hodge, and Leo stormed up the street toward the flame-engulfed tower.

"Shit," cursed Leo as three airships zoomed overhead. "This is bad." Within minutes, military barricades and soldiers were set up along the main street at the temple's entrance. The Brechin military was swift. Leo stopped at the street corner and looked back at Rhys. "What now?"

Panting, Rhys shoved him aside, took aim, and began firing at the soldiers. Bulletproof vests, armor, airships—none of it mattered. Plasma weapons were not just weapons; they were tools meant for the harsh realities of space. Here on Earth, they were mercilessly overpowered. Within seconds, Rhys had carved out a path for them, shot down an airship, and destroyed a solar-powered vehicle being used as a barricade.

"Go!" shouted Rhys, positioning himself at the bottom of the temple stairs. Using his firearm to keep the soldiers at bay and his board as a shield to defend against stray bullets, he covered Hodge and Leo until they cleared the great expanse of stairs.

"Rhys!" yelled Hodge.

With a handful of haphazardly aimed parting shots, Rhys swung himself onto his board and powered up the staircase. Just as he cleared the top, several guards—having heard the commotion—appeared from within. Rhys rotated his board and slammed broadside into the first two, sending them sprawling into their comrades. Shots echoed along the vast veranda as Leo and Hodge opened fire on the remaining guards who scrambled to retaliate.

The guards Rhys had pummeled gaped at him as he dismounted. Rhys fired at the marble floor beside him. "Do you see that? Do you see it melting? That will be your face if you come after us."

He imagined he appeared quite horrible, eyes glowing an eerie blue and silver hair wind-whipped. He was every bit the white god they believed him to be. Rhys called to Hodge and Leo who had been watching the soldiers below.

"They've stopped fighting," remarked Hodge.

"They don't understand why a white god would be attacking the temple," Leo explained breathlessly.

Rhys pushed his board through the open doors of the temple and gazed about the grand entryway which was crowded with nobles, soldiers, and servants. He wanted to scream out to Michael the high priest and to call to Alina, but he knew both would be pointless.

From deep within the building, creaks and moans echoed as the support beams shifted from *Themis'* cannon fire. Murmurs of worry and softly sobbed pleas rose from the temple's inhabitants.

Rhys whirled on Leo. "Why aren't they leaving?"

Leo frowned deeply. "If their faith is strong, the building will remain."

Having had enough of the religious ridiculousness, Rhys leapt onto his board and rose above the crowd. He searched the room for a familiar face but found none, not even the family heads—

The room's magnetic field, which had until a moment ago been glowing bright red in Rhys' vision, began shifting from gray to black to yellow. The magnetic fields were changing? But how? Why? Magnetic fields didn't shift like that, at least, he didn't think they did.

Feeling that something wasn't right, Rhys squatted on his board and then slid off. "What's wrong?" asked Hodge.

"The magnetic fields in the room just changed," cautioned Rhys, looking outside. It was the same. Where there had been red and orange patches of fog, there now extended vast fields of gray and black noise. "I don't know what it means, but this isn't good."

"Is it the high priest?" asked Leo. "What's a magnetic field?"

"Let's get these people out of here." Rhys turned to the crowd. "Move! Now!"

The people nearest him began to trickle out the doors, throwing him terrified looks as they passed.

"Rhys!"

Rhys whirled around at the sound of Alina's voice.

"Rhys?"

Head on a swivel, he began pushing through the throngs of people. "Alina?" he called. "Alina!"

"Rhys!" cried Alina.

Rhys crossed the entire entryway in a matter of seconds. Just as he stepped from the thickest part of the crowd, a flash of silver caught his eye. Before he could properly turn to greet Alina, his sister flung herself at him. Unbalanced, Rhys stumbled backward. He wrapped his arms around Alina and buried his face in her hair. His heart hurt with relief. "Sister."

Rhys looked over Alina's shoulder at Cantia who, oddly enough, was dressed in a boy's trousers, boots, and blouse. Her blond hair was tucked under a cap. Despite the streaks of dirt on her pants and elbows, she beamed at him. Rhys thought he was going to cry. Never before had he been so happy, so overcome with relief.

"Alina!" shouted Hodge, running to them. Alina untangled herself from Rhys and raced to Hodge who swept her into a deep embrace and kissed her face joyously.

"How?" Rhys asked, incredulous.

Cantia pointed to a displaced panel in the wall beside the left elevator. "Air ducts."

"What about the high priest and the others?"

Cantia gazed at Alina, the smile fading from her face. "She wasn't being watched. They had her chained to a table." Cantia dug in her pocket and withdrew the resonance knife Rhys had given Irvine, the Overseer of *Grisle*. "Leo pulled this off that slave trader and gave it to me."

Rhys glanced about the room—the magnetic fields were still in complete disarray—and then at Alina who was speaking enthusiastically to Hodge and Leo. Hodge also must have asked how she had escaped because Alina turned and pointed to the hidden passage.

Able to fully view Alina now, Rhys gaped openly in horror.

Her AI was gone.

"I'm sorry," murmured Cantia. "I didn't get there in time."

Rhys staggered to his sister and clutched at her. Alina looked away, shielding the left side of her face with her hair. "Don't look," she whispered.

"I... Alina... " Rhys reached between them and gently pushed back her hair to reveal a small, bald spot where Logos' external had been and the two injection sites that had connected the unit to her.

"We need to go," called Leo. "The crowd is dispersing. We're going to have a hard time slinking off. Cantia, did anyone see you?"

"No, but they'll know she's missing any moment," replied Cantia, pulling off her cap. "We should leave—"

Suddenly, the floor began shaking, trembling. Overhead, the ceiling cracked loudly, and the building groaned. Cantia groped for Rhys and then stumbled as a violent tremor rocked the ground.

Seismic activity detected, said Pathos.

Seismic activity? Rhys looked at Alina who was gazing about wide-eyed. Of course she didn't know what was going on—she no longer had Logos. A spark of red caught Rhys' eye as the magnetic field present in the building began to swirl in a tempestuous sea of colors.

"Earthquake," breathed Leo. "We need to get out, now."

Hodge grabbed Alina's arm and began running for the massive double doors. All around them, the marble floor cracked. Dust from the ceiling showered them in a fine mist. The walls rattled ominously while the building moaned under the weight of the shifting infrastructure.

Another shock of shivers shook the world around them, and Rhys stumbled. Beside him Cantia staggered to the left and then fell. Rhys glanced ahead at the others who were also having a difficult time remaining standing. Entrusting Alina to Hodge, Rhys grabbed Cantia.

No sooner had he hauled the girl to her feet than the marble floor beneath them shrugged, sending them reeling. Rhys lurched forward and then, tripping over his own feet, fell backward pulling Cantia with him. They landed in a pile.

Over the thunderous rumbling, a gunshot rang out.

Rhys rolled onto Cantia to cover her, frantically searching the chaos for the shooter. His eyes settled on Michael who was braced near one of the elevators ready to fire again.

Hodge's voice rose above the commotion, above the sound of the Earth cracking. "Hey... hey, hey. Alina, hey." Rhys turned to find his sister collapsed against Hodge, blood soaking the back of her robes. "Alina! Alina!" Hodge tapped her face as he sank to the quivering floor with her in his arms. "Hey!"

"You bastard!" screamed Leo, turning and expertly firing a volley at the high priest. A white light blossomed before Michael, and Leo's bullets ricocheted into the surrounding stairs.

As though in response, the walls around them howled menacingly. Somewhere deep in the building, the supports beams shifted, causing a large pile of rubble to separate from the ceiling on the far side of the room and clatter to the floor.

"Sorry! Wrong person," Michael taunted. Leo fired off another round at the high priest.

"Stop," shouted Rhys, gathering himself. "It's a light screen."

Leo stumbled as the floor quaked. "*You* shoot him!"

Plasma weapons didn't work against light screens. Rhys looked back at Alina and at the blood pooling around her and Hodge.

The floor bucked as another wave of tremors tore through the building. Those still inside staggered and fell. Plaster and marble toppled from the ceiling around them, and great fissures large enough to swallow humans ripped at the floor. The air itself shuddered.

"Rhys!" shrieked Cantia, scrambling on her hands and knees to him.

Rhys glanced over his shoulder at Michael, who had also been sent to the ground by the last set of tremors, and then took Cantia's hand. With more strength than he meant to use, he jerked her to her feet.

"Go! Get Alina out of here." Cantia pushed him toward Hodge and Alina. "Go!"

Rhys glanced at the continuously shifting screen of colors around him. He could make it. Another gunshot rang out. Rhys whirled around and returned fire at the high priest at the bottom of the stairs. The light screen that had protected the man before, once again appeared, nullifying Rhys' shot. Michael smirked.

Alina's escape had become a personal insult; her annihilation and Rhys' death were no more than vendettas now. Becoming frantic, Rhys pushed his feet under him and, with Cantia, lunged toward Alina and Hodge.

Yet another series of gun shots rang out and a stinging pain tore at Rhys' upper thigh. He lurched forward but caught himself before hitting the ground. Using Pathos' locking system, Rhys whirled on his good knee and prepared to return fire once more—but Michael was no longer standing. He was slumped on the floor, lying in a pool of his own blood, a bullet wound in his back. Behind him stood Vinz.

Where the Overseer had come from, how he had managed to pass the soldiers outside, how he had been able to get to Michael—Rhys didn't know.

Pistol leveled at the high priest, Vinz approached Michael's body. The Overseer was covered in a heavy sweat, and his chest heaved as he glowered down at the high priest.

Wheezing audibly, Michael rested his cheek on the cracked marble and peered up at Vinz. The man's mouth moved as he spoke, but Rhys could hear nothing.

The expression of triumph on the Overseer's face melted to utter dread. The high priest took a long breath and then collapsed on the trembling floor.

Above the sound of the shifting rubble and clattering plaster, a muted *click* reverberated throughout the room.

The explosion was instantaneous.

Rhys turned his back to the explosion and fell to his knees in an attempt to protect himself. The air in his lungs seized, and his heart slammed into his ribs as the sound blast plowed through him. Dust, debris, plaster, and smoke blanketed him like a quilt of ruin.

A ringing silence ensued.

Rhys coughed, rubbed his deaf right ear, and then breathlessly looked over his shoulder. Heavy clouds of brackish smoke and dust drifted across the staircase and along the floor.

"V-Vinz!" Rhys sputtered as the putrid smell of burning flesh and smoke entered his nose.

"Rhys," called Leo. "Rhys! Get Alina!"

Rhys searched the thick smoke for a moment longer and then motioned for his board which was struggling to maintain altitude in the ever-shifting magnetic fields. When it was close enough, he hobbled to it and pulled it down into a patch of red. "Hodge!" he hoarsely yelled as he swung himself onto the board and locked his feet into the clasps.

Pistol at the ready, Leo wandered into the smoke. "Vinz! Vinz? Answer me!"

Rhys knelt on his uninjured knee and motioned to Hodge. Panic-stricken, Hodge passed Alina's limp body to Rhys. Straining under her weight, Rhys reared back and clutched her in his arms. He instantly became slick with blood.

Once he was sure Alina wasn't going to slip from his grip, he surveyed the area that extended to the front doors. Orange and yellow—he could work with that. He tilted the board toward the door and crouched to urge it forward. At a pace that made his heart plead, the board crept through the orange screen of noise.

"Cantia, where are you?" called Hodge, pulling his shirt over his nose so as not to breathe in the horrible air.

Rhys glanced worriedly over his shoulder as his friend disappeared into the smoke. He couldn't bear thinking that was the last time he would see Hodge.

Outside, he had more magnetic fields to choose from. Glancing at the soldiers below, who were gazing at him in confusion and fear, Rhys climbed sluggishly to gain altitude. Once he hit a dense magnetic field, the board rocketed into the darkness.

The flight to *Themis* was a difficult one. He had thought to take Alina back to the Damien mansion, but the Damiens had helped enough. He could endanger them no more. Undoubtedly, warrants for all of their arrests would be issued within the hour.

Rhys concentrated on the task at hand—flying unhindered by the shifting magnetic waves. Like the earth below, the magnetic fields around him quivered and pulsed as though they were alive. As if he were a god of destruction, he soared through the sky and watched as homes disintegrated into enormous piles of dust and rubble, and hellish plumes of brackish smoke rose into the sky. He could hear people screaming, but the wind threw their distressed cries into the nighttime sky.

Using Pathos, he located *Themis*. The ship was already five kilometers out of port, not a single boat behind her. Panting, Rhys raced toward the ship, his savior. He needed to trust that Leo, Hodge, and Vinz would find a way to meet up with them.

Though he drew ever-closer to *Themis*, his actual arrival seemed to take forever. Andy had the ship at full-throttle. Rhys finally crossed over her bow, pulled back, and set his board on the upper deck. Without stopping, he stepped from the clasps, stumbled from the board, and laid Alina on the deck. "Kallen!" he cried as loudly as he could. "Andy! Kashim!"

Rhys relinquished his hold on the board and traded his sight for night vision. He knelt beside his sister and, using the knowledge he had obtained from her, began checking her vitals. Trembling, he dug his fingers into her wrist. He felt nothing. He moved to her throat. Nothing. "No, no, no… "

"Rhys?" called Kallen from the upper platform.

"Kallen!" His throat closed around her name. "Medical supplies!"

Rhys grabbed the neckline of Alina's robe, which was heavy with blood, and ripped it the length of her torso to reveal the wound. For a moment, he could only gape in horror and panic. There below her left breast was a gaping, sucking hole.

"No!" Rhys jerked his shirt off and fell on her. With his blouse pressed firmly against the wound to stem the bleeding, he began doing compressions. His knowledge told him it was over—Alina was gone— but his heart screamed at him to try.

"Come on, come on," he murmured as he pumped her chest. He felt her ribs crunch under his palms. "Come on, Alina!" He leaned over her, tilted her chin up, covered her nose, and breathed air into her. Frantically, he continued compressions. "Come on! Alina!"

"Rhys!" Kallen rushed to him with the medical pack. Kashim followed behind with three lamps. "I've got—"

Kallen fell still beside him, her eyes set on Alina's body.

Rhys could hear his own rasping breaths as he pressed harder and harder on his sister's bloody chest. With each compression, his hope dwindled. "Come on," he cried. "Pathos, shock her."

"Initiating electric deflection system. Charged," said Pathos. Rhys placed one hand above Alina's right breast and the other near her gaping wound. Alina's torso convulsed upward and then hit the deck with a dull thud. Rhys began compressions again, his sweat and tears mingling on his face and dropping on his sister's lifeless body like rain.

"Alina," he breathed between compressions. "Pathos, again."

"Charged."

Again, Alina shuddered and then fell still. "Come on!" Rhys screamed. "Alina!"

Kashim appeared beside him. "Rhys."

"I can do this!" snapped Rhys, stifling a sob. "I can do this!" He blew air into his sister's mouth and pumped her chest furiously.

Kashim's hand came into his field of vision and stilled his frantic motions. Rhys tried to push him away, but the large man caught his arm and stopped him. Wheezing, Rhys stared at Alina.

She was strong; she had always been strong. Why hadn't she fought more? Why hadn't she tried to stop the bleeding herself? Surely her death hadn't been instant! Had it?

"No!" Rhys jerked his blood-covered arm from Kashim and continued compressions.

"Rhys," Kashim stopped him again. "It's over."

Powerful sobs wracked Rhys' body. He couldn't control his crying, his weeping. His heart hurt; his body hurt. Weakly, he sat back on his heels and lamented the fact that, when it came down to it, he couldn't even save his own sister.

37
REALIZATION

BEFORE COMING TO EARTH, ALINA had just been his half-sibling, the person with whom he shared DNA. Unlike the others on Caelestis who were not told of their siblings, Rhys and Alina had been privileged. They had been given treasured knowledge as a part of their father's ongoing experiments.

Despite knowing their relationship, however, Rhys had never felt much for his sister except contempt and jealousy. From a very early age, he had been continuously compared to her and ridiculed quietly by others for having scored lower on his comprehensive exams. He didn't *hate* his sister; he couldn't. She paid him far too much attention. Even still, when their father called to Rhys and requested that he escape with her on a life pod, Rhys had reservations. Why should he help the one person who had unintentionally made his life a hell? Why should he do anything but leave her behind?

But that day on Caelestis, Doctor Severiano Falkrow had called to Rhys, his Other Child, and asked that he protect Alina. Why? Why hadn't his father asked a fellow colleague to escort Alina aboard a life pod? What was Rhys capable of that the others on Caelestis weren't?

For months, he had wondered these things.

Now, staring into the darkness off the stern of *Themis*, Rhys knew. He knew what his father had only theorized. He knew what he could offer Alina that others on Caelestis never could—kinship.

Once away from Caelestis, their blood bonds had solidified. No longer were they separated by class or occupation. On Earth, everything had turned. It had been them against the world. Despite his own frailty upon their arrival, he had taken it upon himself to defend and protect her.

Driven purely by instinct, he had endeavored to watch over his sister and keep her from harm. He had fought for her, sustained injuries for her, supported her, guided her, killed for her. He had been her brother and greatest confidant. No one else could have done what he had; no one else could have kept her alive for so long.

"Rhys?" Kallen touched his shoulder. "Let's get you cleaned up." After a moment of silence, he let Kallen pull him to his feet and support him across the deck.

Though Kashim and Kallen had transported Alina's body to the forward hatch, her blood remained. Rhys glanced at it as they passed; Kallen ushered him onward. Once inside, Rhys hobbled to the galley. He looked about it despondently and then shifted his gaze to Kallen. Her eyes were red from crying, but he saw no tears in them now. Wearily, she motioned for him to sit.

"Are you hurt?" she asked, kneeling beside him. "Why is this area wet?" She pointed to his left thigh. Unlike Alina's blood, which had dried on him and crusted, his pants leg was soaked.

"I was shot," Rhys murmured.

Kallen pulled his torn pants away and studied the wound. "It just grazed you. You're lucky. Whoever shot you had poor aim."

Rhys swallowed the lump in his throat. The high priest had had good enough aim to kill Alina.

"It doesn't look too deep. You may need stitches though."

Rhys peered over Kallen's hands. A small wedge of his thigh was missing. "I can stitch that."

Kallen looked at him in mild surprise. "You can?"

"Alina taught me."

Kallen stood. "I'm going to fill the bath." She disappeared from the galley.

Rhys stared at the floor and then cautiously examined his wound. It wasn't too bad. Of course, it wasn't pretty, but it was minor compared to his shoulder injury. Kallen returned sometime later and escorted him to the washroom where she scrubbed his hands and arms first in the sink basin before helping him undress. She balanced him as he got into the bathtub and then returned to the galley to boil water in preparation for his surgery.

For a long while, he sat in the bathtub and gazed at his knees miserably. His heart hurt, but he could cry no more. He was mentally, physically, and emotionally exhausted.

When Kallen returned, she scolded him half-heartedly for not having begun washing, knelt by the tub, and drew his hand from the water. She placed soap in it. "Wash," she softly instructed. Rhys obeyed—slowly—until his silver hair was void of all dirt and his skin was no longer dyed red.

Kallen assisted him in standing and, careful not to bump his injured leg, helped him from the tub. With a towel around his waist, Rhys limped from the washroom back to the galley where Kallen had set out several towels and medical tools on the table.

Rhys dragged himself onto the table and watched as she examined his thigh wound once more. "Let it air for a few minutes before we start," she said.

Studying the medical tools left in his care, he asked, "Any... word from Hodge and the others?"

"No, nothing." Kallen took the pot of boiling water from the stove and rested it on the towel-covered table. "Did you run into Vinz?"

"He met us at the temple. Why was he there? I told him to stay with the ship."

"We said the same thing to him, but he told us that he couldn't sit by while his crew was in danger." Kallen thought for a moment. "I think he had been planning to meet you there all along. I know he was wanting to meet the high priest who killed his parents. He left the ship a while before you gave the signal to open fire." Kallen leaned on her knees. "Did that work—us firing?"

"Your aim was perfect, but it didn't have the effect we wanted."

"What do you mean?"

"All the nobles gathered in the bottom of the temple and wouldn't leave because they felt it was their duty to stay by the high priest and defend the temple. Stupid sheep... "

Kallen gazed at her hands and then drew a long breath. "Will you tell me what happened?"

"Later."

"Of course," whispered Kallen. She dunked a cloth in the boiling water, and wrung it out. Rhys took it, gingerly wiped the gaping wound on his leg, and then applied a topical anesthetic. While he waited for the medication to activate on his skin, he prepped the surgical tools—a needle holder and a small pair of forceps as well as the needle and synthetic sutures. Once the anesthetic kicked in, he began the process of sewing his leg. "When did Alina teach you this?" asked Kallen, watching him work.

"Data dump," murmured Rhys. "Last night... Alina gave all of her data to me. *All of it.*"

"I see." Kallen smiled warmly. "I've watched her stitch up people. You're not nearly as good at this as she was."

Rhys fell silent. Kallen had used the past tense: she *was*.

"I'm sorry," whispered Kallen. "I didn't... I didn't mean... "

Rhys finished his sutures—eight in total—and dressed. As Kallen cleaned the galley, Rhys shuffled stiffly to the forward hatch. He found Alina rested on the ramp. Kashim had already wrapped the majority of her body in a drop cloth. Only her head was visible. Groaning, Rhys lowered himself onto the floor beside her.

For an unknown amount of time, he gazed at his sister, reviewing all that had happened.

What could he have done differently? Could he have saved her? If he had gotten to her sooner, perhaps he could have stopped them from stripping her of her AI. But what could he have done? He had already pushed himself to his limit. He had been shot too.

Again and again, he reviewed Alina's death in his mind. He watched repeatedly as she slumped against Hodge, head limp and limbs dangling. If only he hadn't slipped and fallen! That shot was meant for him. That's what Michael had meant by "wrong person."

Rhys was the one who was supposed to have been shot. He was the one who was supposed to have died, not Alina. As tears swelled in his eyes, he buried his face in his arms.

Rhys.

Rhys' heart leapt into his throat and he looked at Alina—but she was still cold and lifeless. Rhys exhaled angrily. *Stop it, Pathos.*

Do you not want to hear her voice? Alina's voice reverberated in his mind.

No, replied Rhys.

As your AI, it is my duty to watch over you, analyze all that you do not consciously process, and help you achieve a better state of being, continued Pathos using Alina's voice. *It is for this reason that I will continue to use Alina Falkrow's voice to share with you the following information.*

Rhys tilted his head in surprise and confusion. This was the first time Pathos had ever disobeyed a direct order; it was the first time that, without prompting either by Rhys or by an external source, it had spoken out.

Rhys, said Pathos. Rhys closed his eyes so he could imagine Alina sitting beside him. *It has come to my attention that your life is in danger.*

When has it not been? he murmured.

You misunderstand. Your life is in danger not from some external source or enemy. With each day, the infection of your synthetic system spreads. You feel no pain right now because you were dosed heavily just a few hours ago. Your connection with the magnetic board for such a long time the other night combined with the time you spent on it this evening has brought your total functioning synthetic synapses down to 45.3 percent. The Monaxin has slowed the progress of the infection; however, once its effects wear off in six hours, you'll be in greater pain than you've ever felt.

Because Monaxin is a habit-forming drug? asked Rhys.

Yes. Kallen gave you a large dose earlier. Though it will keep you from feeling any pain for several hours, once it wears off, the pain will be doubled.

Rhys rested his cheek on his arms. *I'll just make a new medication. Alina bought several promising drugs she thought could act as substitutes. I'll use those.*

Whatever concoction you create will only dull the pain, Pathos explained. *It will not stop the infection.*

So I'm terminal! snapped Rhys. *It doesn't matter anymore.*

Rhys, listen to me, barked Pathos in Alina's voice. Rhys peeked over his knees at his sister's corpse. *The infection stems from your connection to your AI system. If the infection is dealt with, you could live. The infection is only affecting your synthetic processing system—your AI.*

What are you implying? whispered Rhys.

It is possible to live without your AI unit.

Rhys began to object but stopped as his eyes fell on the small bald spot on the left side of Alina's head. Logos had been taken from her and she hadn't seemed any different. The other three from Caelestis had also been stripped of their AIs, yet they seemed able to function.

Trial runs on test subjects were held on Caelestis, said Pathos. *All survived.*

I never saw anyone without a unit, replied Rhys.

They were reattached to their units once the tests were over.

Why didn't you tell us this sooner? growled Rhys. *Because it wasn't relevant?*

No. It was relevant, however, Logos and I agreed that neither of you needed to know until we had more conclusive data. If you knew you could exist without the help of an AI, you would not fight as desperately to protect your units which you needed to survive. Logos told Alina moments before her external AI unit was stripped from her. It seemed to calm her.

Rhys thought for a long moment and then sighed. *Please stop using Alina's voice.*

Very well, replied Pathos in its normal gender-neutral tone.

So... are there side effects to being disconnected from our AI units?

Unknown. The only observable side effects Alina exhibited were weakness and fatigue.

If I disconnect from you, what will I lose? What information? asked Rhys. *Anything?*

The trial runs conducted on Caelestis indicated that some data was lost such as certain skills; memories, however, remained.

I won't be able to pilot the board anymore.

That is correct. Unless you create a device to read the density of the magnetic fields and report it in written expression, you will lose the ability to pilot the magnetic board.

Does... it hurt?

Trial run reports indicate there is no pain, replied Pathos.

What will happen to you once we're separated?

All AI units use biological energy. If an AI is disconnected from its life source, it will cease to function.

Rhys perked up. *Then I could just take you out and reinstall the external unit when I need to pilot the board!*

Negative, Pathos asserted. *After removing the external unit, replacement of it will not be possible. You do not have access to the equipment that would allow for proper disconnect and reconnect. On Caelestis, such equipment was available. Here, no such thing exists because, of course, it's not necessary.*

Can I build it? Create it? Rhys hopefully mused.

No. The materials needed are synthetic and require a mixture of biological substances that have been created through the advancement of technology achieved only by your people in space. Neither the tools nor materials are available here.

What about on the life pod that we came in? Would there be anything there?

The crash site is nearly six weeks' journey. You do not have that long.

Do I just need the equipment for proper reconnect?

No, both disconnect and reconnect must be done via a machine.

Rhys flung himself onto the floor and glared at ceiling. *Then what am I supposed to do? I can't disconnect from you yet. There's a good chance Themis will soon become a target. I need to be able to use the board! I need to be able to fight!*

I have shared with you all that I can. If you decide to disconnect, notify me. There are preparations that can be done to help ease the transition and retain certain pieces of information.

For the next four hours, he lay in the forward hatch and contemplated separation from Pathos. If Alina survived, he could too, right? He pondered on the skills he would try to maintain, the weakness and fatigue that would accompany the disconnect, the loss of his individuality.

He thought of wild plans to take his board and fly ahead at top speeds to return to the life pod and steal whatever AI equipment the escape pod had to offer. Using Pathos' information, he tried to create the blueprints for a machine that would allow him to properly disconnect from his AI. He considered killing himself.

In a trance, he sat in solitude and silence, contemplating his fate. He circled the concepts of life and death numerous times and philosophized about the role he personally played in the universe. He mourned Alina's death and the fact that she would never again be a part of his life.

Two hours before dawn, Kashim's voice echoed through pipe communication system, startling Rhys from his meditation.

"Radar has detected three Brechin airships five liretems out. Prepare for combat."

Rhys glanced at Alina's body and then rolled onto his hands and knees. Wearily, he pushed himself up and then hobbled to the inner door. His left leg was stiff. *Pathos, focus on the leg,* he demanded.

Focusing all healing efforts onto your leg will withdraw said endeavors from your still-recuperating shoulder, Pathos reported.

Do it. Rhys limped from the forward hatch. *I need to be able to move.*

"Hey." Kallen stood in the doorway of her cabin, pulling a shirt on. "How are you feeling?"

"Tired," he replied. Kallen swung his good arm over her shoulders and bolstered him up the stairs to the bridge.

"Four liretems out," announced Kashim as they entered. "They're moving fast."

"And you're sure they're coming after us?" asked Andy.

Kashim studied radar. "Undoubtedly."

"Will they deploy sunboards?"

"No, they don't need them." Kashim looked at Rhys. He must have appeared unreachable because the man's gaze shifted to Kallen. "The engines—where are we on the installation of the new one? Is it done?"

"I've only barely opened the crate. The installation itself will take at least two days of solid work," replied Kallen.

"Also, the sun hasn't risen yet," said Andy. "We're been running on energy reserves since we left port. There's no way we can outrun airships."

"Then we fight," Kashim concluded.

"There's four of us, and two of you are injured." Kallen glanced at Rhys. "There's not much we can do."

"They're after me and Alina," Rhys mused. "Just let them take us."

To his surprise, it was not Kallen who adamantly said, "No," but Kashim. "We can't let them get their hands on you. It will defeat everything that we've worked toward."

"But if it means saving you three, then it's our best option," argued Rhys.

"And what do you think they'll do to the ship once they have you?" Kashim countered. "They'll destroy it and kill us. Your surrender is out of the question. We fight."

Rhys sighed. "Fine, then our weapons—where do we stand on ammo?"

"We have ammo, but they're faster than our targeting system."

"Rhys can track them," offered Kallen.

Kashim leaned on the helm. "Doesn't matter. The cannons are manipulated solely through the bridge."

"Then…" Rhys looked between them. "I'll launch."

"Disable their ships so we can open fire," Kashim provided.

Rhys scrutinized radar. "Fine, I'll disable the airships. Hopefully, the magnetic… fields… What is that?" He pointed to a small blip on the far corner of the radar map. "Do you see it?"

"A merchant ship. Don't worry about it," grunted Kashim. "Your job is to disable the airships. Make it so they can't avoid cannon fire."

Rhys turned and, after ignoring Kallen's offer to help him, limped from the bridge. *Pathos, how much longer before I have to take the next dose of Monaxin?*

Normally it would be another two hours; however, once you connect to the board, that time will be reduced.

If I took a quarter of a vial, would that prevent my body from seizing?

Yes, replied Pathos.

"Kallen," he called over his shoulder. Kallen hurried from the bridge and, without a word, started to help him down the inner staircase. "Get the medication. I need a quarter of a vial."

"That's it?" she asked.

"That's all I can afford."

Kallen left him and jogged down the hallway to her cabin. She met Rhys in the doorway with the injector and administered the medication. Afterward, she pushed him into the galley. "Wrap your leg. Put pressure on it." She opened the medical bag and threw heavy bandages into his waiting hands. As she helped him, she asked, "How's your shoulder?"

"It's fine. The wrapping from earlier is holding." Rhys grimaced as Kallen tied off the bandage. She turned on her knee and rushed from the room. She returned with the resonance cutters, his firearm, and a shirt.

"Two liretems," broadcasted Kashim from the open bridge door.

Kallen threw the shirt over Rhys' head, dragged his arms through, and began strapping the resonance cutters to his back. "I'm sorry," he whispered.

Kallen clenched her jaws. "Don't be. It's them or us. We have to fight." She opened his hand and slid the firearm onto his forearm. Rhys hobbled up the stairs to the upper deck.

"You've got to win this," said Kallen as Rhys clambered onto the board.

"Be ready to fire," he said. With his feet fixed in the clasps, he leaned to the right and began banking away from the ship. Kallen disappeared inside. Rhys turned his attention to the magnetic fields around him. He was pleased to find a nearly flawless array of red.

He gained altitude like an albatross taking to the sea winds and, using Pathos, traced a route to the airships. With some trouble, he crouched, and the board shot forward.

Airships are 1.6 kilometers out, reported Pathos. *Ready to lock-on.*

Rhys slowed the board to a halt, raised his firearm, and steadied it. *Ready for lock-on.*

Locking on.

The moment Pathos' sensors indicated the target had been acquired, Rhys fired rapidly. There was no longer time to consider human lives. He needed to defend *Themis*; he needed to protect Kallen and the others.

In the distant purple sky, a burst of flames blossomed, illuminating one of the airships and the men aboard it. As it started to nosedive, Rhys redirected his fire to the next target. Unsurprisingly, a volley of bullets whizzed around him.

Heart painfully thrumming, Rhys swept farther into the early morning sky, repositioned himself, and opened fire on the next airship, allocating the first few shots to the guns along its bow. Return fire exploded around him and ricocheted off the bottom of his board. He banked hard and sped off into the darkness to escape the barrage. Once he was sure he was out of sight, he straightened himself and took a moment to catch his breath. His leg throbbed.

The remaining airship is breaking away. Its trajectory indicates it is targeting Themis, reported Pathos.

Rhys pushed on the front of the board hard and dove steeply. Thanks to the flames from the first airship and the emergency lighting on the second, his last target was a distinct black silhouette. Beyond the hiss of air in his ears, he heard the sound of gunfire, a cacophonous din. The last airship had opened fire on *Themis.*

With a snarl, Rhys exchanged the shots for a collection of precisely-aimed plasma blasts. He saw a soldier slump—dead—against a comrade before enemy fire once again focused on Rhys. His vision tunneled as he wildly maneuvered through the sky, keeping his board between him the gunfire.

An explosion far below illuminated the early morning sky; the sonic boom that followed sent Rhys scrambling to hang onto his board. He could feel the heat on his face. Squinting against the dimming light, he peered over the side of his board to find the first airship gone. It had been obliterated. He smiled grimly. *Themis* had joined the fight.

Clutching his leg, he banked to gain a better vantage point. Gunfire followed. No matter the maneuvers he pulled or the sudden directional changes he performed, the gunfire never ended. Hoping altitude and the sea winds would alter the course of the bullets, he retreated higher.

How are they following me? he panted, circling far above the flames.

It appears they have an automated tracking system. Currently, you are out of its range, Pathos explained.

So, only that final airship has it?

Below, a deep belch shook the air as *Themis* fired three more shots. The fan of the second airship burst in a brilliant explosion of crimson and orange.

If they have an automated tracking system... Rhys strained to think.

In addition to the three airships currently chasing Themis, it would seem a fourth ship is in pursuit, said Pathos. *The merchant ship Kashim identified earlier has changed its course and is en route to our coordinates.*

It's a merchant ship though, right? It could be coming to help, speculated Rhys.

Possibly.

Can you lock-on to the computer controlling the automated targeting system on the third airship?

If you want a shot that will hit with certainty, you must close the distance between us, Pathos instructed.

Fine, growled Rhys. Once more, he shifted his weight to the front of the board and descended rapidly.

Allowing Pathos full control, Rhys raised his arm at the precise angle and fired. Even from a distance, he could discern the airship's computer release a series of blue sparks and then a cloud of smoke. In response, organized gunfire exploded around him. The soldiers aboard now knew exactly where Rhys was. Board vibrating from the flurry of bullets, Rhys ascended steeply.

Another series of deep, guttural booms burst from *Themis,* and the sea around the airships erupted in enormous fountains of bubbling water. The remaining airship returned fire.

Rhys crouched and sped in the opposite direction. If the final airship was expecting an attack from above, he would instead attack from behind. For several seconds, he rocketed through the black sky away from the battle. When he was certain he was no longer visible, he dropped down to skim along the water's surface.

The merchant ship is approaching Themis, reported Pathos.

One at a time, Rhys replied breathlessly. He squinted ahead; he could just make out the third airship. Visually targeting the ship, he raised his arm and fired multiple times to kill the fans. Like a bird whose wing had suddenly been crippled, the entire vessel tilted precariously in the air. As he sped toward the now maimed unit, Rhys pulled his feet from the clasps on his board and withdrew the resonance cutters. This needed to end before the merchant ship became involved as well.

Keeping his board before him to safeguard against the raging barrage, Rhys approached from the rear. Having only a breath's moment to act, he rocketed over the back of the final airship. His movements masked by the bulk of the board, he slid to the back, balanced himself, and then hurled the board forward. The soldiers followed, firing a near-constant stream of bullets at Rhys' board—unaware that Rhys was now on the stern of the airship.

There was no time for him to grimace or nurse his injured leg. Rhys lunged at the nearest soldiers. Resonance cutters whirring, he tore at the bodies around him. Like a god of war, he blocked attacks and slashed expertly at his attackers, separating limbs from bodies and killing indiscriminately.

One after another, Rhys hacked through the soldiers and their armor. By the time he made it to the command deck, 15 bodies lay around him. The floor was slick with blood.

Wheezing, he stalked up the short, leaning staircase to the command deck where three officers remained. Dressed in thick armor and dripping with weapons, all bravely stood to fight him.

Suddenly, there was a loud bang.

Incoming cannon fire from the merchant ship! Jump, commanded Pathos. In a single, powerful motion, Rhys sheathed the resonance cutters, climbed onto the side of the ship's railing, and leapt. Behind him, there came a deep thud as cannon fire hit the airship.

Remembering what Hodge had told him about falling from great heights, Rhys crossed his legs and arms just before hitting the water. Pathos' instructions were immediate. *Swim!* The water around him quivered violently. *Hurry!*

Rhys broke the surface, gasped, and began frantically swimming, arms flailing and legs kicking. He felt his shoulder wound tear. Panting, he pulled at the water with all his strength.

The board, Pathos alerted. Rhys rolled onto his side to see the board return to him. Gasping, he jerked the black technology into the water and then heaved his torso onto it. Behind him, heat from an explosion burned the back of his neck and arms. All around him pieces from the airship rained down in fiery chunks. Clutching the sides of his board, Rhys jammed his feet into the clasps, stood, and began maneuvering around the debris.

Altitude! shouted Pathos. The board rocketed upward into the purple sky. Twice, Rhys banked hard, first to the right and then to the left to avoid large, burning pieces of metal. By the time he reached a safe altitude, he could hardly breathe.

Panting audibly, he peered down at the final incinerated airship which had crashed into the sea. Smoke blanketed the water; distantly, he could hear men calling to one another.

Rhys shifted his gaze to the approaching merchant ship which was less than a kilometer out. Realizing the shape seemed familiar, he asked Pathos. *Is that what I think it is?*

That is Grisle, his AI confirmed.

Rhys soared toward the slave traders' ship. Had Irvine and his crew been exonerated and released?

"Rhys!" called Kallen from the gaping hole in *Themis'* bridge that had yet to be fixed. She waved to him. "Rhys! It's Hodge and the others! It's Hodge!"

"On *Grisle?*" Rhys shouted, hovering beside the bridge. Kallen nodded. *Pathos, any others on radar?*

No, none.

By the time he reached the slave traders' ship, he was cold, and both his shoulder and leg ached fiercely. In the light of dawn, he could make out someone waving to him. It was Leo.

Rhys stepped off the board onto the upper deck and stumbled as his injured leg gave way. Leo stopped before him, seemingly taken aback by his condition.

"I know," muttered Rhys. "I'm pretty beat up. Who's with you?"

Leo regarded Rhys. "It's just us. Cantia, Hodge, and Terron."

Rhys held his shoulder as a particularly fierce pain shot through it. "And Vinz?"

Leo peered out at the water. "Vinz died in the explosion. I don't know why the high priest... It doesn't make sense. There was nothing left of his body," he murmured. "Even if there was... there's no way we could have carried him out of there. Not with the earthquake and everything." Leo took a long, steadying breath. "I'm sorry."

"I-I just... didn't think... " Rhys glared at the deck. He had mourned Alina's death with tears and heartache. Now though, he felt neither. He felt rage. He felt hatred and anger, bitter fury. Vinz had not been a particularly amazing person nor had he been Rhys' friend, but he had been his Overseer. Despite the fact that both Vinz and Kashim had betrayed him, he had felt that they ultimately belonged on the same side, fighting the powerful Pantarak Empire.

"How's Alina?"

Rhys climbed back onto his board. "She's dead." Without another word, he returned to *Themis*.

When he landed on the upper deck, he disconnected from the board and began pacing. Despite his limp, he moved back and forth across the deck.

First Lyruc and Kyo. Now Alina and Vinz.

How many more people was it going to take? He wanted revenge. He wanted to see Brechin reduced to rubble.

You're losing blood, chided Pathos.

Rhys stopped and looked out at the sea set in the blush of dawn. He needed to bide his time and wait. If he was going to take down Brechin, he needed power, and power only came with time. He needed to be patient; he needed to wait.

He looked at *Grisle* which which now sailed alongside *Themis*. He had two ships with skeleton crews. He needed men. He needed power. If he was going to take on Brechin, he needed *more*.

"Is that it, Alina?" he asked the sunrise. "I have the power to make a difference... but change doesn't come quickly, does it?"

EPILOGUE

AFTER BEING TENDED TO BY Kallen, Rhys retired to his cabin and slept for the majority of the day, skipping midday meal and ignoring Kallen's attempts to coax him awake.

It was late afternoon when he finally rolled from bed, his arm in a sling, and dressed. He slipped on his pants—his back and neck were beginning to hurt again—and wiggled into a fresh shirt. Barefooted, he went to the washroom and washed up. Standing at the sink basin, he gazed at himself in the small mirror which hung above it. His face was worn, his dark silver hair untidy.

His eyes, however, were focused, set.

The path he needed to take lay before him.

He had heard Kallen, Hodge, and Kyo speak often of such revelations. They had used the word "destiny." Of course, he and Alina had always ignored such trivial talk because destiny was not logical; it implied that one did not have control over the future, that a higher power reigned supreme over time.

Now though, Rhys finally understood. "Destiny" was not logical. It was something felt deep within. It did not imply that a higher being controlled his life. He was in control, always. It simply meant that the paths he had taken had led him to the place and time in which he now stood. It meant that because of who he was, because of his experiences, because of his choices, he had been placed on a path that could lead to change.

Pathos, he murmured.

As usual, his AI already knew. *I'm already making preparations.*

Rhys ruffled his hair into place and then went in search of the others. He found Kallen, Kashim, and Andy on the bridge; Kallen was asleep. Rhys looked about for a moment before setting his gaze on Kashim. "Anything on radar?"

"Nothing," replied Kashim.

"I'd like to send off Alina," Rhys said. "Gather the others." Andy went to the radio and began transmitting the message. Once *Themis* and *Grisle* were halted, it took a little over half an hour for everyone to assemble in the forward hatch where Alina's body rested wrapped in a drop cloth on the ramp.

Positioned away from the group, Rhys observed the others' reactions. Kallen remained silent though her eyes were moist. Kashim as usual was stoic, unreadable. Leo gazed at Alina through teary eyes, and Cantia hid her face in Terron's shirt. The only person who joined Alina on the ramp was Hodge. Eyebrows furrowed in heartache and pain, he knelt beside her and rested a hand on her forehead. After several long moments, he backed away.

Kashim picked up a piece of metal debris they had collected from the engine explosion and met Rhys on the ramp next to Hodge. "Help me," the large man murmured to Hodge as he began to tie cord about Alina's ankles.

Rhys looked at the others. All eyes fell on him.

"In my life, there have been very few things that I have had a talent for. I was… regarded as the Other Child on Caelestis and told repeatedly I was a failure. Of course, compared to Alina," he smiled grimly, "I was. As a part of a revolutionizing experiment, Alina and I were told we were siblings. Most people on Caelestis do not know their brothers and sisters. They need only to know their work. What's more, Alina was given a Logos AI—a computer whose core functions were based on logic. I was given a lesser unit, Pathos, which relies primarily on emotion.

"For as long as I can remember, I wondered why I had been disgraced with such a unit. And then we came here. We began experiencing life, what life really is. I grew aware that Alina and I were processing the world around us differently because of our computers. While I became enamored with concepts, ideas, and skills that gave me some sort of emotional fulfillment, Alina pursued those that met her need to think critically. And we diverged. It took time, but I came to accept Pathos. I realized I was experiencing things Alina could never comprehend; and it was the same with her. We were not the same, but we were equal. For the first time in our lives, we were equal." Rhys looked down at his sister. "We were equal."

He thought and then said, "The high priest of Brechin took from us not one but two people. Vinz was... a scholar, an overseer, and a friend. He was forward-thinking and progressive, just like his ideologies. To Vinz, peace was not impossible; it was necessary. The world was against him from the beginning... yet he endeavored. He endeavored because he knew that despite being a single person, he had power. He could start change; he could instigate a revolution." Rhys looked around the forward hatch. "Vinz gave us a direction. Now we're going to take up that mission. We're going to change the world.

"Because peace and freedom do not come without sacrifice, we're going to amass power; we're going to gather strength. We're going to topple the Pantarak Empire and we're going to do it using their own people. Logic doesn't move people. People are moved by endeavors of the heart. We have two ships. We're going to move forward as one." He met each person's gaze. "And—if you'll have me—I will lead you."

There was a moment of silence before Leo chuckled. "We're already following you." He motioned to himself, Cantia, and Terron.

"Agreed," said Hodge. He flashed Rhys a tired smile. "We're already here."

"Agreed," said Kashim.

Andy nodded. "Agreed."

Rhys bowed to his new crew. "You have my gratitude."

Rhys, all preparations are complete, said Pathos.

Thank you, Pathos. Rhys glanced at Alina and then looked at the others. "I am grateful for all that you have done for us... but I think it's time I started standing on my own two feet." Rhys touched the side of his head where Pathos' external unit was attached.

"Rhys," gasped Kallen, lunging at him.

Rhys stopped her with a single look. "It needs to be done."

"But... the board," murmured Hodge.

"The Overseer doesn't need to pilot a board, does he?" His smile faded, and he closed his eyes. "Pathos, I'm ready."

Rhys, one moment. "To the crew members of *Themis,*" continued Pathos aloud. "My purpose was to watch over Rhys, to ensure his safety, and to look after his wellbeing. I am an artificial intelligence enlightenment interface system. By helping Rhys achieve his goals, I fulfill the purpose of my existence. I leave him in your care. Watch over Rhys. Help him learn, guide him along this new path which he will be taking." There was a long pause before Pathos said, "And Rhys?"

Rhys startled. "Yes?"

"I expect great things from your life."

"Pathos... " Rhys placed his hand on his AI's external unit.

All preparations are complete, murmured Pathos. *Rhys Falkrow, in a final declaration of your intention, do you wish to disconnect from your government-issued artificial intelligence enlightenment interface system?*

I do, replied Rhys.

You may now remove the external unit, said Pathos. *Goodbye, Rhys.*

Goodbye, Pathos. Rhys tapped the edge of the external unit. There was a soft hiss in his ear as the nerves connecting the unit detached. Slowly, he pulled the unit from its injectors alongside his head.

His strength escaped through the floor, and his knees buckled. His hands shook and his breathing hastened. No one said anything. Panting, Rhys knelt on the floor and gazed at Pathos' unit. Having lived on Earth for several months now, he appreciated the technology in the palm of his hand. The sheer power contained in the unit was phenomenal—and not necessary here.

Rhys took several more calming breaths and then moved to Alina. "Take care of this for me," he whispered, tucking Pathos deep into the folds of the drop cloth. With Kallen's help, he struggled to his feet and looked at Hodge and Kashim.

"Leo, lower the hatch door," Kashim instructed.

As the hatch door opened, seawater rushed up the ramp and covered Alina. Knee-deep in water, Rhys gazed at his younger sister resting on the bottom of the ramp. In unison, Hodge and Kashim shuffled to the edge of the ramp. Together, they dropped the weight. As it had been with Kyo and Lyruc, in the blink of an eye, Alina vanished into the deep, dark blue of the sea forever.

Rhys leaned against the ramp wall. Without Alina and Pathos, he was no longer tied to Caelestis or his past. He was free. His future was what he made of it. His destiny was his.

"What's the plan, Overseer?" asked Leo.

Rhys' gaze swept over his new crew. "Firekli to resupply and then Paducah. It's time we helped the people fight back."

The Adventure Continues in...

RHYS OF QUADRANT SIX

The Falkrow Narratives
Book II

It's been four months since Rhys Falkrow's life was turned upside down by the events in the capital city of Brechin. At 19, he is now Overseer of the seafaring vessel *Themis* and leader of an ever-growing crew of misfit fighters and diplomats, engineers, and sailors bent on bringing chaos to the Pantarak Empire. Despite his achievements and uncanny abilities, however, Rhys still finds himself without purpose.

Upon coming across a relic, an artificial intelligence unit manufactured over 200 years ago, surprising connections materialize, and his life takes yet another curious turn. As the events of the past become more relevant by the day, Rhys and his crew make a startling discovery that alters their understanding of the world as they know it.

Soon, Rhys finds himself the target of a new enemy, one that has remained silent, hidden for thousands of years. With rebellions against the Pantarak Empire burning around him and war imminent, he takes a calculated risk that will change Earth's destiny—and his—forever.

ACKNOWLEDGMENTS

Since the release of my first book, I've had a number of people randomly jump into various supporting roles, and I'd like to than them for their enduring encouragement.

To Michael Schwartz, who has not only helped place my books in his high school library and encouraged his students to read my works, but who has been a constant source of imagination and creativity. Thank you, Michael.

To my aviator father, who helped flesh out the finer details of the numerous mechanized flying units found in this book. Thank you.

To my husband, Dakota, for reading this book when it was in its rawest form and meticulously picking it apart. Thank you, Husband.

ABOUT THE AUTHOR

Kara has worked toward becoming a young adult (YA)/new adult (NA) fiction author since she was 13. Her first book *The Empress' Consul* was published in 2013 and is the foundation for the expansive world she has created.

Kara graduated in 2012 from the University of Arkansas's prestigious communication department with an MA in Communication with special emphasis in ESL education and mass media. Kara has a double Bachelor's in International Relations and Asian Studies.

When she is not writing her own books, Kara enjoys listening to soundtracks from a myriad of shows and movies, watching anime, playing piano, and beating her husband in video games.

Follow Kara on social media!

www.karadwilson.com
www.facebook.com/karadwilsonbooks